His Share of Glory

The Complete
Short Science Fiction
of C. M. Kornbluth

Edited by Timothy P. Szczesuil

The NESFA Press
Post Office Box 809
Framingham, MA 01701-0203
1997

Acknowledgments

The production of *His Share of Glory* was accomplished through the work of many volunteers. Thanks to Mark Olson and NESFA's Publication Czar Anthony Lewis for their help and guidance on many stylistic and editorial questions. Thanks also to the army of proofreaders: Elisabeth Carey, Ann Crimmins, Irene Harrison, Elisa Hertel, Mark Hertel, Suford Lewis, Tony Lewis, Mark Olson, and Joe Rico. I'm grateful to Tina Le Page-Bradanese for typing several whole stories. For bringing the quality of this book up to professional standards, thanks to our Master Proof-reader George Flynn. Many thanks to Robert A. Madle for supplying the dustjacket photo of Cyril M. Kornbluth, as well as several amusing anecdotes about his run-ins with CMK (and for being a great Boskone guest—thanks Bob!). The dustjacket was designed by Mark and Elisa Hertel from an idea by Suford Lewis. Special thanks to my wife Ann A. Broomhead, who proofread the entire book, and without whom, for many reasons, this book would not be possible. Thank you, my friends.

Colophon

His Share of Glory was produced on a Pentium 100 PC under Windows 95, using Microsoft Word for Windows 6.0, laid out using Aldus PageMaker 6.0, and printed on a HP Laserjet 4M.

This book is set in Adobe Garamond in 11 point on 12, and 9.5 point on 10.5 for the "to spec" section in the back of the book. The display title font is Rockwell Extra Bold. Other casual fonts used were: Futuri, AngloSSK and Zapf Humanist Demi Bold. It is printed on 60# acid-free paper by Bookcrafters of Fredericksburg, Va.

The editor dedicates this book to

All the Members of
The New England Science Fiction Association
without whom this book would not be possible.

Contents

Cyril by Frederik Pohl xiii
Editor's Introduction xix

That Share of Glory 1
The Adventurer 24
Dominoes 35
The Golden Road 42
The Rocket of 1955 59
The Mindworm 61
The Education of Tigress McCardle 72
Shark Ship 80
The Meddlers 105
The Luckiest Man in Denv 108
The Reversible Revolutions 118
The City in the Sofa 129
Gomez 141
Masquerade 160
The Slave 169
The Words of Guru 196
Thirteen O'Clock 202
Mr. Packer Goes to Hell 221
With These Hands 240
Iteration 253
The Goodly Creatures 257
Time Bum 267
Two Dooms 274
Passion Pills 309
The Silly Season 313
Fire-Power 324
The Perfect Invasion 341
The Adventurers 356
Kazam Collects 361
The Marching Morons 372
The Altar at Midnight 396
Crisis! 402
Theory of Rocketry 413
The Cosmic Charge Account 424
Friend to Man 441
I Never Ast No Favors 447
The Little Black Bag 458
What Sorghum Says 479

Table of Contents

MS. Found in a Chinese Fortune Cookie 485
The Only Thing We Learn 494
The Last Man Left in the Bar 502
Virginia 512
The Advent on Channel Twelve 517
Make Mine Mars 520
Everybody Knows Joe 543
The Remorseful 546
Sir Mallory's Magnitude 551
The Events Leading Down to the Tragedy 570

Early "to spec" Stories
King Cole of Pluto 577
No Place to Go 593
Dimension of Darkness 597
Dead Center 605
Interference 620
Forgotten Tongue 627
Return from M-15 632
The Core 648

Cyril

by

Frederik Pohl

In the late 1930s a bunch of us New York City fans, tiring of being members of other people's fan clubs, decided to start our own. We called it "the Futurians." As nearly as I can remember the prime perpetrators were Don Wollheim, Johnny Michel, Bob Lowndes and myself, but we quickly acquired a couple of dozen other like-minded actifans and writer wannabees, and among them was a pudgy, acerbic fourteen-year-old from the far northern reaches of Manhattan whose name was Cyril Kornbluth.

All the Futurians had an attitude; it was what made us so universally loved by other New York fans. Even so, Cyril was special. He had a quick and abrasive wit, and he exercised it on anyone within reach. What he also had, though, was a boundless talent. Even at fourteen, Cyril knew how to use the English language. I think he was born with the gift of writing in coherent, pointed, colorful sentences, and, although I don't think any of his very earliest writing survives, some of the stories in this book were written when he was no more than sixteen.

Most of what Cyril wrote (what all of us Futurians wrote, assiduously and often) was science fiction, but he also had a streak of the poet in him. Cyril possessed a copy of a textbook—written, I think, by one of his high-school teachers —which described all the traditional forms of verse, from haiku to chant royale, and it was his ambition to write one of each. I don't think he made it. I do remember that he did a villanelle and several sonnets, both Shakespearean and Petrarchan, but I don't remember the poems themselves. All I do remember of Cyril's verse is a fragment from the beginning of a long, erotic poem called "Elephanta"—

> *How long, my love, shall I behold this wall*
> *Between our gardens, yours the rose*
> *And mine the swooning lily?*

—and a short piece called "Calisthenics":

> *One, two, three, four,*
> *Flap your arms and prance*
> *In stinky shirt and stinky socks*
> *And stinky little pants.*

By 1939 a few of the Futurians had begun making an occasional sale to the prozines. Then the gates of Heaven opened. In October of that year I fell into a job editing two science-fiction magazines for the great pulp house of Popular Publications; a few months later Don Wollheim persuaded Albing Publications to give him a similar deal, while Bob Lowndes got the call to take over Louis Silberkleit's magazines. These were not major markets. None of us had much to spend in the way of story budgets—Donald essentially had no budget at all—and we were at a disadvantage in competing with magazines like *Amazing, Astounding* and *Thrilling Wonder* for the work of the established pros. What we did have, though, was each other, and all the rest of the Futurians.

I think Cyril's first published story was a collaboration with Dick Wilson, "Stepson of Space," published under the pseudonym of "Ivar Towers" (the Futurian headquarters apartment was called "the Ivory Tower") in my magazine, *Astonishing Stories*. He and I also collaborated on a batch of not very good stories for my own magazines, mostly bylined "S. D. Gottesman" at Cyril's prompting—I think he was getting back at a hated math teacher of that name—but his solo work, under one pen-name or another, generally appeared in Don Wollheim's *Stirring* and *Cosmic*. Most of them are herein.

Then the war came along.

Cyril, who had worked now and then as a machinist, got into uniform as an artillery maintenance man, working in a machine shop far behind the lines to keep the guns going. He probably could have survived the war in relative comfort there, except that the Army had an inspiration. In its wisdom it imagined that the war would go on for a good long time, that it would need educated officers beyond the apparently available supply toward its final stages and that it would be a good idea to send some of its brighter soldiers to school ahead of time. The program was called "ASTP," and Cyril signed up for it at once. It was a very good deal. Cyril went back to school at the Army's expense quite happily ... until the Army noticed that the war was moving toward a close faster than they had expected, with some very big battles yet to be fought. The need was not for future officers but for present combat troops. They met it by canceling ASTP overnight and throwing all its members into the infantry, and so Cyril wound up lugging a 50-caliber machine gun through the snows of the Battle of the Bulge.

The war did finally end. We all got back to civilian life again, and Cyril moved to Chicago to go back to school, at the University of Chicago, on the G.I. Bill. Meanwhile Dick Wilson had also wound up there as a reporter for the news wire service Trans-Radio Press; he was their bureau chief for the city, and when he needed to hire another reporter he gave the job to Cyril. For a couple of years Cyril divided his time between the news bureau and the university, somehow finding enough spare hours to write an occasional short story for the magazines (all of them herein).

Then he came east on a visit. He stayed at our house just outside of Red Bank, New Jersey, for a while, and I was glad to see him because I needed help on a project.

The project was a novel I had begun about the future of the advertising business. I had been working on it desultorily for a year or so and succeeded in getting about the first third of it on paper. I showed that much to Horace Gold, then the editor of *Galaxy,* and Horace said, "Fine. I'll print it as soon as I finish the current serial." "But it isn't finished," I said. "So go home and finish it," said Horace.

I didn't see how that was possible in the time allowed, and so Cyril's arrival was a godsend. When I showed what I had to him and suggested we try collaborating again he agreed instantly; he wrote the next third by himself, and the two of us collaborated, turn and about, on the final section. After some polishing and cleaning up of loose ends we turned it in and Horace ran it as "Gravy Planet"; a little later Ian Ballantine published it in book form as *The Space Merchants* and so it has remained, in many editions and several dozen translations, ever since.

Working with Cyril Kornbluth was one of the great privileges of my life. First to last, we wrote seven novels together: *The Space Merchants, Gladiator-at-Law, Search the Sky* and *Wolfbane* in the field of science fiction, plus our three "mainstream" novels, *Presidential Year, A Town Is Drowning* and *Sorority House* (that last one published under the pseudonym of "Jordan Park"). I can't say that we never quarreled about anything—after all, we were both graduates of the feisty Futurians—but the writing always, *always* went quickly and well. As editor, agent and collaborator I have worked with literally hundreds of writers over the years, in one degree or another of intimacy, but never with one more competent and talented than Cyril. Even when we were not actually collaborating we would now and then help each other out. Once when Cyril complained that he wanted to write a story but couldn't seem to come up with an attractive idea, I reminded him that he had once mentioned to me that he'd like to write a story about medical instruments from the future somehow appearing today; "The Little Black Bag" was the result. And after that was published I urged him to do more with the future background from which those instruments had come, and that turned into "The Marching Morons." And I am indebted to him for any number of details, plot twists and bits of business in my own stories of the time.

All the while we were writing together, of course, he had other irons in the fire. With Judy Merril he wrote two novels, *Marschild* and *Gunner Cade;* he continued to pour out his own wonderful shorter pieces, and he wrote half a dozen novels all his own. Some of them were mainstream—*Valerie, The Naked Storm* and *Man of Cold Rages*—but three were science fiction. They were, of course, brilliant. They are also, however, sadly, somewhat dated; *Takeoff* was all about the first spaceflight, *Not This August* about the results of the anticipated Russian-American World War III, which in his story the Russians had won. By 1958 he had larger plans, with two novels in the works. Neither was science fiction; both were historical. One was to be about the life of St. Dacius, and that is all I know about it; if any part of it was ever on paper it has long since been lost. The other was to be about the battle of the Crater in the Civil War, and for that one Cyril had done an immense quantity of research. He completed several hundred pages of notes and reference material ... but that's as far as it got. The Battle of the Bulge finally took its toll.

By the mid-1950s Cyril began having medical problems. When at last he took them to a doctor the diagnosis was bad. It was essentially malignant hypertension, the doctor said, probably the result of exposure and exhaustion in the Ardennes Forest, and it was likely to be terminal. If Cyril wanted to live much longer, the doctor told him, he would have to give up cigarettes, alcohol and spices of all kinds, and take regular doses of the rauwolfia extracts that were all the pharmacopeia of the day had to offer for that condition.

Cyril did his best to follow orders. When he came out to visit, Carol, my wife at that time, baked him salt-free bread and served him spiceless health foods and we never, never offered him a drink. It wasn't good enough. The dope he was taking relieved his tension, but it also made him stupid; this quick, insightful mind had become woefully slow and fumbling. When I ventured to show him a novel that was giving me trouble in the hope that he could help, he read it over ponderously, then sighed. "Needs salt," he said gloomily, and handed it back.

To live like that, Cyril decided, was no life at all. So he went against the doctor's orders. He stopped the drugs and resumed the cigarettes and the spices. For a while he was the old Cyril again ... and then, on one snowy morning a few months later, I got a despairing phone call from Mary, his wife. Cyril had shoveled snow to get out of the driveway of their home on Long Island, then run to catch a train to the city, and dropped dead of a heart attack on the station platform.

By the time I got there, a few hours later, there was nothing left to do but to try to console his widow and his sons. Mary and I went to the crematorium to watch Cyril's body roll into the chamber; the shutters closed; and that was the last anyone ever saw of Cyril Kornbluth. He was then just thirty-four years old and, I think, only beginning to hit his stride as a writer.

When Cyril died he left behind a few fragments of notes and uncompleted stories. Some of them I completed and published as our final collaborations — "The Quaker Cannon," "Critical Mass" and "Mute, Inglorious Tam" among them. There was one other. That was a very short piece called "The Meeting." For one reason or another it was years before I saw how to deal with that one. But at last I did, and when awards time came around the next year "The Meeting" won a Hugo. It was the only such award ever given to Cyril's work, and it was not enough. He deserved much, much more.

His Share of Glory

Editor's Introduction

"Who is C. M. Kornbluth?" I asked. We had just seen the movie "Robocop" in 1987, and I asked, "Where have I read the line 'I'd buy that for a dollar!'?" To which my wife Ann (my encyclopedia of all SF knowledge) replied without a pause, "It was 'Would you buy it for a quarter?' in 'The Marching Morons.' It's sort of a sequel to 'The Little Black Bag' by ... Kornbluth, C. M. Kornbluth."

I had recognized the tag line but not the author. That was the genesis of this book. Shortly after that I bought a second-hand copy of *The Best of C. M. Kornbluth,* that Fred Pohl edited and Del Rey published in 1976 (by then out-of-print). I inhaled the collection and looked for more. Alas, neither the library nor the bookseller could help me. Eventually, I discovered that some of his other works had been published in even older and more difficult to obtain out-of-print collections: *Thirteen O'Clock and Other Zero Hours, A Mile Beyond the Moon,* and *The Mindworm.* I bought or borrowed these old, yellowed, brittle-paged paperbacks and enjoyed them as well.

In 1990 at a NESFA Other Meeting, Mark Olson first proposed that NESFA publish classic SF authors whose work had gone out of print, and were therefore unavailable to new SF fans or to anyone without a vast library of old pulps. Mark selected Schmitz, and the first of the NESFA's Choice books was published: *The Best of James H. Schmitz.* My proposal was C. M. Kornbluth.

In the preparation of this book I've had the good fortune to speak with many of Cyril M. Kornbluth friends and contemporaries. He seems to have been your typical literary genius: amusing, smart, quick-witted, but acid-tongued. His photograph on the back flyleaf shows a cocky young man, blithely smoking, perfectly confident—yet he is only a boy, sixteen or seventeen years old. Here are cynicism and maturity, characteristics that were present from the beginning of his career to its sudden end.

Why a complete collection? Cyril Kornbluth was widely known for writing under various pseudonyms: Cecil Corwin, S. D. Gottesman, etc. Several of his pennames were house names, used by other writers for the same magazine, some were also collaborations. I searched the usual sources to construct as complete a bibliography of solo Kornbluth stories as possible. Looking at that list and reading the stories, I realized that I couldn't bear to cut out any of them; they all had a unique insight into human nature, and most were very good. A small number had been written hastily, at the last minute to fill space in a pulp magazine being edited by a fellow Futurian, but even the (bad) ones were impressive work for a teenager writing "to spec" on a tight deadline. Some of these early stories I have put in the back section of the book.

Why not include collaborative material? Kornbluth was an extensive collaborator. In the early forties, he collaborated with several of the Futurians: Don Wollheim, Robert A. W. Lowndes, etc. Later, under the pseudonym of Cyril Judd, he collaborated with Judith Merril on the Gunner Cade/Mars Child series. And, of course, throughout his career he collaborated extensively with Fred Pohl. Recently Pohl edited a collection of their collaborative efforts, *Our Best: The Best of Frederik Pohl and C. M. Kornbluth*. Pohl and Kornbluth wrote in a unique voice which was neither Pohl nor Kornbluth. I was interested in presenting Kornbluth's perspective.

To determine which stories were really Kornbluth, I consulted the usual indexes to early SF. The most useful source of bibliographic information I found was, *Cyril M. Kornbluth: The Cynical Scrutineer* by Phil Stephensen-Payne & Gordon Benson, Jr. (ISBN# 1-871133-03-3), a good bibliography that also includes non-SF works. I also conferred with Ken Johnson (an expert on pseudonyms in SF), who had managed to view some of the original receipts from some of the early publishers, and from him I learned that Kornbluth did not write "Hollow of the Moon," a story written under the byline Gabriel Barclay. The Shakespeare quotation at the beginning of "Two Dooms" only appeared in the first occurrence, in the magazine Venture (7/58) and not in any subsequent reprints. In the magazine Galaxy (12/51) there is a variation of the story "With These Hands" with a rather contrived ending, which doesn't appear in other editions of the story. I believe the Galaxy ending to be an editor's addition, and have chosen to include the more widely used variation. There was a heavily abridged version of "The Silly Season" in the collection *The Mindworm*. The complete version appears here.

This book has been part of my life for three years. Throughout this time, it is the stories that hold my attention. Witty, pointed, telling, honest, gutsy. It is through these stories that we see Kornbluth's view the clearest. A universe of intrigue and absurdity, of con-men, of suckers, of justice, his justice, his truth, his vision. The stories that follow are his share of glory.

Timothy P. Szczesuil
Wayland, Mass.
December 1996

[*Astounding* - January 1952]

That Share of Glory

Young Alen, one of a thousand in the huge refectory, ate absent-mindedly as the reader droned into the perfect silence of the hall. Today's lesson happened to be a word-list of the Thetis VIII planet's sea-going folk.

"*Tlon*—a ship," droned the reader.

"*Rtlo*—some ships, number unknown."

"*Long*—some ships, number known, always modified by cardinal."

"*Ongr*—a ship in a collection of ships, always modified by ordinal."

"*Ngrt*—first ship in a collection of ships; an exception to *ongr*."

A lay brother tiptoed to Alen's side. "The Rector summons you," he whispered.

Alen had no time for panic, though that was the usual reaction to a summons from the Rector to a novice. He slipped from the refectory, stepped onto the northbound corridor and stepped off at his cell, a minute later and a quarter-mile farther on. Hastily, but meticulously, he changed from his drab habit to the heraldic robes in the cubicle with its simple stool, washstand, desk, and paper-weight or two. Alen, a level-headed young fellow, was not aware that he had broken any section of the Order's complicated Rule, but he was aware that he could have done so without knowing it. It might, he thought, be the last time he would see the cell.

He cast a glance which he hoped would not be the final one over it; a glance which lingered a little fondly on the reel rack where were stowed: *Nicholson on Martian Verbs*, *The New Oxford Venusian Dictionary*, the ponderous six-reeler *Deutsche Ganymedische Konversatsionslexikon* published long ago and far away in Leipzig. The later works were there, too: *The Tongues of the Galaxy—An Essay in Classification*, *A Concise Grammar of Cephean*, *The Self-Pronouncing Vegan II Dictionary*—scores of them, and, of course, the worn reel of old Machiavelli's *The Prince*.

Enough of that! Alen combed out his small, neat beard and stepped onto the southbound corridor. He transferred to an eastbound at the next intersection and minutes later was before the Rector's lay secretary.

"You'd better review your Lyran irregulars," said the secretary disrespectfully. "There's a trader in there who's looking for a cheap herald on a swindling trip to Lyra VI." Thus unceremoniously did Alen learn that he was not to be ejected from the Order but that he was to be elevated to Journeyman. But as a herald should, he betrayed no sign of his immense relief. He did, however, take the secretary's advice and sensibly reviewed his Lyran.

While he was in the midst of a declension which applied only to inanimate objects, the voice of the Rector—and what a mellow voice it was!—floated through the secretary's intercom.

"Admit the novice, Alen," said the Master Herald.

A final settling of his robes and the youth walked into the Rector's huge office, with the seal of the Order blazing in diamonds above his desk. There was a stranger present; presumably the trader—a black-bearded fellow whose rugged frame didn't carry his Vegan cloak with ease.

Said the Rector: "Novice, this is to be the crown of your toil if you are acceptable to—?" He courteously turned to the trader, who shrugged irritably.

"It's all one to me," growled the blackbeard. "Somebody cheap, somebody who knows the cant of the thievish Lyran gem peddlers, above all, somebody *at once*. Overhead is devouring my flesh day by day as the ship waits at the field. And when we are space-borne, my imbecile crew will doubtless waste liter after priceless liter of my fuel. And when we land the swindling Lyrans will without doubt make my ruin complete by tricking me even out of the minute profit I hope to realize. Good Master Herald, let me have the infant cheap and I'll bid you good day."

The Rector's shaggy eyebrows drew down in a frown. "Trader," he said sonorously, "our mission of galactic utilitarian culture is not concerned with your margin of profit. I ask you to test this youth and, if you find him able, to take him as your Herald on your voyage. He will serve you well, for he has been taught that commerce and words, its medium, are the unifying bonds which will one day unite the cosmos into a single humankind. Do not conceive that the College and Order of Heralds is a mere aid to you in your commercial adventure."

"Very well," growled the trader. He addressed Alen in broken Lyran. "Boy, how you make up Vegan stones of three fires so Lyran women like, come buy, buy again?"

Alen smoothly replied: "The Vegan triple-fire gem finds most favor on Lyra and especially among its women when set in a wide glass anklet if large, and when arranged in the Lyran 'lucky five' pattern in a glass thumb-ring if small." He was glad, very glad, he had come across—and as a matter of course memorized, in the relentless fashion of the Order—a novel which touched briefly on the Lyran jewel trade.

The trader glowered and switched to Cephean—apparently his native tongue. "That was well-enough said, Herald. Now tell me whether you've got guts to man a squirt in case we're intercepted by the thieving so-called Customs collectors of Eyolf's Realm between here and Lyra?"

Alen knew the Rector's eyes were on him. "The noble mission of our Order," he said, "forbids me to use any weapon but the truth in furthering cosmic utilitarian civilization. No, master trader, I shall not man one of your weapons."

The trader shrugged. "So I must take what I get. Good Master Herald, make me a price."

The Rector said casually: "I regard this chiefly as a training mission for our novice; the fee will be nominal. Let us say twenty-five percent of your net as of blastoff from Lyra, to be audited by Journeyman-Herald Alen."

The trader's howl of rage echoed in the dome of the huge room. "It's not fair!" he roared. "Who but you thievish villains with your Order and your catch-'em-young and your years of training can learn the tongues of the galaxy? What chance has a decent merchant busy with profit and loss got to learn the cant of every race between Sirius and the Coalsack? It's not fair! It's not fair and I'll say so until my dying breath!"

"Die outside if you find our terms unacceptable, then," said the Rector. "The Order does not haggle."

"Well I know it," sighed the trader brokenly. "I should have stuck to my own system and my good father's pump-flange factory. But no! I had to pick up a bargain in gems on Vega! Enough of this—bring me your contract and I'll sign it."

The Rector's shaggy eyebrows went up. "There is no contract," he said. "A mutual trust between Herald and trader is the cornerstone upon which cosmos-wide amity and understanding will be built."

"At twenty-five percent of an unlicked pup," muttered blackbeard to himself in Cephean.

None of his instructors had played Polonius as Alen, with the seal of the Journeyman-Herald on his brow, packed for blastoff and vacated his cell. He supposed they knew that twenty years of training either had done their work or had not.

The trader, taking Alen to the field where his ship waited, was less wise. "The secret of successful negotiation," he weightily told his Herald, "is to yield willingly. This may strike you as a paradox, but it is the veritable key to my success in maintaining the profits of my good father's pump-flange trade. The secret is to yield with rueful admiration of your opponent—but *only in unimportant details*. Put up a little battle about delivery date or about terms of credit and then let him have his way. But you never give way a hair's breadth on your asking price unless—"

Alen let him drivel on as they drove through the outer works of the College. He was glad the car was open. For the first time he was being accorded the doffed hat that is the due of Heralds from their inferiors in the Order, and the grave nod of salutation from equals. Five-year-old postulants seeing his brow-seal tugged off their headgear with comical celerity; fellow-novices, equals a few hours before, uncovered as though he were the Rector himself.

The ceremonial began to reach the trader. When, with a final salutation, a lay warder let them through the great gate of the curtain wall, he said with some irritation: "They appear to hold you in high regard, boy."

"I am better addressed as 'Herald'," said Alen composedly.

"A plague descend on the College and Order! Do you think I don't know my manners? Of course I call a Herald 'Herald,' but we're going to be cooped up together and you'll be working for me. What'll happen to ship's discipline if I have to kowtow to you?"

"There will be no problem," said Alen.

Blackbeard grunted and trod fiercely on the accelerator.

"That's my ship," he said at length. "*Starsong*. Vegan registry—it may help passing through Eyolf's Realm, though it cost me overmuch in bribes. A crew of eight, lazy, good-for-nothing wastrels—Agh! Can I believe my eyes?" The car jammed to a halt before the looming ship, and blackbeard was up the ladder and through the port in a second. Settling his robes, Alen followed.

He found the trader fiercely denouncing his chief engineer for using space drive to heat the ship; he had seen the faint haze of a minimum exhaust from the stern tubes.

"For that, dolt," screamed blackbeard, "we have a thing known as electricity. Have you by chance ever heard of it? Are you aware that a chief engineer's responsibility is the efficient and *economical* operation of his ship's drive mechanism?"

The chief, a cowed-looking Cephean, saw Alen with relief and swept off his battered cap. The Herald nodded gravely and the trader broke off in irritation. "We need none of that bowing and scraping for the rest of the voyage," he declared.

"Of course not, sir," said the chief. "O'course not. I was just welcoming the Herald aboard. Welcome aboard, Herald. I'm Chief Elwon, Herald. And I'm glad to have a Herald with us." A covert glance at the trader. "*I've* voyaged with Heralds and without, and I don't mind saying I feel safer indeed with you aboard."

"May I be taken to my quarters?" asked Alen.

"Your—?" began the trader, stupefied.

The chief broke in: "I'll fix you a cabin, Herald. We've got some bulkheads I can rig aft for a snug little space, not roomy, but the best a little ship like this can afford."

The trader collapsed into a bucket seat as the chief bustled aft and Alen followed.

"Herald," the chief said with some embarrassment after he had collared two crewmen and set them to work, "you'll have to excuse our good master trader. He's new to the interstar lanes and he doesn't exactly know the jets yet. Between us we'll get him squared away."

Alen inspected the cubicle run up for him—a satisfactory enclosure affording him the decent privacy he rated. He dismissed the chief and the crewmen with a nod and settled himself on the cot.

Beneath the iron composure in which he had been trained, he felt scared and alone. Not even old Machiavelli seemed to offer comfort or counsel: "There is nothing more difficult to take in hand, more perilous to conduct, or more uncertain in its success, than to take the lead in the introduction of a new order of things," said Chapter Six.

But what said Chapter Twenty-Six? "Where the willingness is great, the difficulties cannot be great."

Starsong was not a happy ship. Blackbeard's nagging stinginess hung over the crew like a thundercloud, but Alen professed not to notice. He walked regularly fore and aft for two hours a day, greeting the crew members in their various native tongues and then wrapping himself in the reserve the Order demanded—though he longed to salute them man-to-man, eat with them, gossip about their native planets, the past misdeeds that had brought them to their berths aboard the miserly *Starsong* and their hopes for the future. The Rule of the College and Order of Heralds decreed otherwise. He accepted the uncoverings of the crew with a nod and tried to be pleased because they stood in growing awe of him that ranged from Chief Elwon's lively appreciation of a Herald's skill to Wiper Jukkl's superstitious reverence. Jukkl was a lowbrowed specimen from a planet of the decadent Sirius system. He outdid the normal slovenliness of an all-male crew on a freighter —a slovenliness in which Alen could not share. Many of his waking hours were spent in his locked cubicle burnishing his metal and cleaning and pressing his robes. A Herald was never supposed to suggest by his appearance that he shared mortal frailties.

Blackbeard himself yielded a little, to the point of touching his cap sullenly. This probably was not so much awe at Alen's studied manner as respect for the incisive, lightning-fast job of auditing the Herald did on the books of the trading venture—absurdly complicated books with scores of accounts to record a simple matter of buying gems cheap on Vega and chartering a ship in the hope of selling them dearly on Lyra. The complicated books and overlapping accounts did tell the story, but they made it very easy for an auditor to erroneously read a number of costs as far higher than they actually were. Alen did not fall into the trap.

On the fifth day after blastoff, Chief Elwon rapped, respectfully but urgently, on the door of Alen's cubicle.

"If you please, Herald," he urged, "could you come to the bridge?"

Alen's heart bounded in his chest, but he gravely said: "My meditation must not be interrupted. I shall join you on the bridge in ten minutes." And for ten minutes he methodically polished a murky link in the massive gold chain that fastened his boat-cloak—the "meditation." He donned the cloak before stepping out; the summons sounded like a full-dress affair in the offing.

The trader was stamping and fuming. Chief Elwon was riffling through his spec book unhappily. Astrogator Hufner was at the plot computer running up trajectories and knocking them down again. A quick glance showed Alen that they were all high-speed trajectories in the "evasive action" class.

"Herald," said the trader grimly, "we have broken somebody's detector bubble." He jerked his thumb at a red-lit signal. "I expect we'll be overhauled shortly. Are you ready to earn your twenty-five percent of the net?"

Alen overlooked the crudity. "Are you rigged for color video, merchant?" he asked.

"We are."

"Then I am ready to do what I can for my client."

He took the communicator's seat, stealing a glance in the still-blank screen. The reflection of his face was reassuring, though he wished he had thought to comb his small beard.

Another light flashed on, and Hufner quit the computer to study the detector board. "Big, powerful and getting closer," he said tersely. "Scanning for us with directionals now. Putting out plenty of energy—"

The loud-speaker of the ship-to-ship audio came to life.

"Which ship are you?" it demanded in Vegan. "We are a Customs cruiser of the Realm of Eyolf. What ship are you?"

"Have the crew man the squirts," said the trader softly to the chief.

Elwon looked at Alen, who shook his head. "Sorry, sir," said the engineer apologetically. "The Herald—"

"We are the freighter *Starsong,* Vegan registry," said Alen into the audio mike as the trader choked. "We are carrying Vegan gems to Lyra."

"They're on us," said the astrogator despairingly, reading his instruments. The ship-to-ship video flashed on, showing an arrogant, square-jawed face topped by a battered naval cap.

"Lyra indeed! We have plans of our own for Lyra. You will heave to—" began the officer in the screen, before he noted Alen. "My pardon, Herald," he said sardonically. "Herald, will you please request the ship's master to heave to for boarding and search? We wish to assess and collect Customs duties. You are aware, of course, that your vessel is passing through the Realm."

The man's accented Vegan reeked of Algol IV. Alen switched to that obscure language to say: "We were not aware of that. Are you aware that there is a reciprocal trade treaty in effect between the Vegan system and the Realm which specifies that freight in Vegan bottoms is dutiable only when consigned to ports in the Realm?"

"You speak Algolian, do you? You Heralds have not been underrated, but don't plan to lie your way out of this. Yes, I am aware of some such agreement as you mentioned. We shall board you, as I said, and assess and collect duty in kind. If, regrettably, there has been any mistake, you are, of course, free to apply to the Realm for reimbursement. Now, heave to!"

"I have no intentions of lying. I speak the solemn truth when I say that we shall fight to the last man any attempt of yours to board and loot us."

Alen's mind was racing furiously through the catalogue of planetary folkways the Rule had decreed that he master. Algol IV—some ancestor-worship; veneration of mother; hand-to-hand combat with knives; complimentary greeting, "May you never strike down a weaker foe"; folk-hero Gaarek unjustly accused of slaying a cripple and exiled but it was an enemy's plot—

A disconcerted shadow was crossing the face of the other as Alen improvised: "You will, of course, kill us all. But before this happens I shall have messaged back to the College and Order of Heralds the facts in the case, with a particular request that your family be informed. Your name, I think, will be remembered as long as Gaarek's—though not in the same way, of course; the Algolian whose hundred-man battle cruiser wiped out a virtually unarmed freighter with a crew of eight."

The officer's face was dark with rage. "You devil!" he snarled. "Leave my family out of this! I'll come aboard and fight you man-to-man if you have the stomach for it!"

Alen shook his head regretfully. "The Rule of my Order forbids recourse to violence," he said. "Our only permissible weapon is the truth."

"We're coming aboard," said the officer grimly. "I'll order my men not to harm your people. We'll just be collecting customs. If your people shoot first, my men will be under orders to do nothing more than disable them."

Alen smiled and uttered a sentence or two in Algolian.

The officer's jaw dropped and he croaked, after a pause: "I'll cut you to ribbons. You can't say that about my mother, you—" and he spewed back some of the words Alen had spoken.

"Calm yourself," said the Herald gravely. "I apologize for my disgusting and unheraldic remarks. But I wished to prove a point. You would have killed me if you could; I touched off a reaction which had been planted in you by your culture. I will be able to do the same with the men of yours who come aboard. For every race of man there is the intolerable insult that must be avenged in blood.

"Send your men aboard under orders not to kill if you wish; I shall goad them into a killing rage. We shall be massacred, yours will be the blame and you will be disgraced and disowned by your entire planet." Alen hoped desperately that the naval crews of the Realm were, as reputed, a barbarous and undisciplined lot—

Evidently they were, and the proud Algolian dared not risk it. In his native language he spat again: "You devil!" and switched back into Vegan. "Freighter *Starsong*," he said bleakly, "I find that my space fix was in error and that you are not in Realm territory. You may proceed."

The astrogator said from the detector board, incredulously: "He's disengaging. He's off us. He's accelerating. Herald, *what* did you say to him?"

But the reaction from blackbeard was more gratifying. Speechless, the trader took off his cap. Alen acknowledged the salute with a grave nod before he started back to his cubicle. It was just as well, he reflected, that the trader didn't know his life and his ship had been unconditionally pledged in a finish fight against a hundred-man battle cruiser.

Lyra's principal spaceport was pocked and broken, but they made a fair-enough landing. Alen, in full heraldic robes, descended from *Starsong* to greet a handful of port officials.

"Any metals aboard?" demanded one of them.

"None for sale," said the Herald. "We have Vegan gems, chiefly triple-fire." He knew that the dull little planet was short of metals and, having made a virtue of necessity, was somehow prejudiced against their import.

"Have your crew transfer the cargo to the Customs shed," said the port official studying *Starsong*'s papers. "And all of you wait there."

All of them—except Alen—lugged numbered sacks and boxes of gems to the low brick building designated. The trader was allowed to pocket a handful for samples before the shed was sealed—a complicated business. A brick was mortared over the simple ironwood latch that closed the ironwood door, a pat of clay was slapped over the brick and the port seal stamped in it. A mechanic with what looked like a pottery blowtorch fed by powdered coal played a flame on the clay seal until it glowed orange-red and that was that.

"Herald," said the port official, "tell the merchant to sign here and make his fingerprints."

Alen studied the document; it was a simple identification form. Blackbeard signed with the reed pen provided and fingerprinted the document. After two weeks in space he scarcely needed to ink his fingers first.

"Now tell him that we'll release the gems on his written fingerprinted order to whatever Lyran citizens he sells to. And explain that this roundabout system is necessary to avoid metal smuggling. Please remove *all* metal from your clothes and stow it on your ship. Then we will seal that, too, and put it under guard until you are ready to take off. We regret that we will have to search you before we turn you loose, but we can't afford to have our economy disrupted by irresponsible introduction of metals." Alen had not realized it was that bad.

After the thorough search that extended to the confiscation of forgotten watches and pins, the port officials changed a sheaf of the trader's uranium-backed Vegan currency into Lyran legal tender based on man-hours. Blackbeard made a partial payment to the crew, and told them to have a good liberty and check in at the port at sunset tomorrow for probable take-off.

Alen and the trader were driven to town in an unlikely vehicle whose power plant was a pottery turbine. The driver, when they were safely out on the open road, furtively asked whether they had any metal they wanted to discard.

The trader asked sharply in his broken Lyran: "What you do you get metal? Where sell, how use?"

The driver, following a universal tendency, raised his voice and lapsed into broken Lyran himself to tell the strangers: "Black market science men pay much, much for little bit metal. Study, use build. Politicians make law no metal, what I care politicians? But you no tell, gentlemen?"

"We won't tell," said Alen. "But we have no metal for you."

The driver shrugged.

"Herald," said the trader, "what do you make of it?"

"I didn't know it was a political issue. We concern ourselves with the basic patterns of a people's behavior, not the day-to-day expressions of the patterns.

The planet's got no heavy metals, which means there were no metals available to the primitive Lyrans. The lighter metals don't occur in native form or in easily-split compounds. They proceeded along the ceramic line instead of the metallic line and appear to have done quite well for themselves up to a point. No electricity, of course, no aviation and no space flight."

"And," said the trader, "naturally the people who make these buggies and that blowtorch we saw are scared witless that metals will be imported and put them out of business. So naturally they have laws passed prohibiting it."

"Naturally," said the Herald, looking sharply at the trader. But blackbeard was back in character a moment later. "An outrage," he growled. "Trying to tell a man what he can and can't import when he sees a decent chance to make a bit of profit."

The driver dropped them at a boardinghouse. It was half-timbered construction, which appeared to be swankier than the more common brick. The floors were plate glass, roughened for traction. Alen got them a double room with a view.

"What's that thing?" demanded the trader, inspecting the view.

The thing was a structure looming above the slate and tile roofs of the town— a round brick tower for its first twenty-five meters and then wood for another fifteen. As they studied it, it pricked up a pair of ears at the top and began to flop them wildly.

"Semaphore," said Alen.

A minute later blackbeard piteously demanded from the bathroom: "*How do you make water come out of the tap? I touched it all over but nothing happened.*"

"You have to turn it," said Alen, demonstrating. "And that thing—you pull it sharply down, hold it and then release."

"Barbarous," muttered the trader. "Barbarous."

An elderly maid came in to show them how to string their hammocks and ask if they happened to have a bit of metal to give her for a souvenir. They sent her away and, rather than face the public dining room, made a meal from their own stores and turned in for the night.

It's going well, thought Alen drowsily: going very well indeed.

He awoke abruptly, but made no move. It was dark in the double room, and there were stealthy, furtive little noises nearby. A hundred thoughts flashed through his head of Lyran treachery and double-dealing. He lifted his eyelids a trifle and saw a figure silhouetted against the faint light of the big window. If a burglar, he was a clumsy one.

There was a stirring from the other hammock, the trader's. With a subdued roar that sounded like "Thieving villains!" blackbeard launched himself from the hammock at the intruder. But his feet tangled in the hammock cords and he belly-flopped on the floor.

The burglar, if it was one, didn't dash smoothly and efficiently for the door. He straightened himself against the window and said resignedly: "You need not fear. I will make no resistance."

Alen rolled from the hammock and helped the trader to his feet. "He said he doesn't want to fight," he told the trader.

Blackbeard seized the intruder and shook him like a rat. "So the rogue is a coward too!" he boomed. "Give us a light, Herald."

Alen uncovered the slow-match, blew it to a flame, squeakily pumped up a pressure torch until a jet of pulverized coal sprayed from its nozzle and ignited it. A dozen strokes more and there was enough heat feeding back from the jet to maintain the pressure cycle.

Through all of this the trader was demanding in his broken Lyran: "What make here, thief? What reason thief us room?"

The Herald brought the hissing pressure lamp to the window. The intruder's face was not the unhealthy, neurotic face of a criminal. Its thin lines told of discipline and thought.

"What did you want here?" asked Alen.

"Metal," said the intruder simply. "I thought you might have a bit of iron."

It was the first time a specific metal had been named by any Lyran. He used, of course, the Vegan word for iron.

"You are particular," remarked the Herald. "Why iron?"

"I have heard that it possesses certain properties—perhaps you can tell me before you turn me over to the police. Is it true, as we hear, that a mass of iron whose crystals have been aligned by a sharp blow will strongly attract another piece of iron with a force related to the distance between them?"

"It is true," said the Herald, studying the man's face. It was lit with excitement. Deliberately Alen added: "This alignment is more easily and uniformly effected by placing the mass of iron in an electric field—that is, a space surrounding the passage of an electron stream through a conductor." Many of the words he used had to be Vegan; there were no Lyran words for "electric," "electron" or "conductor."

The intruder's face fell. "I have tried to master the concept you refer to," he admitted. "But it is beyond me. I have questioned other interstar voyagers and they have touched on it, but I cannot grasp it— But thank you, sir; you have been very courteous. I will trouble you no further while you summon the watch."

"You give up too easily," said Alen. "For a scientist, much too easily. If we turn you over to the watch, there will be hearings and testimony and whatnot. Our time is limited here on your planet; I doubt that we can spare any for your legal processes."

The trader let go of the intruder's shoulder and grumbled: "Why you no ask we have iron, I tell you no. Search, search, take all metal away. We no police you. I sorry hurted you arms. Here for you." Blackbeard brought out a palmful of his sample gems and picked out a large triple-fire stone. "You not be angry me," he said, putting it in the Lyran's hand.

"I can't—" said the scientist.

Blackbeard closed his fingers over the stone and growled: "I give, you take. Maybe buy iron with, eh?"

"That's so," said the Lyran. "Thank you both, gentlemen. Thank you—"

"You go," said the trader. "You go, we sleep again."

The scientist bowed with dignity and left their room.

"Gods of space," swore the trader. "To think that Jukkl, the *Starsong*'s wiper, knows more about electricity and magnetism than a brainy fellow like that."

"And they are the key to physics," mused Alen. "A scientist here is dead-ended forever, because their materials are all insulators! Glass, clay, glaze, wood."

"Funny, all right," yawned blackbeard. "Did you see me collar him once I got on my feet? Sharp, eh? Good night, Herald." He gruntingly hauled himself into the hammock again, leaving Alen to turn off the hissing light and cover the slow-match with its perforated lid.

They had roast fowl of some sort or other for breakfast in the public dining room. Alen was required by his Rule to refuse the red wine that went with it. The trader gulped it approvingly. "A sensible, though backward people," he said. "And now if you'll inquire of the management where the thievish jewel-buyers congregate, we can get on with our business and perhaps be off by dawn tomorrow."

"So quickly?" asked Alen, almost forgetting himself enough to show surprise.

"My charter on *Starsong*, good Herald—thirty days to go, but what might not go wrong in space? And then there would be penalties to mulct me of whatever minute profit I may realize."

Alen learned that Gromeg's Tavern was the gem mart and they took another of the turbine-engined cabs through the brick-paved streets.

Gromeg's was a dismal, small-windowed brick barn with heavy-set men lounging about, an open kitchen at one end and tables at the other. A score of smaller, sharp-faced men were at the tables sipping wine and chatting.

"I am Journeyman-Herald Alen," announced Alen clearly, "with Vegan gems to dispose of."

There was a silence of elaborate unconcern, and then one of the dealers spat and grunted: "Vegan gems. A drug on the market. Take them away, Herald."

"Come, master trader," said Alen in the Lyran tongue. "The gem dealers of Lyra do not want your wares." He started for the door.

One of the dealers called languidly: "Well, wait a moment. I have nothing better to do; since you've come all this way I'll have a look at your stuff."

"You honor us," said Alen. He and blackbeard sat at the man's table. The trader took out a palmful of samples, counted them meaningfully and laid them on the boards.

"Well," said the gem dealer, "I don't know whether to be amused or insulted. I am Garthkint, the gem dealer—not a retailer of *beads*. However, I have no hard feelings. A drink for your frowning friend, Herald? I know you gentry don't indulge." The drink was already on the table, brought by one of the hulking guards.

Alen passed Garthkint's own mug of wine to the trader, explaining politely: "In my master trader's native Cepheus it is considered honorable for the guest to sip the drink his host laid down and none other. A charming custom, is it not?"

"Charming, though unsanitary," muttered the gem dealer—and he did not touch the drink he had ordered for blackbeard.

"I can't understand a word either of you is saying—too flowery. Was this little rat trying to drug me?" demanded the trader in Cephean.

"No," said Alen. "Just trying to get you drunk." To Garthkint in Lyran, he explained, "The good trader was saying that he wishes to leave at once. I was agreeing with him."

"Well," said Garthkint, "perhaps I can take a couple of your gauds. For some youngster who wishes a cheap ring."

"He's getting to it," Alen told the trader.

"High time," grunted blackbeard.

"The trader asks me to inform you," said Alen, switching back to Lyran, "that he is unable to sell in lots smaller than five hundred gems."

"A compact language, Cephean," said Garthkint, narrowing his eyes.

"Is it not?" Alen blandly agreed.

The gem dealer's forefinger rolled an especially fine three-fire stone from the little pool of gems on the table. "I suppose," he said grudgingly, "that this is what I must call the best of the lot. What, I am curious to know, is the price you would set for five hundred equal in quality and size to this poor thing?"

"This," said Alen, "is the good trader's first venture to your delightful planet. He wishes to be remembered and welcomed all of the many times he anticipates returning. Because of this he has set an absurdly low price, counting good will as more important than a prosperous voyage. Two thousand Lyran credits."

"Absurd," snorted Garthkint. "I cannot do business with you. Either you are insanely rapacious or you have been pitifully misguided as to the value of your wares. I am well known for my charity; I will assume that the latter is the case. I trust you will not be too downcast when I tell you that five hundred of these muddy, undersized out-of-round objects are worth no more than two hundred credits."

"If you are serious," said Alen with marked amazement, "we would not dream of imposing on you. At the figure you mention, we might as well not sell at all but return with our wares to Cepheus and give these gems to children in the streets for marbles. Good gem trader, excuse us for taking up so much of your time and many thanks for your warm hospitality in the matter of the wine." He switched to Cephean and said: "We're dickering now. Two thousand and two hundred. Get up; we're going to start to walk out."

"What if he lets us go?" grumbled blackbeard, but he did heave himself to his feet and turn to the door as Alen rose.

"My trader echoes my regrets," the Herald said in Lyran. "Farewell."

"Well, stay a moment," said Garthkint. "I am well known for my soft heart toward strangers. A charitable man might go as high as five hundred and absorb the inevitable loss. If you should return some day with a passable lot of *real* gems, it would be worth my while for you to remember who treated you with such benevolence and give me fair choice."

"Noble Lyran," said Alen, apparently almost overcome, "I shall not easily forget your combination of acumen and charity. It is a lesson to traders. It is a lesson to me. I shall *not* insist on two thousand. I shall cut the throat of my trader's venture by reducing his price to eighteen hundred credits, though I wonder how I shall dare tell him of it."

"What's going on now?" demanded blackbeard.

"Five hundred and eighteen hundred," said Alen. "We can sit down again."

"Up, down—up, down," muttered the trader.

They sat, and Alen said in Lyran: "My trader unexpectedly indorses the reduction. He says, 'Better to lose some than all'—an old proverb in the Cephean tongue. And he forbids any further reduction."

"Come, now," wheedled the gem dealer. "Let us be men of the world about this. One must give a little and take a little. Everybody knows he can't have his own way forever. I shall offer a good, round eight hundred credits and we'll close on it, eh? Pilquis, fetch us a pen and ink!" One of the burly guards was right there with an inkpot and a reed pen. Garthkint had a Customs form out of his tunic and was busily filling it in to specify the size, number and fire of gems to be released to him.

"What's it now?" asked blackbeard.

"Eight hundred."

"Take it!"

"Garthkint," said Alen regretfully, "you heard the firmness and decision in my trader's voice? What can I do? I am only speaking for him. He is a hard man but perhaps I call talk him around later. I offer you the gems at a ruinous fifteen hundred credits."

"Split the difference," said Garthkint resignedly.

"Done at eleven-fifty," said Alen.

That blackbeard understood. "Well done!" he boomed at Alen and took a swig at Garthkint's winecup. "Have him fill in 'Sack eighteen' on his paper. It's five hundred of that grade."

The gem dealer counted out twenty-three fifty-credit notes and blackbeard signed and fingerprinted the release.

"Now," said Garthkint, "you will please remain here while I take a trip to the spaceport for my property." Three or four of the guards were suddenly quite close.

"You will find," said Alen dryly, "that our standard of commercial morality is no lower than yours."

The dealer smiled politely and left.

"Who will be the next?" asked Alen of the room at large.

"I'll look at your gems," said another dealer, sitting at the table.

With the ice-breaking done, the transactions went quicker. Alen had disposed of a dozen lots by the time their first buyer returned.

"It's all right," he said. "We've been tricked before, but your gems are as represented. I congratulate you, Herald, on driving a hard, fair bargain."

"That means," said Alen regretfully, "that I should have asked for more." The guards were once more lounging in corners and no longer seemed so menacing.

They had a mid-day meal and continued to dispose of their wares. At sunset Alen held a final auction to clean up the odd lots that remained over and was urged to stay to dinner.

The trader, counting a huge wad of the Lyran manpower-based notes, shook his head. "We should be off before dawn, Herald," he told Alen. "Time is money, time is money."

"They are very insistent."

"And I am very stubborn. Thank them and let us be on our way before anything else is done to increase my overhead."

Something did turn up—a city watchman with a bloody nose and split lip.

He demanded of the Herald: "Are you responsible for the Cephean maniac known as Elwon?"

Garthkint glided up to mutter in Alen's ear: "Beware how you answer!"

Alen needed no warning. His grounding included Lyran legal concepts— and on the backward little planet touched with many relics of feudalism "responsible" covered much territory.

"What has Chief Elwon done?" he parried.

"As you see," the watchman glumly replied, pointing to his wounds. "And the same to three others before we got him out of the wrecked wineshop and into the castle. Are you responsible for him?"

"Let me speak with my trader for a moment. Will you have some wine meantime?" He signaled and one of the guards brought a mug.

"Don't mind if I do. I can use it," sighed the watchman.

"We are in trouble," said Alen to blackbeard. "Chief Elwon is in the 'castle'— prison—for drunk and disorderly conduct. You as his master are considered responsible for his conduct under Lyran law. You must pay his fines or serve his penalties. Or you can 'disown' him, which is considered dishonorable but sometimes necessary. For paying his fine or serving his time you have a prior lien on his services, without pay—but of course that's unenforceable off Lyra."

Blackbeard was sweating a little. "Find out from the policeman how long all this is likely to take. I don't want to leave Elwon here and I do want us to get off as soon as possible. Keep him occupied, now, while I go about some business."

The trader retreated to a corner of the darkening barnlike tavern, beckoning Garthkint and a guard with him as Alen returned to the watchman.

"Good keeper of the peace," he said, "will you have another?"

He would.

"My trader wishes to know what penalties are likely to be levied against the unfortunate Chief Elwon."

"Going to leave him in the lurch, eh?" asked the watchman a little belligerently. "A fine master you have!"

One of the dealers at the table indignantly corroborated him. "If you foreigners aren't prepared to live up to your obligations, why did you come here in the first place? What happens to business if a master can send his man to steal and cheat and then say: 'Don't blame *me*—it was *his* doing!'"

Alen patiently explained: "On other planets, good Lyrans, the tie of master and man is not so strong that a man would obey if he were ordered to go and steal or cheat."

They shook their heads and muttered. It was unheard-of.

"Good watchman," pressed the Herald, "my trader does not *want* to disown Chief Elwon. Can you tell me what recompense would be necessary—and how long it would take to manage the business?"

The watchman started on a third cup which Alen had unostentatiously signaled for. "It's hard to say," he told the Herald weightily. "For my damages, I would demand a hundred credits at least. The three other members of the watch battered by your lunatic could ask no less. The wineshop suffered easily five hundred credits' damage. The owner of it was beaten, but that doesn't matter, of course."

"No imprisonment?"

"Oh, a flogging, of course"—Alen started before he recalled that the "flogging" was a few half-hearted symbolic strokes on the covered shoulders with a light cane—"but no imprisonment. His Honor, Judge Krarl, does not sit on the night bench. Judge Krarl is a newfangled reformer, stranger. He professes to believe that mulcting is unjust—that it makes it easy for the rich to commit crime and go scot-free."

"But doesn't it?" asked Alen, drawn off-course in spite of himself. There was pitying laughter around him.

"Look you," a dealer explained kindly. "The good watchman suffers battery, the mad Cephean or his master is mulcted for damages, the watchman is repaid for his injuries. What kind of justice is it to the watchman if the mad Cephean is locked away in a cell unfined?"

The watchman nodded approvingly. "Well said," he told the dealer. "Luckily we have on the night bench a justice of the old school, His Honor, Judge Treel. Stern, but fair. You should hear him! 'Fifty credits! A hundred credits and the lash! Robbed a ship, eh? Two thousand credits!'" He returned to his own voice and said with awe: "For a murder, he never assesses less than *ten thousand credits!*"

And if the murderer couldn't pay, Alen knew, he became a "public charge," "responsible to the state"—that is, a slave. If he could pay, of course, he was turned loose.

"And His Honor, Judge Treel," he pressed, "is sitting tonight? Can we possibly appear before him, pay the fines and be off?"

"To be sure, stranger. I'd be a fool if I waited until morning, wouldn't I?" The wine had loosened his tongue a little too far and he evidently realized it. "Enough of this," he said. "Does your master honorably accept responsibility for the Cephean? If so, come along with me, the two of you, and we'll get this over with."

"Thanks, good watchman. We are coming."

He went to blackbeard, now alone in his corner, and said: "It's all right. We can pay off—about a thousand credits—and be on our way."

The trader muttered darkly: "Lyran jurisdiction or not, it's coming out of Elwon's pay. The bloody fool!"

They rattled through the darkening streets of the town in one of the turbine-powered wagons, the watchman sitting up front with the driver, and the trader and the Herald behind.

"Something's burning," said Alen to the trader, sniffing the air.

"This stinking buggy—" began blackbeard. "Oops," he said, interrupting himself and slapping at his cloak.

"Let me, trader," said Alen. He turned back the cloak, licked his thumb and rubbed out a crawling ring of sparks spreading across a few centimeters of the cloak's silk lining. And he looked fixedly at what had started the little fire. It was an improperly covered slow-match protruding from a holstered device that was unquestionably a hand weapon.

"I bought it from one of their guards while you were parleying with the policeman," explained blackbeard embarrassedly. "I had a time making him understand. That Garthkint fellow helped." He fiddled with the perforated cover of the slow-match, screwing it on more firmly.

"A pitiful excuse for a weapon," he went on, carefully arranging his cloak over it. "The trigger isn't a trigger and the thumb-safety isn't a safety. You pump the trigger a few times to build up pressure, and a little air squirts out to blow the match to life. Then you uncover the match and pull back the cocking-piece. This levers a dart into the barrel. *Then* you push the thumb-safety, which puffs coaldust into the firing chamber and also swivels down the slow-match onto a touch-hole. *Poof,* and away goes the dart if you didn't forget any of the steps or do them in the wrong order. Luckily, I also got a knife."

He patted the nape of his neck and said, "That's where they carry 'em here. A little sheath between the shoulderblades—wonderful for a fast draw-and-throw, though it exposes you a little more than I like when you reach. The knife's black glass. Splendid edge and good balance.

"And the thieving Lyrans knew they had me where it hurt. Seven thousand, five hundred credits for the knife and gun—if you can call it that—and the holsters. By rights I should dock Elwon for them, the bloody fool. Still, it's better to buy his way out and leave no hard feelings behind us, eh, Herald?"

"Incomparably better," said Alen. "And I am amazed that you even entertained the idea of an armed jail-delivery. What if Chief Elwon had to serve a few days in a prison? Would that be worse than forever barring yourself from the planet and blackening the names of all traders with Lyra? Trader, do not hope to put down the credits that your weapons cost you as a legitimate expense of the voyage. I will not allow it when I audit your books. It was a piece of folly on which you spent personal funds, as far as the College and Order of Heralds is concerned."

"Look here," protested blackbeard, "you're supposed to be spreading utilitarian civilization, aren't you? What's utilitarian about leaving one of my crewmen here?"

Alen ignored the childish argument and wrapped himself in angry silence. As to civilization, he wondered darkly whether such a trading voyage and his part in it was relevant at all. Were the slanders true? Was the College and Order simply a collection of dupes headed by cynical oldsters greedy for luxury and power?

Such thoughts hadn't crossed his mind in a long time. He'd been too busy to entertain them, cramming his head with languages, folkways, mores, customs, underlying patterns of culture, of hundreds of galactic peoples—and for what? So that this fellow could make a profit and the College and Order take a quarter of that profit. If civilization was to come to Lyra, it would have to come in the form of metal. If the Lyrans didn't want metal, *make* them take it.

What did Machiavelli say? "The chief foundations of all states are good laws and good arms; and as there cannot be good laws where the state is not well-armed, it follows that where they are well-armed, they have good laws." It was odd that the teachers had slurred over such a seminal idea, emphasizing instead the spiritual integrity of the weaponless College and Order—or was it?

The disenchantment he felt creeping over him was terrifying.

"The castle," said the watchman over his shoulder, and their wagon stopped with a rattle before a large but unimpressive brick structure of five stories.

"You wait," the trader told the driver after they got out. He handed him two of his fifty-credit bills. "You wait, you get many, many more money. You understand, wait?"

"I wait plenty much," shouted the driver delightedly. "I wait all night, all day. You wonderful master. You great, great master, I wait—"

"All right," growled the trader, shutting him off. "You wait."

The watchman took them through an entrance hall lit by hissing pressure lamps and casually guarded by a few liveried men with truncheons. He threw open the door of a medium-sized, well-lit room with a score of people in it, looked in, and uttered a despairing groan.

A personage on a chair that looked like a throne said sharply, "Are those the star-travelers? Well, don't just stand there. Bring them in!"

"Yes, Your Honor, Judge Krarl," said the watchman unhappily.

"It's the wrong judge!" Alen hissed at the trader. "This one gives out jail sentences!"

"Do what you can," said blackbeard grimly.

The watchman guided them to the personage in the chair and indicated a couple of low stools, bowed to the chair and retired to stand at the back of the room.

"Your honor," said Alen, "I am Journeyman-Herald Alen, Herald for the trading voyage—"

"Speak when you're spoken to," said the judge sharply. "Sir, with the usual insolence of wealth you have chosen to keep us waiting. I do not take this personally; it might have happened to Judge Treel, who—to your evident dismay—I am replacing because of a sudden illness, or to any other member of the bench. But as an insult to our justice, we cannot overlook it. Sir, consider yourself reprimanded. Take your seats. Watchman, bring in the Cephean."

"Sit down," Alen murmured to the trader. "This is going to be bad."

A watchman brought in Chief Elwon, bleary-eyed, tousled and sporting a few bruises. He gave Alen and the trader a shamefaced grin as his guard sat him on a stool beside them. The trader glared back.

Judge Krarl mumbled perfunctorily: "Letbattlebejoinedamongtheseveral-partiesinthisdisputeletnomanquestionourimpartialawardingofthevictoryspeak-nowifyouyieldinsteadtoourjudgment. *Well?* Speak up, you watchmen!"

The watchman who had brought the Herald and the trader started and said from the back of the room: "Iyieldinsteadtoyourhonorsjudgment."

Three other watchmen and a battered citizen, the wineshop keeper, mumbled in turn: "Iyieldinsteadtoyourhonorsjudgment."

"Herald, speak for the accused," snapped the judge.

Well, thought Alen, I can try. "Your Honor," he said, "Chief Elwon's master does not yield to your honor's judgment. He is ready to battle the other parties in the dispute or their masters."

"What insolence is this?" screamed the judge, leaping from his throne. "The barbarous customs of other worlds do not prevail in this court! Who spoke of battle—?" He shut his mouth with a snap, evidently abruptly realizing that *he* had spoken of battle, in an archaic phrase that harked back to the origins of justice on the planet. The judge sat down again and told Alen, more calmly: "You have mistaken a mere formality. The offer was not made in earnest." Obviously, he didn't like the sound of that himself, but he proceeded, "Now say 'Iyieldinsteadtoyour-honorsjudgment!' and we can get on with it. For your information, trial by combat has not been practiced for many generations on our enlightened planet."

Alen said politely: "Your Honor, I am a stranger to many of the ways of Lyra, but our excellent College and Order of Heralds instructed me well in the underlying principles of your law. I recall that one of your most revered legal maxims declares: 'The highest crime against man is murder; the highest crime against man's society is breach of promise.'"

Purpling, the judge snarled: "Are you presuming to bandy law with me, you slippery-tongued foreigner? Are you presuming to accuse me of the high crime of breaking my promise? For your information, a promise consists of an offer to do, or refrain from doing, a thing in return for a consideration. There must be the five elements of promiser, promisee, offer, substance, and consideration."

"If you will forgive a foreigner," said Alen, suddenly feeling the ground again under his feet, "I maintain that you offered the parties in the dispute your services in awarding the victory."

"An empty argument," snorted the judge. "Just as an offer with substance from somebody to nobody for a consideration is no promise, or an offer without substance from somebody to somebody for a consideration is no promise, so my offer was no promise, for there was no consideration involved."

"Your honor, must the consideration be from the promisee to the promiser?"

"Of course not. A third party may provide the consideration."

"Then I respectfully maintain that your offer was a promise, since a third party, the government, provided you with the considerations of salary and position in return for you offering your services to the disputants."

"Watchmen, clear the room of uninterested persons," said the judge hoarsely. While it was being done, Alen swiftly filled in the trader and Chief Elwon. Blackbeard grinned at the mention of a five-against-one battle royal, and the engineer looked alarmed.

When the doors closed leaving the nine of them in privacy, the judge said bitterly: "Herald, where did you learn such devilish tricks?"

Alen told him: "My College and Order instructed me well. A similar situation existed on a planet called England during an age known as the Victorious. Trial by combat had long been obsolete, there as here, but had never been declared so—there as here. A litigant won a hopeless lawsuit by publishing a challenge to his opponent and appearing at the appointed place in full armor. His opponent ignored the challenge and so lost the suit by default. The English dictator, one Disraeli, hastily summoned his parliament to abolish trial by combat."

"And so," mused the judge, "I find myself accused in my own chamber of high crime if I do not permit you five to slash away at each other and decide who won."

The wineshop keeper began to blubber that he was a peaceable man and didn't intend to be carved up by that black-bearded, bloodthirsty star-traveler. All he wanted was his money.

"Silence!" snapped the judge. "Of course there will be no combat. Will you, shopkeeper, and you watchmen, withdraw if you receive satisfactory financial settlements?"

They would.

"Herald, you may dicker with them."

The four watchmen stood fast by their demand for a hundred credits apiece, and got it. The terrified shopkeeper regained his balance and demanded a thousand. Alen explained that his black-bearded master from a rude and impetuous world might be unable to restrain his rage when he, Alen, interpreted the demand and, ignoring the consequences, might beat him, the shopkeeper, to a pulp. The asking price plunged to a reasonable five hundred, which was paid over. The shopkeeper got the judge's permission to leave and backed out, bowing.

"You see, trader," Alen told blackbeard, "that it was needless to buy weapons when the spoken word—"

"And now," said the judge with a sneer, "we are easily out of *that* dilemma. Watchmen, arrest the three star-travelers and take them to the cages."

"Your honor!" cried Alen, outraged.

"Money won't get you out of *this* one. I charge you with treason."

"The charge is obsolete—" began the Herald hotly, but he broke off as he realized the vindictive strategy.

"Yes, it is. And one of its obsolete provisions is that treason charges must be tried by the parliament at a regular session, which isn't due for two hundred days. You'll be freed and I may be reprimanded, but by my head, for two hundred days you'll regret that you made a fool of *me*. Take them away."

"A trumped up charge against us. Prison for two hundred days," said Alen swiftly to the trader as the watchmen closed in.

"Why buy weapons?" mocked the blackbeard, showing his teeth. His left arm whipped up and down, there was a black streak through the air—and the judge was pinned to his throne with a black glass knife through his throat and the sneer of triumph still on his lips.

The trader, before the knife struck, had the clumsy pistol out, with the cover off the glowing match and the cocking-piece back. He must have pumped and cocked it under his cloak, thought Alen numbly as he told the watchmen, without prompting: "Get back against the wall and turn around." They did. They wanted to live, and the grinning blackbeard who had made meat of the judge with a flick of the arm was a terrifying figure.

"Well done, Alen," said the trader. "Take their clubs, Elwon. Two for you, two for the Herald. Alen, don't argue! I had to kill the judge before he raised an alarm—nothing but death will silence his breed. You may have to kill too before we're out of this. Take the clubs." He passed the clumsy pistol to Chief Elwon and said: "Keep it on their backs. The thing that looks like a thumb-safety is a trigger. Put a dart through the first one who tries to make a break. Alen, tell the fellow on the end to turn around and come to me slowly."

Alen did. Blackbeard swiftly stripped him, tore and knotted his clothes into ropes and bound and gagged him. The others got the same treatment in less than ten minutes.

The trader holstered the gun and rolled the watchmen out of the line of sight from the door of the chamber. He recovered his knife and wiped it on the judge's shirt. Alen had to help him prop the body behind the throne's high back.

"Hide those clubs," blackbeard said. "Straight faces. Here we go."

They went out, single file, opening the door only enough to pass. Alen, last in line, told one of the liveried guards nearby: "His honor, Judge Krarl, does not wish to be disturbed."

"That's news?" asked the tipstaff sardonically. He put his hand on the Herald's arm. "Only yesterday he gimme a blast when I brought him a mug of water he asked me for himself. An outrageous interruption, he called me, and he asked for the water himself. What do you think of that?"

"Terrible," said Alen hastily. He broke away and caught up with the trader and the engineer at the entrance hall. Idlers and loungers were staring at them as they headed for the waiting wagon.

"I wait!" the driver told them loudly. "I wait long, much. You pay more, more?"

"We pay more," said the trader. "You start."

The driver brought out a smoldering piece of punk, lit a pressure torch, lifted the barn-door section of the wagon's floor to expose the pottery turbine and pre-heated it with the torch. He pumped squeakily for minutes, spinning a flywheel with his other hand, before the rotor began to turn on its own. Down went the hatch, up onto the seats went the passengers.

"The spaceport," said Alen. With a slate-pencil screech the driver engaged his planetary gear and they were off.

Through it all, blackbeard had ignored frantic muttered questions from Chief Elwon, who had wanted nothing to do with murder, especially of a judge. "You sit up there," growled the trader, "and every so often you look around and see if we're being followed. Don't alarm the driver. And if we get to the spaceport and blast off without any trouble, keep your story to yourself." He settled down in the back seat with Alen and maintained a gloomy silence. The young Herald was too much in awe of this stranger, so suddenly competent in assorted forms of violence, to question him.

They did get to the spaceport without trouble, and found the crew in the Customs shed, emptied of the gems by dealers with releases. They had built a fire for warmth.

"We wish to leave immediately," said the trader to the port officer. "Can you change my Lyran currency?"

The officer began to sputter apologetically that it was late and the vault was sealed for the night—

"That's all right. We'll change it on Vega. It'll get back to you. Call off your guards and unseal our ship."

They followed the port officer to *Starsong*'s dim bulk out on the field. The officer cracked the seal on her with his club in the light of a flaring pressure lamp held by one of the guards.

Alen was sweating hard through it all. As they started across the field he had seen what looked like two closely spaced green stars low on the horizon towards town suddenly each jerk up and towards each other in minute arcs. The semaphore!

The signal officer in the port administration building would be watching too—but nobody on the field, preoccupied with the routine of departure, seemed to have noticed.

The lights flipped this way and that. Alen didn't know the code and bitterly regretted the lack. After some twenty signals the lights flipped to the "rest" position again as the port officer was droning out a set of take-off regulations: bearing, height above settled areas, permissible atomic fuels while in atmosphere—Alen saw somebody start across the field toward them from the administration building. The guards were leaning on their long, competent-looking weapons.

Alen inconspicuously detached himself from the group around *Starsong* and headed across the dark field to meet the approaching figure. Nearing it, he called out a low greeting in Lyran, using the noncom-to-officer military form.

"Sergeant," said the signal officer quietly, "go and draw off the men a few meters from the star-travelers. Tell them the ship mustn't leave, that they're to cover the foreigners and shoot if—"

Alen stood dazedly over the limp body of the signal officer. And then he quickly hid the bludgeon again and strolled back to the ship, wondering whether he'd cracked the Lyran's skull.

The port was open by then and the crew filing in. He was last. "Close it fast," he told the trader. "I had to—"

"I saw you," grunted blackbeard. "A semaphore message?" He was working as he spoke, and the metal port closed.

"Astrogator and engineer, take over," he told them.

"All hands to their bunks," ordered Astrogator Hufner. "Blast-off immediate."

Alen took to his cubicle and strapped himself in. Blast-off deafened him, rattled his bones and made him thoroughly sick as usual. After what seemed like several wretched hours, they were definitely space-borne under smooth acceleration, and his nausea subsided.

Blackbeard knocked, came in, and unbuckled him.

"Ready to audit the books of the voyage?" asked the trader.

"No," said Alen feebly.

"It can wait," said the trader. "The books are the least important part, anyway. We have headed off a frightful war."

"War? We have?"

"You wondered why I was in such haste to get off Lyra, and why I wouldn't leave Elwon there. It is because our Vegan gems were most unusual gems. I am not a technical man, but I understand they are actual gems which were treated to produce a certain effect at just about this time."

Blackbeard glanced at his wrist chronometer and said dreamily: "Lyra is getting metal. Wherever there is one of our gems, pottery is decomposing into its constituent aluminum, silicon and oxygen. Fluxes and glazes are decomposing into calcium, zinc, barium, potassium, chromium *and iron*. Buildings are crumbling, pants are dropping as ceramic belt-buckles disintegrate—"

"It means chaos!" protested Alen.

"It means civilization and peace. An ugly clash was in the making." Blackbeard paused and added deliberately: "Where neither their property nor their honor is touched, most men live content."

"*The Prince*, Chapter 19. You are—"

"There was another important purpose to the voyage," said the trader, grinning. "You will be interested in this." He handed Alen a document which, unfolded, had the seal of the College and Order at its head.

Alen read in a daze: "Examiner 19 to the Rector—final clearance of Novice—"

He lingered pridefully over the paragraph that described how he had "with coolness and great resource" foxed the battle cruiser of the Realm, "adapting himself readily in a delicate situation requiring not only physical courage but swift recall, evaluation and application of a minor planetary culture."

Not so pridefully he read: "—inclined towards pomposity of manner somewhat ludicrous in one of his years, though not unsuccessful in dominating the crew by his bearing—"

And: "—highly profitable disposal of our gems; a feat of no mean importance, since the College and Order must, after all, maintain itself."

And: "—cleared the final and critical hurdle with some mental turmoil if I am any judge, but did clear it. After some twenty years of indoctrination in unrealistic non-violence, the youth was confronted with a situation where nothing but violence would serve, correctly evaluated this, and applied violence in the form of a truncheon to the head of a Lyran signal officer, thereby demonstrating an ability to learn and common sense as precious as it is rare."

And, finally, simply: "Recommended for training."

"Training?" gasped Alen. "You mean there's more?"

"Not for most, boy. Not for most. The bulk of us are what we seem to be: oily, gun-shy, indispensable adjuncts to trade who feather our nest with percentages. We need those percentages and we need gun-shy Heralds."

Alen recited slowly: "Among other evils which being unarmed brings you, it causes you to be despised."

"Chapter 14," said blackbeard mechanically. "We leave such clues lying by their bedsides for twenty years, and they never notice them. For the few of us who do—more training."

"Will I learn to throw a knife like you?" asked Alen, repelled and fascinated at once by the idea.

"On your own time, if you wish. Mostly it's ethics and morals so you'll be able to weigh the values of such things as knife-throwing."

"Ethics! Morals!"

"We started as missionaries, you know."

"Everybody knows that. But the Great Utilitarian Reform—"

"Some of us," said blackbeard dryly, "think it was neither great, nor utilitarian, nor a reform."

It was a staggering idea. "But we're spreading utilitarian civilization!" protested Alen. "Or if we're not, what's the sense of it all?"

Blackbeard told him: "We have our different motives. One is a sincere utilitarian; another is a gambler—happy when he's in danger and his pulses are pounding. Another is proud and likes to trick people. More than a few conceive themselves as servants of mankind. I'll let you rest for a bit now." He rose.

"But you?" asked Alen hesitantly.

"Me? You will find me in Chapter Twenty-Six," grinned blackbeard. "And perhaps you'll find someone else." He closed the door behind him.

Alen ran through the chapter in his mind, puzzled, until—that was it.

It had a strange and inevitable familiarity to it as if he had always known that he would be saying it aloud, welcomingly, in this cramped cubicle aboard a battered starship:

"God is not willing to do everything, and thus take away our free will and that share of glory which belongs to us."

[*Space SF* - May 1953]

The Adventurer

President Folsom XXIV said petulantly to his Secretary of the Treasury: "Blow me to hell, Bannister, if I understood a single word of that. *Why* can't I buy the Nicolaides Collection? And don't start with the rediscount and the Series W business again. Just tell me *why*."

The Secretary of the Treasury said with an air of apprehension and a thread-like feeling across his throat: "It boils down to—no money, Mr. President."

The President was too engrossed in thoughts of the marvelous collection to fly into a rage. "It's *such* a bargain," he said mournfully. "An archaic Henry Moore figure—really too big to finger, but I'm no culture-snob, thank God—and fifteen early Morrisons and I can't begin to tell you what else." He looked hopefully at the Secretary of Public Opinion: "Mightn't I seize it for the public good or something?"

The Secretary of Public Opinion shook his head. His pose was gruffly professional. "Not a chance, Mr. President. We'd never get away with it. The art-lovers would scream to high heaven."

"I suppose so ... *Why* isn't there any money?" He had swiveled dangerously on the Secretary of the Treasury again.

"Sir, purchases of the new Series W bond issue have lagged badly because potential buyers have been attracted to—"

"Stop it, stop it, *stop* it! You know I can't make head or tail of that stuff. Where's the money *going?*"

The Director of the Budget said cautiously: "Mr. President, during the biennium just ending, the Department of Defense accounted for 78 percent of expenditures—"

The Secretary of Defense growled: "Now wait a minute, Felder! We were voted—"

The President interrupted, raging weakly: "Oh, you rascals! My father would have known what to do with you! But don't think I can't handle it. *Don't* think you can hoodwink me." He punched a button ferociously; his silly face was contorted with rage and there was a certain tension on all the faces around the Cabinet table.

24

Panels slid down abruptly in the walls, revealing grim-faced Secret Servicemen. Each Cabinet officer was covered by at least two automatic rifles.

"Take that—that traitor away!" the President yelled. His finger pointed at the Secretary of Defense, who slumped over the table, sobbing. Two Secret Servicemen half-carried him from the room.

President Folsom XXIV leaned back, thrusting out his lower lip. He told the Secretary of the Treasury: "*Get* me the money for the Nicolaides Collection. Do you understand? I don't care how you do it. *Get* it." He glared at the Secretary of Public Opinion. "Have you any comments?"

"No, Mr. President."

"All right, then." The President unbent and said plaintively: "I don't see why you can't all be more reasonable. I'm a very reasonable man. I don't see why I can't have a few pleasures along with my responsibilities. Really I don't. And I'm sensitive. I don't *like* these scenes. Very well. That's all. The Cabinet meeting is adjourned."

They rose and left silently in the order of their seniority. The President noticed that the panels were still down and pushed the button that raised them again and hid the granite-faced Secret Servicemen. He took out of his pocket a late Morrison fingering-piece and turned it over in his hand, a smile of relaxation and bliss spreading over his face. *Such* amusing textural contrast! *Such* unexpected variations on the classic sequences!

The Cabinet, less the Secretary of Defense, was holding a rump meeting in an untapped corner of the White House gymnasium.

"God," the Secretary of State said, white-faced. "Poor old Willy!"

The professionally gruff Secretary of Public Opinion said: "We should murder the bastard. I don't care what happens—"

The Director of the Budget said dryly: "We all know what would happen. President Folsom XXV would take office. No; we've got to keep plugging as before. Nothing short of the invincible can topple the Republic ..."

"What about a war?" the Secretary of Commerce demanded fiercely. "We've no proof that our program will work. What about a war?"

State said wearily: "Not while there's a balance of power, my dear man. The Io-Callisto Question proved that. The Republic and the Soviet fell all over themselves trying to patch things up as soon as it seemed that there would be real shooting. Folsom XXIV and his excellency Premier Yersinsky know at least that much."

The Secretary of the Treasury said: "What would you all think of Steiner for Defense?"

The Director of the Budget was astonished. "Would he take it?"

Treasury cleared his throat. "As a matter of fact, I've asked him to stop by right about now." He hurled a medicine ball into the budgetary gut.

"Oof!" said the Director. "You bastard. Steiner would be perfect. He runs Standards like a watch." He treacherously fired the medicine ball at the Secretary of Raw Materials, who blandly caught it and slammed it back.

"Here he comes," said the Secretary of Raw Materials. "Steiner! Come and sweat some oleo off!"

Steiner ambled over, a squat man in his fifties, and said: "I don't mind if I do. Where's Willy?"

State said: "The President unmasked him as a traitor. He's probably been executed by now."

Steiner looked grim, and grimmer yet when the Secretary of the Treasury said, dead-pan: "We want to propose you for Defense."

"I'm happy in Standards," Steiner said. "Safer, too. The Man's father took an interest in science, but The Man never comes around. Things are very quiet. Why don't you invite Winch, from the National Art Commission? It wouldn't be much of a change for the worse for him."

"No brains," the Secretary for Raw Materials said briefly. "Heads up!"

Steiner caught the ball and slugged it back at him. "What good are brains?" he asked quietly.

"Close the ranks, gentlemen," State said. "These long shots are too hard on my arms."

The ranks closed and the Cabinet told Steiner what good were brains. He ended by accepting.

The Moon is all Republic. Mars is all Soviet. Titan is all Republic. Ganymede is all Soviet. But Io and Callisto, by the Treaty of Greenwich, are half-and-half Republic and Soviet.

Down the main street of the principal settlement on Io runs an invisible line. On one side of the line, the principal settlement is known as New Pittsburgh. On the other side it is known as Nizhni-Magnitogorsk.

Into a miner's home in New Pittsburgh one day an eight-year-old boy named Grayson staggered, bleeding from the head. His eyes were swollen almost shut.

His father lurched to his feet, knocking over a bottle. He looked stupidly at the bottle, set it upright too late to save much of the alcohol, and then stared fixedly at the boy. "See what you made me do, you little bastard?" he growled, and fetched the boy a clout on his bleeding head that sent him spinning against the wall of the hut. The boy got up slowly and silently—there seemed to be something wrong with his left arm—and glowered at his father.

He said nothing.

"Fighting again," the father said, in a would-be fierce voice. His eyes fell under the peculiar fire in the boy's stare. "Damn fool—"

A woman came in from the kitchen. She was tall and thin. In a flat voice she said to the man: "Get out of here." The man hiccupped and said: "Your brat spilled my bottle. Gimme a dollar."

In the same flat voice: "I have to buy food."

"I said gimme a dollar!" The man slapped her face—it did not change—and wrenched a small purse from the string that suspended it around her neck. The boy suddenly was a demon, flying at his father with fists and teeth. It lasted only a second or two. The father kicked him into a corner where he lay, still glaring, wordless and dry-eyed. The mother had not moved; her husband's handmark was still red on her face when he hulked out, clutching the money bag.

Mrs. Grayson at last crouched in the corner with the eight-year-old boy. "Little Tommy," she said softly. "My little Tommy! Did you cross the line again?"

He was blubbering in her arms, hysterically, as she caressed him. At last he was able to say: "I didn't cross the line, Mom. Not this time. It was in school. They said our name was really Krasinsky. God-damn him!" the boy shrieked. "They said his grandfather was named Krasinsky and he moved over the line and changed his name to Grayson! God-damn him! Doing that to us!"

"Now, darling," his mother said, caressing him. "Now, darling." His trembling began to ebb. She said: "Let's get out the spools, Tommy. You mustn't fall behind in school. You owe that to me, don't you, darling?"

"Yes, Mom," he said. He threw his spindly arms around her and kissed her. "Get out the spools. We'll show him. I mean them."

President Folsom XXIV lay on his death-bed, feeling no pain, mostly because his personal physician had pumped him full of morphine. Dr. Barnes sat by the bed holding the presidential wrist and waiting, occasionally nodding off and recovering with a belligerent stare around the room. The four wire-service men didn't care whether he fell asleep or not; they were worriedly discussing the nature and habits of the President's first-born, who would shortly succeed to the highest office in the Republic.

"A firebrand, they tell me," the A.P. man said unhappily.

"Firebrands I don't mind," the U.P. man said. "He can send out all the inflammatory notes he wants just as long as he isn't a fiend for exercise. I'm not as young as I once was. You boys wouldn't remember the *old* President, Folsom XXII. He used to do point-to-point hiking. He worshipped old F.D.R."

The I.N.S. man said, lowering his voice: "Then he was worshipping the wrong Roosevelt. Teddy was the athlete."

Dr. Barnes started, dropped the presidential wrist and held a mirror to the mouth for a moment. "Gentlemen," he said, "the President is dead."

"O.K.," the A.P. man said. "Let's go, boys. I'll send in the flash. U.P., you go cover the College of Electors. I.N.S., get onto the President-Elect. Trib, collect some interviews and background—"

The door opened abruptly; a colonel of infantry was standing there, breathing hard, with an automatic rifle at port. "Is he dead?" he asked.

"Yes," the A.P. man said. "If you'll let me past—"

"Nobody leaves the room," the colonel said grimly. "I represent General Slocum, Acting President of the Republic. The College of Electors is acting now to ratify—"

A burst of gunfire caught the colonel in the back; he spun and fell, with a single hoarse cry. More gunfire sounded through the White House. A Secret Serviceman ducked his head through the door: "President's dead? You boys stay put. We'll have this thing cleaned up in an hour—" He vanished.

The doctor sputtered his alarm and the newsmen ignored him with professional poise. The A.P. man asked: "Now who's Slocum? Defense Command?"

I.N.S. said: "I remember him. Three stars. He headed up the Tactical Air-borne Force out in Kansas four-five years ago. I think he was retired since then."

A phosphorus grenade crashed through the window and exploded with a globe of yellow flame the size of a basketball; dense clouds of phosphorus pentox-ide gushed from it and the sprinkler system switched on, drenching the room.

"Come on!" hacked the A.P. man, and they scrambled from the room and slammed the door. The doctor's coat was burning in two or three places, and he was retching feebly on the corridor floor. They tore his coat off and flung it back into the room.

The U.P. man, swearing horribly, dug a sizzling bit of phosphorus from the back of his hand with a pen-knife and collapsed, sweating, when it was out. The I.N.S. man passed him a flask and he gurgled down half a pint of liquor. "Who flang that brick?" he asked faintly.

"Nobody," the A.P. man said gloomily. "That's the hell of it. None of this is happening. Just the way Taft the Pretender never happened in '03. Just the way the Pentagon Mutiny never happened in '67."

"'68," the U.P. man said faintly. "It didn't happen in '68, not '67."

The A.P. man smashed a fist into the palm of his hand and swore. "*God* damn," he said. "Some day I'd like to—" He broke off and was bitterly silent.

The U.P. man must have been a little dislocated with shock and quite drunk to talk the way he did. "Me too," he said. "Like to tell the story. Maybe it was '67, not '68. I'm not sure now. Can't write it down, so the details get lost and then after a while it didn't happen at all. Revolution'd be good deal. But it takes people t' make revolution. *People*. With eyes 'n ears. 'N memories. We make things not-happen an' we make people not-see an' not-hear ..." He slumped back against the corridor wall, nursing his burned hand. The others were watching him, very scared.

Then the A.P. man caught sight of the Secretary of Defense striding down the corridor, flanked by Secret Servicemen. "Mr. Steiner!" he called. "What's the picture?"

Steiner stopped, breathing heavily, and said: "Slocum's barricaded in the Oval Study. They don't want to smash in. He's about the only one left. There were only fifty or so. The Acting President's taken charge at the Study. You want to come along?"

They did, and even hauled the U.P. man after them.

The Acting President, who would be President Folsom XXV as soon as the Electoral College got around to it, had his father's face —the petulant lip, the soft jowl—on a hard young body. He also had an auto-rifle ready to fire from the hip. Most of the Cabinet was present. When the Secretary of Defense arrived, he turned on him. "Steiner," he said nastily, "can you explain why there should be a rebel-lion against the Republic in your department?"

"Mr. President," Steiner said, "Slocum was retired on my recommendation two years ago. It seems to me that my responsibility ended there and Security should have taken over."

The President-Elect's finger left the trigger of the auto-rifle and his lip drew in a little. "Quite so," he said curtly, and turned to the door. "Slocum!" he shouted. "Come out of there. We can use gas if we want."

The door opened unexpectedly and a tired-looking man with three stars on each shoulder stood there, bare-handed. "All right," he said drearily. "I was fool enough to think something could be done about the regime. But you fat-faced imbeciles are going to go on and on and—"

The stutter of the auto-rifle cut him off. The President-Elect's knuckles were white as he clutched the piece's forearm and grip; the torrent of slugs continued to hack and plow the general's body until the magazine was empty. "Burn that," he said curtly, turning his back on it. "Dr. Barnes, come here. I want to know about my father's passing."

The doctor, hoarse and red-eyed from the whiff of phosphorus smoke, spoke with him. The U.P. man had sagged drunkenly into a chair, but the other newsmen noted that Dr. Barnes glanced at them as he spoke, in a confidential murmur.

"Thank you, doctor," the President-Elect said at last, decisively. He gestured to a Secret Serviceman. "Take those traitors away." They went, numbly.

The Secretary of State cleared his throat. "Mr. President," he said, "I take this opportunity to submit the resignations of myself and fellow Cabinet members according to custom."

"That's all right," the President-Elect said. "You may as well stay on. I intend to run things myself anyway." He hefted the auto-rifle. "You," he said to the Secretary of Public Opinion. "You have some work to do. Have the memory of my father's—artistic—preoccupations obliterated as soon as possible. I wish the Republic to assume a warlike posture—yes; what is it?"

A trembling messenger said: "Mr. President, I have the honor to inform you that the College of Electors has elected you President of the Republic—unanimously."

Cadet Fourth Classman Thomas Grayson lay on his bunk and sobbed in an agony of loneliness. The letter from his mother was crumpled in his hand: "—prouder than words can tell of your appointment to the Academy. Darling, I hardly knew my grandfather but I know that you will serve as brilliantly as he did, to the eternal credit of the Republic. You must be brave and strong for my sake—"

He would have given everything he had or ever could hope to have to be back with her, and away from the bullying, sneering fellow-cadets of the Corps. He kissed the letter—and then hastily shoved it under his mattress as he heard footsteps.

He popped to a brace, but it was only his roommate Ferguson. Ferguson was from Earth, and rejoiced in the lighter Lunar gravity which was punishment to Grayson's Io-bred muscles.

"Rest, mister," Ferguson grinned.

"Thought it was night inspection."

"Any minute now. They're down the hall. Lemme tighten your bunk or you'll be in trouble—" Tightening the bunk he pulled out the letter and said, calfishly: "Ah-*hah!* Who is she?—" and opened it.

When the cadet officers reached the room they found Ferguson on the floor being strangled black in the face by spidery little Grayson. It took all three of them to pull him off. Ferguson went to the infirmary and Grayson went to the Commandant's office.

The Commandant glared at the cadet from under the most spectacular pair of eyebrows in the Service. "Cadet Grayson," he said, "explain what occurred."

"Sir, Cadet Ferguson began to read a letter from my mother without my permission."

"That is not accepted by the Corps as grounds for mayhem. Do you have anything further to say?"

"Sir, I lost my temper. All I thought of was that it was an act of disrespect to my mother and somehow to the Corps and the Republic too—that Cadet Ferguson was dishonoring the Corps."

Bushwah, the Commandant thought. *A snow job and a crude one.* He studied the youngster. He had never seen such a brace from an Io-bred fourth-classman. It must be torture to muscles not yet toughened up to even Lunar gravity. Five minutes more and the boy would have to give way, and serve him right for showing off.

He studied Grayson's folder. It was too early to tell about academic work, but the fourth-classman was a bear—or a fool—for extra duty. He had gone out for half a dozen teams and applied for membership in the exacting Math Club *and* Writing Club. The Commandant glanced up; Grayson was still in his extreme brace. The Commandant suddenly had the queer idea that Grayson could hold it until it killed him.

"One hundred hours of pack-drill," he barked, "to be completed before quarter-term. Cadet Grayson, if you succeed in walking off your tours, remember that there is a tradition of fellowship in the Corps which its members are expected to observe. Dismiss."

After Grayson's steel-sharp salute and exit the Commandant dug deeper into the folder. Apparently there was something wrong with the boy's left arm, but it had been passed by the examining team that visited Io. Most unusual. Most irregular. But nothing could be done about it now.

The President, softer now in body than on his election day, and infinitely more cautious, snapped: "It's all very well to create an incident. But where's the money to come from? Who wants the rest of Io anyway? And what will happen if there's war?"

Treasury said: "The hoarders will supply the money, Mr. President. A system of percentage-bounties for persons who report currency-hoarders, and then enforced purchase of a bond issue."

Raw Materials said: "We need that iron, Mr. President. We need it desperately."

State said: "All our evaluations indicate that the Soviet Premier would consider nothing less than armed invasion of his continental borders as occasion for all-out war. The consumer-goods party in the Soviet has gained immensely during the past five years and of course their armaments have suffered. Your shrewd directive to put the Republic in a warlike posture has borne fruit, Mr. President ..."

President Folsom XXV studied them narrowly. To him the need for a border incident culminating in a forced purchase of Soviet Io did not seem as pressing as they thought, but they were, after all, specialists. And there was no conceivable way they could benefit from it personally. The only alternative was that they were offering their professional advice and that it would be best to heed it. Still, there was a vague, nagging something ...

Nonsense, he decided. The spy dossiers on his Cabinet showed nothing but the usual. One had been blackmailed by an actress after an affair and railroaded her off the Earth. Another had a habit of taking bribes to advance favorite sons in civil and military service. And so on. The Republic could not suffer at their hands; the Republic and the dynasty were impregnable. You simply spied on everybody— including the spies—and ordered summary executions often enough to show that you meant it, and kept the public ignorant: deaf-dumb-blind ignorant. The spy system was simplicity itself; you had only to let things get as tangled and confused as possible until *nobody* knew who was who. The executions were literally no problem, for guilt or innocence made no matter. And mind-control when there were four newspapers, six magazines and three radio and television stations was a job for a handful of clerks.

No; the Cabinet couldn't be getting away with anything. The system was unbeatable.

President Folsom XXV said: "Very well. Have it done."

Mrs. Grayson, widow, of New Pittsburgh, Io, disappeared one night. It was in all the papers and on all the broadcasts. Some time later she was found dragging herself back across the line between Nizhni-Magnitogorsk and New Pittsburgh in sorry shape. She had a terrible tale to tell about what she had suffered at the hands and so forth of the Nizhni-Magnitogorskniks. A diplomatic note from the Republic to the Soviet was answered by another note which was answered by the dispatch of the Republic's First Fleet to Io which was answered by the dispatch of the Soviet's First and Fifth Fleets to Io.

The Republic's First Fleet blew up the customary deserted target hulk, fulminated over a sneak sabotage attack and moved in its destroyers. Battle was joined.

Ensign Thomas Grayson took over the command of his destroyer when its captain was killed on his bridge. An electrified crew saw the strange, brooding youngster perform prodigies of skill and courage, and responded to them. In one week of desultory action the battered destroyer had accounted for seven Soviet destroyers and a cruiser.

As soon as this penetrated to the flagship Grayson was decorated and given a flotilla. His weird magnetism extended to every officer and man aboard the seven craft. They struck like phantoms, cutting out cruisers and battlewagons in wild unorthodox actions that couldn't have succeeded but did—every time. Grayson was badly wounded twice, but his driving nervous energy carried him through.

He was decorated again and given the battlewagon of an ailing four-striper.

Without orders he touched down on the Soviet side of Io, led out a landing party of marines and bluejackets, cut through two regiments of Soviet infantry, and returned to his battlewagon with prisoners: the top civil and military administrators of Soviet Io.

They discussed him nervously aboard the flagship.

"He had a mystical quality, Admiral. His men would follow him into an atomic furnace. And—and I almost believe he could bring them through safely if he wanted to." The laugh was nervous.

"He doesn't look like much. But when he turns on the charm— watch out!"

"He's—he's a *winner*. Now I wonder what I mean by that?"

"I know what you mean. They turn up every so often. People who can't be stopped. People who have everything. Napoleons. Alexanders. Stalins. Up from nowhere."

"Suleiman. Hitler. Folsom I. Jenghiz Khan."

"Well, let's get it over with."

They tugged at their gold-braided jackets and signaled the honor guard.

Grayson was piped aboard, received another decoration and another speech. This time he made a speech in return.

President Folsom XXV, not knowing what else to do, had summoned his Cabinet. "Well?" he rasped at the Secretary of Defense.

Steiner said with a faint shrug: "Mr. President, there is nothing to be done. He has the fleet, he has the broadcasting facilities, he has the people."

"People!" snarled the President. His finger stabbed at a button and the wall panels snapped down to show the Secret Servicemen standing in their niches. The finger shot tremulously out at Steiner. "Kill that traitor!" he raved.

The chief of the detail said uneasily: "Mr. President, we were listening to Grayson before we came on duty. He says he's *de facto* President now—"

"Kill him! Kill him!"

The chief went doggedly on: "—and we liked what he had to say about the Republic and he said citizens of the Republic shouldn't take orders from you and he'd relieve you—"

The President fell back.

Grayson walked in, wearing his plain ensign's uniform and smiling faintly. Admirals and four-stripers flanked him.

The chief of the detail said: "Mr. Grayson! Are you taking over?"

The man in the ensign's uniform said gravely: "Yes. And just call me Grayson,' please. The titles come later. You can go now."

The chief gave a pleased grin and collected his detail. The rather slight, youngish man who had something wrong with one arm was in charge—*complete* charge.

Grayson said: "Mr. Folsom, you are relieved of the presidency. Captain, take him out and—" He finished with a whimsical shrug. A portly four-striper took Folsom by one arm. Like a drugged man the deposed president let himself be led out.

Grayson looked around the table. "Who are you gentlemen?"

They felt his magnetism, like the hum when you pass a power station.

Steiner was the spokesman. "Grayson," he said soberly, "we were Folsom's Cabinet. However, there is more that we have to tell you. Alone, if you will allow it."

"Very well, gentlemen." Admirals and captains backed out, looking concerned.

Steiner said: "Grayson, the story goes back many years. My predecessor, William Malvern, determined to overthrow the regime, holding that it was an affront to the human spirit. There have been many such attempts. All have broken up on the rocks of espionage, terrorism and opinion-control—the three weapons which the regime holds firmly in its hands.

"Malvern tried another approach than espionage versus espionage, terrorism versus terrorism, and opinion-control versus opinion-control. He determined to use the basic fact that certain men make history: that there are men born to be mold-breakers. They are the Philips of Macedon, the Napoleons, Stalins and Hitlers, the Suleimans—the adventurers. Again and again they flash across history, bringing down an ancient empire, turning ordinary soldiers of the line into unkillable demons of battle, uprooting cultures, breathing new life into moribund peoples.

"There are common denominators among all the adventurers. Intelligence, of course. Other things are more mysterious but are always present. They are foreigners. Napoleon the Corsican. Hitler the Austrian. Stalin the Georgian. Philip the Macedonian. Always there is an Œdipus complex. Always there is physical deficiency. Napoleon's stature. Stalin's withered arm—and yours. Always there is a minority disability, real or fancied.

"This is a shock to you, Grayson, but you must face it. *You were manufactured.*

"Malvern packed the Cabinet with the slyest double-dealers he could find and they went to work. Eighty-six infants were planted on the outposts of the Republic in simulated family environments. Your mother was not your mother but one of the most brilliant actresses ever to drop out of sight on Earth. Your intelligence-heredity was so good that we couldn't turn you down for lack of a physical deficiency. We withered your arm with gamma radiation. I hope you will forgive us. There was no other way.

"Of the eighty-six you are the one that worked. Somehow the combination for you was minutely different from all the other combinations, genetically or environmentally, and it worked. That is all we were after. The mold has been broken, you know now what you are. Let come whatever chaos is to come; the dead hand of the past no longer lies on—"

Grayson went to the door and beckoned; two captains came in. Steiner broke off his speech as Grayson said to them: "These men deny my godhood. Take them out and—" he finished with a whimsical shrug.

"Yes, your divinity," said the captains, without a trace of humor in their voices.

Dominoes

"Money!" his wife screamed at him. "You're killing yourself, Will. Pull out of the market and let's go some place where we can live like human—"

He slammed the apartment door on her reproaches and winced, standing in the carpeted corridor, as an ulcer twinge went through him. The elevator door rolled open and the elevator man said, beaming: "Good morning, Mr. Born. It's a lovely day today."

"I'm glad, Sam," W. J. Born said sourly. "I just had a lovely, lovely breakfast." Sam didn't know how to take it, and compromised by giving him a meager smile.

"How's the market look, Mr. Born?" he hinted as the car stopped on the first floor. "My cousin told me to switch from Lunar Entertainment, he's studying to be a pilot, but the *Journal* has it listed for growth."

W. J. Born grunted: "If I knew I wouldn't tell you. You've got no business in the market. Not if you think you can play it like a craps table."

He fumed all through his taxi ride to the office. Sam, a million Sams, had no business in the market. But they were in, and they had built up the Great Boom of 1975 on which W. J. Born Associates was coasting merrily along. For how long? His ulcer twinged again at the thought.

He arrived at 9:15. Already the office was a maelstrom. The clattering tickers, blinking boards and racing messengers spelled out the latest, hottest word from markets in London, Paris, Milan, Vienna. Soon New York would chime in, then Chicago, then San Francisco.

Maybe this would be the day. Maybe New York would open on a significant decline in Moon Mining and Smelting. Maybe Chicago would nervously respond with a slump in commodities and San Francisco's Utah Uranium would plummet in sympathy. Maybe panic in the Tokyo Exchange on the heels of the alarming news from the States—panic relayed across Asia with the rising sun to Vienna, Milan, Paris, London, and crashing like a shockwave into the opening New York market again.

Dominoes, W. J. Born thought. A row of dominoes. Flick one and they all topple in a heap. Maybe this would be the day.

35

Miss Illig had a dozen calls from his personal crash-priority clients penciled in on his desk pad already. He ignored them and said into her good-morning smile: "Get me Mr. Loring on the phone."

Loring's phone rang and rang while W. J. Born boiled inwardly. But the lab was a barn of a place, and when he was hard at work he was deaf and blind to distractions. You had to hand him that. He was screwy, he was insolent, he had an inferiority complex that stuck out a yard, but he was a worker.

Loring's insolent voice said in his ear: "Who's this?"

"Born," he snapped. "How's it going?"

There was a long pause, and Loring said casually: "I worked all night. I think I got it licked."

"What do you mean?"

Very irritated: "I said I think I got it licked. I sent a clock and a cat and a cage of white mice out for two hours. They came back okay."

"You mean—" W. J. Born began hoarsely, and moistened his lips. "How many years?" he asked evenly.

"The mice didn't say, but I think they spent two hours in 1977."

"I'm coming right over," W. J. Born snapped, and hung up. His office staff stared as he strode out.

If the man was lying—! No; he didn't lie. He'd been sopping up money for six months, ever since he bulled his way into Born's office with his time machine project, but he hadn't lied once. With brutal frankness he had admitted his own failures and his doubts that the thing ever would be made to work. But now, W. J. Born rejoiced, it had turned into the smartest gamble of his career. Six months and a quarter of a million dollars—a two-year forecast on the market was worth a billion! Four thousand to one, he gloated; four thousand to one! Two hours to learn when the Great Bull Market of 1975 would collapse and then back to his office armed with the information, ready to buy up to the very crest of the boom and then get out at the peak, wealthy forever, forever beyond the reach of fortune, good or bad!

He stumped upstairs to Loring's loft in the West Seventies.

Loring was badly overplaying the role of casual roughneck. Gangling, red-headed and unshaved, he grinned at Born and said: "Watcha think of soy futures, W. J.? Hold or switch?"

W. J. Born began automatically: "If I knew I wouldn't—oh, don't be silly. Show me the confounded thing."

Loring showed him. The whining generators were unchanged; the tall Van de Graaff accumulator still looked like something out of a third-rate horror movie. The thirty square feet of haywired vacuum tubes and resistances were still an incomprehensible tangle. But since his last visit a phone booth without a phone had been added. A sheet-copper disk set into its ceiling was connected to the machinery by a ponderous cable. Its floor was a slab of polished glass.

"That's it," Loring said. "I got it at a junkyard and fixed it up pretty. You want to watch a test on the mice?"

"No," W. J. Born said. "I want to try it myself. What do you think I've been paying you for?" He paused. "Do you guarantee its safety?"

"Look, W. J.," Loring said, "I guarantee nothing. I *think* this will send you two years into the future. I *think* if you're back in it at the end of two hours you'll snap back to the present. I'll tell you this, though. If it *does* send you into the future, you had better be back in it at the end of two hours. Otherwise you may snap back into the same space as a strolling pedestrian or a moving car—and an H-bomb will be out of your league."

W. J. Born's ulcer twinged. With difficulty he asked: "Is there anything else I ought to know?"

"Nope," Loring said after considering for a moment. "You're just a paying passenger."

"Then let's go." W. J. Born checked to make sure that he had his memorandum book and smooth-working pen in his pocket and stepped into the telephone booth.

Loring closed the door, grinned, waved and vanished—literally vanished, while Born was looking at him.

Born yanked the door open and said: "Loring! What the devil—" And then he saw that it was late afternoon instead of early morning. That Loring was nowhere in the loft. That the generators were silent and the tubes dark and cold. That there was a mantle of dust and a faint musty smell.

He rushed from the big room and down the stairs. It was the same street in the West Seventies. Two hours, he thought, and looked at his watch. It said 9:55, but the sun unmistakably said it was late afternoon. Something had happened. He resisted an impulse to grab a passing high-school boy and ask him what year it was. There was a newsstand down the street, and Born went to it faster than he had moved in years. He threw down a quarter and snatched a *Post*, dated—September 11th, 1977. He had done it.

Eagerly he riffled to the *Post's* meager financial page. Moon Mining and Smelting had opened at 27. Uranium at 19. United Com at 24. Catastrophic lows! The crash had come!

He looked at his watch again, in panic. 9:59. It had said 9:55. He'd have to be back in the phone booth by 11:55 or—he shuddered. An H-bomb would be out of his league.

Now to pinpoint the crash. "Cab!" he yelled, waving his paper. It eased to the curb. "Public library," W. J. Born grunted, and leaned back to read the *Post* with glee.

The headline said: 25000 RIOT HERE FOR UPPED JOBLESS DOLE. Naturally; naturally. He gasped as he saw who had won the 1976 presidential election. Lord, what odds he'd be able to get back in 1975 if he wanted to bet on the nomination! NO CRIME WAVES, SAYS COMMISSIONER. Things hadn't changed very much after all. BLONDE MODEL HACKED IN TUB; MYSTERY BOYFRIEND SOUGHT. He read that one all the way through, caught by a two-column photo of the blonde model for a hosiery account. And then he noticed that the cab wasn't moving. It was caught in a rock-solid traffic jam. The time was 10:05.

"Driver," he said.

The man turned around, soothing and scared. A fare was a fare; there was a depression on. "It's all right, mister. We'll be out of here in a minute. They turn off the Drive and that blocks the avenue for a couple of minutes, that's all. We'll be rolling in a minute."

They were rolling in a minute, but for a few seconds only. The cab inched agonizingly along while W. J. Born twisted the newspaper in his hands. At 10:13 he threw a bill at the driver and jumped from the cab.

Panting, he reached the library at 10:46 by his watch. By the time that the rest of the world was keeping on that day it was quitting-time in the midtown offices. He had bucked a stream of girls in surprisingly short skirts and surprisingly big hats all the way.

He got lost in the marble immensities of the library and his own panic. When he found the newspaper room his watch said 11:03. W. J. Born panted to the girl at the desk: "File of the *Stock Exchange Journal* for 1975, 1976 and 1977."

"We have the microfilms for 1975 and 1976, sir, and loose copies for this year."

"Tell me," he said, "what year for the big crash? That's what I want to look up."

"That's 1975, sir. Shall I get you that?"

"Wait," he said. "Do you happen to remember the month?"

"I think it was March or August or something like that, sir."

"Get me the whole file, please," he said. Nineteen seventy-five. His year— his real year. Would he have a month? A week? Or—?

"Sign this card, mister," the girl was saying patiently. "There's a reading machine, you just go sit there and I'll bring you the spool."

He scribbled his name and went to the machine, the only one vacant in a row of a dozen. The time on his watch was 11:05. He had fifty minutes.

The girl dawdled over cards at her desk and chatted with a good-looking young page with a stack of books while sweat began to pop from Born's brow. At last she disappeared into the stacks behind her desk.

Born waited. And waited. And waited. Eleven-ten. Eleven-fifteen. Eleven-twenty.

An H-bomb would be out of his league.

His ulcer stabbed him as the girl appeared again, daintily carrying a spool of 35-millimeter film between thumb and forefinger, smiling brightly at Born. "Here we are," she said, and inserted the spool in the machine and snapped a switch. Nothing happened.

"Oh, darn," she said. "The light's out. I *told* the electrician."

Born wanted to scream and then to explain, which would have been just as foolish.

"There's a free reader," she pointed down the line. W. J. Born's knees tottered as they walked to it. He looked at his watch—11:27. Twenty-eight minutes to go. The ground-glass screen lit up with a shadow of the familiar format; January 1st, 1975. "You just turn the crank," she said, and showed him. The shadows spun past on the screen at dizzying speed, and she went back to her desk.

Born cranked the film up to April 1975, the month he had left 91 minutes ago, and to the sixteenth day of April, the very day he had left. The shadow on the ground glass was the same paper he had seen that morning: SYNTHETICS SURGE TO NEW VIENNA PEAK.

Trembling he cranked into a vision of the future; the *Stock Exchange Journal* for April 17th, 1975.

Three-inch type screamed: SECURITIES CRASH IN GLOBAL CRISIS: BANKS CLOSE; CLIENTS STORM BROKERAGES!

Suddenly he was calm, knowing the future and safe from its blows. He rose from the reader and strode firmly into the marble halls. Everything was all right now. Twenty-six minutes was time enough to get back to the machine. He'd have a jump of several hours on the market; his own money would be safe as houses; he could get his personal clients off the hook.

He got a cab with miraculous ease and rolled straight to the loft building in the West Seventies without hindrance. At 11:50 by his watch he was closing the door of the phone booth in the dusty, musty-smelling lab.

At 11:54 he noticed an abrupt change in the sunlight that filtered through the dirt-streaked windows and stepped calmly out. It was April 16th, 1975, again. Loring was sound asleep beside a gas hotplate on which coffee simmered. W. J. Born turned off the gas and went downstairs softly. Loring was a screwy, insolent, insecure young man, but by his genius he had enabled W. J. Born to harvest his fortune at the golden moment of perfection.

Back in his office he called his floor broker and said firmly: "Cronin, get this straight. I want you to sell every share of stock and every bond in my personal account immediately, at the market, and to require certified checks in payment."

Cronin asked forthrightly: "Chief, have you gone crazy?"

"I have not. Don't waste a moment, and report regularly to me. Get your boys to work. Drop everything else."

Born had a light, bland lunch sent in and refused to see anybody or take any calls except from the floor broker. Cronin kept reporting that the dumping was going right along, that Mr. Born must be crazy, that the unheard-of demand for certified checks was causing alarm, and finally, at the close, that Mr. Born's wishes were being carried out. Born told him to get the checks to him immediately.

They arrived in an hour, drawn on a dozen New York banks. W. J. Born called in a dozen senior messengers, and dealt out the checks, one bank to a messenger. He told them to withdraw the cash, rent safe-deposit boxes of the necessary sizes in those banks where he did not already have boxes, and deposit the cash.

He then phoned the banks to confirm the weird arrangement. He was on first-name terms with at least one vice president in each bank, which helped enormously.

W. J. Born leaned back, a happy man. Let the smash come. He turned on his flashboard for the first time that day. The New York closing was sharply off. Chicago was worse. San Francisco was shaky—as he watched, the flashing figures on the composite price index at San Francisco began to drop. In five minutes it was a screaming nosedive into the pit. The closing bell stopped it short of catastrophe.

W. J. Born went out to dinner after phoning his wife that he would not be home. He returned to the office and watched a board in one of the outer rooms that carried Tokyo Exchange through the night hours, and congratulated himself as the figures told a tale of panic and ruin. The dominoes were toppling, toppling, toppling.

He went to his club for the night and woke early, eating alone in an almost-deserted breakfast room. The ticker in the lobby sputtered a good morning as he drew on his gloves against the chilly April dawn. He stopped to watch. The ticker began spewing a tale of disaster on the great bourses of Europe, and Mr. Born walked to his office. Brokers a-plenty were arriving early, muttering in little crowds in the lobby and elevators.

"What do you make of it, Born?" one of them asked.

"What goes up must come down," he said. "*I'm* safely out."

"So I hear," the man told him, with a look that Born decided was envious.

Vienna, Milan, Paris and London were telling their sorry story on the boards in the customers' rooms. There were a few clients silting up the place already, and the night staff had been busy taking orders by phone for the opening. They all were to sell at the market.

W. J. Born grinned at one of the night men and cracked a rare joke: "Want to buy a brokerage house, Willard?"

Willard glanced at the board and said: "No thanks, Mr. Born. But it was nice of you to keep me in mind."

Most of the staff drifted in early; the sense of crisis was heavy in the air. Born instructed his staff to do what they could for his personal clients first, and holed up in his office.

The opening bell was the signal for hell to break loose. The tickers never had the ghost of a chance of keeping up with the crash, unquestionably the biggest and steepest in the history of finance. Born got some pleasure out of the fact that his boys' promptness had cut the losses of his personal clients a little. A very important banker called in midmorning to ask Born into a billion-dollar pool that would shore up the market by a show of confidence. Born said no, knowing that no show of confidence would keep Moon Mining and Smelting from opening at 27 on September 11th, 1977. The banker hung up abruptly.

Miss Illig asked: "Do you want to see Mr. Loring? He's here."

"Send him in."

Loring was deathly pale, with a copy of the *Journal* rolled up in his fist. "I need some money," he said.

W. J. Born shook his head. "You see what's going on," he said. "Money's tight. I've enjoyed our association, Loring, but I think it's time to end it. You've had a quarter of a million dollars clear; I make no claims on your process—"

"It's gone," Loring said hoarsely. "I haven't paid for the damn equipment— not ten cents on the dollar yet. I've been playing the market. I lost a hundred and fifty thousand on soy futures this morning. They'll dismantle my stuff and haul it away. I've got to have some money."

"*No!*" W. J. Born barked. "Absolutely not!"

"They'll come with a truck for the generators this afternoon. I stalled them. My stocks kept going up. And now—all I wanted was enough in reserve to keep working. *I've got to have money.*"

"No," said Born. "After all, it's not my fault."

Loring's ugly face was close to his. "Isn't it?" he snarled. And he spread out the paper on the desk.

Born read the headline—again—of the *Stock Exchange Journal* for April 17th, 1975: SECURITIES CRASH IN GLOBAL CRISIS: BANKS CLOSE; CLIENTS STORM BROKERAGES! But this time he was not too rushed to read on: "A world-wide slump in securities has wiped out billions of paper dollars since it started shortly before closing yesterday at the New York Stock Exchange. No end to the catastrophic flood of sell orders is yet in sight. Veteran New York observers agreed that dumping of securities on the New York market late yesterday by W. J. Born of W. J. Born Associates pulled the plug out of the big boom which must now be consigned to memory. Banks have been hard-hit by the—"

"Isn't it?" Loring snarled. "Isn't it?" His eyes were crazy as he reached for Born's thin neck.

Dominoes, W. J. Born thought vaguely through the pain, and managed to hit a button on his desk. Miss Illig came in and screamed and went out again and came back with a couple of husky customers' men, but it was too late.

[*Stirring Science Stories* - March 1942
as by Cecil Corwin]

The Golden Road

Out of myth of night and language there come strange tales told over wine. There is a man known as The Three-Cornered Scar who frequents a village spot famed for its wine and raconteurs, both of which are above the average.

The Three-Cornered Scar favored us by a visit to my table and ordering, during the course of his story, five half-bottles of house red to my account. The wine is drunk up and the story told.

1

Colt was tired. He was so bone-broke weary that he came near to wishing he was dead. It would have been easy to die in the snow; heaps in the way seemed to beg for the print of his body. He skirted crevasses that were like wide and hungry mouths.

This was Central Asia, High Pamir, a good thousand miles from any permanent habitation of the human race. The nomadic Kirghiz population had been drained away to the Eastern front, civil and military authorities likewise. Colt himself was the tragic, far-strayed end of the First Kuen-Lung Oil Prospecting Expedition, undertaken by a handful of American volunteers on behalf of the Chungking government.

Estimating generously, his assets were five more days of scanty eating. And an eternity of sleep under the glaring stars of the plateau? ...

He had struck, somehow, an easier way across the snow-covered, rocky wastes. There was a route to follow, a winding, mazy route that skirted the Alai Range's jagged foothills and slipped through Tengis-Bai Pass. Old memories of maps and trails swirled through Colt's tired head; he bore north for no better reason than that he could guide himself by Polaris, low on the horizon. Colt was headed, with a laugh and a curse, for Bokhara.

Colt marched through the first watch of the night, before the smiting cold of space descended on this roof of the world; then he would sleep, twitching with frost. He would wake eight hours later, a stone, a block of wood, to unkink his wretched muscles, shoulder his pack and march under the naked, brassy sun.

The Parsees said that this High Pamir was the cradle of human life, that from here had sprung the primals who proliferated into white, yellow, black and brown. To the southwest, at the same thirteen-thousand elevation, was the Valley of the Oxus, a green ribbon in the steel grey and bone white of the plateau. To the northeast were the great peaks—Everest, Kanchinjunga, K-4—that started where other mountains ended, shooting from seventeen thousand up to unthinkable heights, sky-piercing.

Night and day scarcely interrupted the flow of his thoughts. His waking fantasies and his dreams alike were brutish, longing for warmth and comfort, bespelled remembrance of palmier days. He woke to find an ear frostbitten, dead, marble white, without sensation, killed by cold.

It came to him slowly, the idea forcing its way through the numbed machinery of his brain, that he was following a path. This easier way across the plateau could be nothing but one of the historic caravan routes. Over this trail had gone a billion feet of beasts and men, and his own had found their way into the ancient grooves. Colt was content with that; going by the sun and stars was good, compass better, but best of all were the ways that men had taken and found well suited.

There were animal droppings before him now and then, once a fragment of broken crockery. He doubled his pace, from a slow plod to a loping, long-strided walk that took much of his husbanded wind. Finally he saw the print in a snowbank that spelled *man.* It was a shod foot's mark, light and side-stepping. As he watched, a puff of wind drifted it over with dry, gleaming snow.

Colt found a splash of milk against a rock, then the smell of camel clinging about a wiry shrub.

He saw them at last, the tail of a great caravan, and fell fainting into the arms of tall, curious Kirghiz camel drivers.

They carried him in a litter until he awoke and could eat, for nothing was so important or unexpected that it could be allowed to break the schedule of the march. Colt opened his eyes to grunts of satisfaction from his bearers. He accepted the hunks of dried meat and bottle of warm tea they gave him, trying to catch enough of the language to offer thanks.

Coming down the line of the caravan was a large Hindu on one of the small Mongolian ponies. He reined beside Colt and asked in French, "How are you? They passed me word. Can you march with us?"

"But yes! It's like life out of death to find you people here. What can I do to help?"

The Hindu dismounted to walk the pony beside him. "Keep up spirits. Our few Europeans are tired of each other's company. In case of bandit raiding—highly improbable, of course—you'll fight. I'm Raisuli Batar, merchant of the Punjab. I'm caravan master, whose word is law. Not that it's necessary—the boys are well behaved and we have enough food."

"Where are we headed?" asked Colt, gnawing on the hunk of meat.

"We started for Bokhara. Come up the line to meet the better sort with me. They're agog with excitement, of course, don't dare break line without my permission, which I don't choose to grant. By way of payload we have crates of soap on the camels and drums of flavoring essence on the ponies."

Colt sniffed, finding wintergreen and peppermint on the air. "May you find a good price," he said respectfully.

Raisuli smiled and the American was pleased. The caravan master was big and solid, with a grim, handsome face. It was good to please a man like that, Colt thought.

They quickened their pace, overtaking a hundred plodding bearers and a herd of sheep. Colt was introduced to a pale, thoughtful man named McNaughton, a reader in history at the University of Glasgow, who said he had been doing field work in Asia for three years.

Farther on were Lodz and wife, two young Poles from Galicia who were hoping for government work in Bokhara. The man was quiet, his English heavily accented. The wife spoke French only, but with the vivid dash of a Parisienne. Her lips were touched with scarlet; here in the wilderness of the High Pamir she wore a freshly pressed riding habit. Colt was enchanted.

Raisuli cast a glance at the sky. "Bedding down," he snapped. "Excuse me—c'est l'heure."

He left Colt with the Poles, mounting his pony again to gallop down the line barking orders to the various Hindus, Tajiks, Chinese, Abyssinians, Kirghiz and Kroomen who made up the crew. It took no more than a quarter hour to bring the unwieldy line to a halt; in another quarter hour a thousand felt tents were pitched and pegged, fires lighted and animals staked out.

"He times well, that one," smiled M. Lodz. Colt looked up and saw the sky already deepening into black. He shuddered a little and drew nearer to the fire.

"I think," said McNaughton absently, "that I could take a little refreshment." Lodz looked up from under his brows, then clapped his hands. A native boy came running.

"Bring food—some of that cold joint, wallah."

"Yes, sahib."

"Such a night this will be, perhaps," said M. Lodz softly, "as it was in August."

"Just such a night," said McNaughton. "Will you join us, Mr. Colt?"

"Not I," said the American with a sense of guilt. "I was fed when I came to after fainting. Is it safe—may I look about?"

He got no answer. The boy had returned with a great haunch of meat; silently the Occidentals gathered about it, taking out knives. Colt watched in amazement as the dainty Frenchwoman hacked out a great slab of beef and tore at it, crammed it down her throat. Before it was swallowed she was cutting away again.

"Ah—I asked if I ought to look about …"

Lodz shot him a sidewise glance, his mouth crammed with meat, his jaws working busily. Then, as though Colt had never spoken, he returned to the serious business of feeding, with the same animal quality as his wife and McNaughton showed.

"I'll look about then," said Colt forlornly. He wandered away from the fire in the direction of a yellow felt tent. There he was delighted to catch words of

Cantonese.

"Greetings, son of Han," he said to the venerable speaker.

The fine old Mongol head turned; Colt felt himself subjected to a piercing, kindly scrutiny by two twinkling little black eyes. The ruddy little mouth smiled. "Sit down, son. It's a long time between new friends."

Colt squatted by the fire obediently; the venerable one took a long pull from a bottle of *suntori,* a vile synthetic Japanese whisky. Wiping his mouth with the back of a wrinkled, yellow hand, he announced, "I'm Grandfather T'ang. This is my son, T'ang Gaw Yat. If you let him he'll talk you deaf about the time he was on the long march with the Eighth Route Army. He claims General Chu Teh once ate rice with him."

T'ang Gaw Yat smiled obediently and a little tolerantly at his father's whimsy. He was a fine-looking Chinese, big-headed and straight-faced, with little wrinkles of laughter playing about his mouth. "What my father says," he confided, "is strictly true. It was a full thousand miles from—"

"What did I tell you?" broke in the old man. "The slave is his wife, and the smartest one of the lot." He indicated a small Chinese woman of the indeterminate age between twenty and fifty.

She said in English hardly accented, "Hello. You do speak English, don't you? These barbarians don't know anything but their village jargon and Canton talk." The smile took the edge from her harsh words.

Colt introduced himself, and answered endless questions on the state of China, military, political and economic.

"Hold off," ordered the woman at last. "Let him have his turn. Want to know anything, Mr. Colt?"

"Wouldn't mind knowing how long you've been traveling."

"Stupid question," broke in Grandfather Han. "Just what one expects from a foreign devil. The splendor of the night closes about him and he would know how long we've been on the march! Have a drink—a small one." He passed the bottle; Colt politely refused.

"Then maybe you'd like a little game—" There clicked in his palm two ivory cubes.

"Please, Father," said T'ang Gaw Yat. "Put those away."

"Pattern of ancient virtue!" sneered the old man. "O you child of purity!"

"Grandfather is very lucky," said the woman quietly. "He started on the caravan with nothing but those dice and many years of gambling experience. He is now one of the richest men on the line of march. He owns two herds of sheep, a riding camel of his own and the best food there is to be had."

"And drink," said the son somberly.

"Tell you what," said the old man. "You can have some of my V.S.O. stock—stuff I won from a Spaniard a month back." He rummaged for a moment in one of the tent pockets, finally emerged with a slender bottle which caught the firelight like auriferous quartz. "Danziger Goldwasser—*le véritable,* " he gloated. "But I can't drink the stuff. Doesn't bite like this Nipponese hellbroth." He upended the bottle of *suntori* again; passed the brandy to Colt.

The American took it, studied it curiously against the fire. It was a thin, amber liquid, at whose bottom settled little flakes. He shook them up into the neck of the bottle; it was like one of the little globular paperweights that hold a mimic snowstorm. But instead of snow there were bits of purest beaten gold to tickle the palate and fancy of the drinker.

"Thanks," he said inadequately. "Very kind of you."

"Curious, isn't it," said the woman, "how much the caravan life resembles a village? Though the wealth, of course, is not in land but in mercantile prospects—" She stopped as Colt caught her eye. Why, he wondered, had she been rattling on like that?

"The wisdom of the slave is the folly of the master," said Grandfather T'ang amiably. "He is happy who learns to discount the words of a woman."

"Suppose," said the woman slowly and quietly, "you learn to mind your own business, you poisonous old serpent?"

"They can't stand common sense," confided the old man.

Colt felt, painfully, that he had wandered into a family quarrel. He bolted with a mumbled excuse, hanging onto the bottle of brandy. He stood for a moment away from the trail and stared down the long line of fires. There were more than a thousand, snaking nearly out of sight. The spectacle was restful; the fires were a little blue, being kindled largely out of night-soil briquettes.

The sky was quite black; something had overcast the deep-ranked stars of the plateau. No moon shone.

Colt settled against the lee of a rock in a trance. He heard winds and the hiss of voices, soft in the distance. It was the quiet and complaining Tajiki dialect. He could hear it and understand it. It was absurdly simple, he thought abstractedly, to pick out the meanings of words and phrases.

"Such a night," one was saying, "as in August. You remember?"

"I remember." Then, dark and passionate, "The limping, bloody demon! Let him come near and I'll tear his vitals!"

"Surely you will not. He is the tearer in his evil work. We are the torn—"

Colt sat up with a start. What the hell! He couldn't understand Tajiki, not one little word of it! He had been dreaming, he thought. But it didn't melt away as a dream should. The memory of the overheard conversation was as sharp and distinct as it could be, something concrete and mysterious, like a joke that hadn't been explained to him.

Then there was a sort of heavenly grumbling, like a megatherial word or more. Colt twisted and stared at the zenith; could see nothing at all. The rumbling ended. Colt saw black little fingers all down the line rise and attend, twisting and staring and buzzing to each other.

2

He hurried to the fire of his European friends. They were sprawled on blankets, their bodies a little swollen from the enormous meal they had eaten. Colt saw the bare bone of the joint, scraped by knife edges. The Occidentals were unconcernedly smoking.

"What was that racket?" he asked, feeling a little silly. "What was it—do you know?"

"Thunder," said McNaughton noncommittally.

"*Oui,*" agreed M. Lodz, puffing a long, tip-gilt cigarette. "Did it frighten you, the thunder?"

Colt pulled himself together. There was something evasive here, something that sought to elude him. "It was *peculiar* thunder," he said with glacial calm. "There was no lightning preceding it."

"The lightning will come soon," said Lodz furtively. "I tell you so you will not be alarmed."

"You have your lightning after your thunder here? Odd. In my country it's the other way around." He wasn't going to break—he *wasn't* going to swear—

"But how boring," drawled the Pole's wife. "*Never* a change?"

He *wasn't* going to break—

Then the peculiar lightning split the skies. Colt shot one staggered, incredulous glance at it, and was dazzled.

It was a word, perhaps a name, spelled out against the dead-black sky. He knew it. It was in some damned alphabet or other; fretfully he chided himself for not remembering which of the twenty-odd he could recognize it could be.

Colt realized that the Occidentals were staring at him with polite concern. He noticed a shred of meat between the teeth of Mme. Lodz as she smiled reassuringly—white, sharp teeth, they were. Colt rubbed his eyes dazedly. He knew he must be a haggard and unseemly figure to their cultured gaze—but they hadn't seen the words in the sky—*or had they—*?

Politely they stared at him, phrases bubbling from their lips:

"So frightfully sorry, old man—"

"Wouldn't upset you for the world—"

"Hate to see you lose your grip—"

Colt shook his head dazedly, as though he felt strands of sticky silk wind around his face and head. He turned and ran, hearing the voice of Raisuli Batar call after him, "Don't stray too far—"

He didn't know how long he ran or how far he strayed. Finally he fell flat, sprawled childishly, feeling sick and confused in his head. He looked up for a moment to see that the caravan fires were below some curve of rock or other—at any rate, well out of sight. They were such little lights, he thought. Good for a few feet of warm glow, then sucked into the black of High Pamir. They made not even a gleam in the night-heavy sky.

And there, on the other side of him and the caravan, he saw the tall figure of another human being. She stood on black rock between two drifts of snow.

Colt bit out the foil seal of the brandy bottle and pulled the cork with his fingers. After a warm gulp of the stuff, he rose.

"Have a drink?"

She turned. She was young in her body and face, Mongoloid. Her eyes were blue-black and shining like metal. Her nose was short, Chinese, yet her skin was quite white. She did not have the eyefold of the yellow people.

Silently she extended one hand for the bottle, tilted it high. Colt saw a shudder run through her body as she swallowed and passed him the tall flask with its gold-flecked liquor.

"You must have been cold."

"By choice. Do you think I'd warm myself at either fire?"

"Either?" he asked.

"There are two caravans. Didn't you know?"

"No. I'm just here—what's the other caravan?"

"Just here, are you? Did you know that you're dead?"

Colt thought the matter over slowly; finally declared, "I guess I did. And all those others—and you—?"

"All dead. We're the detritus of High Pamir. You'll find, if you look, men who fell to death from airplanes within the past few years walking by the side of Neanderthalers who somehow strayed very far from their tribes and died. The greatest part of the caravans comes, of course, from older caravans of the living who carried their goods from Asia to Europe for thousands of years."

Colt coughed nervously. "Have another drink," he said. "Then let's see this other caravan. I'm not too well pleased with the one I fell into."

She took his hand and guided him across the snow and black rock to back within sight of his own caravan. He stared, eager and hungry to see. As she pointed with one tapering finger it seemed that many things were clearer than they ever had been before. He saw that the long line of lights was not his caravan but another in the opposite direction, paralleling his.

"There you will see *their* caravan master," she said, putting her face next to his. He looked and saw a pot-bellied monster whose turban was half as high as its wearer. Its silhouette, as it passed before a fire, was indescribably unpleasant.

"Evening prayer," said his guide, with a faint tone of mockery.

He studied them as they arranged flares before a platform flung together out of planks and trestles; he also saw them assemble a sort of idol, fitting the various parts together and bolting them securely. When the thing was perhaps two-thirds assembled he turned away and covered his face, repelled.

"I won't look at the rest of it now," he said. "Perhaps later, if you wish me to."

"That's right," she said. "It isn't a thing to look at calmly. But you will see the rest of it one time or another. This is a very long caravan."

She looked down and said, "Now they are worshiping."

Colt looked. "Yes," he said flatly. They were worshiping in their own fashion, dancing and leaping uglily while some dozen of them blew or sawed fantastic discords from musical instruments. Others were arranged in a choir; as they began to sing Colt felt cold nausea stirring at the pit of his belly.

Their singing was markedly unpleasant; Colt, who enjoyed the discords of Ernest Bloch and Jean Sibelius, found them stimulatingly revolting. The choir droned out a minor melody, varying it again and again with what Colt construed to be quarter-tones and split-interval harmonies. He found he was listening intently, nearly fascinated by the ugly sounds.

"Why are they doing it?" he asked at length.

"It is their way," she said with a shrug. "I see you are interested. I, too, am interested. Perhaps I should not discuss this before you have had the opportunity of making up your own mind. But as you may guess, the caravan below us there, where they make the noises, is Bad. It is a sort of marching gallery of demons and the black in heart. On the other hand, the caravan with which you found yourself previously is Good—basically kind and constructive, taking delight in order and precision."

Colt, half-listening, drew her down beside him on the rock. He uncorked the bottle. "You must tell me about yourself," he said earnestly. "It is becoming difficult for me to understand all this. So tell me about yourself, if you may."

She smiled slowly. "I am half-caste," she said. "The Russian Revolution—so many attractive and indigent female aristocrats, quite unable to work with their hands ... many, as you must know, found their way to Shanghai.

"There was a Chinese merchant and my mother, a princess. Not *eine Fürstin*—merely a hanger-on at court. I danced. When I was a small child already I was dancing. My price was high, very high at one time. I lost popularity, and with it income and much self-assurance. I was a very bad woman. Not bad as those people there are bad, but I was very bad in my own way.

"Somehow I learned mathematics—a British actuary who knew me for a while let me use his library, and I learned quickly. So I started for India, where nobody would hire me. I heard that there was a country to the north that wanted many people who knew building and mathematics and statistics. Railway took me through the Khyber and Afghanistan—from there pony and litter—till I died of exposure seven months ago. That is why we meet on High Pamir."

"Listen," said Colt. "Listen to that."

It was again the megatherial voices, louder than before. He looked at the woman and saw that her throat cords were tight as she stared into the black-velvet heavens.

Colt squinted up between two fingers, snapped shut his eyelids after a moment of the glaring word across the sky that followed the voices. He cursed briefly, blinded. Burned into the backs of his eyes were the familiar characters of the lightning, silent and portentous.

"It doesn't do to stare into it that way," said the woman. "Come with me." He felt for her hand and let her pull him to his feet. As sight returned he realized that again they were walking on rock.

"And there's the Good and holy caravan at evening devotions," said the woman, with the same note of bedrock cynicism in her voice. And they were. From his coign of vantage Colt could see Raisuli Batar solemnly prostrating himself before a modestly clad, well-proportioned idol whose face beamed kindly on the congregation through two blue-enameled eyes. There was a choir that sang the old German hymn "Ein Feste Burg."

"Shocking," said the woman, "yet strangely moving to the spirit. One feels a certain longing …."

Bluntly Colt said, "I'd like to join them. You're holding me back, you know. I wouldn't see you as a comrade again if I sang with them." He hummed a few bars of the hymn. "On Earth is not His e-qual—"

"Girding their loins for the good fight," said the woman. She chuckled quietly for a moment. In a ribald tone that seemed barely to conceal heartbreak, she snapped, "Do you care to fall in with the ranks of the Almighty? Or may it be with the Lord of Nothing, Old Angra Mainyu of the sixteen plagues? Pick your sides in the divine sweepstakes! It's for you they do it and of a great love for the soul in you—"

"They want you black and they want you white—"

"How in blazes do you know who's right?"

"It *seems* clear," said Colt doubtfully.

"You think so?" she exploded. "You think so now? Wait and see—with them tearing at your heart two ways and you sure that it'll never hold out but it's going to rip in half, and it never doing that but you going on through the night thirteen thousand meters above the world and never a soft bed and never a bite of real food and never a moment of closing your eyes and sleeping in darkness and night—!"

She collapsed, weeping, into his arms.

3

The long, starless night had not lifted. Three times more the voices had spoken from the heavens and silent lightning scribbled across the sky. The two in-betweeners had chanted back and forth sacred writings of Asia, wretchedly seeking for answers:

"I will incline mine ears to a parable. I will open my dark sayings upon the harp. Wherefore should I fear in the days of evil when the iniquity of my heels shall compass me about?"

"O maker of the material world, thou holy one! When the good waters reach the left instep whereon does the Drukh Nasu rush?"

There was an explosion of cynical laughter above them, old and dry. Grandfather T'ang greeted them, "Be well, Valeska and Colt. And forget the insteps and the heels of the Upanishad. That is my counsel." He upended the *suntori* bottle and flushed his throat with a half-pint of the stuff.

In reply to Colt's surprised glance she said, "He often visits me. Gaw is a terrible old man who thinks nothing of lying and being untrue to himself."

"A little of that would do you no harm, daughter. I belong out here with you, of course. But out here are no likely candidates for the dice box, and this ethereal gullet refuses to do without alcohol. Though this ethereal brain could do with considerably less of the pious nonsense that invariably accompanies winning at dice."

He painfully squatted by them, keeping a death grip on the quart bottle. "They're going to be at it again," said the old man. "It's just such a night as in August. Tooth and nail, hammer and tongs, no holds barred." He spat on the rock. "Pah! These spectacles disgust a man of my mentality."

"You see?" asked the woman. "He lies and cheats at dice. Yet often he sings with the worshipers. And always he says he spits on them in his mind. He is terrible!"

Colt quoted slowly, "Judge me and my cause against the ungodly nation; O deliver me from the deceitful and the unjust man."

"Ah?" asked Grandfather T'ang. "Sacred books? Wisdom of the East? I join your symposium with the following, reverently excerpted from the Shuh King: 'The soil of the province was whitish and mellow. Its contribution of revenue was of the highest, with some proportion of the second. Its fields were of the average of the second class.'" He grinned savagely and drank deeply again.

"You can't be right," said Colt. "You *can't* be. There's something that forbids it being right to lie now that you're dead. It doesn't matter which side you choose— whether it's Raisuli's smiling idol or that thing the other side of the ridge. But you have to choose."

"I'm different," said T'ang smugly. "I'm different, and I'm drunk two thirds of the time, so what's the difference if I'm different?" He began raucously to sing, beating time with the bottle, the one and only Confucian hymn:

> *Superiority in a person*
> *Should better not*
> *Nor should it worsen.*
>
> *It should consider everything*
> *From pussycat to honored king.*
>
> *Inferior people*
> *Need a steeple*
> *To climb and shout*
> *Their views about.*

Colt drew a little aside with Valeska. "Should this matter?" he asked.

"He really ought to choose one caravan or another. It's very wrong of him to pretend to be with one when he's really with neither. Either the Good or the Bad ..." She stared quaintly into Colt's eyes. "Do you think I'm bad?"

"No," said Colt slowly. "I know you're not. And you aren't good either. Not by nature, practice or inclination. I'm the same as you. I want to sing their devil song and a Lutheran hymn at the same time. And it can't be done."

"And you aren't a liar like that lovable old drunk rolling on the rocks there," she said with a gesture. "At least you aren't a liar."

"I congratulate myself. I can appreciate it to the full. Have a drink, Valeska."

"Yes. There is, you know, going to be a holy war. Which side should we be on?"

"Who knows? Let's take another look at the Bad boys."

There was half a pang of terror in his heart—a formless fear that he might find Badness less repugnant to him than Goodness. He knew the feeling: it was the trial of every human soul torn between one thing and another. Doubt was Hell—worse than Hell—and it had to be resolved, even at the risk of this magnificent creature by his side.

Silently he passed the bottle as the sky lightened and the silence spoke out of the heavens.

"As you wish," she said. Colt felt a sort of opening in his mind, as though unspoken words had passed between them. He had heard her think in sorrow and fear of losing him.

She led him over a ridge to the long line of fires of the Bad caravan, fires blue-tipped before the ugly altar. There was a disemboweled sacrifice in its lap. Colt stared his fill, trying to probe what was in his own heart. It was neither pleasure nor pain, neither pompous virtue nor cackling glee in destruction and death. There were techniques of self-searching now open to him that could never be those of a living man; he shuddered to think of how he had groped in darkness and ignorance before his death.

The caravan master, the squat monster in the mighty turban, greeted him warmly, "We've been watching your progress with considerable interest, my son. We have felt that you were warming to our ideas. How do you feel about our community?"

Colt rolled back his consciousness into the dark recesses of his mind, exploring a new stock of knowledge—things that it seemed he must always have known, but never recognized till now for what they were. "Community"—that meant the mutual practice of evil and destruction. One of the tidbits of wisdom newly in his mind was an awareness that the Bad worked together, sealed in a union that bore death as its bond. The Good practiced alone, rising very seldom to a community of any respectable proportions.

"May I enter the bond tentatively?" he asked.

The master looked pained. "My son of abomination," he said kindly, "I'll have to ask you to be very careful. The balance is beautifully precise; it would be a shame to throw them out of kilter. But since you wish to go ahead, very well. Enter!"

Colt squatted on the ground with numerous others of the Bad people. He sent out a consoling line of thought to Valeska, who stood somberly by, fearing to lose her solitary ally. He smiled a little and ran back a signal of reassurance.

He trembled a little with the effort, then threw back his mind like a door. The inverging flood of black, glistening stuff gave him a warm feeling of comradeship with the others; he yielded and allowed himself to drift with them.

He inspected the attitude of which he was a part, found it consisted of a series of aesthetic balances among eye, ear, touch, smell and taste. The viewpoint was multiplex, dirigible, able to rise, enlarge, focus from infinity to zero, split to examine an object from all vantages.

The viewpoint inspected a rock from about a dozen feet in the air, saw it as a smoothly prolate spheroid. There was a moment of dwelling on the seeming fact of its perfection, a painful moment, then the viewpoint descended slowly and with little waves of pleasure as chips and scars became apparent in the rock. The viewpoint split, correlated its observations and registered the fact that the rock was of an eccentric shape, awkward and unbeautiful.

The viewpoint coalesced again and shrank microscopically, then smaller still. For an ecstatic moment it perceived a welter of crashing, blundering molecules, beetling about in blindness.

It shifted again, swiftly, far away to a point in Hong Kong where a lady was entertaining a gentleman. The viewpoint let the two humans' love, hate, disgust, affection and lust slide beneath its gaze. There was a gorgeous magenta jealousy from the man, overlaying the woman's dull-brown, egg-shaped avarice, both swept away in a rushing tide of fluxing, thick-textured, ductile, crimson-black passion.

The viewpoint passed somewhere over a battlefield, dwelt lovingly on the nightmare scene below. There were dim flares of vitality radiating from every crawling figure below; a massing of infantry was like a beacon. From the machinery of war there came a steely radiance which, waxed as it discharged its shell or tripped its bomb, then dimmed to a quiet glow of satisfaction.

A file of tanks crawled over a hill, emitting a purplish radiance which sent out thin cobwebs of illumination. They swung into battle formation, crept down the slope at the infantry mass. Behind the infantry antitank guns were hurrying up—too late. The tanks opened fire, their cobwebs whitening to a demon's flare of death as soldiers, scurrying for cover, one by one, keeled over. As they fell there was a brittle little tingle, the snapping of a thread or wire, and the light of vitality was extinguished, being replaced by a sallow, corpsey glow.

The viewpoint gorged, gloated, bloated on the scene, then seemed to swell immeasurably.

Suddenly, after a wringing transition feeling, it was in a mighty hall, approaching a lightless apse where two little points of radiance gleamed.

There was music, harmonizing ear, eye, taste, touch and smell in a twilit blend of sensations. Colt struggled involuntarily, felt himself bathed in rhythmic complications, subtly off-pleasure, spoiled by the minute introduction of some unharmonious element. With dismay he felt there creeping into his own consciousness, his segment of the viewpoint, a simple little flicker of a theme in C major. He was conscious of a gnat's wing beat of disapproval in response to his untoward disturbance. The viewpoint continued its drift toward the darkened apse.

It lovingly picked out the inhabitant of the lightless space and greeted it, even Colt, even though it was a monster of five legs and incredible teeth which opened wide. Damnably, irritatingly, the little C-major motif persisted; he tried to drive it from his mind, then, in a fatal moment, recognized it as one Oliver's "Flower Song," a sweet little thing suitable for small hands on the pianoforte.

"—lilies, roses, flowers of every hue—"

He couldn't lose it after having recognized it that far; the theme spread and orchestrated through the viewpoint. The whole polysensual off-pleasure matrix broke up, tore wide open as it was about to pass down the gullet of the monster in the apse.

"I'm sorry," he said, rising. "I simply couldn't help—"

"I know," said the caravan master sadly. "I know what it was. But you wrecked a full communion all the same. Go in torment, my son of abomination. May your ways be woeful."

Colt thanked him and left with Valeska.

"How was it?" she asked.

"Indescribable," he exploded. "Loathsome—glorious—terrible. I found myself gloating over—" He went into details.

"So did I," she said absently. "I went through it, too. It has a gorgeous kick to it, no doubt. But it isn't right for us. Me, I broke up their communion with a line from Pushkin: *The aged sorcerer in anger said,/ This queen is evil straight from toe to head.* You know it?"

The sound of singing came from over the ridge, blurred by the megatherial voices. Colt stared abstractedly at the sky as the words were scribbled again in light.

"Their turn," he said. "The Good boys."

4

They stepped over ridges of snowy rock and stood for a moment surveying the other caravan. There was a semicircle of faces, gleaming benevolently in the firelight, handsome smiling faces. They were singing, under the pleasant aspect of the blue-eyed idol, a lusty slab from the great Bach's great Mass in B minor. While Valeska smiled a little cynically, Colt side-stepped into the baritone choir and sounded back tentatively for the words and music. They came easily; he was experiencing again, for the first time in many years, the delights of close harmony that move men to form barbershop quartets and Philharmonic Societies.

He sang the hearty, solid language, the crashing chords, from his chest, standing straight, bouncing the tones from his palate like the old glee-clubber that he was. Beside him he saw Lodz, a beatific smile on his face, chanting sonorously. Why were so many small men bassos?

Colt forgot himself and sang, let his voice swim out into the pool of sound and melt into harmony; when need was, he sang up, playing off against M. Lodz's basso and McNaughton's ringing tenor. And then he sang a sinister quarter-tone. It ended the bar on a gorgeously askew chord and got him very severely looked at. Raisuli Batar, baton in hand, frowned. Colt signaled wildly back that he couldn't help it.

It might have been lack of control, but it wasn't. It seemed that musical virtuosity was a gift to the dead. He had no choice in the matter—it was his nature that had dictated the quarter-tone. Raisuli Batar tapped a rock twice with the baton, then swept down, his left hand signaling volume, cuing in the bassos with his eyes.

The brilliant, crashing unison passage rang out. Damn! As though he had no control over his own voice, Colt sang not in unison but sharping and flatting around the line, botching the grand melody completely.

He strode angrily from the semicircle of singers, back to Valeska. She passed the bottle with a twisted smile on her face.

"You tried to compromise," she said. "It can't be done. They didn't thank you for Stravinskying their Bach."

"Right," he said. *But what do we do?*"

"It doesn't seem right," she brooded. "We shouldn't be the only in-betweeners. Five thousand years—more—they must appear more often. Then something happens to them. And they go away somewhere."

"Right," crowed Grandfather T'ang, drunker than ever. "Right, m'lass. And I know what happens to them. And I'll tell you what to do."

"Why?" asked Colt practically.

"Because I'm not as far outside as you think, children. Once I was as far in-between as you. I had my chance and I missed it—passed it up for the *suntori* and the dice games around the fires. Grandfather was a fool. I can't tell you any more than this: Get into the battle and observe rather closely. When you discover a very important secret, you will ascend to the Eighteenth Orbit and dwell forever, dancing and singing on the rings of Saturn. Or, to discard the gibberish, your psychic tissues so alter that you recognize a plane of existence more tenuous than ours; a plane, one suspects, more delectable. The mythological name for it is Heaven."

He hugged his bottle and crooned affectionately to it:

> *Superiority in a person*
> *Should better not*
> *Nor should it—*

"*Does* he know?" asked Colt, looking out into the long night.

"He wasn't lying this time. Shall we do it?"

"We shall. This waiting blasts my ethereal soul."

"You're an impatient cuss," she smiled at him. "You haven't seen me dance yet. I was a well-paid dancer once. It should be worth your while."

"Dance, then," he said, settling himself against a rock.

"You make the music. You know how."

He thought for a moment, then uncovered another bit of technique known to the dead. He began to send out mentally Debussy's *Clair de Lune*. She heard it, smiled at him as she caught the music, and began to dance.

Her body was not very good; certainly not as good as it had been. But as he studied the dancing, sometimes with eyes closed so that he could hear only the rustle of her feet on the snow and sometimes so abstracted that he could hear only the displacement of air as she moved, Colt was deeply stirred.

He tuned in on her thoughts, picking out the swiftly running stream, the skittering little point of consciousness that danced over them.

"Now I am a swan," said her thoughts while she danced to the music. "Now I am a swan, dying for love of the young prince who has wandered through the courtyard. And now I am the prince, very pretty and as dumb as a prince could be. Now I am his father the King, very wrathy and pompous. And now, and through it all, I was really the great stone gargoyle on the square top tower who saw all and grinned to himself."

She pirouetted to an end with the music, bowing with a stylized, satirically cloying grace. He applauded lustily.

"Unless you have other ideas," she said, "I would like to dance again." Her face was rosy and fresh-looking.

He began to construct music in his mind while she listened in and took little tentative steps. Colt started with a split-log-drum's beat, pulse speed, low and penetrating. He built up another rhythm overlaying it, a little slower, with wood-block timbre. It was louder than the first. Rapidly he constructed a series of seven polyrhythmic layers, from the bottom split-log pulse to a small, incessant snare-drum beat.

"I'm an animal now, a small, very arboreal animal. I can prick up my ears; my toes are opposed, so I can grasp a branch."

He added a bone-xylophone melody, very crude, of only three tones.

"My eyes are both in front of my face. My vision has become stereo-scopic. I can sit up and handle leaves. I can pick insects from the branches I live in."

Colt augmented the xylophone melody with a loud, crude brass.

Valeska thought, "I'm bigger—my arms are longer. And I often walk little distances on the ground, on my feet and my arm knuckles."

Colt added a see-sawing, gutty-sounding string timbre, in a melody opposed to the xylophone and the brass.

"I'm bigger—bigger—too big for trees. And I eat grubs as well as leaves—and I walk almost straight up—see me walk!"

He watched her swinging along the ground, apish, with the memory of bra-chiation stamped in every limb. He modified the bone-xylophone's timbre to a woody ring, increased the melodic range to a full octave.

With tremendous effort Valeska heaved over an imaginary rock, chipped at it. "I'm making flint hand-axes. They kill animals bigger than I am—tigers and bears—see my kitchen heap, high as a mountain, full of their bones!"

He augumented with a unison choir of woodwinds and a jangling ten-string harp.

"I eat bread and drink beer and I pray to the Nile—I sing and I dance, I farm and I bake—see me spin rope! See me paint pictures on plaster!"

A wailing clarinet mourned through the rhythmic sea.

Valeska danced statelily. "Yes—now I'm a man's woman—now I'm on top of the heap of the ages—now I'm a human—now I'm a woman ... ."

Colt stopped short the whole accumulation of percussion, melody and harmony in a score of timbres, cutting in precisely a single blues piano that carried in its minor, sobbing-sad left hand all the sorrow of ages; in the serpentine-stabbing chords splashed gold by the right sang the triumph of man in his glory of metal and stone.

Valeska danced, sending out no words of what the dance was, for it was she, what she dreamed, what she had been, and what she was to be. The dance and the music were Valeska, and they ended when she was in Colt's arms. The brandy bottle dropped from his grip and smashed on the rock.

Their long, wordless communion was broken by a disjointed yell from the two sides of the ridge as fighting forces streamed to battle. From the Bad caravan came the yell, "Kill and maim! Destroy! Destroy!" And the Good caravan cried, "In the name of the right! For sanctity and peace on Earth! Defend the right!"

Colt and Valeska found themselves torn apart in the rush to attack, swept into the thick of the fighting. The thundering voices from above, and the lightning, were almost continuous. The blinding radiance rather than the night hampered the fighting.

They were battling with queer, outlandish things—frying pans, camp stools, table forks. One embattled defender of the right had picked up a piteously bleating kid and was laying about him with it, holding its tiny hooves in a bunch.

Colt saw skulls crack, but nobody gave way or even fell. The dead were immortal. Then what in blazes was this all about? There was something excruciatingly wrong somewhere, and he couldn't fathom what it was.

He saw the righteous and amiable Raisuli Batar clubbing away with a table leg; minutes later he saw the fiendish and amiable chief of the Bad men swinging about him with another.

Vaguely sensing that he ought perhaps to be on the side of the right, he picked up a kettle by the handle and looked about for someone to bean with it. He saw a face that might be that of a fiend strayed from Hell, eyes rolling hideously, teeth locked and grinding with rage as its owner carved away at a small-sized somebody with a broken-bladed axe.

He was on the verge of cracking the fiend out of Hell when it considered itself finished with its victim, temporarily at least, and turned to Colt. "Hello, there," snapped the fiend. "Show some life, will you?"

Colt started as he saw that the fiend was Lodz, one of the Good men. Bewildered, he strayed off, nearly being gouged in the face by Grandfather T'ang, who was happily swinging away with a jagged hunk of *suntori* bottle, not bothering to discriminate.

But how *did* one discriminate? It came over him very suddenly that one didn't and couldn't. The caravaneers were attacking each other. At that moment there came through a mental call from Valeska, who had just made the same discovery on her own. They joined and mounted a table, inspecting the sea of struggling human beings.

"It's all in the way you look at them," said Valeska softly.

Colt nodded. "There was only one caravan," he said in somber tones.

He experimented silently a bit, discovering that by a twiddle of the eyes he could convert Raisuli Batar into the Bad caravan leader, turban and all. And the same went for the Bad idol—a reverse twiddle converted it into the smiling, blue-eyed guardian of the Good caravan. It was like the optical illusion of the three shaded cubes that point one way or the other, depending on how you decide to see them.

"That was what Grandfather T'ang meant," said the woman. Her eyes drifted to the old man. He had just drained another bottle; with a businesslike swing against a rock he shattered the bottom into a splendid cutting tool and set to work again.

"There's no logic to it," Colt said forlornly. "None at all." Valeska smiled happily and hugged him.

Colt felt his cheek laid open.

"Bon soir. Guten Tag. Buon giorno. Buenos dias. Bon soir. Guten Tag. Buon—"

"You can stop that," said Colt, struggling to his feet. He cracked his head against a strut, hung on dazedly. "Where's—"

He inspected the two men standing before him with healthy grins. They wore the Red Army uniform under half-buttoned flying suits. The strut that had got in his way belonged to a big, black helicopter; amidships was blazoned the crimson star of the Soviet Union.

"You're well and all that, I fawncy?" asked one of the flyers. "We spotted you and landed—bunged up your cheek a bit—Volanov heah *would* try to overshoot."

"I'm fine," said Colt, feeling his bandage. "Why'n hell can't you Russians learn to speak American?"

The two soldiers exchanged smiles and glances. They obviously considered Colt too quaint for words. "Pile in, old chap. We can take you as far as Bokhara— we fuel at Samarkand. I—ah—suppose you have papers?"

Colt leaned against the strut and wearily shoved over his credentials. Everything would be all right. Chungking was in solid with the Reds at the moment. Everything would be all right.

"I fawncy," said Volanov, making conversation while his partner handled the helicopter vanes, "youah glad to see the lawst of all that."

Colt looked down, remembered, and wept.

"I find," I said as dryly as possible, "a certain familiarity—a nostalgic ring, as it were—toward the end of your tale." I was just drunk enough to get fancy with The Three-Cornered Scar.

"You do?" he asked. He leaned forward across the table. *"You do?"*

"I've read widely in such matters," I hastily assured him, pouring another glass of red wine.

He grinned glumly, sipping. "If I hadn't left half my spirit with Valeska that night I was dead," he remarked conversationally, "I'd smash your face in."

"That may be," I assented gracefully.

But I should say that he drank less like half a spirit than half a dozen.

[*Stirring Science Stories* - April 1941
as by Cecil Corwin]

The Rocket of 1955

The scheme was all Fein's, but the trimmings that made it more than a pipe-dream, and its actual operation depended on me. How long the plan had been in incubation I do not know, but Fein, one spring day, broke it to me in crude form. I pointed out some errors, corrected and amplified on the thing in general, and told him that I'd have no part of it—and changed my mind when he threatened to reveal certain indiscretions committed by me some years ago.

It was necessary that I spend some months in Europe, conducting research work incidental to the scheme. I returned with recorded statements, old newspapers and photostatic copies of certain documents. There was a brief, quiet interview with that old, bushy-haired Viennese worshipped incontinently by the mob; he was convinced by the evidence I had compiled that it would be wise to assist us.

You all know what happened next—it was the professor's historic radio broadcast. Fein had drafted the thing, I had rewritten it, and told the astronomer to assume a German accent while reading. Some of the phrases were beautiful: "American dominion over the very planets! ... veil at last ripped aside ... man defies gravity ... travel through limitless space ... plant the red-white-and-blue banner in the soil of Mars!"

The requested contributions poured in. Newspapers and magazines ostentatiously donated yard-long checks of a few thousand dollars; the government gave a welcome half-million; heavy sugar came from the "Rocket Contribution Week" held in the nation's public schools; but independent contributions were the largest. We cleared seven million dollars, and then started to build the space-ship.

The virginium that took up most of the money was tin-plate; the monoatomic fluorine that gave us our terrific speed was hydrogen. The take-off was a party for the newsreels: the big, gleaming bullet extravagant with vanes and projections; speeches by the professor; Farley, who was to fly it to Mars, grinning into the cameras. He climbed an outside ladder to the nose of the thing, then dropped into the steering compartment. I screwed down the sound-proof door, smiling as he hammered to be let out. To his surprise, there was no duplicate of the elaborate dummy controls he had been practicing on for the past few weeks.

I cautioned the pressmen to stand back under the shelter, and gave the professor the knife-switch that would send the rocket on its way. He hesitated too long—Fein hissed into his ear: "Anna Pareloff of Cracow, Herr Professor ..."

The triple blade clicked into the sockets. The vaned projectile roared a hundred yards into the air with a wobbling curve—then exploded.

A photographer, eager for an angle-shot, was killed; so were some kids. The steel roof protected the rest of us. Fein and I shook hands, while the pressmen screamed into the telephones which we had provided.

But the professor got drunk, and, disgusted with the part he had played in the affair, told all and poisoned himself. Fein and I left the cash behind and hopped a freight. We were picked off it by a vigilance committee (headed by a man who had lost fifty cents in our rocket). Fein was too frightened to talk or write so they hanged him first, and gave me a paper and pencil to tell the story as best I could.

Here they come, with an insulting thick rope.

[*Worlds Beyond* - December 1950]

The Mindworm

The handsome j.g. and the pretty nurse held out against it as long as they reasonably could, but blue Pacific water, languid tropical nights, the low atoll dreaming
on the horizon—and the complete absence of any other nice young people for
company on the small, uncomfortable parts boat—did their work. On June 30th
they watched through dark glasses as the dazzling thing burst over the fleet and
the atoll. Her manicured hand gripped his arm in excitement and terror. Unfelt
radiation sleeted through their loins.

A storekeeper-third-class named Bielaski watched the young couple with more
interest than he showed in Test Able. After all, he had twenty-five dollars riding
on the nurse. That night he lost it to a chief bosun's mate who had backed the j.g.

In the course of time, the careless nurse was discharged under conditions
other than honorable. The j.g., who didn't like to put things in writing, phoned
her all the way from Manila to say it was a damned shame. When her gratitude
gave way to specific inquiry, their overseas connection went bad and he had to
hang up.

She had a child, a boy, turned it over to a foundling home and vanished
from his life into a series of good jobs and finally marriage.

The boy grew up stupid, puny and stubborn, greedy and miserable. To the home's
hilarious young athletics director he suddenly said: "You hate me. You think I
make the rest of the boys look bad."

The athletics director blustered and laughed, and later told the doctor over
coffee: "I watch myself around the kids. They're sharp—they catch a look or a
gesture and it's like a blow in the face to them, I know that, so I watch myself. So
how did he know?"

The doctor told the boy: "Three pounds more this month isn't bad, but how
about you pitch in and clean up your plate *every* day? Can't live on meat and water; those vegetables make you big and strong."

The boy said: "What's 'neurasthenic' mean?"

The doctor later said to the director: "It made my flesh creep. I was looking at his little spindling body and dishing out the old pep-talk about growing big and strong, and inside my head I was thinking 'we'd call him neurasthenic in the old days' and then out he popped with it. What should we do? Should we do anything? Maybe it'll go away. I don't know anything about these things. I don't know whether anybody does."

"Reads minds, does he?" asked the director. *Be damned if he's going to read my mind about Schultz Meat Market's ten percent.* "Doctor, I think I'm going to take my vacation a little early this year. Has anybody shown any interest in adopting the child?"

"Not him. He wasn't a baby-doll when we got him, and at present he's an exceptionally unattractive-looking kid. You know how people don't give a damn about anything but their looks."

"*Some* couples would take anything, or so they tell me."

"Unapproved for foster-parenthood, you mean?"

"Red tape and arbitrary classifications sometimes limit us too severely in our adoptions."

"If you're going to wish him on some screwball couple that the courts turned down as unfit, I want no part of it."

"You don't have to have any part of it, doctor. By the way, which dorm does he sleep in?"

"West," grunted the doctor, leaving the office.

The director called a few friends—a judge, a couple the judge referred him to, a court clerk. Then he left by way of the east wing of the building.

The boy survived three months with the Berrymans. Hard-drinking Mimi alternately caressed and shrieked at him; Edward W. tried to be a good scout and just gradually lost interest, looking clean through him. He hit the road in June and got by with it for a while. He wore a Boy Scout uniform, and Boy Scouts can turn up anywhere, any time. The money he had taken with him lasted a month. When the last penny of the last dollar was three days spent, he was adrift on a Nebraska prairie. He had walked out of the last small town because the constable was beginning to wonder what on earth he was hanging around for and who he belonged to. The town was miles behind on the two-lane highway; the infrequent cars did not stop.

One of Nebraska's "rivers," a dry bed at this time of year, lay ahead, spanned by a railroad culvert. There were some men in its shade, and he was hungry.

They were ugly, dirty men, and their thoughts were muddled and stupid. They called him "Shorty" and gave him a little dirty bread and some stinking sardines from a can. The thoughts of one of them became less muddled and uglier. He talked to the rest out of the boy's hearing, and they whooped with laughter. The boy got ready to run, but his legs wouldn't hold him up.

He could read the thoughts of the men quite clearly as they headed for him. Outrage, fear and disgust blended in him and somehow turned inside-out and one of the men was dead on the dry ground, grasshoppers vaulting on to his flannel shirt, the others backing away, frightened now, not frightening.

He wasn't hungry any more; he felt quite comfortable and satisfied. He got up and headed for the other men, who ran. The rearmost of them was thinking *Jeez he folded up the evil eye we was only gonna—*

Again the boy let the thoughts flow into his head and again he flipped his own thoughts around them; it was quite easy to do. It was different—this man's terror from the other's lustful anticipation. But both had their points ... .

At his leisure, he robbed the bodies of three dollars and twenty-four cents.

Thereafter his fame preceded him like a death-wind. Two years on the road and he had his growth, and his fill of the dull and stupid minds he met there. He moved to northern cities, a year here, a year there, quiet, unobtrusive, prudent, an epicure.

Sebastian Long woke suddenly, with something on his mind. As night-fog cleared away he remembered, happily. Today he started the Demeter Bowl! At last there was time, at last there was money—six hundred and twenty-three dollars in the bank. He had packed and shipped the three dozen cocktail glasses last night, engraved with Mrs. Klausman's initials—his last commercial order for as many months as the Bowl would take.

He shifted from nightshirt to denims, gulped coffee, boiled an egg but was too excited to eat it. He went to the front of his shop-workroom-apartment, checked the lock, waved at neighbors' children on their way to school, and ceremoniously set a sign in the cluttered window.

It said: "NO COMMERCIAL ORDERS TAKEN UNTIL FURTHER NOTICE."

From a closet he tenderly carried a shrouded object that made a double armful and laid it on his workbench. Unshrouded, it was a glass bowl—*what* a glass bowl! The clearest Swedish lead glass, the purest lines he had ever seen, his secret treasure since the crazy day he had bought it, long ago, for six months' earnings. His wife had given him hell for that until the day she died. From the closet he brought a portfolio filled with sketches and designs dating back to the day he had bought the bowl. He smiled over the first, excitedly scrawled—a florid, rococo conception, unsuited to the classicism of the lines and the serenity of the perfect glass.

Through many years and hundreds of sketches he had refined his conception to the point where it was, he humbly felt, not unsuited to the medium. A strongly molded Demeter was to dominate the piece, a matron as serene as the glass, and all the fruits of the earth would flow from her gravely outstretched arms.

Suddenly and surely, he began to work. With a candle he thinly smoked an oval area on the outside of the bowl. Two steady fingers clipped the Demeter drawing against the carbon black; a hair-fine needle in his other hand traced her lines. When the transfer of the design was done, Sebastian Long readied his lathe. He fitted a small copper wheel, slightly worn as he liked them, into the chuck and with his fingers charged it with the finest rouge from Rouen. He took an ashtray cracked in delivery and held it against the spinning disc. It bit in smoothly, with the *wiping* feel to it that was exactly right.

Holding out his hands, seeing that the fingers did not tremble with excitement, he eased the great bowl to the lathe and was about to make the first tiny cut of the millions that would go into the masterpiece.

Somebody knocked on his door and rattled the doorknob.

Sebastian Long did not move or look towards the door. Soon the busybody would read the sign and go away. But the pounding and the rattling of the knob went on. He eased down the bowl and angrily went to the window, picked up the sign and shook it at whoever it was—he couldn't make out the face very well. But the idiot wouldn't go away.

The engraver unlocked the door, opened it a bit and snapped: "The shop is closed. I shall not be taking any orders for several months. Please don't bother me now."

"It's about the Demeter Bowl," said the intruder.

Sebastian Long stared at him. "What the devil do you know about my Demeter Bowl?" He saw the man was a stranger, undersized by a little, middle-aged—

"Just let me in, please," urged the man. "It's important. Please!"

"I don't know what you're talking about," said the engraver. "But what do you know about my Demeter Bowl?" He hooked his thumbs pugnaciously over the waistband of his denims and glowered at the stranger. The stranger promptly took advantage of his hand being removed from the door and glided in.

Sebastian Long thought briefly that it might be a nightmare as the man darted quickly about his shop, picking up a graver and throwing it down, picking up a wire scratch-wheel and throwing it down. "Here, you!" he roared, as the stranger picked up a crescent wrench which he did not throw down.

As Long started for him, the stranger darted to the workbench and brought the crescent wrench down shatteringly on the bowl.

Sebastian Long's heart was bursting with sorrow and rage; such a storm of emotions as he never had known thundered through him. Paralyzed, he saw the stranger smile with anticipation.

The engraver's legs folded under him and he fell to the floor, drained and dead.

The Mindworm, locked in the bedroom of his brownstone front, smiled again, reminiscently.

Smiling, he checked the day on a wall calendar.

"Dolores!" yelled her mother in Spanish. "Are you going to pass the whole day in there?"

She had been practicing low-lidded, sexy half-smiles like Lauren Bacall in the bathroom mirror. She stormed out and yelled in English: "I don't know how many more times I tell you not to call me that Spick name no more!"

"Dolly!" sneered her mother. "Dah-lee! When was there a Saint Dah-lee that you call yourself after, eh?"

The girl snarled a Spanish obscenity at her mother and ran down the tenement stairs. Jeez, she was gonna be late for sure!

Held up by a stream of traffic between her and her streetcar, she danced with impatience. Then the miracle happened. Just like in the movies, a big convertible pulled up before her and its lounging driver said, opening the door: "You seem to be in a hurry. Could I drop you somewhere?"

Dazed at the sudden realization of a hundred daydreams, she did not fail to give the driver a low-lidded, sexy smile as she said: "Why, *thanks!*" and climbed in. He wasn't no Cary Grant, but he had all his hair ... kind of small, but so was she ... and jeez, the convertible had *leopard-skin seat covers!*

The car was in the stream of traffic, purring down the avenue. "It's a lovely day," she said. "Really too nice to work."

The driver smiled shyly, kind of like Jimmy Stewart but of course not so tall, and said: "I feel like playing hooky myself. How would you like a spin down Long Island?"

"Be wonderful!" The convertible cut left on an odd-numbered street.

"Play hooky, you said. What do you do?"

"Advertising."

"Advertising!" Dolly wanted to kick herself for ever having doubted, for ever having thought in low, self-loathing moments that it wouldn't work out, that she'd marry a grocer or a mechanic and live for ever after in a smelly tenement and grow old and sick and stooped. She felt vaguely in her happy daze that it might have been cuter, she might have accidentally pushed him into a pond or something, but this was cute enough. An advertising man, leopard-skin seat covers ... what more could a girl with a sexy smile and a nice little figure want?

Speeding down the South Shore she learned that his name was Michael Brent, exactly as it ought to be. She wished she could tell him she was Jennifer Brown or one of those real cute names they had nowadays, but was reassured when he told her he thought Dolly Gonzalez was a beautiful name. He didn't, and she noticed the omission, add: "It's the most beautiful name I ever heard!" That, she comfortably thought as she settled herself against the cushions, would come later.

They stopped at Medford for lunch, a wonderful lunch in a little restaurant where you went down some steps and there were candles on the table. She called him "Michael" and he called her "Dolly." She learned that he liked dark girls and thought the stories in *True Story* really were true, and that he thought she was just tall enough, and that Greer Garson was wonderful, but not the way she was, and that he thought her dress was just wonderful.

They drove slowly after Medford, and Michael Brent did most of the talking. He had traveled all over the world. He had been in the war and wounded—just a flesh wound. He was thirty-eight, and had been married once, but she died. There were no children. He was alone in the world. He had nobody to share his town house in the 'fifties, his country place in Westchester, his lodge in the Maine woods. Every word sent the girl floating higher and higher on a tide of happiness; the signs were unmistakable.

When they reached Montauk Point, the last sandy bit of the continent before blue water and Europe, it was sunset, with a great wrinkled sheet of purple and rose stretching half across the sky and the first stars appearing above the dark horizon of the water.

The two of them walked from the parked car out onto the sand, alone, bathed in glorious Technicolor. Her heart was nearly bursting with joy as she heard Michael Brent say, his arms tightening around her: "Darling, will you marry me?"

"Oh, *yes*, Michael!" she breathed, dying.

The Mindworm, drowsing, suddenly felt the sharp sting of danger. He cast out through the great city, dragging tentacles of thought:

"... die if she don't let me ..."

"... six an' six is twelve an' carry one an' three is four ..."

"... gobblegobble madre de dios pero soy gobblegobble ..."

"... parlay Domino an' Missab and shoot the roll on Duchess Peg in the feature ..."

"... melt resin add the silver chloride and dissolve in oil of lavender stand and decant and fire to cone 012 give you shimmering streaks of luster down the walls ..."

"... moiderin' square-headed gobblegobble tried ta poke his eye out wassa matta witta ref ..."

"... O God I am most heartily sorry I have offended thee in ..."

"... talk like a commie ..."

"... gobblegobblegobble two dolla twenny-fi' sense gobble ..."

"... just a nip and fill it up with water and brush my teeth ..."

"... really know I'm God but fear to confess their sins ..."

"... dirty lousy rock-headed claw-handed paddle-footed goggle-eyed snot-nosed hunch-backed feeble-minded pot-bellied son of ..."

"... write on the wall alfie is a stunkur and then ..."

"... thinks I believe it's a television set but I know he's got a bomb in there but who can I tell who can help so alone ..."

"... gabble was ich weiss nicht gabble geh bei Broadvay gabble ..."

"... habt mein daughter Rosie such a fella gobblegobble ..."

"... wonder if that's one didn't look back ..."

"... seen with her in the Medford restaurant ..."

The Mindworm struck into that thought.

"... not a mark on her but the M.E.'s have been wrong before and heart failure don't mean a thing anyway try to talk to her old lady authorize an autopsy get Pancho little guy talks Spanish be best ..."

The Mindworm knew he would have to be moving again—soon. He was sorry; some of the thoughts he had tapped indicated good ... hunting??

Regretfully, he again dragged his net:

"... with chartreuse drinks I mean drapes could use a drink come to think of it ..."

"... reep-beep-reep-beep reepiddy-beepiddy-beep bop man wadda beat ..."

"... $\partial_i^* ex\dot{p} - v^2 x \left(\dot{v} \right) \circ \frac{c-i}{2} \left(\epsilon x^2 x \right) \dot{\circ}$ " *What the Hell was that?*

The Mindworm withdrew, in frantic haste. The intelligence was massive, its overtones those of a vigorous adult. He had learned from certain dangerous children that there was peril of a leveling flow. Shaken and scared, he contemplated traveling. He would need more than that wretched girl had supplied, and it would not be epicurean. There would be no time to find individuals at a ripe emotional crisis, or goad them to one. It would be plain—munching. The Mindworm drank a glass of water, also necessary to his metabolism.

EIGHT FOUND DEAD
IN UPTOWN MOVIE;
"MOLESTER" SOUGHT

Eight persons, including three women, were found dead Wednesday night of unknown causes in widely-separated seats in the balcony of the Odeon Theater at 117th Street and Broadway. Police are seeking a man described by the balcony usher, Michael Fenelly, eighteen, as "acting like a woman-molester."

Fenelly discovered the first of the fatalities after seeing the man "moving from one empty seat to another several times." He went to ask a woman in a seat next to one the man had just vacated whether he had annoyed her. She was dead.

Almost at once, a scream rang out. In another part of the balcony Mrs. Sadie Rabinowitz, forty, uttered the cry when another victim toppled from his seat next to her.

Theater manager I. J. Marcusohn stopped the show and turned on the house lights. He tried to instruct his staff to keep the audience from leaving before the police arrived. He failed to get word to them in time, however, and most of the audience was gone when a detail from the 24th Pct. and an ambulance from Harlem hospital took over at the scene of the tragedy.

The Medical Examiner's office has not yet made a report as to the causes of death. A spokesman said the victims showed no signs of poisoning or violence. He added that it "was inconceivable that it could be a coincidence."

Lt. John Braidwood of the 24th Pct. said of the alleged molester: "We got a fair description of him and naturally we will try to bring him in for questioning."

Clickety-click, clickety-click, clickety-click sang the rails as the Mindworm drowsed in his coach seat.

Some people were walking forward from the diner. One was thinking: "Different-looking fellow. (a) he's aberrant. (b) he's nonaberrant and ill. Cancel (b)—respiration normal, skin smooth and healthy, no tremor of limbs, well-groomed. Is aberrant (1) trivially. (2) significantly. Cancel (1)—displayed no involuntary interest when ... odd! *Running* for the washroom! Unexpected because

(a) neat grooming indicates amour propre inconsistent with amusing others; (b) evident health inconsistent with ..." It had taken one second, was fully detailed.

The Mindworm, locked in the toilet of the coach, wondered what the next stop was. He was getting off at it—not frightened, just careful. Dodge them, keep dodging them and everything would be all right. Send out no mental taps until the train was far away and everything would be all right.

He got off at a West Virginian coal and iron town surrounded by ruined mountains and filled with the offscourings of Eastern Europe. Serbs, Albanians, Croats, Hungarians, Slovenes, Bulgarians and all possible combinations and permutations thereof. He walked slowly from the smoke-stained, brownstone passenger station. The train had roared on its way.

"... ain' no gemmun that's fo sho', fi-cen' tip fo' a good shine lak ah give um ..."

"... dumb bassar don't know how to make out a billa lading yet he ain't never gonna know so fire him get it over with ..."

"... gabblegabblegabble ..." Not a word he recognized in it.

"... gobblegobble dat tam vooman I brek she nack ..."

"... gobble trink visky chin glassabeer gobblegobblegobble ..."

"... gabblegabblegabble ..."

"... makes me so gobblegobble mad little no-good tramp no she ain' but I don' like no standup from no dame ..."

A blond, square-headed boy fuming under a street light.

"... out wit' Casey Oswiak I could kill that dumb bohunk alla time trine ta paw her ..."

It was a possibility. The Mindworm drew near.

"... stand me up for that gobblegobble bohunk I oughtta slap her inna mush like my ole man says ..."

"Hello," said the Mindworm.

"Waddaya wan'?"

"Casey Oswiak told me to tell you not to wait up for your girl. He's taking her out tonight."

The blond boy's rage boiled into his face and shot from his eyes. He was about to swing when the Mindworm began to feed. It was like pheasant after chicken, venison after beef. The coarseness of the environment, or the ancient strain? The Mindworm wondered as he strolled down the street. A girl passed him:

"... oh, but he's gonna be mad like last time wish I came right away so jealous kinda nice but he might bust me one some day be nice to him tonight there he is lam'post leaning on it looks kinda funny gawd I hope he ain't drunk looks kinda funny sleeping sick or bozhe moi gabblegabblegabble ..."

Her thoughts trailed into a foreign language of which the Mindworm knew not a word. After hysteria had gone she recalled, in the foreign language, that she had passed him.

The Mindworm, stimulated by the unfamiliar quality of the last feeding, determined to stay for some days. He checked in at a Main Street hotel.

Musing, he dragged his net:

"... gobblegobblewhompyeargobblecheskygobblegabblechyesh ..."

"... take him down cellar beat the can off the damn chesky thief put the fear of god into him teach him can't bust into no boxcars in *mah* parta the caounty ..."

"... gabblegabble ..."

"... phone ole Mister Ryan in She-cawgo and he'll tell them three-card monte grifters who got the horse-room rights in this necka the woods by damn don't pay protection money for no protection ..."

The Mindworm followed that one further; it sounded as though it could lead to some money if he wanted to stay in the town long enough.

The Eastern Europeans of the town, he mistakenly thought, were like the tramps and bums he had known and fed on during his years on the road—stupid and safe, safe and stupid, quite the same thing.

In the morning he found no mention of the square-headed boy's death in the town's paper and thought it had gone practically unnoticed. It had—by the paper, which was of, by and for the coal and iron company and its native-American bosses and straw bosses. The other town, the one without a charter or police force, with only an imported weekly newspaper or two from the nearest city, noticed it. The other town had roots more than two thousand years deep, which are hard to pull up. But the Mindworm didn't know it was there.

He fed again that night, on a giddy young street-walker in her room. He had astounded and delighted her with a fistful of ten-dollar bills before he began to gorge. Again the delightful difference from city-bred folk was there ... .

Again in the morning he had been unnoticed, he thought. The chartered town, unwilling to admit that there were street-walkers or that they were found dead, wiped the slate clean; its only member who really cared was the native-American cop on the beat who had collected weekly from the dead girl.

The other town, unknown to the Mindworm, buzzed with it. A delegation went to the other town's only public officer. Unfortunately he was young, American-trained, perhaps even ignorant about some important things. For what he told them was: "My children, that is foolish superstition. Go home."

The Mindworm, through the day, roiled the surface of the town proper by allowing himself to be roped into a poker game in a parlor of the hotel. He wasn't good at it, he didn't like it, and he quit with relief when he had cleaned six shifty-eyed, hard-drinking loafers out of about three hundred dollars. One of them went straight to the police station and accused the unknown of being a sharper. A humorous sergeant, the Mindworm was pleased to note, joshed the loafer out of his temper.

Nightfall again, hunger again ... .

He walked the streets of the town and found them empty. It was strange. The native-American citizens were out, tending bar, walking their beats, locking up their newspaper on the stones, collecting their rents, managing their movies —but where were the others? He cast his net:

"... gobblegobblegobble whomp year gobble ..."

"... crazy old pollack mama of mine try to lock me in with Errol Flynn at the Majestic never know the difference if I sneak out the back ..."

That was near. He crossed the street and it was nearer. He homed on the thought:

"... jeez he's a hunka man like Stanley but he never looks at me that Vera Kowalik I'd like to kick her just once in the gobblegobblegobble crazy old mama won't be American so ashamed ..."

It was half a block, no more, down a side-street. Brick houses, two stories, with backyards on an alley. She was going out the back way.

How strangely quiet it was in the alley.

"... ea-sy down them steps fix that damn board that's how she caught me last time what the hell are they all so scared of went to see Father Drugas won't talk bet somebody got it again that Vera Kowalik and her big ..."

"... gobble bozhe gobble whomp year gobble ..."

She was closer; she was closer.

"All think I'm a kid show them who's a kid bet if Stanley caught me all alone out here in the alley dark and all he wouldn't think I was a kid that damn Vera Kowalik her folks don't think she's a kid ..."

For all her bravado she was stark terrified when he said: "Hello."

"Who—who—who?" she stammered.

Quick, before she screamed. Her terror was delightful.

Not too replete to be alert, he cast about, questing.

"... gobblegobblegobble whomp year."

The countless eyes of the other town, with more than two thousand years of experience in such things, had been following him. What he had sensed as a meaningless hash of noise was actually an impassioned outburst in a nearby darkened house.

"Fools! fools! Now he has taken a virgin! I said not to wait. What will we say to her mother?"

An old man with handlebar mustache and, in spite of the heat, his shirt-sleeves decently rolled down and buttoned at the cuffs, evenly replied: "My heart in me died with hers, Casimir, but one must be sure. It would be a terrible thing to make a mistake in such an affair."

The weight of conservative elder opinion was with him. Other old men with mustaches, some perhaps remembering mistakes long ago, nodded and said: "A terrible thing. A terrible thing."

The Mindworm strolled back to his hotel and napped on the made bed briefly. A tingle of danger awakened him. Instantly he cast out:

"... gobblegobble whompyear."

"... whampyir."

"WAMPYIR!"

Close! Close and deadly!

The door of his room burst open, and mustached old men with their shirt-sleeves rolled down and decently buttoned at the cuffs unhesitatingly marched in, their thoughts a turmoil of alien noises, foreign gibberish that he could not wrap his mind around, disconcerting, from every direction.

The sharpened stake was through his heart and the scythe blade through his throat before he could realize that he had not been the first of his kind; and that what clever people have not yet learned, some quite ordinary people have not yet entirely forgotten.

[*Venture* - July 1957 as *The Education of Tigress Macardle*]

The Education of Tigress McCardle

With the unanimity that had always characterized his fans, as soon as they were able to vote they swept him into office as President of the United States. Four years later the 28th Amendment was ratified, republican institutions yielded gracefully to the usages of monarchy, and King Purvis I reigned in the land.

Perhaps even then all would have gone well if it had not been for another major entertainment personage, the insidious Dr. Fu Manchu, that veritable personification of the Yellow Peril, squatting like some great evil spider in the center of his web of intrigue. The insidious doctor appeared to have so much fun on his television series, what with a lovely concubine to paw him and a dwarf to throw knives, that it quite turned the head of Gerald Wang, a hitherto-peaceable antique dealer of San Francisco. Gerald had decided that he too would become a veritable personification of the Yellow Peril, and that he too would squat like some great evil spider in the center of a web of intrigue, and that he would *really* accomplish something. He found it remarkably easy since nobody believed in the Yellow Peril anymore. He grew a mandarin mustache, took to uttering cryptic quotations from the sages, and was generally addressed as "doctor" by the members of his organization, though he made no attempt to practice medicine. His wife drew the line at the concubine, but Gerald had enough to keep him busy with his personifying and squatting.

His great coup occurred in 1986 when, after patient years of squatting and plotting, one of his most insidious ideas reached the attention of His Majesty via a recommendation ridered onto the annual population-resources report. The recommendation was implemented as the Parental Qualifications Program, or P.Q.P., by royal edict. "Ow rackon thet'll make um mahnd they P's and Q's," quipped His Majesty, and everybody laughed heartily—but none more heartily than the insidious Dr. Wang, who was present in disguise as Tuner of the Royal Git-tar.

A typical PQP operation (at least when judged typical by the professor of Chronoscope History Seminar 201 given by Columbia University in 2756 A.D., who ought to know) involved George McCardle ...

72

George McCardle had a *good* deal with his girl friend, Tigress Moone. He dined her and bought her pretties and had the freedom of the bearskin rug in front of her wood-burning fireplace. He had beaten the game; he had achieved a delightful combination of bachelor irresponsibility and marital gratification.

"George," Tigress said thoughtfully one day ... so they got married.

With prices what they were in 1998, she kept her job, of course—at least until she again said thoughtfully; "George ..."

She then had too much time on her hands; it was absurd for a healthy young woman to pretend that taking care of a two-room city apartment kept her occupied ... so she thoughtfully said, "George?" and they moved to the suburbs.

George happened to be a rising young editor in the Civil War Book-of-the-Week Club. He won his spurs when he got *Mightier Than the Sword: A Study of Pens and Pencils in the Army of the Potomac, 1863–1865* whipped into shape for the printer. They then assigned him to the infinitely more difficult and delicate job of handling writers. A temperamental troll named Blount was his special trial. Blount was writing a novelized account of Corporal Piggott's Raid, a deservedly obscure episode which got Corporal Piggott of the 104th New York (Provisional) Heavy Artillery Regiment deservedly court-martialed in the summer of '63. It was George's responsibility to see that Blount novelized the verdict of guilty into a triumphant acquittal followed by an award of the Medal of Honor, and Blount was being unreasonable about it.

It was after a hard day of screaming at Blount, and being screamed back at, that George dragged his carcass off the Long Island Rail Road and into the family car. "Hi, dear," he said to Mrs. McCardle, erstwhile tigress-Diana, and off they drove, and so far it seemed like the waning of another ordinary day. But in the car Mrs. McCardle said thoughtfully: "George ..."

She told him what was on her mind, and he refrained from striking her in the face because they were in rather tricky traffic and she was driving.

She wanted a child.

It was necessary to have a child, she said. Inexorable logic dictated it. For one thing, it was absurd for just the two of them to live in a great barn of a six-room house.

For another thing, she needed a child to fulfill her womanhood. For a third, the brains and beauty of the Moone-McCardle strain should not die out; it was their duty to posterity.

(The students in Columbia's Chronoscope History Seminar 201 retched as one man at the words.)

For a fourth, everybody was having children.

George thought he had her there, but no. The statement was perfectly correct if for "everybody" you substituted "Mrs. Jacques Truro," their next-door neighbor.

By the time they reached their great six-room barn of a place she was consolidating her victory with a rapid drumfire of simple declarative sentences which ended with "Don't you?" and "Won't we?" and "Isn't it?" to which

George, hanging onto the ropes, groggily replied: "We'll see ... we'll see ... we'll see ..."

A wounded thing inside him was soundlessly screaming: *youth! joy! freedom! gone beyond recall, slain by wedlock, coffined by a mortgage, now to be entombed beneath a reeking Everest of diapers!*

"I believe I'd like a drink before dinner," he said. "Had quite a time with Blount today," he said as the Martini curled quietly in his stomach. He was pretending nothing very bad had happened. "Kept talking about his integrity. Writers! They'll never learn. ... Tigress? Are you with me?"

His wife noticed a slight complaining note in his voice, so she threw herself on the floor, began to kick and scream, went on to hold her breath until her face turned blue, and finished by letting George know that she had abandoned her Career to assuage his bachelor misery, moved out to this dreary wasteland to satisfy his whim, and just once in her life requested some infinitesimal consideration for her ghastly drudgery and scrimping.

George, who was a kind and gentle person except with writers, dried her tears and apologized for his brutality. They would have a child, he said contritely. "Though," he added, "I hear there are some complications about it these days."

"For Motherhood," said Mrs. McCardle, getting off the floor, "no complications are too great." She stood profiled like a statue against their picture window, with its view of the picture window of the house across the street.

The next day George asked around at his office.

None of the younger men, married since the P.Q.P. went into effect, seemed to have had children.

A few of them cheerily admitted they had not had children and were not going to have children, for they had volunteered for D-Bal shots, thus doing away with a running minor expense and, more importantly, ensuring a certain peace of mind and unbroken continuity during tender moments.

"Ugh," thought George.

(The Columbia University professor explained to his students, "It is clearly in George's interest to go to the clinic for a painless, effective D-Bal shot and thus resolve his problem, but he does not go; he shudders at the thought. We cannot know what fear of amputation stemming from some early traumatic experience thus prevents him from action, but deep-rooted psychological reasons explain his behavior, we can't be certain." The class bent over the chronoscope.)

And some of George's co-workers slunk away and would not submit to questioning. Young MacBirney, normally open and incisive, muttered vaguely and passed his hand across his brow when George asked him how one went about having a baby—red-tape-wise, that is.

It was Blount, come in for his afternoon screaming match, who spilled the vengeful beans. "You and your wife just phone P.Q.P. for an appointment," he told George with a straight face. "They'll issue you—everything you need." George in his innocence thanked him, and Blount turned away and grinned the twisted, sly grin of an author.

A glad female voice answered the phone on behalf of the P.Q.P. It assured George that he and Mrs. McCardle need only drop in any time at the Empire State Building and they'd be well on their way to parenthood.

The next day Mr. and Mrs. McCardle dropped in at the Empire State Building. A receptionist in the lobby was buffing her nails under a huge portrait of His Majesty. A beautifully lettered sign displayed the words with which His Majesty had decreed that P.Q.P. be enacted: "Ow Racken Theah's a Raht Smaht Ah-dee, Boys."

"Where do we sign up, please?" asked George.

The receptionist pawed uncertainly through her desk. "I *know* there's some kind of book," she said as she rummaged, but she did not find it. "Well, it doesn't matter. They'll give you everything you need in Room 100."

"Will I sign up there?" asked George nervously, conditioned by a lifetime of red tape and uncomfortable without it.

"No," said the receptionist.

"But for the tests—"

"There aren't any tests."

"Then the interviews, the deep probing of our physical and psychological fitness for parenthood, our heredity—"

"No interviews."

"But the evaluation of our financial and moral standing without which no permission can be—"

"No evaluation. Just Room 100." She resumed buffing her nails.

In Room 100 a cheerful woman took a Toddler out of a cabinet, punched the non-reversible activating button between its shoulder blades, and handed it to Mrs. McCardle with a cheery: "It's all yours, madame. Return with it in three months and, depending on its condition, you will, or will not, be issued a breeding permit. Simple, isn't it?"

"The little darling!" gurgled Mrs. McCardle, looking down into the Toddler's pretty face.

It spit in her eye, punched her in the nose and sprang a leak.

"Gracious!" said the cheerful woman. "Get it out of our nice clean office, *if* you please."

"How do you work it?" yelled Mrs. McCardle, juggling the Toddler like a hot potato. "How do you turn it off?"

"Oh, you *can't* turn it off," said the woman. "And you'd better not swing it like that. Rough handling goes down on the tapes inside it and we read them in three months and now if you *please,* you're getting our nice office *all wet*—"

She shepherded them out.

"Do something, George!" yelled Mrs. McCardle. George took the Toddler. It stopped leaking and began a ripsaw scream that made the lighting fixtures tremble.

"Give the poor thing to me!" Mrs. McCardle shouted. "You're hurting it holding it like that—"

She took the Toddler back. It stopped screaming and resumed leaking.

It quieted down in the car. The sudden thought seized them both—*too* quiet? Their heads crashed together as they bent simultaneously over the glassy-eyed little object. It laughed delightedly and waved its chubby fists.

"Clumsy oaf!" snapped Mrs. McCardle, rubbing her head.

"Sorry, dear," said George. "But at least we must have got a good mark out of it on the tapes. I suppose it scores us good when it laughs."

Her eyes narrowed. "Probably," she said. "George, do you think if you fell heavily on the sidewalk—?"

"No," said George convulsively. Mrs. McCardle looked at him for a moment and held her peace.

("Note, young gentlemen," said the history professor, "the turning point, the seed of rebellion." They noted.)

The McCardles and the Toddler drove off down Sunrise Highway, which was lined with filling stations; since their '98 Landcruiser made only two miles to the gallon, it was not long before they had to stop at one.

The Toddler began its ripsaw shriek when they stopped. A hollow-eyed attendant shambled over and peered into the car. "Just get it?" he asked apathetically.

"Yes," said Mrs. McCardle, frantically trying to joggle the Toddler, to change it, to burp it, to do anything that would end the soul-splitting noise.

"Half pint of white 90-octane gas is what it needs," mumbled the attendant. "Few drops of SAE 40 oil. Got one myself. Two weeks to go. I'll never make it. I'll crack. I'll—I'll …" He tottered off and returned with the gasoline in a nursing bottle, the oil in an eye-dropper.

The Toddler grabbed the bottle and began to gulp the gas down contentedly.

"Where do you put the oil?" asked Mrs. McCardle.

He showed her.

"Oh," she said.

"Fill her up," said George. "The car, I mean. I … ah … I'm going to wash my hands, dear."

He cornered the attendant by the cash register. "Look," he said. "What, ah, would happen if you just let it run out of gas? The Toddler, I mean?"

The man looked at him and put a compassionate hand on his shoulder. "It would *scream,* buddy," he said. "The main motors run off an atomic battery. The gas engine's just for a sideshow and for having breakdowns."

"Breakdowns? Oh, my God! How do you fix a breakdown?"

"The best way you can," the man said. "And buddy, when you burp it, watch out for the fumes. I've seen some ugly explosions …"

They stopped at five more filling stations along the way when the Toddler wanted gas.

"It'll be better-behaved when it's used to the house," said Mrs. McCardle apprehensively as she carried it over the threshold.

"Put it down and let's see what happens," said George.

The Toddler toddled happily to the coffee table, picked up a large bronze ashtray, moved to the picture window and heaved the ashtray through it. It gurgled happily at the crash.

"You little—!" George roared, making for the Toddler with his hands clawed before him.

"George!" Mrs. McCardle screamed, snatching the Toddler away. "It's only a machine!"

The machine began to shriek.

They tried gasoline, oil, wiping with a clean lint-free rag, putting it down, picking it up and finally banging their heads together. It continued to scream until it was ready to stop screaming, and then it stopped and gave them an enchanting grin.

"Time to put it to—away for the night?" asked George.

It permitted itself to be put away for the night.

From his pillow George said later: "Think we did pretty well today. Three months? Pah!"

Mrs. McCardle said: "You were wonderful, George."

He knew that tone. "My Tigress," he said.

Ten minutes later, at the most inconvenient time in the world, bar none, the Toddler began its ripsaw screaming.

Cursing, they went to find out what it wanted. They found out. What it wanted was to laugh in their faces.

(The professor explained: "Indubitably, sadism is at work here, but harnessed in the service of humanity. Better a brutal and concentrated attack such as we have been witnessing than long-drawn-out torments." The class nodded respectfully.)

Mr. and Mrs. McCardle managed to pull themselves together for another try, and there was an exact repeat. Apparently the Toddler sensed something in the air.

"Three months," said George, with haunted eyes.

"You'll live," his wife snapped.

"May I ask *just* what kind of a crack that was supposed to be?"

"If the shoe fits, my good *man*—"

So a fine sex quarrel ended the day.

Within a week the house looked as if it had been liberated by a Mississippi National Guard division. George had lost ten pounds because he couldn't digest anything, not even if he seasoned his food with powdered Equanil instead of salt. Mrs. McCardle had gained fifteen pounds by nervous gobbling during the moments when the Toddler left her unoccupied. The picture window was boarded up. On George's salary, and with glaziers' wages what they were, he couldn't have it replaced twice a day.

Not unnaturally, he met his next-door neighbor, Jacques Truro, in a bar.

Truro was rye and soda, he was dry martini; otherwise they were identical.

"It's the little whimper first that gets me, when you know the big screaming's going to come next. I could jump out of my skin when I hear that whimper."

"Yeah. The waiting. Sometimes one second, sometimes five. I count."

"I forced myself to stop. I was throwing up."

"Yeah. Me too. And nervous diarrhea?"

"All the time. Between me and that goddam thing the house is awash. Cheers."
They drank and shared hollow laughter.

"My stamp collection. Down the toilet."

"My fishing pole. Three clean breaks and peanut butter in the reel."

"One thing I'll never understand, Truro. *What* decided you two to have a baby?"

"Wait a minute, McCardle," Truro said. "Marguerite told me that *you* were
going to have one, so *she* had to have one—"

They looked at each other in shared horror.

"Suckered," said McCardle in an awed voice.

"Women," breathed Truro.

They drank a grim toast and went home.

"It's beginning to talk," Mrs. McCardle said listlessly, sprawled in a chair,
her hand in a box of chocolates. "Called me 'old pig-face' this afternoon." She did
look somewhat piggish with fifteen superfluous pounds.

George put down his briefcase. It was loaded with work from the office which
these days he was unable to get through in time. He had finally got the revised
court-martial scene from Blount, and would now have to transmute it into read-
able prose, emending the author's stupid lapses of logic, illiterate blunders of language and raspingly ugly style.

"I'll wash up," he said.

"Don't use the toilet. Stopped up again."

"Bad?"

"He said he'd come back in the morning with an eight-man crew. Something about jacking up a corner of the house."

The Toddler toddled in with a bottle of bleach, made for the briefcase, and
emptied the bleach into it before the exhausted man or woman could comprehend what was going on, let alone do anything about it.

George incredulously spread the pages of the court-martial scene on the
gouged and battered coffee table. His eyes bulged as he watched the thousands of
typed words vanishing before his eyes, turning pale and then white as the paper.

Blount kept no carbons. Keeping carbons called for a minimal quantity of
prudence and brains, but Blount was an author and so he kept no carbons. The
court-martial scene product of six months' screaming, was *gone*.

The Toddler laughed gleefully.

George clenched his fists, closed his eyes and tried to ignore the roaring in
his ears.

The Toddler began a whining chant:

> "*Da*-dy's an *au*-thor!
> *Da*-dy's an *au*-thor!"

"*That did it!*" George shrieked. He stalked to the door and flung it open.
"Where are you going?" Mrs. McCardle quavered.

"To the first doctor's office I find," said her husband in sudden icy calm. "There I will request a shot of D-Bal. When I have had a D-Bal shot, a breeding permit will be of no use whatever to us. Since a breeding permit will be useless, we need not qualify for one by being tortured for another eleven weeks by that obscene little monster, which we shall return to P.Q.P. in the morning. And unless it behaves, it will be returned in a basket, for them to reassemble at their leisure."

"I'm so glad," his wife sighed.

The Toddler said: "May I congratulate you on your decision. By voluntarily surrendering your right to breed, you are patriotically reducing the population pressure, a problem of great concern to His Majesty. We of the P.Q.P. wish to point out that your decision has been arrived at not through coercion but through education; i.e., by presenting you in the form of a Toddler with some of the arguments against parenthood."

"I didn't know you could talk that well," marveled Mrs. McCardle.

The Toddler said modestly: "I've been with the P.Q.P. from the very beginning, ma'am; I'm a veteran Toddler operator, I may say, working out of Room 4567 of the Empire State. And the improved model I'm working through has reduced the breakdown time an average thirty-five percent. I foresee a time, ma'am, when we experienced operators and ever-improved models will do the job in one day!"

The voice was fanatical.

Mrs. McCardle turned around in sudden vague apprehension. George had left for his D-Bal shot.

(*"And thus we see," said the professor to the seminar, "the genius of the insidious Dr. Wang in full flower." He snapped off the chronoscope. "The first boatloads of Chinese landed in California three generations—or should I say non-generations?—later, unopposed by the scanty, elderly population." He groomed his mandarin mustache and looked out for a moment over the great rice paddies of Central Park. It was spring; blue-clad women stooped patiently over the brown water, and the tender, bright-green shoots were just beginning to appear.*)

(*The seminar students bowed and left for their next lecture, "The Hound Dog as Symbol of Juvenile Aggression in Ancient American Folk Song." It was all that remained of the reign of King Purvis I.*)

[*Vanguard* - June 1958
as "Reap the Dark Tide"]

Shark Ship

It was the spring swarming of the plankton; every man and woman and most of the children aboard Grenville's Convoy had a job to do. As the seventy-five gigantic sailing ships plowed their two degrees of the South Atlantic, the fluid that foamed beneath their cutwaters seethed also with life. In the few weeks of the swarming, in the few meters of surface water where sunlight penetrated in sufficient strength to trigger photosynthesis, microscopic spores burst into microscopic plants, were devoured by minute animals which in turn were swept into the maws of barely visible sea monsters almost a tenth of an inch from head to tail; these in turn were fiercely pursued and gobbled in shoals by the fierce little brit, the tiny herring and shrimp that could turn a hundred miles of green water to molten silver before your eyes.

Through the silver ocean of the swarming the Convoy scudded and tacked in great controlled zigs and zags, reaping the silver of the sea in the endlessly reeling bronze nets each ship payed out behind.

The Commodore in *Grenville* did not sleep during the swarming; he and his staff dispatched cutters to scout the swarms, hung on the meteorologists' words, digested the endless reports from the scout vessels and toiled through the night to prepare the dawn signal. The mainmast flags might tell the captains "Convoy course five degrees right," or "Two degrees left," or only "Convoy course: no change." On those dawn signals depended the life for the next six months of the million and a quarter souls of the Convoy. It had not happened often, but it had happened that a succession of blunders reduced a Convoy's harvest below the minimum necessary to sustain life. Derelicts were sometimes sighted and salvaged from such Convoys; strong-stomached men and women were needed for the first boarding and clearing away of human debris. Cannibalism occurred, an obscene thing one had nightmares about.

The seventy-five captains had their own particular purgatory to endure throughout the harvest, the Sail-Seine Equation. It was their job to balance the push on the sails and the drag of the ballooning seines so that push exceeded drag by just the number of pounds that would keep the ship on course and in station, given every conceivable variation of wind force and direction, temperature of water, consistency of brit, and smoothness of hull. Once the catch was salted down it was customary for the captains to converge on *Grenville* for a roaring feast by way of letdown.

Rank had its privileges. There was no such relief for the captains' Net Officers or their underlings in Operations and Maintenance, or for their Food Officers under whom served the Processing and Stowage people. They merely worked, streaming the nets twenty-four hours a day, keeping them bellied out with lines from mast and outriding gigs, keeping them spooling over the great drum amidships, tending the blades that had to scrape the brit from the nets without damaging the nets, repairing the damage when it did occur; and without interruption of the harvest, flash-cooking the part of the harvest to be cooked, drying the part to be dried, pressing oil from the harvest as required, and stowing what was cooked and dried and pressed where it would not spoil, where it would not alter the trim of the ship, where it would not be pilfered by children. This went on for weeks after the silver had gone thin and patchy against the green, and after the silver had altogether vanished.

The routines of many were not changed at all by the swarming season. The blacksmiths, the sailmakers, the carpenters, the water-tenders, to a degree the storekeepers, functioned as before, tending to the fabric of the ship, renewing, replacing, reworking. The ships were things of brass, bronze and unrusting steel. Phosphor-bronze strands were woven into net, lines, and cables; cordage, masts and hull were metal; all were inspected daily by the First Officer and his men and women for the smallest pinhead of corrosion. The smallest pinhead of corrosion could spread; it could send a ship to the bottom before it had done spreading, as the chaplains were fond of reminding worshipers when the ships rigged for church on Sundays. To keep the hellish red of iron rust and the sinister blue of copper rust from invading, the squads of oilers were always on the move, with oil distilled from the catch. The sails and the clothes alone could not be preserved; they wore out. It was for this that the felting machines down below chopped wornout sails and clothing into new fibers and twisted and rolled them with kelp and with glue from the catch into new felt for new sails and clothing.

While the plankton continued to swarm twice a year, Grenville's Convoy could continue to sail the South Atlantic, from ten-mile limit to ten-mile limit. Not one of the seventy-five ships in the Convoy had an anchor.

The Captain's Party that followed the end of Swarming 283 was slow getting under way. McBee, whose ship was Port Squadron 19, said to Salter of Starboard Squadron 30: "To be frank, I'm too damned exhausted to care whether I ever go to another party, but I didn't want to disappoint the Old Man."

The Commodore, trim and bronzed, not showing his eighty years, was across the great cabin from them greeting new arrivals.

Salter said: "You'll feel differently after a good sleep. It was a great harvest, wasn't it? Enough weather to make it tricky and interesting. Remember 276? *That* was the one that wore me out. A grind, going by the book. But this time, on the fifteenth day my foretopsail was going to go about noon, big rip in her, but I needed her for my S-S balance. What to do? I broke out a balloon spinnaker—now wait a minute, let me tell it first before you throw the book at me—and pumped my fore trim tank out. Presto! No trouble; foretopsail replaced in fifteen minutes."

McBee was horrified. "You could have lost your net!"

"My weatherman absolutely ruled out any sudden squalls."

"Weatherman. You could have lost your net!"

Salter studied him. "Saying that once was thoughtless, McBee. Saying it twice is insulting. Do you think I'd gamble with twenty thousand lives?"

McBee passed his hands over his tired face. "I'm sorry," he said. "I told you I was exhausted. Of course under special circumstances it can be a safe maneuver." He walked to a porthole for a glance at his own ship, the nineteenth in the long echelon behind *Grenville*. Salter stared after him. "Losing one's net" was a phrase that occurred in several proverbs; it stood for abysmal folly. In actuality a ship that lost its phosphor-bronze wire mesh was doomed, and quickly. One could improvise with sails or try to jury-rig a net out of the remaining rigging, but not well enough to feed twenty thousand hands, and no fewer than that were needed for maintenance. Grenville's Convoy had met a derelict which lost its net back before 240; children still told horror stories about it, how the remnants of port and starboard watches, mad to a man, were at war, a war of vicious night forays with knives and clubs.

Salter went to the bar and accepted from the Commodore's steward his first drink of the evening, a steel tumbler of colorless fluid distilled from a fermented mash of sargassum weed. It was about forty percent alcohol and tasted pleasantly of iodides.

He looked up from his sip and his eyes widened. There was a man in captain's uniform talking with the Commodore and he did not recognize his face. But there had been no promotions lately!

The Commodore saw him looking and beckoned him over. He saluted and then accepted the old man's hand-clasp. "Captain Salter," the Commodore said, "my youngest and rashest, and my best harvester. Salter, this is Captain Degerand of the White Fleet."

Salter frankly gawked. He knew perfectly well that Grenville's Convoy was far from sailing alone upon the seas. On watch he had beheld distant sails from time to time. He was aware that cruising the two-degree belt north of theirs was another Convoy and that in the belt south of theirs was still another, in fact that the seaborne population of the world was a constant one billion, eighty million. But never had he expected to meet face to face any of them except the one and a quarter million who sailed under Grenville's flag.

Degerand was younger than he, all deeply tanned skin and flashing pointed teeth. His uniform was perfectly ordinary and very queer. He understood Salter's puzzled look. "It's woven cloth," he said. "The White Fleet was launched several decades after Grenville's. By then they had machinery to reconstitute fibers suitable for spinning and they equipped us with it. It's six of one and half a dozen of the other. I think our sails may last longer than yours, but the looms require a lot of skilled labor when they break down."

The Commodore had left them.

"Are we very different from you?" Salter asked.

Degerand said: "Our differences are nothing. Against the dirt men we are brothers—blood brothers."

The term "dirt men" was discomforting; the juxtaposition with "blood" more so. Apparently he was referring to whoever it was that lived on the continents and islands—a shocking breach of manners, of honor, of faith. The words of the Charter circled through Salter's head. "… return for the sea and its bounty … renounce and abjure the land from which we …" Salter had been ten years old before he knew that there *were* continents and islands. His dismay must have shown on his face.

"They have doomed us," the foreign captain said. "We cannot refit. They have sent us out, each upon our two degrees of ocean in larger or smaller convoys as the richness of the brit dictated, and they have cut us off. To each of us will come the catastrophic storm, the bad harvest, the lost net, and death."

It was Salter's impression that Degerand had said the same words many times before, usually to large audiences.

The Commodore's talker boomed out: "Now hear this!" His huge voice filled the stateroom easily; his usual job was to roar through a megaphone across a league of ocean, supplementing flag and lamp signals. "Now hear this!" he boomed. "There's tuna on the table—big fish for big sailors!"

A grinning steward whisked a felt from the sideboard, and there by Heaven it lay! A great baked fish as long as your leg, smoking hot and trimmed with kelp! A hungry roar greeted it; the captains made for the stack of trays and began to file past the steward, busy with knife and steel.

Salter marveled to Degerand: "I didn't dream there were any left that size. When you think of the tons of brit that old-timer must have gobbled!"

The foreigner said darkly: "We slew the whales, the sharks, the perch, the cod, the herring—everything that used the sea but us. They fed on brit and one another and concentrated it in firm savory flesh like that, but we were jealous of the energy squandered in the long food chain; we decreed that the chain would stop with the link brit-to-man."

Salter by then had filled a tray. "Brit's more reliable," he said. "A Convoy can't take chances on fisherman's luck." He happily bolted a steaming mouthful.

"Safety is not everything," Degerand said. He ate, more slowly than Salter. "Your Commodore said you were a rash seaman."

"He was joking. If he believed that, he would have to remove me from command."

The Commodore walked up to them, patting his mouth with a handkerchief and beaming. "Surprised, eh?" he demanded. "Glasgow's lookout spotted that big fellow yesterday half a kilometer away. He signaled me and I told him to lower and row for him. The boat crew sneaked up while he was browsing and gaffed him clean. Very virtuous of us. By killing him we economize on brit and provide a fitting celebration for my captains. Eat hearty! It may be the last we'll ever see."

Degerand rudely contradicted his senior officer. "They can't be wiped out clean, Commodore, not exterminated. The sea is deep. Its genetic potential cannot be destroyed. We merely make temporary alterations of the feeding balance."

"Seen any sperm whale lately?" the Commodore asked, raising his white eyebrows. "Go get yourself another helping, Captain, before it's gone." It was a dismissal; the foreigner bowed and went to the buffet.

The Commodore asked: "What do you think of him?"

"He has some extreme ideas," Salter said.

"The White Fleet appears to have gone bad," the old man said. "That fellow showed up on a cutter last week in the middle of harvest wanting my immediate, personal attention. He's on the staff of the White Fleet Commodore. I gather they're all like him. They've got slack; maybe rust has got ahead of them, maybe they're over-breeding. A ship lost its net and they didn't let it go. They cannibalized rigging from the whole fleet to make a net for it."

"But—"

"But—but—but. Of course it was the wrong thing and now they're all suffering. Now they haven't the stomach to draw lots and cut their losses." He lowered his voice. "Their idea is some sort of raid on the Western Continent, that America thing, for steel and bronze and whatever else they find not welded to the deck. It's nonsense, of course, spawned by a few silly-clever people on the staff. The crews will never go along with it. Degerand was sent to invite us in!"

Salter said nothing for a while and then: "I certainly hope we'll have nothing to do with it."

"I'm sending him back at dawn with my compliments, and a negative, and my sincere advice to his Commodore that he drop the whole thing before his own crew hears of it and has him bowspritted." The Commodore gave him a wintry smile. "Such a reply is easy to make, of course, just after concluding an excellent harvest. It might be more difficult to signal a negative if we had a couple of ships unnetted and only enough catch in salt to feed sixty percent of the hands. Do you think you could give the hard answer under those circumstances?"

"I think so, sir."

The Commodore walked away, his face enigmatic. Salter thought he knew what was going on. He had been given one small foretaste of top command. Perhaps he was being groomed for Commodore—not to succeed the old man, surely, but his successor.

McBee approached, full of big fish and drink. "Foolish thing I said," he stammered. "Let's have drink, forget about it, eh?"

He was glad to.

"Damn fine seaman!" McBee yelled after a couple more drinks. "Best little captain in the Convoy! Not a scared old crock like poor old McBee, 'fraid of every puff of wind!"

And then he had to cheer up McBee until the party began to thin out. McBee fell asleep at last and Salter saw him to his gig before boarding his own for the long row to the bobbing masthead lights of his ship.

Starboard Squadron Thirty was at rest in the night. Only the slowly-moving oil lamps of the women on their ceaseless rust patrol were alive. The brit catch, dried, came to some seven thousand tons. It was a comfortable margin over the 5,670 tons needed for six months' full rations before the autumnal swarming and harvest. The trim tanks along the keel had been pumped almost dry by the ship's current prison population as the cooked and dried and salted cubes were stored in the glass-lined warehouse tier; the gigantic vessel rode easily on a swelling sea before a Force One westerly breeze.

Salter was exhausted. He thought briefly of having his cox'n whistle for a bosun's chair so that he might be hauled at his ease up the fifty-yard cliff that was the hull before them, and dismissed the idea with regret. Rank hath its privileges and also its obligations. He stood up in the gig, jumped for the ladder and began the long climb. As he passed the portholes of the cabin tiers he virtuously kept eyes front, on the bronze plates of the hull inches from his nose. Many couples in the privacy of their double cabins would be celebrating the end of the back-breaking, night-and-day toil. One valued privacy aboard the ship; one's own 648 cubic feet of cabin, one's own porthole, acquired an almost religious meaning, particularly after the weeks of swarming cooperative labor.

Taking care not to pant, he finished the climb with a flourish, springing onto the flush deck. There was no audience. Feeling a little ridiculous and forsaken, he walked aft in the dark with only the wind and the creak of the rigging in his ears. The five great basket masts strained silently behind their breeze-filled sails; he paused a moment beside Wednesday mast, huge as a redwood, and put his hands on it to feel the power that vibrated in its steel latticework.

Six intent women went past, their hand lamps sweeping the deck; he jumped, though they never noticed him. They were in something like a trance state while on their tour of duty. Normal courtesies were suspended for them; with their work began the job of survival. One thousand women, five percent of the ship's company, inspected night and day for corrosion. Sea water is a vicious solvent and the ship had to live in it; fanaticism was the answer.

His stateroom above the rudder waited; the hatchway to it glowed a hundred feet down the deck with the light of a wasteful lantern. After harvest, when the tanks brimmed with oil, one type acted as though the tanks would brim forever. The captain wearily walked around and over a dozen stay-ropes to the hatchway and blew out the lamp. Before descending he took a mechanical look around the deck; all was well—

Except for a patch of paleness at the fantail.

"Will this day never end?" he asked the darkened lantern and went to the fantail. The patch was a little girl in a night dress wandering aimlessly over the deck, her thumb in her mouth. She seemed to be about two years old, and was more than half asleep. She could have gone over the railing in a moment; a small wail, a small splash—

He picked her up like a feather. "Who's your daddy, princess?" he asked.

"Dunno," she grinned. The devil she didn't! It was too dark to read her ID necklace and he was too tired to light the lantern. He trudged down the deck to the crew of inspectors. He said to their chief: "One of you get this child back to her parents' cabin," and held her out.

The chief was indignant. "Sir, we are on watch!"

"File a grievance with the Commodore if you wish. Take the child."

One of the rounder women did, and made cooing noises while her chief glared. "Bye-bye, princess," the captain said. "You ought to be keel-hauled for this, but I'll give you another chance."

"Bye-bye," the little girl said, waving, and the captain went yawning down the hatchway to bed.

His stateroom was luxurious by the austere standards of the ship. It was equal to six of the standard nine-by-nine cabins in volume, or to three of the double cabins for couples. These however had something he did not. Officers above the rank of lieutenant were celibate. Experience had shown that this was the only answer to nepotism, and nepotism was a luxury which no Convoy could afford. It meant, sooner or later, inefficient command. Inefficient command meant, sooner or later, death.

Because he thought he would not sleep, he did not.

Marriage. Parenthood. What a strange business it must be! To share a bed with a wife, a cabin with two children decently behind their screen for sixteen years ... what did one talk about in bed? His last mistress had hardly talked at all, except with her eyes. When these showed signs that she was falling in love with him, Heaven knew why, he broke with her as quietly as possible and since then irritably rejected the thought of acquiring a successor. That had been two years ago when he was thirty-eight, and already beginning to feel like a cabin-crawler fit only to be dropped over the fantail into the wake. An old lecher, a roué, a *user* of women. Of course she had talked a little; what did they have in common to talk about? With a wife ripening beside him, with children to share, it would have been different. That pale, tall, quiet girl deserved better than he could give; he hoped she was decently married now in a double cabin, perhaps already heavy with the first of her two children.

A whistle squeaked above his head; somebody was blowing into one of the dozen speaking tubes clustered against the bulkhead. Then a push-wire popped open the steel lid of Tube Seven, Signals. He resignedly picked up the flexible reply tube and said into it: "This is the captain. Go ahead."

"*Grenville* signals Force Three squall approaching from astern, sir."

"Force Three squall from astern. Turn out the fore-starboard watch. Have them reef sail to Condition Charlie."

"Fore-starboard watch, reef sail to Condition Charlie, aye-aye."

"Execute."

"Aye-aye, sir." The lid of Tube Seven, Signals, popped shut. At once he heard the distant, penetrating shrill of the pipe, the faint vibration as one sixth of the deck crew began to stir in their cabins, awaken, hit the deck bleary-eyed, begin to trample through the corridors and up the hatchways to the deck. He got up himself and pulled on clothes, yawning. Reefing from Condition Fox to Condition Charlie was no serious matter, not even in the dark, and Walters on watch was a good officer. But he'd better have a look.

Being flush-decked, the ship offered him no bridge. He conned her from the "first top" of Friday mast, the rearmost of her five.

The "first top" was a glorified crow's nest fifty feet up the steel basket-work of that great tower; it afforded him a view of all masts and spars in one glance.

He climbed to his command post too far gone for fatigue. A full moon now lit the scene, good. That much less chance of a green topman stepping on a ratline that would prove to be a shadow and hurtling two hundred feet to the deck. That much more snap in the reefing; that much sooner it would be over. Suddenly he was sure he would be able to sleep if he ever got back to bed again.

He turned for a look at the bronze, moonlit heaps of the great net on the fantail. Within a week it would be cleaned and oiled; within two weeks stowed below in the cable tier, safe from wind and weather.

The regiments of the fore-starboard watch swarmed up the masts from Monday to Friday, swarmed out along the spars as bosun's whistles squealed out the drill—

The squall struck.

Wind screamed and tore at him; the captain flung his arms around a stanchion. Rain pounded down upon his head and the ship reeled in a vast, slow curtsey, port to starboard. Behind him there was a metal sound as the bronze net shifted inches sideways, back.

The sudden clouds had blotted out the moon; he could not see the men who swarmed along the yards but with sudden terrible clarity he felt through the soles of his feet what they were doing. They were clawing their way through the sail-reefing drill, blinded and deafened by sleety rain and wind. They were out of phase by now; they were no longer trying to shorten sail equally on each mast; they were trying to get the thing done and descend. The wind screamed in his face as he turned and clung. Now they were ahead of the job on Monday and Tuesday masts, behind the job on Thursday and Friday masts.

So the ship was going to pitch. The wind would catch it unequally and it would kneel in prayer, the cutwater plunging with a great, deep stately obeisance down into the fathoms of ocean, the stern soaring slowly, ponderously, into the air until the topmost rudder-trunnion streamed a hundred-foot cascade into the boiling froth of the wake.

That was half the pitch. It happened, and the captain clung, groaning aloud. He heard above the screaming wind loose gear rattling on the deck, clashing forward in an avalanche. He heard a heavy clink at the stern and bit his lower lip until it ran with blood that the tearing cold rain flooded from his chin.

The pitch reached its maximum and the second half began, after interminable moments when she seemed frozen at a five-degree angle forever. The cutwater rose, rose, rose, the bowsprit blocked out horizon stars, the loose gear countercharged astern in a crushing tide of bales, windlass cranks, water-breakers, stilling coils, steel sun reflectors, lashing tails of bronze rigging—

Into the heaped piles of the net, straining at its retainers on the two great bollards that took root in the keel itself four hundred feet below. The energy of the pitch hurled the belly of the net open, crashing, into the sea. The bollards held for a moment.

A retainer cable screamed and snapped like a man's back, and then the second cable broke. The roaring slither of the bronze links thundering over the fantail shook the ship.

The squall ended as it had come; the clouds scudded on and the moon bared itself, to shine on a deck scrubbed clean. The net was lost.

Captain Salter looked down the fifty feet from the rim of the crow's nest and thought: I should jump. It would be quicker that way.

But he did not. He slowly began to climb down the ladder to the bare deck.

Having no electrical equipment, the ship was necessarily a representative republic rather than a democracy. Twenty thousand people can discuss and decide only with the aid of microphones, loudspeakers and rapid calculators to balance the ayes and noes. With lungpower the only means of communication and an abacus in a clerk's hands the only tallying device, certainly no more than fifty people can talk together and make sense, and there are pessimists who say the number is closer to five than fifty. The Ship's Council that met at dawn on the fantail numbered fifty.

It was a beautiful dawn; it lifted the heart to see salmon sky, iridescent sea, spread white sails of the Convoy ranged in a great slanting line across sixty miles of oceanic blue.

It was the kind of dawn for which one lived—a full catch salted down, the water-butts filled, the evaporators trickling from their thousand tubes nine gallons each sunrise to sunset, wind enough for easy steerageway and a pretty spread of sail. These were the rewards. One hundred and forty-one years ago Grenville's Convoy had been launched at Newport News, Virginia, to claim them.

Oh, the high adventure of the launching! The men and women who had gone aboard thought themselves heroes, conquerors of nature, self-sacrificers for the glory of NEMET! But NEMET meant only Northeastern Metropolitan Area, one dense warren that stretched from Boston to Newport News, built up and dug down, sprawling westward, gulping Pittsburgh without a pause, beginning to peter out past Cincinnati.

The first generation asea clung and sighed for the culture of NEMET, consoled itself with its patriotic sacrifice; any relief was better than none at all, and Grenville's Convoy had drained one and a quarter million population from the huddle. They were immigrants into the sea; like all immigrants they longed for the Old Country. Then the second generation. Like all second generations they had no patience with the old people or their tales. *This* was real, this sea, this gale, this rope! Then the third generation. Like all third generations it felt a sudden desperate hollowness and lack of identity. What was real? Who are we? What is NEMET which we have lost? But by then grandfather and grandmother could only mumble vaguely; the cultural heritage was gone, squandered in three generations, spent forever. As always, the fourth generation did not care.

And those who sat in Council on the fantail were members of the fifth and sixth generations. They knew all there was to know about life. Life was the hull and masts, the sail and rigging, the net and the evaporators. Nothing more. *Nothing less.* Without masts there was no life. Nor was there life without the net.

The Ship's Council did not command; command was reserved to the captain and his officers. The Council governed, and on occasion tried criminal cases. During the black Winter Without Harvest eighty years before it had decreed euthanasia for all persons over sixty-three years of age and for one out of twenty of the other adults aboard. It had rendered bloody judgment on the ringleaders of Peale's Mutiny. It had sent them into the wake and Peale himself had been bowspritted, given the maritime equivalent of crucifixion. Since then no megalomaniacs had decided to make life interesting for their shipmates, so Peale's long agony had served its purpose.

The fifty of them represented every department of the ship and every age-group. If there was wisdom aboard, it was concentrated there on the fantail. But there was little to say.

The eldest of them, Retired Sailmaker Hodgins, presided. Venerably bearded, still strong of voice, he told them:

"Shipmates, our accident has come. We are dead men. Decency demands that we do not spin out the struggle and sink into—unlawful eatings. Reason tells us that we cannot survive. What I propose is an honorable voluntary death for us all, and the legacy of our ship's fabric to be divided among the remainder of the Convoy at the discretion of the Commodore."

He had little hope of his old man's viewpoint prevailing. The Chief Inspector rose at once. She had only three words to say: *"Not my children."*

Women's heads nodded grimly, and men's with resignation. Decency and duty and common sense were all very well until you ran up against that steel bulkhead. *Not my children.*

A brilliant young chaplain asked: "Has the question even been raised as to whether a collection among the fleet might not provide cordage enough to improvise a net?"

Captain Salter should have answered that, but he, murderer of the twenty thousand souls in his care, could not speak. He nodded jerkily at his signals officer.

Lieutenant Zwingli temporized by taking out his signals slate and pretending to refresh his memory. He said: "At 0035 today a lamp signal was made to *Grenville* advising that our net was lost. *Grenville* replied as follows: 'Effective now, your ship no longer part of Convoy. Have no recommendations. Personal sympathy and regrets. Signed, Commodore."

Captain Salter found his voice. "I've sent a couple of other messages to *Grenville* and to our neighboring vessels. They do not reply. This is as it should be. We are no longer part of the Convoy. Through our own—lapse—we have become a drag on the Convoy. We cannot look to it for help. I have no word of condemnation for anybody. This is how life is."

The chaplain folded his hands and began to pray inaudibly.

And then a Council member spoke whom Captain Salter knew in another role. It was Jewel Flyte, the tall, pale girl who had been his mistress two years ago. She must be serving as an alternate, he thought, looking at her with new eyes. He did not know she was even that; he had avoided her since then. And no, she was not married; she wore no ring. And neither was her hair drawn back in the semi-official style of the semi-official voluntary celibates, the super-patriots (or simply sex-shy people, or dislikers of children) who surrendered their right to reproduce for the good of the ship (or their own convenience). She was simply a girl in the uniform of a—a what? He had to think hard before he could match the badge over her breast to a department. She was Ship's Archivist with her crossed key and quill, an obscure clerk and shelf-duster under—far under!—the Chief of Yeomen Writers. She must have been elected alternate by the Yeomen in a spasm of sympathy for her blind-alley career.

"My job," she said in her calm steady voice, "is chiefly to search for precedents in the Log when unusual events must be recorded and nobody recollects offhand the form in which they should be recorded. It is one of those provoking jobs which must be done by someone but which cannot absorb the full time of a person. I have therefore had many free hours of actual working time. I have also remained unmarried and am not inclined to sports or games. I tell you this so you may believe me when I say that during the past two years I have read the Ship's Log in its entirety."

There was a little buzz. Truly an astonishing, and an astonishingly pointless, thing to do! Wind and weather, storms and calms, messages and meetings and censuses, crimes, trials and punishments of a hundred and forty-one years; what a bore!

"Something I read," she went on, "may have some bearing on our dilemma." She took a slate from her pocket and read: "Extract from the Log dated June 30th, Convoy Year 72. 'The Shakespeare-Joyce-Melville Party returned after dark in the gig. They had not accomplished any part of their mission. Six were dead of wounds. all bodies were recovered. The remaining six were mentally shaken but responded to our last ataractics. They spoke of a new religion ashore and its consequences on population. I am persuaded that we seabornes can no longer relate to the continentals. The clandestine shore trips will cease.' The entry is signed 'Scolley, Captain'."

A man named Scolley smiled for a brief proud moment. His ancestor! And then like the others he waited for the extract to make sense. Like the others he found that it would not do so.

Captain Salter wanted to speak, and wondered how to address her. She had been "Jewel" and they all knew it; could he call her "Yeoman Flyte" without looking like, being, a fool? Well, if he was fool enough to lose his net, he was fool enough to be formal with an ex-mistress. "Yeoman Flyte," he said, "where does the extract leave us?"

In her calm voice she told them all: "Penetrating the few obscure words, it appears to mean that until Convoy Year 72 the Charter was regularly violated, with the connivance of successive captains. I suggest that we consider violating it once more, to survive."

The Charter. It was a sort of ground-swell of their ethical life, learned early, paid homage every Sunday when they were rigged for church. It was inscribed in phosphor-bronze plates on Monday mast of every ship at sea, and the wording was always the same.

> IN RETURN FOR THE SEA AND ITS BOUNTY WE RE-
> NOUNCE AND ABJURE FOR OURSELVES AND OUR DECENDANTS
> THE LAND FROM WHICH WE SPRUNG: FOR THE COMMON
> GOOD OF MAN WE SET SAIL FOREVER.

At least half of them were unconsciously murmuring the words.

Retired Sailmaker Hodgins rose, shaking. "Blasphemy!" he said. "The woman should be bowspritted!"

The chaplain said thoughtfully: "I know a little more about what consti-tutes blasphemy than Sailmaker Hodgins, I believe, and assure you that he is mis-taken. It is a superstitious error to believe that there is any religious sanction for the Charter. It is no ordinance of God but a contract between men."

"It is a Revelation!" Hodgins shouted. "A Revelation! It is the newest testa-ment! It is God's finger pointing the way to the clean hard life at sea, away from the grubbing and filth, from the overbreeding and the sickness!"

That was a common view.

"What about my children?" demanded the Chief Inspector. "Does God want them to starve or be—be—" She could not finish the question, but the last un-spoken word of it rang in all their minds.

Eaten.

Aboard some ships with an accidental preponderance of the elderly, aboard other ships where some blazing personality generations back had raised the Char-ter to a powerful cult, suicide might have been voted. Aboard other ships where nothing extraordinary had happened in six generations, where things had been easy and the knack and tradition of hard decision-making had been lost, there might have been confusion and inaction and the inevitable degeneration into sav-agery. Aboard Salter's ship the Council voted to send a small party ashore to in-vestigate. They used every imaginable euphemism to describe the action, took six hours to make up their minds, and sat at last on the fantail cringing a little, as if waiting for a thunderbolt.

The shore party would consist of Salter, Captain; Flyte, Archivist; Pemberton, Junior Chaplain; Graves, Chief Inspector.

Salter climbed to his conning top on Friday mast, consulted a chart from the archives, and gave the order through speaking tube to the tiller gang: "Change course red four degrees."

The repeat came back incredulously.

"Execute," he said. The ship creaked as eighty men heaved the tiller; imper-ceptibly at first the wake began to curve behind them.

Ship Starboard 30 departed from its ancient station; across a mile of sea the bosun's whistles could be heard from Starboard 31 as she put on sail to close the gap.

"They might have signaled something," Salter thought, dropping his glasses at last on his chest. But the masthead of Starboard 31 remained bare of all but its commission pennant.

He whistled up his signals officer and pointed to their own pennant. "Take that thing down," he said hoarsely, and went below to his cabin.

The new course would find them at last riding off a place the map described as New York City.

Salter issued what he expected would be his last commands to Lieutenant Zwingli; the whaleboat was waiting in its davits; the other three were in it.

"You'll keep your station here as well as you're able," said the captain. "If we live, we'll be back in a couple of months. Should we not return, that would be a potent argument against beaching the ship and attempting to live off the conti-nent—but it will be your problem then and not mine."

They exchanged salutes. Salter sprang into the whaleboat, signaled the deck hands standing by at the ropes and the long creaking descent began.

Salter, Captain; age 40; unmarried *ex officio;* parents Clayton Salter, master instrument maintenanceman, and Eva Romano, chief dietician; selected from dame school age 10 for A Track training; seamanship school certificate at age 16, navi-gation certificate at age 20, First Lieutenants School age 24, commissioned en-sign age 24; lieutenant at 30, commander at 32; commissioned captain and suc-ceeded to command of Ship Starboard 30 the same year.

Flyte, Archivist, age 25; unmarried; parents Joseph Flyte, entertainer, and Jessie Waggoner, entertainer; completed dame school age 14, B Track training; Yeoman's School certificate at age 16, Advanced Yeoman's School certificate at age 18; Efficiency rating, 3.5.

Pemberton, Chaplain, age 30; married to Riva Shields, nurse; no children by choice; parents Will Pemberton, master distiller-water tender, and Agnes Hunt, felter-machinist's mate; completed dame school age 12, B Track training; Divin-ity School Certificate at age 20; mid-starboard watch curate, later fore-starboard chaplain.

Graves, Chief Inspector, age 34; married to George Omany, blacksmith third class; two children; completed dame school age 15, Inspectors School Certificate at age 16; inspector third class, second class, first class, master inspector, then chief. Efficiency rating, 4.0; three commendations.

Versus the Continent of North America.

They all rowed for an hour; then a shoreward breeze came up and Salter stepped the mast. "Ship your oars," he said, and then wished he dared coun-termand the order. Now they would have time to think of what they were doing.

The very water they sailed was different in color from the deep water they knew, and different in its way of moving. The life in it—

"Great God!" Mrs Graves cried, pointing astern.

It was a huge fish, half the size of their boat. It surfaced lazily and slipped beneath the water in an uninterrupted arc. They had seen steel-grey skin, not scales, and a great slit of a mouth.

Salter said, shaken: "Unbelievable. Still, I suppose in the unfished offshore waters a few of the large forms survive. And the intermediate sizes to feed them—" And foot-long smaller sizes to feed *them*, and—

Was it mere arrogant presumption that Man had permanently changed the life of the sea?

The afternoon sun slanted down and the tip of Monday mast sank below the horizon's curve astern; the breeze that filled their sail bowled them towards a mist which wrapped vague concretions they feared to study too closely. A shadowed figure huge as a mast with one arm upraised; behind it blocks and blocks of something solid.

"This is the end of the sea," said the captain.

Mrs. Graves said what she would have said if a silly under-inspector had reported to her blue rust on steel: "Nonsense!" Then, stammering: "I beg your pardon, Captain. Of course you are correct."

"But it sounded strange," Chaplain Pemberton said helpfully. "I wonder where they all are?"

Jewel Flyte said in her quiet way: "We should have passed over the discharge from waste tubes before now. They used to pump their waste through tubes under the sea and discharge it several miles out. It colored the water and it stank. During the first voyaging years the captains knew it was time to tack away from land by the color and the bad smell."

"They must have improved their disposal system by now," Salter said. "It's been centuries."

His last word hung in the air.

The chaplain studied the mist from the bow. It was impossible to deny it; the huge thing was an Idol. Rising from the bay of a great city, an Idol, and a female one—the worst kind! "I thought they had them only in High Places," he muttered, discouraged.

Jewel Flyte understood. "I think it has no religious significance," she said. "It's a sort of—huge piece of scrimshaw."

Mrs. Graves studied the vast thing and saw in her mind the glyphic arts as practiced at sea: compacted kelp shaved and whittled into little heirloom boxes, miniature portrait busts of children. She decided that Yeoman Flyte had a dangerously wild imagination. Scrimshaw! Tall as a mast!

There should be some commerce, thought the captain. Boats going to and fro. The Place ahead was plainly an island, plainly inhabited; goods and people should be going to it and coming from it. Gigs and cutters and whaleboats should be plying this bay and those two rivers; at that narrow bit they should be lined up impatiently waiting, tacking and riding under sea anchors and furled sails. There was nothing but a few white birds that shrilled nervously at their solitary boat.

The blocky concretions were emerging from the haze; they were sunset-red cubes with regular black eyes dotting them; they were huge dice laid down side by side by side, each as large as a ship, each therefore capable of holding twenty thousand persons.

Where were they all?

The breeze and the tide drove them swiftly through the neck of water where a hundred boats should be waiting. "Furl the sail," said Salter. "Out oars."

With no sounds but the whisper of the oarlocks, the cries of the white birds and the slapping of the wavelets they rowed under the shadow of the great red dice to a dock, one of a hundred teeth projecting from the island's rim.

"Easy the starboard oars," said Salter; "handsomely the port oars. Up oars. Chaplain, the boat hook." He had brought them to a steel ladder; Mrs. Graves gasped at the red rust thick on it. Salter tied the painter to a corroded brass ring. "Come along," he said, and began to climb.

When the four of them stood on the iron-plated dock Pemberton, naturally, prayed. Mrs. Graves followed the prayer with half her attention or less; the rest she could not divert from the shocking slovenliness of the prospect—rust, dust, litter, neglect. What went on in the mind of Jewel Flyte her calm face did not betray. And the captain scanned those black windows a hundred yards inboard— no; inland!—and waited and wondered.

They began to walk to them at last, Salter leading. The sensation underfoot was strange and dead, tiring to the arches and the thighs.

The huge red dice were not as insane close-up as they had appeared from a distance. They were thousand-foot cubes of brick, the stuff that lined ovens. They were set back within squares of green, cracked surfacing which Jewel Flyte named "cement" or "concrete" from some queer corner of her erudition.

There was an entrance, and written over it: THE HERBERT BROWNELL JR. MEMORIAL HOUSES. A bronze plaque shot a pang of guilt through them all as they thought of The Compact, but its words were different and ignoble.

NOTICE TO ALL TENANTS

A project Apartment is a Privilege and not a Right. Daily Inspection is the Cornerstone of the Project. Attendance at Least Once a Week at the Church or Synagogue of your Choice is Required for Families wishing to remain in Good Standing; Proof of Attendance must be presented on Demand. Possession of Tobacco or Alcohol will be considered Prima Facie Evidence of Undesirability. Excessive Water Use, Excessive Energy Use and Food Waste will be Grounds for Desirability Review. The speaking of Languages other than American by persons over the Age of Six will be considered Prima Facie Evidence of Nonassimilability, though this shall not be construed to prohibit Religious Ritual in Languages other than American.

Below it stood another plaque in paler bronze, an afterthought:

> None of the foregoing shall be construed to condone the Practice of Depravity under the Guise of Religion by Whatever Name, and all Tenants are warned that any Failure to report the Practice of Depravity will result in summary Eviction and Denunciation.

Around this later plaque some hand had painted with crude strokes of a tar brush a sort of anatomical frame at which they stared in wondering disgust.

At last Pemberton said: "They were a devout people." Nobody noticed the past tense, it sounded so right.

"Very sensible," said Mrs. Graves. "No nonsense about them."

Captain Salter privately disagreed. A ship run with such dour coercion would founder in a month; could land people be that much different?

Jewel Flyte said nothing, but her eyes were wet. Perhaps she was thinking of scared little human rats dodging and twisting through the inhuman maze of great fears and minute rewards.

"After all," said Mrs. Graves, "it's nothing but a Cabin Tier. We have cabins and so had they. Captain, might we have a look?"

"This *is* a reconnaissance," Salter shrugged. They went into a littered lobby and easily recognized an elevator which had long ago ceased to operate; there were many hand-run dumbwaiters at sea.

A gust of air flapped a sheet of printed paper across the chaplain's ankles; he stooped to pick it up with a kind of instinctive outrage—leaving paper unsecured, perhaps to blow overboard and be lost forever to the ship's economy! Then he flushed at his silliness. "So much to unlearn," he said, and spread the paper to look at it. A moment later he crumpled it in a ball and hurled it from him as hard and as far as he could, and wiped his hands with loathing on his jacket. His face was utterly shocked.

The others stared. It was Mrs. Graves who went for the paper.

"Don't look at it," said the chaplain.

"I think she'd better," Salter said.

The maintenancewoman spread the paper, studied it and said: "Just some nonsense. Captain, what do you make of it?"

It was a large page torn from a book, and on it was a simple polychrome drawing and some lines of verse in the style of a child's first reader. Salter repressed a shocked guffaw. The picture was of a little boy and a little girl quaintly dressed locked in murderous combat, using teeth and nails. *"Jack and Jill went up the hill,"* said the text, *"to fetch a pail of water. She threw Jack down and broke his crown; it was a lovely slaughter."*

Jewel Flyte took the page from his hands. All she said was, after a long pause: "I suppose they couldn't start them too young." She dropped the page and she too wiped her hands.

"Come along," the captain said. "We'll try the stairs."

The stairs were dust, rat-dung, cobwebs and two human skeletons. Murderous knuckle-dusters fitted loosely the bones of the two right hands. Salter hardened himself to pick up one of the weapons, but could not bring himself to try it on. Jewel Flyte said apologetically: "Please be careful, Captain. It might be poisoned. That seems to be the way they were."

Salter froze. By God, but the girl was right! Delicately, handling the spiked steel thing by its edges, he held it up. Yes; stains—it *would* be stained, and perhaps with poison also. He dropped it into the thoracic cage of one skeleton and said: "Come on." They climbed in quest of a dusty light from above; it was a doorway onto a corridor of many doors. There was evidence of fire and violence. A barricade of queer pudgy chairs and divans had been built to block the corridor, and had been breached. Behind it were sprawled three more heaps of bones.

"They have no heads," the chaplain said hoarsely. "Captain Salter, this is not a place for human beings. We must go back to the ship, even if it means honorable death. This is not a place for human beings."

"Thank you, Chaplain," said Salter. "You've cast your vote. Is anybody with you?"

"Kill your own children, Chaplain," said Mrs. Graves. "Not mine."

Jewel Flyte gave the chaplain a sympathetic shrug and said: "No."

One door stood open, its lock shattered by blows of a fire ax. Salter said: "We'll try that one." They entered into the home of an ordinary middle-class death-worshipping family as it had been a century ago, in the one hundred and thirty-first year of Merdeka the Chosen.

Merdeka the Chosen, the All-Foreigner, the Ur-Alien, had never intended any of it. He began as a retail mail-order vendor of movie and television stills, eight-by-ten glossies for the fan trade. It was a hard dollar; you had to keep an immense stock to cater to a tottery Mae Bush admirer, to the pony-tailed screamer over Rip Torn, and to everybody in between. He would have no truck with pinups. "Dirty, lascivious pictures!" he snarled when broadly-hinting letters arrived. "Filth! Men and women kissing, ogling, pawing each other! Orgies! Bah!" Merdeka kept a neutered dog, a spayed cat, and a crumpled uncomplaining housekeeper who was technically his wife. He was poor; he was very poor. Yet he never neglected his charitable duties, contributing every year to the Planned Parenthood Federation and the Midtown Hysterectomy Clinic.

They knew him in the Third Avenue saloons where he talked every night, arguing with Irishmen, sometimes getting asked outside to be knocked down. He let them knock him down, and sneered from the pavement. Was *this* their argument? *He* could argue. He spewed facts and figures and clichés in unanswerable profusion. Hell, man, the Russians'll have a bomb base on the moon in two years and in two years the Army and the Air Force will still be beating each other over the head with pigs' bladders. Just a minute, let me tell you: the goddammycin's making idiots of us all; do you know of any children born in the past two years that're healthy? And: 'flu be go to hell; it's our own germ warfare from Camp Crowder right outside Baltimore that got out of hand, and it happened the week of the 24th. And: the human animal's obsolete; they've proved at M.I.T., Steinwitz and Kohlmann *proved* that the human animal cannot survive the current radiation levels. And: enjoy your lung cancer, friend; for every automobile and its stinking exhaust there will be two-point-seven-oh-three cases of lung cancer, and we've got to have our automobiles, don't we? And: delinquency my foot; they're insane and it's got to the point where the economy cannot support mass insanity; they've got to be castrated; it's the only way. And: they should dig up the body of Metchnikoff and throw it to the dogs; he's the degenerate who invented venereal prophylaxis and since then vice without punishment has run hog-wild through the world; what we need on the streets is a few of those old-time locomotor ataxia cases limping and drooling to show the kids where vice leads.

He didn't know where he came from. The delicate New York way of establishing origins is to ask: "Merdeka, hah? What kind of a name is that now?" And to this he would reply that he wasn't a lying Englishman or a loudmouthed Irishman or a perverted Frenchman or a chiseling Jew or a barbarian Russian or a toadying German or a thickheaded Scandihoovian, and if his listener didn't like it, what did he have to say in reply?

He was from an orphanage, and the legend at the orphanage was that a policeman had found him, two hours old, in a garbage can coincident with the death by hemorrhage on a trolley car of a luetic young woman whose name appeared to be Merdeka and who had certainly been recently delivered of a child. No other facts were established, but for generation after generation of orphanage inmates there was great solace in having one of their number who indisputably had got off to a worse start than they.

A watershed of his career occurred when he noticed that he was, for the seventh time that year, re-ordering prints of scenes from Mr. Howard Hughes' production *The Outlaw*. These were not the off-the-bust stills of Miss Jane Russell, surprisingly, but were group scenes of Miss Russell suspended by her wrists and about to be whipped. Merdeka studied the scene, growled "Give it to the bitch!" and doubled the order. It sold out. He canvassed his files for other whipping and torture stills from *Desert Song*–type movies, made up a special assortment, and it sold out within a week. Then he knew.

The man and the opportunity had come together, for perhaps the fiftieth time in history. He hired a model and took the first specially posed pictures himself. They showed her cringing from a whip, tied to a chair with a clothesline, and herself brandishing the whip.

Within two months Merdeka had cleared six thousand dollars and he put every cent of it back into more photographs and direct-mail advertising. Within a year he was big enough to attract the post-office obscenity people. He went to Washington and screamed in their faces: "My stuff isn't obscene and I'll sue you if you bother me, you stinking bureaucrats! You show me one breast, you show me one behind, you show me one human being touching another in my pictures! You can't and you know you can't! I don't believe in sex and I don't push sex, so you leave me the hell alone! Life is pain and suffering and being scared so people like to look at my pictures; my pictures are about *them,* the scared little jerks! You're just a bunch of goddam perverts if you think there's anything dirty about my pictures!"

He had them there; Merdeka's girls always wore at least full panties, bras and stockings; he had them there. The post-office obscenity people were vaguely positive that there was *something* wrong with pictures of beautiful women tied down to be whipped or burned with hot irons, but what?

The next year they tried to get him on his income tax; those deductions for the Planned Parenthood Federation and the Midtown Hysterectomy Clinic were preposterous, but he proved them with canceled checks to the last nickel. "In fact," he indignantly told them, "I spend a lot of time at the Clinic and sometimes they let me watch the operations. *That's* how highly they think of me at the Clinic."

The next year he started *DEATH: the Weekly Picture Magazine* with the aid of a half-dozen bright young grads from the new Harvard School of Communicationeering. As *DEATH's* Communicator in Chief (only yesterday he would have been its Publisher, and only fifty years before he would have been its Editor) he slumped biliously in a pigskin-paneled office, peering suspiciously at the closed-circuit TV screen which had a hundred wired eyes throughout *DEATH's* offices, sometimes growling over the voice circuit: "You! What's your name? Boland? You're through, Boland. Pick up your time at the paymaster." For any reason; for no reason. He was a living legend in his narrow-lapel charcoal flannel suit and stringy bullfighter neckties; the bright young men in their Victorian Revival frock coats and pearl-pinned cravats wondered at his—not "obstinacy"; not when there might be a mike even in the corner saloon; say, his "timelessness."

The bright young men became bright young-old men, and the magazine which had been conceived as a vehicle for deadheading house ads of the mail-order picture business went into the black. On the cover of every issue of *DEATH* was a pictured execution-of-the-week, and no price for one was ever too high. A fifty-thousand-dollar donation to a mosque had purchased the right to secretly snap the Bread Ordeal by which perished a Yemenite suspected of tapping an oil pipeline. An interminable illustrated History of Flagellation was a staple of the reading matter, and the Medical Section (in color) was tremendously popular. So too was the weekly Traffic Report.

When the last of the Compact Ships was launched into the Pacific, the event made *DEATH* because of the several fatal accidents which accompanied the launching; otherwise Merdeka ignored the ships. It was strange that he who had unorthodoxies about everything had no opinion at all about the Compact Ships and their crews. Perhaps it was that he really knew he was the greatest manslayer who ever lived, and even so could not face commanding total extinction, including that of the seaborne leaven. The more articulate Sokei-an, who in the name of Rinzei Zen Buddhism was at that time depopulating the immense area dominated by China, made no bones about it: "Even I in my Hate may err; let the celestial vessels be." The opinions of Dr. Spät, European member of the trio, are forever beyond recovery due to his advocacy of the "one-generation" plan.

With advancing years Merdeka's wits cooled and gelled. There came a time when he needed a theory and was forced to stab the button of the intercom for his young-old Managing Communicator and growl at him: "Give me a theory!" And the M.C. reeled out: "The structural intermesh of *DEATH: the Weekly Picture Magazine* with Western culture is no random point-event but a rising world-line. Predecessor attitudes such as the Hollywood dogma 'No breasts—blood!' and the tabloid press's exploitation of violence were floundering and empirical. It was Merdeka who sigma-ized the convergent traits of our times and asymptotically congruentizes with them publication-wise. Wrestling and the roller-derby as blood sports, the routinization of femicide in the detective tale, the standardization at one million per year of traffic fatalities, the wholesome interest of our youth in gang rumbles, all point toward the Age of Hate and Death. The ethic of Love and Life is obsolescent, and who is to say that Man is the loser thereby? Life and Death compete in the marketplace of ideas for the Mind of Man—"

Merdeka growled something and snapped off the set. Merdeka leaned back. Two billion circulation this week, and the auto ads were beginning to Tip. Last year only the suggestion of a dropped shopping basket as the Dynajetic 16 roared across the page, this year a hand, limp on the pictured pavement. Next year, blood. In February the Sylphella Salon chain ads had Tipped, with a crash. "—and the free optional judo course for slenderized Madame or Mademoiselle: learn how to kill a man with your lovely bare hands, with or without mess as desired." Applications had risen 28 percent. By *God* there was a structural intermesh for you!

It was too slow; it was still too slow. He picked up a direct-line phone and screamed into it: "Too slow! What am I paying you people for? The world is wallowing in filth! Movies are dirtier than ever! Kissing! Pawing! Ogling! Men and women together—obscene! Clean up the magazine covers! Clean up the ads!"

The person at the other end of the direct line was Executive Secretary of the Society for Purity in Communications; Merdeka had no need to announce himself to him, for Merdeka was S.P.C.'s principal underwriter. He began to rattle off at once: "We've got the Mothers' March on Washington this week, sir, and a mass dummy pornographic mailing addressed to every Middle Atlantic State female between the ages of six and twelve next week, sir; I believe this one-two punch will put the Federal Censorship Commission over the goal line before recess—"

Merdeka hung up. "Lewd communications," he snarled. "Breeding, breeding, breeding, like maggots in a garbage can. Burning and breeding. But we will make them clean."

He did not need a Theory to tell him that he could not take away Love without providing a substitute.

He walked down Sixth Avenue that night, for the first time in years. In this saloon he had argued; outside that saloon he had been punched in the nose. Well, he was winning the argument, all the arguments. A mother and daughter walked past uneasily, eyes on the shadows. The mother was dressed

Square; she wore a sheath dress that showed her neck and clavicles at the top and her legs from mid-shin at the bottom. In some parts of town she'd be spat on, but the daughter, never. The girl was Hip; she was covered from neck to ankles by a loose, unbelted sack-culotte. Her mother's hair floated; hers was hidden by a cloche. Nevertheless the both of them were abruptly yanked into one of those shadows they prudently had eyed, for they had not watched the well-lit sidewalk for waiting nooses.

The familiar sounds of a Working Over came from the shadows as Merdeka strolled on. "I mean cool!" an ecstatic young voice—boy's, girl's, what did it matter?—breathed between crunching blows.

That year the Federal Censorship Commission was created, and the next year the old Internment Camps in the southwest were filled to capacity by violators, and the next year the First Church of Merdeka was founded in Chicago. Merdeka died of an aortal aneurysm five years after that, but his soul went marching on.

"The Family that Prays together Slays together," was the wall motto in the apartment, but there was no evidence that the implied injunction had been observed. The bedroom of the mother and the father were secured by steel doors and terrific locks, but Junior had got them all the same; somehow he had burned through the steel.

"Thermite?" Jewel Flyte asked herself softly, trying to remember. First he had got the father, quickly and quietly with a wire garotte as he lay sleeping, so as not to alarm his mother. To her he had taken her own spiked knobkerry and got in a mortal stroke, but not before she reached under her pillow for a pistol. Junior's teenage bones testified by their arrangement to the violence of that leaden blow.

Incredulously they looked at the family library of comic books, published in a series called "The Merdekan Five-Foot Shelf of Classics." Jewel Flyte leafed slowly through one called *Moby Dick* and found that it consisted of a near-braining in a bedroom, agonizingly depicted deaths at sea, and for a climax the eating alive of one Ahab by a monster. "Surely there must have been more," she whispered.

Chaplain Pendleton put down *Hamlet* quickly and held onto a wall. He was quite sure that he felt his sanity slipping palpably away, that he would gibber in a moment. He prayed and after a while felt better; he rigorously kept his eyes away from the Classics after that.

Mrs. Graves snorted at the waste of it all, at the picture of the ugly, pop-eyed, busted-nose man labeled MERDEKA THE CHOSEN, THE PURE, THE PURIFIER. There were *two* tables, which was a folly. Who needed two tables? Then she looked closer, saw that one of them was really a bloodstained flogging bench, and felt slightly ill. Its name-plate said *Correctional Furniture Corp. Size 6, Ages 10–14.* She had, God knew, slapped her children more than once when they deviated from her standard of perfection, but when she saw those stains she felt a stirring of warmth for the parricidal bones in the next room.

Captain Salter said: "Let's get organized. Does anybody think there are any of them left?"

"I think not," said Mrs. Graves. "People like that can't survive. The world must have been swept clean. They, ah, killed one another but that's not the important point. This couple had one child, age ten to fourteen. This cabin of theirs seems to be built for one child. We should look at a few more cabins to learn whether a one-child family is—was—normal. If we find out that it was, we can suspect that they are—gone. Or nearly so." She coined a happy phrase: "By race suicide."

"The arithmetic of it is quite plausible," Salter said. "If no factors work except the single-child factor, in one century of five generations a population of two billion will have bred itself down to 125 million. In another century, the population is just under four million. In another, 122 thousand ... by the thirty-second generation the last couple descended from the original two billion will breed one child, and that's the end. And there are the other factors. Besides those who do not breed by choice"—his eyes avoided Jewel Flyte—"there are the things we have seen on the stairs, and in the corridor, and in these compartments."

"Then there's our answer," said Mrs. Graves. She smacked the obscene table with her hand, forgetting what it was. "We beach the ship and march the ship's company onto dry land. We clean up, we learn what we have to get along—" Her words trailed off. She shook her head. "Sorry," she said gloomily. "I'm talking nonsense."

The chaplain understood her, but he said: "The land is merely another of the many mansions. Surely they could learn!"

"It's not politically feasible," Salter said. "Not in its present form." He thought of presenting the proposal to the Ship's Council in the shadow of the mast that bore the Compact, and twitched his head in an involuntary negative.

"There is a formula possible," Jewel Flyte said.

The Brownells burst in on them then, all eighteen of the Brownells. They had been stalking the shore party since its landing. Nine sack-culotted women in cloches and nine men in penitential black, they streamed through the gaping door and surrounded the sea people with a ring of spears. Other factors had indeed operated, but this was not yet the thirty-second generation of extinction.

The leader of the Brownells, a male, said with satisfaction: "Just when we needed new blood." Salter understood that he was not speaking in genetic terms.

The females, more verbal types, said critically: "Evil-doers, obviously. Displaying their limbs without shame, brazenly flaunting the rotted pillars of the temple of lust. Come from the accursed sea itself, abode of infamy, to seduce us from our decent and regular lives."

"We know what to do with the women," said the male leader. The rest took up the antiphon.

"We'll knock them down."

"And roll them on their backs."

"And pull one arm out and tie it fast."

"And pull the other arm out and tie it fast."

"And pull one limb out and tie it fast."

"And pull the other limb out and tie it fast."

"And then—"

"We'll beat them to death and Merdeka will smile."

Chaplain Pemberton stared incredulously. "You must look into your hearts," he told them in a reasonable voice. "You must look deeper than you have, and you will find that you have been deluded. This is not the way for human beings to act. Somebody has misled you dreadfully. Let me explain—"

"Blasphemy," the leader of the females said, and put her spear expertly into the chaplain's intestines. The shock of the broad, cold blade pulsed through him and felled him. Jewel Flyte knelt beside him instantly, checking heartbeat and breathing. He was alive.

"Get up," the male leader said. "Displaying and offering yourself to such as we is useless. We are pure in heart."

A male child ran to the door. "Wagners!" he screamed. "Twenty Wagners coming up the stairs!"

His father roared at him: "Stand straight and don't mumble!" and slashed out with the butt of his spear, catching him hard in the ribs. The child grinned, but only after the pure-hearted eighteen had run to the stairs.

Then he blasted a whistle down the corridor while the sea-people stared with what attention they could divert from the bleeding chaplain. Six doors popped open at the whistle and men and women emerged from them to launch spears into the backs of the Brownells clustered to defend the stairs. "Thanks, pop!" the boy kept screaming while the pure-hearted Wagners swarmed over the remnants of the pure-hearted Brownells; at last his screaming bothered one of the Wagners and the boy was himself speared.

Jewel Flyte said: "I've had enough of this. Captain, please pick the chaplain up and come along."

"They'll kill us."

"You'll have the chaplain," said Mrs. Graves. "One moment." She darted into a bedroom and came back hefting the spiked knobkerry.

"Well, perhaps," the girl said. She began undoing the long row of buttons down the front of her coveralls and shrugged out of the garment, then unfastened and stepped out of her underwear. With the clothes over her arm she walked into the corridor and to the stairs, the stupefied captain and inspector following.

To the pure-hearted Merdekans she was not Phryne winning her case; she was Evil incarnate. They screamed, broke and ran wildly, dropping their weapons. That a human being could do such a thing was beyond their comprehension; Merdeka alone knew what kind of monster this was that drew them strangely and horribly, in violation of all sanity. They ran as she had hoped they would; the other side of the coin was spearing even more swift and thorough than would have been accorded to her fully clothed. But they ran, gibbering with fright and covering their eyes, into apartments and corners of the corridor, their backs turned on the awful thing.

The sea-people picked their way over the shambles at the stairway and went unopposed down the stairs and to the dock. It was a troublesome piece of work for Salter to pass the chaplain down to Mrs. Graves in the boat, but in ten minutes they had cast off, rowed out a little and set sail to catch the land breeze generated by the differential twilight cooling of water and brick. After playing her part in stepping the mast, Jewel Flyte dressed.

"It won't always be that easy," she said when the last button was fastened. Mrs. Graves had been thinking the same thing, but had not said it to avoid the appearance of envying that superb young body.

Salter was checking the chaplain as well as he knew how. "I think he'll be all right," he said. "Surgical repair and a long rest. He hasn't lost much blood. This is a strange story we'll have to tell the Ship's Council."

Mrs. Graves said: "They've no choice. We've lost our net and the land is there waiting for us. A few maniacs oppose us—what of it?"

Again a huge fish lazily surfaced; Salter regarded it thoughtfully. He said: "They'll propose scavenging bronze ashore and fashioning another net and going on just as if nothing had happened. And really, we could do that, you know."

Jewel Flyte said: "No. Not forever. This time it was the net, at the end of harvest. What if it were three masts in midwinter, in mid-Atlantic?"

"Or," said the captain, "the rudder—any time. Anywhere. But can you imagine telling the Council they've got to walk off the ship onto land, take up quarters in those brick cabins, change *everything?* And fight maniacs, and learn to *farm?*"

"There must be a way," said Jewel Flyte. "Just as Merdeka, whatever it was, was a way. There were too many people, and Merdeka was the answer to too many people. There's always an answer. Man is a land mammal in spite of brief excursions at sea. We were seed stock put aside, waiting for the land to be cleared so we could return. Just as these offshore fish are waiting very patiently for us to stop harvesting twice a year so they can return to deep water and multiply. What's the way, Captain?"

He thought hard. "We could," he said slowly, "begin by simply sailing in close and fishing the offshore waters for big stuff. Then tie up and build a sort of bridge from the ship to the shore. We'd continue to live aboard the ship but we'd go out during daylight to try farming."

"It sounds right."

"And keep improving the bridge, making it more and more solid, until before they notice it it's really a solid part of the ship and a solid part of the shore. It might take ... mmm ... ten years?"

"Time enough for the old shellbacks to make up their minds," Mrs. Graves unexpectedly snorted.

"And we'd relax the one-to-one reproduction rule, and some young adults will simply be crowded over the bridge to live on the land—" His face suddenly fell. "And then the whole damned farce starts all over again, I suppose. I pointed out that it takes thirty-two generations bearing one child apiece to run a population of two billion into zero. Well, I should have mentioned that it takes thirty-two generations bearing four children apiece to run a population of two into two billion. Oh, what's the use, Jewel?"

She chuckled. "There was an answer last time," she said. "There will be an answer the next time."

"It won't be the same answer as Merdeka," he vowed. "We grew up a little at sea. This time we can do it with brains and not with nightmares and superstition."

"I don't know," she said. "Our ship will be the first, and then the other ships will have their accidents one by one and come and tie up and build their bridges hating every minute of it for the first two generations and then not hating it, just living it … and who will be the greatest man who ever lived?"

The captain looked horrified.

"Yes, you! Salter, the Builder of the Bridge; Tommy, do you know an old word for 'bridge-builder'? *Pontifex.*"

"Oh, my God!" Tommy Salter said in despair.

A flicker of consciousness was passing through the wounded chaplain; he heard the words and was pleased that somebody aboard was praying.

[*SF Adventures* - September 1953]

The Meddlers

Reev Markon, Continental Weather Chief, swore one of his affected archaic oaths as his pocket transceiver beeped. "By my lousy halidom!" he muttered, turning the signal off and putting the pint-sized set to his face.

"How's that again, chief?" asked the puzzled voice of his assistant Moron Slobb.

"I didn't mean you, Slobb," Markon snapped. "Go ahead. What is so by-our-lady important that I must be dragged from the few pitiful hours of leisure I'm allowed?"

"Meddling," Moron Slobb said in a voice of deepest gloom.

"Ding-bust the consarned villains!" Markon shrieked. "I'll be right down."

He cast a bilious eye over the workshop where he had hoped to relax over the monthend, using his hands, forgetting the wild complexities of modern life while he puttered with his betatron planer, his compact little thermonuclear forming reactor and transmutron. "I'll meddle them," he growled, and stepped through his Transmitter.

There were wild screeches around him.

"I'm sorry, ladies!" he yelled. "It was completely—completely—" One of the ladies hit him with a chair. He abandoned explanations and ducked back through the Transmitter with a rapidly swelling eye. Through the other he read the setting on the Transmitter frame. His wives' athletic club, as he had suspected. Nor had they bothered to clear the setting after using the Transmitter.

"Lollygagging trumpets," he muttered, setting his office combination on the frame and stepping through.

Moron Slobb tactfully avoided staring at the discolored eye. "Glad you're here, chief," he burbled. "Somebody seems to have gimmicked up a private tractor beam in the Mojave area and they're pulling in rainclouds assigned to the Rio Grande eye—I mean Rio Grande Valley."

Reev Markon glared at him and decided to let it pass. "Triangulate for it," he said. "Set up the unilateral Transmitter. We'll burst in and catch them wet-handed."

He went to his private office and computed while the mechanical work was being done outside. A moderately efficient tractor beam, however haywire, could pull down five acre-feet of water a day. Rio Grande was a top-priority area drawing an allotment of eighty acre-feet for the growing season, plus sunships as needed. Plancom had decided that what the Continent needed was natural citrus and that Rio Grande was the area to supply it. Lowest priority for the current season had been assigned to the Idaho turnip acreage. He could divert rainfall from Idaho to Rio Grande. If that wasn't enough, he could seize the precipitation quota of Aspen Recreational with no difficulty since three Plancomembers had broken respectively a leg, a pelvis, and seven ribs on Aspen's beginner's ski trail ... .

Slobb told him: "Chief, we're on it and the Transmitter's set up."

Reev Markon said: "Take a visual first. Those wittold jerks aren't going to booby-trap *me*."

He watched as a camera was thrust through the Transmitter, exposed and snatched back in a thousandth of a second.

The plate showed an improvised-looking tractor-beam generator surrounded by three rustic types in bowler hats and kilts. They obviously hadn't noticed the split-second appearance of the camera and they obviously were unarmed.

"I'm going in," Reev Markon said, cold and courageous. "Slobb, arm yourself and bring me a dazzle gun."

In two minutes the weapons had been signed out of the arsenal. Reev Markon and Moron Slobb walked steadily through the Transmitter, guns at the ready. To the astounded, gaping farmers Reev Markon said: "You're under arrest for meddling. Step through this—"

The rustics stopped gaping and went into action. One of them began ripping at the generator, trying to destroy evidence. The other uncorked an uppercut at Slobb, who intercepted it neatly with his chin. Reev Markon shut his eyes and pulled the trigger of the dazzle gun. When he opened his eyes the farmers and his assistant were all lying limply on the floor. Puffing a good deal, he pitched them one by one through the invisible portal of the unilateral Transmitter. He surveyed the generator, decided it would do as evidence and pitched it through also before he stepped back into the Continental Weather office himself.

When the farmers had recovered, a matter of twenty minutes or so, he tried to interrogate them but got nowhere. "Don't you realize," he asked silkily, "that there are regular channels through which you can petition for heavier rainfall or a changed barometric pressure or more sunlight hours? Don't you realize that you're disrupting continental economy when you try to free-lance?"

They were sullen and silent, only muttering something about their spinach crop needing more water than the damn bureaucrats realized.

"Take them away," Reev Markon sighed to his assistant, and Slobb did. But Slobb rushed back with a new and alarming advisory.

"Chief," he said, "Somebody on Long Island's seeding clouds without a license—"

"The cutpurse crumb!" Reev Markon snarled. Two in a row! He leaned back wearily for a moment. "By cracky, Slobb," he said, "you'd think people would speak up and let us know if they think they've been unjustly treated by Plancom. You'd think they'd tell us instead of haywiring their rise in private and screwing the works."

Slobb mumbled sympathetically, and Reev Markon voiced the ancient complaint of his department: "The trouble with this job is, everybody does things about the weather, but nobody talks about it!"

[*Galaxy* - June 1952
as by Simon Eisner]

The Luckiest Man in Denv

Mayer's man Reuben, of the eighty-third level, Atomist, knew there was something wrong when the binoculars flashed and then went opaque. Inwardly he cursed, hoping that he had not committed himself to anything. Outwardly he was unperturbed. He handed the binoculars back to Rudolph's man Almon, of the eighty-ninth level, Maintainer, with a smile.

"They aren't very good," he said.

Almon put them to his own eyes, glanced over the parapet and swore mildly. "Blacker than the heart of a crazy Angel, eh? Never mind; here's another pair."

This pair was unremarkable. Through it, Reuben studied the thousand setbacks and penthouses of Denv that ranged themselves below. He was too worried to enjoy his first sight of the vista from the eighty-ninth level, but he let out a murmur of appreciation. Now to get away from this suddenly sinister fellow and try to puzzle it out.

"Could we—?" he asked cryptically, with a little upward jerk of his chin.

"It's better not to," Almon said hastily, taking the glasses from his hands. "What if somebody with stars happened to see, you know? How'd *you* like it if you saw some impudent fellow peering up at you?"

"He wouldn't dare!" said Reuben, pretending to be stupid and indignant, and joined a moment later in Almon's sympathetic laughter.

"Never mind," said Almon. "We are young. Some day, who knows? Perhaps we shall look from the ninety-fifth level, or the hundredth."

Though Reuben knew that the Maintainer was no friend of his, the generous words sent blood hammering through his veins; ambition for a moment.

He pulled a long face and told Almon: "Let us hope so! Thank you for being my host. Now I must return to my quarters."

He left the windy parapet for the serene luxury of an eighty-ninth-level corridor and descended slow-moving stairs through gradually less luxurious levels to his own Spartan floor. Selene was waiting, smiling, as he stepped off the stairs.

She was decked out nicely—too nicely. She wore a steely-hued corselet and a touch of scent; her hair was dressed long. The combination appealed to him, and instantly he was on his guard. Why had she gone to the trouble of learning his tastes? What was she up to? After all, she was Griffin's woman.

"Coming *down?*" she asked, awed. "Where have you been?"

"The eighty-ninth, as a guest of that fellow Almon. The vista is immense."

"I've never been ..." she murmured, and then said decisively: "You belong up there. And higher. Griffin laughs at me, but he's a fool. Last night in chamber we got to talking about you, I don't know how, and he finally became quite angry and said he didn't want to hear another word." She smiled wickedly. "I was revenged, though."

Blank-faced, he said: "You must be a good hand at revenge, Selene, and at stirring up the need for it."

The slight hardening of her smile meant that he had scored and he hurried by with a rather formal salutation.

Burn him for an Angelo, but she was easy enough to take! The contrast of the metallic garment with her soft, white skin was disturbing, and her long hair suggested things. It was hard to think of her as scheming something or other; scheming Selene was displaced in his mind by Selene in chamber.

But what was she up to? Had she perhaps heard that he was to be elevated? Was Griffin going to be swooped on by the Maintainers? Was he to kill off Griffin so she could leech on to some rising third party? Was she perhaps merely giving her man a touch of the lash?

He wished gloomily that the binoculars-problem and the Selene-problem had not come together. That trickster Almon had spoken of youth as though it were something for congratulation; he hated being young and stupid and unable to puzzle out the faulty binoculars and the warmth of Griffin's woman.

The attack alarm roared through the Spartan corridor. The Ellays were raiding again. He ducked through the nearest door into a vacant bedroom and under the heavy steel table. Somebody else floundered under the table a moment later, and a third person tried to join them.

The second-comer roared: "Get out and find your own shelter! I don't propose to be crowded out by you or to crowd you out either and see your ugly blood and brains if there's a hit. Go, now!"

"Forgive me, sir! At once, sir!" the late-comer wailed and scrambled away as the alarm continued to roar.

Reuben gasped at the "sirs" and looked at his neighbor. It was Mayer himself. The general had been trapped, no doubt, on an inspection tour of the level.

"Sir," he said respectfully, "if you wish to be alone, I can find another room."

"You may stay with me for company. Are you one of mine?" There was power in the general's voice and on his craggy face.

"Yes, sir. Mayer's man Reuben, of the eighty-third level. Atomist."

Mayer surveyed him, and Reuben noted that there were pouches of skin depending from cheekbones and the jaw line—dead-looking, coarse-pored skin.

"You're a well-made boy, Reuben! Do you have women?"

"Yes, sir," said Reuben hastily. "One after another—I *always* have women. I'm making up at this time to a charming thing called Selene. Well-rounded, yet firm, soft but supple, with long red hair and long white legs—"

"Spare me the details," muttered the general. "It takes all kinds. An Atomist, you said. That has a future, to be sure. I myself was a Controller long ago. The calling seems to have gone out of fashion—"

Abruptly the alarm stopped. The silence was hard to bear.

Mayer swallowed and went on: "... for some reason or other. Why don't youngsters elect for Controller any more? Why didn't you, for instance?"

Reuben wished he could be saved by a direct hit. The binoculars, Selene, the enemy raid, and now he was supposed to make intelligent conversation with a general.

"I really don't know, sir," he said miserably. "At the time there seemed to be very little difference—Controller, Atomist, Missiler, Maintainer. We have a saying, 'The buttons are different,' which usually ends any conversation on the subject."

"Indeed?" asked Mayer distractedly. His face was thinly filmed with sweat. "Do you suppose Ellay intends to clobber us this time?" he asked almost hoarsely. "It's been some weeks since they made a maximum effort, hasn't it?"

"Four," said Reuben. "I remember because one of my best Servers was killed by a falling corridor roof—the only fatality and it had to happen to my team."

He laughed nervously and realized that he was talking like a fool, but Mayer seemed not to notice.

Far below them, there was a series of screaming whistles as the interceptors were loosed to begin their intricate, double basketwork wall of defense in a towering cylinder about Denv.

"Go on, Reuben!" said Mayer. "That was most interesting." His eyes were searching the underside of the steel table.

Reuben averted his own eyes from the frightened face, feeling some awe drain out of him. Under a table with a general! It didn't seem so strange now.

"Perhaps, sir, you can tell me what a puzzling thing, that happened this afternoon, means? A fellow—Rudolph's man Almon, of the eighty-ninth level—gave me a pair of binoculars that flashed in my eyes and then went opaque. Has your wide experience—"

Mayer laughed hoarsely and said in a shaky voice: "That old trick! He was photographing your retinas for the blood-vessel pattern. One of Rudolph's men, eh? I'm glad you spoke to me; I'm old enough to spot a revival like that. Perhaps my good friend Rudolph plans—"

There was a thudding volley in the air and then a faint jar. An enemy bomb had got through, exploding, from the feel of it, far down at the foot of Denv.

The alarm roared again, in bursts that meant all clear; only one flight of missiles and that disposed of.

The Atomist and the general climbed out from under the table; Mayer's secretary popped through the door. The general waved him out again and leaned heavily on the table, his arms quivering. Reuben hastily brought a chair.

"A glass of water," said Mayer.

The Atomist brought it. He saw the general wash down what looked like a triple dose of xxx—green capsules which it was better to leave alone.

Mayer said after a moment: "That's better. And don't look so shocked, youngster; you don't know the strain we're under. It's only a temporary measure which I shall discontinue as soon as things ease up a bit. I was saying that perhaps my good friend Rudolph plans to substitute one of his men for one of mine. Tell me, how long has this fellow Almon been a friend of yours?"

"He struck up an acquaintance with me only last week. I should have realized—"

"You certainly should have. One week. Time enough and more. By now you've been photographed, your fingerprints taken, your voice recorded and your gait studied without your knowledge. Only the retinascope is difficult, but one must risk it for a real double. Have you killed your man, Reuben?"

He nodded. It had been a silly brawl two years ago over precedence at the refectory; he disliked being reminded of it.

"Good," said Mayer grimly. "The way these things are done, your double kills you in a secluded spot, disposes of your body and takes over your role. We shall reverse it. You will kill the double and take over *his* role."

The powerful, methodical voice ticked off possibilities and contingencies, measures and counter-measures. Reuben absorbed them and felt his awe return. Perhaps Mayer had not really been frightened under the table; perhaps it had been he reading his own terror in the general's face. Mayer was actually talking to him of backgrounds and policies. "Up from the eighty-third level!" he swore to himself as the great names were uttered.

"My good friend Rudolph, of course, wants the five stars. You would not know this, but the man who wears the stars is now eighty years old and failing fast. I consider myself a likely candidate to replace him. So, evidently, must Rudolph. No doubt he plans to have your double perpetrate some horrible blunder on the eve of the election, and the discredit would reflect on me. Now what you and I must do—"

You and I—Mayer's man Reuben and Mayer himself—up from the eighty-third! Up from the bare corridors and cheerless bedrooms to marble halls and vaulted chambers! From the clatter of the crowded refectory to small and glowing restaurants where you had your own table and servant and where music came softly from the walls! Up from the scramble to win this woman or that, by wit or charm or the poor bribes you could afford, to the eminence from which you could calmly command your pick of the beauty of Denv! From the moiling intrigue of tripping your fellow Atomist and guarding against him tripping you to the heroic thrust and parry of generals!

Up from the eighty-third!

Then Mayer dismissed him with a speech whose implications were deliriously exciting. "I need an able man and a young one, Reuben! Perhaps I've waited too long looking for him. If you do well in this touchy business, I'll consider you very seriously for an important task I have in mind."

Late that night, Selene came to his bedroom.

"I know you don't like me," she said pettishly, "but Griffin's such a fool and I wanted somebody to talk to. Do you mind? What was it like up there today? Did you see carpets? I wish I had a carpet."

He tried to think about carpets and not the exciting contrast of metallic cloth and flesh.

"I saw one through an open door," he remembered. "It looked odd, but I suppose a person gets used to them. Perhaps I didn't see a very good one. Aren't the good ones very thick?"

"Yes," she said. "Your feet sink into them. I wish I had a *good* carpet and four chairs and a small table as high as my knees to put things on and as many pillows as I wanted. Griffin's such a fool. Do you think I'll ever get those things? I've never caught the eye of a general. Am I pretty enough to get one, do you think?"

He said uneasily: "Of course you're a pretty thing, Selene. But carpets and chairs and pillows—" It made him uncomfortable, like the thought of peering up through binoculars from a parapet.

"I want them," she said unhappily. "I like you very much, but I want so many things and soon I'll be too old even for the eighty-third level, before I've been up higher, and I'll spend the rest of my life tending babies or cooking in the crèche or the refectory."

She stopped abruptly, pulled herself together and gave him a smile that was somehow ghastly in the half-light.

"You bungler," he said, and she instantly looked at the door with the smile frozen on her face. Reuben took a pistol from under his pillow and demanded, "When do you expect him?"

"What do you mean?" she asked shrilly. "Who are you talking about?"

"My double. Don't be a fool, Selene! Mayer and I—" he savored it—"Mayer and I know all about it. He warned me to beware of a diversion by a woman while the double slipped in and killed me. When do you expect him?"

"I really *do* like you," Selene sobbed. "But Almon promised to take me up there and I *knew* when I was where they'd see me that I'd meet somebody really important. I really do like you, but soon I'll be too old—"

"Selene, listen to me! Listen to me! You'll get your chance. Nobody but you and I will know that the substitution didn't succeed!"

"Then I'll be spying for you on Almon, won't I?" she asked in a choked voice. "All I wanted was a few nice things before I got too old. All right, I was supposed to be in your arms at 2350 hours!"

It was 2349. Reuben sprang from bed and stood by the door, his pistol silenced and ready. At 2350 a naked man slipped swiftly into the room, heading for the bed as he raised a ten-centimeter poignard. He stopped in dismay when he realized that the bed was empty.

Reuben killed him with a bullet through the throat.

"But he doesn't look a bit like me," he said in bewilderment, closely examining the face. "Just in a general way."

Selene said dully: "Almon told me people always say that when they see their doubles. It's funny, isn't it? He looks just like you, really."

"How was my body to be disposed of?"

She produced a small flat box. "A shadow suit. You were to be left here and somebody would come tomorrow."

"We won't disappoint him." Reuben pulled the web of the shadow suit over his double and turned on the power. In the half-lit room, it was a perfect disappearance; by daylight it would be less perfect. "They'll ask why the body was shot instead of knifed. Tell them you shot me with the gun from under the pillow! Just say I heard the double come in and you were afraid there might have been a struggle."

She listlessly asked: "How do you know I won't betray you?"

"You won't, Selene." His voice bit. "You're *broken*."

She nodded vaguely, started to say something and then went out without saying it.

Reuben luxuriously stretched in his narrow bed. Later, his beds would be wider and softer, he thought. He drifted into sleep on a half-formed thought that some day he might vote with other generals on the man to wear the five stars—or even wear them himself, Master of Denv.

He slept healthily through the morning alarm and arrived late at his regular twentieth-level station. He saw his superior, Mayer's man Oscar of the eighty-fifth level, Atomist, ostentatiously take his name. Let him!

Oscar assembled his crew for a grim announcement: "We are going to even the score, and perhaps a little better, with Ellay. At sunset there will be three flights of missiles from Deck One."

There was a joyous murmur and Reuben trotted off on his task.

All forenoon he was occupied with drawing plutonium slugs from hyper-suspicious storekeepers in the great rock-quarried vaults, and seeing them through countless audits and assays all the way to Weapons Assembly. Oscar supervised the scores there who assembled the curved slugs and the explosive lenses into sixty-kilogram warheads.

In mid-afternoon there was an incident. Reuben saw Oscar step aside for a moment to speak to a Maintainer whose guard fell on one of the Assembly Servers, and dragged him away as he pleaded innocence. He had been detected in sabotage. When the warheads were in and the Missilers seated, waiting at their boards, the two Atomists rode up to the eighty-third's refectory.

The news of a near-maximum effort was in the air; it was electric. Reuben heard on all sides in tones of self-congratulation: "We'll clobber them tonight."

"That Server you caught," he said to Oscar. "What was he up to?"

His commander stared. "Are you trying to learn my job? Don't try it, I warn you! If my black marks against you aren't enough, I could always arrange for some fissionable material in your custody to go astray."

"No, no! I was just wondering why people do something like that."

Oscar sniffed doubtfully. "He's probably insane, like all the Angelos. I've heard the climate does it to them. You're not a Maintainer or a Controller. Why worry about it?"

"They'll brain-burn him, I suppose?"

"I suppose. *Listen!*"

Deck one was firing. One, two, three, four, five, six. One, two, three, four, five, six. One, two, three, four, five, six.

People turned to one another and shook hands, laughed and slapped shoulders heartily. Eighteen missiles were racing through the stratosphere, soon to tumble on Ellay. With any luck, one or two would slip through the first wall of interceptors and blast close enough to smash windows and topple walls in the enemy city by the ocean. It would serve the lunatics right.

Five minutes later an exultant voice filled most of Denv.

"Recon missile report," it said. "Eighteen launched, eighteen perfect trajectories. Fifteen shot down by Ellay first-line interceptors, three shot down by Ellay second-line interceptors. Extensive blast damage observed in Griffith Park area of Ellay."

There were cheers.

And eight Full Maintainers marched into the refectory silently, and marched out with Reuben.

He knew better than to struggle or ask futile questions. Any question you asked of a Maintainer was futile. But he goggled when they marched him onto an upward-bound stairway.

They rode past the eighty-ninth level and Reuben lost count, seeing only the marvels of the upper reaches of Denv. He saw carpets that ran the entire length of corridors, and intricate fountains, and mosaic walls, stained-glass windows, more wonders than he could recognize, things for which he had no name.

He was marched at last into a wood-paneled room with a great polished desk and a map behind it. He saw Mayer, and another man who must have been a general—Rudolph?—but sitting at the desk was a frail old man who wore a circlet of stars on each khaki shoulder.

The old man said to Reuben: "You represent an enemy. You are an Ellay spy and saboteur."

Reuben looked at Mayer. Did one speak directly to the man who wore the stars, even in reply to such an accusation?

"Answer him, Reuben!" Mayer said kindly.

"I am Mayer's man Reuben, of the eighty-third level, an Atomist," he said.

"Explain," said the other general heavily, "if you can, why all eighteen of the warheads you procured today failed to fire."

"But they did," gasped Reuben. "The Recon missile report said there was blast damage from the three that got through and it didn't say anything about the others failing to fire."

The other general suddenly looked sick and Mayer looked even kindlier. The man who wore the stars turned inquiringly to the chief of the Maintainers, who nodded and said: "That was the Recon missile report, sir."

The general snapped: "What I said was that he would *attempt* to sabotage the attack. Evidently he failed. I also said he is a faulty double, somehow slipped with great ease into my good friend Mayer's organization. You will find that his left thumb print is a clumsy forgery of the real Reuben's thumb print and that his hair has been artificially darkened."

The old man nodded at the chief of the Maintainers, who said: "We have his card, sir."

Reuben abruptly found himself being fingerprinted and deprived of some hair.

"The f.p.'s check, sir," one Maintainer said. "He's Reuben."

"Hair's natural, sir," said another.

The general began a rearguard action: "My information about his hair seems to have been inaccurate. But the fingerprint means only that Ellay spies substituted his prints for Reuben's prints in the files—"

"Enough, sir," said the old man with the stars. "Dismissed. All of you. Rudolph, I am surprised. All of you, go!"

Reuben found himself in a vast apartment with Mayer, who was bubbling and chuckling uncontrollably until he popped three of the green capsules into his mouth hurriedly.

"This means the eclipse for years of my good friend Rudolph," he crowed. "His game was to have your double sabotage the attack warheads and so make it appear that my organization is rotten with spies. The double must have been under post-hypnotic suggestion, primed to admit everything. Rudolph was so sure of himself that he made his accusations before the attack, the fool!"

He fumbled out the green capsules again.

"Sir," said Reuben, alarmed.

"Only temporary," Mayer muttered, and swallowed a fourth. "But you're right. You leave them alone! There are big things to be done in your time, not in mine. I told you I needed a young man who could claw his way to the top. Rudolph's a fool. He doesn't need the capsules because he doesn't ask questions. Funny, I thought a coup like the double affair would hit me hard, but I don't feel a thing. It's not like the old days. I used to plan and plan, and when the trap went *snap* it was better than this stuff. But now I don't feel a thing."

He leaned forward from his chair; the pupils of his eyes were black bullets.

"Do you want to *work?*" he demanded. "Do you want your world stood on its head and your brains to crack and do the only worthwhile job there is to do? Answer me!"

"Sir, I am a loyal Mayer's man. I want to obey your orders and use my ability to the full."

"Good enough," said the general. "You've got brains, you've got push. I'll do the spade work. I won't last long enough to push it through. You'll have to follow. Ever been outside of Denv?"

Reuben stiffened.

"I'm not accusing you of being a spy. It's really all right to go outside of Denv. I've been outside. There isn't much to see at first—a lot of ground pocked and torn up by shorts and overs from Ellay and us. Farther out, especially east, it's different. Grass, trees, flowers. Places where you could grow food.

"When I went outside, it troubled me. It made me ask questions. I wanted to know how we started. Yes—started. *It wasn't always like this.* Somebody built Denv. Am I getting the idea across to you? *It wasn't always like this.*

"Somebody set up the reactors to breed uranium and make plutonium. Somebody tooled us-up for the missiles. Somebody wired the boards to control them. Somebody started the hydroponics tanks.

"I've dug through the archives. Maybe I found something. I saw mountains of strength reports, ration reports, supply reports, and yet I never got back to the beginning. I found a piece of paper and maybe I understood it and maybe I didn't. It was about the water of the Colorado River and who should get how much of it. How can you divide water in a river? But it could have been the start of Denv, Ellay, and the missile attacks."

The general shook his head, puzzled, and went on: "I don't see clearly what's ahead. I want to make peace between Denv and Ellay, but I don't know how to start or what it will be like. I think it must mean not firing, not even making any more weapons. Maybe it means that some of us, or a lot of us, will go out of Denv and live a different kind of life. That's why I've clawed my way up. That's why I need a young man who can claw with the best of them. Tell me what you think!"

"I think," said Reuben measuredly, "it's magnificent—the salvation of Denv. I'll back you to my dying breath if you'll let me."

Mayer smiled tiredly and leaned back in the chair as Reuben tiptoed out.

What luck, Reuben thought—what unbelievable luck to be at a fulcrum of history like this!

He searched the level for Rudolph's apartment and gained admission.

To the general, he said: "Sir, I have to report that your friend Mayer is insane. He has just been raving to me, advocating the destruction of civilization as we know it, and urging me to follow in his footsteps. I pretended to agree— since I can be of greater service to you if I'm in Mayer's confidence."

"So?" said Rudolph thoughtfully. "Tell me about the double. How did that go wrong?"

"The bunglers were Selene and Almon, Selene because she alarmed me instead of distracting me, Almon because he failed to recognize her incompetence."

"They shall be brain-burned. That leaves an eighty-ninth-level vacancy in my organization, doesn't it?"

"You're very kind, sir, but I think I should remain a Mayer's man—outwardly. If I earn any rewards, I can wait for them. I presume that Mayer will be elected to wear the five stars. He won't live more than two years after that, at the rate he is taking drugs."

"We can shorten it," grinned Rudolph. "I have pharmacists who can see that his drugs are more than normal strength."

"That would be excellent, sir. When he is too enfeebled to discharge his duties, there may be an attempt to rake up the affair of the double to discredit you. I could then testify that I was your man all along and that Mayer coerced me."

They put their heads together, the two saviors of civilization as they knew it, and conspired ingeniously long into the endless night.

[*Cosmic Stories* - March 1941
as by Cecil Corwin]

The Reversible Revolutions

J. C. Battle, late of the Foreign Legion, Red Army, United States Marines, Invincibles de Bolivia and Coldstream Guards, alias Alexandre de Foma, Christopher Jukes, Burton Macauly and Joseph Hagstrom—*né* Etzel Bernstein—put up his hands.

"No tricks," warned the feminine voice. The ample muzzle of the gun in his back shifted slightly, seemingly from one hand to another. Battle felt his pockets being gone through. "Look out for the left hip," he volunteered. "That gat's on a hair-trigger."

"Thanks," said the feminine voice. He felt the little pencilgun being gingerly removed. "Two Colts," said the voice admiringly, "a Police .38, three Mills grenades, pencilgun, brass knuckles, truncheons of lead, leather and rubber, one stiletto, tear-gas gun, shells for same, prussic-acid hypo kit, thuggee's braided cord, sleeve Derringer and a box of stink bombs. Well, you walking armory! Is that all?"

"Quite," said Battle. "Am I being taken for a ride?" He looked up and down the dark street and saw nothing in the way of accomplices.

"Nope. I may decide to drop you here. But before you find out, suppose you tell me how you got on my trail?" The gun jabbed viciously into his back. "Talk!" urged the feminine voice nastily.

"How *I* got on *your* trail?" exploded Battle. "Dear lady, I can't see your face, but I assure you that I don't recognize your voice, that I'm not on anybody's trail, that I'm just a soldier of fortune resting up during a slack spell in the trade. And anyway, I don't knock off ladies. We—we have a kind of code."

"Yeah?" asked the voice skeptically. "Let's see your left wrist." Mutely Battle twitched up the cuff and displayed it. Aside from a couple of scars it was fairly ordinary. "What now?" he asked.

"I'll let you know," said the voice. Battle's hand was twisted behind his back, and he felt a cold, stinging liquid running over the disputed wrist. "What the—?" he began impatiently.

"Oh!" ejaculated the voice, aghast. "I'm sorry! I thought—" The gun relaxed and Battle turned. He could dimly see the girl in the light of the merc lamp far

118

down the deserted street. She appeared to be blushing. "Here I've gone and taken you apart," she complained, "and you're not even from Breen at all! Let me help you." She began picking up Battle's assorted weapons from the sidewalk where she had deposited them. He stowed them away as she handed them over.

"There," she said. "That must be the last of them."

"The hypo kit," he reminded her. She was holding it, unconsciously, in her left hand. He hefted the shoulder holster under his coat and grunted. "That's better," he said.

"You must think I'm an awful silly," said the girl shyly.

Battle smiled generously as he caught sight of her face. "Not at all," he protested. "I've made the same mistake myself. Only I've not always caught myself in time to realize it." This with a tragic frown and sigh.

"*Really?*" she breathed. "You must be awfully important —all these guns and things."

"Tools of the trade," he said noncommittally. "My card." He handed her a simple pasteboard bearing the crest of the United States Marines and the legend:

LIEUTENANT J. C. BATTLE
SOLDIER OF FORTUNE
REVOLUTIONS A SPECIALTY

She stared, almost breathless. "How wonderful!" she said.

"In every major insurrection for the past thirty years," he assured her complacently.

"That must make you—let's see—" she mused.

"Thirty years, did I say?" he quickly interposed. "I meant twenty. In case you were wondering, I'm just thirty-two years old." He tweaked his clipped, military mustache.

"Then you were in your first at—"

"Twelve. Twelve and a half, really. Shall we go somewhere for a cup of coffee, Miss—er—ah—?"

"McSweeney," she said, and added demurely, "but my friends all call me Spike."

"China? Dear me, yes! I was with the Eighth Route Army during the celebrated long trek from Annam to Szechuan Province. And I shouldn't call it boasting to admit that without me—"

Miss Spike McSweeney appeared to be hanging on his every word. "Have you ever," she asked, "done any technical work?"

"Engineering? Line of communication? Spike, we fighters leave that to the 'greaseballs,' as they are called in most armies. I admit that I fly a combat fighter as well as the next—assuming that he's pretty good—but as far as the engine goes, I let that take care of itself. Why do you ask?"

"Lieutenant," she said earnestly, "I think I ought to tell you what all this mess is about."

"Dear lady," he said gallantly, "the soldier does not question his orders."

"Anyway," said Miss McSweeney, "I need your help. It's a plot—a big one. A kind of revolution. You probably know more about them than I do, but this one seems to be the dirtiest trick that was ever contemplated."

"How big is it?" asked Battle, lighting a cigarette.

"Would you mind not smoking?" asked the girl hastily, shrinking away from the flame. "Thanks. How big is it? World-scale. A world revolution. Not from the Right, not from the Left, but, as near as I can make out, from Above."

"How's that?" asked Battle, startled.

"The leader is what you'd call a scientist-puritan, I guess. His name's Breen—Dr. Malachi Breen, formerly of every important university and lab in the world. And now he's got his own revolution all planned out. It's for a world without smoking, drinking, swearing, arguing, dancing, movies, music, rich foods, steam heat—all those things."

"Crackpot!" commented the lieutenant.

She stared at him grimly. "You wouldn't think so if you knew him," said Spike. "I'll tell you what I know. I went to work for him as a stenographer. He has a dummy concern with offices in Rockefeller Plaza and a factory in New Jersey. He's supposed to be manufacturing Pot-O-Klutch, a device to hold pots on the stove in case of an earthquake. With that as a front, he goes on with his planning. He's building machines of some kind in his plant—and with his science and his ambition, once he springs his plans, the world will be at his feet!"

"The field of action," said Battle thoughtfully, "would be New Jersey principally. Now, you want me to break this insurrection?"

"Of course!" agonized the girl. "As soon as I found out what it really was, I hurried to escape. But I knew I was being followed by *his* creatures!"

"Exactly," said Battle. "Now, what's in this for me?"

"I don't understand. You mean—?"

"Money," said Battle. "The quartermaster's getting short-handed. Say twenty thousand?"

The girl only stared. "I haven't any money," she finally gasped. "I thought—"

"You thought I was a dilettante?" asked Battle. "Dear lady, my terms are fifty percent cash, remainder conditional on the success of the campaign. I'm sorry I can't help you—"

"Look out!" screamed the girl. Battle spun around and ducked under the table as a bomb crashed though the window of the coffee shop and exploded in his face.

"Open your eyes, damn you!" growled a voice.

"Stephen—the profanity—" objected another voice mildly.

"Sorry, Doc. Wake, friend! The sun is high."

Battle came to with a start and saw a roast-beef face glowering into his. He felt for his weapons. They were all in place. "What can I do for you, gentlemen?" he asked.

"Ah," said the second voice gently. "Our convert has arisen. On your feet, Michael."

"My name is Battle," said the lieutenant. "J. C. Battle. My card."

"Henceforth you shall be known as Michael, the Destroying Angel," said the second voice. "It's the same name, really."

Battle looked around him. He was in a kind of factory, dim and vacant except for himself and the two who had spoken. They wore pure white military uniforms; one was a tough boy, obviously. It hurt Battle to see how clumsily he carried his guns. The bulges were plainly obvious through his jacket and under his shoulder. The other either wore his more skillfully or wasn't heeled at all. That seemed likely, for his gentle blue eyes carried not a trace of violence, and his rumpled, pure white hair was scholarly and innocent.

"Will you introduce yourselves?" asked the lieutenant calmly.

"Steve Haglund, outta Chi," said the tough.

"Malachi Breen, manufacturer of Pot-O-Klutch and temporal director of Sweetness and Light, the new world revolution," said the old man.

"Ah," said Battle, sizing them up. "What happened to Miss McSweency?" he asked abruptly, remembering.

"She is in good hands," said Breen. "Rest easy on her account, Michael. You have work to do."

"Like what?" asked the lieutenant.

"Trigger work," said Haglund. "Can you shoot straight?"

In answer there roared out three flat crashes, and Battle stood with his smoking police special in his hand. As he reloaded he said, "Get yourself a new lathe, Dr. Breen. And if you'll look to see how close together the bullets were—"

The old man puttered over to Battle's target. "Extraordinary," he murmured. "A poker chip would cover them." His manner grew relatively brisk and businesslike. "How much do you want for the job?" he asked. "How about a controlling factor in the world of Sweetness and Light?"

Battle smiled slowly. "I *never* accept a proposition like that," he said. "Twenty thousand is my talking point for all services over a six-month period."

"Done," said Breen promptly, counting out twenty bills from an antiquated wallet. Battle pocketed them without batting an eyelash. "Now," he said, "what's my job?"

"As you may know," said Breen, "Sweetness and Light is intended to bring into being a new world. Everybody will be happy, and absolute freedom will be the rule and not the exception. All carnal vices will be forbidden and peace will reign. Now, there happens to be an enemy of this movement at large. He thinks he has, in fact, a rival movement. It is your job to convince him that there is no way but mine. And you are at absolute liberty to use any argument you wish. Is that clear?"

"Perfectly, sir," said Battle. "What's his name?"

"Lenninger Underbottam," said Breen, grinding his teeth. "The most unprincipled faker that ever posed as a scientist and scholar throughout the long history of the world. His allegedly rival movement is called 'Devil Take the Hindmost.' The world he wishes to bring into being would be one of the most revolting excesses—all compulsory, mark you! I consider it my duty to the future to blot him out!"

His rage boiled over into a string of expletives. Then, looking properly ashamed, he apologized. "Underbottam affects me strangely and horribly. I believe that if I were left alone with him I should—I, exponent of Sweetness and Light!—resort to violence. Anyway, Lieutenant, you will find him either at his offices in the Empire State Building where the rotter cowers under the alias of the Double-Action Kettlesnatcher Manufacturing Corporation, or in his upstate plant where he is busy turning out not only weapons and defenses but also his ridiculous Kettlesnatcher, a device to remove kettles from the stove in case of hurricane or typhoon."

Battle completed his notes and stowed away his memo book. "Thank you, sir," he said. "Where shall I deliver the body?"

"Hello!" whispered a voice.

"Spike!" Battle whispered back. "What are you doing here?" He jerked a thumb at the illuminated ground glass of the door and the legend, *Double-Action Kettlesnatcher Manufacturing Corp., Lenninger Underbottam, Pres.*

"They told me where to find you."

"They?"

"Mr. Breen, of course. Who did you think?"

"But," expostulated the lieutenant, "I thought you hated him and his movement."

"Oh, that," said the girl casually. "It was just a whim. Are you going to knock him off?"

"Of course. But how did you get here?"

"Climbed one of the elevator shafts. The night watchman never saw me. How did you make it?"

"I slugged the guard and used a service lift. Let's go."

Battle applied a clamp to the doorknob and wrenched it out like a turnip from muddy ground. The door swung open as his two Colts leaped into his hands. The fat man at the ornate desk rose with a cry of alarm and began to pump blood as Battle drilled him between the eyes.

"Okay. That's enough," said a voice. The lieutenant's guns were snatched from his hands with a jerk that left them stinging, and he gaped in alarm as he saw, standing across the room, an exact duplicate of the bleeding corpse on the floor.

"You Battle?" asked the duplicate, who was holding a big, elaborate sort of radio tube in his hand.

"Yes," said the lieutenant feebly. "My card—"

"Never mind that. Who's the dame?"

"Miss McSweeney. And you, sir, are—?"

"I'm Underbottam, Chief of Devil Take the Hindmost. You from Breen?"

"I was engaged by the doctor for a brief period," admitted Battle. "However, our services were terminated—"

"Liar," snapped Underbottam. "And if they weren't, they will be in a minute or two. Lamp this!" He rattled the radio tube, and from its grid leaped a fiery radiance that impinged momentarily on the still-bleeding thing that Battle had shot down. The thing was consumed in one awful blast of heat. "End of a robot," said Underbottam, shaking the tube again. The flame died down, and there was nothing left of the corpse but a little fused lump of metal.

"Now, you going to work for me, Battle?"

"Why not?" shrugged the lieutenant.

"Okay. Your duties are as follows: Get Breen. I don't care how you get him, but get him soon. He posed for twenty years as a scientist without ever being apprehended. Well, I'm going to do some apprehending that'll make all previous apprehending look like no apprehending at all. You with me?"

"Yes," said Battle, very much confused. "What's that thing you have?"

"Piggy-back heat ray. You transpose the air in its path into an unstable isotope which tends to carry all energy as heat. Then you shoot your juice, light or whatever along the isotopic path and you burn whatever's on the receiving end. You want a few?"

"No," said Battle. "I have my gats. What else have you got for offense and defense?"

Underbottam opened a cabinet and proudly waved an arm. "Everything," he said. "Disintegrators, heat rays, bombs of every type. And impenetrable shields of energy, massive and portable. What more do I need?"

"Just as I thought," mused the lieutenant. "You've solved half the problem. How about tactics? Who's going to use your weapons?"

"Nothing to that," declaimed Underbottam airily. "I just announce that I have the perfect social system. My army will sweep all before it. Consider: Devil Take the Hindmost promises what every person wants—pleasure, pure and simple. Or vicious and complex, if necessary. Pleasure will be compulsory; people will be so happy that they won't have time to fight or oppress or any of the other things that make the present world a caricature of a madhouse."

"What about hangovers?" unexpectedly asked Spike McSweeney.

Underbottam grunted. "My dear young lady," he said, "if you had a hangover, would you want to do anything except die? It's utterly automatic. Only puritans—damn them!—have time enough on their hands to make war. You see?"

"It sounds reasonable," confessed the girl.

"Now, Battle," said Underbottam. "What are your rates?"

"Twen—" began the lieutenant automatically. Then, remembering the ease with which he had made his last twenty thousand, he paused. "Thir—" he began again. "Forty thousand," he said firmly, holding out his hand.

"Right," said Underbottam, handing him two bills.

Battle scanned them hastily and stowed them away. "Come on," he said to Spike. "We have a job to do."

The lieutenant courteously showed Spike a chair. "Sit down," he said firmly. "I'm going to unburden myself." Agitatedly Battle paced his room. "I don't know where in hell I'm at!" he yelled frantically. "All my life I've been a soldier. I know military science forward and backward, but I'm damned if I can make head or tail of this bloody mess. Two scientists, each at the other's throat, me hired by both of them to knock off the other—and incidentally, where do you stand?" He glared at the girl.

"Me?" she asked mildly. "I just got into this by accident. Breen manufactured me originally, but I got out of order and gave you that fantastic story about me being a steno at his office—I can hardly believe it was me!"

"What do you mean, manufactured you?" demanded Battle.

"I'm a robot, Lieutenant. Look." Calmly she took off her left arm and put it on again.

Battle collapsed into a chair. "Why didn't you tell me?" he groaned.

"You didn't ask me," she retorted with spirit. "And what's wrong with robots? I'm a very superior model, by the way—the Seduction Special, designed for diplomats, army officers (that must be why I sought you out) and legislators. Part of Sweetness and Light. Breen put a lot of work into me himself. I'm only good for about three years, but Breen expects the world to be his by then."

Battle sprang from his chair. "Well, this pretty much decides me, Spike. I'm washed up. I'm through with Devil Take the Hindmost and Sweetness and Light both. I'm going back to Tannu-Tuva for the counterrevolution. Damn Breen, Underbottam and the rest of them!"

"That isn't right, Lieutenant," said the robot thoughtfully. "Undeterred, one or the other of them is bound to succeed. And that won't be nice for you. A world without war?"

"Awk!" grunted Battle. "You're right, Spike. Something has to be done. But not by me. That heat ray—ugh!" He shuddered.

"Got any friends?" asked Spike.

"Yes," said Battle, looking at her hard. "How did you know?"

"I just guessed—" began the robot artlessly.

"Oh, no, you didn't," gritted the lieutenant. "I was just going to mention them. Can you read minds?"

"Yes," said the robot in a small voice. "I was built that way. Governor Burly—faugh! It was a mess."

"And—and you know all about me?" demanded Battle.

"Yes," she said. "I know you're forty-seven and not thirty-two. I know that you were busted from the Marines. And I know that your real name is—"

"That's enough," he said, white-faced.

"But," said the robot softly, "I love you anyway."

"What?" sputtered the lieutenant.

"And I know that you love me, too, even if I am—what I am."

Battle stared at her neat little body and her sweet little face. "Can you be kissed?" he asked at length.

"Of course, Lieutenant," she said. Then, demurely, "I told you I was a very superior model."

To expect a full meeting of the Saber Club would be to expect too much. In the memory of the oldest living member, Major Breughel, who had been to the Netherlands Empire what Clive and Warren Hastings had been to the British, two thirds—nearly—had gathered from the far corners of the earth to observe the funeral services for a member who had been embroiled in a gang war and shot in the back. The then mayor of New York had been reelected for that reason.

At the present meeting, called by First Class Member Battle, about a quarter of the membership appeared.

There was Peasely, blooded in Tonkin, 1899. He had lost his left leg to the thigh with Kolchak in Siberia. Peasely was the bombardier of the Saber Club. With his curious half-lob he could place a Mills or potato masher or nitro bottle on a dime.

Vaughn, he of the thick Yorkshire drawl, had the unique honor of hopping on an Axis submarine and cleaning it out with a Lewis gun from stem to stern, then, single-handed, piloting it to Liverpool, torpedoing a German mine layer on the way.

The little Espera had left a trail of bloody revolution through the whole of South America; he had a weakness for lost causes. It was worth his life to cross the Panama Canal; therefore he made it a point to do so punctually, once a year. He never had his bullets removed. By latest tally three of his ninety-seven pounds were lead.

"When," demanded Peasely fretfully, "is that lug going to show up? I had an appointment with a cabinetmaker for a new leg. Had to call it off for Battle's summons. Bloody shame—he doesn't give a hang for my anatomy."

"Ye'll coom when 'e wish, bate's un," drawled Vaughn unintelligibly. Peasely snarled at him.

Espera sprang to his feet. "Miss Millicent," he said effusively.

"Don't bother to rise, gentlemen," announced the tall, crisp woman who had entered. "As if you would anyway. I just collected on that Fiorenza deal, Manuel," she informed Espera. "Three gees. How do you like that?"

"I could have done a cleaner job," said Peasely snappishly. He had cast the only blackball when this first woman to enter the Saber Club had been voted a member. "What did you use?"

"Lyddite," she said, putting on a pale lipstick.

"Thot's pawky explaw-seeve," commented Vaughn. "I'd noat risk such."

She was going to reply tartly when Battle strode in. They greeted him with a muffled chorus of sighs and curses.

"Hi," he said briefly. "I'd like your permission to introduce a person waiting outside. Rules do not apply in her case for—for certain reasons. May I?"

There was a chorus of assent. He summoned Spike, who entered. "Now," said Battle, "I'd like your help in a certain matter of great importance to us all."

"Yon's t' keenin' tool," said the Yorkshireman.

"Okay, then. We have to storm and take a plant in New Jersey. This plant is stocked with new weapons—dangerous weapons—weapons that, worst of all, are intended to effect a world revolution which will bring an absolute and complete peace within a couple of years, thus depriving us of our occupations without compensation. Out of self-defense we must take this measure. Who is with me?"

All hands shot up in approval. "Good. Further complications are as follows: This is only one world revolution; there's another movement which is in rivalry to it, and which will surely dominate if the first does not. So we will have to split our forces—"

"No, you won't," said the voice of Underbottam.

"Where are you?" asked Battle, looking around the room.

"In my office, you traitor. I'm using a wire screen in your clubroom for a receiver and loudspeaker in a manner you couldn't possibly understand."

"I don't like that traitor talk," said Battle evenly. "I mailed back your money— and Breen's. Now what was that you said?"

"We'll be waiting for you together in Rockefeller Center. Breen and I have pooled our interests. After we've worked our revolution we're going to flip a coin. That worm doesn't approve of gambling, of course, but he'll make this exception."

"And if I know you, Underbottam," said Battle heavily, "it won't be gambling. What time in Rockefeller Center?"

"Four in the morning. Bring your friends—nothing like a showdown. By heaven, I'm going to save the world whether you like it or not!"

The wire screen from which the voice had been coming suddenly fused in a flare of light and heat.

Miss Millicent broke the silence. "Scientist!" she said in a voice heavy with scorn. Suddenly there was a gun in her palm. "If he's human I can drill him," she declared.

"Yeah," said Battle gloomily. "That was what I thought."

The whole length of Sixth Avenue not a creature was stirring, not even a mouse, as the six crept through the early morning darkness under the colossal shadow of the RCA building. The vertical architecture of the Center was lost in the sky as they hugged the wall of the Music Hall.

"When do you suppose they'll finish it?" asked Peasely, jerking a thumb at the boarding over the Sixth Avenue subway under construction.

"What do you care?" grunted Battle. "We need a scout to take a look at the plaza. How about you, Manuel? You're small and quick."

"Right," grinned Espera. "I could use a little more weight." He sped across the street on silent soles, no more than a shadow in the dark. But he had been spotted, for a pale beam of light hissed for a moment on the pavement beside him. He flattened and gestured.

"Come on—he says," muttered Miss Millicent. They shot across the street and flattened against the building. "Where are they, Manuel?" demanded Battle.

"Right there in the plaza beside the fountain. They have a mess of equipment. Tripods and things. A small generator."

"Shall I try a masher?" asked Peasely.

"Do," said Miss Millicent. "Nothing would be neater."

The man with the wooden leg unshipped a bomb from his belt and bit out the pin. He held it to his ear for just a moment to hear it sizzle. "I love the noise," he explained apologetically to Spike. Then he flung it with a curious twist of his arm.

Crash!

Battle looked around the corner of the building. "They haven't been touched. And that racket's going to draw the authorities," he said. "They have some kind of screen, I guess."

"Darling," whispered Spike.

"What is it?" asked Battle, sensing something in her tone.

"Nothing," she said, as women will.

"Close in under heavy fire, maybe?" suggested the little Espera.

"Yep," snapped Battle. "Ooops! There goes a police whistle."

Pumping lead from both hips, the six of them advanced down the steps to the Plaza, where Breen and Underbottam were waiting behind a kind of shimmering illumination.

The six ducked behind the waist-high stone wall of the Danish restaurant, one of the eateries which rimmed the Plaza. Hastily, as the others kept up their fire, Vaughn set up a machine gun.

"Doon, a' fu' leef!" he ordered. They dropped behind the masking stone. "Cae oot, yon cawbies," yelled Vaughn.

His only answer was a sudden dropping of the green curtain and a thunderbolt or something like it that winged at him and went way over his head, smashing into the RCA building and shattering three stories.

"Haw!" laughed Peasely. "They can't aim! Watch this." He bit another grenade and bowled it underhand against the curtain. The ground heaved and bucked as the crash of the bomb sounded. In rapid succession he rolled over enough to make the once-immaculate Plaza as broken a bit of terrain as was ever seen, bare pipes and wires exposed underneath. Underbottam's face was distorted with rage.

The curtain dropped abruptly and the two embattled scientists and would-be saviors of the world squirted wildly with everything they had—rays in every color of the spectrum, thunderbolts and lightning flashes, some uncomfortably near.

The six couldn't face up to it; what they saw nearly blinded them. They flattened themselves to the ground and prayed mutely in the electric clash and spatter of science unleashed.

"Darling," whispered Spike, her head close to Battle's.

"Yes?"

"Have you got a match?" she asked tremulously. "No—don't say a word." She took the match pack and kissed him awkwardly and abruptly. "Stay under cover," she said. "Don't try to follow. When my fuel tank catches it'll be pretty violent."

Suddenly she was out from behind the shelter and plastered against one of the tumbled rocks, to leeward of the worldsavers' armory. A timid bullet or two was coming from the Danish restaurant.

In one long, staggering run she made nearly seven yards, then dropped, winged by a heat ray that cauterized her arm. Cursing, Spike held the matches in her mouth and tried to strike one with her remaining hand. It lit, and she applied it to the match pack, dropping it to the ground. Removing what remained of her right arm, she lit it at the flaring pack. It blazed like a torch; her cellulose skin was highly inflammable.

She used the arm to ignite her body at strategic points and then, a blazing, vengeful figure of flame, hurled herself on the two scientists in the Plaza.

From the restaurant Battle could see, through tear-wet eyes, the features of the fly-by-night worldsavers. Then Spike's fuel tank exploded and everything blotted out in one vivid sheet of flame.

"Come on! The cops!" hissed Miss Millicent. She dragged him, sobbing as he was, into the Independent subway station that let out into the Center. Aimlessly he let her lead him onto an express, the first of the morning.

"Miss Millicent, I loved her," he complained.

"Why don't you join the Foreign Legion to forget?" she suggested amiably.

"What?" he said, making a wry face. "Again?"

[*Cosmic Stories* - July 1941
as by Cecil Corwin]

The City in the Sofa

Lieutenant J. C. Battle tweaked the ends of his trim little military mustache and smiled brilliantly at the cashier.

"Dear lady," he said, "there seems to have been some mistake. I could have sworn I'd put my wallet in this suit—"

The superblonde young lady looked bored and crooked a finger at the manager of the cafeteria. The manager crooked a finger at three muscular busboys, who shambled over to the exit.

"Now," said the manager, "what seems to be the trouble?"

The lieutenant bowed. "My name," he said, "is Battle. My card, sir." He presented it.

"A phony," said the manager with the wickedest of smiles. "A deadbeat. The check says thirty cents, Major—do you cough up or wash dishes?" He flung the card aside, and an innocent-appearing old man, white-haired, wrinkled of face and shabbily dressed, who had been patiently waiting to pay his ten-cent check, courteously stooped and tapped the manager on the shoulder.

"You dropped this," he said politely, extending the card.

"Keep it," snarled the manager. The innocent old man scanned the card and stiffened as though he had been shot.

"If you will allow me," he said, interrupting Battle's impassioned plea for justice, "I shall be glad to pay this young man's check." He fished out an ancient wallet and dropped a half dollar into the superblonde's hand.

"May I have your address, sir?" asked Battle when they were outside. "I shall mail you the money as soon as I get back to my club."

The old man raised a protesting hand. "Don't mention it," he smiled toothlessly. "It was a pleasure. In fact I should like you to come with me to *my* club." He looked cautiously around. "I think," he half-whispered, "that I have a job for you, Lieutenant—if you're available."

"Revolution?" asked Battle, skeptically surveying the old man, taking in every wrinkle in the suit he wore. "I'm rather busy at the moment, sir, but I can recom-

129

mend some very able persons who might suit you as well. They do what might be called a cut-rate business. My price is high, sir—very high."

"Be that as it may, Lieutenant. My club is just around the corner. Will you follow me, please?"

Only in New York could you find a two-bit cafeteria on a brightly lit avenue around the corner from the homes of the wealthy on one side and the poor on the other. Battle fully expected the old man to cross the street and head riverwards; instead he led the soldier of fortune toward Central Park.

Battle gasped as the old man stopped and courteously gestured him to enter a simple door in an old-style marble-faced building. Disbelievingly he read the house number.

"But this is—" said Battle, stuttering a little in awe.

"Yes," said the old man simply. "This is the Billionaire's Club."

In the smoking room, Battle eased himself dazedly into a chair upholstered with a priceless Gobelin tapestry shot through by wires of pure gold. Across the room he saw a man with a vast stomach and a nose like a pickled beet whom he recognized as Old Jay. He was shaking an admonishing finger at the stock-market plunger known as The Cobra of Wall Street.

"Where you should put your money—" Old Jay rumbled. As Battle leaned forward eagerly, the rumble dropped to a whisper. The Cobra jotted down a few notes in a solid-silver memo pad and smiled gratefully. As he left the room he nodded at a suave young man whom the lieutenant knew to be the youngest son of the Atlantis Plastic and Explosives Dynasty.

"I didn't," said Battle breathlessly, "I didn't catch the name, sir."

"Cromleigh," snapped the old man who had brought him through the fabulous portals. "Ole Cromleigh, 'Shutter-shy,' they call me. I've never been photographed, and for a very good reason. All will be plain in a moment. Watch this." He pressed a button.

"Yessir?" snapped a page, appearing through a concealed door as if by magic.

Cromleigh pointed at a rather shabby mohair sofa. "I want that fumigated, sonny," he said. "I'm afraid it's crummy."

"Certainly, sir," said the page. "I'll have it attended to right away, sir." He marched through the door after a smart salute.

"Now study that sofa," said Cromleigh meditatively. "Look at it carefully and tell me what you think of it."

The lieutenant looked at it carefully. "Nothing," he said at length, and quite frankly. "I can't see a thing wrong with it, except that beside all this period furniture it looks damned shabby."

"Yes," said Ole Cromleigh. "I see." He rubbed his hands meditatively. "You heard me order that page to fumigate it, eh? Well—he's going to forget all about those orders as completely as if I'd never delivered them."

"I don't get it," confessed Battle. "But I'd like you to check—for my benefit."

Cromleigh shrugged and pressed the button again. To the page who appeared, he said irascibly, "I told you to have that sofa fumigated—didn't I?"

The boy looked honestly baffled. "No, sir," he said, wrinkling his brows. "I don't think so, sir."

"All right, sonny. Scat." The boy disappeared with evident relief.

"That's quite a trick," said Battle. "How do you do it?" He was absolutely convinced that it was the same boy and that he had forgotten all about the incident.

"You hit the nail on the head, young man," said Cromleigh, leaning forward. "I didn't do it. I don't know who did, but it happens regularly." He looked about him sharply and continued, "I'm owing-gay oo-tay eek-spay in ig-pay atin-lay. Isten-lay."

And then, in the smoking room of the Billionaire's Club, the strangest story ever told was unreeled—in pig-Latin!—for the willing ears of Lieutenant J. C. Battle, Soldier of Fortune. And it was the prelude to his strangest job—the strangest job any soldier of fortune was ever hired for throughout the whole history of the ancient profession.

Battle was bewildered. He stared about himself with the curious feeling of terrified uncertainty that is felt in nightmares. At his immediate left arose a monstrous spiral mountain, seemingly of metal-bearing ore, pitted on the surface and crusted with red rust.

From unimaginable heights above him filtered a dim, sickly light ... beneath his feet was a coarse stuff with great ridges and interstices running into the distance. Had he not known, he would never have believed that he was standing on wood.

"So this," said Battle, "is what the inside of a mohair sofa is like."

Compressed into a smallness that would have made a louse seem mastodonic, he warily trod his way across huge plains of that incredible worm's-eye wood, struggled over monstrous tubes that he knew were the hairy padding of the sofa.

From somewhere far off in the dusk of this world of near night, there was a trampling of feet, many feet. Battle drew himself on the alert, snapped out miniature revolvers, one in each hand. He thought briskly that these elephant-pistols had been, half an hour ago, the most dangerous handguns on Earth, whereas here—well?

The trampling of feet attached itself to the legs of a centipede, a very small centipede that was only about two hundred times the length of the lieutenant. Its many sharp eyes sighted him, and rashly the creature headed his way.

The flat crash of his guns echoing strangely in the unorthodox construction of this world, Battle stood his ground, streaming smoke from both pistols. The centipede kept on going.

He drew a smoke bomb and hurled it delicately into the creature's face. The arthropod reared up and thrashed for a full second before dying. As Battle went a long way around it, it switched its tail, nearly crushing the diminished soldier of fortune.

After the equivalent of a two-mile walk he saw before him a light that was not the GE's filtering down from the smoking room of the Billionaire's Club, but a bright, chemical flare of illumination.

"It's them," breathed the lieutenant. "In person!" He crouched behind a towering wood shaving and inspected the weird scene. It was a city that spread out before him, but a city the like of which man's eyes had never seen before.

A good, swift kick would have sent most of it crashing to the ground, but to the tiny lieutenant it was impressive and somehow beautiful. It was built mostly of wood splinters quarried from the two-by-fours which braced the sofa; the base of the city was more of the same, masticated into a sort of papier-mâché platform. As the soldier of fortune looked down on it from the dizzy height of two feet, he felt his arms being very firmly seized.

"What do we do about this?" demanded a voice, thin and querulous. "I never saw one this size."

"Take him to the Central Committee, stupid," snapped another. Battle felt his guns being hoisted from their holsters and snickered quietly. They didn't know—

Yes, they did. A blindfold was whipped about his eyes and his pockets and person were given a thorough going-over. They even took the fulminate of mercury that he kept behind his molars.

"Now what?" asked the first voice. Battle could picture its owner gingerly handling the arsenal that he habitually carried with him.

"Now," said the second voice, "now freedom slowly broadens down." *Clunk!* Battle felt something—with his last fighting vestige of consciousness, he realized that it was one of his own gun butts—contact his head, then went down for the count.

The next thing he knew, a dulcet voice was cooing at him. The lieutenant had never heard a dulcet voice before, he decided. There had been, during his hitch with the Foreign Legion, one Messoua whose voice he now immediately classified as a sort of hoarse cackle. The blonde Hedvig, the Norwegian spy he had encountered in service with Los Invincibles de Bolivia, had seemed at the time capable of a dulcet coo; Battle reallocated the Norse girl's tones as somewhere between a rasp and a metallic gurgle.

The voice cooed at him, "Get up, stupid. You're conscious."

He opened his eyes and looked for the voice as he struggled to his feet. As he found the source of the coo he fell right flat on his back again. J. C. Battle, soldier of fortune extraordinary, highest-priced insurrectionnaire in the world, had seen many women in the course of his life. Many women had looked on him and found him good, and he had followed the lead with persistence and ingenuity. His rep as a Lothario stretched over most of the Earth's surface. Yet never, he swore fervently to himself, never had he seen anything to match this little one with the unfriendly stare.

She was somewhat shorter than the lieutenant and her coloring was the palest, most delicate shade of apple green imaginable. Her eyes were emerald and her hair was a glorious lushness like the hue of a high-priced golf club's putting green on a summer morning. And she was staring at him angrily, tapping one tiny foot.

"Excuse me, madame," said Battle as he rose with a new self-possession in his bearing. He noted that she was wearing what seemed to be a neat little paper frock of shell pink. "Excuse me—I had no notion that it was a lady whom I was keeping waiting."

"Indeed," said the lady coldly. "We'll dispense with introductions, whoever you are. Just tell your story. Are you a renegade?" She frowned. "No, you couldn't be that. Begin talking."

Battle bowed. "My card," he said, tendering it. "I presume you to be in a position of authority over the—?" He looked around and saw that he was in a room of wood, quite unfurnished.

"Oh, sit down if you wish," snapped the woman. She folded herself up on the floor and scrutinized the card.

"What I am doesn't concern you," she said broodingly. "But since you seem to know something about our plans, know that I am the supreme commander of the—" She made a curious, clicking noise. "That's the name of my people. You can call us the Invaders."

"I shall," began Battle. "To begin at the beginning, it is known that your—Invaders—plan to take over this world of ours. I congratulate you on your location of your people in a mohair sofa; it is the most ingenious place of concealment imaginable. However, so that the sofa will not be fumigated, you must perform operations at long range—posthypnotic suggestion, I imagine—on the minds of the servants at the Billionaire's Club. Can you explain to me why you cannot perform these operations on the club members themselves?"

"Very simple," said the woman sternly, with the ghost of a smile. "Since all the billionaire members are self-made men, they insist that even the lowest busboys have advanced degrees and be Phi Beta Kappas. This betokens a certain type of academic mind which is very easy to hypnotize. But even if we worked in twenty-four-hour relays on Old Jay, we couldn't put a dent in him. The psychic insensitivity of a billionaire is staggering.

"And," she added, looking at Battle through narrowed eyes, "there was one member who noticed that the busboys never fumigated the sofa. We tried to work on him while he slept, but he fought us back. He even subconsciously acquired knowledge of our plans. Thought he'd dreamed it and forgot most of the details."

Battle sighed. "You're right," he admitted. "Cromleigh was his name, and he tipped me off. Where are you Invaders from?"

"None of your business," she tartly retorted. "And where, precisely, do *you* come from?"

"This Cromleigh," said Battle, "was—and is—no fool. He went to a psychologist friend and had his mind probed. The result was a complete outline of your civilization and plans—including that ingenious device of yours, the minifier. He had one built in his lab and paid me very highly to go into it. Then I was dropped by him personally into this sofa with a pair of tweezers."

"How much does he know?" snapped the woman.

"Not much. Only what one of your more feeble-minded citizens let him know. He doesn't know the final invasion plans and he doesn't know the time schedule—if there is any as yet."

"There isn't," she said with furrowed brow. "And if there were, you imbecile monsters would never learn it from *us*." Suddenly she blazed at him, "Why must you die the hard way? Why don't you make room for the superrace while you have the chance? But no! We'd never be able to live in peace with you—you—cretins!" Then her lip trembled. "I'm sorry," she said. "I don't mean to be harsh—but there are so few of us and so many of you—" The dam broke, and the little lady dissolved in a flood of tears.

Battle leaped into the breach like a veteran. He scored 99.9807 on the firing range consistently and that was pretty good, but when it came to comforting weeping female soldiers of fortune Battle *really* shone.

Some minutes later they were chummily propped up against the wall of the wooden room. Her weeps over, the little lady—who had identified herself as Miss Aktying *click!* Byam—began:

"We came—you could have guessed this from our size—from an asteroid near Jupiter. Don't ask me why my people are so much like yours except for size; after all, why shouldn't they be? Spores of life, you know.

"Our spaceship's somewhere in your New Jersey; we landed there two years ago and sized up the situation. We'd been driven from our own planet by nasty creatures from Ceres who had the damndest war machines you ever saw—flame guns, disintegrator rays—and they're going to mop up the universe when they get around to it. By your standards they were three inches tall; to us they were twenty-foot horrors.

"We sent out a few agents who learned the language in two or three days; we could live on the spaceship and keep out of sight. The agents came back to us all steamed up. They'd been riding in coat pockets and things, listening in on private wires. They found out that most of the wealth in the world is concentrated in the Billionaire's Club, right here where we are. So we moved *en masse*, all three hundred of us, into this sofa and built our city.

"It isn't as easy as it sounds, of course. To listen in on a conversation means that you have to weigh yourself down with almost an ounce of equipment for raising the octaves of the voice and scaling it down to fit our ears. But now we have our listening posts and we eavesdrop in relays to every word that's spoken. If you knew what I know about Atlantis Plastic and Explosives—

"Anyway, Battle, we have our fingers on the economic pulse of the planet. We could release information through dreams and hunches that would wreck the market, as you call it, and create the most staggering panic of all times. Once that happens, Battle ..."

"Go on," snapped the lieutenant.

"Once that happens, Battle," she said in a small, tense voice, "we turn on a little machine we have and every human being that walks the Earth turns into pocket fuzz."

She faced his horrified stare with a pitying smile. "It's true," she said. "We can do it. When we're ready, when we're convinced that science and research are so disorganized that they can't possibly do anything about it, we turn on the machine, technically known as a protoplasmo high carbon proteidic discellular converter, and *it* happens."

"Not," grated Battle, "if I can stop it."

"That's the rub, my dear," she said with a frown. "You can't. You're my prisoner." And she smiled exquisitely, baring apple-green teeth, so that Battle was constrained to agree with the little lady.

"It seems fitting," he brooded absently. "A superrace indeed is come to humble Man."

"Darling," said Battle, "it's the strange mixture of ruthlessness and sentimentality that makes your people perpetually amazing to me. It's a pitched battle in the dark on our part; my people have no notion of what's going on behind their backs, and you see nothing evil or dark in the situation."

Busily Miss Aktying *click!* Byam kissed him and returned to her desk. "My sweet," she said, "if you trouble your head over our alien morality you'll never get to the end of it. Enough that you are accepted into our midst as a noncombatant worker and the very special charge of the Expediter-in-Chief—that's me. Now, go away, please. I'll see you tonight."

Battle pocketed the seal he had lifted from her desk and blew a kiss at her back as he closed the door behind him.

The week he had been imprisoned had been no great hardship; he had been privileged to roam within the limits of the city and examine the marvelously complicated life these tiny invaders had made for themselves. There had been other privileges as well ...

The lieutenant, professional and romanticized killer, could not get over the appalling technique of the invaders. It was not inefficient, it was not cold-blooded; somehow to him it was worse. Like all right-minded military men of the old school, he deplored the occasional necessity of spying. What then could he think of a campaign that was spying and nothing else but?

He had been allowed to see—under guard—the wonderful listening posts of the tiny people. From little speakers boomed the voices of Old Jay and the other titans of finance who worked off steam in the smoking room of the Billionaire's Club. And nobody ever sat on the sofa or moved it; it simply would never occur to a member to do so, and in the minds of the servants there had been built up a myth that it was the very first sofa that the celebrated and deceased founder of the club, Nicholas van Bhoomenbergen, had installed and that it would be a breach of the club's rules to move it. The fact was that it had been brought in by two men from Airways Express who had had their minds taken over for the nonce by the invaders. A Mrs. Pinsky, for whom it had been originally consigned, never did find out what happened to it.

Battle ascertained by judicious inquiry that the pocket-fuzz machine actually did exist. It had been a swipe from the war science of the invaders from

Ceres. The thing was broken down at the moment, but when they got it into shape again—!

He had uneasy pictures of a vast number of speculators all waking up with the same hunch on which way the market would jump. All bidding simultaneously for the same securities would make a ticklish situation that could be touched off by judicious inspiration of an investment banker—any investment banker—who could be dreamed into thinking his bank was without assets.

Bank closes and banker commits suicide. Panic on the market; the vast number of speculators find themselves with securities at fantastically high prices and worth fantastically near nothing at all. Vast numbers of speculators sell out and are ruined, for then three more banks close and three more bankers commit suicide. President declares bank holiday; the great public withdraws savings as soon as the banks open again; therefore the banks close again. The great public holes up for a long, hard winter. With loose cash lying around, crime is on the upswing and martial law is declared, at which Leftist organizations explode and start minor insurrections in industrial cities.

Mexico attacks across the Rio Grande; the invaders from the asteroid have a contingent of expert hypnotists ready to leave for Chihuahua, where the southern republic's army is stationed.

And then the protoplasmo high carbon proteidic discellular converter would be turned on. The population of Manhattan would turn into pocket fuzz—or at least separate large-molecule units resembling very closely the stuff you find in pockets or handbags after two or three weeks of use.

Manhattan is fortified by the wee folk from the asteroid, who build several more of the flug machines, aiming them at the other boroughs and moving their twenty-mile field of effectiveness at the rate of a state each day. The North American continent would be clear of any and all protoplasmic life at the end of two months, they estimated.

And the hell of it was that they were right. But Battle was whistling cheerily as he forged a pass with the aid of the seal from his lady's desk.

He had crept out into the open, been perceived by the eagle eye of Ole Cromleigh, lifted on a pair of tweezers and whisked into a waiting Rolls.

Once again his natural size in the New Jersey lab, he stretched comfortably. "Thanks for being so prompt," he yawned. "Thanks a lot. They were coming after me, by the sound of the footsteps in the distance."

"Now you see why I had to be quiet and do this thing on the sly?" demanded the financier. "If I'd told all I know, they'd have called me mad and locked me up the way his family treated poor old John D.—but don't let that get out, Lieutenant. Now tell me what you found there—begin at the beginning. How much do they know about finance and manipulation? Have they got their records in a safe place?"

Battle lit a cigarette; he hadn't taken any with him for fear of firing the sofa. Luxuriously he drew in a draft of the smoke clear down to his toenails and let it trickle from the corners of his mouth. "One question at a time," he said. "And I'll ask the first few of them. Mr. Cromleigh, why won't you let me bomb the sofa?"

The old man twisted his hands nervously together. "Because a bomb in the smoking room would kill Old Jay when he hears about it; the man always goes to Lhasa in Tibet when July Fourth rolls around. He's been that way since the Wall Street Massacre in '24 or '25. Because I'm not cold-blooded. And because, dammit, those little people I saw were *cute*."

"Yeah," agreed Battle reminiscently. "That she was. To begin at the beginning, your dream was substantially correct. They're little people from an asteroid. They have war machinery and no hearts whatsoever. They're listening twenty-four hours a day. Not a word spoken in the room escapes them and it all goes onto records."

"Good—good God!" whispered Cromleigh, cracking his freckled knuckles. "What that information must be worth!" He rose. "Let's get back to Manhattan for a drink, Lieutenant," he said shakily. "And there's another aspect I want to discuss with you. Your first trip was a sort of foray. It was mostly to convince me that I wasn't mad. And to size up the ground as well. Now can we discuss planting a permanent spy in the sofa? To keep tabs on them and move only when necessary?"

"Delightful," said Battle thoughtfully. "I have friends. My own club you probably do not know of, but it is the best of its kind."

Cromleigh, nervously tapping his desk with a pencil, was alone in the great New Jersey lab as far as could be seen. Grotesque machinery lined the walls; during the day there would be eight score technicians working, checking and double-checking their results, bringing new honor and glory to the Cromleigh Vacumaxic Sweeper and the rest of the string of electric products. His sugar plants and labs were far away in Pasadena; the Cromleigh Ironworks were going full blast in the ore basin of the continent. He looked like a very worried man.

From the shadows, with completely noiseless tread, stole a figure. "Good evening, sir," said Battle. "I've brought all of the Saber Club that's available on two hours' notice.

"Miss Millicent, this is Mr. Cromleigh," he announced, leading forth from the shadows a tall, crisp woman.

When she spoke it was with a faint Southern drawl. "Pleased t'know you. Any frien' of Lieutenant Battle's ..." She trailed back into the darkness and vanished completely.

"Dr. Mogilov, former Professor of Philosophy at the University of Kazan."

A slight, smiling man bowed out from the darkness; he was smooth-shaven and looked very un-Russian. In a pronounced Cambridge dialect he said, "Delighted," and put one hand on the butt of a revolver slung from his slender waist.

"And Alex Vaughn, Yorkshire born and bred."

The Englishman said thickly, in the peculiar speech that makes the clear-headed, big-boned men of York sound always a little intoxicated, "Ah coom wi' russi-*veh*-shins, soor. Lut thawt bay oondair-stud."

"He says," interpreted the lieutenant, "that he comes with reservations; let that be understood. And that completes the present roster of the Saber Club present in New York."

"Only three?" complained Cromleigh. "And one a woman? You gave me to understand that they could completely smash the invaders."

"Yes," said the lieutenant, his voice heavy with added meaning. "*Any* invaders."

"No doubt—" said Cromleigh. Then some message in Battle's eyes alarmed him unaccountably; his hand trembled on the desk top and gripped the edge to steady itself.

"That did it!" snapped Battle. He swung on Ole Cromleigh. "How long have we?" he grated, pulling a gun and aiming it for the financier's throat.

In a voice hoarse with hatred Cromleigh yelled, "Just two minutes more, you meddling scum! Then—"

"Lights!" yelled Battle. "Turn the damned lights on, Miss Millicent!" As the overhead indirects flared up, bathing the huge lab in a lambent, flaming radiance, the four figures of the Saber Club members, the Billionaire Clubman and one other leaped into sharp reality.

It was the figure of the sofa. "We took the liberty," said Battle, his gun swerving not an inch, "of removing this object from the smoking room. It's going lock, stock and barrel into the enlarging machine you have here."

"You fool!" roared Cromleigh. "Don't you know—" The descending gun butt cut off any further conversation.

"Hurry up!" grated the lieutenant. He hefted the sofa to his broad shoulders. "That trembling hand was a signal if ever I saw one. His friends'll be here any minute. Open that damned machine and plug in the power!"

The Russian philosopher, muttering wildly to himself, swung wide the gates of the boxlike magnifier through which Battle had come only a few hours before.

"Thank God there's plenty of room!" groaned Battle. "And if this doesn't work, prepare for Heaven, friends!" He turned on the machine full power and speed, took Miss Millicent by the arm, and dragged her to the far end of the vast lab.

During the incredibly long three minutes that ensued, they made ready their weapons for what might prove to be a siege, while Battle explained in rapid-fire undertones what he had had no time for during the plane ride from Manhattan.

As he checked the load of his quick firers he snapped, "Invaders—phooey! Anybody could tell that those women were fresh from an office. They had the clerical air about them. The only invader—as a carefully logical process of deduction demonstrated—was the gruesome creature who's been posing as Cromleigh. Just murdered the old guy—I suppose—and took over his body. He and his friends whom he just signaled. He's the only baby who hypnotized the Phi Beta Kappas they use for busboys.

"Why did he risk sending me in there? The inevitable mark of a louse. Doesn't trust anybody, not even his own office staff dyed a pale green and reduced to half-gnat size. So he sent me in to spy on them. The whole cock-and-bull story of the creatures from an asteroid was so that there'd be no suspicion directed at him in case some bright waiter should find the louse people. Wouldn't be surprised if he's from an asteroid himself. Crazy business! Craziest damned business!"

"How about the financial angle?" asked Vaughn, who could be intelligible when money was involved.

"I picked that bird's pocket slick as a whistle just after I conked him. Feels like a hundred grand."

"Here they come!" snapped Miss Millicent.

"They" were creatures of all sizes and shapes who were streaming through the only door to the lab, at the other end of the room.

"Awk!" gulped the lady involuntarily. "They" were pretty awful. There were a hundred or so of them, many much like men, a few in an indescribable liquid-solid state that sometimes was gaseous. The luminous insides of these churned wildly about; there were teeth inside them two feet long. Others were gigantic birds, still others snakes, still others winged dragons.

"That settles it," grunted the Russian philosopher as he flicked his gun into and out of its holster faster than the eye could follow. "That settles it. They are amœbic, capable of assuming any shape at all. One is changing now—awk!" He persevered. "Indubitably possessed of vast hypnotic powers over unsuspecting minds only. Otherwise they would be working on us."

"They" were rolling in a flood of shifting, slimy flesh down the floor of the lab.

"The machine! The sofa!" cried Miss Millicent. Battle breathed a long sigh of relief as the cabinetlike expander exploded outward and the sofa it held kept on growing—and growing—and *growing!* It stopped just as it filled the segment of the lab that it occupied.

With a squeaking of tortured timbers the laws of cross-sectional sufferance power asserted themselves and the hundred-yard-high sofa collapsed in a monstrous pile of rubble.

"Sit very still," said the lieutenant. "Be quite quiet and blow the head off any hundred-foot centipede that wanders our way."

There were agonized yells from the other side of the couch's ruins. "That couch," Battle informed them, "was just plain lousy. Full of centipedes, lice, what have you. Naturally; never been fumigated. And when a louse smells blood—God help any invaders around, be they flesh, fish, fowl or amœbic!"

After ten minutes there was complete quiet.

"What abaht th' boogs?" asked Vaughn.

"They're dead," said Battle, rising and stretching. "Their respiratory systems can't keep up with the growth. They were good for about ten minutes, then they keeled over. Their tracheæ can't take in enough oxygen to keep them going, which is a very good thing for the New Jersey countryside."

He strolled over to the vast pile of rubble and began turning over timbers, Miss Millicent assisting him.

"Ah!" he grunted. "Here it is!" He had found the body of an apple-green young lady whose paint was beginning to peel, revealing a healthy pink beneath.

With many endearing terms he brought her out of her swoon as Miss Millicent's eyebrows went higher and higher.

Finally she exploded, as the two were cosily settled on a mountainous upholstery needle that had, at some time, got lost in the sofa.

"Just *when,* Lieutenant, did you find out that these people weren't invaders from an asteroid?"

Battle raised his eyebrows and kissed the girl.

"Have no fear, darling," he said. "A gentleman never—er—kisses—and tells."

Gomez

Now that I'm a cranky, constipated old man I can afford to say that the younger generation of scientists makes me sick to my stomach. Short order fry-cooks of destruction, they hear through the little window the dim order: "Atom bomb rare, with cobalt 60!" and sing it back and rattle their stinking skillets and sling the deadly hash—just what the customer ordered, with never a notion invading their smug, too-heated havens that there's a small matter of right and wrong that takes precedence even over their haute cuisine.

There used to be a slew of them who yelled to high heaven about it. Weiner, Urey, Szilard, Morrison—dead now, and worse. Unfashionable. The greatest of them you have never heard of. Admiral MacDonald never did clear the story. He was Julio Gomez, and his story was cleared yesterday by a fellow my Jewish friends call Malach Hamovis, the Hovering Angel of Death. A black-bordered letter from Rosa advised me that Malach Hamovis had come in on runway six with his flaps down and picked up Julio at the age of 39. Pneumonia.

"But," Rosa painfully wrote, "Julio would want you to know he died not too unhappy, after a good though short life with much satisfaction—"

I think it will give him some more satisfaction, wherever he is, to know that his story at last is getting told.

It started twenty-two years ago with a routine assignment on a crisp October morning. I had an appointment with Dr. Sugarman, the head of the physics department at the University. It was the umpth anniversary of something or other—first atomic pile, the test A-bomb, Nagasaki—I don't remember what, and the Sunday editor was putting together a page on it. My job was to interview the three or four University people who were Manhattan District grads.

I found Sugarman in his office at the top of the modest physics building's square Gothic tower, brooding through a pointed-arch window at the bright autumn sky. He was a tubby, jowly little fellow. I'd been seeing him around for a couple of years at testimonial banquets and press conferences, but I didn't expect him to remember me. He did, though, and even got the name right.

"Mr. Vilchek?" he beamed. "From the *Tribune?*"

141

"That's right, Dr. Sugarman. How are you?"

"Fine; fine. Sit down, please. Well, what shall we talk about?"

"Well, Dr. Sugarman, I'd like to have your ideas on the really fundamental issues of atomic energy, A-bomb control and so on. What in your opinion is the single most important factor in these problems?"

His eyes twinkled; he was going to surprise me. "Education!" he said, and leaned back waiting for me to register shock.

I registered. "That's certainly a different approach, doctor. How do you mean that, exactly?"

He said impressively: "Education—*technical* education—is the key to the underlying issues of our time. I am deeply concerned over the unawareness of the general public to the meaning and accomplishments of science. People underrate me—underrate *science,* that is—because they do not *understand* science. Let me show you something." He rummaged for a moment through papers on his desk and handed me a sheet of lined tablet paper covered with chicken-track handwriting. "A letter I got," he said. I squinted at the penciled scrawl and read:

October 12

Esteemed Sir:

Beg to introduce self to you the atomic Scientist as a youth 17 working with diligence to perfect self in Mathematical Physics. The knowledge of English is imperfect since am in New-York 1 year only from Puerto Rico and due to Father and Mother poverty must wash the dishes in the restaurant. So esteemed sir excuse imperfect English which will better.

I hesitate intruding your valuable Scientist time but hope you sometime spare minutes for diligents such as I. My difficulty is with neutron cross-section absorption of boron steel in Reactor which theory I am working out. Breeder reactors demand

$$u = \frac{x}{1} + \frac{x^5}{1} + \frac{x^{10}}{1} + \frac{x^{15}}{1} + \cdots$$

for boron steel, compared with neutron cross-section absorption of

$$v = \frac{x^{2/5}}{1} + \frac{x}{1} + \frac{x^2}{1} + \frac{x^3}{1} + \cdots$$

for any concrete with which I familiarize myself. Whence arises relationship

$$v^5 = u \frac{1 - 2u + 4u^2 - 3u^3 + u^4}{1 + 3u + 4u^2 + 2u^3 + u^4}.$$

indicating only a fourfold breeder gain. Intuitively I dissatisfy
with this gain and beg to intrude your time to ask wherein I neglect.
With the most sincere thanks.

J. Gomez
c/o Porto Bello Lunchroom
124th Street & St. Nicholas Avenue
New York, New York

I laughed and told Dr. Sugarman appreciatively: "That's a good one. I wish
our cranks kept in touch with us by mail, but they don't. In the newspaper business they come in and demand to see the editor. Could I use it, by the way? The
readers ought to get a boot out of it."

He hesitated and said: "All right—if you don't use my name. Just say 'a prominent physicist.' I didn't think it was too funny myself though, but I see your point,
of course. The boy may be feeble-minded—and he probably is—but he believes,
like too many people, that science is just a bag of tricks which any ordinary person can acquire—"

And so on and so on.

I went back to the office and wrote the interview in twenty minutes. It took
me longer than that to talk the Sunday editor into running the Gomez letter in a
box on the atom-anniversary page, but he finally saw it my way. I had to retype it.
If I'd just sent the letter down to the composing room as it was, we would have
had a strike on our hands.

On Sunday morning, at a quarter past six, I woke up to the tune of fists thundering on my hotel-room door. I found my slippers and bathrobe and lurched
blearily across the room. They didn't wait for me to unlatch. The door opened.
I saw one of the hotel clerks, the Sunday editor, a frosty-faced old man and
three hard-faced, hard-eyed young men. The hotel clerk mumbled and retreated
and the others moved in. "Chief," I asked the Sunday editor hazily, "what's
going—?"

A hard-faced young man was standing with his back to the door; another
was standing with his back to the window and the third was blocking the bathroom door. The icy old man interrupted me with a crisp authoritative question
snapped at the editor. "You identify this man as Vilchek?"

The editor nodded.

"Search him," snapped the old man. The fellow standing guard at the window slipped up and frisked me for weapons while I sputtered incoherently and
the Sunday editor avoided my eye.

When the search was over, the frosty-faced old boy said to me: "I am Rear
Admiral MacDonald, Mr. Vilchek. I'm here in my capacity as deputy director of
the office of Security and Intelligence, U.S. Atomic Energy Commission. Did
you write this?" He thrust a newspaper clipping at my face.

I read, blearily:

WHAT'S SO TOUGH ABOUT A-SCIENCE?
TEENAGE POT-WASHER DOESN'T KNOW

A letter received recently by a prominent local atomic scientist points up Dr. Sugarman's complaint (see adjoining column) that the public does not appreciate how hard a physicist works. The text, complete with "mathematics" follows:

Esteemed Sir:

Beg to introduce self to you the Atomic Scientist as youth 17 working—

"Yes," I told the admiral. "I wrote it, except for the headline. What about it?"

He snapped: "The letter is purportedly from a New York youth seeking information, yet there is no address for him given. Why is that?"

I said patiently: "I left it off when I copied it for the composing room. That's *Trib.* style on readers' letters. *What* is all this about?"

He ignored the question and asked: "Where is the purported original of the letter?"

I thought hard and told him: "I think I stuck it in my pants pocket. I'll get it—" I started for the chair with my suit draped over it.

"Hold it, mister!" said the young man at the bathroom door. I held it and he proceeded to go through the pockets of the suit. He found the Gomez letter in the inside breast pocket of the coat and passed it to the admiral. The old man compared it, word for word, with the clipping and then put them both in his pocket.

"I want to thank you for your cooperation," he said coldly to me and the Sunday editor. "I caution you not to discuss, and above all not to publish, any account of this incident. The national security is involved in the highest degree. Good day."

He and the boys started for the door, and the Sunday editor came to life. "Admiral," he said, 'this is going to be on the front page of tomorrow's *Trib.*"

The admiral went white. After a long pause he said: "You are aware that this country may be plunged into global war at any moment. That American boys are dying every day in border skirmishes. Is it to protect civilians like you who won't obey a reasonable request affecting security?"

The Sunday editor took a seat on the edge of my rumpled bed and lit a cigarette. "I know all that, admiral," he said. "I also know that this is a free country and how to keep it that way. Pitiless light on incidents like this of illegal search and seizure."

The admiral said: "I personally assure you, on my honor as an officer, that you would be doing the country a grave disservice by publishing an account of this."

The Sunday editor said mildly: "Your honor as an officer. You broke into this room without a search warrant. Don't you realize that's against the law? And I saw your boy ready to shoot when Vilchek started for that chair." I began to sweat a little at that, but the admiral was sweating harder.

With an effort he said: "I should apologize for the abruptness and discourtesy with which I've treated you. I do apologize. My only excuse is that, as I've said, this is a crash-priority matter. May I have your assurance that you gentlemen will keep silent?"

"On one condition," said the Sunday editor. "I want the *Trib.* to have an exclusive on the Gomez story. I want Mr. Vilchek to cover it, with your full cooperation. In return, we'll hold it for your release and submit it to your security censorship."

"It's a deal," said the admiral, sourly. He seemed to realize suddenly that the Sunday editor had been figuring on such a deal all along.

On the plane for New York, the admiral filled me in. He was precise and unhappy, determined to make the best of a bad job. "I was awakened at three this morning by a phone call from the chairman of the Atomic Energy Commission. *He* had been awakened by a call from Dr. Monroe of the Scientific Advisory Committee. Dr. Monroe had been up late working and sent out for the Sunday *Tribune* to read before going to sleep. He saw the Gomez letter and went off like a 16-inch rifle. The neutron cross-section absorption relationship expressed in it happens to be, Mr. Vilchek, his own work. It also happens to be one of the nation's most closely guarded—er—atomic secrets. Presumably this Gomez stumbled on it somehow, as a janitor or something of the sort, and is feeding his ego by pretending to be an atomic scientist."

I scratched my unshaved jaw. "Admiral," I said, "you wouldn't kid me? How can three equations be a top atomic secret?"

The admiral hesitated. "All I can tell you," he said slowly, "is that breeder reactors are involved."

"But the letter said that. You mean this Gomez not only swiped the equations but knew what they were about?"

The admiral said grimly: "Somebody has been incredibly lax. It would be worth many divisions to the Soviet for their man Kapitza to see those equations and realize that they are valid."

He left me to chew that one over for a while as the plane droned over New Jersey. Finally the pilot called back: "E.T.A. five minutes, sir. We have landing priority at Newark."

"Good," said the admiral. "Signal for a civilian-type car to pick us up without loss of time."

"Civilian," I said.

"Of course civilian!" he snapped. "That's the hell of it. Above all we must not arouse suspicion that there is anything special or unusual about this Gomez or his letter. Copies of the *Tribune* are on their way to the Soviets now as a matter of routine—they take all American papers and magazines they can get. If we tried to stop shipment of *Tribune*s, that would be an immediate give-away that there was something of importance going on."

We landed and the five of us got into a late-model car, neither drab nor flashy. One of the admiral's young men relieved the driver, a corporal with Signal Corps insignia. There wasn't much talk during the drive from Newark to Spanish

Harlem, New York. Just once the admiral lit a cigarette, but he flicked it through the window after a couple of nervous puffs.

The Porto Bello Lunchroom was a store-front restaurant in the middle of a shabby tenement block. Wide-eyed, graceful, skinny little kids stared as our car parked in front of it and then converged on us purposefully. "Watch your car, mister?" they begged. The admiral surprised them—and me—with a flood of Spanish that sent the little extortionists scattering back to their stickball game in the street and their potsy layouts chalked on the sidewalks.

"Higgins," said the admiral, "see if there's a back exit." One of his boys got out and walked around the block under the dull, incurious eyes of black-shawled women sitting on their stoops. He was back in five minutes, shaking his head.

"Vilchek and I will go in," said the admiral. "Higgins, stand by the restaurant door and tackle anyone who comes flying out. Let's go, reporter. And remember that I do the talking."

The noon-hour crowd at the Porto Bello's ten tables looked up at us when we came in. The admiral said to a woman at a primitive cashier's table: *"Nueva York* Board of Health, *señora."*

"Ah!" she muttered angrily. *"Por favor, no aquí!* In back, understand? Come." She beckoned a pretty waitress to take over at the cash drawer and led us into the steamy little kitchen. It was crowded with us, an old cook and a young dishwasher. The admiral and the woman began a rapid exchange of Spanish. He played his part well. I myself couldn't keep my eyes off the kid dishwasher who somehow or other had got hold of one of America's top atomic secrets.

Gomez was seventeen, but he looked fifteen. He was small-boned and lean, with skin the color of bright Virginia tobacco in an English cigarette. His hair was straight and glossy-black and a little long. Every so often he wiped his hands on his apron and brushed it back from his damp forehead. He was working like hell, dipping and swabbing and rinsing and drying like a machine, but he didn't look pushed or angry. He wore a half-smile that I later found out was his normal, relaxed expression, and his eyes were far away from the kitchen of the Porto Bello Lunchroom. The elderly cook was making it clear by the exaggerated violence of his gesture and a savage frown that he resented these people invading his territory. I don't think Gomez even knew we were there. A sudden, crazy idea came into my head.

The admiral had turned to him. *"Como se llama, chico?"*

He started and put down the dish he was wiping. "Julio Gomez, *señor. Por que, por favor? Qué pasa?"*

He wasn't the least bit scared.

"Nueva York Board of Health," said the admiral. *"Con su permiso—"* He took Gomez' hands in his and looked at them gravely, front and back, making *tsk-tsk* noises. Then, decisively: *"Vámonos, Julio. Siento mucho. Usted está muy enfermo."* Everybody started talking at once, the woman doubtless objecting to the slur on her restaurant and the cook to losing his dishwasher and Gomez to losing time from the job.

The admiral gave them broadside for broadside and outlasted them. In five minutes we were leading Gomez silently from the restaurant. *"La lotería!"* a woman customer said in a loud whisper. *"O las mutas,"* somebody said back. Arrested for policy or marihuana, they thought. The pretty waitress at the cashier's table looked stricken and said nervously: "Julio?" as we passed, but he didn't notice.

Gomez sat in the car with the half-smile on his lips and his eyes a million miles away as we rolled downtown to Foley Square. The admiral didn't look as though he'd approve of any questions from me. We got out at the Federal Building and Gomez spoke at last. He said in surprise: "This, it is not the hospital!"

Nobody answered. We marched him up the steps and surrounded him in the elevator. It would have made anybody nervous—it would have made *me* nervous—to be herded like that; everybody's got something on his conscience. But the kid didn't even seem to notice. I decided that he must be a half-wit or—there came that crazy notion again.

The glass door said "U.S. Atomic Energy Commission, Office of Security and Intelligence." The people behind it were flabbergasted when the admiral and party walked in. He turned the head man out of his office and sat at his desk, with Gomez getting the caller's chair. The rest of us stationed ourselves uncomfortably around the room.

It started. The admiral produced the letter and asked in English: "Have you ever seen this before?" He made it clear from the way he held it that Gomez wasn't going to get his hands on it.

"*Sí, seguro.* I write it last week. This is funny business. I am not really sick like you say, no?" He seemed relieved.

"No. Where did you get these equations?"

Gomez said proudly: "I work them out."

The admiral gave a disgusted little laugh. "Don't waste my time, boy. Where did you get these equations?"

Gomez was beginning to get upset. "You got no right to call me liar," he said. "I not so smart as the big physicists, *seguro,* and maybe I make mistakes. Maybe I waste the *profesór* Soohar-man his time but he got no right to have me arrest. I tell him right in letter he don't have to answer if he don't want. I make no crime and you got no right!"

The admiral looked bored. "Tell me how you worked the equations out," he said.

"Okay," said Gomez sulkily. "You know the random paths of neutron is expressed in matrix mechanics by *profesór* Oppenheim five years ago, all okay. I transform his equations from path-prediction domain to cross-section domain and integrate over absorption areas. This gives u series and v series. And from there, the u-v relationship is obvious, no?"

The admiral, still bored, asked: "Got it?"

I noticed that one of his young men had a shorthand pad out. He said: "Yes."

The admiral picked up the phone and said: "This is MacDonald. Get me Dr. Mines out at Brookhaven right away." He told Gomez blandly: "Dr. Mines is the chief of the A.E.C. Theoretical Physics Division. I'm going to ask him what he thinks of the way you worked the equations out. He's going to tell me that you were just spouting a lot of gibberish. And then you're going to tell me where you *really* got them."

Gomez looked mixed up, and the admiral turned back to the phone. "Dr. Mines? This is Admiral MacDonald of Security. I want your opinion on the following." He snapped his fingers impatiently and the stenographer passed him his pad. "Somebody has told me that he discovered a certain relationship by taking"— he read carefully—"by taking the random paths of a neutron expressed in matrix mechanics by Oppenheim, transforming his equations from the path-prediction domain to the cross-section domain and integrating over the absorption areas."

In the silence of the room I could hear the faint buzz of the voice on the other end. And a great red blush spread over the admiral's face from his brow to his neck. The faintly-buzzing voice ceased, and after a long pause the admiral said slowly and softly: "No, it wasn't Fermi or Szilard. I'm not at liberty to tell you who. Can you come right down to the Federal Building Security Office in New York? I—I need your help. Crash priority." He hung up the phone wearily and muttered to himself: "Crash priority. Crash." And wandered out of the office looking dazed.

His young men stared at one another in frank astonishment. "Five years," said one, "and—"

"Nix," said another, looking pointedly at me.

Gomez asked brightly: "What goes on anyhow? This is damn funny business, I think."

"Relax, kid," I told him. "Looks as if you'll make out all—"

"Nix," said the nixer again savagely, and I shut up and waited.

After a while somebody came in with coffee and sandwiches and we ate them. After another while the admiral came in with Dr. Mines. Mines was a white-haired, wrinkled Connecticut Yankee. All I knew about him was that he'd been in mild trouble with Congress for stubbornly plugging world government and getting on some of the wrong letterheads. But I learned right away that he was all scientist and didn't have a phony bone in his body.

"Mr. Gomez?" he asked cheerfully. "The admiral tells me that you are either a well-trained Russian spy or a phenomenal self-taught nuclear physicist. He wants me to find out which."

"Russia?" yelled Gomez, outraged. "He crazy! I am American United States citizen!"

"That's as may be," said Dr. Mines. "Now, the admiral tells me you describe the *u-v* relationship as 'obvious.' I should call it a highly abstruse derivation in the theory of continued fractions and complex multiplication."

Gomez strangled and gargled helplessly trying to talk, and finally asked, his eyes shining: *"Por favor,* could I have piece paper?"

They got him a stack of paper and the party was on.

For two unbroken hours Gomez and Dr. Mines chattered and scribbled. Mines gradually shed his jacket, vest and tie, completely oblivious to the rest of us. Gomez was even more abstracted. He *didn't* shed his jacket, vest and tie. He didn't seem to be aware of anything except the rapid-fire exchange of ideas via scribbled formulæ and the terse spoken jargon of mathematics. Dr. Mines shifted on his chair and sometimes his voice rose with excitement. Gomez didn't shift or wriggle or cross his legs. He just sat and scribbled and talked in a low, rapid mono- tone, looking straight at Dr. Mines with his eyes very wide-open and lit up like searchlights.

The rest of us just watched and wondered.

Dr. Mines broke at last. He stood up and said: "I can't take any more, Gomez. I've got to think it over—" He began to leave the room, mechanically scooping up his clothes, and then realized that we were still there.

"Well?" asked the admiral grimly.

Dr. Mines smiled apologetically. "He's a physicist, all right," he said. Gomez sat up abruptly and looked astonished.

"Take him into the next office, Higgins," said the admiral. Gomez let him- self be led away, like a sleepwalker.

Dr. Mines began to chuckle. "Security!" he said. "Security!"

The admiral rasped: "Don't trouble yourself over my decisions, if you please, Dr. Mines. My job is keeping the Soviets from pirating American science and I'm doing it to the best of my ability. What I want from you is your opinion on the possibility of that young man having worked out the equations as he claimed."

Dr. Mines was abruptly sobered. "Yes," he said. "Unquestionably he did. And will you excuse my remark? I was under some strain in trying to keep up with Gomez."

"Certainly," said the admiral, and managed a frosty smile. "Now if you'll be so good as to tell me how this completely impossible thing can have happened— ?"

"It's happened before, admiral," said Dr. Mines. "I don't suppose you ever heard of Ramanujan?"

"No."

"*Srinivasa* Ramanujan?"

"*No!*"

"Oh. Well, Ramanujan was born in 1887 and died in 1920. He was a poor Hindu who failed twice in college and then settled down as a government clerk. With only a single obsolete textbook to go on, he made himself a very great math- ematician. In 1913 he sent some of his original work to a Cambridge professor. He was immediately recognized and called to England, where he was accepted as a first-rank man, became a member of the Royal Society, a Fellow of Trinity and so forth."

The admiral shook his head dazedly.

"It happens," Dr. Mines said. "Oh, yes, it happens. Ramanujan had only one out-of-date book. But this is New York. Gomez has access to all the math- ematics he could hope for and a great mass of unclassified and declassified nuclear data. And—genius. The way he puts things together ... he seems to have only the vaguest notion of what a proof should be. He *sees* relationships as a whole. A most convenient faculty which I envy him. Where I have to take, say, a dozen painful steps from one conclusion to the next, he achieves it in one grand flying leap. Ramanujan was like that too, by the way—very strong on intuition, weak on what we call 'rigor.'" Dr. Mines noted with a start that he was holding his tie, vest and coat in one hand and began to put them on. "Was there anything else?" he asked politely.

"One thing," said the admiral. "Would you say he's—he's a better physicist than you are?"

"Yes," said Dr. Mines. "Much better." And he left.

The admiral slumped, uncharacteristically, at the desk for a long time. Finally he said to the air: "Somebody get me the General Manager. No, the Chairman of the Commission." One of his boys grabbed the phone and got to work on the call.

"Admiral," I said, "where do we stand now?"

"Eh? Oh, it's you. The matter's out of my hands now since no security violation is involved. I consider Gomez to be in my custody and I shall turn him over to the Commission so that he may be put to the best use in the nation's interest."

"Like a machine?" I asked, disgusted.

He gave me both barrels of his ice-blue eyes. "Like a weapon," he said evenly.

He was right, of course. Didn't I know there was a war on? Of course I did. Who didn't? Taxes, housing shortage, somebody's cousin killed in Korea, everybody's kid brother sweating out the draft, prices sky-high at the supermarket. Uncomfortably I scratched my unshaved chin and walked to the window. Foley Square below was full of Sunday peace, with only a single girl stroller to be seen. She walked the length of the block across the street from the Federal Building and then turned and walked back. Her walk was dragging and hopeless and tragic.

Suddenly I knew her. She was the pretty little waitress from the Porto Bello; she must have hopped a cab and followed the men who were taking her Julio away. Might as well beat it, sister, I told her silently. Julio isn't just a good-looking kid any more; he's a military asset. The Security office is turning him over to the policy-level boys for disposal. When that happens you might as well give up and go home.

It was as if she'd heard me. Holding a silly little handkerchief to her face, she turned and ran blindly for the subway entrance at the end of the block and disappeared into it.

At that moment the telephone rang.

"MacDonald here," said the admiral. "I'm ready to report on the Gomez affair, Mr. Commissioner."

Gomez was a minor, so his parents signed a contract for him. The job description on the contract doesn't matter, but he got a pretty good salary by government standards and a per-diem allowance too.

I signed a contract, too—"Information Specialist." I was partly companion, partly historian and partly a guy they'd rather have their eyes on than not. When somebody tried to cut me out on the grounds of economy, Admiral MacDonald frostily reminded him that he had given his word. I stayed, for all the good it did me.

We didn't have any name. We weren't operation Anything or Project Whoozis or Task Force Dinwiddie. We were just five people in a big fifteen-room house on the outskirts of Milford, New Jersey. There was Gomez, alone on the top floor with a lot of books, technical magazines and blackboards and a weekly visit from Dr. Mines. There were the three Security men, Higgins, Dalhousie and Leitzer, sleeping by turns and prowling the grounds. And there was me.

From briefing sessions with Dr. Mines I kept a diary of what went on. Don't think from that that I knew what the score was! War correspondents have told me of the frustrating life they led at some close-mouthed commands. So-and-so-many air sorties, the largest number since January 15th. Casualties a full fifteen percent lighter than expected. Determined advance in an active sector against relatively strong enemy opposition. And so on—all adding up to nothing in the way of real information.

That's what it was like in my diary because that's all they told me. Here are some excerpts: "On the recommendation of Dr. Mines, Mr. Gomez today began work on a phase of reactor design theory to be implemented at Brookhaven National Laboratory. The work involves the setting-up of thirty-five pairs of partial differential equations ... Mr. Gomez announced tentatively today that in checking certain theoretical work in progress at the Los Alamos Laboratory of the A.E.C. he discovered a fallacious assumption concerning neutron-spin which invalidates the conclusions reached. This will be communicated to the Laboratory ... Dr. Mines said today that Mr. Gomez has successfully invoked a hitherto unexploited aspect of Minkowski's tensor analysis to crack a stubborn obstacle towards the control of thermonuclear reactions—"

I protested at one of the briefing sessions with Dr. Mines against this gobble-dygook. He didn't mind my protesting. He leaned back in his chair and said calmly: "Vilchek, with all friendliness I assure you that you're getting everything you can understand. Anything more complex than the vague description of what's going on would be over your head. And anything more specific would give away exact engineering information which would be of use to foreign countries."

"This isn't the way they treated Bill Lawrence when he covered the atomic bomb," I said bitterly.

Mines nodded, with a pleased smile. "That's it exactly," he said. "Broad principles were being developed then—interesting things that could be told without any great harm being done. If you tell somebody that a critical mass of U-235 or Plutonium goes off with a big bang, you really haven't given away a great deal. He still has millions of man-hours of engineering before him to figure out how much is critical mass, to take only one small point."

So I took his word for it, faithfully copied the communiqués he gave me and wrote what I could on the human-interest side for release some day.

So I recorded Gomez' progress with English, his taste for chicken-pot pie and rice pudding, his habit of doing his own housework on the top floor and his old-maidish neatness. "You live your first fifteen years in a tin shack, Beel," he told me once, "and you find out you like things nice and clean." I've seen Dr. Mines follow Gomez through the top floor as the boy swept and dusted, talking at him in their mathematical jargon.

Gomez worked in forty-eight-hour spells usually, and not eating much. Then for a couple of days he'd live like a human being, grabbing naps, playing catch on the lawn with one or another of the Security people, talking with me about his childhood in Puerto Rico and his youth in New York. He taught me a little Spanish and asked me to catch him up on bad mistakes in English.

"But don't you ever want to get out of here?" I demanded one day.

He grinned: "Why should I, Beel? Here I eat good, I can send money to the parents. Best, I find out what the big professors are up to without I have to wait five-ten years for damn de-classifying."

"Don't you have a girl?"

He was embarrassed and changed the subject back to the big professors.

Dr. Mines drove up then, with his chauffeur who looked like a G-man and almost certainly was. As usual, the physicist was toting a bulging briefcase. After a few polite words with me, he and Julio went indoors and upstairs.

They were closeted for five hours—a record. When Dr. Mines came down I expected the usual briefing session. But he begged off. "Nothing serious," he said. "We just sat down and kicked some ideas of his around. I told him to go ahead. We've been—ah—using him very much like a sort of computer, you know. Turning him loose on the problems that were too tough for me and some of the other men. He's got the itch for research now. It would be very interesting if his forte turned out to be creative."

I agreed.

Julio didn't come down for dinner. I woke up in darkness that night when there was a loud bump overhead, and went upstairs in my pajamas.

Gomez was sprawled, fully dressed, on the floor. He'd tripped over a footstool. And he didn't seem to have noticed. His lips were moving and he stared straight at me without knowing I was there.

"You all right, Julio?" I asked, and started to help him to his feet.

He got up mechanically and said: "... real values of the zeta function vanish."

"How's that?"

He saw me then and asked, puzzled: "How you got in here, Beel? Is dinner-time?"

"Is four A.M., *por dios*. Don't you think you ought to get some sleep?" He looked terrible.

No; he didn't think he ought to get some sleep. He had some work to do. I went downstairs and heard him pacing overhead for an hour until I dozed off.

This splurge of work didn't wear off in forty-eight hours. For a week I brought him meals and sometimes he ate absently, with one hand, as he scribbled on a yellow pad. Sometimes I'd bring him lunch to find his breakfast untouched. He didn't have much beard, but he let it grow for a week—too busy to shave, too busy to talk, too busy to eat, sleeping in chairs when fatigue caught up with him.

I asked Leitzer, badly worried, if we should do anything about it. He had a direct scrambler-phone connection with the New York Security and Intelligence office, but his orders didn't cover anything like a self-induced nervous breakdown of the man he was guarding.

I thought Dr. Mines would do something when he came—call in an M.D., or tell Gomez to take it easy, or take some of the load off by parceling out whatever he had by the tail.

But he didn't. He went upstairs, came down two hours later and absently tried to walk past me. I headed him off into my room. "What's the word?" I demanded.

He looked me in the eye and said defiantly: "He's doing fine. I don't want to stop him."

Dr. Mines was a good man. Dr. Mines was a humane man. And he wouldn't lift a finger to keep the boy from working himself into nervous prostration. Dr. Mines liked people well enough, but he reserved his love for theoretical physics. "How important can this thing be?"

He shrugged irritably. "It's just the way some scientists work," he said. "Newton was like that. So was Sir William Rowan Hamilton—"

"Hamilton-Schmamilton," I said. "What's the sense of it? *Why* doesn't he sleep or eat?"

Mines said: "*You* don't know what it's like."

"Of course," I said, getting good and sore. "I'm just a dumb newspaper man. Tell me, Mr. Bones, what is it like?"

There was a long pause, and he said mildly: "I'll try. That boy up there is using his brain. A great chess player can put on a blindfold and play a hundred opponents in a hundred games simultaneously, remembering all the positions of his pieces and theirs and keeping a hundred strategies clear in his mind. Well, that stunt simply isn't in the same league with what Julio's doing up there.

"He has in his head some millions of facts concerning theoretical physics. He's scanning them, picking out one here and there, fitting them into new relationships, checking and rejecting when he has to, fitting the new relationships together, turning them upside-down and inside-out to see what happens, comparing them with known doctrine, holding them in his memory while he repeats the whole process and compares—and all the while he has a goal firmly in mind against which he's measuring all these things." He seemed to be finished.

For a reporter, I felt strangely shy. "What's he driving at?" I asked.

"I think," he said slowly, "he's approaching a unified field theory."

Apparently that was supposed to explain everything. I let Dr. Mines know that it didn't.

He said thoughtfully: "I don't know whether I can get it over to a layman—no offense, Vilchek. Let's put it this way. You know how math comes in waves, and how it's followed by waves of applied science based on the math. There was a big wave of algebra in the Middle Ages—following it came navigation, gunnery, surveying and so on. Then the Renaissance and a wave of analysis—what you'd call calculus. That opened up steam power and how to use it, mechanical engineers, electricity. The wave of *modern* mathematics since say 1875 gave us atomic energy. That boy upstairs may be starting off the next big wave."

He got up and reached for his hat.

"Just a minute," I said. I was surprised that my voice was steady. "What comes next? Control of gravity? Control of personality? Sending people by radio?"

Dr. Mines wouldn't meet my eye. Suddenly he looked old and shrunken. "Don't worry about the boy," he said.

I let him go.

That evening I brought Gomez chicken-pot pie and a non-alcoholic eggnog. He drank the eggnog, said "Hi, Beel," and continued to cover yellow sheets of paper.

I went downstairs and worried.

Abruptly it ended late the next afternoon. Gomez wandered into the big first-floor kitchen looking like a starved old rickshaw coolie. He pushed his lank hair back from his forehead, said: "Beel, what is to eat—" and pitched forward onto the linoleum. Leitzer came when I yelled, expertly took Gomez' pulse, rolled him onto a blanket and threw another one over him. "It's just a faint," he said. "Let's get him to bed."

"Aren't you going to call a doctor, man?"

"Doctor couldn't do anything we can't do," he said stolidly. "And I'm here to see that security isn't breached. Give me a hand."

We got him upstairs and put him to bed. He woke up and said something in Spanish, and then, apologetically: "Very sorry, fellows. I ought to taken it easier."

"I'll get you some lunch," I said, and he grinned.

He ate it all, enjoying it heartily, and finally lay back gorged. "Well," he asked me, "what it is new, Beel?"

"What *is* new. And you should tell me. You finish your work?"

"I got it in shape to finish. The hard part it is over." He rolled out of bed.

"Hey!" I said.

"I'm okay now," he grinned. "Don't write this down in your history, Beel. Everybody will think I act like a woman."

I followed him into his work room where he flopped into an easy chair, his eyes on a blackboard covered with figures. He wasn't grinning any more.

"Dr. Mines says you're up to something big," I said.

"*Sí.* Big."

"Unified field theory, he says."

"That is it," Gomez said.

"Is it good or bad?" I asked, licking my lips. "The application, I mean."

His boyish mouth set suddenly in a grim line. "That, it is not my business," he said. "I am American citizen of the United States." He stared at the blackboard and its maze of notes.

I looked at it too—*really* looked at it for once—and was surprised by what I saw. Mathematics, of course, I don't know. But I had soaked up a very little *about* mathematics. One of the things I had soaked up was that the expressions of higher mathematics tend to be complicated and elaborate, involving English, Greek and Hebrew letters, plain and fancy brackets and a great variety of special signs besides the plus and minus of the elementary school.

The things on the blackboard weren't like that at all. The board was covered with variations of a simple expression that consisted of five letters and two symbols: a right-handed pothook and a left-handed pothook.

"What do they mean?" I asked, pointing.

"Somethings I made up," he said nervously. "The word for that one is 'enfields.' The other one is 'is enfielded by.'"

"What's *that* mean?"

His luminous eyes were haunted. He didn't answer.

"It looks like simple stuff. I read somewhere that all the basic stuff is simple once it's been discovered."

"Yes," he said almost inaudibly. "It is simple, Beel. Too damn simple, I think. Better I carry it in my head, I think." He strode to the blackboard and erased it. Instinctively I half rose to stop him. He gave me a grin that was somehow bitter and unlike him. "Don't worry," he said. "I don't forget it." He tapped his forehead. "I *can't* forget it." I hope I never see again on any face the look that was on his.

"Julio," I said, appalled. "Why don't you get out of here for a while? Why don't you run over to New York and see your folks and have some fun? They can't keep you here against your will."

"They told me I shouldn't—" he said uncertainly. And then he got tough. "You're damn right, Beel. Let's go in together. I get dressed up. Er—You tell Leitzer, hah?" He couldn't quite face up to the hard-boiled security man.

I told Leitzer, who hit the ceiling. But all it boiled down to was that he sincerely wished Gomez and I wouldn't leave. We weren't in the Army, we weren't in jail. I got hot at last and yelled back that we were damn well going out and he couldn't stop us. He called New York on his direct wire and apparently New York confirmed it, regretfully.

We got on the 4:05 Jersey Central, with Higgins and Dalhousie tailing us at a respectful distance. Gomez didn't notice them and I didn't tell him. He was having too much fun. He had a shine put on his shoes at Penn Station and worried about the taxi fare as we rode up to Spanish Harlem.

His parents lived in a neat little three-room apartment. A lot of the furniture looked brand new, and I was pretty sure who had paid for it. The mother and father spoke only Spanish, and mumbled shyly when *"mi amigo Beel"* was introduced. I had a very halting conversation with the father while the mother and Gomez rattled away happily and she poked his ribs to point up the age-old complaint of any mother anywhere that he wasn't eating enough.

The father, of course, thought the boy was a janitor or something in the Pentagon and, as near as I could make out, he was worried about his Julio being grabbed off by a man-hungry government girl. I kept reassuring him that his Julio was a good boy, a very good boy, and he seemed to get some comfort out of it.

There was a little spat when his mother started to set the table. Gomez said reluctantly that we couldn't stay, that we were eating somewhere else. His mother finally dragged from him the admission that we were going to the Porto Bello so he could see Rosa, and everything was smiles again. The father told me that Rosa was a good girl, a very good girl.

Walking down the three flights of stairs with yelling little kids playing tag around us, Gomez asked proudly: "You not think they in America only a little time, hey?"

I yanked him around by the elbow as we went down the brownstone stoop into the street. Otherwise he would have seen our shadows for sure. I didn't want to spoil his fun.

The Porto Bello was full, and the pretty little girl was on duty as cashier at the table. Gomez got a last-minute attack of cold feet at the sight of her. "No table," he said. "We better go someplace else."

I practically dragged him in. "We'll get a table in a minute," I said.

"Julio," said the girl, when she saw him.

He looked sheepish. "Hello, Rosa. I'm back for a while."

"I'm glad to see you again," she said tremulously.

"I'm glad to see you again too—" I nudged him. "Rosa, this is my good friend Beel. We work together in Washington."

"Pleased to meet you, Rosa. Can you have dinner with us? I'll bet you and Julio have a lot to talk over."

"Well, I'll see … look, there's a table for you. I'll see if I can get away."

We sat down and she flagged down the proprietress and got away in a hurry.

All three of us had *arróz con pollo*—rice with chicken and lots of other things. Their shyness wore off and I was dealt out of the conversation, but I didn't mind. They were a nice young couple. I liked the way they smiled at each other, and the things they remembered happily—movies, walks, talks. It made me feel like a benevolent uncle with one foot in the grave. It made me forget for a while the look on Gomez' face when he turned from the blackboard he had covered with too-simple math.

Over dessert I broke in. By then they were unselfconsciously holding hands. "Look," I said, "why don't you two go on and do the town? Julio, I'll be at the Madison Park Hotel." I scribbled the address and gave it to him. "And I'll get a room for you. Have fun and reel in any time." I rapped his knee. He looked down and I slipped him four twenties. I didn't know whether he had money on him or not, but anything extra the boy could use he had coming to him.

"Swell," he said. "Thanks." And looked shame-faced while I looked paternal.

I had been watching a young man who was moodily eating alone in a corner, reading a paper. He was about Julio's height and build and he wore a sports jacket pretty much like Julio's. And the street was pretty dark outside.

The young man got up moodily and headed for the cashier's table. "Gotta go," I said. "Have fun."

I went out of the restaurant right behind the young man and walked as close behind him as I dared, hoping we were being followed.

After a block and a half of this, he turned on me and snarled: "Wadda you, mister? A wolf? Beat it!"

"Okay," I said mildly, and turned and walked the other way. Higgins and Dalhousie were standing there, flat-footed and open-mouthed. They sprinted back to the Porto Bello, and *I* followed *them*. But Julio and Rosa had already left.

"Tough, fellows," I said to them as they stood in the doorway. They looked as if they wanted to murder me. "He won't get into any trouble," I said. "He's just going out with his girl." Dalhousie made a strangled noise and told Higgins: "Cruise around the neighborhood. See if you can pick them up. I'll follow Vilchek." He wouldn't talk to me. I shrugged and got a cab and went to the Madison Park Hotel, a pleasantly unfashionable old place with big rooms where I stay when business brings me to New York. They had a couple of adjoining singles; I took one in my own name and the other for Gomez.

I wandered around the neighborhood for a while and had a couple of beers in one of the ultra-Irish bars on Third Avenue. After a pleasant argument with a gent who thought the Russians didn't have any atomic bombs and faked their demonstrations and that we ought to blow up their industrial cities tomorrow at dawn, I went back to the hotel.

I didn't get to sleep easily. The citizen who didn't believe Russia could maul the United States pretty badly or at all had started me thinking again—all kinds of ugly thoughts. Dr. Mines, who had turned into a shrunken old man at the mention of applying Gomez' work. The look on the boy's face. My layman's knowledge that present-day "atomic energy" taps only the smallest fragment of the energy locked up in the atom. My layman's knowledge that once genius has broken a trail in science, mediocrity can follow the trail.

But I slept at last, for three hours.

At four-fifteen A.M. according to my watch the telephone rang long and hard. There was some switchboard and long-distance-operator mumbo-jumbo and then Julio's gleeful voice: "Beel! Congratulate us. We got marriage!"

"Married," I said fuzzily. "You got *married,* not marriage. How's that again?"

"We got *married.* Me and Rosa. We get on the train, the taxi driver takes us to the justice of peace, we got *married,* we go to hotel here."

"Congratulations," I said, waking up. "Lots of congratulations. But you're under age, there's a waiting period—"

"Not in this state," he chuckled. "Here is no waiting periods and here I have twenty-one years if I say so."

"Well," I said. "Lots of congratulations, Julio. And tell Rosa she's got herself a good boy."

"Thanks, Beel," he said shyly. "I call you so you don't worry when I don't come in tonight. I think I come in with Rosa tomorrow so we tell her mama and my mama and papa. I call you at the hotel, I still have the piece of paper."

"Okay, Julio. All the best. Don't worry about a thing." I hung up, chuckling, and went right back to sleep.

Well, sir, it happened again.

I was shaken out of my sleep by the strong, skinny hand of Admiral MacDonald. It was seven-thirty and a bright New York morning. Dalhousie had pulled a blank canvassing the neighborhood for Gomez, got panicky and bucked it up to higher headquarters.

"Where is he?" the admiral rasped.

"On his way here with his bride of one night," I said. "He slipped over a couple of state lines and got married."

"By God," the admiral said, "we've got to do something about this. I'm going to have him drafted and assigned to special duty. This is the last time—"

"*Look,*" I said. "You've got to stop treating him like a chesspiece. You've got duty-honor-country on the brain and thank God for that. Somebody has to; it's your profession. But can't you get it through your head that Gomez is a kid and that you're wrecking his life by forcing him to grind out science like a machine? And I'm just a stupe of a layman, but have you professionals worried once about digging too deep and blowing up the whole shebang?"

He gave me a piercing look and said nothing.

I dressed and had breakfast sent up. The admiral, Dalhousie and I waited grimly until noon, and then Gomez phoned up.

"Come on up, Julio," I said tiredly.

He breezed in with his blushing bride on his arm. The admiral rose automatically as she entered, and immediately began tongue-lashing the boy. He spoke more in sorrow than in anger. He made it clear that Gomez wasn't treating his country right. That he had a great talent and it belonged to the United States. That his behavior had been irresponsible. That Gomez would have to come to heel and realize that his wishes weren't the most important thing in his life. That he could and would be drafted if there were any more such escapades.

"As a starter, Mr. Gomez," the admiral snapped, "I want you to set down, immediately, the enfieldment matrices you have developed. I consider it almost criminal of you to arrogantly and carelessly trust to your memory alone matters of such vital importance. Here!" He thrust pencil and paper at the boy, who stood, drooping and disconsolate. Little Rosa was near crying. She didn't have the ghost of a notion as to what it was about.

Gomez took the pencil and paper and sat down at the writing-table silently. I took Rosa by the arm. She was trembling. "It's all right," I said. "They can't do a thing to him." The admiral glared briefly at me and then returned his gaze to Gomez.

The boy made a couple of tentative marks. Then his eyes went wide and he clutched his hair. *"Dios mío!"* he said. *"Está perdido! Olvidado!"*

Which means: "My God, it's lost! Forgotten!"

The admiral turned white beneath his tan. "Now, boy," he said slowly and soothingly. "I didn't mean to scare you. You just relax and collect yourself. Of course you haven't forgotten, not with that memory of yours. Start with something easy. Write down a general biquadratic equation, say."

Gomez just looked at him. After a long pause he said in a strangled voice: "*No puedo.* I can't. It too I forget. I don't think of the math or physics at all since—" He looked at Rosa and turned a little red. She smiled shyly and looked at her shoes.

"That is it," Gomez said hoarsely. "Not since then. Always before in the back of my head is the math, but not since then."

"My God," the admiral said softly. "Can such a thing happen?" He reached for the phone.

He found out that such things can happen.

Julio went back to Spanish Harlem and bought a piece of the Porto Bello with his savings. I went back to the paper and bought a car with *my* savings. MacDonald never cleared the story, so the Sunday editor had the satisfaction of bulldozing an admiral, but didn't get his exclusive.

Julio and Rosa sent me a card eventually announcing the birth of their first-born: a six-pound boy, Francisco, named after Julio's father. I saved the card and when a New York assignment came my way—it was the National Association of Dry Goods Wholesalers; dry goods are important in our town—I dropped up to see them.

Julio was a little more mature and a little more prosperous. Rosa—alas!— was already putting on weight, but she was still a pretty thing and devoted to her man. The baby was a honey-skinned little wiggler. It was nice to see all of them together, happy with their lot.

Julio insisted that he'd cook *arróz con pollo* for me, as on the night I practically threw him into Rosa's arms, but he'd have to shop for the stuff. I went along.

In the corner grocery he ordered the rice, the chicken, the garbanzos, the peppers and, swept along by the enthusiasm that hits husbands in groceries, about fifty other things that he thought would be nice to have in the pantry.

The creaking old grocer scribbled down the prices on a shopping bag and began painfully to add them up while Julio was telling me how well the Porto Bello was doing and how they were thinking of renting the adjoining store.

"Seventeen dollars, forty-two cents," the grocer said at last.

Julio flicked one glance at the shopping bag and the upside-down figures. "Should be seventeen thirty-nine," he said reprovingly. "Add up again."

The grocer painfully added up again and said, "Is seventeen thirty-nine. Sorry." He began to pack the groceries into the bag.

"Hey," I said.

We didn't discuss it then or ever. Julio just said: "Don't tell, Beel." And winked.

[*Stirring Science Stories* - March 1942
as by Kenneth Falconer]

Masquerade

A man can wake one morning to read in his tabloid that his father has been shot fleeing the scene of a bank robbery. In these times there is no guarantee against the unexpected striking one down harder than a thunderbolt and almost as quick. From the vast-spreading matrix of the ordinary there may fly into your face the grotesque, the shocking, even the horrible.

Why did Leonard die?

Who were the Whelmers, silent partners in the most horrid nightmare that ever rose to walk the streets of New York?

Mac Leonard, who is now compressed into the small confines of a crematory urn, had always seemed to me to be one of the chosen of the Lord. In Columbia University, where we both studied, he was a shining campus light. I said *both studied*, but that is a misconception. Keeping the profligate's hours that he did, tumbling into bed dead drunk four nights out of the seven, Leonard could not possibly have studied in the ordinary sense.

Revolving the matter carefully, I realize that Leonard could not possibly have done anything in the ordinary sense. He was a blinding flash of a man; the hardest liver, the most brilliant scholar and the coolest head on the blocks-long campus was his. If he had gone to a smaller school he would have stood out like a beacon. He would probably, furthermore, have been thrown out like a bum for his vices and dissipations. As far as I was concerned, of course, they were his business. He drank and went with the Joe College set, but had no illusions about their capacities.

This was, you will remember, in the Flaming Youth era, when skirts were short and gin was aged in the porcelain for about five minutes. Mac drank with them, but he talked with men and the rest of the grinds on the school daily and the *Journal of the Columbia Philosophical Society*.

It comes back to me like a nightmare that was almost funny—the deadly seriousness of the kids. Mac himself had been almost completely taken in by Mr. James Branch Cabell, who had been fortunate enough to have one of his recent puerilities barred from the mails.

Perhaps the business of the mysterious Whelmers was all my fault, for one day I made it my business to catch Mac on the fly between classes. "Leonard," I yelled, overtaking him.

Looking at me with the glazed eyes of a hangover, he said: "Hi. Going in for track, old son of the lamp?" He focussed on the book I was holding out to him. "What's that mouse-colored tome?"

"Take it. I want you to read it. My very own personally-annotated copy of Kant's *Critique of Pure Reason*. It's about time you learned something in college."

"Very truly yours," he said, pocketing it and weaving off down the red brick walk. That, of course, wasn't the last of it. He came around that night—standing up his gin and jazz crowd—to chew the rug about Kant. He had actually read the book in six hours, and assimilated most of the meat.

"It is," he said, "quite a change-over from math and science to beat one's brow against a thing like this. Have I been neglecting the eternal verities in my pursuit of hard facts? Speak, O serpent of the thousand diamond scales."

Modestly I assured him that that had been the idea. And what did he think of Kant in the light of his scientific attainments?

"Stinking," said Mac briefly. "But—at least a googolplex advanced above Mr. Cabell. Imbued with that quasi-mystic hogwash I could do naught but agree with the simple-minded laddie that the world is what you make it and that the eternal verity is to get along with one's neighbors. Your friend Kant is all wet, but by no means as wet as that."

With that he wandered away. When I saw him next he had enrolled in several philosophy courses at the same time. In the Philosophical Society we pinned his ears back with ease whenever he tried to enter into debate, but that was only because he didn't quite know how to use the quaint language of the gentle science.

I've been rambling badly. The point that I wanted to bring out was that Mac Leonard was brilliant, as brilliant as they come in the current mortal mold. Also that he was a student of the physical sciences and the only philosophy they have, mathematics.

By a kind of miracle I survived the crash of 1929 with a young fortune in gold certificates. The miracle was an uncle who had burned his fingers in the crash of 1922 and warned me: "When you see the board rooms crowded with people who have no business there—laundrymen, grocers, taxi drivers—then *sell!*" Ignoring the optimistic fictions of Mr. Roger W. Babson, prophet of the stock exchange, now, I believe, candidate for the presidency on the Prohibition Party's ticket, I sold and came out on top. I didn't even trust to the safe deposit vaults the money I had made; it went into the fireproof, burglarproof, earthquakeproof warrens of the Manhattan Storage and Warehouse Corporation. Quick-money imbeciles who had been stuck considered me a traitor not to have lost by the crash. For years I was as good as ostracized by former friends. That was all right with me—I was a scholar and intended to remain one while my capital lasted, which it did.

A man can be a recluse in the middle of New York; that much I found out in ten years of study. It wasn't in any of the books I read; it was what I proved with my own quiet life. And at the end of many years I heard again from Mac Leonard—a scenic postal card marked Uvalde, Mexico. Characteristically laconic, the message was: "—and wife." That and his signature was supposed to be all I wanted to know about him and his fortunes since we had parted at commencement.

Hoping that he would not already be gone—who but a tourist would write on a scenic postal card?—I mailed a long letter giving my own story to date and demanding his.

His answer came very much later, three months or more, from Council Bluffs, Iowa:

> Dear Vulcan, [the nickname in reference to my slight limp]
> So the plumy anaconda has found his forked tongue after these long years? I should be hurt at your neglect of me—failing to write when a simple matter like not knowing my address stood in your way. You're right—I was on my honeymoon in the vastly overrated country of Mexico. And she is a very nice girl, in a rowdy sort of way.
> I'm still playing with paper boxes and numbers. The chair of mathematics at one of our little high schools out here is all mine, and very uncomfortable it is. Still, Civil Service is nothing to be sneezed at in these troubled times.
> My life seems to have slipped into a slap-happy routine of examination papers and recitations; the really heart-breaking part is that none of my excessively brilliant students get my jokes. Aside from that all is milk and honey. I live in a bungalow with my wife—seems damned strange to write that down; as though it never really happened!—and we are like a pair of larks in the springtime. Whenever quarrels come I demonstrate by the calculus of symbolic logic that she's wrong and I'm right, and that settles the matter. Theoretically, at least.
> Honestly, old dish towel, I'm *happy*—a truly representative specimen of that rarest work of God, the man who is contented with his lot in life. It may sound idiotic to you, but I hope I never change from what I am. If time stood still this very minute I wouldn't have a kick coming in the world.
>   Mac

Other letters followed that; there was an erratic quality to his correspondence that made it completely delightful. I found in my mailbox or resting on my doorstep anything from postal cards to bundles of year-old exams in Geometry One, neatly rated with mean, average and modes. For three years it kept up; at one time we were waging half a dozen chess games simultaneously as well as a discussion of Hegelian dialectics. "One of these days" he kept carelessly promising, he would blow into the city to see me.

Then, abruptly, he did. And it wasn't as an honored guest but as a man flee-ing from disgrace. Never a coward, not one now in the nastiest position that any man could face, he sent me a note giving the arrival-time of his bus. And he en-closed a bunch of clippings from the local press.

To say that I was shocked would be putting it mildly. He had been no angel in his college days, but a man grows out of that, especially when he marries. The clippings didn't make it any easier. With an obscene, missish reticence oddly com-bined with the suggestive vulgarity that is the specialty of the tabloid press, they told the sordid and familiar story of a male teacher in a co-ed school—you know what I mean. It happens.

I met them at the terminal. He was the picture of a hunted man, eyes sunken and hair lank down his temples. He'd kept his shape; there wasn't a sign of the usual professorial pot-belly. But his mouth was very tight. His nose wrinkled as though he could still smell those headlines. Yes, they were so nasty they actually stank.

He mumbled a brief introduction, and I smiled wildly at his wife in acknowl-edgment. No self-respecting woman would—

They came to my apartment to get their luggage settled. They were traveling light. He explained, as we all three lit cigarettes, that he had left his bungalow in the hands of an agent, and that when the business died down somebody would buy it furnished and ready for occupancy. "But," he added grimly, "that won't be for a long while."

"Do you want to talk about it?" I asked, with my damned morbid curiosity.

"You saw the papers. To correct a popular misconception, which our jour-nals tended to foster, she was not fifteen but nineteen. Big and dumb. And despite their hinting, she was the only one. And anybody in the school could have told you that I wasn't her first boyfriend—as it were."

"I'm sorry, Mac. It's a lousy thing to happen. I know how it is—" That pe-culiar noise was me, making like I was broad-minded. But I still didn't see how anybody in his right mind would do a thing like that. I shot a glance at his wife, and luck would have it that she met my eyes squarely.

With the Midwest twang she said: "I can see that you're wondering what I think about the whole matter." I took a good look at her then, my first. She wasn't a very beautiful woman. Her face was the kind you call intelligent. She had a figure that, with cultivation, could be glorious; as it was it was only superb. But I'm easy to please.

"My husband made a fool of himself, that's plain enough. If he learned his lesson as well as he teaches—it's *over*. Am I right, Len?"

"Right," he said dispiritedly.

"I'll make some coffee," I said, rising, beginning to walk across the floor. I felt the way the lame do, her eyes on my twisted right foot. She had reached the kitchen door before I was well under way.

"Please let me," she said. "You men will want to talk."

"Thanks," I said, wondering angrily if she was going to be sickeningly sweet and sympathetic about my very minor disability. "Go right ahead." I sat down facing Mac. "Not many women would be that understanding," I said.

His answer nearly paralyzed me. He leaped across the distance between us, his face desperate and contorted, whispering: "We're going to some hotel. I'll come back and see you tonight. Have to explain. You don't know—"

"Coffee!" gaily announced Mrs. Leonard, carrying in the tray.

I rose gallantly, and very much surprised. "How in Heaven's name did you make it so quickly?" I demanded.

"You don't think I made it with that fancy glass thing of yours, do you?" she laughed. "I have more sense than that."

"But you couldn't have had time to boil the water!"

"Silly—there was a pan of water seething. Oh!" Her hand flew to her mouth. "I hope there wasn't salt or anything in it!" I seemed to remember something about water boiling—perhaps I had meant to prepare a hot cloth for my ankle before going to meet the bus.

"And this," she said, pouring, "is Iowa pan coffee the way my grandmother made it in a covered wagon."

I got a mouthful of grounds and swallowed convulsively. "Those pioneers had courage," I said inanely.

Working on a learned monograph revealing factors in the sociology of the Bronx that Fordham University had not even touched, I was baffled by what I had written a few months later. It was done in the style peculiar to some textbooks and degree themes; that is, it was no style at all but an attempt to set down without emotion or effect certain facts in their natural order.

That was the effect which Mac's talk with me that night had. He had come about nine o'clock, panting from the climb up the stairs and perspiring profusely. He wouldn't take anything to drink but water.

"It was partly drink that got me into trouble in Council Bluffs," he said. "I'm never going to touch it again." He looked up at the indirect light from the ceiling and blinked. "Would you mind—?" he asked inarticulately. "Eyestrain—"

I turned off the big light and lit a table-lamp which spread a bright pool on the console, leaving the rest of the room obscured. "Now shoot," I said. "And I'm not making any promises about anything tonight. Not one way or another."

"Don't worry," he almost snarled. "I'm not after your damned money." As I started up angrily—and God knows I had a right to be angry—he buried his face in his hands. I sank back into my chair, inexpressibly shocked to hear him weeping.

"Easy," I muttered. "No need to go on like that, Mac. What would Nicholas Butler say to hear a Columbia man crying?" The ridiculous joke didn't stop him; he sobbed like a child. No; sobbed like a man, from the diaphragm, where it hurts as if your ribs are being torn out one by one.

He looked up, his eyes streaming, and wiped his face. Returning the handkerchief to his breast pocket, he said in a very steady voice: "It isn't the dreams that get you; it's when you know you're awake and they keep on coming."

"Yes?" I asked, leaning back. I thought he was delirious.

"Shut up. I'm telling you everything—don't you see? It's your fault anyway—waking me up when I was dreaming James Branch Cabell—showing me the way things happen."

"Go on," I said after a long pause. He didn't seem to hear me, for it was an equally long time before he made a curious choking sound and said:

"I think I have been in Hell for the past few years, old ink-blotter. But I recall a very special chapter of the book. Allow me to describe it. There is, first of all, a large, rocky cavern." He paused again and leaned back, speaking in a very faint, rasping voice, as though he could not bear the sounds of the words he was saying.

"And there is very foolish talk going on. There are people in the cavern who think they are Satanists, or something like it. They have prepared fantastic things—a long table, various dyes and pigments. Very foolish. They are well-dressed people; it is true, as a rule, that the poor are on the side of God.

"One of the foolish, wealthy people is a woman. She finds it necessary to undress and begin to dance as the others clap their hands. Did I mention that there were fires lighting this cavern? She spins close by the fires, one by one, and makes it a point to burn herself badly in various places. Then, as she falls to the floor, another, a man, has reasons for doing, essentially, what she has done. But the man wears a chain around his neck which he does not remove, and from this chain hangs a small medallion. When the man is very badly burned, another woman makes a fool of herself in the same manner, and after her a man.

"Would you believe it if I told you that in all twenty-four people willingly subjected themselves to widespread first-degree burns? After hours of this folly they sat in a circle, still without their clothes, and mumbled gibberish for twenty minutes or more.

"At that point they had conjured up Satan, theoretically. My guess is that they did nothing of the sort. The incarnation of Evil? No! He would not have let them live or praise him. Something they did conjure up. What it was I do not know, but this is what happened.

"There was, first of all, a noticeable diminution of the firelight. Then appeared a definite blue glow at what would be the apex of the cone about whose basal circumference they were sitting. As that glow grew, the fires went out. There was definitely a Presence there ...

"I don't know what to call it. It was not Satan. There probably is no Satan. But there was a Presence, and it had horns and a tail and great, shining teeth and lustful, shining eyes."

I stood up from my chair. "That's enough!" I yelled at him.

He looked at me and then, shockingly, suddenly, gave a low chuckle. "Quaint tale, isn't it? What's the matter?"

"You tell me!" I snapped. "What's on your mind?"

"Allow me to get on with the story. I'm afraid I was becoming hypnotized by my own rhetoric. And interrupt if you feel too weak to stand it." I flushed suddenly as I felt his eyes on my twisted foot. Where did the damned slander start that cripples are loose in the head?

"Go on," I growled.

"To be brief, direct and—crude—the women then proceed to caress this creature. And then—!

"There appears a man in that cavern who does not wear a pendant from his neck. He is no demonologist. He is, God knows, not wealthy. He is but a simple mathematician who made the horrid mistake of attempting to tie in his mathematics with occult philosophy."

Another very long pause. "Go on," I said.

"Don't get me wrong," said Mac. "Don't do that. I didn't know what I was doing. If I'd known I would have cut off my hand before I wrote the supersonic equations. But it's so simple. All you need is a scale of tuning forks—then you modify them the right way and you find yourself in the nearest occult vortex. It's so simple! The clue is in several of Madame Blavatsky's *Meditations*. That old hag didn't know what she was writing, I suppose. You need money, millions, to get into the circle. I was an outsider.

"The Presence vanished, and I was cursed by those people—cursed while I was waking, sleeping, talking, walking, dancing, writing and reading. Then they opened a door and threw me out."

"A *door?*" I asked. "In a cavern?"

He laughed like the closing of a lock. "The rocks," he said, "were papier mâché. The cavern was the third-floor ballroom of a hotel on 32nd Street."

"And so?" I asked.

"I wired back to Council Bluffs for bus fare. I was back there in two days with a tale of urgent business in New York."

"That's plenty, Leonard. Now you can get the hell out of my house. Yes, even before you build up to the touch for the rare herbs that'll take the curse off you."

"Sorry," he said, rising. "I tried to let you know. It wasn't a touch. I remembered that you have a cousin, or had, the one you wrote that Bronx monograph on—"

"He's up the river. Dewey got him, with the rest of Murder Incorporated. Did you want a bodyguard against the demons? Or do you want to become a policy banker?"

He had his hat on. From the door he said: "I wanted to have a murder done for me. But now I suppose I'll have to do it myself ..."

I locked the door and went to bed, fuming like a tea-kettle. I'm from a short-lived clan; we break down early and live in the fear of death. That night I found myself with a hacking cough, which didn't add to my sense of well-being, for my father and sister had died of throat infections. You could accurately say that between Mac's turning out to be a chiseling phony and my fears that in a week I'd be a dead man, I bordered on distraction. There was a heightening of the sensory powers—*all* the sensory powers. The darkest room was not dark enough for me, and the traffic below jerked me up in bed repressing shrieks of pain. It was as though I had been flayed alive, for the silk bedsheets I use for that very reason were like sacking-cloth—or sandpaper.

How I managed to fall asleep I didn't know. Certainly the quality of my dreams was horrid enough to wake me up screaming.

I got disconnected scraps and images from Leonard's story of that night. I saw over again, in the most damnably vivid colors, the lie he had told of the ceremonial in the hotel. Details he had omitted were plentifully supplied by my subconscious— revolting details. Cripples, I am told, are generally stews of repression and fear.

Quite the most awful part was the Presence turning to me and stating, in a language of snarls and drooling grunts, the following message:

"A curse is no mouthing of words. That worries at a man but does not kill. A curse is no juggling of hands. That worries at a man, but does not maim. A curse is no thinking of evil. That worries at a man, but does not blind, tear, crush, char and slash. A curse is something you can see, hear, feel, hate and love."

That was not the end of the dream, but it was near. After I—subconsciously doubling for Mac—had been thrown out of that ballroom, it ended and I awoke. My throat irritation was gone, which was good. That night I did not sleep any more, but read and re-read the clippings Mac had sent me. I wanted to look at his letters, but they were in no kind of order.

I saw the sun rise and made myself a breakfast of bacon and eggs. It was interrupted by a telegram slipped under my door. The yellow slip read: "Please phone me. Not a touch. Mac Leonard." The telegram was because I have no phone; if you want to hear my dulcet voice, you have to coerce me into going down to the corner drug store to call you up.

Frankly, I didn't know what to do. I was still mad, half because of his ridiculous story, half because of his continuous rude staring at my right foot. I long ago passed the point where I allowed people to indulge their curiosity at the cost of much personal anguish to me. I decided that I might as well.

I threw some clothes on and went down to the corner where a tubercular young clerk was dispensing a few early-morning Cokes. "Hi," he said. "Nice day." Avoiding his conversational spray I got change and slid into the booth.

A woman's voice answered the phone in their room at a nearby hotel.

"Mrs. Leonard?" I asked. "I got a telegram from Mac—he wanted me to call him."

"He must have gone out," she said. "He wasn't here when I woke up. Must have gone for breakfast—wouldn't wait for me, the barbarian!"

I mumbled some inanity or other, wondering what I ought to do.

"Listen," she said, suddenly urgent. "This is the first chance I've had to talk to you, really. I'm just a dumb woman, so they tell me, but there are some things I want to know. That foot of yours—what's wrong with it?"

"I don't want to talk about it," I snarled. "Since you began it, it was run over sidewise by a car when I was about twenty. Is there anything else?"

"Yes. What do you do for a living?"

The damnable impudence of the woman! I didn't answer; just slammed the receiver down on the hook and stormed out.

Mac was waiting for me in my apartment. The landlady had let him in, she told me as I was going up.

"Now what's this?" I asked, as I found him nervously smoking on the edge of my bed.

"Sorry I broke in," he said. Damn him! His eyes were on my twisted foot again!

"What do you want? I was just talking with your wife."

"You might want to know why I did a damned foolish thing like trying to make a student. It was because my wife wouldn't treat me like a husband. I was nearly crazy. I loved her so." His voice was thin and colorless.

"I don't care about your personal affairs, Mac. Get out of here."

He rose slowly and dangerously, and as he moved towards me I began to realize how big he was and how small I was. He grabbed me by the coat lapels; as he twisted them into a tight knot and lifted me so that my dragging foot cleared the ground, he snarled: "You tell me what's wrong with your foot or I'll break your neck!"

"Car ran over it!" I gasped. I was shocked to find out that I was a physical coward; never before had I been subjected to an assault like this. I feared that man with the lunatic gleam in his eyes as I had never feared anything before.

"Car," he growled. "Now how do you make a living? Don't give me that 'retired capitalist' bull you tried in your letters. I've been looking you up and you haven't got a single bank-account anywhere. Where do you get your money from?"

A voice from my door sounded. "Put him down," it said. "He's no friend of mine. Maybe of yours." I fell in a heap and turned to see Leonard's wife. "The Whelmers," she said, "disavowed him."

Mac turned away. "You know that I know!" he gasped, his face quite dead, dirty white. It was absolutely bloodless.

"I saw two of the Whelmers in the street. They know nothing of this." She gestured contemptuously at me. "That foot of his is no mark. Now, Mr. Leonard—" She advanced slowly on him, step by step.

He backed away, to before a window. "Only a few days ago," he gasped, "only a few days ago I put it all together. *I never knew your parents. You are the curse of the Whelmers.* And last night I—we—my God!" His eyes were dilated with terror.

"Last night," said the woman, "you were my husband and I was your wife."

With the beginning of a musical laugh she slumped and bloated strangely, quietly, a bluish glare shining from her skin.

With the glare came a momentary paralysis of my limbs. I would have run rather than have seen what I had to see. I would have died rather than have seen that Presence that had horns and a tail and great, shining teeth and lustful, shining eyes.

Leonard took his dry dive through the window just a second before I fainted. When I awoke, there was nobody at all in the room except myself and the friendly, curious police.

[*SF Adventures* - September 1957]

The Slave

1

The drunken bum known as Chuck wandered through the revelry of the New Year's Eve crowd. Times Square was jammed with people; midnight and a whole new millennium were approaching. Horns tooted, impromptu snake-dances formed and dissolved, bottles were happily passed from hand to hand; it was minutes to A.D. 2000. One of those bottles passed to Chuck and passed no further. He scowled at a merry-maker who reached for it after he took his swig, and jammed it into a pocket. He had what he came for; he began to fight his way out of the crowd, westward to the jungle of Riveredge.

The crowd thinned out at Ninth Avenue, and by Tenth Avenue he was almost alone, lurching through the tangle of transport machinery that fed Manhattan its daily billion tons of food, freight, clothes, toys. Floodlights glared day and night over Riveredge, but there was darkness there too, in patches under a 96-inch oil main or in the angle between a warehouse wall and its inbound roofed freightway. From these patches men looked out at him with sudden suspicion and then dull lack of care. One or two called at him aimlessly, guessing that he had a bottle on him. Once a woman yelled her hoarse invitation at him from the darkness, but he stumbled on. Ten to one the invitation was to a lead pipe behind the ear.

Now and then losing his bearings, he stopped and turned his head peeringly before stumbling on. He never got lost in Riveredge, which was more than most transport engineers, guided by blueprints, could say. T.G. was *that* way.

He crashed at last into his own shared patch of darkness: the hollow on one side of a titanic I-beam. It supported a freightway over which the heaviest castings and forgings for the city rumbled night and day. A jagged sheet of corrugated metal leaned against the hollow, enclosing it as if by accident.

"Hello, Chuck," T.G. croaked at him from the darkness as he slid under the jagged sheet and collapsed on a pallet of nylon rags.

"Yeh," he grunted.

"Happy New Year," T.G. said. "I heard it over here. It was louder than the freightway. You scored."

"Good guess," Chuck said skeptically, and passed him the bottle. There was a long gurgle in the dark. T.G. said at last: "Good stuff." The gurgle again. Chuck reached for the bottle and took a long drink. It was good stuff. Old Huntsman. He used to drink it with—

T.G. said suddenly, pretending innocent curiosity: "Jocko who?"

Chuck lurched to his feet and yelled: "God damn you, I told you not to do that! If you want any more of my liquor, keep the hell out of my head—and I *still* think you're a phony!"

T.G. was abject. "Don't take it that way, Chuck," he whined. "I get a belt of good stuff in me and I want to give the talent a little workout, that's all. You know I would not do anything bad to you."

"You'd better not … Here's the bottle."

It passed back and forth. T.G. said at last: "You've got it too."

"You're crazy."

I would be if it wasn't for liquor … but you've got it too.

"Oh, shut up and drink."

Innocently: "I didn't say anything, Chuck."

Chuck glared in the darkness. It was true; he hadn't. His imagination was hounding him. His imagination or something else he didn't want to think about.

The sheet of corrugated metal was suddenly wrenched aside and blue-white light stabbed into their eyes. Chuck and the old man cowered instinctively back into the hollow of the I-beam, peering into the light and seeing nothing but dazzle.

"God, look at them!" a voice jeered from the other side of the light. "Like turning over a wet rock."

"What the hell's going on?" Chuck asked hoarsely. "Since when did you clowns begin to pull vags?"

T.G. said: "They aren't the clowns, Chuck. They want you—I can't see why."

The voice said: "Yeah? And just who are you, grampa?"

T.G. stood up straight, his eyes watering in the glare. "The Great Hazleton," he said, with some of the old ring in his voice. "At your service. Don't tell me who you are, sir. The Great Hazleton knows. I see a man of authority, a man who works in a large white building—"

"Knock it off, T.G.," Chuck said.

"You're Charles Barker," the voice said. "Come along quietly."

Chuck took a long pull at the bottle and passed it to T.G. "Take it easy," he said. "I'll be back sometime."

"No," T.G. quavered. "I see danger. I see terrible danger."

The man behind the dazzling light took his arm and yanked him out of the shelter of the I-beam.

"Cut out the mauling," Chuck said flatly.

"Shut up, Barker," the man said with disgust. "*You* have no beefs coming."

So he knew where the man had come from and could guess where the man was taking him.

At 1:58 A.M. of the third millennium Chuck was slouching in a waiting room on the 89th floor of the New Federal Building. The man who had pulled him out of Riveredge was sitting there too, silent and aloof.

Chuck had been there before. He cringed at the thought. He had been there before, and not to sit and wait. Special Agent Barker of Federal Security and Intelligence had been ushered right in with the sweetest smile a receptionist could give him ... .

A door opened and a spare, well-remembered figure stood there. "Come in, Barker," the Chief said.

He stood up and went in, his eyes on the grey carpeting. The office hadn't changed in three years; neither had the Chief. But now Chuck waited until he was asked before sitting down.

"We had some trouble finding you," the Chief said absently. "Not much, but some. First we ran some ads addressed to you in the open Service code. Don't you read the papers any more?"

"No," Chuck said.

"You look pretty well shot. Do you think you can still work?"

The ex-agent looked at him piteously.

"Answer me."

"Don't play with me," Chuck said, his eyes on the carpet. "You never reinstate."

"Barker," the Chief said, "I happen to have an especially filthy assignment to deal out. In my time, I've sent men into an alley at midnight after a mad-dog killer with a full clip. This one is so much worse and the chances of getting a sliver of usable information in return for an agent's life are so slim that I couldn't bring myself to ask for volunteers from the roster. Do you think you can still work?"

"Why me?" the ex-agent demanded sullenly.

"That's a good question. There are others. I thought of you because of the defense you put up at your departmental trial. Officially, you turned and ran, leaving Jocko McAllester to be cut down by the gun-runners. Your story was that somehow you knew it was an ambush and when that dawned on you, you ran to cover the flank. The board didn't buy it and neither do I—not all the way. You let a hunch override standard doctrine, and you were wrong and it looked like cowardice under fire. We can't have that; you had to go. But you've had other hunches that worked out better. The Bruni case. Locating the photostats we needed for the Wayne County civil rights indictment. Digging up that louse Sherrard's wife in Birmingham. Unless it's been a string of lucky flukes, you have a certain talent I need right now. If you have that talent, you may come out alive. And cleared."

Barker leaned forward and said savagely: "That's good enough for me. Fill me in."

2

The woman was tall, quietly dressed and a young forty-odd. Her eyes were serene and guileless as she said: "You must be curious as to how I know about your case.

It's quite simple—and unethical. We have a tipster in the clinic you visited. May I sit down?"

Dr. Oliver started and waved her to the dun-colored chair. A reaction was setting in. It was a racket—a cold-blooded racket preying on weak-minded victims silly with terror. "What's your proposition?" he asked, impatient to get it over with. "How much do I pay?"

"Nothing," the woman said calmly. "We usually pay poorer patients a little something to make up for the time they lose from work, but I presume you have a nest-egg. All this will cost you is a pledge of secrecy—and a little time."

"Very well," said Oliver stiffly. He had been hooked often enough by salesmen on no-money-down, free-trial-for-thirty-days, demonstration-for-consumer-reaction-only deals. He was on his guard.

"I find it's best to begin at the beginning," the woman said. "I'm an investment counselor. For the past five years I've also been a field representative for something called the Moorhead Foundation. The Moorhead Foundation was organized in 1915 by Oscar Moorhead, the patent-medicine millionaire. He died very deeply embittered by the attacks of the muckrakers; they called him a baby-poisoner and a number of other things. He always claimed that his preparations did just as much good as a visit to an average doctor of the period. Considering the state of medical education and licensing, maybe he was right.

"His will provided for a secret search for the cure of cancer. He must have got a lot of consolation daydreaming about it. One day the Foundation would announce to a startled world that it had cracked the problem and that old Oscar Moorhead was a servant of humanity and not a baby-poisoner after all.

"Maybe secrecy is good for research. I'm told that we know a number of things about neoplasms that the pathologists haven't hit on yet, including how to cure most types by radiation. My job, besides clipping coupons and reinvesting funds for the Foundation, is to find and send on certain specified types of cancer patients. The latest is what they call a Rotino 707-G. You. The technical people will cure you without surgery in return for a buttoned lip and the chance to study you for about a week. Is it a deal?"

Hope and anguish struggled in Dr. Oliver. *Could* anybody invent such a story? *Was* he saved from the horror of the knife?

"Of course," he said, his guts contracting. "I'll be expected to pay a share of the expenses, won't I? In common fairness?"

The woman smiled. "You think it's a racket, don't you? Well, it isn't. You don't pay a cent. Come with your pockets empty and leave your checkbook at home if you like. The Foundation gives you free room and board. I personally don't know the ins and outs of the Foundation, but I have professional standing of my own and I assure you I'm not acting as a transmission belt to a criminal gang. I've *seen* the patients, Dr. Oliver. I send them on sick, and I see them a week or so later well. It's like a miracle."

Dr. Oliver went distractedly to his telephone stand, picked up the red book and leafed through it.

"ROosevelt 4-19803," the woman said with amusement in her voice.

Doggedly he continued to turn the "W" pages. He found her. "Mgrt WIN-STON invstmnt cnslr RO4-19803." He punched the number.

"Winston Investments," came the answer.

"Is Miss Winston there?" he asked.

"No, sir. She should be back by three if you wish to call again. May I take a message?"

"No message. But—would you describe Miss Winston for me?"

The voice giggled. "Why not? She's about five-eight, weighs about 135, brown hair and eyes, and when last seen was wearing a tailored navy culotte suit with white cuffs and collar. What're you up to, mister?"

"Not a thing," he said. "Thanks." He hung up.

"Look," the woman said. She was emptying her wallet. "Membership card in the Investment Counselors' Guild. U.M.T. honorable discharge, even if it is a reduced photostat. City license to do business. Airline credit card. Residential rental permit. Business rental permit. City motor vehicle parking permit. Blood-donor card."

He turned them over in his hands. The plastic-laminated things were unanswerable, and he gave himself up to relief and exultation. "I'm in, Miss Winston," he said fervently. "You should have seen the fellow they showed me after an operation like mine." He shuddered as he remembered Jimmy and his "splendid adjustment."

"I don't have to," the woman said, putting her wallet away. "I saw my mother die. From one of the types of cancer they haven't licked yet. I get the usual commission on funds I handle for them, but I have a little personal interest in promoting the research end ... ."

"Oh. I see."

Suddenly she was brisk. "Now, Dr. Oliver, you've got to write whatever letters are necessary to explain that you're taking a little unplanned trip to think things out, or whatever you care to say. And pack enough things for a week. You can be on the jet in an hour if you're a quick packer and a quick letter-writer."

"Jet to where?" he asked, without thinking.

She smiled and shook her head.

Dr. Oliver shrugged and went to his typewriter. This was one gift horse he would not look in the mouth. Not after Jimmy.

Two hours later the fat sophomore Gillespie arrived full of lies and explanations with his overdue theme on the Elizabethan dramatists, which was full of borrowings and evasions. On Dr. Oliver's door was pinned a small note in the doctor's handwriting: *Dr. Oliver will be away for several days for reasons of health.*

Gillespie scratched his head and shrugged. It was all right with him; Dr. Oliver was practically impossible to get along with, in spite of his vague reputation for brilliance. A schizoid, his girl called him. She majored in Psych.

3

The Moorhead Foundation proved to be in Mexico, in a remote valley of the state of Sonora. A jetliner took Dr. Oliver and Miss Winston most of the way very fast.

Buses and finally an obsolete gasoline-powered truck driven by a Mexican took them the rest of the way very slowly. The buildings were a remodeled *ranchería* enclosed by a low, thick adobe wall.

Dr. Oliver, at the door of his comfortable bedroom, said: "Look, will I be treated immediately?" He seemed to have been asking that question for two days, but never to have got a plain yes or no answer.

"It all depends," Miss Winston said. "Your type of growth is definitely curable, and they'll definitely cure it. But there may be a slight holdup while they're studying it. That's your part of the bargain, after all. Now I'll be on my way. I expect you're sleepy, and the lab people will take over from here. It's been a great pleasure."

They shook hands and Dr. Oliver had trouble suppressing a yawn. He was very sleepy, but he tried to tell Miss Winston how grateful he was. She smiled deprecatingly, almost cynically, and said: "We're using you too, remember? Well, good-bye."

Dr. Oliver barely made it to his bed.

His nightmares were terrible. There was a flashing light, a ringing bell, and a wobbling pendulum that killed him, killed him, killed him, inch by inch, burying him under a mountain of flashes and clangs and blows while he was somehow too drugged to fight his way out.

He reached fuzzily in the morning for the Dialit, which wasn't there. Good God! he marveled. Was one expected to get *up* for breakfast? But he found a button that brought a grinning Mexican with a breakfast tray. After he dressed the boy took him to *los médicos*.

The laboratory, far down a deserted corridor, was staffed by two men and a woman. "Dr. Oliver," the woman said briskly. "Sit there." It was a thing like a dentist's chair with a suggestion of something ugly and archaic in a cup-shaped headrest.

Oliver sat, uneasily.

"The carcinoma," one of the men said to the other.

"Oh, yes." The other man, quite ignoring Oliver as a person, wheeled over a bulky thing not much different in his eyes from a television camera. He pointed it at Oliver's throat and played it noiselessly over his skin. "That should do it," he said to the first man.

Oliver asked incredulously: "You mean I'm cured?" And he started to rise.

"*Silence!*" the woman snarled, rapping a button. Dr. Oliver collapsed back into the chair with a moan. Something had happened to him; something terrible and unimaginable. For a hideous split-second he had known undiluted pain, pure and uniform over every part of his body, interpreted variously by each. Blazing headache, eyeache and earache, wrenching nausea, an agony of itching, colonic convulsions, stabbing ache in each of his bones and joints.

"But—" he began piteously.

"*Silence!*" the woman snarled, and rapped the button again.

He did not speak a third time but watched them with sick fear, cringing into the chair.

They spoke quite impersonally before him, lapsing occasionally into an unfamiliar word or so.

"Not more than twenty-seven *vistch,* I should say. Cardiac."

"Under a good—master, would you call it?—who can pace him, more."

"Perhaps. At any rate, he will not be difficult. See his record."

"Stimulate him again."

Again there was the split-second of hell on earth. The woman was studying a small sphere in which colors played prettily. "A good surge," she said, "but not a good recovery. What is the order?"

One of the men ran his finger over a sheet of paper—but he was looking at the woman. "Three military."

"What kind of military, *sobr'?*"

The man hastily rechecked the sheet with his index finger. "All for *igr' i khom.* I do not know what you would call it. A smallship? A killship?"

The other man said scornfully: "Either a light cruiser or a heavy destroyer."

"According to functional analogy I would call it a heavy destroyer," the woman said decisively. "A good surge is important to *igr' i khom.* We shall call down the destroyer to take on this Oliver and the two Stosses. Have it done."

"Get up," one of the men said to Oliver.

He got up. Under the impression that he could be punished only in the chair he said: "What—?"

"Silence!" the woman snarled, and rapped the button. He was doubled up with the wave of pain. When he recovered, the man took his arm and led him from the laboratory. He did not speak as he was half-dragged through endless corridors and shoved at last through a door into a large, sunlit room. Perhaps a dozen people were sitting about and turned to look.

He cringed as a tall, black-haired man said to him: "Did you just get out of the chair?"

"It's all right," somebody else said. "You can talk. We aren't—them. We're in the same boat as you. What's the story—heart disease? Cancer?"

"Cancer," he said, swallowing. "They promised me—"

"They come through on it," the tall man said. "They do come through on the cures. Me, I have nothing to show for it. I was supposed to survey for minerals here— my name's Brockhaus. And this is Johnny White from Los Angeles. He was epileptic—bad seizures every day. But not any more. And this—but never mind. You can meet the rest later. You better sit down. How many times did they give it to you?"

"Four times," Dr. Oliver said. "What's all this about? Am I going crazy?"

The tall man forced him gently into a chair. "Take it easy," he said. "We don't know what it's all about."

"Goddamn it," somebody said, "the hell we don't. It's the Commies, as plain as the nose on your face. Why else should they kidnap an experienced paper salesman like me?"

Brockhaus drowned him out: "Well, maybe it's the Reds, though I doubt it. All we *know* is that they get us here, stick us in the chair and then—take us away. And the ones they take away don't come back."

"They said something about cruisers and destroyers," Oliver mumbled. "And surges."

"You mean," Brockhaus said, "you stayed conscious all the way through?"

"Yes. Didn't you?"

"No, my friend. Neither did any of us. What are you, a United States Marine?"

"I'm an English professor. Oliver, of Columbia University."

Johnny White from Los Angeles threw up his hands. "He's an English professor!" he yelled to the room. There was a cackle of laughter.

Oliver flushed, and White said hastily: "No offense, prof. But naturally we've been trying to figure out what—they—are after. Here we've got a poetess, a preacher, two lawyers, a salesman, a pitchman, a mining engineer, a dentist—and now an English professor."

"*I* don't know," Oliver mumbled. "But they did say something about cruisers and destroyers and surges."

Brockhaus was looking skeptical. "I didn't imagine it," Oliver said stubbornly. "And they said something about 'two Stosses.'"

"I guess you didn't imagine it," the tall man said slowly. "Two Stosses we've got. Ginny! This man heard something about you and your old man."

A white-haired man, stocky in build and with the big, mobile face of an actor, thrust himself past Brockhaus to confront Oliver. "What did they say?" he demanded.

A tired-looking blonde girl said to him: "Take it easy, Mike. The man's beat."

"It's all right," Oliver said to her. "They talked about an order. One of the men seemed to be reading something in Braille—but he didn't seem to have anything wrong with his eyes. And the woman said they'd call down the destroyer to take on me and the two Stosses. But don't ask me what it means."

"We've been here a week," the girl said. "They tell me that's as long as anybody stays."

"Young man," Stoss said confidentially, "since we're thrown together in this informal fashion I wonder if I could ask whether you're a sporting man? The deadly dullness of this place—" He was rattling a pair of dice casually.

"*Please,* Mike!" the girl said in a voice near hysteria. "Leave the man alone. What good's money here?"

"I'm a sporting man, Ginny," he said mildly. "A friendly game of chance to break the monotony—"

"You're a crook on wheels," the girl said bitterly, "and the lousiest monte operator that ever hit the road."

"My own daughter," the man said miserably. "My own daughter that got me into this lousy can—"

"How was I supposed to know it was a fake?" she flared. "And if you do die you won't die a junkie, by God!"

Oliver shook his head dazedly at their bickering.

"What will this young man think?" asked Stoss, with a try at laughing it off. "I can see he's a person of indomitable will behind his mild exterior, a person who won't let the chance word of a malicious girl keep him from indulging in a friendly—"

"Yeah! I might believe that if I hadn't been hearing you give that line to farm-hands and truck-drivers since I was seven. Now you're a cold-reader. My aching torso."

"Well," Stoss said with dignity, "*this* time I happened to have meant it."

Oliver's head was throbbing. An indomitable will behind a mild exterior. It rang a bell somewhere deep inside him—a bell that clanged louder and louder until he felt his very body dissolve under its impact.

He dismissed the bizarre fantasy. He was Dr. Oliver of Columbia. He was Dr. Oliver of Columbia. He had always been.

The Stosses had drifted to a window, still quarreling. Brockhaus said after a pause: "It's a funny thing. He was on heroin. You should see his arms. When he first got here he went around begging and yelling for a fix of dope because he *expected* that he'd want it. But after a few hours he realized that he didn't want it at all. For the first time in twelve years, he says. Maybe it was the shocks in the chair. Maybe they did it intentionally. I don't know. The girl—there's nothing wrong with her. She just came along to keep the old man company while he took the marvelous free cure."

A slight brunette woman with bangs was saying to him shyly: "Professor, I'm Mitty Worth. You may have heard of me—or not. I've had some pieces in the *New New Review*."

"Delighted," Dr. Oliver said. "How did they get *you?*"

Her mouth twisted. "I was doing the Michoacán ruins. There was a man—a very handsome man—who persuaded me that he had made an archaeological find, that it would take the pen of a poet to do it justice—" She shrugged. "What's your field, professor?"

"Jacobean prose writers."

Her face lit up. "Thank God for somebody to talk to. I'm specially interested in Tom Fuller myself. I have a theory, you know, about the *Worthies of England.* Everybody automatically says it's a grab-bag, you know, of everybody who happened to interest Fuller. But I think I can detect a definite *structure* in the book—"

Dr. Oliver of Columbia groped wildly in his memory. What was the woman running on about?

"I'm afraid I'm not familiar with the work," he said.

Mitty Worth was stunned.

"Or perhaps," Oliver said hastily, "I'm still groggy from the—the laboratory. Yes, I think that must be it."

"Oh," Mitty Worth said, and retreated.

Oliver sat and puzzled. Of course his specialty was the Jacobean prose writers. The foolish woman had made a mistake. Tom Fuller must be in another period. The *real* writers of Jacobean prose were—

Were—?

Dr. Oliver of Columbia, whose field was the Jacobean prose writers, didn't know any of them by name.

I'm going crazy, he decided wildly. I'm Oliver of Columbia. I wrote my thesis on—

What?

The old faker was quite right. He was an indomitable will behind a mild exterior, and a ringing bell had something to do with it, and so did a flashing light and a wobbling pendulum, and so did Marty Braun who could keep a tin can bouncing ten yards ahead of him as he walked firing from the hip, but Marty had a pair of star-gauge .44's and he wasn't a gun nut himself even if he could nip the ten-ring four out of five—

The world of Dr. Oliver was dissolving into delirium when his name was sharply called.

Everybody was looking at him as if he were something to be shunned, something with a curse laid on it. One of—them—was standing in the door. Dr. Oliver remembered what they could do. He got up hastily and hastily went through an aisle that cleared for him to the door as if by magic.

"Stand there," the man said to him. "The two Stoss people," he called. The old man and his daughter silently joined him.

"You must walk ahead of me," said the man.

They walked down the corridor and turned left at a command, and went through a handsome oak door into the sunlight. Gleaming in the sunlight was a vast disk-shaped thing.

Dr. Oliver of Columbia smiled suddenly and involuntarily. He knew now who he was and what was his mission.

He was Special Agent Charles Barker of Federal Security and Intelligence. He was in disguise—the most thorough disguise ever effected. His own personality had been obliterated by an unbroken month of narcohypnosis, and for another unbroken month a substitute personality, that of the ineffectual Dr. Oliver, had been shoved into his head by every mechanical and psychological device that the F.S.I. commanded. Twenty-four hours a day, waking and sleeping, records had droned in his ears and films had unreeled before his glazed drugged eyes, all pointing toward this moment of post-hypnotic revelation.

People vanished. People had always vanished. Blind Homer heard vague rumors and incorporated them in his repertory of songs about the recent war against the Trojans: vague rumors about a one-eyed thing that kidnapped men—to eat, of course.

People continued to vanish through the Roman Empire, the Middle Ages, the Renaissance, the growth of population and the invention of census machines. When the census machines were perfected, everything was known statistically about everybody, though without invasion of privacy, for the machines dealt in percentages and not personalities. Population loss could be accounted for; such and such a percentage died, and this percentage pigged it drunkenly in Riveredge, and that percentage deserted wife and kids for a while before it was inevitably, automatically traced—

And there was a percentage left over. People still vanished.

The F.S.I. noted that three cancer patients in Morningside Heights, New York, had vanished last year, so they gave (Temporary) Special Agent Charles Barker a cancer by nagging a harmless throat polyp with dyes and irritants, and installed him in Morningside Heights to vanish—and do something about it.

The man marched the two Stosses and Barker-Oliver into the spaceship.

Minutes later a smashing takeoff acceleration dashed them unconscious to the deck.

4

In an Earthly navy they would have called Gori "Guns" in the wardroom. He didn't look like an officer and a gentleman, or a human being for that matter, and the batteries of primary and secondary weapons he ruled over did not look like cannon. But Gori had a pride and a class feeling that would have made familiar sense in any navy. He voiced it in his needling of Lakhrut: a brother officer but no fighting man; a sweat-soaked ruler of the Propulsion Division whose station was between decks, screwing the last flicker of drive from the units.

Languidly Gori let his fingertips drift over a page of text; he was taking a familiarization course in propulsion. "I don't understand," he said to Lakhrut, "why one shouldn't treat the units with a little more formality. My gun-pointers, for example—"

Lakhrut knew he was being needled, but had to pretend otherwise. Gori was somewhat his senior. "Gun-pointers are one thing," he said evenly. "Propulsion units are another. I presume you've worked the globes."

Gori raised his fingers from the page in surprise. "Evidently you—people between decks don't follow the Games," he said. "I have a Smooth Award from the last meet but one."

"What class vessel?"

"Single-seater. And a beauty! Built to my orders, stripped to a bare hull microns in thickness."

"Then you know working the globes isn't easy. But—with all respect—I don't believe you know that working a globe under orders, shift after shift, with no stake in the job and no hope or relief ever is most infernally heartbreaking. You competed for the Smooth Award and won it and slept for a week, I dare say, and are still proud—don't misunderstand me: *rightly* proud—of the effort. But the propulsion units aren't competing for anything. They've been snatched away from their families—I'm not certain; I believe a family system prevails—and they *don't* like it. We must break them of that. Come and see the new units."

Gori reluctantly followed Lakhrut to the inport where unconscious figures were being stacked.

"Pah! They stink!" he said.

"A matter of diet. It goes away after they've been on our rations for a while."

Gori felt one of the figures curiously. "Clothes," he said in surprise. "I thought—"

Lakhrut told him wearily: "They have been wearing clothes for quite a while now. Some five thousand of their years." That had been a dig too. Gori had been reminding him that he was not greatly concerned with the obscure beasts between decks; that he, Lakhrut, must clutter his mind with such trivial details while Gori was splendidly free to man his guns if there should be need. "I'll go and see my driver," he snapped.

When he left, Gori sat down and laughed silently.

Lakhrut went between decks to the banks of units and swiftly scanned them. Number Seven was sleeping, with deep lines of fatigue engraved on his mind. He would be the next to go; indeed he should have been shot through the spacelock with Three, Eight-Female and Twelve. At the first opportunity— His driver approached.

"Baldwin," he snapped at the driver, "will you be able to speak with the new units?"

Baldwin, a giant who had been a mere propulsion unit six months ago and was fiercely determined never to be one again, said in his broken speech: "Believe it. Will make to understand somewise. They may not—converse—my language called English. Will make to understand somewise."

Barker awoke staring into dull-red lights that looked unbelievably like old-fashioned incandescent lamps. Beside him a girl was moaning with shock and fear. In the dull light he could make out her features: Ginny Stoss. Her father was lying unconscious with his head in her lap.

A brutal hand yanked him to his feet—there was gravity! But there was no time to marvel over it. A burly giant in a grey kilt was growling at him: "You speak English?"

"Yes. What's all this about? Where are we?"

He was ignored. The giant yanked Ginny Stoss to her feet and slapped her father into consciousness as the girl winced and Barker balled his fists helplessly. The giant said to the three of them: "My name's Baldwin. You call me mister. Come on."

He led them, the terrified girl, the dazed old man and the rage-choked agent, through spot-polished metal corridors to—

A *barber shop*, Barker thought wildly. Rows and rows of big adjustable chairs gleaming dully under the red lights, people sitting in them, at least a hundred people. And then you saw there was something archaic and ugly about the cup-shaped headrests fitted to the chairs. And then you saw that the people, men and women, were dirty, unkempt and hopeless-eyed, dressed in rags or nothing at all.

Ginny Stoss screamed sharply when she saw Lakhrut. He was not a pretty sight with his single bulging orb above the nose. It pointed at her and Lakhrut spat guttural syllables at Baldwin. The burly giant replied, cringing and stammering. The monster's orb aimed at Barker, and he felt a crawling on the surface of his brain—as if fingers were trying to grasp it.

Barker knew what to do; more important, he did it. He turned off Barker. He turned on Dr. Oliver, the erudite scared rabbit.

Lakhrut scanned them suspiciously. The female was radiating sheer terror; good. The older male was frightened too, but his sense of reality was clouded; he detected a faint undertone of humor. *That* would go. The younger man—Lakhrut stooped forward in a reflex associated with the sense of smell. The younger man—men?—no; man—the younger man—

Lakhrut stopped trying to scan him. He seemed to be radiating on two bands simultaneously, which was not possible. Lakhrut decided that he wasn't focusing properly, that somebody else's radiation was leaking and that the younger man's radiation was acting as a carrier wave for it. And felt vaguely alarmed and ashamed of himself. He ought to be a better scanner than he was.

"Baldwin," he said, "question that one closely."

The hulking driver asked: "You want name?"

"Of course not, fool! Question him about anything. I want to scan his responses."

Baldwin spoke to the fellow unintelligibly and the fellow replied unintelligibly. Lakhrut almost smiled with relief as the questioning progressed. The odd double-band effect was vanishing and the young man radiated simple fright.

Baldwin said laboriously: "Says is teacher of language and—tales of art. Says where is this and why have—"

"That's enough," he told the driver. "Install them." None of this group was dangerous enough to need killing.

"Sit there," Baldwin told Barker, jerking his thumb at an empty chair.

Barker felt the crawling fingers withdraw, and stifled a thought of triumph. They *had* him, this renegade and his cyclops boss. They had him like a bug underfoot to be squashed at a whim, but there had been some kind of test and he had bluffed them. Wearing the persona of Oliver, he quavered: "What *is* this terrible place, Mr. Baldwin? *Why* should I sit there?"

Baldwin moved in with a practiced ring shuffle and swung his open palm against the side of Barker's head. The agent cried out and nursed the burning cheek. Baldwin would never know how close he came that moment to a broken back ... .

He collapsed limply into the chair and felt it mold to him almost like a living thing. Plates slid under his thighs and behind his shoulder blades, accommodating themselves to his body.

"Just to show you nobody's fooling," Baldwin said grimly. He pressed a button on the chair and again something indescribably painful happened, wringing his bones and muscles to jelly for a timeless instant of torment. He did not faint; it was there and gone too quickly for the vascular system to make such an adjustment. He slumped in the chair, gasping.

Baldwin said: "Take hold of the two handles." He was surprised to find that he could move. He took hold of two spherical handles. They were cold and slimy-dry. Baldwin said: "You have to make the handles turn rough, like abrasive paper. You do it different ways. I can't tell you how. Everybody has a different way. Some people just concentrate on the handles. Other people just try to make their

minds a blank and that works for them. You just find your own way and do it
when we tell you to. Or you get the Pain again. That's all."

Barker heard him move down the line and repeat the speech in substantially
the same words to the Stosses.

Baldwin was no puzzle. He was just a turncoat bastard. The wrecked, ragged
men and women with lackluster eyes sitting around him were no puzzle. Not after the Pain. Baldwin's boss, the cyclops—

How long had this been going on? Since Homer?

He bore down on the spherical handles. Amazingly they went from silk-
smooth to paper-coarse and then to sandstone-gritty. Baldwin was back, peering
to look at an indicator of some unimaginable kind. "That's very good," the big
man said. "You keep that up and some day you'll get out of the chair like me."

Not like you, you bastard. Not like you. He choked down the thought. If the
boss were here it would have undone him.

There were mechanical squeals and buzzers. Those who were sleeping in their
chairs awoke instantly, with panic on their faces, visible even in the dim red light.

"All right," Baldwin was shouting. "*Give,* you bastards! Five seconds and we
cut you in. *Give,* Morgan, or it's the Pain! Silver, make it move! I ain't forgetting
anything, Silver—next time it's three jolts. Give, you bastards! *Give!*"

Barker gave in a frenzy of concentration. Under his sweaty palms the globes
became abrasive. In five seconds there was a thudding shock through his body
that left him limp. The globes went smooth and Baldwin was standing over him:
"Make it go, Oliver, or it's the Pain. Make it go."

Somehow, he did.

It seemed to go on for hours while the world rocked and reeled about him,
whether subjectively or objectively he could not tell. And at last there was the
roar: "Let it go now. Everybody off."

Racking vibration ceased and he let his head nod forward limply.

From the chair in front of him came an exhausted whisper: "He's gone now.
Some day I'm going to—"

"Can we talk?" Barker asked weakly.

"Talk, sing, anything you want." There was a muttering and stirring through
the big room. From the chair in front, hopefully: "You happen to be from Rupp
City? My family—"

"No," Barker said. "I'm sorry. What is all this? What are we doing?"

The exhausted whisper said: "All this is an armed merchantman of the
A'rkhov-Yar. We're running it. We're galley slaves."

5

Three feedings later the man from Rupp City leaped from his chair, howling, and
threw himself on a tangle of machinery in the center aisle. He was instantly elec-
trocuted.

Before he died he had told Barker in rambling, formless conversations that
he had it figured out; the star-people simply knew how to amplify psychokinetic

energy. He thought he could trace eighteen stages of amplification through the drive machinery.

The death was—a welcome break in the monotony. Barker was horrified to discover that was his principal reaction to it, but he was not alone.

They were fed water and moist yellow cakes that tasted like spoiled pork. Normally they worked three shifts in rotation. Only now and then were they all summoned for a terrific surge; usually they had only to keep steerage way on the vessel. But eight hours spent bearing down on the spherical handles, concentrating, was an endless agony of boredom and effort. If your attention wandered, you got the Pain. Barker got it five times in fifteen feedings. Others got it ten or twelve. Ginny Stoss was flighty of mind; she got it twenty times, and after that, never. She mumbled continuously after that and spent all her time in practice, fingering the handles and peering into the bad light with dim, monomaniac eyes.

There was an efficient four-holer latrine, used without regard to sex or privacy. Sex was a zero in their lives, despite the mingling of men and women. When they slept in their chairs, they slept. The Pain and then death were the penalties for mating, and also their energy was low. The men were not handsome and the women were not beautiful. Hair and beards grew and straggled—why not? Their masters ignored them as far as clothing went. If the things they wore when they came aboard fell apart, very well, they fell apart. They weren't going any place.

It was approximately eight hours working the globular handles, eight hours sleeping, and eight hours spent in rambling talk about the past, with many lies told of riches and fame. Nobody ever challenged a lie; why should they?

Bull-necked Mr. Baldwin appeared for feedings, but he did not eat with them. The feedings were shift-change time, and he spent them in harangues and threats.

Barker sucked up to Baldwin disgustingly, earning the hatred of all the other "units." But they knew next to nothing, and what he desperately needed was information. All they knew was that they had been taken aboard—a year ago? Six years ago? A month ago? They could only guess. It was impossible to keep track of time within the changeless walls of the room. Some of them had been taken directly aboard. Some had been conveyed in a large craft with many others and then put aboard. Some had served in other vessels, with propulsion rooms that were larger or smaller, and then put aboard. They had been told at one time or another that they were in the A'rkhov-Yar fleet, and disputed feebly about the meaning and pronunciation. It was more of a rumor than a fact.

Barker picked a thread from his tie each day to mark the days, and sucked up to Baldwin.

Baldwin liked to be liked, and pitied himself. "You think," he asked plaintively, "I'm inhuman? You think I want to drive the units like I do? I'm as friendly as the next guy, but it's dog eat dog, isn't it? If I wasn't driving I'd be in a chair getting driven, wouldn't I?"

"*I* can see that, Mr. Baldwin. And it takes character to be a leader like you are."

"You're Goddamned right it does. And if the truth was known, I'm the best friend you people have. If it wasn't me it'd be somebody else who'd be worse.

Lakhrut said to me once that I'm too easy on the units and I stood right up to him and said there wasn't any sense to wearing them out and not having any drive when the going gets hot."

"I think it's amazing, Mr. Baldwin, the way you picked up the language. That takes *brains*."

Baldwin beamed modestly. "Oh, it ain't too hard. For instance—"

Instruction began. It was not too hard, because Baldwin's vocabulary consisted of perhaps four hundred words, all severely restricted to his duties. The language was uninflected; it could have been an old and stable speech. The grammar was merely the word-order of logic: subject, verb, object. Outstandingly, it was a guttural speech. There were remnants of "tonality" in it. Apparently it had once been a sung language like Chinese, but had evolved even out of that characteristic. Phonemes that once had been low-toned were now sounded back in the throat; formerly high-toned phonemes were now forward in the throat. That sort of thing he had picked up from "Oliver."

Barker hinted delicately at it, and Baldwin slammed a figurative door in his face. "I don't know," he growled. "I don't go asking smart questions. You better not either."

Four more threads were snapped from the fringe of Barker's tie before Baldwin came back, hungry for flattery. Barker was on shift, his head aching with the pointless, endless, unspeakably dull act of concentration when the big man shook his shoulder and growled: "You can lay off. Seven, eight—it don't matter. The others can work harder."

He slobbered thanks.

"Ah, that's all right. I got a good side to me too, see? I said to Lakhrut once—"

And so on, while the other units glared.

"Mr. Baldwin, this word *khesor*, does it mean the whole propulsion set-up or the energy that makes it work? You say, '*Lakhrut a'g khesor-takh*' for 'Lakhrut is the boss of propulsion,' right?"

Baldwin's contempt was kindly. "For a smart man you can ask some God-damned stupid questions. What difference does it make?" He turned to inspect the globes for a moment and snarl at Ginny Stoss: "What's the matter with you? You want the Pain again? *Give!*"

Her lips moved in her endless mutter and her globe flared bright.

The bull-necked man said confidingly: "Of course I wouldn't really give her the Pain again. But you have to scare them a little from time to time."

"Of course, Mr. Baldwin. You certainly know psychology." *One of these days I'm going to murder you, you bastard.*

"Sure; it's the only way. Now, you know what *ga'lt* means?

"No, Mr. Baldwin."

The bull-necked pusher was triumphant. "There is no word for it in English. It's something they can do and we can't. They can look right into your head if they want to. '*Lakhrut ga'lt takh-lyur-Baldwin*' means 'Lakhrut looks right into underchief Baldwin's head and reads his mind.'"

"Do they do it all the time?"

"No. I think it's something they learn. I don't think all of them can do it either—or maybe not all of them learn to do it. I got a theory that Lakhrut's a *ga'lt* specialist."

"Why, Mr. Baldwin?"

Baldwin grinned. "To screen out troublemakers. No hard feelings, Oliver, but do you notice what a gutless bunch of people you got here? Not a rebel in a carload. Chicken-livered. Don't take it personal—either you got it or you don't."

"But *you*, Mr. Baldwin—why didn't the screening stop you?"

"I got a theory about that. I figure he let me through on purpose because they needed a hard guy to do just what I'm doing. After I got broke in on the globes it wasn't hardly any time at all before I got to be *takh-lyur*."

You're wrong, you bastard. You're the yellowest coward aboard.

"That must be it, Mr. Baldwin. They know a leader when they see one."

Four threads later he knew that he had acquired all of the language Baldwin had to give him. During his sleep period he went to old Stoss's chair. Stoss was on rest. He was saying vaguely to a grey-haired woman in the chair in front of his: "Boston, Atlanta, Kansas City—all the prominent cities of the nation, my dear lady. I went in with a deck of cards and came out of each with a diamond ring and a well-filled wallet. My hands were sure, my voice was friendly—"

"Atlanta," the woman sighed. "The Mathematics Teachers Association met there in '87, or was it '88? I remember gardens with old brick walls—or was that Charleston? Yes, I think it was Charleston."

"—In one memorable session of stud behind locked doors in the old Muehlebach Hotel I was high on the third card with the jack of clubs and the ten of diamonds, with the ace of clubs for my hole-card. Well, madam—"

"—We had terrible trouble in the school one year with the boys and girls gambling in the reactor room, and worse if you can believe it. The reactor man was their 'look-out,' so to speak, so naturally we tried to have him discharged. But the union wouldn't let—"

"—Well, madam, there was seven hundred-odd dollars in the pot—"

"Mr. Stoss," Barker said.

The old man studied him coolly for a moment and then said: "I don't believe I care to talk to you, sir. As I was saying, ma'am, there was—"

"I'm going to kill Baldwin," Barker told him.

He was instantly alert, and instantly scared. "But the danger," he whispered. "Won't they take it out on all of us? And he's a big brute—"

"So maybe he'll kill me. But I'm going to try. I want you to go to the latrine when Baldwin shows up next. Don't quite go in. Watch the corridor. If there's anybody coming, lift your hand. I'll only need a few seconds. Either way, it'll be finished by then."

"The danger," whispered Stoss. His eyes wandered to his daughter's chair. She was asleep. And her lips still moved in her endless muttering. "All right," the old man said at last. "I'll help you."

"Can you imagine that?" the woman said, still amazed after all these years. "The man was caught *in flagrante delicto,* so to speak, and the union wouldn't let the principal discharge him without a full public hearing, and naturally the publicity would have been most distasteful so we were forced to—"

Barker padded back to his chair, a gaunt man in stinking rags, wild-haired and sporting a beard in which grey hairs were beginning to appear.

There had to be a lookout. Three times since takeoff Lakhrut had appeared in the doorway for a moment to stare at the units. Twice other people had actually come into the room with Baldwin to probe through the tangle of machinery down the center aisle with long, slender instruments.

It might have been one hour; it might have been seven. Baldwin appeared, followed by the little self-propelled cart. It began to make its rounds, stopping at each chair long enough for the bottle of water and the dish of soggy cake to be picked off. Stoss, looking perfectly innocent, passed Barker's chair.

Barker got up and went to the pusher. Stoss was looking through the door, and did not wave. The cart clicked and rolled to the next chair. "Something wrong, Oliver?" Baldwin asked.

"I'm going to kill you, you bastard."

"*What?*" Baldwin's mouth was open, but he dropped into a fighter's crouch instinctively.

His ankle hooked behind Baldwin's foot. The bull-necked man threw a punch which he ducked, and tried to clinch when he butted him in the chest. Baldwin went sprawling into the tangle of machinery at the same spot where the man from Rupp City had fried. There were sparks and stench. Then it was over.

Baldwin's mouth was still open and his body contorted. Barker could imagine him saying: "You think I'm inhuman? You think I want to drive the units like I do?" And he could also imagine him roaring: "*Give,* Goddamn you!"

Steadily Barker went back to his seat in time for the cart to click by. Stoss, his face a perfect blank, padded back from the latrine. A murmur and stir grew louder in the big rectangular room.

6

Lakhrut was lying in his hammock in the dark, his fingers idly reading. It should have been a manual; instead it was a historical romance. His fingers skipped a half-page describing an old-style meal and slowed to absorb the description of the fight in which it ended.

"Yar raises his revolver charged with powder and ball. Who is so brave as Yar? He pulls back the trigger and presses the hammer of the death-dealing tube! The flash of flame shows the face of Lurg! But smoke from the tube obscures—"

His fingers jerked from the page as the commander's voice roared through his cubicle: "*Lakhrut!* Look to your units! We have no steerage way!"

He leaped from the hammock and raced through the vessel cursing Baldwin, the maintenance crew, the units and every soul on board.

He took in the situation at a glance. Baldwin lying spread-eagled and charred against the conversion grids. The units yammering and terrified in their chairs, none of them driving. Into a wall mike he snapped to the bridge: "My driver's dead, Commander. He got the charge from the conversion grids—"

"Stop your gabbing and give me power, you fool!"

Deathly pale, Lakhrut turned to the disorganized units and tried to talk to them in remembered scraps of English. (He should have worked more with his driver on it. He should have worked more.) They only gawked at him, and he swore in A'rkhov—

But one of the units was doing something that made sense. He was yelling in English, pointing to the chairs. And a dozen of the units resumed their places and began to drive, feebly at first and then better.

That was taken care of. He turned to the machinery and checked rapidly through the stages of amplification. They were clear; the commander, curse him, was getting his power. The fellow who had yelled at the units was standing by him when the inspection was completed. Startlingly, he said in A'rkhov, though with a fearsome accent: "Can I serve Lakhrut-*takh?*"

With considerable effort, Lakhrut scanned him. Obedience, fear, respect, compliance. All was well. He asked him coldly: "Who are you that you should speak the tongue?"

"Name is Oliver. I studied languages. Baldwin-*takh-lyur* taught me the tongue." Lakhrut scanned; it all was true.

"How did he die?"

"I did not see. Oliver was not looking. I was in darkness."

Asleep, was he trying clumsily to say? Lakhrut scanned. There was no memory of the death-scene in the scared, compliant mind of this unit. But something nagged Lakhrut and teased at his mind. "Did you kill him?" he snapped.

The flood of horror and weakness he scanned was indubitable. The unit babbled brokenly: "No, Lakhrut-*takh!* No! I could not kill! I could not kill!" Well, *that* was true enough. It had been a silly thing to ask.

"Take me," he said, "to each unit in turn and ask them whether they killed the *takh-lyur.*"

This Oliver did, and reported twenty-two denials while Lakhrut scanned each. Each was true; none of the twenty-two minds into which he peered was shuddering with the aftermath of murder; none seemed to have the killer's coldness and steel.

Lakhrut said to the wall mike: "Power is restored. I have established that my driver's death was accidental. I have selected a new driver from among the units." He turned off the mike after a curt acknowledgment and said to Oliver: "Did you understand? I meant you." At the mike again he called two maintenance men to clear the conversion grid and space the body.

"Establish unit shifts and then come with me," he told Oliver, and waited for the new driver to tell off the gangs. He ceased scanning; his head was aching abominably.

Barker felt the fingers leave his brain and breathed deeper. Dr. Oliver of Columbia, the whining incubus on him, was bad company. His own memory of the past few minutes was vague and fragmentary. In jittery terror Dr. Oliver had yelled at the units to man their chairs before they all were killed for disobedience. In abject compliance Dr. Oliver had placed himself at Lakhrut's orders. And he had heard that he would be the new slave-driver with almost tearful gratitude. To be shaved and clean again! To dine again! Barker wanted to spit. Instead he divided the units into new shifts and followed Lakhrut from the oblong room.

He washed and used a depilatory powder that burned horribly as the cyclops monster called Lakhrut silently watched. Somebody brought him shorts that fit. Apparently the concept of a uniform was missing—so even was style. He saw passing on the upper decks crew "men" in trousers, gowns, kilts and indescribable combinations of these. The only common note was simplicity and a queer, vulgar absence of dash, as if nobody cared what he looked like as long as the clothes didn't get in his way.

"That's enough," Lakhrut said, as Barker was trying to comb his wetted hair with his fingers. "Come with me."

Back between decks they went to a cubicle near the drive room—a combination of kitchen, cramped one-man office and hammock-space. Lakhrut briskly showed Barker how to draw and prepare the food for the units—it was the first time he suspected that Baldwin had cooked for them—and how to fill in a daily report on the condition of the units. It was hardly writing; he simply had to check a box in the appropriate column next to the unit's number. His "pen" flowed clear plastic which bonded to the paper in a raised ridge. The "printed" form was embossed with raised lines. Barker could make nothing of the numerals that designated the units or the column-headings; the alphabet rang no bells in his memory or the Oliver-memory. But that would come later.

The commander was winding up his critique, and his division officers were perspiring freely.

"As to the recent gun-drill, I have very little to say. What, gentlemen, *is* there to say about the state of training, the peak of perfection which enabled Gori-*takh*'s crews to unlimber, train and dryfire their primary and secondary batteries in a mere two hundred and thirty-six and eleven-twelfths *vistch?* I am sure the significance of this figure will be clear to us all when I point out that the average space engagement lasts one hundred and eighteen *vistch.* Is the significance clear to you, Gori-*takh?*"

"Yes, Commander," said the division officer, very pale.

"*Perfectly* clear?"

"Yes, Commander," Gori said, wishing he were dead.

"Good. Then we will go on to pleasanter subjects. Propulsion has been excellent and uninterrupted since our last meeting. Steerage way has been satisfactorily maintained, units are in reasonable health, mechanical equipment checks out between Satisfactory and Excellent. The surprise-drill calls for driving surges were responded to promptly and with vigor. Lakhrut-*takh,* you are to be commended."

He left the compartment on that note, and the division officers sprawled, sighed and gave other signs of release from tension.

Lakhrut said to Gori, with the proper blend of modesty and sympathetic blandness: "It's just luck, you know. Your bad luck and my good luck. I happen to have stumbled on the most extraordinary driver in the fleet. The fellow is amazing. He speaks the tongue, he's pitiless to the units, and he's wild to anticipate my every wish. He's even trying to learn the mechanism."

A *takh* vaguely corresponding to the Paymaster of a British naval vessel, with a touch of Chaplain and Purser thrown in, said: "What's that? Isn't there a *Yongsong* order about that? Perhaps I'd better—"

Lakhrut hastily balanced the benefit of a lie at this point against the chance that the *takh,* a master-scanner because of his office, might scan him for veracity. Since scanning of equals was bad manners and he felt himself the *takh's* equal at least after the commander's sweet words of praise, he lied. "'Trying' does not mean succeeding,'" he said, letting his voice sound a little hurt. "I'm surprised that you should think I'd let an Outworlder into our secrets. No; the man is merely cracking his brains over an obsolete manual or two of advanced theory. He can barely read, as I've repeatedly verified by scanning. His tactile memory barely exists. What brutes these Outlanders are! I doubt that they can tell fur from marble."

The *takh* said: "That is extremely unlikely in view of their fairly-advanced mechanical culture. Take me to him; I shall scan him."

Gori tried not to look exultant as Lakhrut, crestfallen, led the *takh* from the room.

The *takh* was somehow alarmed when he saw Lakhrut's driver. Even before scanning he could see that the fellow was tough. Vague thoughts of a spotter from Fleet Command or a plant from some enemy— or nominally friendly—fleet drifted through his head before he could clamp down on them. He said to the driver: "Who are you and what was your occupation?" And simultaneously he scanned deep.

The driver said: "Name is Oliver, *takh*. Teacher of language and letters."

The personality-integral included: Inferiority. ? Self-deprecation/Neurosis. ? … Weakling's job/Shame. ? Traumata … A light. A bell. A pendulum. Fear. Fear. Being buried, swallowed, engulfed.

The *takh* was relieved. There was no danger in such a personality-integral. But the matter of security—he handed the driver a fingering-piece, a charming abstraction by the great Kh'hora. It had cost him his pay for an entire tour of duty and it was quite worth it. Kh'hora had carved it at the height of his power, and his witty juxtapositions of textures were unsurpassed to this day. It could be fingered a dozen ways, each a brilliant variation on a classic theme.

The driver held it stupidly.

"Well?" demanded the *takh,* his brows drawing together. He scanned.

The driver said: "Please, *takh,* I don't know what to do with it."

The personality-integral included: Fear. Bewilderment. Ignorance. Blankness.

"Finger it, you fool!"

The driver fumbled at the piece and the *takh* scanned. The tactile impressions were unbelievably obtuse and blurry. There was no emotional response to them whatsoever except a faint, dull gratification at a smooth boss on the piece. And the imbecile kept *looking* at it.

It was something like sacrilege. The *takh* snatched the piece back indignantly. "Describe it," he said, controlling himself.

The fellow began to maunder about its visual appearance while the *takh* scanned. It was true; he had practically no tactile memory.

The *takh* left abruptly with Lakhrut. "You were right," he said. "If it amuses the fellow to pretend that he can read, I see no obstacle. And if it contributes to the efficiency of your department, we all shine that much brighter." (More literally, with fuller etymological values, his words could be rendered: "If it amuses the fellow to pretend that he fingers wisdom, my hands are not grated. And if it smoothes your quarry wall, we all hew more easily.")

Lakhrut's hands were not grated either; it was a triumphant vindication of his judgment.

And so, for departmental efficiency, he let his marvelous driver have all the books he wanted.

7

Barker's head ached and his eyes felt ready to fall out of their sockets. He did not dare take rubbings of the books, which would have made them reasonably legible. He had to hold them slantwise to the light in his cubicle and read the shadows of the characters. Lakhrut had taught him the Forty-Three Syllables, condescendingly; and the rest was up to him. He had made the most of it.

An imagery derived more from tactile than visual sense-impressions sometimes floored him with subtleties—as, he was sure, an intensely visual English nature poem would have floored Lakhrut. But he progressed.

Lakhrut had brought him a mish-mash of technical material and trashy novelettes—and a lexicon. The *takh* who had made such a fuss about the chipped pebble had brought him something like a Bible. Pay dirt!

It seems that in the beginning Spirit had created Man—which is what the A'rkhov-Yar called the A'rkhov-Yar—and set him to rule over all lesser creation. Man had had his ups and downs on the Planet, but Spirit had seen to it that he annihilated, after sanguinary, millennium-long battles, his principal rivals for the Planet. These appeared to have been twelve-footed brutes who fought with flint knives in their first four feet.

And then Spirit had sent the Weak People to the Planet in a spaceship. Schooled to treachery in the long struggle against the knife-wielding beasts, Man had greeted the Weak People with smiles, food and homage. The Weak People had foolishly taught them the art of writing, had foolishly taught Man their sciences. And then the Weak People had been slain, all twelve of them, in an hour of blood.

Barker somehow saw the Weak People as very tired, very gentle, very guile-less survivors of a planetary catastrophe beyond guessing. But the book didn't say.

So the A'rkhov-Yar stole things. Science. People. Let George do it, appeared to be their morality, and then steal it from George. Well, they'd had a hard up-bringing fighting down the Knifers, which was no concern of his. They'd been man-stealing for God knows how long; they'd made turncoats like the late Mister Baldwin, and judas goats like neat Miss Winston, disgusting creatures preying on their own kind.

From the varied reading matter he built up a sketchy picture of the A'rkhov-Yar universe. There were three neighboring stars with planetary systems, and the cyclopes had swarmed over them once the guileless Weak People had shown them spaceflight. First they had driven their own ships with their own wills. Then they had learned that conquered races could be used equally well, so they had used them. Then they learned that conquered races tended to despair and die out.

"Then," he said savagely to old man Stoss, "they showed the one flash of creative intelligence in their career—unless they stole it from one of their subjects. They invaded Earth—secretly. Without knowing it, we're their slave-breeding pen. If we knew it, we'd either fight and win, or fight and lose—and die out in despair."

"The one flash?" Stoss asked dryly, looking about them at the massive ma-chinery.

"Stolen. All stolen. They have nations, trades and wars—but this is a copy of the Weak People's ship; all their ships are. And their weapons are the meteor screens and sweepers of the Weak People. With stolen science they've been steal-ing people, I think at a rate of thousands per year. God knows how long it's been going on—probably since the neolithic age. You want proof of their stupidity? The way they treat us. It leads to a high death rate and fast turnover. That's bad engineering, bad economics and bad housekeeping. Look at the lights they use—low-wattage incandescents! As inefficient lamps as were ever designed—"

"I've got a thought about those lights," Stoss said. "The other day when Lakhrut was inspecting and you were passing out the food I took two cakes in-stead of one—just to keep in practice. I used sleight of hand, misdirection—but Lakhrut didn't misdirect worth a damn. He slapped the pain button and I put the extra cake back. What does it mean when the hand is quicker than the eye but the sucker isn't fooled?"

"I don't get you."

"What if those aren't very inefficient lamps but very efficient heaters?"

"They're blind," whispered Barker. "My God, you've got to be right! The lamps, the tactile culture, the embossed writing. And that thing that looks like an eye—it's their mind-reading organ, so it can't be an eye after all. You can't perform two radically different functions with the same structure."

"It's worth thinking about," old man Stoss said.

"I could have thought about it for a million years without figuring that out, Stoss. How did you do it?"

The old man looked modest. "Practice. Long years of it. When you want to take a deacon for a long score on the con game, you study him for his weaknesses. You don't assume he hasn't got any just because he's a deacon, or a doctor, or a corporation treasurer. Maybe it's women, or liquor, or gambling, or greed. You just play along, what interests him interests you, everything he says is wise and witty, and sooner or later he lets you know what's his soft spot. Then, lad, you've got him. You make his world revolve around his little weakness. You cater to it and play it up and by and by he gets to thinking that you're the greatest man in the world, next to him, and the only real friend he'll ever have. Then you 'tell the tale,' as we say. And the next sound you hear is the sweetest music this side of Heaven, the squealing of a trimmed sucker."

"You're a revolting old man," said Barker, "and I'm glad you're here."

"I'm glad you're here too," the old man said. And he added with a steady look: "Whoever you are."

"You might as well know. Charles Barker—F.S.I. agent. They fished me out of the Riveredge gutter because I may or may not have telepathic flashes, and they put me on the disappearance thing."

Stoss shook his head unhappily. "At my age, cooperating with the F.S.I. I'll never live it down."

Barker said: "They've got sound to go on, of course. They hear movements, air currents. They carry in their heads a sound picture—but it isn't a 'picture'; damn language!—of their environment. They can't have much range or discrimination with that sense; too much noise hashing up the picture. They're probably heat-detectors, too. If bedbugs and mosquitoes can use heat for information, so can these things. Man could do it too if he had to, but we have eyes. The heat-sense must be short range too; black-body radiation falls off proportional to the fourth power of the distance. It's beginning to fit together. They don't go *very* near those incandescent bulbs ever, do they? They keep about a meter distant?"

"Yes, I've noticed that. Anything closer must be painful to the heat sense— 'blinding,' you might say."

"Then that leaves their telepathy. That specialist came into this room to examine me, which tells us something about the range. Something—but not enough."

Stoss said: "A person might pretend to throw something at one of them from a distance of ten yards. If the creature didn't notice, we'd know they don't have a ten-yard range with sound, heat or telepathy. And the next day he could try it at nine yards. And so on, until it noticed."

"And blew the person in half with those side-arms they carry," said Barker. "Who volunteers for the assignment, Stoss?"

"Not I," the old man said hastily. "Let's be practical. But perhaps I could persuade Miss Trimble?"

"The math teacher? Hell, no. If things work out, we're going to need all the mathematical talent we've got."

They conferred quietly, deciding which of their fellow-Earthmen could be persuaded to sacrifice himself. The choice fell on a nameless, half-mad youngster in the third seat of the second tier; he spoke to nobody and glared suspiciously over his food and drink.

"But can you do it?" asked Barker.

Stoss was offended. "In my time," he said, "I've taken some fifty-five really big scores from suckers. I've persuaded people who love money better than life itself to turn their money over to me, and I've sent them to the bank for more."

"Do your best," Barker said.

What approach the old swindler did use, he never learned. But the next day Third Seat, Second Tier, rose during the doling out of the food and pretended to hurl his plate at Lakhrut. The cyclops, ten meters away, stalked serenely on and the young man collapsed in an ecstasy of fright.

The next day it was eight yards.

The next day six.

And other things filled the days: the need for steady driving of the ship, and whispered consultations up and down the benches.

They needed a heat source, something that would blaze at 500 degrees, jangling, dazzling and confusing the senses of their captors. But it was an armed merchantman, a warship, and warships have nothing on board that will burn. Their poor clothing heaped together and somehow ignited would make a smoldering little fire, doing more damage to the human beings by its smoke than to the A'rkhov-Yar by its heat.

Barker went exploring in the cargo spaces. Again and again he was passed in the corridors by crew "men." Huddling against the glowing bulbs, choking down his rage and fear, he imitated the paint on the walls, and sometimes they broke their stride for a puzzled moment, sometimes not.

In a cargo space on the next day he found cases labeled with worms of plastic as "attention sticks" or possibly "arresting or halting tubes."

They were the close equivalent of railroad flares in appearance. He worked the tight-fitting cap of one to the point where he felt gritty friction. A striking surface—but he did not dare strike and test it. These things would have to put out hundreds of degrees of heat, or, if they were intended for use at any appreciable distance, thousands. They were thermal shrieks; they would be heard from one end of the ship to the other. In three trips he smuggled 140 of the sticks back to the propulsion room. Stoss helped him distribute them among the seats. He grimly told the lackluster eyes and loose mouths: "If anybody pulls off one of the caps before I say so, I am going to hit the pain button and hold it down for five minutes."

They understood it for the death threat it was.

"Today's the day, I think," said Stoss in a whisper as Lakhrut made his benevolent entrance. "He sensed something yesterday at four meters. Today it's going to be three."

Barker pushed his little food cart, fingering the broken-off knob of a propulsion chair resting on its lower tray. He moved past Third Seat, Second Tier,

Lakhrut behind him. The mad young man rose, picked up his plate and pretended to throw it at the cyclops.

Lakhrut drew his side-arm and blew the young man's head into a charred lump. "Oliver!" he cried, outraged. "Why did you not report that one of your units was becoming deranged? You should have put him through the spacelock days ago!"

"Oliver's" reply was to pace off a precise four meters and hurl the broken-off knob at the monster. He took a full windup, and rage for five thousand years of slavery and theft drove his muscles. The cyclops eye broke and spilled; the cyclops staggered in circles; screaming. Barker closed in, twisted the side-arm from the monster's convulsed hand and gave him what Third Seat, Second Tier, had got.

The roomful of men and women rose in terror, screaming.

"Quiet!" he yelled at them. "I've talked to some of you about this. You saw what happened. Those things are blind! You can strike them from five yards away and they'll never know what hit them."

He snatched up one of the fusees and rasped off the cap; it began to flare pulsatingly, not very bright, but intensely hot. He held it at arm's length and it scorched the hair on the back of his hand. "These things will dazzle what sensory equipment they do have," he yelled, "and you can confuse them with noise. They'll be coming to get us in a minute. All you have to do is make noise and mill around. You'll see what happens when they come for us—and then we'll go hunting!"

In less than a minute his prediction was verified. A squad of the cyclops crew burst in, and the screaming of the Earth people left nothing to be desired; the creatures recoiled as if they had struck a wall. From six meters away Barker and the Stosses carefully ignited the flares and tossed them into the squad. They made half-hearted efforts to fire into the source of the trouble, but they were like men in a darkened boiler works—whose darkness was intermittently relieved by intolerable magnesium flares. Lakhrut's side-arm made short work of the squad.

Barker ripped their weapons from their fingers and demanded: "Who wants one? Who wants to go hunting? Not you, Miss Trimble; we'll need you for later. Stay in a safe place. Who's ready for a hunting party?"

One by one, twitching creatures remembered they were men and came up to take their weapons.

The first hunting party worked its way down a corridor, hurling fusees, yelling and firing. The bag was a dozen cyclopes, a dozen more weapons.

They met resistance at a massive door with a loophole. Blasts from a hand weapon leaped through the loophole, blind but deadly. Three of them fell charging the door.

"Warm it up for them," Stoss said. He snatched a dozen fusees, ducked under the fire and plastered himself against the door. Meticulously he uncapped the sticks and leaned them against the door, one by one. The blast of heat drove Barker and his party back down the corridor. Stoss did not collapse until he had ignited the last flare and wrenched open the door with a seared hand.

Through the door could be seen staggering cyclops figures, clawing blindly at the compartment walls. The Earthmen leaped through the brief, searing heat of the dozen flares and burned them down.

In the A'rkhov-Yar language, a terrified voice spoke over the ship public address system: "To the leader of the rebels! To the leader of the rebels! Return to your propulsion room and your crimes will be forgiven! Food will be doubled and the use of the Pain discontinued!"

Barker did not bother to translate. "Let's head for the navigation room," he said. "Try to save a couple of them."

One hour later he was telling the commander and Gori: "You two will set courses for Earth. You will work separately, and if your results don't agree we will put you each in a chair and hold down the button until you produce results that do agree. We also have a lady able to check on your mathematics, so don't try anything."

"You are insane," said the commander. "Other ships will pursue and destroy you."

"Other ships," Barker corrected him, "will pursue and fail to overtake us. I doubt very much that slave ships can overtake a ship driven by free men and women going home."

"We will attack openly for this insolence," snorted Gori. "Do you think you can stand against a battle fleet? We will destroy your cities until you've had enough, and then use you as the slaves you are."

"I'm sure you'll try," said Barker. "However, all I ask is a couple of weeks for a few first-rate Ph.D.'s to go over this ship and its armaments. I believe you'll find you have a first-rate war on your hands, gentlemen. We don't steal; we *learn*.

"And now, if you please, start figuring that course. *You're* working for *us* now."

[*Stirring Science Stories* - June 1941
as by Kenneth Falconer]

The Words of Guru

Yesterday, when I was going to meet Guru in the woods a man stopped me and said: "Child, what are you doing out at one in the morning? Does your mother know where you are? How old are you, walking around this late?"

I looked at him, and saw that he was white-haired, so I laughed. Old men never see; in fact men hardly see at all. Sometimes young women see part, but men rarely ever see at all. "I'm twelve on my next birthday," I said. And then, because I would not let him live to tell people, I said, "and I'm out this late to see Guru."

"Guru?" he asked. "Who is Guru? Some foreigner, I suppose? Bad business mixing with foreigners, young fellow. Who is Guru?"

So I told him who Guru was, and just as he began talking about cheap magazines and fairy-tales I said one of the words that Guru taught me and he stopped talking. Because he was an old man and his joints were stiff, he didn't crumple up but fell in one piece, hitting his head on the stone. Then I went on.

Even though I'm going to be only twelve on my next birthday, I know many things that old people don't. And I remember things that other boys can't. I remember being born out of darkness, and I remember the noises that people made about me. Then when I was two months old I began to understand that the noises meant things like the things that were going on inside my head. I found out that I could make the noises too, and everybody was very much surprised. "Talking!" they said, again and again. "And so very young! Clara, what do you make of it?" Clara was my mother.

And Clara would say: "I'm sure I don't know. There never was any genius in my family, and I'm sure there was none in Joe's." Joe was my father.

Once Clara showed me a man I had never seen before, and told me that he was a reporter—that he wrote things in newspapers. The reporter tried to talk to me as if I were an ordinary baby, I didn't even answer him, but just kept looking at him until his eyes fell and he went away. Later Clara scolded me and read me a little piece in the reporter's newspaper that was supposed to be funny—about the reporter asking me very complicated questions and me answering with baby-noises.

196

It was not true, of course. I didn't say a word to the reporter, and he didn't ask me even one of the questions.

I heard her read the little piece, but while I listened I was watching the slug crawling on the wall. When Clara was finished I asked her: "What is that grey thing?"

She looked where I pointed, but couldn't see it. "What grey thing, Peter?" she asked. I had her call me by my whole name, Peter, instead of anything silly like Petey. "What grey thing?"

"It's as big as your hand, Clara, but soft. I don't think it has any bones at all. It's crawling up, but I don't see any face on the topwards side. And there aren't any legs."

I think she was worried, but she tried to baby me by putting her hand on the wall and trying to find out where it was. I called out whether she was right or left of the thing. Finally she put her hand right through the slug. And then I realized that she really couldn't see it, and didn't believe it was there. I stopped talking about it then and only asked her a few days later: "Clara, what do you call a thing which one person can see and another person can't?"

"An illusion, Peter," she said. "If that's what you mean." I said nothing, but let her put me to bed as usual, but when she turned out the light and went away I waited a little while and then called out softly. "Illusion! Illusion!"

At once Guru came for the first time. He bowed, the way he always has since, and said: "I have been waiting."

"I didn't know that was the way to call you," I said.

"Whenever you want me I will be ready. I will teach you, Peter—if you want to learn. Do you know what I will teach you?"

"If you will teach me about the grey thing on the wall," I said, "I will listen. And if you will teach me about real things and unreal things I will listen."

"These things," he said thoughtfully, "very few wish to learn. And there are some things that nobody ever wished to learn. And there are some things that I will not teach."

Then I said: "The things nobody has ever wished to learn I will learn. And I will even learn the things you do not wish to teach."

He smiled mockingly. "A master has come," he said, half-laughing. "A master of Guru."

That was how I learned his name. And that night he taught me a word which would do little things, like spoiling food.

From that day to the time I saw him last night, he has not changed at all, though now I am as tall as he is. His skin is still as dry and shiny as ever it was, and his face is still bony, crowned by a head of very coarse, black hair.

When I was ten years old I went to bed one night only long enough to make Joe and Clara suppose I was fast asleep. I left in my place something which appears when you say one of the words of Guru and went down the drainpipe outside my window. It always was easy to climb down and up, ever since I was eight years old.

I met Guru in Inwood Hill Park. "You're late," he said.

"Not too late," I answered. "I know it's never too late for one of these things."

"How do you know?" he asked sharply. "This is your first."

"And maybe my last," I replied. "I don't like the idea of it. If I have nothing more to learn from my second than my first, I shan't go to another."

"You don't know," he said. "You don't know what it's like—the voices, and the bodies slick with unguent, leaping flames; mind-filling ritual! You can have no idea at all until you've taken part."

"We'll see," I said. "Can we leave from here?"

"Yes," he said. Then he taught me the word I would need to know, and we both said it together.

The place we were in next was lit with red lights, and I think that the walls were of rock. Though of course there was no real seeing there, and so the lights only seemed to be red, and it was not real rock.

As we were going to the fire one of them stopped us. "Who's with you?" she asked, calling Guru by another name. I did not know that he was also the person bearing that name, for it was a very powerful one.

He cast a hasty, sidewise glance at me and then said: "This is Peter of whom I have often told you."

She looked at me then and smiled, stretching out her oily arms. "Ah," she said, softly, like the cats when they talk at night to me. "Ah, this is Peter. Will you come to me when I call you, Peter? And sometimes call for me—in the dark—when you are alone?"

"Don't do that!" said Guru, angrily pushing past her. "He's very young—you might spoil him for his work."

She screeched at our backs: "Guru and his pupil—fine pair! Boy, he's no more real than I am—you're the only real thing here!"

"Don't listen to her," said Guru. "She's wild and raving. They're always tight-strung when this time comes around."

We came near the fires then, and sat down on rocks. They were killing animals and birds and doing things with their bodies. The blood was being collected in a basin of stone, which passed through the crowd. The one to my left handed it to me. "Drink," she said, grinning to show me her fine, white teeth. I swallowed twice from it and passed it to Guru.

When the bowl had passed all around we took off our clothes. Some, like Guru, did not wear them, but many did. The one to my left sat closer to me, breathing heavily at my face. I moved away. "Tell her to stop, Guru," I said. "This isn't part of it, I know."

Guru spoke to her sharply in their own language, and she changed her seat, snarling.

Then we all began to chant, clapping our hands and beating our thighs. One of them rose slowly and circled about the fires in a slow pace, her eyes rolling wildly. She worked her jaws and flung her arms about so sharply that I could hear the elbows crack. Still shuffling her feet against the rock floor, she bent her body backwards down to her feet. Her belly-muscles were bands nearly standing out from her skin, and the oil rolled down her body and legs. As the palms of her hands touched the ground, she collapsed in a twitching heap and began to set up a thin wailing noise against the steady chant and hand beat that the rest of us were keeping up. Another of them did the same as the first, and we chanted louder for her and still louder for the third. Then, while we still beat our hands and thighs, one of them took up the third, laid her across the altar and made her ready with a stone knife. The fire's light gleamed off the chipped edge of obsidian. As her blood drained down the groove, cut as a gutter into the rock of the altar, we stopped our chant and the fires were snuffed out.

But still we could see what was going on, for these things were, of course, not happening at all—only seeming to happen, really, just as all the people and things there only seemed to be what they were. Only I was real. That must be why they desired me so.

As the last of the fires died Guru excitedly whispered: "The Presence!" He was very deeply moved.

From the pool of blood from the third dancer's body there issued the Presence. It was the tallest one there, and when it spoke its voice was deeper, and when it commanded its commands were obeyed.

"Let blood!" it commanded, and we gashed ourselves with flints. It smiled and showed teeth bigger and sharper and whiter than any of the others.

"Make water!" it commanded, and we all spat on each other. It flapped its wings and rolled its eyes, which were bigger and redder than any of the others.

"Pass flame!" it commanded, and we breathed smoke and fire on our limbs. It stamped its feet, let blue flames roar from its mouth, and they were bigger and wilder than any of the others.

Then it returned to the pool of blood and we lit the fires again. Guru was staring straight before him; I tugged his arm. He bowed as though we were meeting for the first time that night.

"What are you thinking of?" I asked. "We shall go now."

"Yes," he said heavily. "Now we shall go." Then we said the word that had brought us there.

The first man I killed was Brother Paul, at the school where I went to learn the things that Guru did not teach me.

It was less than a year ago, but it seems like a very long time. I have killed so many times since then.

"You're a very bright boy, Peter," said the brother.

"Thank you, brother."

"But there are things about you that I don't understand. Normally I'd ask your parents but—I feel that they don't understand either. You were an infant prodigy, weren't you?"

"Yes, brother."

"There's nothing very unusual about that—glands, I'm told. You know what glands are?"

Then I was alarmed. I had heard of them, but I was not certain whether they were the short, thick green men who wear only metal or the things with many legs with whom I talked in the woods.

"How did you find out?" I asked him.

"But Peter! You look positively frightened, lad! I don't know a thing about them myself, but Father Frederick does. He has whole books about them, though I sometimes doubt whether he believes them himself."

"They aren't good books, brother," I said. "They ought to be burned."

"That's a savage thought, my son. But to return to your own problem—"

I could not let him go any further knowing what he did about me. I said one of the words Guru taught me and he looked at first very surprised and then seemed to be in great pain. He dropped across his desk and I felt his wrist to make sure, for I had not used that word before. But he was dead.

There was a heavy step outside and I made myself invisible. Stout Father Frederick entered, and I nearly killed him too with the word, but I knew that that would be very curious. I decided to wait, and went through the door as Father Frederick bent over the dead monk. He thought he was asleep.

I went down the corridor to the book-lined office of the stout priest and, working quickly, piled all his books in the center of the room and lit them with my breath. Then I went down to the schoolyard and made myself visible again when there was nobody looking. It was very easy. I killed a man I passed on the street the next day.

There was a girl named Mary who lived near us. She was fourteen then, and I desired her as those in the Cavern out of Time and Space had desired me.

So when I saw Guru and he had bowed, I told him of it, and he looked at me in great surprise. "You are growing older, Peter," he said.

"I am, Guru. And there will come a time when your words will not be strong enough for me."

He laughed. "Come, Peter," he said. "Follow me if you wish. There is something that is going to be done—" He licked his thin, purple lips and said: "I have told you what it will be like."

"I shall come," I said. "Teach me the word." So he taught me the word and we said it together.

The place we were in next was not like any of the other places I had been to before with Guru. It was No-place. Always before there had been the seeming passage of time and matter, but here there was not even that. Here Guru and the others cast off their forms and were what they were, and No-place was the only place where they could do this.

It was not like the Cavern, for the Cavern had been out of Time and Space, and this place was not enough of a place even for that. It was No-place.

What happened there does not bear telling, but I was made known to certain ones who never departed from there. All came to them as they existed. They had not color or the seeming of color, or any seeming of shape.

There I learned that eventually I would join with them; that I had been selected as the one of my planet who was to dwell without being forever in that No-place.

Guru and I left, having said the word.

"Well?" demanded Guru, staring me in the eye.

"I am willing," I said. "But teach me one word now—"

"Ah," he said grinning. "The girl?"

"Yes," I said. "The word that will mean much to her."

Still grinning, he taught me the word.

Mary, who had been fourteen, is now fifteen and what they call incurably mad.

Last night I saw Guru again and for the last time. He bowed as I approached him. "Peter," he said warmly.

"Teach me the word," said I.

"It is not too late."

"Teach me the word."

"You can withdraw—with what you master you can master also this world. Gold without reckoning; sardonyx and gems, Peter! Rich crushed velvet—stiff, scraping, embroidered tapestries!"

"Teach me the word."

"Think, Peter, of the house you could build. It could be of white marble, and every slab centered by a winking ruby. Its gate could be of beaten gold within and without and it could be built about one slender tower of carven ivory, rising mile after mile into the turquoise sky. You could see the clouds float underneath your eyes."

"Teach me the word."

"Your tongue could crush the grapes that taste like melted silver. You could hear always the song of the bulbul and the lark that sounds like the dawnstar made musical. Spikenard that will bloom a thousand thousand years could be ever in your nostrils. Your hands could feel the down of purple Himalayan swans that is softer than a sunset cloud."

"Teach me the word."

"You could have women whose skin would be from the black of ebony to the white of snow. You could have women who would be as hard as flints or as soft as a sunset cloud."

"Teach me the word!"

Guru grinned and said the word.

Now, I do not know whether I will say that word, which was the last that Guru taught me, today or tomorrow or until a year has passed.

It is a word that will explode this planet like a stick of dynamite in a rotten apple.

[*Stirring Science Stories* - February 1941
as by Cecil Corwin]

Thirteen O'Clock

1

Peter Packer excitedly dialed his slide rule, peering through a lens as one of the minutely scored lines met with another. He rose from his knees, brushing dust from the neat crease of his serge trousers. No doubt of it—the house had a secret attic room. Peter didn't know anything about sliding panels or hidden buttons; in the most direct way imaginable he lifted the axe he had brought and crunched it into the wall.

On his third blow he holed through. The rush of air from the darkness was cool and sweet. Smart old boy, his grandfather, thought Peter. Direct ventilation all over the house—even in a false compartment. He chopped away heartily, the hollow strokes ringing through the empty attic and down the stairs.

He could have walked through the hole erect when he was satisfied with his labors; instead he cautiously turned a flashlight inside the space. The beam was invisible; all dust had long since settled. Peter grunted. The floor seemed to be sound. He tested it with one foot, half in, half out of the hidden chamber. It held.

The young man stepped through easily, turning the flash on walls and floor. The room was not large, but it was cluttered with a miscellany of objects—chests, furniture, knickknacks and whatnots. Peter opened a chest, wondering about pirate gold. But there was no gold, for the thing was full to the lid with chiffons in delicate hues. A faint fragrance of musk filled the air; sachets long since packed away were not entirely gone.

Funny thing to hide away, thought Peter. But Grandfather Packer had been a funny man—having this house built to his own very sound plans, waiting always on the Braintree docks for the China and India clippers and what rare cargo they might have brought. Chiffons! Peter poked around in the box for a moment, then closed the lid again. There were others.

He turned the beam of the light on a wall lined with shelves. Pots of old workmanship—spices and preserves, probably. And a clock. Peter stared at the clock. It was about two by two by three feet—an unusual and awkward size. The workmanship was plain, the case of crudely finished wood. And yet there was something about it—his eyes widened as he realized what it was. The dial showed thirteen hours!

Between the flat figures XII and I there was another—an equally flat XIII. What sort of freak this was the young man did not know. Vaguely he conjectured on prayer time, egg boiling and all the other practical applications of chronometry. But nothing he could dredge up from his well-stored mind would square with this freak. He set the flash on a shelf and hefted the clock in his arms, lifting it easily.

This, he thought, would bear looking into. Putting the light in his pocket, he carried the clock down the stairs to his second-floor bedroom. It looked strangely incongruous there, set on a draftsman's table hung with rules and T-squares. Determinedly, Peter began to pry open the back with a chisel, when it glided smoothly open without tooling. There was better construction in the old timepiece than he had realized. The little hinges were still firm and in working order. He peered into the works and ticked his nail against one of the chimes. It sounded sweet and clear.

The young man took up a pair of pliers. Lord knew where the key was, he thought, as he began to wind the clock. Slowly it got under way, ticking loudly. The thing had stopped at 12:59. That would be nearly one o'clock on any other timepiece; on this, the minute hand crept slowly toward the enigmatic XIII.

Peter wound the striking mechanism carefully, and watched as a little whir sounded. The minute hand met the Roman numeral, and with a click the chimes sounded out in an eerie, jangling discord. Peter thought with sudden confusion that all was not as well with the clock as he had thought. The chimes grew louder, filling the little bedroom with their clang.

Horrified, the young man put his hands on the clock as though he could stop off the noise. As he shook the old cabinet, the peals redoubled until they battered against the eardrums of the draftsman, ringing in his skull and resounding from the walls, making instruments dance and rattle on the drawing board. Peter drew back, his hands to his ears. He was filled with nausea, his eyes bleared and smarting. As the terrible clock thundered out its din without end, he reached the door feebly, the room swaying and spinning about him, nothing real but the suddenly glowing clock dial and the clang and thunder of its chimes.

As he opened the door it ceased, and he closed his eyes in relief as his nausea passed. He looked up again, and his eyes widened with horror. Though it was noon outside, a night wind fanned his face, and though he was on the second-story landing of his Grandfather Packer's house, dark trees rose about him, stretching as far as the eye could see.

For three hours—by his wristwatch's luminous dial—Peter had wandered, aimless and horrified, waiting for dawn. The aura of strangeness that hung over the forest in which he walked was bearable; it was the gnawing suspicion that he had gone mad that shook him to his very bones. The trees were no ordinary things, of that he was sure. For he had sat under one forest giant and leaned back against its bole only to rise with a cry of terror. He had felt its pulse beat slowly and regularly under the bark. After that he did not dare to rest, but he was a young and normal male. Whether he would or not, he found himself blundering into ditches and stones from sheer exhaustion. Finally, sprawled on the ground, he slept.

Peter awoke stiff and sore from his nap on the bare ground, but he felt better for it. The sun was high in the heavens; he saw that it was about eleven o'clock. Remembering his terrors of the night, he nearly laughed at himself. This was a forest, and there were any number of sane explanations of how he had got here. An attack of amnesia lasting about twelve hours would be one cause. And there were probably others less disturbing.

He thought the country might be Maine. God knew how many trains or buses he had taken since he lost his memory in his bedroom. Beginning to whistle, he strode through the woods. Things were different in the daytime.

There was a sign ahead! He sprinted up to its base. The thing was curiously large, painted in red characters on a great slab of wood, posted on a dead tree some twelve feet from the ground. The sign said: ELLIL. He rolled the name over in his mind and decided that he didn't recognize it. But he couldn't be far from a town or house.

Ahead of him sounded a thunderous grunt.

Bears! he thought in a panic. They had been his childhood bogies; he had been frightened of them ever since. But it was no bear, he saw. He almost wished it was. For the thing that was veering on him was a frightful composite of every monster of mythology, menacing him with saber-like claws and teeth and gusts of flame from its ravening throat. It stood only about as high as the man, and its legs were long, but to the engineer it seemed ideally styled for destruction.

Without ado he jumped for a tree and dug his toes into the grooves of the bark, shinning up it as he used to as a child. But there was nothing childlike about it now. With the creature's flaming breath scorching his heels, he climbed like a monkey, stopping only at the third set of main branches, twenty-five feet from the ground. There he clung, limp and shuddering, and looked down.

The creature was hopping grotesquely about the base of the tree, its baleful eyes on him. The man's hand reached for a firmer purchase on the branch, and part came away in his hand. He had picked a sort of coconut—heavy, hard, and with sharp corners. Peter raised his eyebrows. Why not? Carefully noting the path that the creature below took around the trunk, he poised the fruit carefully. Wetting a finger, he adjusted the placing. On a free drop that long you had to allow for windage, he thought.

Twice more around went the creature, and then its head and the murderous fruit reached the same point at the same time. There was a crunching noise which Peter could hear from where he was, and the insides of its head spilled on the forest sward.

"Clever," said a voice beside him on the branch.

He turned with a cry. The speaker was only faintly visible—the diaphanous shadow of a young girl, not more than eighteen, he thought.

Calmly it went on, "You must be very mancic to be able to land a fruit so accurately. Did he give you an extra sense?" Her tone was light, but from what he could see of her dim features, they were curled in an angry smile.

Nearly letting go of the branch in his bewilderment, he answered as calmly as he could, "I don't know whom you mean. And what is mancic?"

"Innocent," she said coldly. "Eh? I could push you off this branch without a second thought. But first you tell me where Almarish got the model for you. I might turn out a few myself. Are you a doppelgänger or a golem?"

"Neither," he spat, bewildered and horrified. "I don't even know what they are!"

"Strange," said the girl. "I can't read you." Her eyes squinted prettily and suddenly became solid, luminous wedges in her transparent face. "Well," she sighed, "let's get out of this." She took the man by his elbow and dropped from the branch, hauling him after her. Ready for a sickening impact with the ground, Peter winced as his heels touched it light as a feather. He tried to disengage the girl's grip, but it was hard as steel.

"None of that," she warned him. "I have a blast finger. Or didn't he tell you?"

"What's a blast finger?" demanded the engineer.

"Just so you won't try anything," she commented. "Watch." Her body solidified then, and she pointed her left index finger at a middling-sized tree. Peter hardly saw what happened, being more interested in the incidental miracle of her face and figure. But his attention was distracted by a flat crash of thunder and sudden glare. And the tree was riven as if by a terrific stroke of lightning. Peter smelled ozone as he looked from the tree to the girl's finger and back again.

"No nonsense?" she asked.

"Okay," he said.

"Come on."

They passed between two trees, and the vista of forest shimmered and tore, revealing a sort of palace—all white stone and maple timbers.

"That's my place," said the girl.

2

"Now," she said, settling herself into a cane-backed chair.

Peter looked about the room. It was furnished comfortably with pieces of antique merit, in the best New England tradition. His gaze shifted to the girl, slender and palely luminous, with a half-smile playing about her chiseled features.

"Do you mind," he said slowly, "not interrupting until I'm finished with what I have to say?"

"A message from Almarish? Go on."

And at that he completely lost his temper. "Listen, you snip!" he raged. "I don't know who you are or where I am, but I'd like to tell you that this mystery isn't funny or even mysterious—just downright rude. Do you get that? Now—my name is Peter Packer. I live in Braintree, Mass. I make my living as a consulting and industrial engineer. This place obviously isn't Braintree, Mass. Right? Then where is it?"

"Ellil," said the girl simply.

"I saw that on a sign," said Packer. "It still doesn't mean anything to me. Where is Ellil?"

Her face became suddenly grave. "You may be telling the truth," she said thoughtfully. "I do not know yet. Will you allow me to test you?"

"Why should I?" he snapped.

"Remember my blast finger?"

Packer winced. "Yes," he said. "What are the tests?"

"The usual," she smiled. "Rosemary and garlic, crucifixes and the secret name of Jehovah. If you get through those you're okay."

"Then get on with it," the man said confusedly.

"Hold these." She passed him a flowery sprig and a clove of garlic. He took them, one in each hand.

"All right?" he asked.

"Oh, those, yes. Now take the cross and read this name. You can put the vegetables down now."

He followed instructions, stammering over the harsh Hebrew word.

In a cold fury the girl sprang to her feet and leveled her left index finger at him. "Clever," she blazed. "But you can't get away with it! I'll blow you so wide open—"

"Wait," he pleaded. "What did I do?" The girl, though sweet-looking, seemed to be absolutely irresponsible.

"Mispronounced the name," she snapped. "Because you can't say it straight without crumbling into dust!"

He looked at the paper again, and read aloud, slowly and carefully. "Was that right?" he asked.

Crestfallen, the girl sat down. "Yes," she said. "I'm sorry. You seem to be okay. A real human. Now what do you want to know?"

"Well—who are you?"

"My name's Millicent." She smiled deprecatingly. "I'm a—sort of a sorceress."

"I can believe that," grunted the man. "Now, why should you take me for a demon, or whatever you thought I was?"

"Doppelgänger," she corrected him. "I was sure—well, I'd better begin at the beginning.

"You see, I haven't been a sorceress very long—only two years. My mother was a witch—a real one, and pretty first class. I've heard it said that she brewed the neatest spells in Ellil. All I know I learned from her—never studied it formally. My mother didn't die a natural sort of death, you see. Almarish got her."

"Who's Almarish?"

She wrinkled her mouth with disgust. "That thug!" she spat. "He and his gang of half-breed demons are out to get control of Ellil. My mother wouldn't stand for it—she told him so, right out flat over a multiplex apparition. And after that he was gunning for her steadily—no letup at all. And believe me, there are mighty few witches who can stand up under much of that, but Mother stood him off for fifteen years. They got my father—he wasn't much good—a little while after I was born. Vampires.

"Mother got caught alone in the woods one morning without her tools—unguents, staffs and things—by a whole flock of golems and zombies." The girl shuddered. "Some of them—well, Mother finished about half before they overwhelmed her and got a stake of myrtle through her heart. That finished her—she lost all her magic, of course, and Almarish sent an ordinary plague of ants against her. Adding insult to injury, I call it!" There were real tears of rage in her eyes.

"And what's this Almarish doing now?" asked Peter, fascinated.

Millicent shrugged. "He's after me," she said simply. "The bandur you killed was one of my watchdogs. And I thought he'd sent you. I'm sorry."

"I see," breathed the man slowly. "What powers has he?"

"The usual, I suppose. But he has no principles about using them. And he has his gang—I can't afford real retainers. Of course I whip up some simulacra whenever I hold a reception or anything of that sort. Just images to serve and take wraps. They can't fight."

Peter tightened his jaw: "You must be in a pretty bad way," he volunteered diffidently.

The girl looked him full in the eye, her lip trembling. She choked out, "I'm in such a hell of a spot!" and then the gates opened and she was weeping as if her heart would break.

The man stared frozenly, wondering how he could comfort a despondent sorceress. "There, there," he said tentatively.

She wiped her eyes and looked at him. "I'm sorry," she said, sniffling. "But it's seeing a fairly friendly face again after all these years—no callers but leprechauns and things. You don't know what it's like."

"I wonder," said Peter, "how you'd like to live in Braintree."

"I don't know," she said brightly. "But how could I get there?"

"There should be at least one way," reflected the man.

"But why— What was that?" shot out the girl, snatching up a wand.

"Knock on the door," said Peter. "Shall I open it?"

"Please," said Millicent nervously, holding up the slender staff.

The man stood aside and swung the door wide. In walked a curious person of mottled red and white coloring. One eye was small and blue, the other large and savagely red. His teeth were quite normal—except that the four canines protruded two inches each out of his mouth. He walked with a limp; one shoe seemed curiously small. And there was a sort of bulge in the trousers that he wore beneath his formal morning coat.

"May I introduce myself?" said this individual, removing his sleek black topper. "I am Balthazar Pike. You must be Miss Millicent? And this—ah—zombie?" He indicated Peter with a dirty leer.

"Mr. Packer, Mr. Pike," said the girl.

Peter simply stared in horror while the creature murmured, "Enchanted."

Millicent drew herself up proudly. "And this, I suppose," she said, "is the end?"

"I fear so, Miss Millicent," said the creature regretfully. "I have my orders. Your house has been surrounded by picked forces; any attempt to use your blast finger or any other weapon of offense will be construed as resistance. Under the laws of civilized warfare we are empowered to reduce you to ashes should such resistance be forthcoming. May I have your reply?"

The girl surveyed him haughtily, then, with a lightning-like sweep of her wand, seemed to blot out every light in the room. Peter heard her agitated voice. "We're in a neutral screen, Mr. Packer. I won't be able to keep it up for long. Listen! That was one of Almarish's stinkers—the big cheese. He didn't expect any trouble from me. He'll take me captive as soon as they break the screen down. Do you want to help me?"

"Of course!" exploded the man.

"Good. Then you find the third oak from the front door on the left and walk widdershins three times. You'll find out what to do from them."

"Walk how?" asked Peter.

"Widdershins—counterclockwise. Lord, you're dumb!"

Then the lights seemed to go on again, and Peter saw that the room was filled with the half-breed creatures. With an expression of injured dignity, the formally attired Balthazar Pike asked, "Are you ready to leave now, Miss Millicent? Quite ready?"

"Thank you, General, yes," said the girl coldly. Two of the creatures took her arms and walked her from the room. Peter saw that as they stepped over the threshold they vanished, all three.

The last to leave was Pike, who turned and said to the man, "I must remind you, Mister—er—ah—that you are trespassing. This property now belongs to the Almarish Realty Corporation. All offenders will be prosecuted to the fullest extent of the law. Good day, Mister—er—ah—" With which he stepped over the doorsill and vanished.

Hastily Peter followed him across the line, but found himself alone outside the house. For which he was grateful. "Third oak left from the door," he repeated. Simple enough. Feeling foolish, he walked widdershins three times around and stopped dead, waiting for something.

What a sweet, brave kid she had been! He hoped nothing would really happen to her—before he got there.

He felt a sort of tugging at his serge trousers and stepped back in alarm. "Well?" shrilled a small voice. Peter looked down and winced. The dirtiest, most bedraggled little creature he had ever seen was regarding him with tiny, sharp eyes. There were others, too, squatting on pebbles and toadstools.

"Miss Millicent told me to ask you what I should do," said Peter. As the little leader of the troop glared at him, he added hastily, "If you please."

"Likely tale," piped the voice of the creature. "What's in it for us?"

"I dunno," said the man, bewildered. "What do you want?"

"Green cloth," the creature answered promptly. "Lots of it. And if you have any small brass buttons, them, too."

Peter hastily conducted an inventory of his person. "I'm sorry," he said hesitantly. "I haven't any green. How about blue? I can spare my vest." He carefully lowered the garment to the ground among the little people.

"Looks all right," said the leader. "Jake!" One of the creatures advanced and fingered the cloth. "Hmm—" he said. "Good material." Then there was a whispered consultation with the leader, who at last shouted up to Peter, "Head east for water. You can't miss it!"

"Hey!" said Peter, blinking. But they were already gone. And though he widdershin-walked for the next half hour, and even tried a few incantations remembered from his childhood, they did not come back—nor did his vest.

So, with his back to the sinking sun, he headed east for water.

3

The sign said: MAHOORA CITY LIMITS.

Peter scratched his head and passed it. He had hit the stretch of highway a few miles back, once he had got out of the forest, and it seemed to be leading straight into a city of some kind. There was a glow ahead in the sky—a glow which abruptly became a glare.

"Jeepers!" the man gasped. "Buildings—skyscrapers!" Before him reared a sort of triple Wall Street with which were combined the most spectacular features of Rockefeller Center. In the sudden way in which things happened in Ellil, he turned a sort of blind corner in the road and found himself in the thick of it.

A taxi roared past him; with a muttered imprecation he jumped out of the way. The bustling people on the sidewalks ignored him completely. It was about six o'clock; they were probably going home from their offices. There were all sorts of people—women and girls, plain and pretty, men and boys, slim, fat, healthy and dissipated. And there, Peter saw striding along in lordly indifference, was a cop.

"Excuse me," said Peter, elbowing his way through the crowd to the member of Mahoora's finest. "Can you tell me where I can find water?" That was, he realized, putting it a bit crudely. But he was hopelessly confused by the traffic and swarms of pedestrians.

The cop turned on him with a glassy stare. "Water?" he rumbled. "Would yez be wantin' tap, ditch, fire—or cologne?"

The man hesitated. He didn't know, he realized in a sudden panic. The elves, or whatever they had been, hadn't specified. Cagily he raised his hand to his brow and muttered, "'Scuse me—previous engagement—made the appointment for today—just forgot—" He was edging away from the cop when he felt a hand on his arm.

"What was that about water?" asked the cop hoarsely, putting his face near Peter's.

Desperately the man blurted, "The water I have to find to lick Almarish!" Who could tell? Maybe the cop would help him.

"What?" thundered M.P.D. Shield No. 2435957607. "And me a loyal supporter of the Mayor Almarish Freedom, Peace and Progress Reform Administration?" He frowned. "You look subversive to me—come on!" He raised his night-stick suggestively, and Peter meekly followed him through the crowds.

"How'd they get you in here?" asked Peter's cellmate.

Peter inspected him. He was a short, dark sort of person with a pair of disconcertingly bright eyes. "Suspicion," said Peter evasively. "How about you?"

"Practicing mancy without a license, theoretically. Actually because I tried to buck the Almarish machine. You know how it is."

"Can't say I do," answered Peter. "I'm a stranger here."

"Yeah? Well—like this. Few years ago we had a neat little hamlet here. Mahoora was the biggest little city in these parts of Ellil, though I say it myself. A little industry—magic chalices for export, sandals of swiftness, invisibility cloaks, invincible weapons—you know?"

"Um," said Peter noncommittally.

"Well, I had a factory—modest little chemical works. We turned out love philters from my own prescription. It's what I call a neat dodge—eliminates the *balneum mariae* entirely from the processing, cuts down drying time—maybe you aren't familiar with the latest things in the line?"

"Sorry, no."

"Oh—well, then, in came these plugs of Almarish's. Flying goon squads that wrecked plants and shops on order, labor spies, provocateurs, everything. Soon they'd run out every racketeer in the place and hijacked them lock, stock and barrel. Then they went into politics. There was a little scandal about buying votes with fairy gold—people kicked when it turned into ashes. But they smoothed that over when they got in.

"And then—! Graft right and left, patronage, unemployment, rotten-food scandals, bribery, inefficiency—everything that's on the list. And this is their fifth term. How do you like that?"

"Lord," said Peter, shocked. "But how do they stay in office?"

"Oh," grinned his friend. "The first thing they did was to run up some pretty imposing public works—tall buildings, bridges, highways and monuments. Then they let it out that they were partly made of half-stuff. You know what that is?"

"No," said Peter. "What is it?"

"Well—it's a little hard to describe. But it isn't really there and it isn't really not there. You can walk on it and pick it up and things, but—well, it's a little hard to describe. The kicker is this: half-stuff is there only as long as you—the one who prepared a batch of it, that is—keep the formula going. So if we voted those leeches out of office, they'd relax their formula and the half-stuff would vanish and the rest of the buildings and bridges and highways and monuments would fall with a helluva noise and damage. How do you like that?"

"Efficiency plus," said Peter. "Where's this Almarish hang out?"

"The mayor?" asked his cellmate sourly. "You don't think he'd be seen in the city, do you? Some disgruntled citizen might sic a flock of vampires on His Honor. He was elected in absentia. I hear he lives around Mal-Tava way."

"Where's that?" asked Peter eagerly.

"You don't know? Say, you're as green as they come! That's a pretty nasty corner of Ellil—the nastiest anywhere, I guess. It's a volcanic region, and those lava nymphs are pretty tough molls. Then there's a dragon ranch down there. The owner got careless and showed up missing one day. The dragons broke out and ran wild; they're the killingest you could hope to see. Anything else?"

"No," said Peter, heavyhearted. "I guess not."

"That's good. Because I think we're going to trial right now."

A guard was opening the door, club poised. "His Honor, Judge Balthazar Pike, will see you now," said the warden. Peter groaned.

The half-breed demon, his sartorial splendor of the preceding afternoon replaced by judiciary black silk, smiled grimly on the two prisoners. "Mr. Morden," he said, indicating the erstwhile love-philter manufacturer, "and Mister er—ah—?"

"Packer!" exploded the man. "What are you doing here?"

"Haw!" laughed the judge. "That's what I was going to ask you. But first we have this matter of Mr. Morden to dispose of. Excuse me a moment? Clerk, read the charges."

A cowed-looking little man picked an index card from a stack and read, "Whereas Mr. Percival Morden of Mahoora has been apprehended in the act of practicing mancy and whereas this Mr. Morden does not possess an approved license for such practice it is directed that His Honor Chief Judge Balthazar Pike declare him guilty of the practice of mancy without a license. Signed, Mayor Almarish. Vote straight Freedom Peace and Progress Reform Party for a clean and efficient administration." He paused for a moment and looked timidly at the judge, who was cleaning his talons. "That's it, Your Honor," he said.

"Oh—thank you. Now, Morden—guilty or not guilty?"

"What's the difference?" asked the manufacturer sourly. "Not guilty, I guess."

"Thank you." The judge took a coin from his pocket. "Heads or tails?" he asked.

"Tails," answered Morden. Then, aside to Peter, "It's magic, of course. You can't win."

The half-breed demon spun the coin dexterously on the judicial bench; it wobbled, slowed, and fell with a tinkle. The judge glanced at it. "Sorry, old man," he said sympathetically. "You seem to be guilty. Imprisonment for life in an oak tree. You'll find Merlin de Bleys in there with you. You'll like him, I rather fancy. Next case," he called sharply as Morden fell through a trapdoor in the floor.

Peter advanced before the bar of justice. "Can't we reason this thing out?" he asked agitatedly. "I mean, I'm a stranger here and if I've done anything I'm sorry—"

"Tut!" exclaimed the demon. He had torn the cuticle of his left index talon, and it was bleeding. He stanched the green liquid with a handkerchief and looked down at the man. "Done anything?" he asked mildly. "Oh—dear me, no! Except for a few trifles like felonious impediment of an officer in the course of his duty, indecent display, seditious publication, high treason and unlawful possession of military and naval secrets—done anything?" His two odd eyes looked reproachfully down on the man.

Peter felt something flimsy in his hand. Covertly he looked down and saw a slip of blue paper on which was written in green ink: *This is Hugo, my other watchdog. Feed him once a day on green vegetables. He does not like tobacco. In haste, Millicent.*

There was a stir in the back of the courtroom, and Peter turned to see one of the fire-breathing horrors which had first attacked him in the forest tearing down the aisle, lashing out to right and left, incinerating a troop of officers with one blast of its terrible breath. Balthazar Pike was crawling around under his desk, bawling for more police.

Peter cried, "You can add one more—possession of a bandur without a license! Sic 'em, Hugo!"

The monster flashed an affectionate look at him and went on with the good work of clearing the court. The man sprang aside as the trapdoor opened beneath his feet, and whirled on a cop who was trying to swarm over him. With a quick one-two he laid him out and proceeded to the rear of the courtroom, where Hugo was standing off a section of the fire department that was trying to extinguish his throat. Peter snatched an axe from one and mowed away heartily. Resistance melted away in a hurry, and Peter pushed the hair out of his eyes to find that they were alone in the court.

"Come on, boy," he said. Whistling cheerily, he left the building, the bandur at his heels, smoking gently. Peter collared a cop—the same one who had first arrested him. "Now," he snarled, "where do I find water?"

Stuttering with fright, and with two popping eyes on the bandur, the officer said, "The harbor's two blocks down the street if you mean—"

"Never mind what I mean!" growled Peter, luxuriating in his new-found power. He strode off pugnaciously, Hugo following.

4

"I beg your pardon—are you looking for water?" asked a tall, dark man over Peter's shoulder. Hugo growled and let loose a tongue of flame at the stranger's foot.

"Shuddup, Hugo," said Peter. Then, turning to the stranger, "As a matter of fact, I was. Do you—?"

"I heard about you from them," said the stranger. "You know. The little people."

"Yes," said Peter. "What do I do now?"

"Underground railroad," said the stranger. "Built after the best Civil War model. Neat, speedy and efficient. Transportation at half the usual cost. I hope you weren't planning to go by magic carpet?"

"No," Peter assured him hastily. "I never use them."

"That's great," said the stranger, swishing his long black cloak. "Those carpet people—stifling industry, I call it. They spread a whispering campaign that our road was unsafe! Can you imagine it?"

"Unsafe," scoffed Peter. "I'll bet they wish their carpets were half as safe as your railroad!"

"Well," said the stranger thoughtfully, "perhaps not half as safe ... . No, I wouldn't say half as safe ... ." He seemed likely to go on indefinitely.

Peter asked, "Where do I get the Underground?"

"A little east of here," said the stranger. He looked about apprehensively. "We'd better not be seen together," he muttered out of the corner of his mouth. "Meet you over there by the clock tower—you can get it there."

"Okay," said Peter. "But why the secrecy?"

"We're really underground," said the stranger, walking away.

Peter rejoined him at the corner of the clock tower. With an elaborate display of unconcern the stranger walked off, Peter following at some distance. Soon they were again in the forest that seemed to border the city of Mahoora.

Once they were past the city-limits sign the stranger turned, smiling. "I guess we're safe now," he said. "They could try a raid and drag us back across the line, but they wouldn't like to play with your bandur, I think. Here's the station."

He pressed a section of bark on a huge tree; silently it slid open like a door. Peter saw a row of steps leading down into blackness. "Sort of spooky," he said.

"Not at all! I have the place ghostproofed once a year." The stranger led the way, taking out what looked like a five-branched electric torch.

"What's that?" asked Peter, fascinated by the weird blue light it shed.

"Hand of glory," said the stranger casually. Peter looked closer and shuddered, holding his stomach. Magic, he thought, was probably all right up to the point where it became grave robbery.

They arrived at a neatly tiled station; Peter was surprised to find that the trains were tiny things. The one pulled up on the tracks was not as high as he was.

"You'll have to stoke, of course," said the stranger.

"What?" demanded Peter indignantly.

"Usual arrangement. Are you coming or aren't you?"

"Of course—but it seems strange," complained Peter, climbing into the engine. Hugo climbed into the coal car and curled up, emitting short smoky bursts of flame, which caused the stranger to keep glancing at him in fear for his fuel.

"What's in the rest of the train?" asked Peter.

"Freight. This is the through cannonball to Mal-Tava. I have a special shipment for Almarish. Books and things, furniture, a few cases of liquor—you know?"

"Yes. Any other passengers?"

"Not this month. I haven't much trouble with them. They're usually knights and things out to kill sorcerers like Almarish. They take their horses along or send them ahead by carpet. Do you plan to kill Almarish?"

Peter choked. "Yes," he finally said. "What's it to you?"

"Nothing—I take your money and leave you where you want to go. A tradesman can't afford opinions. Let's get up some steam, eh?"

Amateurishly Peter shoveled coal into the little furnace while the stranger in the black cloak juggled with steam valves and levers. "Don't be worried," he advised Peter. "You'll get the hang of things after a while." He glanced at a watch. "Here we go," he said, yanking the whistle cord.

The train started off into its tunnel, sliding smoothly and almost silently along, the only noise being from the driving rods. "Why doesn't it clack against the rails?" asked Peter.

"Levitation. Didn't you notice? We're an inch off the track. Simple, really."

"Then why have a track?" asked Peter.

The stranger smiled and said, "Without—" then stopped abruptly and looked concerned and baffled. And that was all the answer Peter got.

"Wake up," shouted the stranger, nudging Peter. "We're in the war zone!"

"Zasso?" asked Peter, blinking. He had been napping after hours of steady travel. "What war zone?"

"Trolls—you know."

"No, I don't!" snapped Peter. "What side are we on?"

"Depends on who stops us," said the stranger, speeding the engine. They were out of the tunnel now, Peter saw, speeding along a couple of inches above the floor of an immense dim cave. Ahead, the glittering double strand of the track stretched into the distance.

"Oh—oh!" muttered the cloaked stranger. "Trouble ahead!"

Peter saw a vague, stirring crowd before them. "Those trolls?" he asked.

"Yep," answered the engineer resignedly, slowing the train. "What do you want?" he asked a solid-looking little man in a ragged uniform.

"To get the hell out of here," said the little man. He was about three feet tall, Peter saw.

"What happened?" he asked.

"The lousy Insurgents licked us," said the troll. "Will you let us on the train before they cut us down?"

"First," said the engineer methodically, "there isn't room. Second, I have to keep friends with the party in power. Third, you know very well that you can't be killed."

"What if we are immortal?" asked the troll agitatedly. "Would you like to live forever scattered in little pieces?"

"Second," said Peter abruptly, "you can get out of it as best you can." He was speaking to the engineer. "And first, you can dump all the freight you have for Almarish. He won't want it anyway when I'm through with him."

"That right?" asked the troll.

"Not by me!" exploded the engineer. "Now get your gang off the track before I plow them under!"

"Hugo," whispered Peter. With a lazy growl the bandur scorched the nape of the engineer's neck.

"All right," said the engineer. "All right. Use force—all right." Then, to the leader of the trolls, "You tell your men they can unload the freight and get as comfortable as they can."

"Wait!" interjected Peter. "Inasmuch as I got you out of this scrape—I think—would you be willing to help me out in a little affair of honor with Almarish?"

"Sure!" said the troll. "Anything at all. You know, for a surface-dweller you're not half bad." With which he began to spread the good news among his army.

Later, when they were all together in the cab, taking turns with the shovel, the troll introduced himself as General Skaldberg of the Third Loyalist Army. They were steaming ahead again at full speed.

The end of the cavern was in sight when another swarm of trolls blocked the path. "Go through them!" ordered Peter coldly.

"For pity's sake," pleaded the stranger. "Think of what this will do to my franchise!"

"That's your worry," said the general. "You fix it up with the Insurgents. We gave you the franchise anyway—they have no right of search."

"Maybe," muttered the engineer. He closed his eyes as they went slapping into the band of trolls under full steam. When it was all over and they were again tearing through the tunnel, he looked up. "How many?" he asked brokenly.

"Only three," said the general regretfully. "Why didn't you do a good job while you were at it?"

"You should have had your men fire from the freight cars," said the engineer coldly.

"Too bad I didn't think of it. Could you turn back and take them in a surprise attack?"

The engineer cursed violently, giving no direct answer. But for the next half hour he muttered to himself distraitly, groaning "Franchise!" over and over again.

"How much farther before we get to Mal-Tava?" asked Peter glumly.

"Very soon now," said the troll. "I was there once. Very broken terrain—fine for guerrilla work."

"Got any ideas on how to handle the business of Almarish?"

The general scratched his head. "As I remember," he said slowly, "I once thought it was a pushover for some of Clausewitz's ideas. It's a funny tactical problem—practically no fortifications within the citadel—everything lumped outside in a wall of steel. Of course Almarish probably has a lot on the ball personally. All kinds of direct magic at his fingertips. And that's where I get off with my men. We trolls don't even pretend to know the fine points of thaumaturgy. Mostly straight military stuff with us."

"So I have to face him alone?"

"More or less," said the general. "I have a couple of guys that majored in Military Divination at Ellil Tech Prep. They can probably give you a complete layout of the citadel, but they won't be responsible for illusions, multiplex apparitions or anything else Almarish might decide to throw in the way. My personal advice to you is—be skeptical."

"Yes?" asked Peter miserably.

"Exactly," said Skaldberg. "The real difficulty in handling arcane warfare is in knowing what's there and what ain't. Have you any way of sneaking in a confederate? Not a spy, exactly—we military men don't approve of spying—but a sort of—ah—one-man intelligence unit."

"I have already," said Peter diffidently. "She's a sorceress, but not much good, I think. Has a blast finger, though."

"Very good," grunted Skaldberg. "Very good indeed. God, how we could have used her against the Insurgents! The hounds had us in a sort of peninsular spot—with only one weak line of supply and communication between us and the main force—and I was holding a hill against a grand piquet of flying carpets that were hurling thunderbolts at our munitions supply. But their sights were away off and they only got a few of our snipers. God, what a blast finger would have done to those bloody carpets!"

The engineer showed signs of interest. "You're right!" he snapped. "Blow 'em out of the sky—menace to life and limb! I have a bill pending at the All Ellil Conference on Communication and Transportation—would you be interested?"

"No," grunted the general. The engineer, swishing his long black cloak, returned to his throttle, muttering about injunctions and fair play.

5

"Easy, now!" whispered the general.

"Yessir," answered a troll, going through obvious mental strain while his hand, seemingly of its own volition, scrawled lines and symbols on a sheet of paper. Peter was watching, fascinated and mystified, as the specialist in military divination was doing his stuff.

"There!" said the troll, relaxing. He looked at the paper curiously and signed it: *Borgenssen, Capt.*

"Well?" asked General Skaldberg excitedly. "What was it like?"

The captain groaned. "You should see for yourself, sir!" he said despondently. "Their air force is flying dragons and their infantry's a kind of Kraken squad. What they're doing out of water I don't know."

"Okay," said the general. He studied the drawing. "How about their mobility?"

"They haven't got any and they don't need any," complained the diviner. "They just sit there waiting for you—in a solid ring. And the air force has a couple of auxiliary rocs that pick up the Krakens and drop them behind your forces. Pincer stuff—very bad."

"I'll be the judge of that!" thundered the general. "Get out of my office!" The captain saluted and stumbled out of the little cave which the general had chosen to designate as GHQ. His men were "barracked" on the bare rock outside. Volcanoes rumbled and spat in the distance. There came one rolling crash that stood Peter's hair on end.

"Think that was for us?" he asked nervously.

"Nope—I picked this spot for lava drainage. I have a hundred men erecting a shutoff at the only exposed point. We'll be safe enough." He turned again to the map, frowning. "This is our real worry—what I call impregnable, or damn near it.

If we could get them to attack us—but those rocs smash anything along that line. We'd be cut off like a rosebud. And with our short munitions we can't afford to be discovered and surrounded. Ugh! What a spot for an army man to find himself in!"

A brassy female voice asked, "Somep'n bodderin' you, shorty?"

The general spun around in a fine purple rage. Peter looked in horror and astonishment on the immodest form of a woman who had entered the cave entirely unperceived—presumably by some occult means. She was a slutty creature, her hair dyed a vivid red and her satin skirt quite a few inches above the knee. She was violently made up with flame-colored rouge, lipstick and even eye shadow.

"Well," she complained stridently, puffing on a red cigarette, "wadda you joiks gawkin' at? Aincha nevva seen a lady befaw?"

"Madam—" began the general, outraged.

"Can dat," she advised him easily. "I hoid youse guys chewin' da fat—I wanna help youse out." She seated herself on an outcropping of rock and adjusted her skirt—northward.

"I concede that women," spluttered the general, "have their place in activities of the military—but that place has little or nothing to do with warfare as such! I demand that you make yourself known. Where did you come from?"

"Weh did I come from?" she asked mockingly. "Weh, he wansa know. Lookit dat!" She pointed one of her bright-glazed fingernails at the rocky floor of the cave, which grew liquid in a moment, glowing cherry red. She leered at the two and spat at the floor. It grew cold in another moment. "Don't dat mean nothin' to youse?" she asked.

The general stared at the floor. "You must be a volcano nymph."

"Good fa you, shorty!" she sneered. "I represent da goils from Local Toity-Tree. In brief, chums, our demands are desc: one, dat youse clear away from our union hall pronto; two, dat youse hang around in easy reach—in case we want youse fa poiposes of our own. In retoin fa dese demands we—dat's me an' da goils—will help youse guys out against Almarish. Dat lousy fink don't give his hands time off no more. Dis place might as well be a goddam desert fa all da men around. Get me?"

"These—ah—purposes of your own in clause two," said the general hesitantly. "What would they be?"

She smiled dirtily and half-closed her eyes. "Escort soivice, ya might call it. Nuttin' harmful ta yer men, Cap. We'll probably get tired of dem in a munt' or two and send dem off safe. You trolls are kinda cute."

The general stared, too horrified even to resent being called "Cap."

"Well?" demanded the nymph.

"Well—yes," said the general.

"Okay, shorty," she said, crushing out her cigarette against her palm. "Da goils'll be aroun' at dawn fa da attack. I'll try ta keep 'em off yer army until da battle's over. So long!" She sank into the earth, leaving behind only a smell of fleur-de-floozy perfume.

"God!" whispered General Skaldberg. "The things I do for the army!"

In irregular open formation the trolls advanced, followed closely by the jeering mob of volcano nymphs.

"How about it, General?" asked Peter. He and the old soldier were surveying the field of battle from a hill in advance of their forces; the hideous octopoid forms of the defenders of Almarish could be plainly seen, lumbering onward to meet the trolls with a peculiar sucking gait.

"Any minute now—any second," said Skaldberg. Then, "Here it comes!" The farthest advanced of the trolls had met with the first of the Krakens. The creature lashed out viciously; Peter saw that its tentacles had been fitted with studded bands and other murderous devices. The troll dodged nimbly and pulled an invincible sword on the octopoid myth. They mixed it; when the struggle went behind an outcropping of rock the troll was in the lead, unharmed, while the slow-moving Kraken was leaking thinly from a score of punctures.

"The dragons," said Peter, pointing. "Here they are." In V formation the monsters were landing on a far end of the battlefield, then coming at a scrabbling run.

"If they make it quicker than the nymphs—" breathed the general. Then he sighed relievedly. They had not. The carnage among the dragons was almost funny; at will the nymphs lifted them high in the air on jets of steam and squirted melted rock in their eyes. Squalling in terror, the dragons flapped into the air, and lumbered off southward.

"That's ocean," grinned the general. "They'll never come back—trying to find new homes, I suspect."

In an incredibly short time the field was littered with the flopping chunks that had been hewed from the Krakens. Living still they were, but powerless. The general shook his hand warmly. "You're on your own now," he said. "Good luck, boy. For a civilian, you're not a bad sort of egg at all." He walked away.

Glumly Peter surveyed the colossal fortress of Almarish. He walked aimlessly up to its gate, a huge thing of bronze and silver, and pulled at the silken cord hanging there. A gong sounded and the door swung open. Peter advanced hopelessly into a sort of audience chamber.

"So!" thundered a mighty voice.

"So what?" asked Peter despondently. He saw on a throne high above him an imposing figure. "You Almarish?" he asked listlessly.

"I am. And who are you?"

"It doesn't matter. I'm Peter Packer of Braintree, Mass. I don't even expect you to believe me." The throne lowered slowly and jerkily, as if on hydraulic pumps. The wizard descended and approached Peter. He was a man of about forty, with a full brown beard reaching almost to his belt.

"Why," asked the sorcerer, "have you come bearing arms?"

"It's the only way I could come," said Peter. "Let me first congratulate you on an efficient, well-oiled set of political machinery. Not even back in the United States have I seen graft carried to such a high degree. Second, your choice of assistants is an eye-opener. Your Mr. Pike is the neatest henchman I've ever seen. Third, produce the person of Miss Millicent or I'll have to use force."

"Is that so?" rumbled Almarish. "Young puppy! I'd like to see you try it. Wrestle with me—two falls out of three. I dare you!"

Peter took off his coat of blue serge. "I never passed up a dare yet," he said. "How about a mat?"

"Think I'm a sissy?" the sorcerer jeered.

Peter was stripped for action. "Okay," he said. Slowly Almarish advanced on him, grappling for a hold. Peter let him take his forearm, then shifted his weight so as to hurl the magician over his shoulder. A moment later Peter was astonished to find himself on the floor underneath the wizard.

"Haw!" grunted Almarish, rising. "You still game?" He braced himself.

"Yep!" snapped Peter. He hurled himself in a flying tackle that began ten feet away from the wizard and ended in a bone-crushing grip about the knees. Peter swarmed up his trunk and cruelly twisted an arm across his chest. The magician yelped in sudden agony, and let himself fall against the floor. Peter rose, grinning. "One all," he said cheerfully.

Almarish grappled for the third fall; Peter cagily backed away. The wizard hurled himself in a bruising body block against Peter, battering him off his feet and falling on the young man. Instinctively Peter bridged his body, arching it off the floor. Almarish, grunting fiercely, gripped his arm and turned it slowly, as though he were winding a clock. Peter snapped over, rolling on the wizard's own body as a fulcrum. He had his toe in his hand, and closed his fist with every ounce of mustle he had. The sorcerer screamed and fell over on his face. Peter jammed his knee in the wizard's inside socket and bore down terribly. He could feel the bones bend in his grip.

"Enough!" gasped the wizard. Peter let him loose.

"You made it," said Almarish. "Two out of three."

Peter studied his face curiously. Take off that beard and you had—

"You said it, Grandfather Packer," said Peter, grinning.

Almarish groaned. "It's a wise child that knows its own father—grandfather, in this case," he said. "How could you tell?"

"Everything just clicked," said Peter simply. "You disappearing—that clock—somebody applying American methods in Ellil—and then I shaved you mentally and there you were. Simple?"

"Sure is. But how do you think I made out here, boy?"

"Shamefully. That kind of thing isn't tolerated any more. It's gangsterism—you'll have to cut it out, Gramp."

"Gangsterism be damned!" snorted the wizard. "It's business. Business and common sense."

"Business maybe—certainly not common sense. My boys wiped out your guard, and I might have wiped out you if I had magic stronger than yours."

Grandfather Packer chuckled in glee. "Magic? I'll begin at the beginning. When I got that dad-blamed clock back in '63, I dropped right into Ellil—onto the head of an assassin who was going for a real magician. Getting the setup, I pinned the killer with a half nelson and the magician dispatched him. Then he got grateful—said he was retiring from public life and gave me a kind of token—good for any three wishes.

"So I took it, thanking him kindly, and wished for a palace and a bunch of gutty retainers. It was in my mind to run Ellil like a business, and I did it the only way I knew how—force. And from that day to this I used only one wish and I haven't a dab of magic more than that!"

"I'll be damned!" whispered Peter.

"And you know what I'm going to do with those other two wishes? I'm going to take you and me right back into the good old U.S.A.!"

"Will it only send two people?"

"So the magician said."

"Grandfather Packer," said Peter earnestly, "I am about to ask a very great sacrifice of you. It is also your duty to undo the damage which you have done."

"Oh," said Almarish glumly. "The girl? All right."

"You don't mind?" asked Peter incredulously.

"Far be it from me to stand in the way of young love," grunted the wizard sourly. "She's up there."

Peter entered timidly; the girl was alternately reading a copy of the *Braintree Informer* and staring passionately at a photograph of Peter. "Darling," said Peter.

"Dearest," said Millicent, catching on almost immediately.

A short while later Peter was asking her, "Do you mind, dearest, if I ask for one favor of you—a very great sacrifice?" He produced a small, sharp penknife.

And all the gossip for a month in Braintree was of Peter Packer's stunning young wife, though some people wondered how it was that she had only nine fingers.

[*Stirring Science Stories* - June 1941
as by Cecil Corwin]

Mr. Packer Goes to Hell

1

"Drat it!" cursed Almarish, enchanter supreme and master of all Ellil. "Drat the sizzling dingus!" Lifting his stiffly embroidered robes of imperial purple, he was dashing to left and right about his bedroom, stooping low, snatching with his jeweled hands at an elusive something that skidded about the floor with little, chuckling snickers.

Outside, beyond the oaken door, there was a sinister thud of footsteps, firm and normal slaps of bare sole against pavement alternating with sinister tappings of bone. "Slap-click. Slap-click. Slap-click," was the beat. Almarish shot a glance over his shoulder at the door, his bearded face pale with strain.

"Young 'un," he snapped to an empty room, "this ain't the silly season. Come out, or when I find you I'll jest take your pointed ears and twist them till they come off in my hands."

Again there was the chuckling snicker, this time from under the bed. Almarish, his beard streaming, dove headlong, his hands snapping shut. The snicker turned into a pathetic wail.

"Leggo!" shrilled a small voice. "You're crushing me, you ox!"

Outside the alternating footsteps had stopped before his door. A horny hand pounded on the solid oak.

"Be with ye in a minute," called the bearded enchanter. Sweat had broken out on his brow. He drew out his clenched fists from under the bed.

"Now, young lady!" he said grimly, addressing his prize.

The remarkable creature in his hands appeared to be young; at least she was not senile. But if ever a creature looked less like a lady it was she. From tiny feet, shod in rhinestone, high-heeled pumps, to softly waved chestnut hair at her very crown, she was an efficient engine of seduction and disaster. And to omit what came between would be a sin: her voluptuous nine inches were encased in a *lamé* that glittered with the fire of burnished silver, cut and fitted in the guise of an evening gown. Pouting and sullen as she was in Almarish's grasp, she hadn't no-

221

ticed that the hem was scarcely below her ankles, as was intended by the unknown couturier who had spared no pains on her. That hem, or the maladjustment of it, revealed, in fact, that she had a pretty, though miniature, taste in silks and lacework.

"Ox!" she stormed at the bearded sorcerer. "Beastly oaf—you'll squeeze me out of shape with your great, clumsy hands!"

"That would be a pity," said Almarish. "It's *quite* a shape, as you seem to know."

The pounding on the door redoubled. "Lord Almarish!" shouted a voice, clumsily feigning anxiety. "Are you all right?"

"Sure, Pike," called the sorcerer. "Don't bother me now. I have a lady with me. We're looking at my potted plants."

"Oh," said the voice of Pike. "All right—my business can wait."

"That stalled him," grunted Almarish. "But not for long. You, what's your name?"

She stuck out a tiny tongue at him.

"Look here," said Almarish gently. He contracted his fist a little and the creature let out an agonized squawk on a small scale. "What's your name?" he repeated.

"Moira," she snapped tartly. "And if your throat weren't behind all that hay I'd cut it."

"Forget that, kid," he said. "Let me give you a brief *résumé* of pertinent facts:

"My name is Packer and I'm from Braintree, Mass., which you never heard of. I came to Ellil by means of a clock with thirteen hours. Unusual, eh? Once here I sized things up and began to organize on a business basis with the assistance of a gang of half-breed demons. I had three wishes, but they're all used up now. I had to send back to Braintree my grandson Peter, who got here the same way I did, and with him a sweet young witch he picked up.

"Before leaving he read me a little lecture on business reform and the New Deal. What I thought was commercial common sense—little things like bribes, subornation of perjury, arson, assassination and the like—he claimed was criminal. So I, like a conscientious Packer, began to set things right. This my gang didn't like. The best testimony of that fact is that the gentleman outside my door is Balthazar Pike, my trusted lieutenant, who has determined to take over.

"I learned that from Count Hacza, the vampire, when he called yesterday, and he said that I was to be wiped out today. He wrung my hand with real tears in his eyes—an affectionate chap—as he said goodbye."

"And," snarled the creature, "ain't that too damn' bad?"

"No," said Almarish mildly. "No, because you're going to get me out of this. I knew you were good luck the moment you poked your nose through the wall and began to snicker."

Moira eyed him keenly. "What's in it for me?" she finally demanded.

There was again the pounding on the door. "Lord Almarish," yelled Balthazar Pike, "aren't you through with those potted plants yet?"

"No," called the sorcerer. "We've just barely got to the gladioli."

"Pretty slow working," grumbled the trusted lieutenant. "Get some snap into it."

"Sure, Pike. Sure. Only a few minutes more." He turned on the little creature. "What do you want?" he asked.

There was a curious catch in her voice as she answered, "A vial of tears from *la Bête Joyeux*."

"Cut out the bunk," snapped Almarish impatiently. "Gold, jewels—anything at all. Name it."

"Look, whiskers," snarled the little creature. "I told you my price and I'll stick to it. What's more, I'll take you to the right place."

"And on the strength of that," grinned the sorcerer, "I'm supposed to let you out of my hands?"

"That's the idea," snapped Moira. "You have to trust somebody in this lousy world—why not me? After all, mister, I'm taking your word—if you'll give it."

"Done," said Almarish with great decision. "I hereby pledge myself to do everything I can to get you that whatever-it-was's tears, up to and including risk and loss of life."

"Okay, whiskers," she said. "Put me down." He obliged, and saw her begin to pace out pentacles and figures on the mosaic floor. As she began muttering to herself with great concentration, he leaned his head against the door. There were agitated murmurs without.

"Don't be silly," Pike was saying. "He told me with his own mouth he had a woman—"

"Look, Bally," said another voice, one that Almarish recognized as that of a gatekeeper, "I ain't sayin' you're wacked up, but they ain't even no mice in his room. I ain't let no one in and the ectoplasmeter don't show nothin' on the grounds of the castle."

"Then," said Pike, "he must be stalling. Rourke, you get the rest of the 'breeds and we'll break down the door and settle Lord Almarish's hash for good. The lousy weakling!"

Lord Almarish began to sweat afresh and cast a glance at Moira, who was standing stock-still to one side of the mosaic design in the floor. He noted abruptly a series of black tiles in the center that he had never seen before. Then others surrounding them turned black, and he saw that they were not coloring but ceasing to exist. Apparently something of a bottomless pit was opening up beneath his palace.

Outside the padding and clicking of feet sounded. "Okay, boys! Get it in line!"

They would be swinging up a battering ram, Almarish surmised. The shivering crash of the first blow against the oaken door made his ears ring. Futilely he braced his own brawny body against the planking and felt the next two blows run through his bones.

"One more!" yelled his trusted lieutenant. And with that one more the door would give way, he knew, and what they would do to him would be no picnic. He had schooled them well, though crudely, in the techniques of strikebreaking practiced by employers of the 1880s.

"Hurry it up!" he snapped at Moira. She didn't answer, being wholly intent, it seemed, on the enlargement of the pit which was growing in the floor. It would now admit the passage of a slimmer man than the sorcerer, but his own big bones would never make it.

With agonizing slowness the pit grew, tile by tile, as the tiny creature frowned into it till her face was white and bloodless. Almarish fancied he could hear through the door the labored breathing of the half-breed demons as they made ready to swing again.

Crash! It came again, and only his own body kept the door from falling in fragments.

"Right—*dive!*" shrilled the little voice of Moira as the battering ram poked through into the room. He caught her up in one hand and squeezed through into the blackness of the pit. He looked up and could see a circle of faces snarling with rage as he slid down a kind of infinitely smooth inclined tunnel. Abruptly the patch of light above him was blotted out and there was absolutely nothing to be seen.

All Almarish knew was that he was gliding in utter blackness at some terrifying speed in excess of anything sane down to a place he knew nothing of in the company of a vicious little creature whose sole desire seemed to be to cut his throat and drink his blood with glee.

2

"Where," asked Almarish, "does this end?"

"You'll find out," snarled the little creature. "Maybe you're yellow already?"

"Don't say that," he warned. "Not unless you want to get playfully pinched—in half."

"Cold-blooded," she marveled. "Like a snake or lizard. Heart's probably three-ventricled, too."

"Our verbal contract," said the sorcerer, delicately emphasizing *verbal,* "didn't include an exchange of insults."

"Yeah," she said abstractedly. And though they were in the dark, he could sense that she was worried. "Yeah, that's right."

"What's the matter?" he demanded.

"It's your fault," she shrilled. "It's your own damned fault hurrying me up so I did this!" The man knew that she was near distraction with alarm. And he could feel the reason why. They were slowing down, and this deceleration, presumably, was not on Moira's schedule.

"We on the wrong line?" he asked coolly.

"Yes. That's about it. And don't ask me what happens now, because I don't know, you stupid cow!" Then she was sniffling quietly in his hand, and the sorcerer was wondering how he could comfort her without breaking her in two.

"There now," he soothed tentatively, stroking her hair carefully with the tip of a finger. "There, now, don't get all upset—"

It occurred to him to worry on his own account. They had slowed to a mere snail's pace, and at the dramatically, psychologically correct moment a light appeared ahead. A dull chanting resounded through the tube:

> *Slimy flesh,*
> *Clotted blood,*
> *Fat, white worms,*
> *These are food.*

From Moira there was a little, strangled wail. "Ghouls!"

"Grave robbers?" asked the sorcerer. "I can take care of them—knock a few heads together."

"No," she said in thin, hopeless tones. "You don't understand. These are the real thing. You'll see."

As they slid from the tube onto a sort of receiving table, Almarish hastily pocketed the little creature. Then, staring about him in bewilderment, he dropped his jaw and let it hang.

The amiable dietary ditty was being ground out by a phonograph, tending which there was a heavy-eyed person dressed all in grey. He seemed shapeless, lumpy, like a half-burned tallow candle on whose sides the drops of wax have congealed in half teardrops and cancerous clusters. He had four limbs and, on the upper two, hands of a sort, and wore what could roughly be described as a face.

"You," said Almarish. "What's—where—?" He broke off in confusion as a lackluster eye turned on him.

From a stack beside him the creature handed him a pamphlet. The sorcerer studied the title:

WORKERS!
FIGHT TO *PRESERVE* AND *EXTEND*
the GLORIOUS REVOLUTION which has BEFALLEN *YOU!*

He read further:

> There are those among you who still can remember the haphazard days of individual enterprise and communal wealth. Those days were bad; many starved for lack of nutritious corpses. And yet people died Above; why this poverty in the midst of plenty?
>
> There were Above as usual your scouts who cast about for likely members of your elite circle, those who wished to live forever on the traditional banquets of the Immortal Eaters. Fortunate indeed was the scout who enrolled Ingvar Hemming. For it was he who, descending to the Halls of the Eaters, saw the pitiful confusion which existed.

Even as he had brought order into the vast holdings which had been his when Above, he brought order to the Halls. A ratio was established between production and consumption and civilized habits of life-in-death were publicized. Nowadays no Immortal Eater would be seen barbarously clawing the flesh from a corpse as in the bad old days; in these times your Safety-Tasty cans are the warrant of cleanliness and flavor.

Bug-eyed, Almarish turned to the back of the booklet and scanned the advertisements:

> There's STRENGTH
> s-p-e-e-d
> *grace*
> In A HEMMING HEARSE
> "To serve we strive
> The dead-alive."

> For Those Guests Tonight!
> *Why Not*
> A Bottle of SAFETY-TASTY EYES
> 10 per bottle—Hemming-Pakt
> "5 blue, 5 brown—remember?"

He tore his eyes from the repulsive pages. "Chum," he demanded hoarsely of the phonograph attendant, "what the hell goes on here?"

"Hell?" asked the ghoul in a creaky, slushy voice. "You're way off. You'll never get there now. I buzzed the receiving desk—they'll come soon."

"I mean this thing." Gingerly he held it up between thumb and forefinger.

"Oh—that. I'm supposed to give it to each new arrival. It's full of bunk. If you could possibly get out of here, you'd do it. This ain't no paradise, not by a long shot."

"I thought," said Almarish, "that you all had enough to eat now. And if you can afford hearses you must be well off."

"You think so?" asked the attendant. "I can remember back when things was different. And then this Hemming man—he comes down from Above, corners the supply, hires men to can it and don't pay them enough to buy it in cans. I don't understand it, but I know it ain't right."

"But who buys the—the eyes and hearses?"

"Foremen an' ex-ex-ekky-tives. And whut they are I don't know. It jest ain't jolly down here no more."

"Where you from?" asked Almarish.

"Kentucky. Met a scout, 1794. Liked it and been here ever since. You change—cain't git back. It's a sad thing naow." He dummied up abruptly as a squad of ghouls approached. They were much less far gone—"changed"—than the attendant. One snapped out a notebook.

"Name?" he demanded.

"Packer, Almarish—what you will," he said, fingering an invincible dagger in his sleeve.

"Almarish—*the* Almarish?"

"Overlord of Ellil," he modestly confessed, assuming, and rightly, that the news of his recent deposition had not yet reached the Halls of the Eternal Eaters. "Come on a tour of inspection. I was wondering if I ought to take over this glorified cafeteria."

"I assume," said one of the reception committee—for into such it had hastily resolved itself—"you'll want to see our vice-president in charge of Inspection and Regulation?"

"You assume wrongly," said the sorcerer coldly. "I want to see the president."

"Mr. Hemming?" demanded the spokesman. All heads save that of Almarish bowed solemnly. "You—you haven't an appointment, you know."

"Lead on," ordered the sorcerer grimly. "To *Mr. Hemming.*" Again the heads bowed.

Almarish strode majestically through the frosted-glass door simply lettered with the name and title of the man who owned the nation of ghouls body and soul.

"Hello, Hemming," said he to the man behind the desk, sitting down unbidden.

The president was scarcely "changed" at all. It was possible that he had been eating food that he had been used to when Above. What Almarish saw was an ordinary man in a business suit, white-haired, with a pair of burning eyes and a stoop forward that gave him the aspect of a cougar about to pounce.

"Almarish," he said, "I welcome you to my—corporation."

"Yes—thank you," said the sorcerer. He was vaguely worried. Superb businessman that he was, he could tell with infallible instinct that something was wrong—that his stupendous bluff was working none too well.

"I've just received an interesting communication," said Hemming casually. "A report via rock signals that there was some sort of disturbance in your Ellil. A sort of—palace revolution. Successful, too, I believe."

Almarish was about to spring at his throat and bring down guards about his head when he felt a stirring in his pocket. Over the top of it peeked the head of Moira.

"Won't you," she said, "introduce me to the handsome man?"

Almarish, grinning quietly, brought her out into full view. With a little purr she gloriously stretched her lithe body. Hemming was staring like an old goat.

"This," said the sorcerer, "is Moira."

"For sale?" demanded the president, clenching his hands till the knuckles whitened on the top of his desk.

"Of course," she drawled amiably. "At the moment a free agent. Right?" She tipped Almarish a wink.

"Of course," he managed to say regretfully, "you know your own mind, Moira, but I wish you'd stay with me a little longer."

"I'm tired of you," she said. "A lively girl like me needs them young and handsome to keep my interest alive. There are some men"—she cast a sidelong, slumbrous glance at Hemming—"*some men* I'd never grow tired of."

"Bring her over," said the president, trying to control his voice.

Almarish realized that there was something in the combination of endemic desirability and smallness which was irresistible. He didn't know it, but that fact was being demonstrated in his own Braintree, Mass., at that very time by a shop which had abandoned full-sized window dummies and was using gorgeous things a little taller than Moira but scarcely as sexy. In the crowds around their windows there were four men to every woman.

His Moira pirouetted on the desk top, displaying herself. "And," she said, "for *some men* I'll do a really extraordinary favor."

"What's that?" asked Hemming, fighting with himself to keep his hands off her. He was plainly terrified of squashing this gorgeous creature.

"I could make you," she said, "my size. Only a little taller, of course. Women like that."

"You can?" he asked, his voice breaking. "Then go ahead!"

"I have your full consent?"

"Yes," he said. "Full consent."

"Then—" A smile curved her lips as she swept her hands through the air in juggling little patterns.

A lizard about ten inches long reared up on its hind legs, then frantically skittered across the tabletop. Almarish looked for Hemming; could not see him anywhere. He picked up Moira. In a sleepy, contented voice she was saying:

"My size. Only a little taller, of course."

3

Back in the tube from which they had been shunted into the Halls of the Eternal Eaters, as the ghouls fancied calling themselves, Almarish couldn't get sense out of Moira. She had fallen asleep in his pocket and was snoring quietly, like a kitten that purred in its sleep.

And more than ever he marveled at this cold-blooded little creature. She had had the routine of seduction and transformation down so pat that he was sure she had done it a hundred times—or a thousand. You couldn't tell ages in any of these unreal places; he, who should be a hundred and eight, looked just thirty-five and felt fifteen years younger than that.

All the same, it would be a good thing not to give Moira full and clear consent to anything at all. That must be an important part of the ceremony.

He hoped that the ghouls would straighten themselves out now that their president was a ten-inch lizard. But there were probably twenty villainous vice-presidents, assorted as to size, shape and duties, to fill his place. Maybe they'd get to fighting over it, and the ghouls-in-ordinary would be able to toss them all over.

Just like Ellil. A good thing he'd gotten out of *that*.

Not that he liked this way of traveling, he assured himself. It couldn't be anything half so honest as it seemed—a smooth-lined tube slanting down through solid rock. It was actually, of course, God-knew-what tricky path between the planes of existence. That thirteen-hour clock was one way, this was another, but more versatile.

Lights ahead again—red lights. He took Moira from his pocket and shook her with incredible delicacy.

"You ox!" she snapped. "Trying to break my back?"

"Sorry," he said. "Lights—red ones. What about them?"

"That's it," she said grimly. "Do you feel like a demigod—particularly?"

"No," he admitted. "Not—particularly."

"Then that's too damn bad," she snapped. "Remember, you have a job to do. When you get past the first trials and things, wake me up."

"Trials?"

"Yes, always. Egyptian, Greek, Roman, Norse—they all have a Weigher of Souls. It's always the same place, of course, but they like the formality. Now let me sleep."

He put her back into his pocket and tried to brake with his hands and feet. No go. But soon he began to decelerate. Calling up what little he knew of such things, he tried to draw a desperate analogy between molecules standing radially instead of in line and whatever phenomenon this was which made him—who was actually, he knew, not moving at all—not-move more slowly than before, when he had been standing still at an inconceivably rapid pace.

The lights flared ahead into a bloody brilliance, and he skidded onto another of the delivery tables of sardonyx.

A thing with a hawk face took his arm.

"Stwm stm!" it said irritably.

"Velly solly," said the sorcerer. "Me no spik—whatever in Hades you're speaking."

"R khrt sr tf mtht," it said with a clash of its beak. Almarish drew his invincible dirk, and the thing shrugged disarmingly.

"Chdl nfr," it grinned, sauntering off.

A Chinese approached, surveying him. "Sholom aleichim," he greeted Almarish, apparently fooled by the beard.

"Aleichim sholom," replied the enchanter, "but you've made a mistake."

"Sorry," said the Chinese. "We'll put you on the calendar at General Sessions. Take him away!" he called sharply.

Almarish was hustled into a building and up a flight of stairs by two men in shiny blue uniforms before he had a chance to ask what the charge was. He was hustled through a pen, through innumerable corridors, through a sort of chicken-wire cage, and finally into a courtroom.

"*Hurrah!*" yelled thousands of voices. Dazedly he looked over a sea of faces, mostly bloodthirsty.

"Tough crowd," one of the attendants muttered. "We better stick around to take care of you. They like to collect souvenirs. Arms ... scalps ..."

"See him?" demanded the other attendant, pointing at the judge. "Used to be a Neminant Divine. This is his punishment. This and dyspepsia. Chronic."

Almarish could read the sour lines in the judge's face like a book. And the book looked as though it had an unhappy ending.

"Prisoner to the bar," wheezed the justice.

THE COURT: Prisoner, give your name and occupation.

PRISONER: Which ones, Your Honor? There are so many.

       (Laughter and hisses.)

A VOICE: Heretic—burn him!

THE COURT: Order! Prisoner, give the ones you like best. And remember—We Know All.

PRISONER: Yes, Your Honor. Packer, ex-overlord of Ellil.

THE COURT: Read the accusation, clerk.

CLERK: *(several words lost)* did willfully conspire to transform said Hemming into a lizard ten inches long.

       (Laughter in the court.)

THE COURT: Poppycock!

RECORDING CLERK: How do you spell that, Your Honor?

THE COURT: Silence! I said *Poppycock!*

RECORDING CLERK: Thank you, Your Honor.

PRISONER'S COUNSEL: Your Honor, *(several words lost),* known *(several words lost)* childhood *(several words lost).*

THE COURT: Prisoner's counsel is very vague.

PRISONER: My God—is *he* my lawyer?

THE COURT: So it would appear.

PRISONER: But I never saw the man before, and he's obviously drunk, Your Honor!

THE COURT: Hic! What of it, prisoner?

PRISONER: Nothing. Nothing at all. Move to proceed.

PROSECUTING ATT'Y: I object! Your Honor, I object!

THE COURT: Sustained.

       (A long silence. Hisses and groans.)

THE COURT: Mr. Prosecutor, *you* got us into this—what have you to say for yourself?

PROSECUTING ATT'Y: Your Honor, I—I—I move to proceed.

PRISONER: It's my turn, Your Honor. *I* object.

THE COURT: Overruled.

       (Cheers and whistles.)

VOICES: Hang him by the thumbs!

       Cut his face off!

          Heretic—burn him!

THE COURT: I wish it to go on record that I am much gratified by the intelligent interest which the public is taking in this trial.

(Cheers and whistles.)

PROSECUTING ATT'Y: Your Honor, I see no need further to dillydally. This is a clear-cut case and the state feels no hesitation in demanding that the Court impose maximum penalty under law—which, if I remember aright, is death *per flagitionem extremum, peine forte et dure, crucifictio ultima* and *inundation sub aqua regia*—in that order.

(Cheers and screams. Wild demonstration.)

THE COURT: I so—

A VOICE: Hey, blue-eyes!

THE COURT: I so—

A VOICE (the same): Hey, you, cutie-pants!

THE COURT: Prisoner.

PRISONER: Yes, Your Honor?

THE COURT: Prisoner, are you aware of what you have in your pocket?

PRISONER: Oh—*her.* Cute, isn't she?

THE COURT: Bring it closer. I shall make it Exhibit A.

A VOICE (the same): Hey—that tickles!

THE COURT: Exhibit A, have you any testimony to give?

(Demonstration, mostly whistles.)

EXHIBIT A: Yes, Your Honor. Take me away from this horrible man! The things he's done to me—

THE COURT: Yes? Yes?

EXHIBIT A: You can't imagine. But, Your Honor, you're not like him. You know, Your Honor, there are *some men (rest of testimony lost).*

THE COURT: *(comments lost).*

EXHIBIT A: *(testimony lost).*

THE COURT: Really! You don't mean it! Well, go ahead.

EXHIBIT A: Have I your full consent?

THE COURT: You have—free, clear and legal.

EXHIBIT A: *(gestures with both hands).*

THE COURT: *(turns into lizard approx. 10 in. long).*

EXHIBIT A: Come on, whiskers—let's beat it!

PRISONER: I hear you talkin'!

PROSECUTING ATT'Y: Go after them, you damfools!

COURT ATTACHÉS: Not us, bud. What kind of dopes do we look like to you?

(Screams, howls, whistles, yells, demonstrations, complete pandemonium.)

4

"How will I know," demanded Almarish, "when I'm supposed to turn left?"

"When the three moons show up as an equilateral triangle," said Moira, "will be high time. Now, damn you, let me go to sleep."

"Why are you always so tired after these little transformation acts of yours?"

"You, not being a real sorcerer, wouldn't understand. But suffice it to say that any magic-worker would have to do as much. Watch out for ghosts. Good night."

She was in his pocket again, either purring or snoring. He never could decide which was the right word. And Almarish realized that this little lady had somehow become very dear to him.

He was walking along a narrow, sullen strip of desert bordered on either side by devil trees that lashed out with poisonous, thorny branches. The things must have had sharp ears, for they would regularly lie in wait for him and lash up as he stepped past. Fortunately, they could not make the extra yard or two of leeway he had.

Above, the three moons of the present night were shifting in a stately drill, more like dancers than celestial bodies, sometimes drawing near to an equilateral triangle but never quite achieving it. And she had been most specific about it.

There was still *la Bête Joyeux* to face, from whose eyes had to be wrung a vial of tears for purpose or purposes unknown to the sorcerer. His French was a little weak, but he surmised that the thing was a happy beast, and that to make it weep would bear looking into. He made a mental note to ask her about it. He was always asking her about things.

The devil trees were at it again, this time with a new twist. They would snap their tentacles at him like whips, so that one or more of the darts would fly off and whiz past his face. And it was just as well that they did. One of those things would drop a rhino in full charge, Moira had told him. Odd name, Moira. Sounded Irish.

He looked up and drew his breath in sharply. The moons had formed their triangle and held it for a long, long five minutes. Time to turn left. The way was blocked, of course, by ill-tempered trees. He drew the invincible dirk, hoping that the trees did not know enough magic to render the thing just an innocent little brand, and deliberately stepped within reach of one of the trees.

It lashed out beautifully; Almarish did not have to cut at it. The tentacle struck against the blade and lopped itself clean off. The tree uttered a mournful squeal and tried to find and haul in the severed tentacle with the others. They had a way of sticking them back on again.

He slashed away heartily, counting them as they fell. With each fresh gush of pussy sap the tree wailed more and more weakly. Finally it drooped, seemingly completely done in. Treachery, of course. He flung a lump of sandstone into the nest of arms and saw them close, slowly and with little crushing power, around it. Were it he instead of the stone, he could have hacked himself free before the thing burst into sand.

Quite boldly, therefore, he picked his way among the oozing tendrils, now and then cutting at one from the wrist. He gumshoed past the trunk itself and saw the pulsing membranes quiver malevolently at his step. They had things like this back in Ellil; he felt more than competent to deal with them.

But ghosts, now—ghosts were something else again. He had never seen a ghost, though the rumors did go about. And if ever ghosts were to be seen, it was in this spot.

Here the moons did not send their light—he didn't know why—and the grass underfoot was fatty, round rods. From shrubs shone a vague, reddish light that frayed on a man's nerves. There was the suggestion of a sound in the air, like the ghost itself of a noise dispersed.

"Moira," he said softly. "Snap out of it. I'm scared."

A tiny head peeked over the top of his pocket. "Yellow already?" she insultingly asked. "The master of all Ellil's turning green?"

"Look," he said. "Just you tell me what we're up against and I'll go ahead. Otherwise, no."

"Ghosts," she said. "This place is a den of them. I suppose you've heard all the stories about them and don't quite believe. Well, the stories are true. Just forget about the whimsy à la John Kendrick Bangs. Ghosts aren't funny; they're the most frightening things that ever were. There's nothing you can do about them; none of the magical formulas work, because they aren't even magical. They are distilled essence of terror in tactile form. There's absolutely nothing you can do with, to or about them. I can't give you a word of advice. You know what you have to do, whiskers. We're after that vial of tears."

"Right," he said. "Keep your head out—here we go."

He—they—walked into a vast glob of darkness that saturated their minds, seeped between their molecules and into their lungs and hearts.

"Oh, my God!" wailed a voice. "Oh, my God!"

Almarish didn't turn his head; kept walking straight on.

"Stranger—help me—here they come —" the voice shrilled. There was a sickening sound of crackling, then a mushy voice that spoke a few indistinguishable words.

"They're at it," said Moira tremulously. "Don't let it get you down."

"A big man like you," said the sweet voice of a young girl, "consorting with that evil little creature! You ought to be ashamed of yourself. I'm *ever* so much nicer ... ."

In the gooey blackness appeared a figure—wispy, luminous—of a charming maiden whose head was a skull and whose hair was a convolution of pink, writhing worms. Gently they hissed in chorus:

> *Bold, big master,*
> *Come to terms;*
> *Feed the dainty*
> *Maid of Worms.*

The last line of the ditty echoed from all sides in a variety of voices, ranging from a new-born wail to the hoarseness of a death rattle.

Almarish shut his eyes and walked ahead as the Maid reached out her arms. He walked into her and felt a clammy, gelid coldness, the tightness of arms around him, and ropy things fumbling on his face. Repressing a shriek, breathing heavily, he strode on, finally opening his eyes. Again he—they—were in the blackness, without a sound or light. Fumbling for a handkerchief, he swabbed at his brow and cheeks, dripping with cold sweat. As he thought of the Maid again, his back rose into little prickles of ice.

"It was me," he said, trembling violently, "who could never stand mice and roaches, Moira."

"Keep going," she snapped coldly. "This isn't a picnic." The little creature was upset again. Almarish walked on, missed his footing and fell, sprawling grotesquely. Slowly he drifted down through unimaginable depths of blackness, reaching out frantically for holds, and there were none.

"Stop it!" shrilled Moira. "Stop struggling!"

Obediently he relaxed. His fall ended with a bump, on a twilit road sloping gently downward as far as the eye could see. There was a vague, rumbling noise underfoot, as if there were heavy carts on the road.

He looked up along the road. Something was coming, and it was brutally big. Legless, it rolled along on iron wheels, coming at him. The thing was a flattened ovoid of dark, sharkish grey, and like a shark it had a gruesome, toothy slit of mouth. Growing bigger and bigger, it thundered down the road as he watched, petrified, his own mouth open in childish alarm.

A shrill scream from his pocket brought him to. "Jump, you dummy!" shrieked Moira. *"Jump!"* He leaped into the air as the thing, its triangular mouth snapping savagely, teeth clashing, thundered beneath him.

He watched it go on down the road, still cold with terror.

"Can it come back?" he asked.

"Of course not," said Moira. "Could *you* roll uphill?"

"You're right," he said. "Quite right. But what do we do now?" He mopped his brow again.

"Look," said the little creature kindly, "I know how you feel, but don't worry. You're doing a lot better than you think you are. We'll be out of this in a minute, if you don't break down." She looked sharply into his face.

"Maybe I won't," he said. "I'm not making promises, the way I feel. What—what in Hades—?"

He—they—were snatched up by a gigantic wind and were sucked through the air like flies in an air-conditioning plant.

"Close your eyes," said Moira. "Close them tight and think of something—anything—except what's going to happen to you. Because if you think of something else, it won't happen."

Almarish squeezed his eyes tight shut as a thunderous droning noise filled his ears. "Ex sub one sub two," he gabbled, "equals ei square plus two ei plus the square root of bee plus and minus ei square minus two ei bee over two ei." The droning roar was louder; he jammed his thumbs into his ears.

He felt a hideous impulse to open his eyes. Little, stinging particles of dust struck against his neck.

Flying through the air, turning over and over, the droning roar became one continual crash that battered against his body with physical force. There was one indescribable, utterly, incomparably violent noise that nearly blew his brain out like an overload of electricity. Then things became more or less quiet, and he tumbled onto a marshy sort of ground.

"All clear?" he asked, without opening his eyes.

"Yes," said Moira. "You were magnificent."

He lifted his lids warily and saw that he sat on a stretch of forest sward. Looking behind him—

"My God!" he screamed. "Did we go through *that?*"

"Yes," said Moira. "It's a ghost—unless you're afraid of it, it can't hurt you."

Behind them, the thousand-foot blades of a monstrous electric fan swirled brilliantly at several hundred r.p.s. The noise reached them in a softening blur of sound. Gently it faded away.

Almarish of Ellil leaned back quietly.

"The big calf!" muttered Moira. "*Now* he faints on me!"

5

"Now," said Almarish, "what about this happy animal?"

"*La Bête Joyeux?*" asked the little creature.

"If that's what its name is. Why this damned nonsense about tears?"

"It's a curse," said Moira grimly. "A very terrible curse."

"Then it'll keep. Who's in there?"

He pointed to a stony hut that blocked the barely-defined trail they were following. Moira shaded her tiny eyes and wrinkled her brow as she stared. "I don't know," she admitted at last. "It's something new."

Almarish prepared to detour. The stone door slid open. Out looked a wrinkled, weazened face, iron-rimmed spectacles slid down over the nose. It was whiskered, but not as resplendently as Almarish's, whose imposing mattress spread from his chin to his waist. And the beard straggling from the face was not the rich mahogany hue of the sorcerer's, but a dirty white, streaked with grey and soup stains.

"Hello," said Almarish amiably, getting his fingers around the invincible dirk.

"Beaver!" shrilled the old man, pointing a dirty-yellow, quavering, derisive finger at Almarish. Then he lit a cigarette with a big, apparently homemade match and puffed nervously.

"Is there anything," inquired the sorcerer, "we can do for you? Otherwise we'd like to be on our way."

"We?" shrilled the old man.

Almarish realized that Moira had retreated into his pocket again. "I mean I," he said hastily. "I was a king once—you get into the habit."

"Come in," said the old man quaveringly. By dint of extraordinarily hard puffing, he had already smoked down the cigarette to his yellowed teeth. Carefully he lit another from its butt.

Almarish did not want to come in. At least he had not wanted to, but there was growing in his mind a conviction that this was a very nice old man, and that it would be a right and proper thing to go in. That happy-animal nonsense could wait. Hospitality was hospitality.

He went in and saw an utterly revolting interior, littered with the big, clumsy matches and with cigarette butts smoked down to eighth-inches and stamped out. The reek of nicotine filled the air; ashtrays deep as water buckets overflowed everywhere onto the floor.

"Perhaps," said the sorcerer, "we'd better introduce ourselves. I'm Almarish, formerly of Ellil."

"Pleased to meet you," shrilled the ancient. Already he was chain-smoking his third cigarette. "My name's Hopper. I'm a geasan."

"What?"

"Geasan—layer-on of geases. A geas is an injunction which can't be disobeyed. Sit down."

Almarish felt suddenly that it was about time he took a little rest. "Thanks," he said, sitting in a pile of ashes and burned matches. "But I don't believe that business about you being able to command people."

The geasan started his sixth cigarette and cackled shrilly. "You'll see. Young man, I want that beard of yours. My mattress needs restuffing. You'll let me have it, of course."

"Of course," said Almarish. Anything at all for a nice old man like this, he thought. But that business about geases was too silly for words.

"And I may take your head with it. You won't object."

"Why, no," said the sorcerer. What in Hades was the point of living, anyway?

Lighting his tenth cigarette from the butt of the ninth, the geasan took down from the wall a gigantic razor.

A tiny head peeked over the top of the sorcerer's pocket.

"Won't you," said a little voice, "introduce me, Almarish, to your handsome friend?"

The eleventh cigarette dropped from the lips of the ancient as Almarish brought out Moira and she pirouetted on his palm. She cast a meaningful glance at the geasan. "Almarish is *such* a boor," she declared. "Not one bit like *some* men ... ."

"It was the cigarettes that gave him his power, of course," decided the sorcerer as he climbed the rocky bluff.

"My size," purred Moira, "only a little taller, of course. Women like that." She began to snore daintily in his pocket.

Almarish heaved himself over the top of the bluff, and found himself on a stony plain or plateau scattered with tumbled rocks.

"Vials, sir?" demanded a voice next to his ear.

"Ugh!" he grunted, rapidly sidestepping. "Where are you?"

"Right here." Almarish stared. "No—*here*." Still he could see nothing.

"What was that about vials?" he asked, fingering the dirk.

Something took shape in the air before his eyes. He picked it out of space and inspected the thing. It was a delicate bottle, now empty, designed to hold only a few drops. Golden wires ran through the glass forming patterns suggestive of murder and other forms of sudden death.

"How much?" he asked.

"That ring?" suggested the voice. Almarish felt his hand being taken and one of his rings being twisted off.

"Okay," he said. "It's yours."

"Thanks ever so much," replied the voice gratefully. "Miss Megaera will *love* it."

"Keep away from those Eumenides, boy," Almarish warned. "They're tricky sluts."

"I'll thank you to mind your own business, sir," snapped the voice. It began to whistle an air, which trailed away into the distance.

From behind one of the great, tumbled cairns of rock slid, with a colossal clashing of scales, a monster.

"Ah, there," said the monster.

Almarish surveyed it carefully. The thing was a metallic cross among the octopus, scorpion, flying dragon, tortoise, ape and toad families. Its middle face smiled amiably, almost condescendingly, down on the sorcerer.

"You the *Bête Joyeux?*" asked Almarish.

"See here," said the monster, snorting a bit and dribbling lava from a corner of its mouth. "See here—I've been called many things, some unprintable, but that's a new one. What's it mean?"

"Happy animal, I think," said Almarish.

"Then I probably am," said the monster. It chuckled. "Now what do you want?"

"See this vial? It has to be filled with your tears."

"So what?" asked the monster, scratching itself.

"Will you weep for me?"

"Out of sheer perversity, no. Shall we fight now?"

"I suppose so," said Almarish, heavy-hearted. "There's only one other way to get your tears that I can think of. Put up your dukes, chum."

The monster squared off slowly. It didn't move like a fighter; it seemed to rely on static firepower, like a battle tank. It reached out a tentacle whose end opened slowly into a steaming nozzle. Almarish snapped away as a squirt of sulfurous matter gushed from the tip.

With a lively blow the sorcerer slashed off the tentacle, which scuttled for shelter. The monster proper let out a yell of pain. One of its lionlike paws slapped down and sidewise at Almarish; he stood his ground and let the thing run into the dirk its full length, then jumped inside the thing's guard and scaled its shoulder.

"No fair!" squalled the monster.

He replied with a slash that took off an ear. The creature scratched frantically for him, but he easily eluded the clumsy nails that raked past its hide. As he danced over the skin, stabbing and slashing more like a plowman than a warrior, the nails did fully as much damage as he did.

Suddenly, treacherously, the monster rolled over. Almarish birled it like a log in a pond, harrowing up its exposed belly as it lay on its back.

Back on its feet again, the thing was suddenly still. The sorcerer, catching his breath, began to worry. The squawking pants that had been its inhalations and exhalations had stopped. But it wasn't dead, he knew. The thing was holding its breath. But why was it doing that?

The temperature of the skin began to rise, sharply. So, thought Almarish, it was trying to smoke him off by containing all its heat! He scrambled down over its forehead. The nostril flaps were tight shut. Seemingly, it breathed only by its middle head, the one he was exploring.

His heels were smoking, and the air was growing super-heated. Something had to be done, but good and quick.

With a muttered prayer, Almarish balanced the dirk in his hand and flung it with every ounce of his amazing brawn. Then, not waiting to see the results, he jumped down and ran frantically to the nearest rock. He dodged behind it and watched.

The dirk had struck home. The nostril flaps of the monster had been *pinned* shut. He chuckled richly to himself as the thing pawed at its nose. The metallic skin was beginning to glow red-hot, then white.

He ducked behind the rock, huddled close to it as he saw the first faint hairline of weakness on the creature's glowing hide.

Crash! It exploded like a thunderclap. Parts whizzed past the rock like bullets, bounced and skidded along the ground, fusing rocks as they momentarily touched.

Almarish looked up at last. *La Bête Joyeux* was scattered over most of the plateau.

Almarish found the head at last. It had cooled down considerably; he fervently hoped that it had not dried out. With the handle of his dirk he pried up the eyelid and began a delicate operation.

Finally the dead-white sac was in his hands. Unstoppering the vial, he carefully milked the tear gland into it.

"Moira," he said gently, shaking her.

"You ox!"

She was awake in a moment, ill-tempered as ever.

"What is it now?"

"Your vial," he said, placing it on his palm beside her.

"Well, set it down on the ground. Me, too." He watched as she tugged off the stopper and plunged her face into the crystal-clear liquid.

Then, abruptly, he gasped. "Here," he said, averting his eyes. "Take my cloak."

"Thanks," said the tall young lady with a smile. "I didn't think, for the moment, that my clothes wouldn't grow when I did."

"Now—would you care to begin at the beginning?"

"Certainly. Moira O'Donnel's my name. Born in Dublin. Located in Antrim at the age of twenty-five, when I had the ill luck to antagonize a warlock named McGinty. He shrank me and gave me a beastly temper. Then, because I kept plaguing him, he banished me to these unreal parts.

"He was hipped on the Irish literary renaissance—Yeats, AE, Joyce, Shaw and the rest. So he put a tag on the curse that he found in one of Lord Dunsany's stories, about the tears of *la Bête Joyeux*. In the story it was 'the gladsome beast,' and Mac's French was always weak.

"What magic I know I picked up by eavesdropping. You can't help learning things knocking around the planes, I guess. There were lots of bits that I filed away because I couldn't use them until I achieved full stature again. And now, Almarish, they're all yours. I'm very grateful to you."

He stared into her level green eyes. "Think you could get us back to Ellil?"

"Like *that!*" She snapped her fingers.

"Good. Those rats—Pike and the rest—caught me unawares, but I can raise an army anywhere on a week's notice and take over again."

"I knew you could do it. I'm with you, Almarish, Packer, or whatever your name is."

Diffidently he said, "Moira, you grew very dear to me as you used to snore away in my pocket."

"I don't snore!" she declared.

"Anyway—you can pick whichever name you like. It's yours if you'll have it."

After a little while she said, smiling into his eyes:

"My size. Only a little taller, of course."

[*Galaxy* - December 1951]

With These Hands

1

Halvorsen waited in the Chancery office while Monsignor Reedy disposed of three persons who had preceded him. He was a little dizzy with hunger and noticed only vaguely that the prelate's secretary was beckoning to him. He started to his feet when the secretary pointedly opened the door to Monsignor Reedy's inner office and stood waiting beside it.

The artist crossed the floor, forgetting that he had leaned his portfolio against his chair, remembered at the door and went back for it, flushing. The secretary looked patient.

"Thanks," Halvorsen murmured to him as the door closed.

There was something wrong with the prelate's manner.

"I've brought the designs for the Stations, Padre," he said, opening the portfolio on the desk.

"Bad news, Roald," said the monsignor. "I know how you've been looking forward to the commission—"

"Somebody else get it?" asked the artist faintly, leaning against the desk. "I thought his eminence definitely decided I had the—"

"It's not that," said the monsignor. "But the Sacred Congregation of Rites this week made a pronouncement on images of devotion. Stereopantograph is to be licit within a diocese at the discretion of the bishop. And his eminence—"

"S.P.G.—slimy imitations," protested Halvorsen. "Real as a plastic eye. No texture. No guts. *You* know that, Padre!" he said accusingly.

"I'm sorry, Roald," said the monsignor. "Your work is better than we'll get from a stereopantograph—to my eyes, at least. But there are other considerations."

"Money!" spat the artist.

"Yes, money," the prelate admitted. "His eminence wants to see the St. Xavier U. building program through before he dies. Is that wrong, Roald? And there are our schools, our charities, our Venus mission. S.P.G. will mean a considerable saving on procurement and maintenance of devotional images.

240

Even if I could, I would not disagree with his eminence on adopting it as a matter of diocesan policy."

The prelate's eyes fell on the detailed drawings of the Stations of the Cross and lingered.

"Your St. Veronica," he said abstractedly. "Very fine. It suggests one of Caravaggio's careworn saints to me. I would have liked to see her in the bronze."

"So would I," said Halvorsen hoarsely. "Keep the drawings, Padre." He started for the door.

"But I can't—"

"That's all right."

The artist walked past the secretary blindly and out of the Chancery into Fifth Avenue's spring sunlight. He hoped Monsignor Reedy was enjoying the drawings and was ashamed of himself and sorry for Halvorsen. And he was glad he didn't have to carry the heavy portfolio any more. Everything was heavy lately—chisels, hammer, wooden palette. Maybe the padre would send him something and pretend it was for expenses or an advance, as he had in the past.

Halvorsen's feet carried him up the Avenue. No, there wouldn't be any advances any more. The last steady trickle of income had just been dried up, by an announcement in *Osservatore Romano*. Religious conservatism had carried the Church as far as it would go in its ancient role of art patron.

When all Europe was writing on the wonderful new vellum, the Church stuck to good old papyrus. When all Europe was writing on the wonderful new paper, the Church stuck to good old vellum. When all architects and municipal monument committees and portrait bust clients were patronizing the stereopantograph, the Church stuck to good old expensive sculpture. But not any more.

He was passing an S.P.G. salon now, where one of his Tuesday night pupils worked: one of the few men in the classes. Mostly they consisted of lazy, moody, irritable girls. Halvorsen, surprised at himself, entered the salon, walking between asthenic semi-nude stereos executed in transparent plastic that made the skin of his neck and shoulders prickle with gooseflesh.

Slime! he thought. *How can they ...*

"May I help—oh, hello, Roald. What brings you here?"

He knew suddenly what had brought him there. "Could you make a little advance on next month's tuition, Lewis? I'm strapped." He took a nervous look around the chamber of horrors, avoiding the man's condescending face.

"I guess so, Roald. Would ten dollars be any help? That'll carry us through to the 25th, right?"

"Fine, right, sure," he said, while he was being unwillingly towed around the place.

"I know you don't think much of S.P.G., but it's quiet now, so this is a good chance to see how we work. I don't say it's Art with a capital A, but you've got to admit it's *an* art, something people like at a price they can afford to pay. Here's where we sit them. Then you run out the feelers to the reference points on the face. You know what they are?"

He heard himself say dryly: "I know what they are. The Egyptian sculptors used them when they carved statues of the pharaohs."

"Yes? I never knew that. There's nothing new under the sun, is there? But *this* is the heart of the S.P.G." The youngster proudly swung open the door of an electronic device in the wall of the portrait booth. Tubes winked sullenly at Halvorsen.

"The esthetikon?" he asked indifferently. He did not feel indifferent, but it would be absurd to show anger, no matter how much he felt it, against a mindless aggregation of circuits that could calculate layouts, criticize and correct pictures for a desired effect—and that had put the artist of design out of a job.

"Yes. The lenses take sixteen profiles, you know, and we set the esthetikon for whatever we want—cute, rugged, sexy, spiritual, brainy, or a combination. It fairs curves from profile to profile to give us just what we want, distorts the profiles themselves within limits if it has to, and there's your portrait stored in the memory tank waiting to be taped. You set your ratio for any enlargement or reduction you want and play it back. I wish we were reproducing today; it's fascinating to watch. You just pour in your cold-set plastic, the nozzles ooze out a core and start crawling over to scan—a drop here, a worm there, and it begins to take shape.

"We mostly do portrait busts here, the Avenue trade, but Wilgus, the foreman, used to work in a monument shop in Brooklyn. He did that heroic-size war memorial on the East River Drive—hired Garda Bouchette, the TV girl, for the central figure. And what a figure! He told me he set the esthetikon plates for three-quarters sexy, one-quarter spiritual. Here's something interesting—standing figurine of Orin Ryerson, the banker. He ordered twelve. Figurines are coming in. The girls like them because they can show their shapes. You'd be surprised at some of the poses they want to try—"

Somehow, Halvorsen got out with the ten dollars, walked to Sixth Avenue and sat down hard in a cheap restaurant. He had coffee and dozed a little, waking with a guilty start at a racket across the street. There was a building going up. For a while he watched the great machines pour walls and floors, the workmen rolling here and there on their little chariots to weld on a wall panel, stripe on an electric circuit of conductive ink, or spray plastic finish over the "wired" wall, all without leaving the saddles of their little mechanical chariots.

Halvorsen felt more determined. He bought a paper from a vending machine by the restaurant door, drew another cup of coffee and turned to the help-wanted ads.

The tricky trade-school ads urged him to learn construction work and make big money. Be a plumbing-machine set-up man. Be a house-wiring machine tender. Be a servotruck driver. Be a lumber-stacker operator. Learn pouring-machine maintenance.

Make big money!

A sort of panic overcame him. He ran to the phone booth and dialed a Passaic number. He heard the *ring-ring-ring* and strained to hear old Mr. Krehbeil's stumping footsteps growing louder as he neared the phone, even though he knew he would hear nothing until the receiver was picked up.

Ring-ring-ring. "Hello?" grunted the old man's voice, and his face appeared on the little screen. "Hello, Mr. Halvorsen. What can I do for you?"

Halvorsen was tongue-tied. He couldn't possibly say: I just wanted to see if you were still there. I was afraid you weren't there any more. He choked and improvised: "Hello, Mr. Krehbeil. It's about the banister on the stairs in my place. I noticed it's pretty shaky. Could you come over some time and fix it for me?"

Krehbeil peered suspiciously out of the screen. "I could do that," he said slowly. "I don't have much work nowadays. But you can carpenter as good as me, Mr. Halvorsen, and frankly you're very slow pay and I like cabinet work better. I'm not a young man and climbing around on ladders takes it out of me. If you can't find anybody else, I'll take the work, but I got to have some of the money first, just for the materials. It isn't easy to get good wood any more."

"All right," said Halvorsen. "Thanks, Mr. Krehbeil. I'll call you if I can't get anybody else."

He hung up and went back to his table and newspaper. His face was burning with anger at the old man's reluctance and his own foolish panic. Krehbeil didn't realize they were both in the same leaky boat. Krehbeil, who didn't get a job in a month, still thought with senile pride that he was a journeyman carpenter and cabinet-maker who could make his solid way anywhere with his tool-box and his skill, and that he could afford to look down on anything as disreputable as an artist—even an artist who could carpenter as well as he did himself.

Labuerre had made Halvorsen learn carpentry, and Labuerre had been right. You build a scaffold so you can sculp up high, not so it will collapse and you break a leg. You build your platforms so they hold the rock steady, not so it wobbles and chatters at every blow of the chisel. You build your armatures so they hold the plasticine you slam onto them.

But the help-wanted ads wanted no builders of scaffolds, platforms and armatures. The factories were calling for set-up men and maintenance men for the production and assembly machines.

From upstate, General Vegetables had sent a recruiting team for farm help—harvest set-up and maintenance men, a few openings for experienced operators of tank-caulking machinery. Under "office and professional" the demand was heavy for computer men, for girls who could run the I.B.M. Letteriter, esp. familiar sales and collections corresp., for office machinery maintenance and repair men. A job printing house wanted an esthetikon operator for letterhead layouts and the like. A.T.&T. wanted trainees to earn while learning telephone maintenance. A direct-mail advertising outfit wanted an artist—no, they wanted a sales-executive who could scrawl picture-ideas that would be subjected to the criticism and correction of the esthetikon.

Halvorsen leafed tiredly through the rest of the paper. He knew he wouldn't get a job, and if he did he wouldn't hold it. He knew it was a terrible thing to admit to yourself that you might starve to death because you were bored by anything except art, but he admitted it.

It had happened often enough in the past—artists undergoing preposterous hardships, not, as people thought, because they were devoted to art, but because nothing else was interesting. If there were only some impressive, sonorous word that summed up the aching, oppressive futility that overcame him when he tried to get out of art—only there wasn't.

He thought he could tell which of the photos in the tabloid had been corrected by the esthetikon.

There was a shot of Jink Bitsy, who was to star in a remake of *Peter Pan*. Her ears had been made to look not pointed but pointy, her upper lip had been lengthened a trifle, her nose had been pugged a little and tilted quite a lot, her freckles were cuter than cute, her brows were innocently arched, and her lower lip and eyes were nothing less than pornography.

There was a shot, apparently uncorrected, of the last Venus ship coming in at La Guardia and the average-looking explorers grinning. Caption: "Austin Malone and crew smile relief on safe arrival. Malone says Venus colonies need men, machines. See story on p. 2."

Petulantly, Halvorsen threw the paper under the table and walked out. What had space travel to do with him? Vacations on the Moon and expeditions to Venus and Mars were part of the deadly encroachment on his livelihood and no more.

2

He took the subway to Passaic and walked down a long-still traffic beltway to his studio, almost the only building alive in the slums near the rusting railroad freight yard.

A sign that had once said "F. Labuerre, Sculptor—Portraits and Architectural Commissions" now said "Roald Halvorsen; Art Classes—Reasonable Fees." It was a grimy two-story frame building with a shopfront in which were mounted some of his students' charcoal figure studies and oil still-lifes. He lived upstairs, taught downstairs front, and did his own work downstairs, back behind dirty, ceiling-high drapes.

Going in, he noticed that he had forgotten to lock the door again. He slammed it bitterly. At the noise, somebody called from behind the drapes: "Who's that?"

"Halvorsen!" he yelled in a sudden fury. "I live here. I own this place. Come out of there! What do you want?"

There was a fumbling at the drapes and a girl stepped between them, shrinking from their dirt.

"Your door was open," she said firmly, "and it's a shop. I've just been here a couple of minutes. I came to ask about classes, but I don't think I'm interested if you're this bad-tempered."

A pupil. Pupils were never to be abused, especially not now.

"I'm terribly sorry," he said. "I had a trying day in the city." Now turn it on. "I wouldn't tell everybody a terrible secret like this, but I've lost a commission. You understand? I thought so. Anybody who'd traipse out here to my dingy abode would be *simpatica*. Won't you sit down? No, not there—humor an artist and sit over there. The warm background of that still-life brings out your color—quite good color. Have you ever been painted? You've a very interesting face, you know. Some day I'd like to—but you mentioned classes.

"We have figure classes, male and female models alternating, on Tuesday nights. For that I have to be very stern and ask you to sign up for an entire course of twelve lessons at sixty dollars. It's the models' fees—they're exorbitant. Saturday afternoons we have still-life classes for beginners in oils. That's only two dollars a class, but you might sign up for a series of six and pay ten dollars in advance, which saves you two whole dollars. I also give private instructions to a few talented amateurs."

The price was open on that one—whatever the traffic would bear. It had been a year since he'd had a private pupil and she'd taken only six lessons at five dollars an hour.

"The still-life sounds interesting," said the girl, holding her head self-consciously the way they all did when he gave them the patter. It was a good head, carried well up. The muscles clung close, not yet slacked into geotropic loops and lumps. The line of youth is heliotropic, he confusedly thought. "I saw some interesting things back there. Was that your own work?"

She rose, obviously with the expectation of being taken into the studio. Her body was one of those long-lined, small-breasted, coltish jobs that the pre-Raphaelites loved to draw.

"Well—" said Halvorsen. A deliberate show of reluctance and then a bright smile of confidence. "*You'll* understand," he said positively and drew aside the curtains.

"What a curious place!" She wandered about, inspecting the drums of plaster, clay and plasticine, the racks of tools, the stands, the stones, the chisels, the forge, the kiln, the lumber, the glaze bench.

"I *like* this," she said determinedly, picking up a figure a half-meter tall, a Venus he had cast in bronze while studying under Labuerre some years ago. "How much is it?"

An honest answer would scare her off, and there was no chance in the world that she'd buy. "I hardly ever put my things up for sale," he told her lightly. "That was just a little study. I do work on commission only nowadays."

Her eyes flicked about the dingy room, seeming to take in its scaling plaster and warped floor and see through the wall to the abandoned slum in which it was set. There was amusement in her glance.

I am not being honest, she thinks. She thinks that is funny. Very well, I will be honest. "Six hundred dollars," he said flatly.

The girl set the figurine on its stand with a rap and said, half angry and half amused: "I don't understand it. That's more than a month's pay for me. I could get an S.P.G. statuette just as pretty as this for ten dollars. Who do you artists think you are, anyway?"

Halvorsen debated with himself about what he could say in reply:

An S.P.G. operator spends a week learning his skill and I spend a lifetime learning mine.

An S.P.G. operator makes a mechanical copy of a human form distorted by formulæ mechanically arrived at from psychotests of population samples. I take full responsibility for my work; it is mine, though I use what I see fit from Egypt, Greece, Rome, the Middle Ages, the Renaissance, the Augustan and Romantic and Modern Eras.

An S.P.G. operator works in soft, homogeneous plastic; I work in bronze that is more complicated than you dream, that is cast and acid-dipped today so it will slowly take on rich and subtle coloring many years from today.

An S.P.G. operator could not make an Orpheus Fountain ...

He mumbled, "Orpheus," and keeled over.

Halvorsen awoke in his bed on the second floor of the building. His fingers and toes buzzed electrically and he felt very clear-headed. The girl and a man, unmistakably a doctor, were watching him.

"You don't seem to belong to any Medical Plans, Halvorsen," the doctor said irritably. "There weren't any cards on you at all. No Red, no Blue, no Green, no Brown."

"I used to be on the Green Plan, but I let it lapse," the artist said defensively. "And look what happened!"

"Stop nagging him!" the girl said. "I'll pay you your fee."

"It's supposed to come through a Plan," the doctor fretted.

"We won't tell anybody," the girl promised. "Here's five dollars. Just stop nagging him."

"Malnutrition," said the doctor. "Normally I'd send him to a hospital, but I don't see how I could manage it. He isn't on any Plan at all. Look, I'll take the money and leave some vitamins. That's what he needs—vitamins. And food."

"I'll see that he eats," the girl said, and the doctor left.

"How long since you've had anything?" she asked Halvorsen.

"I had some coffee today," he answered, thinking back. "I'd been working on detail drawings for a commission and it fell through. I told you that. It was a shock."

"I'm Lucretia Grumman," she said, and went out.

He dozed until she came back with an armful of groceries.

"It's hard to get around down here," she complained.

"It was Labuerre's studio," he told her defiantly. "He left it to me when he died. Things weren't so run-down in his time. I studied under him; he was one of the last. He had a joke—'They don't really want my stuff, but they're ashamed to let me starve.' He warned me that they wouldn't be ashamed to let *me* starve, but I insisted and he took me in."

Halvorsen drank some milk and ate some bread. He thought of the change from the ten dollars in his pocket and decided not to mention it. Then he remembered that the doctor had gone through his pockets.

"I can pay you for this," he said. "It's very kind of you, but you mustn't think I'm penniless. I've just been too preoccupied to take care of myself."

"Sure," said the girl. "But we can call this an advance. I want to sign up for some classes."

"Be happy to have you."

"Am I bothering you?" asked the girl. "You said something odd when you fainted—'Orpheus.'"

"Did I say that? I must have been thinking of Milles' Orpheus Fountain in Copenhagen. I've seen photos, but I've never been there."

"Germany? But there's nothing left of Germany."

"Copenhagen's in Denmark. There's quite a lot of Denmark left. It was only on the fringes. Heavily radiated, but still there."

"I want to travel, too," she said. "I work at La Guardia and I've never been off, except for an orbiting excursion. I want to go to the Moon on my vacation. They give us a bonus in travel vouchers. It must be wonderful dancing under the low gravity."

Spaceport? Off? Low gravity? Terms belonging to the detested electronic world of the stereopantograph in which he had no place.

"Be very interesting," he said, closing his eyes to conceal disgust.

"I *am* bothering you. I'll go away now, but I'll be back Tuesday night for the class. What time do I come and what should I bring?"

"Eight. It's charcoal—I sell you the sticks and paper. Just bring a smock."

"All right. And I want to take the oils class, too. And I want to bring some people I know to see your work. I'm sure they'll see something they like. Austin Malone's in from Venus—he's a special friend of mine."

"Lucretia," he said. "Or do some people call you Lucy?"

"Lucy."

"Will you take that little bronze you liked? As a thank you?"

"I can't do that!"

"Please. I'd feel much better about this. I really mean it."

She nodded abruptly, flushing, and almost ran from the room.

Now why did I do that? he asked himself. He hoped it was because he liked Lucy Grumman very much. He hoped it wasn't a cold-blooded investment of a piece of sculpture that would never be sold, anyway, just to make sure she'd be back with class fees and more groceries.

3

She was back on Tuesday, a half-hour early and carrying a smock. He introduced her formally to the others as they arrived: a dozen or so bored young women who, he suspected, talked a great deal about their art lessons outside, but in class used any excuse to stop sketching.

He didn't dare show Lucy any particular consideration. There were fierce little miniature cliques in the class. Halvorsen knew they laughed at him and his line among themselves, and yet, strangely, were fiercely jealous of their seniority and right to individual attention.

The lesson was an ordeal, as usual. The model, a muscle-bound young graduate of the barbell gyms and figure-photography studios, was stupid and argumentative about ten-minute poses. Two of the girls came near a hair-pulling brawl over the rights to a preferred sketching location. A third girl had discovered Picasso's cubist period during the past week and proudly announced that she didn't *feel* perspective.

But the two interminable hours finally ticked by. He nagged them into cleaning up—not as bad as the Saturdays with oils—and stood by the open door. Otherwise they would have stayed all night, cackling about absent students and snarling sulkily among themselves. His well-laid plans went sour though. A large and flashy car drove up as the girls were leaving.

"That's Austin Malone," said Lucy. "He came to pick me up and look at your work."

That was all the wedge her fellow-pupils needed.

"Aus-tin Ma-*lone! Well!"*

"Lucy, darling, I'd love to meet a real *spaceman.*"

"Roald, darling, would you mind very much if I stayed a moment?"

"I'm certainly not going to miss this and I don't care if you mind or not, Roald, darling!"

Malone was an impressive figure. Halvorsen thought: he looks as though he's been run through an esthetikon set for "brawny" and "determined." Lucy made a hash of the introductions and the spaceman didn't rise to conversational bait dangled enticingly by the girls.

In a clear voice, he said to Halvorsen: "I don't want to take up too much of your time. Lucy tells me you have some things for sale. Is there any place we can look at them where it's quiet?"

The students made sulky exits.

"Back here," said the artist.

The girl and Malone followed him through the curtains. The spaceman made a slow circuit of the studio, seeming to repel questions.

He sat down at last and said: "I don't know what to think, Halvorsen. This place stuns me. Do you *know* you're in the Dark Ages?"

People who never have given a thought to Chartres and Mont St. Michel usually call it the Dark Ages, Halvorsen thought wryly. He asked, "Technologically, you mean? No, not at all. My plaster's better, my colors are better, my metal is better—tool metal, not casting metal, that is."

"I mean *hand* work," said the spaceman. "Actually working by *hand.*"

The artist shrugged. "There have been crazes for the techniques of the boiler works and the machine shop," he admitted. "Some interesting things were done, but they didn't stand up well. Is there anything here that takes your eye?"

"I like those dolphins," said the spaceman, pointing to a perforated terra-cotta relief on the wall. They had been commissioned by an architect, then later refused for reasons of economy when the house had run way over estimate. "They'd look bully over the fireplace in my town apartment. Like them, Lucy?"

"I think they're wonderful," said the girl.

Roald saw the spaceman go rigid with the effort not to turn and stare at her. He loved her and he was jealous.

Roald told the story of the dolphins and said: "The price that the architect thought was too high was three hundred and sixty dollars."

Malone grunted. "Doesn't seem unreasonable—if you set a high store on inspiration."

"I don't know about inspiration," the artist said evenly. "But I was awake for two days and two nights shoveling coal and adjusting drafts to fire that thing in my kiln."

The spacemen looked contemptuous. "I'll take it," he said. "Be something to talk about during those awkward pauses. Tell me, Halvorsen, how's Lucy's work? Do you think she ought to stick with it?"

"Austin," objected the girl, "don't be so blunt. How can he possibly know after one day?"

"She can't draw yet," the artist said cautiously. "It's all coordination, you know—thousands of hours of practice, training your eye and hand to work together until you can put a line on paper where you want it. Lucy, if you're really interested in it, you'll learn to draw well. I don't think any of the other students will. They're in it because of boredom or snobbery, and they'll stop before they have their eye-hand coordination."

"I *am* interested," she said firmly.

Malone's determined restraint broke. "Damned right you are. In—" He recovered himself and demanded of Halvorsen: "I understand your point about coordination. But thousands of hours when you can buy a camera? It's absurd."

"I was talking about drawing, not art," replied Halvorsen. "Drawing is putting a line on paper where you want it, I said." He took a deep breath and hoped the great distinction wouldn't sound ludicrous and trivial. "So let's say that art is knowing how to put the line in the right place."

"Be practical. There isn't any art. Not any more. I get around quite a bit and I never see anything but photos and S.P.G.s. A few heirlooms, yes, but nobody's painting or carving any more."

"There's some art, Malone. My students—a couple of them in the still-life class—are quite good. There are more across the country. Art for occupational therapy, or a hobby, or something to do with the hands. There's trade in their work. They sell them to each other, they give them to their friends, they hang them on the walls. There are even some sculptors like that. Sculpture is prescribed by doctors. The occupational therapists say it's even better than drawing and painting, so some of these people work in plasticine and soft stone, and some of them get to be good."

"Maybe so. I'm an engineer, Halvorsen. We glory in doing things the easy way. Doing things the easy way got me to Mars and Venus and it's going to get me to Ganymede. You're doing things the hard way, and your inefficiency has no place in this world. Look at you! You've lost a fingertip—some accident, I suppose."

"I never noticed—" said Lucy, and then let out a faint "Oh!"

Halvorsen curled the middle finger of his left hand into the palm, where he usually carried it to hide the missing first joint.

"Accidents are a sign of inadequate mastery of material and equipment," said Malone sententiously. "While you stick to your methods and I stick to mine, *you can't compete with me.*"

His tone made it clear that he was talking about more than engineering.

"Shall we go now, Lucy? Here's my card, Halvorsen. Send those dolphins along and I'll mail you a check."

4

The artist walked the half-dozen blocks to Mr. Krehbeil's place the next day. He found the old man in the basement shop of his fussy house, hunched over his bench with a powerful light overhead. He was trying to file a saw.

"Mr. Krehbeil!" Halvorsen called over the shriek of metal.

The carpenter turned around and peered with watery eyes. "I can't see like I used to,' he said querulously. "I go over the same teeth on this damn saw, I skip teeth, I can't see the light shine off it when I got one set. The glare." He banged down his three-cornered file petulantly. "Well, what can I do for you?"

"I need some crating stock. Anything. I'll trade you a couple of my maple four-by-fours."

The old face became cunning. "And will you set my saw? My *saws,* I mean. It's nothing to you—an hour's work. You have the eyes."

Halvorsen said bitterly: "All right." The old man had to drive his bargain, even though he might never use his saws again. And then the artist promptly repented of his bitterness, offering up a quick prayer that his own failure to conform didn't make him as much of a nuisance to the world as Krehbeil was.

The carpenter was pleased as they went through his small stock of wood and chose boards to crate the dolphin relief. He was pleased enough to give Halvorsen coffee and cake before the artist buckled down to filing the saws.

Over the kitchen table, Halvorsen tried to probe. "Things pretty slow now?"

It would be hard to spoil Krehbeil's day now. "People are always fools. They don't know good handwork. Some day," he said apocalyptically, "I laugh on the other side of my face when their foolish machine-buildings go falling down in a strong wind, all of them, all over the country. Even my boy—I used to beat him good, almost every day—he works a foolish concrete machine and his house should fall on his head like the rest."

Halvorsen knew it was Krehbeil's son who supported him by mail, and changed the subject. "You get some cabinet work?"

"Stupid women! What they call antiques—they don't know Meissen, they don't know Biedermeier. They bring me trash to repair sometimes. I make them pay; I swindle them good."

"I wonder if things would be different if there were anything left over in Europe—"

"People will still be fools, Mr. Halvorsen," said the carpenter positively. "Didn't you say you were going to file those saws today?"

So the artist spent two noisy hours filing before he carried his crating stock to the studio.

Lucy was there. She had brought some things to eat. He dumped the lumber with a bang and demanded: "Why aren't you at work?"

"We get days off," she said vaguely. "Austin thought he'd give me the cash for the terra-cotta and I could give it to you."

She held out an envelope while he studied her silently. The farce was beginning again. But this time he dreaded it.

It would not be the first time that a lonesome, discontented girl chose to see him as a combination of romantic rebel and lost pup, with the consequences you'd expect.

He knew from books, experience and Labuerre's conversation in the old days that there was nothing novel about the comedy—that there had even been artists, lots of them, who had counted on endless repetitions of it for their livelihood.

The girl drops in with groceries and the artist is pleasantly surprised; the girl admires this little thing or that after payday and buys it and the artist is pleasantly surprised; the girl brings her friends to take lessons or make little purchases and the artist is pleasantly surprised. The girl may be seduced by the artist or vice versa, which shortens the comedy, or they may get married, which lengthens it somewhat.

It had been three years since Halvorsen had last played out the farce with a manic-depressive divorcée from Elmira: three years during which he had crossed the mid-point between thirty and forty; three more years to get beaten down by being unwanted and working too much and eating too little.

Also, he knew, he was in love with this girl.

He took the envelope, counted three hundred and twenty dollars and crammed it into his pocket. "That was your idea," he said. "Thanks. Now get out, will you? I've got work to do."

She stood there, shocked.

"I said get out. I have work to do."

"Austin was right," she told him miserably. "You don't care how people feel. You just want to get things out of them."

She ran from the studio, and Halvorsen fought with himself not to run after her.

He walked slowly into his workshop and studied his array of tools, though he paid little attention to his finished pieces. It would be nice to spend about half of this money on open-hearth steel rod and bar stock to forge into chisels; he thought he knew where he could get some—but she would be back, or he would break and go to her and be forgiven, and the comedy would be played out, after all.

He couldn't let that happen.

5

Aalesund, on the Atlantic side of the Dourefeld mountains of Norway, was in the lee of the blasted continent. One more archaeologist there made no difference, as long as he had the sense to recognize the propeller-like international signposts that said with their three blades, *Radiation Hazard,* and knew what every schoolboy knew about protective clothing and reading a personal Geiger counter.

The car Halvorsen rented was for a brief trip over the mountains to study contaminated Oslo. Well-muffled, he could make it and back in a dozen hours and no harm done.

But he took the car past Oslo, Wennersborg and Göteborg, along the Kattegat coast to Helsinborg, and abandoned it there, among the three-bladed polyglot signs, crossing to Denmark. Danes were as unlike Prussians as they could be, but their unfortunate little peninsula was a sprout off Prussia which radio-cobalt dust couldn't tell from the real thing. The three-bladed signs were most specific.

With a long way to walk along the rubble-littered highways, he stripped off the impregnated coveralls and boots. He had long since shed the noisy counter and the uncomfortable gloves and mask.

The silence was eerie as he limped into Copenhagen at noon. He didn't know whether the radiation was getting to him or whether he was tired and hungry and no more. As though thinking of a stranger, he liked what he was doing.

I'll be my own audience, he thought. *God knows I learned there isn't any other, not any more. You have to know when to stop. Rodin, the dirty old, wonderful old man, knew that. He taught us not to slick it and polish it and smooth it until it looked like liquid instead of bronze and stone. Van Gogh was crazy as a loon, but he knew when to stop and varnish it, and he didn't care if the paint looked like paint instead of looking like sunset clouds or moonbeams. Up in Hartford, Brown and Sharpe stop when they've got a turret lathe; they don't put caryatids on it. I'll stop while my life is a life, before it becomes a thing with distracting embellishments such as a wife who will come to despise me, a succession of gradually less worthwhile pieces that nobody will look at.*

Blame nobody, he told himself, lightheadedly.

And then it was in front of him, terminating a vista of weeds and bomb rubble—Milles' Orpheus Fountain.

It took a man, he thought. Esthetikon circuits couldn't do it. There was a gross mixture of styles, a calculated flaw that the esthetikon couldn't be set to make. Orpheus and the souls were classic or later; the three-headed dog was archaic. That was to tell you about the antiquity and invincibility of Hell, and that Cerberus knows Orpheus will never go back into life with his bride.

There was the heroic, tragic central figure that looked mighty enough to battle with the gods, but battle wasn't any good against the grinning, knowing, hateful three-headed dog it stood on. You don't battle the pavement where you walk or the floor of the house you're in; you can't. So Orpheus, his face a mask of controlled and suffering fury, crashes a great chord from his lyre that moved trees and stones. Around him the naked souls in Hell start at the chord, each in its own way: the young lovers down in death; the mother down in death; the musician, deaf and down in death, straining to hear.

Halvorsen, walking uncertainly towards the fountain, felt something break inside him, and a heaviness in his lungs. As he pitched forward among the weeds, he didn't care that the three-headed dog was grinning its knowing, hateful grin down at him. He had heard the chord from the lyre.

Iteration

I punched IIIAA24 and heard over my bonephone, wincing: "Darling—you're ... *back!*"

I cut the wince short and threw in the life lever. Joe Henderson, standing in the actor's dock, said broodingly: "Yes, dear ..." He registered worry, then gallantry and cheerfulness. I threw out the life lever and punched IVTG13, which was a young couple, summer clothes, seen walking into their suburban bungalow.

I could've played that score in my sleep; I don't know how many times the soapies have used it—

I asked you not to interrupt me damn it! You wanted to know why I ran out, and I said I'd tell you—oh, dinner?

What's this stuff—beep—oh, *beef?* 'S good. Hard on the jaws first time, though—I'll go on with the story.

You want to know why they don't punch it on rolls like a jacquard loom, do you? Once they used to, but even a weaving machine makes mistakes. When there's a mistake they just rip it out and go on. But when the soapies go out—

Their pattern either got punched wrong or the machine slipped or something. So when Old Ma Whiddicomb came into the screen, instead of lavender from the grill you got IXWQO9, which is used in stable scenes. And once, on *When a Man Marries Joan's Big Sister* everything was going fine on a big renunciation scene—Joan was giving up David—she kept up a brave front and walked away smiling. When she turned the corner she was supposed to run for her bedroom and burst into tears, but instead of her bedroom door closing, the machine cut in a shot of a two-holer from *Uncle Eb of Gobbler's Nob.*

That's what the present system evolved out of, and it's foolproof. I took three years at the Rochester Conservatory and did PG at the Juilliard. Give me any score, one with a hundred sets, landscapes, weather, twenty actors in the dock, scents to match everything, mood music changing every two seconds—I can handle it.

Pay is right, brother—didn't catch your name?—how'd'y'do, Mr. Osgood. I got two thousand a month and a pension plan for a twelve-hour week.

Okay, okay—I'm *telling* you why I ran out. In fact I've told you already. It was that line: "Darling—you're ... *back!*"

It's a dramatic convention, I suppose, like the property man in the Chinese theater, or a Chorus in the Greek, or asides in the big tub-thumping Victorian days. If an Athenian Greek didn't have a chorus to explain what was going on, he'd feel bewildered and cheated. If the housewife watching a soapie didn't see the heroine say to her husband when he comes home: "Darling—you're ... *back!*" she'd think there was something wrong and worry about it.

No, don't ask me why they say it. I don't know why a dame who just saw her husband leave for work at ten should register surprise, delight and wonder when he comes back home at fifteen o'clock. They just do, in the soapies.

Anyway, I was telling you about the day before yesterday. In a nice blend of canned shots by me and close-ups by Henderson and his babe, we ground our way through the next ten minutes. It was established that Henderson had lost his job because of an inexplicable decline in his efficiency index; he groaned that he was no good and would run out because it would be better that way.

Then we cut to Henderson's mother-in-law and established that she'd slipped him some phenylethylbarbituric acid instead of his vitamins, so he'd lose his job and run out and she could marry her daughter off to a man she had her eye on. Some nice canned stuff in that sequence of her hands opening a capsule and changing the powder in it, all with the appropriate chemical scents.

Cut back to Henderson, making his will before running out. His wife shyly comes in and shows him a tiny identification tag she's been making.

"You don't mean—?" cries Henderson and she lowers her eyes. I step down hard on the benzedrine pedal, throw in the *Hallelujah Chorus,* set up Abstraction 17 for two seconds and cut to the announcer, who's been combing his beard and worrying about a blackhead he just noticed.

"Ladies!" he cries—big smile—"How often lately have you been making the FT?" He lowers his voice, winks a little and coos: "FT, as of course you all know, stands for the famous Cam Brothers Flatulence Test—"

Pete Laurie comes to relieve me on the console and I'm through for the day; I walk out on the Commercial and head for the *Olde Tyme Speake,* down the street.

I don't know if any of you are New Yorkers—maybe you know the *Speake?* It's a really quaint place with authentic atmosphere, early twentieth century—old oak rafters and red-leather bar-stools, a rack of shaving mugs, lots of chromium. They have mottoes on the wall from the period—*Landlord, Fill the Flowing Bowl, Nuts to You,* and things like that.

Can I have some more of that beep stuff? I mean *beef.* I'll learn, quit the kidding—I only ran out last night, fella!

Anyway, I met Sam Caldicott at the *Speake.* Could've knocked me over with a feather. We were classmates at Chicago Metaphysical before I went to Rochester. He was going to go in for dietetics or something.

"Hello, Sam!" I said.

"You too," he growled, looking up. "Go to Dachau." He was nasty-drunk, but he finally recognized me. I got him a wake-up and had a buttered rum myself. When the stuff worked on him, he apologized and asked me politely what I was doing with myself. I told him I was a soapie consolist; he gave me a funny look.

He had switched from dietetics to psychiatry pretty late and so had to start learning almost from the beginning again. He'd been in practice only six years, but he said he was doing nicely.

"Well," I said. "If I'm ever tempted to run out I'll give you a ring and you can talk me out of it."

"Are you so sure I would?"

I shuddered at the thought. "If you're any kind of friend, you will; the hell with that Reserve stuff!"

"Ever been there?"

"No," I told him, "and I never will. A bunch of howling barbarians that couldn't stand the gaff, thought they were higher-strung than anybody else—sissies is what they are. They slip back culturally to the twentieth or fifteenth century and they think they're rugged he-men!"

"It could be worse," he said tolerantly. His eyes narrowed as he seemed to remember something: "I'm treating a woman now—pitiful case; hopeless, I fear. She'd be a hell of a lot better off if she'd been in the Utah Reserve for the past few years."

I gave him some stuff from a talk I'd had with Mr. Administrator Etterson. He'd had it absolutely firsthand that they were practicing human sacrifice in the Reserve. Caldicott just laughed; he simply didn't believe it. I asked him what he meant by that crack about the woman who should have run out. He said he'd show me. I had to get home to my wife, but he got me mad enough to forget about it for the time being. We took a flit to Bronnix, the Morrisania Hospital where he was Resident Psychiatrist.

He warned me outside the patient's room that I'd better keep my mouth shut—the least little thing could send her off into one of her spasms. We went in.

The woman was knitting, her eye on a soapie screen. She turned to us—not bad looking—and said to Caldicott: "Darling—you're ... *back!*" Just like that. Then she registered alarm, apprehension and curiosity and said, batting her eyes at me: "But—won't you ... *introduce* me?"

It was hard to keep from looking around for the mike and the console. I've played and seen that situation a thousand times and now I was meeting it in real life!

"This is my associate," said Caldicott ambiguously. He snapped off the soapie just as Vera Venable, the Alienist's niece, was pleading with Professor Sykes not to fire her uncle from the clinic staff.

"Turn it on!" she screamed. "You've left poor Vera hanging in the ether! Call her back! Don't leave her out there!"

Caldicott resignedly turned the soapie back on, and the woman said, arching her brows: "Why—*thank* you, darling! That was ... very sweet!" Running the last two words together and simultaneously lowering her eyes with a shy little smile. The line was another oldie, used several times a day to cover everything from passing an ashtray to a diamond ring.

We left and went to the hospital refectory.

The refectory soapie screen was on, of course, and I was alarmed to find I was alarmed at the number of people who were watching it. Caldicott read my expression, and gave a sour grin.

"She's the first," he said simply.

"Go to Dachau! I don't believe it!"

"You will soon. I tell you, she's the first. There are going to be more—and more—*and more*."

"Consider: as long ago as the twentieth century there were housewives who never differentiated between real persons and the audio-performers whom they listened to daily. They worried with them, laughed with them, discussed them as though they were absent neighbors. With the slow development of the additional circuits—video, oleo, full-color and tactile for those who like it—the effect was magnified. With the Krebski Formula of the last century, which related the numerical quantities of music to the numerical quantities of the electroencephalogram curves produced by the music, the effect was perfected.

"The housewife of today, frankly, has a soft touch. She dusts, washes dishes, waxes floors and so on by tapping buttons. With her spare time she watches the soapie screen, and she has a *lot* of spare time. I've drawn a graph—"

He took out a sheet of paper and smoothed it carefully. I don't pretend to understand such things; I'm a consolist, not a tube-jockey, and I told him so.

"But look," he urged. "Here's the abscissa meaning 'log-log of number of Caldicott Syndrome cases at one time'—"

"Caldicott Syndrome?"

"That's what I call it," he said modestly. "And this red circle indicates where we stand on the time-axis now. You see the rise—"

I finally looked and laughed at what I saw. "You really think," I said, "that the saturation point's been reached?"

"I predicted it a year ago," he said solemnly. "I was actually waiting for the case you just saw to turn up. I believe that there will be five hundred cases tomorrow, two thousand cases the next day, and so on. Pfannkuchen's studies in mass hysteria—"

I got up. "If you're right," I said, "I'll be the first man to run out and join the wild-men in the Utah Reserve. But, Caldicott, I think you're all wet. That woman upstairs is weak-minded and that's all there is to it. I work with the soapies; I can't believe that any normal person, like my wife, say, could be knocked off the trolley by them. I've got to go now; I'll be seeing you around."

I left and took a flit for Linden, where I live. Pfannkuchen's studies in mass hysteria, my eye!

But my wife met me at the door and said, with surprise, delight and apprehension: "Darling—you're ... *back!*"

Would you pass me some more of that beef stuff?

[Fantasy and Science Fiction - December 1952]

The Goodly Creatures

How many goodly creatures are there here!
How beauteous mankind is! O brave new world,
That has such people in it!
—Shakespeare, "The Tempest"

Farwell suddenly realized that his fingers had been trembling all morning, with a hair-fine vibration that he couldn't control. He looked at them in amazement and rested them on the keys of his typewriter. The tremor stopped and Farwell told himself to ignore it; then it would go away. The copy in the typewriter said: *Kumfyseets—add I* in the upper left-hand corner and under it: *hailed by veteran space-men as the greatest advance in personal comfort and safety on the spaceways since ...*

Since what? It was just another pneumatic couch. Why didn't he ever get anything he could *work* with? This one begged for pix—a stripped-down model in a Kumfyseet, smiling under a pretended seven-G take-off acceleration—but the Chicago Chair Company account didn't have an art budget. No art, and they were howling for tear-sheets already.

... comfort and safety on the spaceways since ...

He could take Worple to a good lunch and get a shirt-tail graf in his lousy "Stubby Says" column and that should hold Chicago Chair for another week. They wouldn't know the difference between Worple and ...

Farwell's intercom buzzed. "Mr. Henry Schneider to see you about employment."

"Send him in, Grace."

Schneider was a beefy kid with a practiced smile and a heavy handshake. "I saw your ad for a junior copywriter," he said, sitting down confidently. He opened an expensive, new-looking briefcase and threw a folder on the desk.

Farwell leafed through it—the standard presentation. A fact sheet listing journalistic honors in high school and college, summer jobs on weeklies, "rose to sergeantcy in only ten months during U.M.T. period." Copies of by-line pieces pasted neatly, without wrinkles, onto heavy pages. A TV scenario for the college station. A letter from the dean of men, a letter from the dean of the journalism school.

"As you see," Schneider told him, "I'm versatile. Sports, travel, science, human-interest, spot news—anything."

"Yes. Well, you wouldn't be doing much actual writing to start, Schneider. When …"

"I'm glad you mentioned that, Mr. Farwell. What exactly would be the nature of my work?"

"The usual *cursus honorum* …" Schneider looked blank and then laughed heartily. Farwell tried again: "The usual success story in public relations is, copy boy to junior copywriter to general copywriter to accounts man to executive. If you last that long. For about three months you can serve Greenhough and Brady best by running copy, emptying waste baskets and keeping your eyes open. After you know the routine we can try you on …"

Schneider interrupted: "What's the policy on salaries?" He didn't seem to like the policy on promotions.

Farwell told him the policy on salaries and Schneider tightened his mouth disapprovingly. "That's not much for a starter," he said. "Of course, I don't want to haggle, but I think my presentation shows I can handle responsibility."

Farwell got up with relief and shook his hand. "Too bad we couldn't get together," he said, talking the youngster to the door. "Don't forget your briefcase. If you want, you can leave your name with the girl and we'll get in touch with you if anything comes up. As you say, you might do better in another outfit that has a more responsible job open. It was good of you to give us a try, Schneider …" A warm clap on the shoulder got him out.

Next time, Farwell thought, feeling his forty-five years, it would be better to mention the starting salary in the ad and short-stop the youngsters with inflated ideas. He was pretty sure he hadn't acted like that beefy hotshot when he was a kid—or had he?

… comfort and safety on the spaceways since …

He turned on the intercom and said: "Get me Stubby Worple at the *Herald*."

Worple was in.

"Jim Farwell, Stub. I was looking at the column this morning and I made myself a promise to buzz you and tell you what a damn fine job it is. The lead graf was sensational."

Modest protests.

"No, I mean it. Say, why don't we get together? You got anything on for lunch?"

He did, but how about dinner? Hadn't been to the Mars Room for a coon's age.

"Oh, Mars Room. Sure enough, all right with me. Meet you in the bar at 7:30?"

He would.

Well, he'd left himself wide open for that one. He'd be lucky to get off with a $30 tab. But it was a sure tear-sheet for the Chicago Chair people.

Farwell said to the intercom: "Get me a reservation for eight tonight at the Mars Room, Grace. Dinner for two. Tell Mario it's got to be a good table."

He ripped the Kumfyseets first ad out of the typewriter and dropped it into the wastebasket. Fifty a week from Chicago Chair less thirty for entertainment. Mr. Brady wasn't going to like it; Mr. Brady might call him from New York about it to say gently: "Anybody can *buy* space, Jim. You should know by now that we're not in the business of *buying* space. Sometimes I think you haven't got a grasp of the big picture the way a branch manager should. Greenhough asked about you the other day and I really didn't know what to tell him." And Farwell would sweat and try to explain how it was a special situation and maybe try to hint that the sales force was sometimes guilty of overselling a client, making promises that Ops couldn't possibly live up to. And Mr. Brady would close on a note of gentle melancholy with a stinging remark or two "for your own good, Jim."

Farwell glanced at the clock on his desk, poured one from his private bottle; Brady receded a little into the background of his mind.

"Mr. Angelo Libonari to see you," said the intercom. "About employment."

"Send him in."

Libonari stumbled on the carpeting that began at the threshold of Farwell's office. "I saw your ad," he began shrilly, "your ad for a junior copywriter."

"Have a seat." The boy was shabby and jittery. "Didn't you bring a presentation?"

He didn't understand. "No, I just saw your ad. I didn't know I had to be introduced. I'm sorry I took up your time ..." He was on his way out already.

"*Wait* a minute, Angelo! I meant, have you got any copies of what you've done, where you've been to school, things like that."

"Oh." The boy pulled out a sheaf of paper from his jacket pocket. "This stuff isn't very good," he said. "As a matter of fact, it isn't really finished. I wrote it for a magazine, *Integration*, I don't suppose you ever heard of it; they were going to print it but they folded up, it's a kind of prose poem." Abruptly he ran dry and handed over the wad of dog-eared, interlined copy. His eyes said to Farwell: *please don't laugh at me.*

Farwell read at random: "... and then the Moon will drift astern and out of sight, the broken boundary that used to stand between the eye and the mind." He read it aloud and asked: "Now, what does that mean?"

The boy shyly and proudly explained: "Well, what I was trying to bring out there was that the Moon used to be as far as anybody could go with his eyes. If you wanted to find out anything about the other celestial bodies you had to guess and make inductions—that's sort of the whole theme of the piece—liberation, broken boundaries."

"Uh-huh," said Farwell, and went on reading. It was a rambling account of an Earth–Ganymede flight. There was a lot of stuff as fuzzy as the first bit, there were other bits that were hard, clean writing. The kid might be worth developing if only he didn't look and act so *peculiar*. Maybe it was just nervousness.

"So you're specially interested in space travel?" he asked.

"Oh, very much. I know I failed to get it over in this; it's all second-hand. I've never been off. But nobody's really written well about it yet—" He froze.

His terrible secret, Farwell supposed with amusement, was that he hoped to be the laureate of space flight. Well, if he wasn't absolutely impossible, Greenhough and Brady could give him a try. Shabby as he was, he wouldn't dare quibble about the pay.

He didn't quibble. He told Farwell he could get along on it nicely, he had a room in the run-down sub-Bohemian near the north side of town. He was from San Francisco, but had left home years ago—Farwell got the idea that he'd run away— and been in a lot of places. He'd held a lot of menial jobs and picked up a few credits taking night college courses here and there. After a while Farwell told him he was hired and to see the girl for his withholding tax and personnel data forms.

He buzzed his copy chief about the boy and leaned back in good humor. Angelo could never get to be an accounts man, of course, but he had some talent and imagination. Tame it and the kid could grow into a good producer. A rocket fan would be handy to have around if Sales stuck Ops with any more lemons like Chicago Chair.

Worple drank that night at the Mars Room like a man with a hollow leg and Farwell more or less had to go along with him. He got the Kumfyseets item planted but arrived at the office late and queasy as McGuffy, the copy chief, was bawling out Angelo for showing up in a plaid shirt, and a dirty one at that.

McGuffy came in to see him at 4:30 to ask about Angelo. "He just doesn't seem to be a Greenhough and Brady man, J. F. Of course if you think he's got something on the ball, that's good enough for me. But, honestly, can you see him taking an account to lunch?"

"Is he really getting in your hair, Mac? Give him a few days."

McGuffy was back at the end of the week, raging. "He showed me a poem, J. F. A sonnet about Mars. And he acted as if he was doing me a favor! As if he was handing me a contract with Pan-American Steel!"

Farwell laughed; it was exactly what he would expect Angelo to do. "It was his idea of a compliment, Mac. It means he thinks you're a good critic. I know these kids. I used to—" He broke off, dead-pan.

McGuffy grumbled: "You know I'm loyal, J. F. If you think he's got promise, all right. But he's driving me nuts."

After the copy chief left, Farwell shook his head nervously. What had he almost said? "I used to be one myself." Why, so he had—just about twenty-five years ago, a quarter of a century ago, when he went into radio work temporarily. *Temporarily!* A quarter-century ago he had been twenty years old. A quarter-century ago he had almost flunked out of college because he sat up all night trying to write plays instead of studying.

He hazily remembered saying to somebody, a girl, something like: "I am aiming for a really creative synthesis of Pinero and Shaw." Somehow that stuck, but he couldn't remember what the girl looked like or whether she'd been impressed. Farwell felt his ears burning: "A really creative synthesis of Pinero and Shaw." What a little—!

He told the intercom: "Send in Libonari."

The boy was more presentable; his hair was cut and he wore a clean blue shirt. "I've had a couple of complaints," said Farwell. "Suppose we get this clear: you are the one who is going to conform if you want to stay with us. Greenhough and Brady isn't going to be remolded nearer to the heart's desire of Angelo Libonari. Are you going out of your way to be difficult?"

The boy shrugged uneasily and stammered: "No, I wouldn't do anything like that. It's just, it's just that I find it hard to take all this seriously—but don't misunderstand me. I mean I can't help thinking that I'm going to do more important things some day, but honestly, I'm trying to do a good job here."

"Well, honestly you'd better try harder," Farwell said, mimicking his nervous voice. And then, more agreeably: "I'm not saying this for fun, Angelo. I just don't want to see you wasted because you won't put out a little effort, use a little self-discipline. You've got a future here if you work with us instead of against us. If you keep rubbing people the wrong way and I have to fire you, what's it going to be? More hash-house jobs, more crummy furnished rooms, hot in the summer, cold in the winter. You'll have something you call 'freedom,' but it's not the real thing. And it's all you'll have. Now beat it and try not to get on Mr. McGuffy's nerves."

The boy left, looking remorseful, and Farwell told himself that not everybody could handle an out-of-the-way type that well. If he pasted the little sermon in his hat, he'd be all right.

"Really creative synthesis!" Farwell snorted and poured himself a drink before he buckled down to planning a series of releases for the International Spacemen's Union. The space lines, longing for the old open-shop days, were sniping at the I.S.U. wherever they found an opening. They had a good one in the union's high initiation fee. The union said the high fee kept waifs and strays out and insured that anybody who paid it meant business and would make the spaceways his career. The union said the benefits that flowed from this were many and obvious. The companies said the union just wanted the money.

Farwell started blocking out a midwestern campaign. It might start with letters to the papers signed by SPACEMAN'S WIFE, WIDOW OF SCAB SPACER and other folks; the union could locate them to sign the letters. Next thing to do was set up a disinterested outfit. He tentatively christened it "The First Pan-American Conference on Space Hazards" and jotted down the names of a few distinguished chronic joiners and sponsors for the letterheads. They could hold a three-day meeting in Chicago, and conclude that the most important factor in space safety is experienced crewmen, and the longer their service the better. No mention of the I.S.U. initiation fee policy out of the F.P.A.C.S.H., but the union could use their conclusions in *its* material.

The union could use it to get a couple of state legislatures to pass resolutions endorsing the initiation fee policy. G. and B. would write the resolutions, but the

I.S.U.—an independent union—would have to swing the big federations into putting pressure on the legislatures in the name of labor unity.

Numerically the spacemen were insignificant.

He pawed through stacks of material forwarded to him as ammo by the union looking for the exact amount of the fee but couldn't locate it. The coyness was not surprising; it recalled the way corporation handouts bannered the "profit per dollar of sales" and buried the total profit in dollars and cents. He buzzed Copy.

"Mac, does anybody there know exactly what the I.S.U. initiation fee is?"

"I'll see, J. F."

A moment later he heard Angelo's voice. "It's kind of complicated. Mr. Farwell—maybe to keep anybody from saying it's exactly this or exactly that. Here's the way it works: base fee, $1,000, to be paid before they issue you a work card. What they call "accrual fee" on top of that—$100 if you're twenty years old, $200 if you're twenty-two, $300 if you're twenty-four and so on up to thirty, and after that you can't join. You can pay accrual fee out of your first voyage. From the accrual fee you can deduct $50 for each dependent. On top of that there's a five percent assessment of your first-voyage pay only, earmarked for the I.S.U. Space Medicine Research Foundation at Johns Hopkins. And that's all."

Farwell had been jotting it down. "Thanks, Angelo," he said absently. The Space Medicine Research thing was good, but he'd have to be careful that they weren't represented at the F.P.A.C.S.H.; you didn't want a direct union tie-in there. Now what could you do about the fee? Get the union to dig up somebody who's paid only the $1,000 base because of age and the right number of dependents. Forget the accrual and the assessment. How many people on a spaceship—50, 60? Make it 60 to get a plausibly unround number. Sixty into 1,000 is 16 $^{67}/_{100}$.

> *Dear Editor: Is there anybody riding the spaceways who would not cheerfully pay $16.67 to insure that the crewmen who hold his life in their hands are thoroughly experienced veterans of interplanetary flight? Is there anybody so short-sighted that he would embark with a green crew to save $16.67? Of course not! And yet that is what certain short-sighted persons demand! Throwing up a smoke-screen of loose charges to divert the public from the paramount issue of SAFETY, they accuse ...*

That wasn't exactly it. He had made it look as though the passengers paid the I.S.U. initiation fee. Well, he'd struck a keynote; Copy could take it from there.

And then there ought to be a stunt—a good, big stunt with pix possibilities. Girls, or violence, or both. Maybe a model demonstrating an escape hatch or something at a trade show, something goes wrong, a heroic I.S.U. member in good standing who happens to be nearby dashes in ...

He was feeling quite himself again.

The switchboard girl must have been listening in on the New York call. As Farwell stepped from his office he felt electricity in the air; the word had been passed already. He studied the anteroom, trying to see it through Greenhough's eyes.

"Grace," he told the switchboard girl, "get your handbag off the PBX and stick it in a drawer somewhere. Straighten that picture. And put on your bolero— you have nice shoulders and we all appreciate them, but the office is air-conditioned."

She tried to look surprised as he went on into Art.

Holloway didn't bother to pretend. "What time's he getting in?" he asked worriedly. "Can I get a shave?"

"They didn't tell me," said Farwell. "Your shave's all right. Get things picked up and get ties on the boys." The warning light was off; he looked into the dark-room. "A filthy mess!" he snapped. "How can you get any work done in a litter like that? Clean it up."

"Right away, J. F.," Holloway said, hurt.

Copy was in better shape; McGuffy had a taut hand.

"Greenhough's coming in today, I don't know what time. Your boys here look good."

"I can housebreak anything, J. F. Even Angelo. He bought a new suit!"

Farwell allowed a slight puzzled look to cross his face. "Angelo? Oh, the Libonari boy. How's he doing?"

"No complaints. He'll never be an accounts man if I'm any judge, but I've been giving him letters to write the past couple weeks. I don't know how you spotted it, but he's got talent. I have to hand it to you for digging him up, J. F."

Farwell saw the boy now at the last desk on the windowless side of the room, writing earnestly in longhand. Two months on a fair-enough salary hadn't filled him out as much as Farwell expected, but he did have a new suit on his back.

"It was just a gamble," he told McGuffy and went back to his office.

He had pretended not to remember the kid. Actually he'd been in his thoughts off and on since he hired him. There had been no trouble with Angelo since his grim little interview with the boy. Farwell hoped, rather sentimentally, he knew, that the interview had launched him on a decent career, turned him aside from the rocky Bohemian road and its pitfalls. As he had been turned aside himself. The nonsensical "really creative synthesis of Pinero and Shaw" pattered through his head again and he winced, thoroughly sick of it. For the past week the thought of visiting a psychiatrist had pattered after Pinero and Shaw every time, each time to be dismissed as silly.

His phone buzzed and he mechanically said, "Jim Farwell."

"Farwell, why didn't you check with me?" rasped Greenhough's voice.

"I don't understand, Mr. Greenhough. Where are you calling from?"

"The Hotel Greybar down the street, of course! I've been sitting here for an hour waiting for your call."

"Mr. Greenhough, all they told me from New York was that you were coming to Chicago."

"Nonsense. I gave the instructions myself."

"I'm sorry about the mixup—I must have misunderstood. Are you going to have a look at the office?"

"No. Why should I do anything like that? I'll call you back." Greenhough hung up.

Farwell leaned back, cursing whoever in New York had crossed up the message. It had probably been done deliberately, he decided—Pete Messler, the New York office manager, trying to make him look bad.

He tried to work on an account or two, but nervously put them aside to wait for Greenhough's call. At five he tried to reach Greenhough to tell him he was going home and give him his home number. Greenhough's room didn't answer the call or his next four, so he phoned a drugstore to send up a sandwich and coffee.

Before he could get started on the sandwich Greenhough phoned again to invite him to dinner at the Mars Room. He was jovial as could be: "Get myself some of that famous Chicago hospitality, hey, Jim? You know I'm just a hick from Colorado, don't you?" He went on to give Farwell about ten minutes of chuckling reminiscence and then hung up without confirming the dinner date. It turned out that it didn't matter. As Farwell was leaving the deserted office his phone buzzed again. It was Greenhough abruptly calling off the Mars Room. He told Farwell: "I've got somebody important to talk to this evening."

The branch manager at last dared to pour himself a heavy drink and left.

His bedside phone shrilled at three in the morning. "Jim Farwell," he croaked into it while two clock dials with the hands making two luminous L's wavered in front of him. His drink at the office had been the first of a series.

"This is Greenhough, Farwell," snarled the voice of the senior partner. "You get over here right away. Bring Clancy, whatever his name is—the lawyer." *Click.*

Where was "here"? Farwell phoned the Greybar. "*Don't* connect me with his room—I just want to know if he's in." The floor clerk said he was and Farwell tried to phone the home of the Chicago branch's lawyer, but got no answer. Too much time lost. He soaked his head in cold water, threw his clothes on and drove hell-for-leather to the Greybar.

Greenhough was in one of the big two-bedroom suites on the sixteenth floor. A frozen-faced blonde girl in an evening gown let Farwell in without a word. The senior partner was sprawled on the sofa in dress trousers and stiff shirt. He had a bruise under his left eye.

"I came as quickly as I could, Mr. Greenhough," said Farwell. "I couldn't get in touch with—"

The senior partner coughed thunderously, twitched his face at Farwell in a baffling manner, and then stalked into a bedroom. The blonde girl's frozen mask suddenly split into a vindictive grin. "*You're* going to get it!" she jeered at Farwell. "I'm supposed to think his name's Wilkins. Well, go on after him, pappy."

Farwell went into the bedroom. Greenhough was sitting on the bed dabbing at the bruise and muttering. "I told you I wanted our lawyer!" he shouted at the branch manager. "I was attacked by a drunkard in that damned Mars Room of yours and by God booked by the police like a common criminal! I'm going to get satisfaction if I have to turn the city upside-down! Get on that phone and get me Clancy or whatever his name is!"

"But I *can't!*" said Farwell desperately. "He won't answer his phone, and in the second place he isn't that kind of lawyer. I *can't* ask Clarahan to fight a disorderly-conduct charge—he's a big man here. He only does contract law and that kind of thing. You posted bond, didn't you, Mr. Greenhough?"

"Twenty dollars," said the senior partner bitterly, "and they only wanted ten from that drunken ape."

"Then why not just forget about it? Forfeit the bond and probably you'll never hear of it again, especially since you're an out-of-towner. I'll do what I can to smooth it over if they don't let it slide."

"Get out of here," said Greenhough, dabbing at the bruise again.

The blonde was reading a TV magazine in the parlor; she ignored Farwell as he let himself out.

The branch manager drove to an all-night barber shop near one of the terminals and napped through "the works." A slow breakfast killed another hour and by then it wasn't too ridiculously early to appear at the office.

He dawdled over copy until nine and phoned the Greybar. They told him Mr. Greenhough had checked out leaving no forwarding address. The morning papers came and he found nothing about a scuffle at the Mars Room or the booking of Greenhough. Maybe the senior partner had given a false name—Wilkins?—or maybe the stories had been killed because Greenhough and Brady did some institutional advertising. Maybe there was some mysterious interlock between Greenhough and Brady and the papers, high up on some misty alp that Farwell had never glimpsed.

Don't worry about it, he told himself savagely. You gave him good advice, the thing's going to blow over, Clarahan wouldn't have taken it, anyway. He hoped Pete Messler in New York wouldn't hear about it and try to use it as a lever to pry him out of the spot he held, the spot Pete Messler coveted. Maybe there was some way he could get somebody in the New York office to keep an eye on Messler and let him know how he was doing, just to get something he could counter-punch with when Messler pulled something like that garbled message stunt.

The intercom buzzed and Grace said, "Angelo wants to see you. He says it's personal."

"Send him in."

The kid was beaming. He looked pretty good—not raw and jumpy; just happy.

"I want to say thanks and good-bye, Mr. Farwell," he told the branch manager. "Look!"

The plastic-laminated card said "WORK PERMIT" and "Brother Angelo Libonari" and "International Union of Spacemen, Spacedockworkers and Rocket Maintenance Men, Unaffiliated (ISU-IND)" and "Member in Good Standing" and other things.

"So that was the game," said Farwell slowly. "We take you and we train you at a loss, hoping that some day you'll turn out decent copy for us and as soon as you have a thousand bucks saved up you quit like a shot and buy a work card to be a wiper on a rocket. Well, I hope you show a little more loyalty to your space line than you showed us."

Angelo's face drooped in miserable surprise. "I never thought—" he stuttered. "I didn't mean to run out, Mr. Farwell. I'll give two weeks notice if you want—a month? How about a month?"

"It doesn't matter," said Farwell. "I should have known. I thought I pounded some sense into your head, but I was wrong. You're forgiven, Angelo. I hope you have a good time. What are your plans?" He wasn't really interested, but why go out of his way to kick the kid in the teeth? Obviously he'd meant it when he registered surprise—he didn't have the boss's viewpoint and his other jobs had been one-week stands in hash-houses.

The boy carefully put his work card in his breast pocket and beamed again at what he was saying—partly to Farwell, it appeared, mostly to himself in wonder at its coming true at last. "I'll be a wiper at the start, all right," he said. "I don't care if I never get higher than that. I want to see it and feel it, all of it. That's the only way the real thing's ever going to get written. Higgins and Delare and Beeman and the rest of them—passengers. You can feel it in your bones when you read their stuff. One-trippers or two-trippers.

"They aren't soaked in it. The big passage in Delare's *Planetfall,* the take-off from Mars: he's full of the wonder of it, sure. Who wouldn't be the first time? And he kept his eyes open, watching himself and the others. But I'm going to take off from Earth and Mars and Venus and Ganymede and the Moon twenty times before I dare to write about it. I'm going to get it *all*—brains, bone, muscle, and belly—take-off, landings, free flight, danger, monotony—*all* of it."

"Sonnets? Prose poems?" asked Farwell, just to be saying something.

Angelo flushed a little, but his eyes didn't have the old pleading look. He didn't have to plead; he had what he wanted. "They were good exercise," he said stoutly. "I suppose I was trying to write form because I didn't have content. I think it's going to be novels—if I feel like it. And they can publish them or not publish them, just as they please." He meant it, Farwell thought. He had what he wanted.

"I'll look forward to them," he said, and shook hands with the boy. He didn't notice him leave. Angelo Messler, he thought; Pete Libonari. "... really creative synthesis of Pinero and Shaw—" pattered through his head, and the psychiatrist-thought followed naggingly after. He looked at his hands in amazement, suddenly realizing that they had been trembling all morning uncontrollably.

Time Bum

Harry Twenty-Third Street suddenly burst into laughter. His friend and some-times roper Farmer Brown looked inquisitive.

"I just thought of a new con," Harry Twenty-Third Street said, still chuckling.

Farmer Brown shook his head positively. "There's no such thing, my man," he said. "There are only new switches on old cons. What have you got—a store con? Shall you be needing a roper?" He tried not to look eager as a matter of principle, but everybody knew the Farmer needed a connection badly. His girl had two-timed him on a badger game, running off with the chump and marrying him after an expensive, month-long buildup.

Harry said, "Sorry, old boy. No details. It's too good to split up. I shall rip and tear the suckers with this con for many a year, I trust, before the details become available to the trade. Nobody, but nobody, is going to call copper after I take him. It's beautiful and it's mine. I will see you around, my friend."

Harry got up from the booth and left, nodding cheerfully to a safeblower here, a fixer there, on his way to the locked door of the hangout. Naturally he didn't nod to such small fry as pickpockets and dope peddlers. Harry had his pride.

The puzzled Farmer sipped his lemon squash and concluded that Harry had been kidding him. He noticed that Harry had left behind him in the booth a copy of a magazine with a space ship and a pretty girl in green bra and pants on the cover.

"A furnished ... bungalow?" the man said hesitantly, as though he knew what he wanted but wasn't quite sure of the word.

"Certainly, Mr. Clurg," Walter Lachlan said. "I'm sure we can suit you. Wife and family?"

"No," said Clurg. "They are ... far away." He seemed to get some secret amusement from the thought. And then, to Walter's horror, he sat down calmly in empty air beside the desk and, of course, crashed to the floor looking ludicrous and astonished.

Walter gaped and helped him up, sputtering apologies and wondering privately what was wrong with the man. There wasn't a chair there. There was a chair on the other side of the desk and a chair against the wall. But there just wasn't a chair where Clurg had sat down.

Clurg apparently was unhurt; he protested against Walter's apologies, saying: "I should have known, Master Lachlan. It's quite all right; it was all my fault. What about the bang—the bungalow?"

Business sense triumphed over Walter's bewilderment. He pulled out his listings and they conferred on the merits of several furnished bungalows. When Walter mentioned that the Curran place was especially nice, in an especially nice neighborhood—he lived up the street himself—Clurg was impressed. "I'll take that one," he said. "What is the … feoff?"

Walter had learned a certain amount of law for his real-estate license examination; he recognized the word. "The *rent* is seventy-five dollars," he said. "You speak English very well, Mr. Clurg." He hadn't been certain that the man was a foreigner until the dictionary word came out. "You have hardly any accent."

"Thank you," Clurg said, pleased. "I worked hard at it. Let me see— seventy-five is six twelves and three." He opened one of his shiny-new leather suitcases and calmly laid six heavy little paper rolls on Walter's desk. He broke open a seventh and laid down three mint-new silver dollars. "There I am," he said. "I mean, there you are."

Walter didn't know what to say. It had never happened before. People paid by check or in bills. They just didn't pay in silver dollars. But it was money—why shouldn't Mr. Clurg pay in silver dollars if he wanted to? He shook himself, scooped the rolls into his top desk drawer and said: "I'll drive you out there if you like. It's nearly quitting time anyway."

Walter told his wife Betty over the dinner table: "We ought to have him in some evening. I can't imagine where on Earth he comes from. I had to show him how to turn on the kitchen range. When it went on he said, 'Oh, yes—electricity!' and laughed his head off. And he kept ducking the question when I tried to ask him in a nice way. Maybe he's some kind of a political refugee."

"Maybe …" Betty began dreamily, and then shut her mouth. She didn't want Walter laughing at her again. As it was, he made her buy her science-fiction magazines downtown instead of at neighborhood newsstands. He thought it wasn't becoming for his wife to read them. He's so eager for success, she thought sentimentally.

That night, while Walter watched a television variety show, she read a story in one of her magazines. (Its cover, depicting a space ship and a girl in green bra and shorts, had been prudently torn off and thrown away.) It was about a man from the future who had gone back in time, bringing with him all sorts of marvelous inventions. In the end the Time Police punished him for unauthorized time traveling. They had come back and got him, brought him back to his own time. She smiled. It *would* be nice if Mr. Clurg, instead of being a slightly eccentric foreigner, were a man from the future with all sorts of interesting stories to tell and a satchelful of gadgets that could be sold for millions and millions of dollars.

After a week they did have Clurg over for dinner. It started badly. Once more he managed to sit down in empty air and crash to the floor. While they were brushing him off he said fretfully: "I *can't* get used to not—" and then said no more.

He was a picky eater. Betty had done one of her mother's specialties, veal cutlet with tomato sauce, topped by a poached egg. He ate the egg and sauce, made a clumsy attempt to cut up the meat, and abandoned it. She served a plate of cheese, half a dozen kinds, for dessert, and Clurg tasted them uncertainly, breaking off a crumb from each, while Betty wondered where that constituted good manners. His face lit up when he tried a ripe cheddar. He popped the whole wedge into his mouth and said to Betty: "I will have that, please."

"Seconds?" asked Walter. "Sure. Don't bother, Betty. I'll get it." He brought back a quarter-pound wedge of the cheddar.

Walter and Betty watched silently as Clurg calmly ate every crumb of it. He sighed. "Very good. Quite like—" The word, Walter and Betty later agreed, was *see-mon-joe.* They were able to agree quite early in the evening, because Clurg got up after eating the cheese, said warmly, "Thank you so much!" and walked out of the house.

Betty said, *"What—on—Earth!"*

Walter said uneasily, "I'm sorry, doll. I didn't think he'd be quite that peculiar—"

"—But after *all!*"

"—Of course he's a foreigner. What was that word?"

He jotted it down.

While they were doing the dishes Betty said, "I think he was drunk. Falling-down drunk."

"No," Walter said. "It's exactly the same thing he did in my office. As though he expected a chair to come to him instead of him going to a chair." He laughed and said uncertainly, "Or maybe he's royalty. I read once about Queen Victoria never looking around before she sat down, she was so sure there'd be a chair there."

"Well, there isn't any more royalty, not to speak of," she said angrily, hanging up the dish towel. "What's on TV tonight?"

"Uncle Miltie. But ... uh ... I think I'll read. Uh ... where do you keep those magazines of yours, doll? Believe I'll give them a try."

She gave him a look that he wouldn't meet, and she went to get him some of her magazines. She also got a slim green book which she hadn't looked at for years. While Walter flipped uneasily through the magazines, she studied the book.

After about ten minutes she said: "Walter. *Seemonjoe.* I think I know what language it is."

He was instantly alert. "Yeah? What?"

"It should be spelled c-i-m-a-n-g-o, with little jiggers over the C and G. It means 'universal food' in Esperanto."

"Where's Esperanto?" he demanded.

"Esperanto isn't anywhere. It's an artificial language. I played around with it a little once. It was supposed to end war and all sorts of things. Some people called it 'the language of the future'." Her voice was tremulous.

Walter said, "I'm going to get to the bottom of this."

He saw Clurg go into the neighborhood movie for the matinee. That gave him about three hours.

Walter hurried to the Curran bungalow, remembered to slow down and tried hard to look casual as he unlocked the door and went in. There wouldn't be any trouble—he was a good citizen, known and respected—he could let himself into a tenant's house and wait for him to talk about business if he wanted to.

He tried not to think of what people would think if he should be caught rifling Clurg's luggage, as he intended to do. He had brought along an assortment of luggage keys. Surprised by his own ingenuity, he had got them at a locksmith's by saying his own key was lost and he didn't want to haul a heavy packed bag downtown.

But he didn't need the keys. In the bedroom closet the two suitcases stood, unlocked.

There was nothing in the first except uniformly new clothes, bought locally at good shops. The second was full of the same. Going through a rather extreme sports jacket, Walter found a wad of paper in the breast pocket. It was a newspaper page. A number had been penciled on a margin; apparently the sheet had been torn out and stuck into the pocket and forgotten. The dateline on the paper was July 18th, 2403.

Walter had some trouble reading the stories at first, but found it was easy enough if he read them aloud and listened to his voice.

One said:

TAIM KOP NABD:
PROSKYOOTR ASKS DETH

Patrolm'n Oskr Garth 'v thi Taim Polis w'z arest'd toodei at hiz hom, 4365 9863th Strit, and bookd at 9768th Prisint on tchardg'z 'v Polis-Ekspozh'r. Thi aledjd Ekspozh'r okur'd hwaile Garth w'z on dooti in thi Twenti-Furst Sentch'ri. It konsist'd 'v hiz admish'n too a sit'zen 'v thi Twenti-Furst Sentch'ri that thi Taim Polis ekzisted and woz op'rated fr'm thi Twenti-Fifth Sentch'ri. Thi Proskyoot'rz Ofis sed thi deth pen'lti wil be askt in vyoo 'v thi heinus neitch'r 'v thi ofens, hwitch thret'nz thi hwol fabrik 'v Twenti-Fifth-Sentch'ri eksiztens.

There was an advertisement on the other side:

BOIZ 'ND YUNG MEN!
SERV EUR SENTCH'RI!
ENLIST IN THI TAIM POLIS RISURV NOW!
RIMEMB'R—
ONLI IN THI TAIM POLIS KAN EU SI THI PAJENT 'V THI AJEZ! ONLY IN THI TAIM POLIS KAN EU PROTEKT EUR SIVILIZASH'N FR'M VARI'NS! THEIR IZ NO HAIER SERVIS TOO AR KULTCH'R! THEIR IZ NO K'REER SO FAS'NATING AZ A K'REER IN THI TAIM POLIS!

Underneath it another ad asked:

HWAI BI ASHEIM'D 'V EUR TCHAIRZ? GET ROLFASTS!
No uth'r tcheir haz thi immidjit respons 'v a Rolfast.
Sit enihweir—eor Rolfast iz their!

Eur Rolfast met'l partz ar solid gold to avoid tairsum pol-ishing. Eur Rolfast beirings are thi fain'st six-intch dupliks di'mondz for long wair.

Walter's heart pounded. Gold—to avoid tiresome polishing! Six-inch diamonds— for long wear!

And Clurg must be a time policeman. "Only in the time police can you see the pageant of the ages!" What did a time policeman do? He wasn't quite clear about that. But what they *didn't* do was let anybody else—anybody earlier—know that the Time Police existed. He, Walter Lachlan of the Twentieth Century, held in the palm of his hand Time Policeman Clurg of the Twenty-Fifth Century—the Twenty-Fifth Century where gold and diamonds were common as steel and glass in this!

He was there when Clurg came back from the matinee.

Mutely, Walter extended the page of newsprint. Clurg snatched it incredu-lously, stared at it and crumpled it in his fist. He collapsed on the floor with a groan. "I'm done for!" Walter heard him say.

"Listen, Clurg," Walter said. "Nobody ever needs to know about this—*no-body.*"

Clurg looked up with sudden hope in his eyes. "You will keep silent?" he asked wildly. "It is my life!"

"What's it worth to you?" Walter demanded with brutal directness. "I can use some of those diamonds and some of that gold. Can you get it into this century?"

"It would be missed. It would be over my mass-balance," Clurg said. "But I have a duplix. I can copy diamonds and gold for you; that was how I made my feoff money."

He snatched an instrument from his pocket—a fountain pen, Walter thought. "It is low in charge. It would duplix about five kilograms in one operation—"

"You mean," Walter demanded, "that if I brought you five kilograms of diamonds and gold you could duplicate it? And the originals wouldn't be harmed? Let me see that thing. Can I work it?"

Clurg passed over the "fountain pen." Walter saw that within the case was a tangle of wires, tiny tubes, lenses—he passed it back hastily. Clurg said, "That is correct. You could buy or borrow jewelry and I could duplix it. Then you could return the originals and retain the copies. You swear by your contemporary God that you would say nothing?"

Walter was thinking. He could scrape together a good thirty thousand dollars by pledging the house, the business, his own real estate, the bank account, the life insurance, the securities. Put it all into diamonds, of course, and then—*doubled! Overnight!*

"I'll say nothing," he told Clurg. "If you come through." He took the sheet from the twenty-fifth-century newspaper from Clurg's hands and put it securely in his own pocket. "When I get those diamonds duplicated," he said, "I'll burn this and forget the rest. Until then, I want you to stay close to home. I'll come around in a day or so with the stuff for you to duplicate."

Clurg nervously promised.

The secrecy, of course, didn't include Betty. He told her when he got home and she let out a yell of delight. She demanded the newspaper, read it avidly, and then demanded to see Clurg.

"I don't think he'll talk," Walter said doubtfully. "But if you really want to ..."

She did, and they walked to the Curran bungalow. Clurg was gone, lock, stock and barrel, leaving not a trace behind. They waited for hours, nervously.

At last Betty said, "He's gone back."

Walter nodded. "He wouldn't keep his bargain, but by God I'm going to keep mine. Come along. We're going to the *Enterprise.*"

"Walter," she said. "You wouldn't—would you?"

He went alone, after a bitter quarrel.

At the *Enterprise* office he was wearily listened to by a reporter, who wearily looked over the twenty-fifth-century newspaper. "I don't know what you're peddling, Mr. Lachlan," he said, "but we like people to buy their ads in the *Enterprise.* This is a pretty barefaced publicity grab."

"But—" Walter sputtered.

"Sam, would you please ask Mr. Morris to come up here if he can?" the reporter was saying into the phone. To Walter he explained, "Mr. Morris is our press-room foreman."

The foreman was a huge, white-haired old fellow, partly deaf. The reporter showed him the newspaper from the twenty-fifth century and said, "How about this?"

Mr. Morris looked at it and smelled it and said, showing no interest in the reading matter: "American Type Foundry Futura number nine, discontinued about ten years ago. It's been hand-set. The ink—hard to say. Expensive stuff, not a news ink. A book ink, a job-printing ink. The paper, now, I know. A nice linen rag that Benziger jobs in Philadelphia."

"You see, Mr. Lachlan? It's a fake." The reporter shrugged.

Walter walked slowly from the city room. The press-room foreman *knew*. It was a fake. And Clurg was a faker. Suddenly Walter's heels touched the ground after twenty-four hours and stayed there. Good God, the diamonds! Clurg was a conman! He would have worked a package switch! He would have had thirty thousand dollars' worth of diamonds for less than a month's work!

He told Betty about it when he got home and she laughed unmercifully. "Time Policeman" was to become a family joke between the Lachlans.

Harry Twenty-Third Street stood, blinking, in a very peculiar place. Peculiarly, his feet were firmly encased, up to the ankles, in a block of clear plastic.

There were odd-looking people and a big voice was saying: "May it please the court. The People of the Twenty-Fifth Century versus Harold Parish, alias Harry Twenty-Third Street, alias Clurg, of the Twentieth Century. The charge is impersonating an officer of the Time Police. The Prosecutor's Office will ask the death penalty in view of the heinous nature of the offense, which threatens the whole fabric—"

[*Venture* - July 1958]

Two Dooms

... Why should we be tender
To let an arrogant piece of flesh threat us,
Play judge and executioner all himself?
　　　　　—Shakespeare, "Cymbeline"

It was May, not yet summer by five weeks, but the afternoon heat under the corrugated roofs of Manhattan Engineer District's Los Alamos Laboratory was daily less bearable. Young Dr. Edward Royland had lost fifteen pounds from an already meager frame during his nine-month hitch in the desert. He wondered every day while the thermometer crawled up to its 5:45 peak whether he had made a mistake he would regret the rest of his life in accepting work with the Laboratory rather than letting the local draft board have his carcass and do what they pleased with it. His University of Chicago classmates were glamorously collecting ribbons and wounds from Saipan to Brussels; one of them, a first-rate mathematician named Hatfield, would do no more first-rate mathematics. He had gone down, burning, in an Eighth Air Force Mitchell bomber ambushed over Lille.

"And what, Daddy, did you do in the war?"

"Well, kids, it's a little hard to explain. They had this stupid atomic bomb project that never came to anything, and they tied up a lot of us in a Godforsaken place in New Mexico. We figured and we calculated and we fooled with uranium and some of us got radiation burns and then the war was over and they sent us home."

Royland was not amused by this prospect. He had heat rash under his arms and he was waiting, not patiently, for the Computer Section to send him his figures on Phase 56c, which was the (goddamn childish) code designation for Element Assembly Time. Phase 56c was Royland's own particular baby. He was under Rotschmidt, supervisor of WEAPON DESIGN TRACK III, and Rotschmidt was under Oppenheimer, who bossed the works. Sometimes a General Groves came through, a fine figure of a man, and once from a window Royland had seen the venerable Henry L. Stimson, Secretary of War, walking slowly down their dusty street, leaning on a cane and surrounded by young staff officers. That's what Royland was seeing of the war.

274

Laboratory! It had sounded inviting, cool, bustling but quiet. So every morning these days he was blasted out of his cot in a barracks cubicle at seven by "Oppie's whistle," fought for a shower and shave with thirty-seven other bachelor scientists in eight languages, bolted a bad cafeteria breakfast and went through the barbed-wire Restricted Line to his "office"—another matchboard-walled cubicle, smaller and hotter and noisier, with talking and typing and clack of adding machines all around him.

Under the circumstances he was doing good work, he supposed. He wasn't happy about being restricted to his one tiny problem, Phase 56c, but no doubt he was happier than Hatfield had been when his Mitchell got it.

Under the circumstances ... they included a weird haywire arrangement for computing. Instead of a decent differential analyzer machine they had a human sea of office girls with Burroughs desk calculators; the girls screamed "Banzai!" and charged on differential equations and swamped them by sheer volume; they clicked them to death with their little adding machines. Royland thought hungrily of Conant's huge, beautiful analog differentiator up at M.I.T.; it was probably tied up by whatever the mysterious "Radiation Laboratory" there was doing. Royland suspected that the "Radiation Laboratory" had as much to do with radiation as his own "Manhattan Engineer District" had to do with Manhattan engineering. And the world was supposed to be trembling on the edge these days of a New Dispensation of Computing which would obsolete even the M.I.T. machine—tubes, relays and binary arithmetic at blinding speed instead of the suavely turning cams and the smoothly extruding rods and the elegant scribed curves of Conant's masterpiece. He decided that he wouldn't like that; he would like it even less than he liked the little office girls clacking away, pushing lank hair from their dewed brows with undistracted hands.

He wiped his own brow with a sodden handkerchief and permitted himself a glance at his watch and the thermometer. Five-fifteen and 103 Fahrenheit.

He thought vaguely of getting out, of fouling up just enough to be released from the project and drafted. No; there was the post-war career to think of. But one of the big shots, Teller, had been irrepressible; he had rambled outside of his assigned mission again and again until Oppenheimer let him go; now Teller was working with Lawrence at Berkeley on something that had reputedly gone sour at a reputed quarter of a billion dollars—

A girl in khaki knocked and entered. "Your material from the Computer Section, Dr. Royland. Check them and sign here, please." He counted the dozen sheets, signed the clipboarded form she held out and plunged into the material for thirty minutes.

When he sat back in his chair, the sweat dripped into his eyes unnoticed. His hands were shaking a little, though he did not know that either. Phase 56c of WEAPON DESIGN TRACK III was finished, over, done, successfully accomplished. The answer to the question "Can U_{235} slugs be assembled into a critical mass within a physically feasible time?" was in. The answer was "Yes."

Royland was a theory man, not a Wheatstone or a Kelvin; he liked the numbers for themselves and had no special passion to grab for wires, mica and bits of graphite so that what the numbers said might immediately be given flesh in a wonderful new gadget. Nevertheless he could visualize at once a workable atomic bomb assembly within the framework of Phase 56c. You have so many microseconds to assemble your critical mass without it boiling away in vapor; you use them by blowing the subassemblies together with shaped charges; lots of microseconds to spare by that method; practically foolproof. Then comes the Big Bang.

Oppie's whistle blew; it was quitting time. Royland sat still in his cubicle. He should go, of course, to Rotschmidt and tell him; Rotschmidt would probably clap him on the back and pour him a jigger of Bols Geneva from the tall clay bottle he kept in his safe. Then Rotschmidt would go to Oppenheimer. Before sunset the project would be redesigned! Track I, Track II, Track IV and Track V would be shut down and their people crammed into Track III, the one with the paydirt! New excitement would boil through the project; it had been torpid and souring for three months. Phase 56c was the first good news in at least that long; it had been one damned blind alley after another. General Groves had looked sour and dubious last time around.

Desk drawers were slamming throughout the corrugated, sun-baked building; doors were slamming shut on cubicles; down the corridor, somebody roared with laughter, strained laughter. Passing Royland's door somebody cried impatiently: "—aber was kann man tun?"

Royland whispered to himself: "You damned fool, what are you thinking of?"

But he knew—he was thinking of the Big Bang, the Big Dirty Bang, and of torture. The judicial torture of the old days, incredibly cruel by today's lights, stretched the whole body, or crushed it, or burned it, or shattered the fingers and legs. But even that old judicial torture carefully avoided the most sensitive parts of the body, the generative organs, though damage to these, or a real threat of damage to these, would have produced quick and copious confessions. You have to be more or less crazy to torture somebody that way; the sane man does not think of it as a possibility.

An M.P. corporal tried Royland's door and looked in. "Quitting time, professor," he said.

"Okay," Royland said. Mechanically he locked his desk drawers and his files, turned his window lock and set out his wastepaper basket in the corridor. Click the door; another day, another dollar.

Maybe the project was breaking up. They did now and then. The huge boner at Berkeley proved that. And Royland's barracks was light two physicists now; their cubicles stood empty since they had been drafted to M.I.T. for some anti-submarine thing. Groves had not looked happy last time around; how did a general make up his mind anyway? Give them three months, then the axe? Maybe Stimson would run out of patience and cut the loss, close the District down. Maybe F.D.R. would say at a cabinet meeting, "By the way, Henry, what ever became of—?" and that would be the end if old Henry could say only that the scientists appear to be optimistic of eventual success, Mr. President, but that as yet there seems to be nothing concrete—

He passed through the barbed wire of the Line under scrutiny of an M.P. lieutenant and walked down the barracks-edged company street of the maintenance troops to their motor pool. He wanted a jeep and a trip ticket; he wanted a long desert drive in the twilight; he wanted a dinner of *frijoles* and eggplant with his old friend Charles Miller Nahataspe, the medicine man of the adjoining Hopi reservation. Royland's hobby was anthropology; he wanted to get a little drunk on it—he hoped it would clear his mind.

Nahataspe welcomed him cheerfully to his hut; his million wrinkles all smiled. "You want me to play informant for a while?" he grinned. He had been to Carlisle in the 1880's and had been laughing at the white man ever since; he admitted that physics was funny, but for a real joke give him cultural anthropology every time. "You want some nice unsavory stuff about our institutionalized homosexuality? Should I cook us a dog for dinner? Have a seat on the blanket, Edward."

"What happened to your chairs? And the funny picture of McKinley? And—and everything?" The hut was bare except for cooking pots that simmered on the stone-curbed central hearth.

"I gave the stuff away," Nahataspe said carelessly. "You get tired of things."

Royland thought he knew what that meant. Nahataspe believed he would die quite soon; these particular Indians did not believe in dying encumbered by possessions. Manners, of course, forbade discussing death.

The Indian watched his face and finally said: "Oh, it's all right for *you* to talk about it. Don't be embarrassed."

Royland asked nervously: "Don't you feel well?"

"I feel terrible. There's a snake eating my liver. Pitch in and eat. You feel pretty awful yourself, don't you?"

The hard-learned habit of security caused Royland to evade the question. "You don't mean that literally about the snake, do you, Charles?"

"Of course I do," Miller insisted. He scooped a steaming gourd full of stew from the pot and blew on it. "What would an untutored child of nature know about bacteria, viruses, toxins and neoplasms? What would I know about break-the-sky medicine?"

Royland looked up sharply; the Indian was blandly eating. "Do you hear any talk about break-the-sky medicine?" Royland asked.

"No talk, Edward. I've had a few dreams about it." He pointed with his chin toward the Laboratory. "You fellows over there shouldn't dream so hard; it leaks out."

Royland helped himself to stew without answering. The stew was good, far better than the cafeteria stuff, and he did not *have* to guess the source of the meat in it.

Miller said consolingly: "It's only kid stuff, Edward. Don't get so worked up about it. We have a long dull story about a horned toad who ate some loco-weed and thought he was the Sky God. He got angry and he tried to break the sky but he couldn't, so he slunk into his hole ashamed to face all the other animals and died. But they never knew he tried to break the sky at all."

In spite of himself Royland demanded: "Do you have any stories about any-body who did break the sky?" His hands were shaking again and his voice almost hysterical. Oppie and the rest of them were going to break the sky, kick humanity right in the crotch, and unleash a prowling monster that would go up and down by night and day peering in all the windows of all the houses in the world, leaving no sane man ever unterrified for his life and the lives of his kin. Phase 56c, God damn it to blackest hell, made sure of that! Well done, Royland; you earned your dollar today!

Decisively the old Indian set his gourd aside. He said: "We have a saying that the only good paleface is a dead paleface, but I'll make an exception for you, Edward. I've got some strong stuff from Mexico that will make you feel better. I don't like to see my friends hurting."

"Peyote? I've tried it. Seeing a few colored lights won't make me feel better, but thanks."

"Not peyote, this stuff. It's God Food. I wouldn't take it myself without a month of preparation; otherwise the Gods would scoop me up in a net. That's because my people see clearly, and your eyes are clouded." He was busily rummaging through a clay-chinked wicker box as he spoke; he came up with a covered dish. "You people have your sight cleared just a little by the God Food, so it's safe for you."

Royland thought he knew what the old man was talking about. It was one of Nahataspe's biggest jokes that Hopi children understood Einstein's relativity as soon as they could talk—and there was some truth to it. The Hopi language—and thought—had no tenses and therefore no concept of time-as-an-entity; it had nothing like the Indo-European speech's subjects and predicates, and therefore no built-in metaphysics of cause and effect. In the Hopi language and mind all things were frozen together forever into one great relationship, a crystalline structure of space-time events that simply were because they were. So much for Nahataspe's people "seeing clearly." But Royland gave himself and any other physicist credit for seeing as clearly when they were working a four-dimensional problem in the X Y Z space variables and the T time variable.

He could have spoiled the old man's joke by pointing that out, but of course he did not. No, no; he'd get a jag and maybe a bellyache from Nahataspe's herb medicine and then go home to his cubicle with his problem unresolved: to kick or not to kick?

The old man began to mumble in Hopi, and drew a tattered cloth across the door-frame of his hut; it shut out the last rays of the setting sun, long and slanting on the desert, pink-red against the adobe cubes of the Indian settlement. It took a minute for Royland's eyes to accommodate to the flickering light from the hearth and the indigo square of the ceiling smoke hole. Now Nahataspe was "dancing," doing a crouched shuffle around the hut holding the covered dish before him. Out of the corner of his mouth, without interrupting the rhythm, he said to Royland: "Drink some hot water now." Royland sipped from one of the pots on the hearth; so far it was much like peyote ritual, but he felt calmer.

Nahataspe uttered a loud scream, added apologetically: "Sorry, Edward," and crouched before him whipping the cover off the dish like a headwaiter. So

God Food was dried black mushrooms, miserable, wrinkled little things. "You swallow them all and chase them with hot water," Nahataspe said.

Obediently Royland choked them down and gulped from the jug; the old man resumed his dance and chanting.

A little old self-hypnosis, Royland thought bitterly. Grab some imitation sleep and forget about old 56c, as if you could. He could see the big dirty one now, a hell of a fireball, maybe over Munich, or Cologne, or Tokyo, or Nara. Cooked people, fused cathedral stone, the bronze of the big Buddha running like water, perhaps lapping around the ankles of a priest and burning his feet off so he fell prone into the stuff. He couldn't see the gamma radiation, but it would be there, invisible sleet doing the dirty unthinkable thing, coldly burning away the sex of men and women, cutting short so many fans of life at their points of origin. Phase 56c could snuff out a family of Bachs, or five generations of Bernoullis, or see to it that the great Huxley-Darwin cross did not occur.

The fireball loomed, purple and red and fringed with green—

The mushrooms were reaching him, he thought fuzzily. He could really see it. Nahataspe, crouched and treading, moved through the fireball just as he had the last time, and the time before that. Déjà vu, extraordinarily strong, stronger than ever before, gripped him. Royland knew all this had happened to him before, and remembered perfectly what would come next; it was on the very tip of his tongue, as they say—

The fireballs began to dance around him and he felt his strength drain suddenly out; he was lighter than a feather; the breeze would carry him away; he would be blown like a dust mote into the circle that the circling fireballs made. And he knew it was wrong. He croaked with the last of his energy, feeling himself slip out of the world: "Charlie! Help!"

Out of the corner of his mind as he slipped away he sensed that the old man was pulling him now under the arms, trying to tug him out of the hut, crying dimly into his ear: "You should have told me you did not see through smoke! You see clear; I never knew; I nev—"

And then he slipped through into blackness and silence.

Royland awoke sick and fuzzy; it was morning in the hut; there was no sign of Nahataspe. Well. Unless the old man had got to a phone and reported to the Laboratory, there were now jeeps scouring the desert in search of him and all hell was breaking loose in Security and Personnel. He would catch some of that hell on his return, and avert it with his news about assembly time.

Then he noticed that the hut had been cleaned of Nahataspe's few remaining possessions, even to the door cloth. A pang went through him; had the old man died in the night? He limped from the hut and looked around for a funeral pyre, a crowd of mourners. They were not there; the adobe cubes stood untenanted in the sunlight, and more weeds grew in the single street than he remembered. And his jeep, parked last night against the hut, was missing.

There were no wheel-tracks, and uncrushed weeds grew tall where the jeep had stood.

Nahataspe's God Food had been powerful stuff. Royland's hand crept uncertainly to his face. No; no beard.

He looked about him, looked hard. He made the effort necessary to see details. He did not glance at the hut and because it was approximately the same as it had always been, concluded that it was unchanged, eternal. He looked and saw changes everywhere. Once-sharp adobe corners were rounded; protruding roof beams were bleached bone-white by how many years of desert sun? The wooden framing of the deep fortress-like windows had crumbled; the third building from him had wavering soot-stains above its window-boles and its beams were charred.

He went to it, numbly thinking: Phase 56c at least is settled. Not old Rip's baby now. They'll know me from fingerprints, I guess. One year? Ten? I *feel* the same.

The burnt-out house was a shambles. In one corner were piled dry human bones. Royland leaned dizzily against the door-frame; its charcoal crumbled and streaked his hand. Those skulls were Indian—he was anthropologist enough to know that. Indian men, women and children, slain and piled in a heap. Who kills Indians? There should have been some sign of clothes, burnt rags, but there were none. Who strips Indians naked and kills them?

Signs of a dreadful massacre were everywhere in the house. Bulletpocks in the walls, high and low. Savage nicks left by bayonets—and swords? Dark stains of blood; it had run two inches high and left its mark. Metal glinted in a rib cage across the room. Swaying, he walked to the boneheap and thrust his hand into it. The thing bit him like a razor blade; he did not look at it as he plucked it out and carried it to the dusty street. With his back turned to the burnt house he studied his find. It was a piece of swordblade six inches long, hand-honed to a perfect edge with a couple of nicks in it. It had stiffening ribs and the usual blood gutters. It had a perceptible curve that would fit into only one shape: the Samurai sword of Japan.

However long it had taken, the war was obviously over.

He went to the village well and found it choked with dust. It was while he stared into the dry hole that he first became afraid. Suddenly it all was real; he was no more an onlooker but a frightened and very thirsty man. He ransacked the dozen houses of the settlement and found nothing to his purpose—a child's skeleton here, a couple of cartridge cases there.

There was only one thing left, and that was the road, the same earth track it had always been, wide enough for one jeep or the rump-sprung station wagon of the Indian settlement that once had been. Panic invited him to run; he did not yield. He sat on the well-curb, took off his shoes to meticulously smooth wrinkles out of his khaki G.I. socks, put the shoes on and retied the laces loosely enough to allow for swelling, and hesitated a moment. Then he grinned, selected two pebbles carefully from the dust and popped them in his mouth. "Beaver Patrol, forward march," he said, and began to hike.

Yes, he was thirsty; soon he would be hungry and tired; what of it? The dirt road would meet state-maintained blacktop in three miles and then there would be traffic and he'd hitch a ride. Let them argue with his fingerprints if they felt like it. The Japanese had got as far as New Mexico, had they? Then God help their home islands when the counterblow had come. Americans were a ferocious people when trespassed on. Conceivably, there was not a Japanese left alive …

He began to construct his story as he hiked. In large parts it was a repeated "I don't know." He would tell them: "I don't expect you to believe this, so my feelings won't be hurt when you don't. Just listen to what I say and hold everything until the F.B.I. has checked my fingerprints. My name is—" And so on.

It was midmorning then, and he would be on the highway soon. His nostrils, sharpened by hunger, picked up a dozen scents on the desert breeze: the spice of sage, a whiff of acetylene stink from a rattler dozing on the shaded side of a rock, the throat-tightening reek of tar suggested for a moment on the air. That would be the highway, perhaps a recent hotpatch on a chuckhole. Then a startling tang of sulfur dioxide drowned them out and passed on, leaving him stung and sniffling and groping for a handkerchief that was not there. What in God's name had that been, and where from? Without ceasing to trudge he studied the horizon slowly and found a smoke pall to the far west dimly smudging the sky. It looked like a small city's, or a fair-sized factory's, pollution. A city or a factory where "in his time"—he formed the thought reluctantly—there had been none.

Then he was at the highway. It had been improved; it was a two-laner still, but it was nicely graded now, built up by perhaps three inches of gravel and tar beyond its old level, and lavishly ditched on either side.

If he had a coin he would have tossed it, but you went for weeks without spending a cent at Los Alamos Laboratory; Uncle took care of everything, from cigarettes to tombstones. He turned left and began to walk westward toward that sky-smudge.

I am a reasonable animal, he was telling himself, and I will accept whatever comes in a spirit of reason. I will control what I can and try to understand the rest—

A faint siren scream began behind him and built up fast. The reasonable animal jumped for the ditch and hugged it for dear life. The siren howled closer, and motors roared. At the ear-splitting climax Royland put his head up for one glimpse, then fell back into the ditch as if a grenade had exploded in his middle.

The convoy roared on, down the *center* of the two-lane highway, straddling the white line. First the three little recon cars with the twin-mount machine guns, each filled brimful with three helmeted Japanese soldiers. Then the high-profiled, armored car of state, six-wheeled, with a probably ceremonial gun turret astern— nickel-plated gunbarrels are impractical—and the Japanese admiral in the fore-and-aft hat taking his lordly ease beside a rawboned, hatchet-faced SS officer in gleaming black. Then, diminuendo, two more little recon jobs …

"We've lost," Royland said in his ditch meditatively. "Ceremonial tanks with glass windows—we lost a *long* time ago." Had there been a Rising Sun insignia or was he now imagining that?

He climbed out and continued to trudge westward on the improved blacktop. You couldn't say "I reject the universe"; not when you were as thirsty as he was.

He didn't even turn when the put-putting of a westbound vehicle grew loud behind him and then very loud when it stopped at his side.

"Zeegail," a curious voice said. "What are you doing here?"

The vehicle was just as odd in its own way as the ceremonial tank. It was minimum motor transportation, a kid's sled on wheels, powered by a noisy little air-cooled outboard motor. The driver sat with no more comfort than a cleat to back his coccyx against, and behind him were two twenty-five-pound flour sacks that took up all the remaining room the little buckboard provided. The driver had the leathery Southwestern look; he wore a baggy blue outfit that was obviously a uniform and obviously unmilitary. He had a name-tape on his breast above an incomprehensible row of dull ribbons: MARTFIELD, E., 1218824, P/7 NQOTD43. He saw Royland's eyes on the tape and said kindly: "My name is Martfield—Paymaster Seventh, but there's no need to use my rank here. Are you all right, my man?"

"Thirsty," Royland said. "What's the NQOTD43 for?"

"You can read!" Martfield said, astounded. "Those clothes—"

"Something to drink, please," Royland said. For the moment nothing else mattered in the world. He sat down on the buckboard like a puppet with cut strings.

"See here, fellow!" Martfield snapped in a curious, strangled way, forcing the words through his throat with a stagy, conventional effect of controlled anger. "You can stand until I invite you to sit!"

"Have you any water?" Royland asked dully.

With the same bark: "Who do you think you are?"

"I happen to be a theoretical physicist—" tiredly arguing with a dim seventh-carbon-copy imitation of a drill sergeant.

"Oh-*hoh!*" Martfield suddenly laughed. His stiffness vanished; he actually reached into his baggy tunic and brought out a pint canteen that gurgled. He then forgot all about the canteen in his hand, roguishly dug Royland in the ribs and said: "I should have suspected. You scientists! Somebody was supposed to pick you up—but he was another scientist, eh? Ah-hah-hah-hah!"

Royland took the canteen from his hand and sipped. So a scientist was supposed to be an idiot-savant, eh? Never mind now; drink. People said you were not supposed to fill your stomach with water after great thirst; it sounded to him like one of those puritanical rules people make up out of nothing because they sound reasonable. He finished the canteen while Martfield, Paymaster Seventh, looked alarmed, and wished only that there were three or four more of them.

"Got any food?" he demanded.

Martfield cringed briefly. "Doctor, I regret extremely that I have nothing with me. However if you would do me the honor of riding with me to my quarters—"

"Let's go," Royland said. He squatted on the flour sacks and away they chugged at a good thirty miles an hour; it was a fair little engine. The Paymaster Seventh continued deferential, apologizing over his shoulder because there was no windscreen, later dropped his cringing entirely to explain that Royland was seated on flour—"*white* flour, understand?" An over-the-shoulder wink. He had a friend in the bakery at Los Alamos. Several buckboards passed the other way as they traveled. At each encounter there was a peering examination of insignia to decide who saluted. Once they met a sketchily-enclosed vehicle which furnished its driver with a low seat instead of obliging him to sit with legs straight out, and Paymaster Seventh Martfield almost dislocated his shoulder saluting first. The driver of that one was a Japanese in a kimono. A long curved sword lay across his lap.

Mile after mile the smell of sulfur and sulfides increased; finally there rose before them the towers of a Frasch Process layout. It looked like an oilfield, but instead of ground-laid pipelines and bass-drum storage tanks there were foothills of yellow sulfur. They drove between them—more salutes from baggily-uniformed workers with shovels and yard-long Stillson wrenches. Off to the right were things that might have been Solvay Process towers for sulfuric acid, and a glittering horror of a neo-Roman administration-and-labs building. The Rising Sun banner fluttered from its central flagstaff.

Music surged as they drove deeper into the area; first it was a welcome counterirritant to the pop-pop of the two-cycle buckboard engine, and then a nuisance by itself. Royland looked, annoyed, for the loudspeakers, and saw them everywhere—on power poles, buildings, gateposts. Schmaltzy Strauss waltzes bathed them like smog, made thinking just a little harder, made communication just a little more blurry even after you had learned to live with the noise.

"I miss music in the wilderness," Martfield confided over his shoulder. He throttled down the buckboard until they were just rolling; they had passed some line unrecognized by Royland beyond which one did not salute everybody—just the occasional Japanese walking by in business suit with blueprint-roll and slide rule, or in kimono with sword. It was a German who nailed Royland, however: a classic jack-booted German in black broadcloth, black leather, and plenty of silver trim. He watched them roll for a moment after exchanging salutes with Martfield, made up his mind, and said: "Halt."

The Paymaster Seventh slapped on the brake, killed the engine, and popped to attention beside the buckboard. Royland more or less imitated him. The German said, stiffly but without accent: "Whom have you brought here, Paymaster?"

"A scientist, sir. I picked him up on the road returning from Los Alamos with personal supplies. He appears to be a minerals prospector who missed a rendezvous, but naturally I have not questioned the Doctor."

The German turned to Royland contemplatively. "So, Doctor. Your name and specialty."

"Dr. Edward Royland," he said. "I do nuclear power research." If there was no bomb he'd be damned if he'd invent it now for these people.

"So? That is very interesting, considering that there is no such thing as nuclear power research. Which camp are you from?" The German threw an aside to the Paymaster Seventh, who was literally shaking with fear at the turn things had taken. "You may go, Paymaster. Of course you will report yourself for harboring a fugitive."

"At once, sir," Martfield said in a sick voice. He moved slowly away pushing the little buckboard before him. The Strauss waltz oom-pah'd its last chord and instantly the loudspeakers struck up a hoppity-hoppity folk dance, heavy on the brass.

"Come with me," the German said, and walked off, not even looking behind to see whether Royland was obeying. This itself demonstrated how unlikely any disobedience was to succeed. Royland followed at his heels, which of course were garnished with silver spurs. Royland had not seen a horse so far that day.

A Japanese stopped them politely inside the administration building, a rimless-glasses, office-manager type in a grey suit. "How nice to see you again, Major Kappel! Is there anything I might do to help you?"

The German stiffened. "I didn't want to bother your people, Mr. Ito. This fellow appears to be a fugitive from one of our camps; I was going to turn him over to our liaison group for examination and return."

Mr. Ito looked at Royland and slapped his face hard. Royland, by the insanity of sheer reflex, cocked his fist as a red-blooded boy should, but the German's reflexes operated also. He had a pistol in his hand and pressed against Royland's ribs before he could throw the punch.

"All right," Royland said, and put down his hand.

Mr. Ito laughed. "You are at least partly right, Major Kappel; he certainly is not from one of *our* camps! But do not let me delay you further. May I hope for a report on the outcome of this?"

"Of course, Mr. Ito," said the German. He holstered his pistol and walked on, trailed by the scientist. Royland heard him grumble something that sounded like "Damned extraterritoriality!"

They descended to a basement level where all the door signs were in German, and in an office labeled WISSENSCHAFTSLICHESICHERHEITSLIAISON Royland finally told his story. His audience was the major, a fat officer deferentially addressed as Colonel Biederman, and a bearded old civilian, a Dr. Piqueron, called in from another office. Royland suppressed only the matter of bomb research, and did it easily with the old security habit. His improvised cover story made the Los Alamos Laboratory a research center only for the generation of electricity.

The three heard him out in silence. Finally, in an amused voice, the colonel asked: "Who was this Hitler you mentioned?"

For that Royland was not prepared. His jaw dropped.

Major Kappel said: "Oddly enough, he struck on a name which does figure, somewhat infamously, in the annals of the Third Reich. One Adolf Hitler was an early Party agitator, but as I recall it he intrigued against the Leader during the War of Triumph and was executed."

"An ingenious madman," the colonel said. "Sterilized, of course?"

"Why, I don't know. I suppose so. Doctor, would you—?"

Dr. Piqueron quickly examined Royland and found him all there, which astonished them. Then they thought of looking for his camp tattoo number on the left bicep, and found none. Then, thoroughly upset, they discovered that he had no birth number above his left nipple either.

"And," Dr. Piqueron stammered, "his shoes are odd, sir—I just noticed. Sir, how long since you've seen sewn shoes and braided laces?"

"You must be hungry," the colonel suddenly said. "Doctor, have my aide get something to eat for—for the doctor."

"Major," said Royland, "I hope no harm will come to the fellow who picked me up. You told him to report himself."

"Have no fear, er, doctor," said the major. "Such humanity! You are of German blood?"

"Not that I know of; it may be."

"It *must* be!" said the colonel.

A platter of hash and a glass of beer arrived on a tray. Royland postponed everything. At last he demanded: "Now. Do you believe me? There must be fingerprints to prove my story still in existence."

"I feel like a fool," the major said. "You still could be hoaxing us. Dr. Piqueron, did not a German scientist establish that nuclear power is a theoretical and practical impossibility, that one always must put more into it than one can take out?"

Piqueron nodded and said reverently: "Heisenberg. 1953, during the War of Triumph. His group was then assigned to electrical weapons research and produced the blinding bomb. But this fact does not invalidate the doctor's story; he says only that his group was *attempting* to produce nuclear power."

"We've got to research this," said the colonel. "Dr. Piqueron, entertain this man, whatever he is, in your laboratory."

Piqueron's laboratory down the hall was a place of astounding simplicity, even crudeness. The sinks, reagents and balance were capable only of simple qualitative and quantitative analyses; various works in progress testified that they were not even strained to their modest limits. Samples of sulfur and its compounds were analyzed here. It hardly seemed to call for a "doctor" of anything, and hardly even for a human being. Machinery should be continuously testing the products as they flowed out; variations should be scribed mechanically on a moving tape; automatic controls should at least stop the processes and signal an alarm when variation went beyond limits; at most it might correct whatever was going wrong. But here sat Piqueron every day, titrating, precipitating and weighing, entering results by hand in a ledger and telephoning them to the works!

Piqueron looked about proudly. "As a physicist you wouldn't understand all this, of course," he said. "Shall I explain?"

"Perhaps later, doctor, if you'd be good enough. If you'd first help me orient myself—"

So Piqueron told him about the War of Triumph (1940–1955) and what came after.

In 1940 the realm of der Fuehrer (Herr Göbbels, of course—that strapping blond fellow with the heroic jaw and eagle's eye whom you can see in the picture there) was simultaneously and treacherously invaded by the misguided French, the sub-human Slavs and the perfidious British. The attack, for which the shocked Germans coined the name *Blitzkrieg*, was timed to coincide with an internal eruption of sabotage, well-poisoning and assassination by the *Zigeunerjuden,* or Jewpsies, of whom little is now known; there seem to be none left.

By Nature's ineluctable law, the Germans had necessarily to be tested to the utmost so that they might fully respond. Therefore Germany was overrun from East and West, and Holy Berlin itself was taken; but Göbbels and his court withdrew like Barbarossa into the mountain fastnesses to await their day. It came unexpectedly soon. The deluded Americans launched a million-man amphibious attack on the homeland of the Japanese in 1945. The Japanese resisted with almost Teutonic courage. Not one American in twenty reached shore alive, and not one in a hundred got a mile inland. Particularly lethal were the women and children who lay in camouflaged pits hugging artillery shells and aircraft bombs, which they detonated when enough invaders drew near to make it worthwhile.

The second invasion attempt, a month later, was made up of second-line troops scraped up from everywhere, including occupation duty in Germany.

"Literally," Piqueron said, "the Japanese did not know how to surrender, so they did not. They could not conquer, but they could and did continue suicidal resistance, consuming manpower of the allies and their own womanpower and childpower—a shrewd bargain for the Japanese! The Russians refused to become involved in the Japanese war; they watched with apish delight while two future enemies, as they supposed, were engaged in mutual destruction.

"A third assault wave broke on Kyushu and gained the island at last. What lay ahead? Only another assault on Honshu, the main island, home of the Emperor and the principal shrines. It was 1946; the volatile, child-like Americans were war weary and mutinous; the best of them were gone by then. In desperation the Anglo-American leaders offered the Russians an economic sphere embracing the China coast and Japan as the price of participation."

The Russians grinned and assented; they would take that—at *least* that. They mounted a huge assault for the spring of 1947; they would take Korea and leap off from there for Northern Honshu while the Anglo-American forces struck in the south. Surely this would provide at last a symbol before which the Japanese might without shame bow down and admit defeat!

And then, from the mountain fastnesses, came the radio voice: "Germans! Your Leader calls upon you again!" Followed the Hundred Days of Glory during which the German Army reconstituted itself and expelled the occupation troops— by then, children without combat experience, and leavened by not-quite-disabled veterans. Followed the seizure of the airfields; the Luftwaffe in business again. Followed the drive, almost a dress parade, to the Channel Coast, gobbling up immense munition dumps awaiting shipment to the Pacific Theater, millions of warm uniforms, good boots, mountains of rations, piles of shells and explosives that lined the French roads for scores of miles, thousands of two-and-a-half-ton trucks, and lakes of gasoline to fuel them. The shipyards of Europe, from Hamburg to Toulon, had been turning out, furiously, invasion barges for the Pacific. In April of 1947 they sailed against England in their thousands.

Halfway around the world, the British Navy was pounding Tokyo, Nagasaki, Kobe, Hiroshima, Nara. Three quarters of the way across Asia the Russian Army marched stolidly on; let the decadent British pickle their own fish; the glorious motherland at last was gaining her long-sought, long-denied, warm-water seacoast. The British, tired women without their men, children fatherless these eight years, old folks deathly weary, deathly worried about their sons, were brave but they were not insane. They accepted honorable peace terms; they capitulated.

With the Western front secure for the first time in history, the ancient Drive to the East was resumed; the immemorial struggle of Teuton against Slav went on.

His spectacles glittering with rapture, Dr. Piqueron said: "We were worthy in those days of the Teutonic Knights who seized Prussia from the sub-men! On the ever-glorious Twenty-First of May, Moscow was ours!"

Moscow and the monolithic state machinery it controlled, and all the roads and rail lines and communication wires which led only to—and from—Moscow. Detroit-built tanks and trucks sped along those roads in the fine, bracing spring weather; the Red Army turned one hundred and eighty degrees at last and countermarched halfway across the Eurasian landmass, and at Kazan it broke exhausted against the Frederik Line.

Europe at last was one and German. Beyond Europe lay the dark and swarming masses of Asia, mysterious and repulsive folk whom it would be better to handle through the non-German, but chivalrous, Japanese. The Japanese were reinforced with shipping from Birkenhead, artillery from the Putilov Works, jet fighters from Châteauroux, steel from the Ruhr, rice from the Po valley, herring from Norway, timber from Sweden, oil from Romania, laborers from India. The American forces were driven from Kyushu in the winter of 1948, and bloodily back across their chain of island steppingstones that followed.

Surrender they would not; it was a monstrous affront that shield-shaped North America dared to lie there between the German Atlantic and the Japanese Pacific threatening both. The affront was wiped out in 1955.

For one hundred and fifty years now the Germans and the Japanese had uneasily eyed each other across the banks of the Mississippi. Their orators were fond of referring to that river as a vast frontier unblemished by a single fortification. There was even some interpenetration; a Japanese colony fished out of Nova Scotia on the very rim of German America; a sulfur mine which was part of the Farben system lay in New Mexico, the very heart of Japanese America—this was where Dr. Edward Royland found himself, being lectured to by Dr. Piqueron, Dr. Gaston Pierre Piqueron, true-blue German.

"Here, of course," Dr. Piqueron said gloomily, "we are so damned provincial. Little ceremony and less manners. Well, it would be too much to expect them to assign *German* Germans to this dreary outpost, so we French Germans must endure it somehow."

"You're all French?" Royland asked, startled.

"French *Germans*," Piqueron stiffly corrected him. "Colonel Biederman happens to be a French German also; Major Kappel is—hrrmph—an Italian German." He sniffed to show what he thought of that.

The Italian German entered at that point, not in time to shut off the question: "And you all come from Europe?"

They looked at him in bafflement. "My grandfather did," Dr. Piqueron said. Royland remembered; so Roman legions used to guard their empire—Romans born and raised in Britain, or on the Danube, Romans who would never in their lives see Italy or Rome.

Major Kappel said affably: "Well, this needn't concern us. I'm afraid, my dear fellow, that your little hoax has not succeeded." He clapped Royland merrily on the back. "I admit you've tricked us all nicely; now may we have the facts?"

Piqueron said, surprised: "His story is false? The shoes? The missing *Geburtsnummer?* And he appears to understand some chemistry!"

"Ah-h-h—but he said his specialty was *physics,* doctor! Suspicious in itself!"

"Quite so. A discrepancy. But the rest—?"

"As to his birth number, who knows? As to his shoes, who cares? I took some inconspicuous notes while he was entertaining us and have checked thoroughly. There *was* no Manhattan Engineering District. There *was* no Dr. Oppenheimer, or Fermi, or Bohr. There *is* no theory of relativity, or equivalence of mass and energy. Uranium has one use only—coloring glass a pretty orange. There is such a thing as an isotope but it has nothing to do with chemistry; it is the name used in Race Science for a permissible variation within a subrace. And what have you to say to *that,* my dear fellow?"

Royland wondered first, such was the positiveness with which Major Kappel spoke, whether he had slipped into a universe of different physical properties and history entirely, one in which Julius Caesar discovered Peru and the oxygen molecule was lighter than the hydrogen atom. He managed to speak. "How did you find all that out, major?"

"Oh, don't think I did a skimpy job," Kappel smiled. "I looked it all up in the *big* encyclopedia."

Dr. Piqueron, chemist, nodded grave approval of the major's diligence and thorough grasp of the scientific method.

"You still don't want to tell us?" Major Kappel asked coaxingly.

"I can only stand by what I said."

Kappel shrugged. "It's not my job to persuade you; I wouldn't know how to begin. But I can and will ship you off forthwith to a work camp."

"What—is a work camp?" Royland unsteadily asked.

"Good heavens, man, a camp where one works! You're obviously an *Ungleichgeschaltling* and you've got to be *Gleichgeschaltet.* " He did not speak these words as if they were foreign; they were obviously part of the everyday American working vocabulary. *Gleichgeschaltet* meant to Royland something like "coordinated, brought into tune with." So he would be brought into tune—with what, and how?

The Major went on: "You'll get your clothes and your bunk and your chow, and you'll work, and eventually your irregular vagabondish habits will disappear and you'll be turned loose on the labor market. And you'll be damned glad we took the trouble with you." His face fell. "By the way, I was too late with your friend the Paymaster. I'm sorry. I sent a messenger to Disciplinary Control with a stop order. After all, if you took us in for an hour, why should you not have fooled a Pay-Seventh?"

"Too late? He's *dead*? For picking up a *hitchhiker*?"

"I don't know what that last word means," said the Major. "If it's dialect for 'vagabond', the answer is ordinarily 'yes'. The man, after all, was a Pay-Seventh; he could read. Either you're keeping up your hoax with remarkable fidelity or you've been living in isolation. Could that be it? Is there a tribe of you somewhere? Well, the interrogators will find out; that's their job."

"The Dogpatch legend!" Dr. Piqueron burst out, thunderstruck. "He may be an Abnerite!"

"By Heaven," Major Kappel said slowly, "that might be it. What a feather in my cap to find a living Abnerite."

"*Whose* cap?" demanded Dr. Piqueron coldly.

"I think I'll look the Dogpatch legend up," said Kappel, heading for the door and probably the big encyclopedia.

"So will I," Dr. Piqueron announced firmly. The last Royland saw of them they were racing down the corridor, neck and neck.

Very funny. And they had killed simple-minded Paymaster Martfield for picking up a hitchhiker. The Nazis always had been pretty funny—fat Hermann pretending he was young Siegfried. As blond as Hitler, as slim as Göring and as tall as Göbbels. Immature guttersnipes who hadn't been able to hang a convincing frame on Dimitrov for the Reichstag fire; the world had roared at their bungling. Huge, corny party rallies with let's-play-detectives nonsense like touching the local flags to that hallowed banner on which the martyred Horst Wessel had had a nosebleed. And they had rolled over Europe, and they killed people ... .

One thing was certain: life in the work camp would at least bore him to death. He was supposed to be an illiterate simpleton, so things were excused him which were not excused an exalted Pay-Seventh. He poked through a closet in the corner of the laboratory—he and Piqueron were the same size—

He found a natty change of uniform and what must be a civilian suit: somewhat baggy pants and a sort of tunic with the neat, sensible Russian collar. Obviously it would be all right to wear it because here it was; just as obviously, it was all wrong for him to be dressed in chinos and a flannel shirt. He did not know exactly what this made him, but Martfield had been done to death for picking up a man in chinos and a flannel shirt. Royland changed into the civilian suit, stuffed his own shirt and pants far back on the top shelf of the closet; this was probably concealment enough from those murderous clowns. He walked out, and up the stairs, and through the busy lobby, and into the industrial complex. Nobody saluted him and he saluted nobody. He knew where he was going—to a good, sound Japanese laboratory where there were no Germans.

Royland had known Japanese students at the University and admired them beyond words. Their brains, frugality, doggedness and good humor made them, as far as he was concerned, the most sensible people he had ever known. Tojo and his warlords were not, as far as Royland was concerned, essentially Japanese but just more damfool soldiers and politicians. The real Japanese would courteously listen to him, calmly check against available facts—

He rubbed his cheek and remembered Mr. Ito and his slap in the face. Well, presumably Mr. Ito was a damfool soldier and politician—and demonstrating for the German's benefit in a touchy border area full of jurisdictional questions.

At any rate, he would *not* go to a labor camp and bust rocks or refinish furniture until those imbeciles decided he was *Gleichgeschaltet;* he would go mad in a month.

Royland walked to the Solvay towers and followed the glass pipes containing their output of sulfuric acid along the ground until he came to a bottling shed where beetle-browed men worked silently filling great wicker-basketed carboys and heaving them outside. He followed other men who levered them up onto hand trucks and rolled them in one door of a storage shed. Out the door at the other end more men loaded them onto enclosed trucks which were driven up from time to time.

Royland settled himself in a corner of the storage shed behind a barricade of carboys and listened to the truck dispatcher swear at his drivers and the carboy handlers swear at their carboys.

"Get the goddam Frisco shipment *loaded,* stupid! I don't *care* if you gotta go, we gotta get it out by *midnight!*"

So a few hours after dark Royland was riding west, without much air, and in the dangerous company of one thousand gallons of acid. He hoped he had a careful driver.

A night, a day, and another night on the road. The truck never stopped except to gas up; the drivers took turns and ate sandwiches at the wheel and dozed off shift. It rained the second night. Royland, craftily and perhaps a little crazily, licked the drops that ran down the tarpaulin flap covering the rear. At the first crack of dawn, hunched between two wicker carcasses, he saw they were rolling through irrigated vegetable fields, and the water in the ditches was too much for him. He heard the transmission shift down to slow for a curve, swarmed over the tailgate and dropped to the road. He was weak and limp enough to hit like a sack.

He got up, ignoring his bruises, and hobbled to one of the brimming five-foot ditches; he drank, and drank, and drank. This time puritanical folklore proved right; he lost it all immediately, or what had not been greedily absorbed by his shriveled stomach. He did not mind; it was bliss enough to *stretch*.

The field crop was tomatoes, almost dead ripe. He was starved for them; as he saw the rosy beauties he knew that tomatoes were the only thing in the world he craved. He gobbled one so that the juice ran down his chin; he ate the next two delicately, letting his teeth break the crispness of their skin and the beautiful taste ravish his tongue. There were tomatoes as far as the eye could see, on either side of the road, the green of the vines and the red dots of the ripe fruit graphed by the checkerboard of silvery ditches that caught the first light. Nevertheless he filled his pockets with them before he walked on.

Royland was happy.

Farewell to the Germans and their sordid hash and murderous ways. *Look* at these beautiful fields! The Japanese are an innately artistic people who bring beauty to every detail of daily life. And they make damn good physicists, too. Confined in their stony home, cramped as he had been in the truck, they grew twisted and painful; why should they not have reached out for more room to grow, and what other way is there to reach but to make war? He could be very understanding about any people who had planted these beautiful tomatoes for him.

A dark blemish the size of a man attracted his attention. It lay on the margin of one of the swirling five-foot ditches out there to his right. And then it rolled slowly into the ditch with a splash, floundered a little and proceeded to drown.

In a hobbling run Royland broke from the road and across the field. He did not know whether he was limber enough to swim. As he stood panting on the edge of the ditch, peering into the water, a head of hair surfaced near him. He flung himself down, stretched wildly and grabbed the hair—and yet had detachment enough to feel a pang when the tomatoes in his tunic pocket smashed.

"Steady," he muttered to himself, yanked the head toward him, took hold with his other hand and lifted. A surprised face confronted him and then went blank and unconscious.

For half an hour Royland, weak as he was, struggled, cursed feebly, and sweated to get that body out of the water. At last he plunged in himself, found it only chest-deep, and shoved the carcass over the mudslick bank. He did not know by then whether the man was alive or dead or much care. He knew only that he couldn't walk away and leave the job half-finished.

The body was that of a fat, middle-aged oriental, surely Chinese rather than Japanese, though Royland could not say why he thought so. His clothes were soaked rags except for a leather wallet the size of a cigar box which he wore on a wide cloth belt. Its sole content was a handsome blue-glazed porcelain bottle. Royland sniffed at it and reeled. Some kind of super-gin! He sniffed again, and then took a conservative gulp of the stuff. While he was still coughing he felt the bottle being removed from his hand. When he looked he saw the Chinese, eyes still closed, accurately guiding the neck of the bottle to his mouth. The Chinese drank and drank and drank, then returned the bottle to the wallet and finally opened his eyes.

"Honorable sir," said the Chinese in flat, California American speech, "you have deigned to save my unworthy life. May I supplicate your honorable name?"

"Ah, Royland. Look, take it easy. Don't try to get up; you shouldn't even talk."

Somebody screamed behind Royland: "There has been thieving of tomatoes! There has been smasheeng and deestruction of thee vines! Chil-dren you, will bee weet-ness be-fore the Jappa-neese!"

Christ, now what?

Now a skinny black man, not a Negro, in a dirty loin-cloth, and beside him like a pan-pipes five skinny black loin-clothed offspring in descending order. All were capering, pointing and threatening. The Chinese groaned, fished in his tattered robes with one hand and pulled out a soggy wad of bills. He peeled one off, held it out and said: "Begone pestilential barbarians from beyond Tian-Shang. My master and I give you alms, not tribute."

The Dravidian, or whatever he was, grabbed the bill and keened. "Een-suffee-cient for the terrible dommage! The Jappa-neese—"

The Chinese waved them away boredly. He said: "If my master will conde-scend to help me arise?"

Royland uncertainly helped him up. The man was wobbly, whether from the near-drowning or the terrific belt of alcohol he'd taken there was no knowing. They proceeded to the road, followed by shrieks to be careful about stepping on the vines.

On the road, the Chinese said: "My unworthy name is Li Po. Will my mas-ter deign to indicate in which direction we are to travel?"

"What's this master business?" Royland demanded. "If you're grateful, swell, but I don't *own* you."

"My master is pleased to jest," said Li Po. Politely, face-saving and third-personing Royland until hell wouldn't have it, he explained that Royland, having meddled with the Celestial decree that Li Po should, while drunk, roll into the irri-gation ditch and drown, now had Li Po on his hands, for the Celestial Ones had washed theirs of him. "As my master of course will recollect in a moment or two." Understandingly, he expressed his sympathy with Royland's misfortune in acquiring him as an obligation, especially since he had a hearty appetite, was known to be dis-honest, and suffered from fainting fits and spasms when confronted with work.

"I don't *know* about all this," Royland said fretfully. "Wasn't there another Li Po? A poet?"

"Your servant prefers to venerate his namesake as one of the greatest drunk-ards the Flowery Kingdom has ever known," the Chinese observed. And a mo-ment later he bent over, clipped Royland behind the knees so that he toppled for-ward and bumped his head, and performed the same obeisance himself, more gracefully. A vehicle went sputtering and popping by on the road as they kow-towed.

Li Po said reproachfully: "I humbly observe that my master is unaware of the etiquette our noble overlords exact. Such negligence cost the head of my in-significant elder brother in his twelfth year. Would my master be pleased to ex-plain how he can have reached his honorable years without learning what babes in their cradles are taught?"

Royland answered with the whole truth. Li Po politely begged clarification from time to time, and a sketch of his mental horizons emerged from his ques-tioning. That "magic" had whisked Royland forward a century or more he did not doubt for an instant, but he found it difficult to understand why the proper *feng shui* precautions had not been taken to avert a disastrous outcome to the God Food experiment. He suspected, from a description of Nahataspe's hut, that a simple wall at right angles to the door would have kept all really important demons out. When Royland described his escape from German territory to Japanese, and why he had effected it, he was very bland and blank. Royland judged that Li Po pri-vately thought him not very bright for having left *any* place to come here.

And Royland hoped he was not right. "Tell me what it's like," he said.

"This realm," said Li Po, "under our benevolent and noble overlords, is the haven of all whose skin is not the bleached-bone hue which indicates the undying curse of the Celestial Ones. Hither flock men of Han like my unworthy self, and the sons of Hind beyond the Tian-Shang, that we may till new soil and raise up sons, and sons of sons to venerate us when we ascend."

"What was that bit," Royland demanded, "about the bleached bones? Do they shoot, ah, white men on sight here, or do they not?"

Li Po said evasively: "We are approaching the village where I unworthily serve as fortune teller, doctor of *feng shui,* occasional poet and storyteller. Let my master have no fear about his color. This humble one will roughen his master's skin, tell a circumstantial and artistic lie or two, and pass his master off as merely a leper."

After a week in Li Po's village Royland knew that life was good there. The place was a wattle-and-clay settlement of about two hundred souls on the bank of an irrigation ditch large enough to be dignified by the name of "canal." It was situated nobody knew just where; Royland thought it must be the San Fernando Valley. The soil was thick and rich and bore furiously the year round. A huge kind of radish was the principal crop. It was too coarse to be eaten by man; the villagers understood that it was feed for chickens somewhere up north. At any rate they harvested the stuff, fed it through a great hand-powered shredder and shade-cured the shreds. Every few days a Japanese of low caste would come by in a truck, they would load tons of the stuff onto it, and wave their giant radish good-by forever. Presumably the chickens ate it, and the Japanese then ate the chickens.

The villagers ate chicken too, but only at weddings and funerals. The rest of the time they ate vegetables which they cultivated, a quarter-acre to a family, the way other craftsmen facet diamonds. A single cabbage might receive, during its ninety days from planting to maturity, one hundred work-hours from grandmother, grandfather, son, daughter, eldest grandchild and on down to the smallest toddler. Theoretically the entire family line should have starved to death, for there are not one hundred energy-hours in a cabbage; somehow they did not. They merely stayed thin and cheerful and hard-working and fecund.

They spoke English by Imperial decree; the reasoning seemed to be that they were as unworthy to speak Japanese as to paint the Imperial Chrysanthemum Seal on their houses, and that to let them cling to their old languages and dialects would have been politically unwise.

They were a mixed lot of Chinese, Hindus, Dravidians and, to Royland's surprise, low-caste and outcaste Japanese; he had not known there were such things. Village tradition had it that a *samurai* named Ugetsu long ago said, pointing at the drunk tank of a Hong Kong jail, "I'll have that lot," and "that lot" had been the ancestors of these villagers transported to America in a foul hold practically as ballast and settled here by the canal with orders to start making their radish quota. The place was at any rate called the Ugetsu Village, and if some of the descendants were teetotalers, others like Li Po gave color to the legend of their starting point.

After a week the cheerful pretense that he was a sufferer from Hansen's disease evaporated and he could wash the mud off his face. He had merely to avoid the upper-caste Japanese and especially the *samurai*. This was not exactly a stigma; in general it was a good idea for *everybody* to avoid the *samurai*.

In the village Royland found his first love and his first religion both false.

He had settled down; he was getting used to the Oriental work rhythm of slow, repeated, incessant effort; it did not surprise him any longer that he could count his ribs. When he ate a bowl of artfully-arranged vegetables, the red of pimiento played off against the yellow of parsnip, a slice of pickled beet adding visual and olfactory tang to the picture, he felt full enough; he *was* full enough for the next day's feeble work in the field. It was pleasant enough to play slowly with a wooden mattock in the rich soil; did not people once buy sand so their children might do exactly what he did, and envy their innocent absorption? Royland was innocently absorbed, then, and the radish truck had collected six times since his arrival, when he began to feel stirrings of lust. On the edge of starvation (but who knew this? For everybody was) his mind was dulled, but not his loins. They burned, and he looked about him in the fields, and the first girl he saw who was not repulsive he fell abysmally in love with.

Bewildered, he told Li Po, who was also Ugetsu Village's go-between. The storyteller was delighted; he waddled off to seek information and returned. "My master's choice is wise. The slave on whom his lordly eye deigned to rest is known as Vashti, daughter of Hari Bose, the distiller. She is his seventh child and so no great dowry can be expected (I shall ask for fifteen kegs toddy, but would settle for seven), but all this humble village knows that she is a skilled and willing worker in the hut as in the fields. I fear she has the customary lamentable Hindu talent for concocting curries, but a dozen good beatings at the most should cause her to reserve it to appropriate occasions, such as visits from her mother and sisters."

So, according to the sensible custom of Ugetsu, Vashti came that night to the hut which Royland shared with Li Po, and Li Po visited with cronies by his master's puzzling request. He begged humbly to point out that it would be dark in the hut, so this talk of lacking privacy was inexplicable to say the least. Royland made it an order, and Li Po did not really object, so he obeyed it.

It was a damnably strange night during which Royland learned all about India's national sport and most highly developed art-form. Vashti, if she found him weak on the theory side, made no complaints. On the contrary, when Royland woke she was doing something or other to his feet.

"More?" he thought incredulously. "With *feet?*" He asked what she was doing. Submissively she replied: "Worshipping my lord husband-to-be's big toe. I am a pious and old-fashioned woman."

So she painted his toe with red paint and prayed to it, and then she fixed breakfast—curry, and excellent. She watched him eat, and then modestly licked his leavings from the bowl. She handed him his clothes, which she had washed while he still slept, and helped him into them after she helped him wash. Royland thought incredulously: "It's not possible! It must be a show, to sell me on marrying her—as if I had to be sold!" His heart turned to custard as he saw her, without a moment's pause, turn from dressing him to polishing his wooden rake. He asked that day in the field, roundabout fashion, and learned that this was the kind of service he could look forward to for the rest of his life after marriage. If the woman got lazy he'd have to beat her, but this seldom happened more than every year or so. We have good girls here in Ugetsu Village.

So an Ugetsu Village peasant was in some ways better off than anybody from "his time" who was less than a millionaire!

His starved dullness was such that he did not realize this was true for only half the Ugetsu Village peasants.

Religion sneaked up on him in similar fashion. He went to the part-time Taoist priest because he was a little bored with Li Po's current after-dinner saga. He could have sat like all the others and listened passively to the interminable tale of the glorious Yellow Emperor, and the beautiful but wicked Princess Emerald, and the virtuous but plain Princess Moon Blossom; it just happened that he went to the priest of Tao and got hooked hard.

The kindly old man, a toolmaker by day, dropped a few pearls of wisdom which, in his foggy starvation-daze, Royland did not perceive to be pearls of undemonstrable nonsense, and showed Royland how to meditate. It worked the first time. Royland bunged right smack through into a 200-proof state of *samadhi*—the Eastern version of self-hypnotized Enlightenment—that made him feel wonderful and all-knowing and left him without a hangover when it wore off. He had despised, in college, the type of people who took psychology courses and so had taken none himself; he did not know a thing about self-hypnosis except as just demonstrated by this very nice old gentleman. For several days he was offensively religious and kept trying to talk to Li Po about the Eightfold Way, and Li Po kept changing the subject.

It took murder to bring him out of love and religion.

At twilight they were all sitting and listening to the storyteller as usual. Royland had been there just one month and for all he knew would be there forever. He soon would have his bride officially; he knew he had discovered The Truth About the Universe by way of Tao meditation; why should he change? Changing demanded a furious outburst of energy, and he did not have energy on that scale. He metered out his energy day and night; one had to save so much for tonight's love-play, and then one had to save so much for tomorrow's planting. He was a poor man; he could not afford to change.

Li Po had reached a rather interesting bit where the Yellow Emperor was declaiming hotly: "Then she shall die! Whoever dare transgress Our divine will—"

A flashlight began to play over their faces. They perceived that it was in the hand of a *samurai* with kimono and sword. Everybody hastily kowtowed, but the *samurai* shouted irritably (all *samurai* were irritable, all the time): "Sit up, you fools! I want to see your stupid faces. I hear there's a peculiar one in this flea-bitten dungheap you call a village."

Well, by now Royland knew his duty. He rose and with downcast eyes asked: "Is the noble protector in search of my unworthy self?"

"Ha!" the *samurai* roared. "It's true! A big nose!" He hurled the flashlight away (all *samurai* were nobly contemptuous of the merely material), held his scabbard in his left hand and swept out the long curved sword with his right.

Li Po stepped forward and said in his most enchanting voice: "If the Heaven-born would only deign to heed a word from this humble—" What he must have known would happen happened. With a contemptuous backhand sweep of the blade the *samurai* beheaded him and Li Po's debt was paid.

The trunk of the storyteller stood for a moment and then fell stiffly forward. The *samurai* stooped to wipe his blade clean on Li Po's ragged robes.

Royland had forgotten much, but not everything. With the villagers scattering before him he plunged forward and tackled the *samurai* low and hard. No doubt the *samurai* was a Brown Belt judo master; if so he had nobody but himself to blame for turning his back. Royland, not remembering that he was barefoot, tried to kick the *samurai's* face in. He broke his worshipful big toe, but its untrimmed horny nail removed the left eye of the warrior and after that it was no contest. He never let the *samurai* get up off the ground; he took out his other eye with the handle of a rake and then killed him an inch at a time with his hands, his feet, and the clownish rustic's traditional weapon, a flail. It took easily half an hour, and for the final twenty minutes the *samurai* was screaming for his mother. He died when the last light left the western sky, and in darkness Royland stood quite alone with the two corpses. The villagers were gone.

He assumed, or pretended, that they were within earshot and yelled at them brokenly: "I'm sorry, Vashti. I'm sorry, all of you. I'm going. Can I make you understand?

"Listen. You aren't living. This isn't life. You're not making anything but babies, you're not changing, you're not growing up. That's not enough! You've got to read and write. You can't pass on anything but baby-stories like the Yellow Emperor by word of mouth. The village is growing. Soon your fields will touch the fields of Sukoshi Village to the west, and then what happens? You won't know what to do, so you'll fight with Sukoshi Village.

"Religion. No! It's just getting drunk the way you do it. You're set up for it by being half-starved and then you go into *samadhi* and you feel better so you think you understand everything. No! You've got to *do* things. If you don't grow up, you die. All of you.

"Women. *That's* wrong. It's good for the men, but it's wrong. Half of you are slaves, do you understand? Women are people too, but you use them like animals and you've convinced them it's right for them to be old at thirty and discarded for the next girl. For God's sake, can't you try to think of yourselves in their place?

"The breeding, the crazy breeding—it's got to stop. You frugal Orientals! But you aren't frugal; you're crazy drunken sailors. You're squandering the whole world. Every mouth you breed has got to be fed by the land, and the land isn't infinite.

"I hope some of you understood. Li Po would have, a little, but he's dead.

"I'm going away now. You've been kind to me and all I've done is make trouble. I'm sorry."

He fumbled on the ground and found the *samurai's* flashlight. With it he hunted the village's outskirts until he found the Japanese's buckboard car. He started the motor with its crank and noisily rolled down the dirt track from the village to the highway.

Royland drove all night, still westward. His knowledge of southern California's geography was inexact, but he hoped to hit Los Angeles. There might be a chance of losing himself in a great city. He had abandoned hope of finding present-day counterparts of his old classmates like Jimmy Ichimura; obviously they had lost out. Why shouldn't they have lost? The soldier-politicians had won the war by happenstance, so all power to the soldier-politicians! Reasoning under the great natural law *post hoc ergo propter hoc,* Tojo and his crowd had decided: fanatic feudalism won the war; therefore fanatic feudalism is a good thing, and it necessarily follows that the more fanatical and feudal it is, the better a thing it is. So you had Sukoshi Village, and Ugetsu Village; Ichi Village, Ni Village, San Village, Shi Village, dotting that part of Great Japan formerly known as North America, breeding with the good old fanatic feudalism and so feudally averse to new thought and innovations that it made you want to scream at them—which he had.

The single weak headlight of his buckboard passed few others on the road; a decent feudal village is self-contained.

Damn them and their suicidal cheerfulness! It was a pleasant trait; it was a fool in a canoe approaching the rapids saying: "Chin up! Everything's going to be all right if we just keep smiling."

The car ran out of gas when false dawn first began to pale the sky behind him. He pushed it into the roadside ditch and walked on; by full light he was in a tumble-down, planless, evil-smelling, paper-and-galvanized-iron city whose name he did not know. There was no likelihood of him being noticed as a "white" man by anyone not specifically looking for him. A month of outdoor labor had browned him, and a month of artistically-composed vegetable plates had left him gaunt.

The city was carpeted with awakening humanity. Its narrow streets were paved with sprawled-out men, women and children beginning to stir and hawk up phlegm and rub their rheumy eyes. An open sewer-latrine running down the center of each street was casually used, ostrich-fashion—the users hid their own eyes while in action.

Every mangled variety of English rang in Royland's ears as he trod between bodies.

There had to be something more, he told himself. This was the shabby industrial outskirts, the lowest marginal-labor area. Somewhere in the city there was beauty, science, learning!

He walked aimlessly plodding until noon, and found nothing of the sort. These people in the cities were food-handlers, food-traders, food-transporters. They took in one another's washing and sold one another chop suey. They made automobiles (Yes! There were one-family automobile factories which probably made six buckboards a year, filing all metal parts by hand out of bar stock!) and orange crates and baskets and coffins; abacuses, nails and boots.

The Mysterious East has done it again, he thought bitterly. The Indians-Chinese-Japanese won themselves a nice sparse area. They could have laid things out neatly and made it pleasant for everybody instead of for a minute speck of aristocracy which he was unable even to detect in this human soup ... but they had done it again. They had bred irresponsibly just as fast as they could until the land was *full*. Only famines and pestilence could "help" them now.

He found exactly one building which owned some clear space around it and which would survive an earthquake or a flicked cigarette butt. It was the German Consulate.

I'll give them the Bomb, he said to himself. Why not? None of this is mine. And for the Bomb I'll exact a price of some comfort and dignity for as long as I live. *Let* them blow one another up! He climbed the consulate steps.

To the black-uniformed guard at the swastika-trimmed bronze doors he said: "*Wenn die Lichtstärke der von einer Fläche kommenden Strahlung dem Cosinus des Winkels zwischen Strahlrichtung und Flächennormalen proportional ist, so nennen wir die Fläche eine volkommen streuende Fläche.*" Lambert's Law, Optics I. All the Goethe he remembered happened to rhyme, which might have made the guard suspicious.

Naturally the German came to attention and said apologetically: "I don't speak German. What is it, sir?"

"You may take me to the consul," Royland said, affecting boredom.

"Yes, sir. At once, sir. Er, you're an *agent* of course, sir?"

Royland said witheringly: "*Sicherheit, bitte!*"

"Yessir. This way, sir!"

The consul was a considerate, understanding gentleman. He was somewhat surprised by Royland's true tale, but said from time to time: "I see; I see. Not impossible. Please go on."

Royland concluded: "Those people at the sulfur mine were, I hope, unrepresentative. One of them at least complained that it was a dreary sort of backwoods assignment. I am simply gambling that there is intelligence in your Reich. I ask you to get me a real physicist for twenty minutes of conversation. You, Mr. Consul, will not regret it. I am in a position to turn over considerable information on—atomic power." So he had not been able to say it after all; the Bomb was still an obscene kick below the belt.

"This has been very interesting, Dr. Royland," said the consul gravely. "You referred to your enterprise as a gamble. I too shall gamble. What have I to lose by putting you *en rapport* with a scientist of ours if you prove to be a plausible lunatic?" He smiled to soften it. "Very little indeed. On the other hand, what have I to gain if your extraordinary story is quite true? A great deal. I will go along with you, doctor. Have you eaten?"

The relief was tremendous. He had lunch in a basement kitchen with the Consulate guards—a huge lunch, a rather nasty lunch of stewed *Lungen* with a floured gravy, and cup after cup of coffee. Finally one of the guards lit up an ugly little spindle-shaped cigar, the kind Royland had only seen before in the carica-tures of George Grosz, and as an afterthought offered one to him.

He drank in the rank smoke and managed not to cough. It stung his mouth and cut the greasy aftertaste of the stew satisfactorily. One of the blessings of the Third Reich, one of its gross pleasures. They were just people, after all—a certain censorious, busy-body type of person with altogether too much power, but they were human. By which he meant, he supposed, members of Western Industrial Culture like him.

After lunch he was taken by truck from the city to an airfield by one of the guards. The plane was somewhat bigger than a B-29 he had once seen, and lacked propellers. He presumed it was one of the "jets" Dr. Piqueron had mentioned. His guard gave his dossier to a Luftwaffe sergeant at the foot of the ramp and said cheerfully: "Happy landings, fellow. It's all going to be all right."

"Thanks," he said. "I'll remember you, Corporal Collins. You've been very helpful." Collins turned away.

Royland climbed the ramp into the barrel of the plane. A bucket-seat job, and most of the seats were filled. He dropped into one on the very narrow aisle. His neighbor was in rags; his face showed signs of an old beating. When Royland addressed him, he simply cringed away and began to sob.

The Luftwaffe sergeant came up, entered and slammed the door. The "jets" began to wind up, making an unbelievable racket; further conversation was im-possible. While the plane taxied, Royland peered through the windowless gloom at his fellow-passengers. They all looked poor and poorly.

God, were they so quickly and quietly airborne? They were. Even in the bucket seat, Royland fell asleep.

He was awakened, he did not know how much later, by the sergeant. The man was shaking his shoulder and asking him: "Any joolery hid away? Watches? Got some nice fresh water to sell to people that wanna buy it."

Royland had nothing, and would not take part in the miserable little racket if he had. He shook his head indignantly and the man moved on with a grin. He would not last long!—petty chiselers were leaks in the efficient dictatorship; they were rapidly detected and stopped up. Mussolini made the trains run on time, after all. (But naggingly Royland recalled mentioning this to a Northwestern University English professor, one Bevans. Bevans had coldly informed him that from 1931 to 1936 he had lived under Mussolini as a student and tourist guide, and therefore had extraordinary opportunities for observing whether the trains ran on time or not, and could definitely state that they did not; that railway time-tables under Mussolini were best regarded as humorous fiction.)

And another thought nagged at him, a thought connected with a pale, scarred face named Bloom. Bloom was a young refugee physical chemist working on WEAPONS DEVELOPMENT TRACK I, and he was somewhat crazy, perhaps. Royland, on TRACK III, used to see little of him and could have done with even less. You couldn't say hello to the man without it turning into a lecture on the horrors of Nazism. He had wild stories about "gas chambers" and crematoria which no reasonable man could believe, and was a blanket slanderer of the German medical profession. He claimed that trained doctors, certified men, used human beings in experiments which terminated fatally. Once, to try and bring Bloom to reason, he asked what sort of experiments these were, but the monomaniac had had that worked out: piffling nonsense about reviving mortally frozen men by putting naked women into bed with them! The man was probably sexually deranged to believe that; he naively added that one variable in the series of experiments was to use women immediately after sexual intercourse, one hour after sexual intercourse, et cetera. Royland had blushed for him and violently changed the subject.

But that was not what he was groping for. Neither was Bloom's crazy story about the woman who made lampshades from the tattooed skin of concentration camp prisoners; there were people capable of such things, of course, but under no regime whatever do they rise to positions of authority; they simply can't do the work required in positions of authority because their insanity gets in the way.

"Know your enemy," of course—but making up pointless lies? At least Bloom was not the conscious prevaricator. He got letters in Yiddish from friends and relations in Palestine, and these were laden with the latest wild rumors supposed to be based on the latest word from "escapees."

Now he remembered. In the cafeteria about three months ago Bloom had been sipping tea with somewhat shaking hand and rereading a letter. Royland tried to pass him with only a nod, but the skinny hand shot out and held him.

Bloom looked up with tears in his eyes: "It's cruel, I'm tellink you, Royland, it's cruel. They're not givink them the right to scream, to strike a futile blow, to sayink prayers *Kiddush ha Shem* like a Jew should when he is dyink for Consecration of the Name! They trick them, they say they go to farm settlements, to labor camps, so four-five of the stinkink bastards can handle a whole trainload Jews. They trick the clothes off of them at the camps, they sayink they delouse them. They trick them into room says showerbath over the door and then is too late to sayink prayers; *then goes on the gas.*"

Bloom had let go of him and put his head on the table between his hands. Royland had mumbled something, patted his shoulder and walked on, shaken. For once the neurotic little man might have got some straight facts. That was a very circumstantial touch about expediting the handling of prisoners by systematic lies—always the carrot and the stick.

Yes, everybody had been so goddam agreeable since he climbed the Consulate steps! The friendly door guard, the Consul who nodded and remarked that his story was not an impossible one, the men he'd eaten with—all that quiet optimism. "Thanks. I'll remember you, Corporal Collins. You've been very helpful." He had felt positively benign toward the corporal, and now remembered that the corporal had turned around *very* quickly after he spoke. *To hide a grin?*

The guard was working his way down the aisle again and noticed that Royland was awake. "Changed your mind by now?" he asked kindly. "Got a good watch, maybe I'll find a piece of bread for you. You won't need a watch where you're going, fella."

"What do you mean?" Royland demanded.

The guard said soothingly: "Why, they got clocks all over them work camps, fella. Everybody knows what time it is in them work camps. You don't need no watches there. Watches just get in the way at them work camps." He went on down the aisle, quickly.

Royland reached across the aisle and, like Bloom, gripped the man who sat opposite him. He could not see much of him; the huge windowless plane was lit only by half a dozen stingy bulbs overhead. "What are you here for?" he asked.

The man said shakily: "I'm a Laborer Two, see? A Two. Well, my father he taught me to read, see, but he waited until I was ten and knew the score? See? So I figured it was a family tradition, so I taught my own kid to read because he was a pretty smart kid, ya know? I figured he'd have some fun reading like I did, no harm done, who's to know, ya know? But I should of waited a couple years, I guess, because the kid was too young and got to bragging he could read, ya know how kids do? I'm from St. Louis, by the way. I should of said first I'm from St. Louis, a track maintenance man, see, so I hopped a string of returning empties for San Diego because I was scared like you get."

He took a deep sigh. "Thirsty," he said. "Got in with some Chinks, nobody to trouble ya, ya stay outta the way, but then one of them cops-like seen me and he took me to the Consul place like they do, ya know? Had me scared, they always tole me illegal reading they bump ya off, but they don't, ya know? Two years work camp, how about that?"

Yes, Royland wondered. How about it?

The plane decelerated sharply; he was thrown forward. Could they brake with those "jets" by reversing the stream or were the engines just throttling down? He heard gurgling and thudding; hydraulic fluid to the actuators letting down the landing gear. The wheels bumped a moment later and he braced himself; the plane was still and the motors cut off seconds later.

Their Luftwaffe sergeant unlocked the door and bawled through it: "Shove that goddam ramp, willya?" The sergeant's assurance had dropped from him; he looked like a very scared man. He must have been a very brave one, really, to have let himself be locked in with a hundred doomed men, protected only by an eight-shot pistol and a chain of systematic lies.

They were herded out of the plane onto a runway of what Royland immediately identified as the Chicago Municipal Airport. The same reek wafted from the stockyards; the row of airline buildings at the eastern edge of the field was ancient and patched but unchanged; the hangars though were now something that looked like inflated plastic bags. A good trick. Beyond the buildings surely lay the dreary red-brick and painted-siding wastes of Cicero, Illinois.

Luftwaffe men were yapping at them: "Form up, boys; make a line! Work means freedom! Look tall!" They shuffled and were shoved into columns of fours. A snappy majorette in shiny satin panties and white boots pranced out of an administration building twirling her baton; a noisy march blared from louvers in her tall fur hat. Another good trick.

"Forward march, boys," she shrilled at them. "Wouldn't y'all just like to follow me?" Seductive smile and a wiggle of the rump; a Judas ewe. She strutted off
in time to the music; she must have been wearing earstopples. They shuffled after
her. At the airport gate they dropped their blue-coated Luftwaffe boys and picked
up a waiting escort of a dozen black-coats with skulls on their highpeaked caps.

They walked in time to the music, hypnotized by it, through Cicero. Cicero
had been bombed to hell and not rebuilt. To his surprise Royland felt a pang for
the vanished Poles and Slovaks of Al's old bailiwick. There were *German* Germans,
French Germans and even Italian Germans, but he knew in his bones that there
were no Polish or Slovakian Germans. ... And Bloom had been right all along.

Deathly weary after two hours of marching (the majorette was indefatigable),
Royland looked up from the broken pavement to see a cockeyed wonder before
him. It was a Castle; it was a Nightmare; it was the Chicago Parteihof. The thing
abutted Lake Michigan; it covered perhaps sixteen city blocks. It frowned down
on the lake at the east and at the tumbled acres of bombed-out Chicago at the
north, west and south. It was made of steel-reinforced concrete grained and grooved
to look like medieval masonry. It was walled, moated, portcullis-ed, towered,
ramparted, crenellated. The death's-head guards looked at it reverently and the
prisoners with fright. Royland wanted only to laugh wildly. It was a Disney production. It was as funny as Hermann Göring in full fig, and probably as deadly.

With a mumbo-jumbo of passwords, heils and salutes they were admitted,
and the majorette went away, no doubt to take off her boots and groan.

The most bedecked of the death's-head lined them up and said affably: "Hot
dinner and your beds presently, my boys; first a selection. Some of you, I'm afraid,
aren't well and should be in sick bay. Who's sick? Raise your hands, please."

A few hands crept up. Stooped old men.

"That's right. Step forward, please." Then he went down the line tapping a
man here and there—one fellow with glaucoma, another with terrible varicose
sores visible through the tattered pants he wore. Mutely they stepped forward.
Royland he looked thoughtfully over. "You're thin, my boy," he observed. "Stomach pains? Vomit blood? Tarry stools in the morning?"

"Nossir!" Royland barked. The man laughed and continued down the line.
The "sick bay" detail was marched off. Most of them were weeping silently; they
knew. Everybody knew; everybody pretended that the terrible thing would not,
might not, happen. It was much more complex than Royland had realized.

"Now," said the death's-head affably, "we require some competent cement
workers—"

The line of remaining men went mad. They surged forward almost touching the officer but never stepping over an invisible line surrounding him. "Me!"
some yelled. "Me! Me!" Another cried: "I'm good with my hands, I can learn, I'm
a machinist too, I'm strong and young, I can learn!" A heavy middle-aged one
waved his hands in the air and boomed: "Grouting and tile-setting! Grouting and
tile-setting!" Royland stood alone, horrified. They knew. They knew this was an
offer of real work that would keep them alive for a while.

He knew suddenly how to live in a world of lies.

The officer lost his patience in a moment or two, and whips came out. Men with their faces bleeding struggled back into line. "Raise your hands, you cement people, and no lying, please. But you wouldn't lie, would you?" He picked half a dozen volunteers after questioning them briefly, and one of his men marched them off. Among them was the grouting-and-tile man, who looked pompously pleased with himself; such was the reward of diligence and virtue, he seemed to be proclaiming; pooh to those grasshoppers back there who neglected to learn A Trade.

"Now," said the officer casually, "we require some laboratory assistants." The chill of death stole down the line of prisoners. Each one seemed to shrivel into himself, become poker-faced, imply that he wasn't really involved in all this.

Royland raised his hand. The officer looked at him in stupefaction and then covered up quickly. "Splendid," he said. "Step forward, my boy. You," he pointed at another man. "You have an intelligent forehead; you look as if you'd make a fine laboratory assistant. Step forward."

"Please, no!" the man begged. He fell to his knees and clasped his hands in supplication. "Please, no!" The officer took out his whip meditatively; the man groaned, scrambled to his feet and quickly stood beside Royland.

When there were four more chosen, they were marched off across the concrete yard into one of the absurd towers, and up a spiral staircase and down a corridor, and through the promenade at the back of an auditorium where a woman screamed German from the stage at an audience of women. And through a tunnel, and down the corridor of an elementary school with empty classrooms full of small desks on either side. And into a hospital area where the fake-masonry walls yielded to scrubbed white tile and the fake flagstones underfoot to composition flooring and the fake pinewood torches in bronze brackets that had lighted their way to fluorescent tubes.

At the door marked RASSENWISSENSCHAFT the guard rapped and a frosty-faced man in a laboratory coat opened up. "You requisitioned a demonstrator, Dr. Kalten," the guard said. "Pick any one of these."

Dr. Kalten looked them over. "Oh, this one, I suppose," he said. Royland. "Come in, fellow."

The Race Science Laboratory of Dr. Kalten proved to be a decent medical setup with an operating table, intricate charts of the races of men and their anatomical, mental and moral makeups. There was also a phrenological head diagram and a horoscope on the wall, and an arrangement of glittering crystals on wire which Royland recognized. It was a model of one Hans Hörbiger's crackpot theory of planetary formation, the *Welteislehre*.

"Sit there," the doctor said, pointing to a stool. "First I've got to take your pedigree. By the way, you might as well know that you're going to end up dissected for my demonstration in Race Science III for the Medical School, and your degree of co-operation will determine whether the dissection is performed under anaesthesia or not. Clear?"

"Clear, doctor."

"Curious—no panic. I'll wager we find you're a proto-Hamitoidal hemi-Nordic of at *least* degree five … but let's get on. Name?"

"Edward Royland."

"Birthdate?"

"July second, 1923."

The doctor threw down his pencil. "If my previous explanation was inadequate," he shouted, "let me add that if you continue to be difficult I may turn you over to my good friend Dr. Herzbrenner. Dr. Herzbrenner happens to teach interrogation technique at the Gestapo School. *Do—you—now—understand?*"

"Yes, doctor. I'm sorry I cannot withdraw my answer."

Dr. Kalten turned elaborately sarcastic. "How then do you account for your remarkable state of preservation at your age of approximately 180 years?"

"Doctor, I am twenty-three years old. I have traveled through time."

"Indeed?" Kalten was amused. "And how was this accomplished?"

Royland said steadily: "A spell was put on me by a satanic Jewish magician. It involved the ritual murder and desanguination of seven beautiful Nordic virgins."

Dr. Kalten gaped for a moment. Then he picked up his pencil and said firmly: "You will understand that my doubts were logical under the circumstances. Why did you not give me the sound scientific basis for your surprising claim at once? Go ahead; tell me all about it."

He was Dr. Kalten's prize; he was Dr. Kalten's treasure. His peculiarities of speech, his otherwise-inexplicable absence of a birth number over his left nipple, when they got around to it the gold filling in one of his teeth, his uncanny knowledge of old America, now had a simple scientific explanation. He was from 1944. What was so hard to grasp about that? Any sound specialist knew about the lost Jewish Kabbalah magic, golems and such.

His story was that he had been a student Race Scientist under the pioneering master William D. Pully. (A noisy whack who used to barnstorm the chaw-and-gallus belt with the backing of Deutsches Neues Büro; sure enough they found him in Volume VII of the standard *Introduction to a Historical Handbook of Race Science*.) The Jewish fiends had attempted to ambush his master on a lonely road; Royland persuaded him to switch hats and coats; in the darkness the substitution was not noticed. Later, in their stronghold he was identified, but the Nordic virgins had already been ritually murdered and drained of their blood, and it wouldn't keep. The dire fate destined for the master had been visited upon the disciple.

Dr. Kalten loved that bit. It tickled him pink that the sub-men's "revenge" on their enemy had been to precipitate him into a world purged of the sub-men entirely, where a Nordic might breathe freely!

Kalten, except for discreet consultations with such people as Old America specialists, a dentist who was stupefied by the gold filling, and a dermatologist who established that there was not and never had been a *Geburtsnummer* on the subject examined, was playing Royland close to his vest. After a week it became apparent that he was reserving Royland for a grand unveiling which would climax the reading of a paper. Royland did not want to be unveiled; there were too many holes in his story. He talked with animation about the beauties of Mexico in the spring, its fair mesas, cactus and mushrooms. Could they make a short trip there? Dr. Kalten said they could not. Royland was becoming restless? Let him study, learn, profit by the matchless arsenal of the sciences available here in Chicago Parteihof. Dear old Chicago boasted distinguished exponents of the World Ice Theory, the Hollow World Theory, Dowsing, Homeopathic Medicine, Curative Folk Botany—

This last did sound interesting. Dr. Kalten was pleased to take his prize to the Medical School and introduce him as a protégé to Professor Albiani, of Folk Botany.

Albiani was a bearded gnome out of the Arthur Rackham illustrations for *Das Rheingold*. He loved his subject. "Mother Nature, the all-bounteous one! Wander the fields, young man, and with a seeing eye in an hour's stroll you will find the ergot that aborts, the dill that cools fever, the tansy that strengthens the old, the poppy that soothes the fretful teething babe!"

"Do you have any hallucinogenic Mexican mushrooms?" Royland demanded.

"We may," Albiani said, surprised. They browsed through the Folk Botany museum and pored over dried vegetation under glass. From Mexico there were peyote, the buttons and the root, and there was marihuana, root, stem, seed and stalk. No mushrooms.

"They may be in the storeroom," Albiani muttered.

All the rest of the day Royland mucked through the storeroom where specimens were waiting for exhibit space on some rotation plan. He went to Albiani and said, a little wild-eyed: "They're not there."

Albiani had been interested enough to look up the mushrooms in question in the reference books. "See?" he said happily, pointing to a handsome color plate of the mushroom: growing, mature, sporing and dried. He read: "'… superstitiously called *God Food*,'" and twinkled through his beard at the joke.

"They're not there," Royland said.

The professor, annoyed at last, said: "There might be some uncatalogued in the basement. Really, we don't have room for everything in our limited display space—just the *interesting* items."

Royland pulled himself together and charmed the location of the department's basement storage space out of him, together with permission to inspect it. And, left alone for a moment, ripped the color plate from the professor's book and stowed it away.

That night Royland and Dr. Kalten walked out on one of the innumerable tower-tops for a final cigar. The moon was high and full; its light turned the cratered terrain that had been Chicago into another moon. The sage and his disciple from another day leaned their elbows on a crenellated rampart two hundred feet above Lake Michigan.

"Edward," said Dr. Kalten, "I shall read my paper tomorrow before the Chicago Academy of Race Science." The words were a challenge; something was wrong. He went on: "I shall expect you to be in the wings of the auditorium, and to appear at my command to answer a few questions from me and, if time permits, from our audience."

"I wish it could be postponed," Royland said.

"No doubt."

"Would you explain your unfriendly tone of voice, doctor?" Royland demanded. "I think I've been completely co-operative and have opened the way for you to win undying fame in the annals of Race Science."

"Co-operative, yes. Candid—I wonder? You see, Edward, a dreadful thought struck me today. I have always thought it amusing that the Jewish attack on Reverend Pully should have been for the purpose of precipitating him into the future and that it should have mis-fired." He took something out of his pocket: a small pistol. He aimed it casually at Royland. "Today I began to wonder *why* they should have done so. Why did they not simply murder him, as they did thousands, and dispose of him in their secret crematoria, and permit no mention in their controlled newspapers and magazines of the disappearance?

"Now, the blood of seven Nordic virgins can have been no cheap commodity. One pictures with ease Nordic men patrolling their precious enclaves of humanity, eyes roving over every passing face, noting who bears the stigmata of the sub-men, and following those who do most carefully indeed lest race-defilement be committed with a look or an 'accidental' touch in a crowded street. Nevertheless the thing was done; your presence here is proof of it. It must have been done at enormous cost; hired Slavs and Negroes must have been employed to kidnap the virgins, and many of them must have fallen before Nordic rage.

"This merely to silence one small voice crying in the wilderness? *I—think—not.* I think, Edward Royland, or whatever your real name may be, that Jewish arrogance sent you, a Jew yourself, into the future as a greeting from the Jewry of that day to what it foolishly thought would be the triumphant Jewry of this. At any rate, the public questioning tomorrow will be conducted by my friend Dr. Herzbrenner, whom I have mentioned to you. If you have any little secrets, they will not remain secrets long. No, no! Do not move towards me. I shall shoot you disablingly in the knee if you do."

Royland moved toward him and the gun went off; there was an agonizing hammer blow high on his left shin. He picked up Kalten and hurled him, screaming, over the parapet two hundred feet into the water. And collapsed. The pain was horrible. His shinbone was badly cracked if not broken through. There was not much bleeding; maybe there would be later. He need not fear that the shot and scream would rouse the castle. Such sounds were not rare in the Medical Wing.

He dragged himself, injured leg trailing, to the doorway of Kalten's living quarters; he heaved himself into a chair by the signal bell and threw a rug over his legs. He rang for the diener and told him very quietly: "Go to the medical storeroom for a leg U-brace and whatever is necessary for a cast, please. Dr. Kalten has an interesting idea he wishes to work out."

He should have asked for a syringe of morphine—no, he shouldn't. It might affect the time-distortion.

When the man came back, he thanked him and told him to turn in for the night.

He almost screamed getting his shoe off; his trouser leg he cut away. The gauze had arrived just in time; the wound was beginning to bleed more copiously. Pressure seemed to stop it. He constructed a sloppy walking cast on his leg. The directions on the several five-pound cans of plaster helped.

His leg was getting numb; good. His cast probably pinched some major nerve, and a week in it would cause permanent paralysis; who cared about *that?*

He tried it out and found he could get across the floor inefficiently. With a strong-enough banister he could get downstairs but not, he thought, up them. That was all right. He was going to the basement.

God-damning the medieval Nazis and their cornball castle every inch of the way, he went to the basement; there he had a windfall. A dozen drunken SS men were living it up in a corner far from the censorious eyes of their company commander; they were playing a game which might have been called Spin the Corporal. They saw Royland limping and wept sentimental tears for poor ol' doc with a bum leg; they carried him two winding miles to the storeroom he wanted, and shot the lock off for him. They departed, begging him to call on ol' Company K any time, bes' fellas in Chicago, doc. Ol' Bruno here can tear the arm off a Latvik shirker with his bare hands, honest, doc! Jus' the way you twist a drumstick off a turkey. You wan' us to get a Latvik an' show you?

He got rid of them at last, clicked on the light and began his search. His leg was now ice cold, painfully so. He rummaged through the uncatalogued botanicals and found after what seemed like hours a crate shipped from Jalasco. Royland opened it by beating its corners against the concrete floor. It yielded and spilled plastic envelopes; through the clear material of one he saw the wrinkled black things. He did not even compare them with the color plate in his pocket. He tore the envelope open and crammed them into his mouth, and chewed and swallowed.

Maybe there had to be a Hopi dancing and chanting, maybe there didn't have to be. Maybe one had to be calm, if bitter, and fresh from a day of hard work at differential equations which approximated the Hopi mode of thought. Maybe you only had to fix your mind savagely on what you desired, as his was fixed now. Last time he had hated and shunned the Bomb; what he wanted was a world without the Bomb. He had got it, all right!

… his tongue was thick and the fireballs were beginning to dance around him, the circling circles …

Charles Miller Nahataspe whispered: "Close. Close. I was so frightened."

Royland lay on the floor of the hut, his leg unsplinted, unfractured, but aching horribly. Drowsily he felt his ribs; he was merely slender now, no longer gaunt. He mumbled: "You were working to pull me back from this side?"

"Yes. You, you were there?"

"I was there. God, let me sleep."

He rolled over heavily and collapsed into complete unconsciousness.

When he awakened it was still dark and his pains were gone. Nahataspe was crooning a healing song very softly. He stopped when he saw Royland's eyes open. "Now you know about break-the-sky medicine," he said.

"Better than anybody. What time is it?"

"Midnight."

"I'll be going then." They clasped hands and looked into each other's eyes.

The jeep started easily. Four hours earlier, or possibly two months earlier, he had been worried about the battery. He chugged down the settlement road and knew what would happen next. He wouldn't wait until morning; a meteorite might kill him, or a scorpion in his bed. He would go directly to Rotschmidt in his apartment, defy Vrouw Rotschmidt and wake her man up to tell him about 56c, tell him we have the Bomb.

We have a symbol to offer the Japanese now, something to which they can surrender, and will surrender.

Rotschmidt would be philosophical. He would probably sigh about the Bomb: "Ah, do we ever act responsibly? Do we ever know what the consequences of our decisions will be?"

And Royland would have to try to avoid answering him very sharply: "Yes. This once we damn well do."

Passion Pills

The only dignified thing about Richard Claxton Hanbury III was his name, and it served only to underscore the grotesqueness of his appearance. Richard at 23 years was of average height but stooped by a mild spinal curvature into shrimphood; his face thrust boldly forward from a negligible chin and a raked forehead toward what could have been an impressive corvine mask if he had only nose enough to sustain the effect, but Richard's nose was an uncute button.

He had, of course, brains. The Great Kidder does not vouchsafe spectacular ugliness to anybody who is unable to appreciate it fully.

Richard knew perfectly well Bernard Shaw's dictum that there is nobody so ugly or disagreeable that he or she cannot find a spouse, but it happened that a spouse was not what he wanted. What he wanted was Girls. The author admits that this was not very intelligent of Richard, but pleads that he was brainwashed by Twentieth Century Western Culture. A shy and unattractive man like he would in simpler times have found himself in a monastery doing at least no harm and not worrying about bosoms. In a more vicious day he would have found himself now and then in a Place of Ill Repute with nothing more to worry him than the possibility of contracting a ludicrous minor tribulation thought to be no worse than a bad cold. In more practical times he would have arranged with the parent (*the* parent then!) of a "female" to take said female off said parent's hands and board bill in exchange for a cash settlement; the female would have called him "Mr. Hanbury" even after the marriage, and it would not have occurred to either of them to worry about love.

The era in which Richard had been raised, however, was neither vicious, simple nor practical. The iconographer of Richard's era was Mr. Jon Whitcomb, and the ritual illustration he has done for a thousand ritual magazine stories sums up the age. There is a yellow convertible with the top down, and there is a tanned blonde girl in the convertible. She is plainly about sixteen years old for her skin is that of an unblemished child, and she is plainly a new mother for her bosom is of a size functional only in a lactating woman; who has committed this crime upon her? Yet the text says she is a virgin! She smiles, and she is plainly an Innocent who has escaped from three-nurse custodial care in the first auto she found, for in that smile there is no trace of human intelligence but only the animal bliss of a bear who has found honey. Yet the text says she is a Ph.D. in astrophysics! She is plainly a narcissistic she-monster, for every hair of every wisp is in its calculated place and her garb is tight where tight and loose where loose to the predetermined thousandth of an inch at the cost of nightly toil, mad self-love and abnegation of all other activity. Yet the text calls her casual, vital, warm!

She was the girl whom Richard wanted, poor fellow, and he wanted lots of her—blonde, red-haired, brunette, tanned and pale, playtime, daytime and gaytime, tall and rangy, cute and cuddly, the sophisticate who learns in the back pages that brains are not enough, the naïve thing who turns out in the back pages to have brains enough to save the day.

My readers have of course all seen through the pitiful sham, and will feel only amused compassion for Richard.

Through grammar school and high school Richard met several dozen versions of The Girl, and for each one he carefully thought out the witty opening phrase of a campaign that would end only with her as helpless putty in his hands. It happened, however, that he never got to speak the carefully-composed phrase. He would choke up; or the girl would say "Well, dig you later" and breeze off wobbling tantalizingly; or a football player would roar up out of nowhere and slap him on the back; or the class bell would ring—always something.

That was the way it went through college too, except for one evening when he got carried away and attempted near-assault on a field-hockey-playing version of The Girl. They patched him up at the infirmary and believed him when he said he had been hit by a runaway three-quarter-ton truck.

After his bones had knit Richard said to himself: "The hell with this noise. Charm I do not have. Muscle too I lack. What I do possess, some knowledge of biochemistry, seems irrelevant to the problem. Or—or *is* it?" For Richard was majoring in biochemistry because of an aptitude test he had taken, in the course of which his punch card had been put into a machine upside-down.

Richard leaped to his feet and cried "*Thalassa!*" since his talent for languages was almost as slight as his aptitude for biochemistry. Then, more collectedly, he schemed: "The girl shall be mine through the science which I am learning, and specifically through those certain pills and fluids of which one has heard!"

Forthwith he plunged into a reading program to establish the basis for his research. The first thing he learned in his quest for what are euphemistically called "love philtres" was the discouraging fact that there are no such things, vulgar superstition to the contrary notwithstanding. Such diverse substances as cabbage juice, powdered mandrake, muscatel wine, oysters on the half-shell, and frog spawn have had their vogues, he learned, but proved to have no effect except an imaginary one. The notorious Spanish Fly, he discovered, is about as effective a love potion as a kick in the stomach, which is to say not very.

Richard concluded his first week of reading by slamming his books shut, hurling them into the corner of his dormitory room and stalking with agitation out into the campus night. "Thunderation!" he growled. "I'm going to have to start from scratch and invent this whole science in the lab with my own two hands!" From this the reader may gauge the depths of his determination.

After that it was no unusual thing to see the lights burning late in the biochemistry building, or to behold a single shadow moving busily against the drawn blind, ever pouring, mixing, distilling, titrating, centrifuging. "A good lad, Hanbury," his professors took to telling one another. "Pity he's such a gargoyle."

It will be a little difficult for the lay reader to follow the ensuing passage without the utmost concentration, so the author requests that the television set be turned off, the mind be cleared, the lamp adjusted to shine over the left shoulder without glare and the feet slightly elevated on a stool or hassock to promote a stimulating flow of blood to the brain.

Richard began his attempts at synthesis of an aphrodisiac by hooking two benzene rings symmetrically to one end of a long-chain hydrocarbon, mainly because the molecular diagram of this compound looked reasonably suggestive. He found, however, that it was instantly toxic to the laboratory hamsters even though it made a fair fuel for his motor scooter, and so was forced to abandon this line. Next he isolated the congenerics of muscatel wine, that is, the trace substances responsible for muscatel's peculiar flavor, using in the process several gallons of the stuff. His attempt to win the radium of truth from the pitchblende of folklore was a failure. The isolated congenerics proved to be a malodorous sludge which caused the hamsters to turn blue and die as if relieved to have done with the awful taste in their little mouths; also, his heavy purchases at the liquor shop gained him an undeserved reputation as a wino which almost resulted in his expulsion from the college.

But as we learn from the illustrious histories of Robert the Bruce, Thomas the Dewey and Adlai the Stevenson, "If at first you don't succeed, try, try, try again." Richard did, and by catalyzing hexylmethyldiethylstilbestrol in the presence of, oddly enough, tri-tri-tri-ethylmermanotic acid he precipitated two five-grain tablets, each one stamped INSTANT LUST.

Obviously success was his at last, and obviously there was no question of testing the pills on a hamster; they were too precious. For days he went about the campus absently juggling his pills in his hand, his eye roving from blonde to brunette to redhead. All unaware, they paraded for him in their youth and beauty.

As if by inspiration the answer came to him after a pleasant week spent in the first eliminations, the finals, and the semi-finals. In a blow the two campus queens (they knew it not) who were vying for his dear smile were swept aside and undone. Studs Flanagan would be his choice.

At first blush this would appear an odd choice, for Studs was moon-faced, stringy-haired, bony of figure and awkward of movement. Studs proceeding along the gravel walks of the campus reminded students from the great Dakota wheat fields of a steam thresher in full career across the golden harvest bounty. Studs appropriately was in economics. Economics is known as "the dismal science," and it seemed to suit her. Her social life consisted of arguing bitterly with other economics majors about the rediscount rate and the validity of bat-guano tonnage importations as an index of agricultural prosperity.

Start small, a little voice had told Richard; that was why he chose Studs to be the first to taste his pills. Were he suddenly to become the adored one of a reigning campus queen, there would be no end of talk. He could not immediately afford the luxury of a great beauty; he would have to start small—and who smaller than Studs?—and work his way up while people slowly got used to the idea of him as a successful lover.

He hailed Studs one afternoon at the co-op; she was alone and reading gloomily; untasted cocoa stood before her. "Hi," said Richard, his throat sealed almost shut by *globus hystericus.* "Wanted to talk to you about the bat-guano situation."

She eyed him coldly. "What about it?"

"Well, the effects of synthetic fertilizer, ah, man-made guano so to speak— I'm in biochem, you know—isn't that Professor Guano—I mean Granotto—over there?"

She looked over there; splash-splash went the two little pills into her cocoa. She looked back. "No," she said.

"Have your cocoa," he invited her largely.

"Thanks," she said satirically, and sipped. "Tastes odd," she said, and took a larger gulp, rolled it unattractively around her mouth, and swallowed.

Richard sat back complacently waiting for it to begin.

It began. His pulses started to pound; his eyes popped a little; his heart convulsed in his breast. He was in love with Studs Flanagan.

"Watcha staring at me for?" she demanded. "You chemistry creeps been synthesizing cocaine again?"

"Studs," he said hoarsely, "darling Studs, did anybody ever tell you that you have the most beautiful case of acne in the world?"

"Insults from a monkey like you I don't have to take," she snorted, and stalked out of the co-op. Richard Claxton Hanbury III trailed after her like an arbutus plant.

Eventually he persuaded her of his sincerity and they were married.

Everybody cautiously said that they were well matched. Sometimes Richard would see a tanned, long-limbed blonde lounging in a yellow convertible and suffer an anachronistic pang, but it did not happen often. He was happy in the dear presence of his Studs, and at all times profoundly grateful that he had not tried out the pills on a hamster. Some things are practically impossible to explain, and that would have been one of them.

[*Fantasy and Science Fiction* - Fall 1950]

The Silly Season

It was a hot summer afternoon in the Omaha bureau of the World Wireless Press Service, and the control bureau in New York kept nagging me for copy. But, since it was a hot summer afternoon, there was no copy. A wrapup of local baseball had cleared about an hour ago, and that was that. Nothing but baseball happens in the summer. During the dog days, politicians are in the Maine woods fishing and boozing, burglars are too tired to burgle and wives think it over and decide not to decapitate their husbands.

I pawed through some press releases. One sloppy stencil-duplicated sheet began: "Did you know that the lemonade way to summer comfort and health has been endorsed by leading physiotherapists from Maine to California? The Federated Lemon-Growers Association revealed today that a survey of 2,500 physiotherapists in 57 cities of more than 25,000 population disclosed that 87 percent of them drink lemonade at least once a day between June and September, and that another 72 percent no only drink the cooling and healthful beverage but actually prescribe it—"

Another note tapped out on the news circuit printer from New York: "960M-HW KICKER? ND SNST-NY"

That was New York saying they needed a bright and sparkling little news item immediately—"soonest." I went to the eastbound printer and punched out: "96NY-UPCMNG FU MINS-OM".

The lemonade handout was hopeless; I dug into the stack again. The State University summer course was inviting the governor to attend its summer conference on aims and approaches in adult secondary education. The Agricultural College wanted me to warn farmers that white-skinned hogs should be kept from the direct rays of the summer sun. The manager of a fifth-rate local pug sent a write-up of his boy and a couple of working press passes to his next bout in the Omaha Arena. The Schwartz and White Bandage Company contributed a glossy eight-by-ten of a blonde in a bathing suit improvised from two S. and W. Redi-Dressings.

Accompanying text: "Pert starlet Miff McCoy is ready for any seaside emergency. That's not only a darling swimsuit she has on—it's two standard all-pur-

313

pose Redi-Dressing bandages made by the Schwartz and White Bandage Company of Omaha. If a broken rim results from too-strenuous beach athletics, Miff's dress can supply the dressing." Yeah. The rest of the stack wasn't even that good. I dumped them all in the circular file, and began to rack my brains in spite of the heat.

I'd have to fake one, I decided. Unfortunately, there had been no big running silly season story so far this summer—no flying saucers, or monsters in the Florida Everglades, or chloroform bandits terrifying the city. If there had, I could have hopped on and faked a "with." As it was, I'd have to fake a "lead," which is harder and riskier.

The flying saucers? I couldn't revive them; they'd been forgotten for years, except by newsmen. The giant turtle of Lake Huron had been quiet for years, too. If I started a chloroform bandit scare, every old maid in the state would back me up by swearing she heard the bandit trying to break in and smelled chloroform—but the cops wouldn't like it. Strange messages from space received at the State University's radar lab? That might do it. I put a sheet of copy paper in the typewriter and sat, glaring at it and hating the silly season.

There was a slight reprieve—the Western Union tie-line printer by the desk dinged at me, and its sickly-yellow bulb lit up. I tapped out: "WW GA PLS," and the machine began to eject yellow, gummed tape which told me this:

> WU CO62-DPR COLLECT—FT HICKS ARK AUG 22 105P—
> WORLDWIRELESS OMAHA—TOWN MARSHAL PINKNEY
> CRAWLES DIED MYSTERIOUS CIRCUMSTANCES FISH-TRIP-
> PING OZARK HAMLET RUSH CITY TODAY. RUSHERS
> PHONED HICKSERS "BURNED DEATH SHINING DOMES
> APPEARED YESTERWEEK." JEEPING BODY HICKS-WARD.
> QUERIED RUSH CONSTABLE P.C. ALLENBY LEARNING
> "SEVEN GLASSY DOMES EACH HOUSESIZE CLEARING MILE
> SOUTH TOWN. RUSHERS UNTOUCHED, UNAPPROACHED.
> CRAWLES WARNED BUT TOUCHED AND DIED BURNS."
> NOTE DESK—RUSH FONECALL 1.85. SHALL I UPFOLLOW?—
> BENSON—FISHTRIPPING RUSHERS HICKSERS YESTER-
> WEEK JEEPING HICKWARD HOUSESIZE 1.85 428P CLR …

It was just what the doctor ordered. I typed an acknowledgment for the message and pounded out a story, fast. I punched it and started the tape wiggling through the eastbound transmitter before New York could send any more irked notes. The news circuit printer from New York clucked and began relaying my story immediately:

> WW72 (KICKER)
>   FORT HICKS, ARKANSAS, AUG 22—(WW)—MYSTERIOUS
> DEATH TODAY STRUCK DOWN A LAW ENFORCEMENT
> OFFICER IN A TINY OZARK MOUNTAIN HAMLET. MARSHAL
> PINKNEY CRAWLES OF FORT HICKS, ARKANSAS, DIED OF
> BURNS WHILE ON A FISHING TRIP TO THE LITTLE VILLAGE
> OF RUSH CITY. TERRIFIED NATIVES OF RUSH CITY BLAMED

THE TRAGEDY ON WHAT THEY CALLED "SHINING
DOMES." THEY SAID THE SO-CALLED DOMES APPEARED
IN A CLEARING LAST WEEK ONE MILE SOUTH OF TOWN.
THERE ARE SEVEN OF THE MYSTERIOUS OBJECTS—EACH
ONE THE SIZE OF A HOUSE. THE INHABITANTS OF RUSH
CITY DID NOT DARE APPROACH THEM. THEY WARNED
THE VISITING MARSHAL CRAWLES—BUT HE DID NOT
HEED THEIR WARNING. RUSH CITY'S CONSTABLE P.C.
ALLENBY WAS A WITNESS TO THE TRAGEDY. SAID HE:—
"THERE ISN'T MUCH TO TELL. MARSHAL CRAWLES JUST
WALKED UP TO ONE OF THE DOMES AND PUT HIS HAND
ON IT. THERE WAS A BIG FLASH, AND WHEN I COULD SEE
AGAIN, HE WAS BURNED TO DEATH." CONSTABLE ALLEN-
BY IS RETURNING THE BODY OF MARSHAL CRAWLES TO
FORT HICKS. 602P220M

That, I thought, should hold them for a while. I remembered Benson's "note desk" and put through a long distance call to Fort Hicks, person to person. The Omaha operator asked for Fort Hicks information, but there wasn't any. The Fort Hicks operator asked whom she wanted. Omaha finally admitted that we wanted to talk to Mr. Edwin C. Benson. Fort Hicks figured out loud and then decided that Ed was probably at the police station if he hadn't gone home for supper yet. She connected us with the police station, and I got Benson. He had a pleasant voice, not particularly backwoods Arkansas. I gave him some old oil about a fine dispatch, and a good, conscientious job, and so on. He took it with plenty of dry reserve, which was odd. Our rural stringers always ate that kind of stuff up. Where, I asked was he from?

"Fort Hicks," he told me, "but I've moved around. I did the courthouse beat in Little Rock—" I nearly laughed out loud at that, but the laugh died out as he went on— "rewrite for the A.P. in New Orleans, got to be bureau chief there but I didn't like wire service work. Got an opening on the Chicago *Trib* desk. That didn't last—they sent me to head up their Washington bureau. There I switched to the New York *Times*. They made me a war correspondent and I got hurt—back to Fort Hicks. I do some magazine writing now. Did you want a follow-up on the Rush City story?"

"Sure," I told him weakly. "Give it a real ride—use your own judgment! Do you think it's a fake?"

"I saw Pink's body a little while ago at the undertaker's parlor, and I had a talk with Allenby, from Rush City. Pink got burned, all right, and Allenby didn't make his story up. Maybe somebody else did—he's pretty dumb—but as far as I can tell, this is the real thing. I'll keep the copy coming. Don't forget about that dollar eighty-five phone call, will you?"

I told him I wouldn't, and hung up. Mr. Edwin C. Benson had handed me quite a jolt. I wondered how badly he had been hurt, that he had been forced to abandon a brilliant news career and bury himself in the Ozarks.

Then there came a call from God, the board chairman of World Wireless. He was fishing in Canada, as all good board chairmen do during the silly season, but he had caught a news broadcast which used my Rush City story. He had a mobil phone in his trailer, and it was but the work of a moment to ring Omaha and louse up my carefully-planned vacation schedules and rotation of night shifts. He wanted me to go down to Rush City and cover the story personally. I said yes and began trying to round up the rest of the staff. My night editor was sobered up by his wife and delivered to the bureau in fair shape. A telegrapher on vacation was reached at his summer resort and talked into checking out. I got a taxi company on the phone and told them to have a cross-country cab on the roof in an hour. I specified their best driver, and told them to give him maps of Arkansas.

Meanwhile, tw "with domes" dispatches arrived from Benson and got moved on the wire. I monitored a couple of newscasts; the second on carried a story by another wire service on the domes—a pickup of our stuff, but they'd have their own men on the scene fast enough. I filled in the night editor, and went up to the roof for the cab.

The driver took off in the teeth of a gathering thunderstorm. We had to rise above it, and by the time we could get down to sight-pilotage altitude, we were lost. We circled most of the night until the driver picked up a beacon he had on his charts at about 3:30 A.M. We landed at Fort Hicks as day was breaking, not on speaking terms.

The Fort Hicks field clerk told me where Benson lived, and I walked there. It was a white frame house. A quiet, middle-aged woman let me in. She was his widowed sister, Mrs. McHenry. She got me some coffee and told me she had been up all night waiting for Edwin to come back from Rush City. He had started out about 8 P.M., and it was only a two-hour trip by car. She was worried. I tried to pump her about her brother, but she'd only say that he was the bright one of the family. She didn't want to talk about his work as war correspondent. She did show me some of his magazine stuff—boy-and-girl stories in national weeklies. He seemed to sell one every couple of months.

We had arrived at a conversational stalemate when her brother walked in, and I discovered why his news career had been interrupted. He was blind. Aside from a long, puckered brown scar that ran from his left temple back over his ear and on to the nape of his neck, he was a pleasant-looking fellow in his mid-forties.

"Who is it, Vera?" he asked.

"It's Mr. Williams, the gentleman who called you from Omaha today—I mean yesterday."

"How do you do, Williams. Don't get up," he added, hearing, I suppose, the chair squeak as I leaned forward to rise.

"You were so *long*, Edwin," his sister said with relief and reproach.

"That young jackass Howie—my chauffeur for the night"—he added an aside to me—"got lost going there and coming back. But I did spend more time than I'd planned at Rush City." He sat down, facing me. "Williams, there is some difference of opinion about the shining domes. The Rush City people say that they exist, and I say they don't."

His sister brought him a cup of coffee.

"What happened, exactly?" I asked.

"That Allenby took me and a few other hardy citizens to see them. They told me just what they looked like. Seven hemispheres in a big clearing, glassy, looming up like houses, reflecting the gleam of the headlights. But they weren't there. Not to me, and not to any blind man. I know when I'm standing in front of a house or anything else that big. I can feel a little tension on the skin of my face. It works unconsciously, but the mechanism is thoroughly understood.

"The blind get—because they have to—an aural picture of the world. We hear a little hiss of air that means we're at the corner of a building; we hear and feel big, turbulent air currents that mean we're coming to a busy street. Some of the boys can thread their way through an obstacle course and never touch a single obstruction. I'm not that good, maybe because I haven't been blind as long as they have, but by hell, I know when there are seven objects the size of houses in front of me, and there just were no such things in the clearing at Rush City."

"Well"—I shrugged—"there goes a fine piece of silly-season journalism. What kind of a gag are the Rush City people trying to pull, and why?"

"No kind of gag. My driver saw the domes too—and don't forget the late marshal. Pink not only saw them but touched them. All I know is that people see them and I don't. If they exist, they have a kind of existence like nothing else I've ever met."

"I'll go up there myself," I decided.

"Best thing," said Benson. "I don't know what to make of it. You can take our car." He gave me directions and I gave him a schedule of deadlines. We wanted the coroner's verdict, due today, an eye-witness story—his driver would do for that—some background stuff on the area, and a few statements from local officials.

I took his car and got to Rush City in two hours. It was an unpainted collection of dog-trot homes, set down in the big pine forest that covers all that rolling Ozark country. There was a general store that had the place's only phone. I suspected it had been kept busy by the wire services and a few enterprising newspapers. A state trooper in a flashy uniform was lounging against a fly-specked tobacco counter when I got there.

"I'm Sam Williams, from World Wireless," I said. "You come to have a look at the domes?"

"World Wireless broke that story, didn't they?" he asked me, with a look I couldn't figure out.

"We did. Our Fort Hicks stringer wired it to us."

The phone rang, and the trooper answered it. It seemed to have been a call he had placed with the governor's office.

"No, sir," he said over the phone. "No, sir. They're all sticking to the story, but I didn't see anything. I mean, they don't see them any more, but they say they *were* there, and now they aren't any more." A couple more "No, sirs" and he hung up.

"When did that happen?" I asked.

"About a half hour ago. I just came from there on my bike to report."

The phone rang again, and I grabbed it. It was Benson, asking for me. I told him to phone a flash and bulletin to Omaha on the disappearance and then took off to find Constable Allenby. He was a stage reuben with a nickel-plated badge and a six-shooter. He cheerfully climbed into the car and guided me to the clearing.

There was a definite little path worn between Rush City and the clearing by now, but there was a disappointment at the end of it. The clearing was empty. A few small boys sticking carefully to its fringes told wildly contradictory stories about the disappearance of the domes, and I jotted down some kind of dispatch out of the most spectacular versions. I remember it involved flashes of blue fire and a smell like sulphur candles. That was all there was to it.

I drove Allenby back. By then a mobile unit from a TV network had arrived. I said hello, waited for an A.P. man to finish a dispatch on the phone, and then dictated my lead direct to Omaha. The hamlet was beginning to fill up with newsmen from the wire services, the big papers, the radio and TV nets and the newsreels. Much good they'd get out of it. The story was over—I thought. I had some coffee at the general store's two-table restaurant corner and drove back to Fort Hicks.

Benson was tirelessly interviewing by phone and firing off copy to Omaha. I told him he could begin to ease off, thanked him for his fine work, paid him for his gas, said good-bye and picked up my taxi at the field. Quite a bill for waiting had been run up.

I listened to the radio as we were flying back to Omaha, and wasn't at all surprised. After baseball, the shining domes were top news. Shining domes had been seen in twelve states. Some vibrated with a strange sound. They came in all colors and sizes. One had strange writing on it. One was transparent, and there were big green men and women inside. I caught a women's mid-morning quiz show, and the M.C. kept gagging about the domes. One crack I remember was a switch on the "pointed-head" joke. He made it "dome-shaped head" and the ladies in the audience laughed until they nearly burst.

We stopped in Little Rock for gas, and I picked up a couple of afternoon papers. Both papers had shining-dome cartoons on their editorial pages, hastily drawn and slapped it. One paper, anti-Administration, showed the President cautiously reaching out a finger to touch the dome of the Capitol, which was rendered as a shining dome and labeled: "Shining Dome of Congressional Immunity to Executive Dictatorship." A little man labeled "Mr. and Mrs. Plain, Self-Respecting Citizens of the United States of America" was in one corner of the cartoon saying: "CAREFUL, MR. PRESIDENT! REMEMBER WHAT HAPPENED TO PINKNEY CRAWLES!"

The other paper, pro-Administration, showed a shining dome that had the President's face. A band of fat little men in Prince Albert coats, string ties and broad-brimmed hats labelled "Congressional Smear Artists and Hatchet-men" were creeping up the dome with the President's face, their hands reaching out as if to strangle. Above the cartoon a cut line said: "WHO'S GOING TO GET HURT?"

We landed at Omaha, and I checked into the office. Things were clicking right along. The clients were happily gobbling up our dome copy and sending wires asking for more. I dug into the morgue for the "Flying Disc" folder, and the "Huron Turtle" and the "Bayou Vampire" and a few others even further back. I spread out the old clippings and tried to shuffle and arrange them into some kind of underlying sense. I picked up the latest dispatch to come out of the tie-line printer from Wertern Union. It was from our man in Owosso, Michigan, and told how Mrs. Lettie Overholtzer, aged sixty-one, saw a shining dome in her own kitchen at midnight. It grew like a soap bubble until it was as big as her refrigerator, and then disappeared.

I went over to the desk man and told him: "Let's have a downhold on stuff like Lettie Overholtzer! We can move a sprinkling of it, but I don't want to run this into the ground. Those things might turn up again, and then we wouldn't have any room left to play around with them. We'll have everybody's credulity used up."

He looked mildly surprised. "You mean," he asked, "there really *was* something there?"

"I don't know. Maybe. I didn't see anything myself, and the only man down there I trust can't make up his mind. Anyhow, hold it down as far as the clients let us!"

I went home to get some sleep. When I went back to work, I found the clients hadn't let us work the downhold after all. Nobody at the other wire services seemed to believe seriously that there had been anything out of the ordinary at Rush City, so they merrily pumped out solemn stories like the Lettie Overholtzer item, and wire-photo maps of locations where domes were reported, and tabulations of number of domes reported.

We had to string along. Our Washington bureau badgered the Pentagon and the A.E.C. into issuing statements, and there was a race between a navy and an air force investigating mission to see who could get to Rush City first. After they got there, there was a race to see who could get the first report out. The Air Force won that contest. Before the week was out, "Domies" had appeared. They were hats for juveniles—shining-dome skull-caps molded from a transparent plastic. We had to ride with it. I'd started the mania, but it was out of hand and a long time dying down.

The World Series, the best in years, finally killed off the domes. By an unspoken agreement among the services, we simply stopped running stories every time a hysterical woman thought she saw a dome or wanted to get her name in the paper. And of course when there was no longer publicity to be had for the asking, people stopped seeing domes. There was no percentage in it. Brooklyn won the series, international tension climbed as the thermometer dropped, burglars began burgling again, and a bulky folder labeled "Domes, Shining," went into our morgue. The shining domes were history, and earnest graduate students in psychology would shortly begin to bother us with requests to borrow that folder.

The only thing that had come of it, I thought, was that we had somehow got through another summer without too much idle wire time, and that Ed Benson and I had struck up a casual correspondence.

A newsman's strange and weary year wore on. Baseball gave way to football. An off-year election kept us on the run. Christmas loomed ahead, with its feature stories and its kickers about Santa Claus, Indiana. Christmas passed, and we began to clear jolly stories about New Year hangovers, and tabulate the great news stories of the year. New Year's Day, a ghastly rat-race of covering one hundred and three bowl games—record snowfalls in the Great Plains and Rockies—spring floods in Ohio and the Columbia River Valley—twenty-one tasty Lenten menus, and Holy Week around the world—baseball again, daylight-saving time, Mother's Day, Derby Day, the Preakness, and the Belmont Stakes.

It was about then that a disturbing letter arrived from Benson. I was concerned not about its subject-matter but because I thought no sane man would write such a thing. It seemed to me that Benson was slipping his trolley. All he said was that he expected a repeat performance of the domes, or of something like the domes. He said that "they" probably found the tryout a smashing success and would continue according to plan. I replied cautiously, which amused him.

He wrote back:

> I wouldn't put myself out on a limb like this if I had anything to lose by it, but you know my station in life. It was just an intelligent guess, based on a study of power politics and Æsop's fables. And if it does happen, you'll find it a trifle harder to put over, won't you?

I guessed he was kidding me, but I wasn't certain. When people begin to talk about "them" and what "they" are doing, it's a bad sign. But, guess or not, something pretty much like domes did turn up in late July, during a crushing heat wave.

This time it was big black spheres rolling across the countryside. The spheres were seen by a Baptist congregation in central Kansas which had met in a prairie to pray for rain. About eighty Baptists took their Bible oaths that they saw large black spheres some ten feet high rolling along the prairie. They had passed within five yards of one man. The rest had run from them as soon as they could take in the fact that they really were there.

World Wireless didn't break that story, but we got on it fast enough as soon as we were tipped. Being now the recognized silly-season authority in the W.W. Central Division, I took off for Kansas.

It was much the way it had been in Arkansas. The Baptists really thought they had seen the things—with one exception. The exception was an old gentleman with a patriarchal beard. He had been the one man who hadn't run, the man the objects passed nearest to. He was blind. He told me with a great deal of heat that he would have known all about it, blind or not, if any large spheres had rolled within five yards of him—or twenty-five, for that matter.

Old Mr. Emerson didn't go into the matter of air currents and turbulence, as Benson had. With him, it was all well below the surface. He took the position that the Lord had removed his sight, and in return had given him another sense which would do for emergency use.

"You just try me out, son!" he piped angrily. "You come stand over here, wait awhile and put your hand up in front of my face! I'll tell you when you do it, no matter how quiet you are." He did it, too, three times, and then took me out into the main street of his little prairie town. There were several wagons drawn up before the grain elevator, and he put on a show for me by threading his way around and between them without touching once.

That—and Benson—seemed to prove that whatever the things were, they had some connection with the domes. I filed a thoughtful dispatch on the blind-man angle, and got back to Omaha to find that it had been cleared through our desk but killed in New York before relay.

We tried to give the black spheres the usual ride, but it didn't last as long. The political cartoonists tired of it sooner, and fewer old maids saw them. People got to jeering at them as newspaper hysteria, and a couple of highbrow magazines ran articles on "the irresponsible press." Only the radio comedians tried to milk the new mania as usual, but they were disconcerted to find their ratings falling. A network edict went out to kill all sphere gags. People were getting sick of them.

> It makes sense [Benson wrote to me]. An occasional exercise of the sense of wonder is refreshing, but it can't last forever. That, plus the ingrained American cynicism towards all sources of public information, has worked against the black spheres being greeted with the same naïf delight with which the domes were received. Nevertheless, I predict—and I'll thank you to remember that my predictions have been right so far one hundred percent of the time—that next summer will see another mystery comparable to the domes and the black things. And I also predict that the new phenomenon will be imperceptible to any blind person in the immediate vicinity, if there should be any.

I managed to wait out the year—the same interminable round I felt I could do in my sleep. Staffers got ulcers and resigned, staffers got tired and were fired, libel suits were filed and settled, one of our desk men got a Nieman Fellowship and went to Harvard, one of our telegraphers got his working hand mashed in a car door and jumped from a bridge but lived with a broken back. Then, in mid-August, when the weather bureau had been correctly predicting "fair and warmer" for sixteen straight days, it turned up. It wasn't anything on whose nature a blind man could provide a negative check, but it had what I had come to think of as "their" trademark.

A summer seminar was meeting outdoors, because of the frightful heat, at our own State University. Twelve trained schoolteachers testified that a series of perfectly circular pits opened up in the grass before them, one directly under the education professor teaching the seminar. They testified further that the professor, with an astonished look and a heartrending cry, plummeted down into that perfectly circular pit. They testified further that the pits remained there for some thirty seconds and then suddenly were there no longer. The scorched summer grass was back where it had been, the pits were gone and so was the professor.

I interviewed every one of them. They weren't yokels, but intelligent men and women, all with master's degrees, working toward their doctorates during the summers. They agreed closely on their stories, as I would expect trained and capable persons to do.

The police, however, did not expect agreement, being used to dealing with the lower I.Q. brackets. They arrested the twelve on some technical charge—"obstructing peace officers in the performance of their duties," I believe—and were going to beat the living hell out of them when an attorney arrived with twelve writs of habeas corpus. The cops' unvoiced suspicion was that the teachers had conspired to murder their professor, but nobody ever tried to explain why they'd do a thing like that.

The cops' reaction was typical of the way the public took it. Newspapers—which had reveled wildly in the shining domes story and less so in the black spheres story—were cautious. Some went overboard and gave the black pits a ride, in the old style, but they didn't pick up any sales that way. People declared that the press was insulting their intelligence, and also that they were bored with marvels.

The few papers who had played up the pits were soundly spanked in very dignified editorials printed by other sheets which played down the pits.

At World Wireless we sent out a memo to all stringers: "File no more enterpriser dispatches on black-pit story. Mail queries should be sent to regional desk if a new angle breaks in your territory." We got about ten mail queries, mostly from journalism students acting as string men, and we turned them all down. The older hands didn't bother to file it to us when the town drunk or the village old maid loudly reported that she saw a pit open up on High Street across from the drugstore. They knew it was probably untrue, and that, furthermore, nobody cared.

I wrote Benson about all this, and humbly asked him what his prediction for next summer was. He replied, obviously having the time of his life, that there would be at least one more summer phenomenon like the last three, and possibly two more—but none after that.

It's so easy now to reconstruct, with our bitterly earned knowledge.

Any youngster could whisper now of Benson: "Why, the damned fool! Couldn't anybody with the brains of a louse see that they wouldn't keep it up for two years?" One did whisper that to me the other day, when I told this story to him. And I whispered back that, far from being a damned fool, Benson was the one person on the face of the Earth, as far as I knew, who had bridged with logic the widely separated phenomena with which this reminiscence deals.

Another year passed. I gained three pounds, drank too much, rowed incessantly with my staff and got a tidy raise. A telegrapher took a swing at me midway through the office Christmas party, and I fired him. My wife and the kids didn't arrive in April when I expected them. I phoned Florida, and she gave me some excuse or other about missing the plane. After a few more missed planes and a few more phone calls, she got around to telling me that she didn't want to come back. That was okay with me. In my own intuitive way I knew that the upcoming silly season was more important than who stayed married to whom.

In July a dispatch arrived by wire while a new man was working the night desk. It was from Hood River, Oregon. Our stringer there reported that more than one hundred "green capsules" about fifty yards long had appeared in and around an apple orchard. The new desk man was not so new that he did not recall the downhold policy on silly-season items. He killed it, but left it on the spike for my amused inspection in the morning. I suppose exactly the same thing happened in every wire service newsroom in the region. I rolled in at 10:30 and riffled through the stuff on the spike. When I saw the "green capsules" dispatch I tried to phone Portland but couldn't get a connection. Then the phone buzzed and a correspondent of ours in Seattle began to yell at me, but the line went dead.

I shrugged and phoned Benson, in Fort Hicks. He was at the police station and asked me: "Is this it?"

"It is," I told him. I read him the telegram from Hood River and told him about the line trouble in Seattle.

"So," he said wonderingly, "I called the turn, didn't I?"

"Called what turn?"

"On the invaders. I don't know who they are—but it's the story of the boy who cried wolf. Only this time the wolves realized—" Then the phone went dead.

But he was right.

The people of the world were the sheep.

We newsmen—radio, TV, press and wire services—were the boy, who should have been ready to sound the alarm.

But the cunning wolves had tricked us into sounding the alarm so many times that the villagers were weary, and would not come when there was real peril.

The wolves who were then burning their way through the Ozarks, utterly without opposition—the wolves were the Martians under whose yoke and lash we now endure our miserable existences.

[*Cosmic Stories* - July 1941
as by S. D. Gottesman]

Fire-Power

1

Tiny, trim Babe MacNeice descended the very secret staircase that led into the very private office of Intelligence Wing Commander Bartok.

"Hello!" he gasped as the wall panel slid aside. "You're on Magdeburg's 83— or aren't you?"

"There was very little doing there," she smiled, seating herself. "Except a bustle and roiling about as I left. It seems that someone had kidnapped their HQ secretary and sweated him for some information relative to their new interceptors."

"Have they any idea," asked Bartok anxiously, "who that someone was?"

Babe laughed. "They have the finger on him. From some confidential instructions he dropped while making a getaway, they learned that he was a secret agent for some Venusian colony or other. He was described as a thin old man of effeminate carriage and manner."

Bartok smiled, relieved. "Your number twelve. Report, please." He started a phonograph turning and pointed the mike at Babe.

The girl said chattily: "MacNeice went per orders to Magdeburg's 83 for confirmation or denial of rumors concerning a planned uprising against Terrestrial authority. There she found widespread reports of similar character; the entire planet was flooded with propaganda.

"Information was conclusively—ah—secured—from an official to the effect that the colonial governor, Allison by name, was fomenting an insurrection by means of which he would be able to assume supreme authority over the planet and defend it against terrestrial forces. That is all." She lit a cigarette and stared dully at the floor as the wing commander sealed and labeled the report record.

"That," said Bartok, "sews up Allison in a very uncomfortable sack. We'll send a cruiser tonight."

"Sure," said the girl. "He hasn't got a chance. None of them have against the insidious Commander Bartok and his creatures of evil. That's me."

"And don't tell me you don't love it," he grinned. "I know better. In the blood, that's where it is—the congenital urge to pry into other people's affairs and never be suspected. It gives us a kick like two ounces of *novadyne*."

"Speaking of which," said Babe, "are you dining alone tonight?"

"Nope. I have a standing date with my favorite little *voyeur* whenever she comes back to Earth. Scamper along to get dressed; I'll meet you in two hours at the living statues."

The show-place of New Metropole, capital of the All Earth Union and Colonies, was the Square of Living Statues. Bathed in ever-changing lights, the groups of three men and three women, molded from the purest gold and silver and assembled with every artifice of the year A.D. 3880, changed steps and partners, moving through the hours of the day in a stately dance that was never twice the same in even the smallest step.

Grouped on a lofty platform, the heroically proportioned figures were the focus of every visitor to the wonder-city of all time and space. There was absolutely nothing like them in the universe, nothing like their marvelous grace that would balance a three-ton male on his toes while whirling a two-ton female partner in a vast arc, all to the most subtly exquisite music that could be evolved from supertheramins and electroviolas. The music too was completely automatic. The divine harmonies came from nothing more than a revolving drum which selected at random sequences of tones and the companion coloring of the lights that flooded the statues in their dance.

In a glassed restaurant Bartok and Babe were dining. Through the walls filtered enough of the music to furnish a subdued background to lovers' talk. But when these two got together it was business. As the wing commander had said, it was something in the blood.

"MacNeice," snapped Bartok, "I am not arguing with you, I'm telling you. You are not going to do any such damfool thing as walk in on our piratical friends and confront them with what you doubtless think of as 'The Papers.' I'm going to get this melodrama out of your head if I have to beat it out."

The girl's face was flushed and angry. "Try that and you'll get yours with an Orban," she snapped. "I say that if you bring it right home to them that we're on their tails they'll give up without a struggle, and we've saved so many lives and so much fuel that a medal for me will be in order."

"The cruiser," said Bartok, "leaves tonight. And that settles everything. Forget, child, that this wing of the service was once its brains instead of its eyes and ears. We are now officially an appendage devoted to snooping, and the glorious history of the Intelligence Division is behind us."

"Fitzjames," she muttered, gritting her teeth. "I'd like to take that Admiral of the Fleet by his beard and tear his head off. And don't tell me you aren't in the project body and soul." Mocking his tones she said: "I know better."

"Off the record," admitted Bartok, "I may opine that our tiny suite of offices has more brains in its charladies' little fingers than the entire fighting forces have in all the heads of all the commanders of all their mile-long battlewagons.

That is, naturally, gross overstatement and pure sentimentality on my part. Eat your Marsapples and shut up."

She bit viciously into one of the huge fruit and swallowed convulsively, her eyes drifting through the glass wall to the living statues. They were performing a sort of minuet, graceful beyond words, to an accompaniment from the theremins in the manner of Mozart.

"And what's more," barked the wing commander in an angry afterthought, "the body of the space navy could dispense with us at will, whereas without them we'd be lost. You can't exist for the purpose of making reports to nobody. What good would your spying have done if there hadn't been any cruiser to be sent off to bomb Allison's capital city?"

"None at all," she snapped at him. "Only I don't like the job if it has to mean taking guff from every half-witted ensign who graduated because he knows how to work an Auto-Crammer. Barty, you know and I know that they hate us and check up on everything we send in. The—the sneaks!" Abruptly she was weeping. The wing commander, indecisively, passed her a handkerchief. *Women!* he was thinking. Sometimes they could be thoroughly opaque to reason. Any man could see through his sardonic recital of rules. The wing commander detested the well-set-up officers and gentlemen who would not and could not move until he had charted the course. The wing commander had a healthy contempt for any and all formality and routine, with which the naval service was weighed down as with tons of lead. But the wing commander was, first, last and always, of that unalterable cast of mind which makes the superb, chilled-steel military spy.

In all the records of the All Earth Union and Colonies navy, there had probably been no such man as Bartok. Back to the days of the Herkimer scandal there had been a succession of brilliantly proved men in his office, but for resourcefulness and the spy's temperament he had had no equal.

He would have gone far in the old days; further than any intelligence man now could. Many years ago, when Earth had only a few hundred colonial planets, the news suddenly broke that there was a virtual dictatorship over the navy by the Intelligence Wing. Herkimer, since painted as a scoundrel of the deepest dye, had been merely an exceptionally enthusiastic officer.

The course his enthusiasm ran included incidentally the elimination of much red tape in the form of unfriendly fleet officers; that he regretted as unfortunate and even tragic. But his mission of expanding Earth's culture and civilization to the stars would not brook interference. Classic scholars could scarcely avoid a comparison with the Roman emperor Trajan, who pushed the bounds of the Empire to the absolute limits of the Western world, and created a situation which hastened the fall of Rome by centuries.

Since the Herkimer affair they had been very careful with the Intelligence Wing. Once it was almost abolished for good; a few years of operation of the fleet practically blind, with no ground laid for them or information of enemy movements, proved that to be impractical. But they did what they could to keep the spies within bounds. It was an actually heartbreaking situation to the executives of the Wing. But you can't keep the *voyeur* instinct down; that was what they were chosen for and that was how they operated.

Take this affair on Magdeburg's 83. It was an insignificant outer planet very far away from New Metropole. Yet the filtering of rumors brought it into the brilliant limelight of the Wing. The body of the fleet could not move less than a mile-long battlewagon at one time; the Wing—personified by Commander Bartok —dispatched tiny, trim Babe MacNeice. She returned with the information that a hitherto trusted colonial officer had decided to play Napoleon and was secretly fortifying the planet.

In the last analysis, lives were saved. The single cruiser could send a landing party and take the trusted colonial officer back to Earth for trial; surely a preferable alternative to a minor war with the propaganda-inflamed ophidians that were native to the planet.

Wing executives did not speak—in private—of their love for the body of the fleet. They held to the stubborn conviction that there was nothing dumber than a flagship commander, nothing less beautiful than a flagship.

2

At about that time, things were popping on the lineship *Stupendous,* two million miles off the orbit of Venus. On it was jammed the entire Headquarters Wing of the All Earth and Colonies navy. In the very heart of the ship, inside almost a cubic mile of defensive and offensive power, was Wing Commander Fitzjames, by virtue of his command Admiral of the Fleet.

"Not a murmur," he said to his confidential secretary, a man named Voss. "Not a murmur from the crew." He lolled back in his chair and breathed easier under his chestful of medals.

"They don't know," said Voss. "When they find out—!"

"Stick to your shorthand, son," snapped the Admiral. "When they find out, they'll keep on carrying out orders very much the way they always have. They're picked men on this ship. Now take this down: General Order to all lineship Commanders. By authority of the Admiral you are empowered to govern any and all citizens and subjects of All Earth. An emergency has arisen which makes it absolutely necessary to eliminate opposition to this program. Your direct superior is your Wing Commander, who is responsible only to ranking members of the Headquarters Wing. A list of proscribed persons will follow."

The Admiral lit a cigar with an unsteady hand. "Code that," he said. "Send it in twenty minutes."

"Anything else?" asked the secretary. "How about the Wing Commanders? Are you coming clean with them?"

Fitzjames stared at the metal ceiling. "Take this: Confidential Memorandum to Wing Commanders. From Admiral of the Fleet Fitzjames. You are hereby notified that the Headquarters Wing of the fleet has voted to take over power from the hands of the Executive Committee of All Earth. You are on your honor as officers and gentlemen to support this move by your brothers in arms. You will continue to patrol your regular sectors, having dispatched details to attend to the physical acts of taking power. No planet must be left under a Colonial Governor acting by right of a charter from the Exec All Earth. Details follow. Report to *Stupendous* immediately in code. We are seizing Venus as a base."

"Right," said Voss. "So go ahead and seize it."

"We're on our way," said the Admiral heavily.

Depending on where you were to see the affair, the seizing of Venus was either a trivial or a Jovian episode. From space, for example, all there was to see was the bulk of the lineship slipping its length into the clouds above the dawnstar and vanishing from sight. But from the city of Astarte, principal freight port of the planet, it was vastly impressive.

Above the towers and loading peaks of the yards there appeared the most gigantic of all the spaceships in the universe, covering the town like a roof over its roofs.

There were a couple of smoke-bombs dropped into the streets and a few old-fashioned radios exploded under the power of the monster ship's sending tubes that announced that the city was taken and would be hostage for the rest of the planet's good behavior. Landing parties went down by lighter ships to establish order and arrange several necktie parties in which the Colonial Governor had the stellar role, minor parts being taken by his subordinates and clerks. Venusian natives were warned off the streets; henceforth none but the Earthborn could show their faces by daylight. Plans were announced to transport the verminous natives to the Darkside District. All this took exactly six hours, Earth time.

A brief résumé of the life of Alexander Hertford III, Captain of the Fleet and Commander of Patrol Wing Twenty-Three, would include many revealing facts relative to the situation of the moment.

As he lay comfortably sprawled on a divan aboard his lineship *Excalibur*, a capital fighting vessel of standard offensive and defensive equipment, he was a fine figure of a man in his uniform of purple and gold. The collar was open, which, with his tumbled curls hanging over his brow in the manner of an ancient Irish *glib*, gave him a dashing, devil-may-care expression. At least Miss Beverly deWinder thought so, for she was smoothing those tumbled curls and smiling maternally.

Leaving the commander's ship—which was stationed off Rigel—for a moment, we take a brief survey of his career. He was thirty years old, and his grandfather, the first of his name, was also in the Navy. His father was not as bright as his grandfather, but appointments were easily got from the sentimental All Earth Exec, which wished to breed a race of fighting men, true, loyal and hard as nails. Alexander Hertford II just got through Prep Wing and Training Wing by the skin of his teeth, lived on a lineship and died at his post quelling an uprising among the outer planets of Alpha Centauri.

The third of the name was definitely dull. However, by virtue of the anonymous genius who invented the Auto-Cram and peddled them to students, he got through with what could easily be mistaken for flying colors, won his commission, saw service and was promoted to a Wing Command.

Life in Prep Wing and Training Wing was Spartan in the extreme. Tradition was extensively cultivated; for example, it was legitimate to steal anything edible and criminal to steal anything drinkable. Another of the blunders of the career-molding branch of the Navy was the policy of rigidly excluding females from the lives of the boys and men for the duration of the course. Thus it was no more than natural that after graduating they got their romance in heavy doses.

The end-product of this was sprawling off Rigel when a discreet tapping sounded on the door of the Commander's lounge.

"I'll see, sweetie," said Miss deWinder, who was a good-hearted girl. She took the slip of paper that poked through the slot and carried it to Alexander Hertford III.

He opened it and read.

"Damn," said Alexander Hertford III.

"Wassa matta, sweetie pie? Did bad ol' Admiral sen' sweetie pie away f'om li'l Bevvie-wevvie?"

Sweetie pie opened a closet whose inner face was a mirror and adjusted his collar and hair. As he cocked his cap at the right fraction of an angle, he said: "Nothing to worry about. You just sit tight. I may not be back for a few days—we're seeing action again." He reread the slip of paper.

"Damn," he marveled again. "When we used to talk about it around the mess-tables I never thought it'd come in my time. But here it is. Beverly, sweet, the Navy's taking over. Your lover-boy isn't a flying policeman anymore." He buckled on his belt and opened the lap of the handgun holster. There was a look of strain on his dumb, handsome face. "From now on," he said, "your lover-boy is ruler, and no questions asked, over Cosmic Sector Twenty-Three, with full power of life and death."

Miss deWinder echoed after him, fascinated: "And no questions asked ..."

The decode clerk at Intelligence Wing read off the message he had just received and set into English. Working like an automaton, he was grasping its meaning for the first time, though it had been a full quarter-hour's labor to untangle the quadruply alternating cipher. He read; he understood at last; he whistled a long, slow whistle of amazement.

In agitated tones he snapped at an office girl: "This is for Barty and nobody else. Give it to him and run, because there's going to be an explosion."

He reread the slip of paper: "—hereby notified that the Headquarters Wing has ..." He folded and sealed the slip.

The office girl stood back a few yards to watch the Commander's face. Alternately it registered disgust and amazement as he read and reread the slip. "Scat!" he finally choked at her, with an imperious gesture.

Alone in his office with Babe MacNeice he shoved the slip across his desk, his face working.

She read it and looked up, frankly puzzled. "So what?" Babe demanded. "It's a general order, memo—whatever you want to call it. Why the skillful simulation of epilepsy?"

"You don't know," he groaned, burying his head in his hands. "Women, children, imbeciles and men who haven't passed through the Prep and Training Wings. I'd be just like them if I hadn't had the spy kink from birth and been through the Training Section of the Wing I now command. You don't know, Babe, what your typical Navy officer is like.

"Once for an experiment they tried sending some Rigelians—who are very much like genus homo except that they haven't any internal organs—all highly organized custard inside—to Training. Would those long-headed beauties let them stay? Nope—tradition. It was a school for gentlemen, scholars—by virtue of the Autocram—and Terrestrials exclusively. Things are so bad now that you have to be a direct descendant of a previous student before they admit you. All Earth Exec— blah! Democratic, but soft-headed and sentimental.

"When these prize beauties get into power they'll make such a hash of our beautiful colonial system—!" He was nearly weeping.

Babe MacNeice rose from her chair with gleaming eyes. "Well," she yelled at the man, "don't just sit there! What are you going to *do* about it?" He looked up. "Yes," she snapped, "I said *do*. Here you are sitting pretty with a corner on all the brains in the Navy, with the most loyal staff of any commander, and you just snivel about what those imbeciles plan for the future. If you feel so damn broken-up about it why don't you stop them?"

Bartok was looking at her with amazed eyes. Women, he decided, were wonderful. No false sentiment about them; something about their ugly biological job must make them innate fact-facers. Of course some man would have to find them the facts to face, but neither sex was perfect.

"Babe," he said wonderingly, "I believe you have it." He sprang to his feet. "Fitzjames," he barked, "and the rest of his crew are going to curse the days they were born when I'm through with them. Now let's get down to brass tacks, kid. I have under me about three thousand first-class Intelligence men, one thousand women. My office staff is four hundred. Lab resources—all my men have private labs; for big-scale work we borrow equipment from the University. Armament, every first-class operative owns a hand-gun and shells. Most of them carry illegal personal electric stunners. Rolling stock—two thousand very good one-man ships that can make it from here to Orion without refueling and about five hundred larger ships of various sizes. All ships unarmed. Servicing for the ships is in the hands of the local civilian authorities wherever we land. Good thing that we take fuel like civilian and private ships. Oh, yes—our personnel is scattered pretty widely through the cosmos. But we can call them in any time by the best conference-model communications hookup in space. And that's that."

"It sounds good, Barty," said the girl. "It sounds very good to me. How about the rest of them?"

The Wing Commander looked very sick suddenly. "Them," he brooded. "Well, to our one division they have twenty-six, each with a flagship of the line.

They have twenty-six bases—including graving-docks, repair-shops, maintenance crews, fuel, ammunition and what-have-you—and innumerable smaller ships and boats.

"And, Babe, they have one thing we haven't got at all. Each and every ship in the numbered Patrol Wings of the Navy mounts at least one gun. The lineships, of which there are eighty-two, mount as many as a hundred quick-fire repeaters and twenty loading ordnance pieces, each of which could blow a minor planet to hell and gone. They have guns and we have minds."

The girl rested her chin in her hands. "Brainpower versus fire-power," she brooded. "Winner take all."

3

The first clash came two weeks later off Rigel. Alexander Hertford III, Commander of Patrol Wing Twenty-Three, was apprised of the startling facts as he awoke from a night (theoretically) of revelry with Miss deWinder.

Rubbing the sleep from his baby-blue eyes, he yawned: "Impossible. There aren't any capital ships other than those in the Navy. There's some silly mistake. You must have decoded it all wrong."

"Impossible, Commander," said the orderly respectfully. "And it wasn't sent wrong either. They repeated several times."

The commander stared at the slip which bore the incredible message from Cruiser DM 2. "As regards orders to pacify star-cluster eight, your district, impossible to proceed. Unrecognizable lineship heavily armed warned us away. When asked for section and command they replied, 'Section One, Command of Reason.' Instruct. The Commanding Officer, DM 2."

With one of those steel-spring decisions for which the Navy personnel is famous, he abruptly ordered: "My compliments to what's his name, the pilot and navigator. We're going to relieve DM 2 and see what those asses think they've found."

In just the time he took to dress and bid Miss deWinder a cheery though strained good morning, the ship was hauling alongside the cruiser. After an exchange of salutations, the commanding officer of the cruiser, frankly angry, yelled at Hertford (over the communications system): "Use your own damned eyes, commander. You can't miss the damned thing—biggest damned ship I ever saw in my damned life!"

"Captain," said the commander, "you're over-wrought. Lie down and we'll look about." He was on what they called the bridge, a vast arc of a room which opened, for effect, on the very hull of the ship. Vast, sweepingly curved plates of lucostruc opened on the deeps of space, though scanner discs would have been structurally sounder.

Taking an angry turn about the bridge he snapped at the lookout: "Have you found that lunatic's chimera yet?" For, be it known, there is no such thing as blundering on a spaceship. You have to do some very involved calculating to blunder on a sun, and even so luck must be on your side. In short, unless this mythical lineship chose to show itself, there wasn't one chance in a thousand thousand of its being located.

"Can't see any chimera, commander," said the lookout, one straining eye glued to a telescope. "But right there's the biggest, meanest fighting ship I've ever struck eyes to." He yielded to the commander, who stared incredulously through the 'scope.

By God, it was there. By all the twelve planets, so it was. The thing was bigger than the *Excalibur,* Hertford's ship. It floated very far away and could be spotted only by the superb display of illumination they'd put on, with taunting intent, it seemed to the commander.

"Battle stations!" he yelled immediately. "Ready full fire-power."

The lookout spoke into a mike and stood by.

"Get in touch with him," snapped the commander. "When you get his wavelength give me the speaker. I'll talk to him direct, whoever he is." Through his mind were running confused visions of the glorious old days of piracy, when his grandfather had so nobly fought in a ship a tenth the size of his own, to crush the mighty federation of the gentlemen of fortune. "And," he said aloud, "by God they did it."

The entire ship was buzzing confusedly with rumor. Each and every one of the crew of a thousand and the marines who numbered half that had his own private theory half an hour after the strange lineship had been sighted. These ranged from the improbably accurate notion that it was a rebel against the Navy who were going to raise some hell, to the equally absurd notion that the commander himself was the rebel and that the Admiral had sent his best ship to punish him. The truth, of course, was too obvious to be guessed by anybody.

As the ship was readied for battle it seemed to draw in on itself, like a crouching tiger. Its skin seemed to be too small for it. Men stood as if rooted to the metal floor-plates, but they quivered in tune with the accumulating mass-energy of the drivers.

A fighting ship is built around its guns, therefore a word about these may not be out of place. The *Excalibur* had the most modern of armaments. From every imaginable spot in its hide there could extrude the spaceship equivalent of old seagoing "murder guns." Disgusted gunners gave that name to the little quick-firers with which they picked off floating men and boats.

The *Excalibur's* "murder guns" were about a yard long with a caliber of three inches between the lands. They were loaded with shells exploding on time; it would be murder indeed to leave a score or more of contact shells floating unexploded in space. The rate of fire from these little killers was adjusted from single-shot to ten a second and never a jam from the loading mechanism.

There were intermediate guns as well, but more for their own sake than for any practical use. The twelve-inch shells from these could blow a destroyer out of space, but who ever heard of a lineship fighting a destroyer? However, if the occasion should arise, they were there, about twenty of them scattered throughout the ship, covering every second of curved surface.

Finally there were the Big Guns. These were the reason for building the *Excalibur* or anything like it. The rest of the ship was designed to service those guns, store their ammunition, shelter the men who worked them, move them about in space, and protect them from harm. The Big Guns were really big, so there was no need for more than four of them. Two fore and two aft were sufficiently heavy armament for any ship. One of these four happened to be out of commission on Hertford's ship. That, he thought bitterly, would count heavily against him in the fight that was coming.

"Aim gun II, aft," said the commander. There had been no answer from the mocking fighting ship that had suicidally turned on every light it had. The thing was still in plain view. Hertford did not draw nearer or even move for fear he would be spotted. It was enough that he knew where his nameless foe was.

"Fire," said Hertford, "when ready."

From the magazine in the heart of the ship there slid along frictionless runways barrel-like capsules of propulsive burner compound, which consisted of big-moleculed acid and base which combined, in the presence of a catalyst, and released monstrous clouds of gas in the fraction of a second. Following the capsules there slid the Shell, approximately the size of a three-story suburban villa.

Loading machinery, that looked as though it could be utilized in off moments to build universes, fitted the shell into the breech and rammed it home, shoved after it the burner compound that would shoot it on its way.

And all this while, in the quarter of the ship devoted to fire-control, two hundred men had been sighting, resighting, calculating and recalculating at batteries of machines to whom the integraph was as the amœba is to the mastodon.

The point is this: that Shell couldn't possibly miss, because to avoid it, the colossal bulk of the nameless enemy would have had to begin moving only a second after the order to fire when ready had been delivered. It was violating every rule of warfare, and, the fire-control men were confident, it would not survive the error.

The Gun finally moved on delicately jeweled bearings. This was going to be the most direct hit of all time. Cubic yards of metal locked it in position.

Metallically, over the loudspeaker: "Ready to fire, commander."

The commander: "Then *fire!*"

There are no words to describe the discharge of a Big Gun and the progress of a Shell through space towards a goal. But that mile-long battlewagon was rocked like a sapling in a hurricane. When the initial shock was over the reeling commander clung to a stanchion and glued his eye to the telescope fixed on the nameless enemy.

It still glowed with lights; it still seemed to be a shade bigger than the *Excalibur*. The feelings of the commander, subtly schooled to brutality and murder, were mostly of exultation as he saw the Shell enter the field of the telescope. Now, he thought, they would be frantically dashing about as it drew nearer and desperately trying and trying to move a mass that could not be moved in less time than it would take the Shell to contact it and explode.

Two seconds ... one second ... half—quarter—eighth—

"What the hell?" asked the commander with a childishly hurt air. He scratched his head, and as he scratched it his lineship, the *Excalibur*, disintegrated in a tangled, pulverized hell of metal, plastic, flesh, bone, Miss Beverly deWinder, two hundred fire-control men, operating crew of a thousand, half that number of marines and Commander Alexander Hertford III. They never knew what hit them, but it was their own Shell.

4

New Metropole, capital of Earth and, before the Navy took over, capital of the All Earth Union and Colonies, was being pacified. This is done by lighter-loads of marines and fighting sailors who descend from a lineship hanging ominously over the most highly populated portion of the city. The lineship itself does not descend because an uncalled bluff is worth more than a called one and because the battlewagons cannot land from the moment they are launched to the moment they are scrapped except in graving docks, and the nearest to Earth was at Alpha Centauri.

Marines swarmed through the streets in the traditional manner of rightist revolutionaries. Should a face appear that hinted of Rigelian blood, or should a half-breed with the abnormally long hands and black teeth of a Betelgeusian pass the marines, there would be bloodshed and no questions asked. After a few hours of the reign of terror, the extraterrestrials crept into cellars and stayed there for the duration.

The All Earth Executive Committee was imprisoned pending trial; trial for what was never made clear. Communications sending sets were declared provisionally illegal; anyone caught with one in working commission would suffer death. The only etheric voice that could be legally heard was the light, mocking one of Voss, personal secretary to Admiral Fitzjames, and that only from the powerful sender aboard the Admiral's ship *Stupendous,* floating grimly above the Bronx.

The receiving code set in the communications room of the little suite of offices once occupied by the Intelligence Wing was clicking like a mad thing, and never an answer came, for the Wing had moved out lock, stock and barrel. The message that kept repeating (Admiral Fitzjames had said "Keep trying" two days ago) was: "Why don't you answer, Intelligence Wing? Bartok, report immediately aboard *Stupendous* to show cause why you should not be removed from office and the Wing disbanded. Why don't you answer, Intelligence Wing? Bartok, report—" et cetera.

A squad of marines would shortly break into the office and find nothing of interest to anybody.

But there were two people who seemed to be partly Rigelian from the greenish patches on their faces and their peculiar scalp-lines, shaped like tipsy S's. They were cowering in a cellar as many other Rigelians were doing during those lunatic days when the Navy had first taken over, but there was something purposeful and grim about their behavior that didn't fit the disguises.

Babe MacNeice was tinkering despondently with the central control panel of the conference-type communications system exclusive to the Intelligence Wing. The panel was a little thing, like a book in size and shape, but its insides were so fearfully complicated that nothing short of an installations engineer could make anything of them. And the panel was definitely shot to hell.

She said as much, and burst into a flood of tears. Bartok, the other Rigelian, snarled softly and handed over a mussy handkerchief. "Take it easy," he snapped, his own nerves raw and quick with strain. "We're sitting pretty compared with the rest of the office staff."

The brave smile that always ended the weeping spells flashed out as she returned the handkerchief. "What now?" she demanded tremulously. "Now that we can't keep in touch with the rest of the men?"

"Now," he said slowly, "I don't know. But—" He snatched at her wrist and dragged her behind a pillar as the door of their cellar swung open and a streak of light shot through the gloom. The profile of a marine's cap showed against the light. Bartok raised his handgun, resting the long barrel across his left forearm, pioneer-sharpshooter style.

The door opened fully. The marine called: "Come on out or I'll shoot!" That was on general principles. It was surprising how many fell for the centuries-old dodge. Then when the hider came out the marines would have a little innocent fun with their handguns and depart for other cellars.

Babe sneezed. The marine started and Bartok shot him through the head. "Come on," he snapped in an undertone as he tore off the Rigelian wig. "Through the window, Babe, and try to forget you're a lady!"

The hue and cry has been called the most shameful tradition of genus homo; for generations it had been abandoned in favor of more civilized and efficient methods, such as teletype alarms and radio squad cars. Now, in the taking-over by the Navy, the dishonorable tradition was revived as a further testimony that this taking-over was nothing short of barbarism once you sheared it of the nickelplate of the lineships and the gold braid dripping from officers' shoulders.

Behind the two fleeing people poured a ragged mob of marines and sailors, roaring inarticulate things about what they would do to the sneaking murderers when they caught them.

Luckily—in a way—an officer of the Navy popped from a doorway armed to the teeth and charging them to surrender. This they gladly did as he stood off the mob with his weapons.

They found themselves at last in a lighter, one of the small boats connected to the *Stupendous*. In an off-hand way, as the boat left the ground, the officer said: "I recognized you, you know."

"Really?" asked Babe, frozen-faced.

"Not you," he hastily explained. "But Commander Bartok—I've seen his picture. Did you know you were proscribed, Commander?"

"I assumed so," answered the commander dryly. The officer—an ensign—was very young and callow. The hard lines were growing about his mouth, though. When he could call this "pacification" without laughing out loud, thought Bartok, he'd be a real Navy man.

"How's everything going?" asked the commander. "Would you know how the campaign's progressing in other parts?"

The ensign, seemingly delighted to converse on equal terms with a Wing Commander, even though a proscribed one, drew nearer—or as much nearer as he could, in the windowless, tiny, completely enclosed compartment that was the load-space of the lighter, and grinned: "Some dashed mysterious things have been happening, and I wouldn't be a bit surprised if you johnnies in Intelligence were behind them."

He shifted uneasily beneath Bartok's steady, piercing stare. "You needn't look at me like that," he complained. "Even if it isn't true, it's the official non-official news—if you understand me." He chuckled.

Bartok moved swiftly then, clutching the ensign by the throat and bringing an elbow into his midriff. The ensign, not wholly taken by surprise, apparently, drew his gun and fired.

They dragged his bloody body—he had been shot in the face, and it had run all over the enclosed space—from the lighter a few minutes later. Babe was having a hysterical attack and the ensign frantically signaled to the sailors who took in the boat to relieve him of her. The engineer of the little craft came from his cubbyhole in the bow and took her by the arm, led her away from the mess on the floor.

"Poor girl," said the ensign. "She must have loved him terribly."

To follow Babe MacNeice, after the first torrential outburst she was dry-eyed, but there was a catch in her voice when she spoke: "Where are you taking me?"

"To the O.D., lady. He'll route you."

The Officer of the Day decided that she was important enough to go directly to the Admiral.

In the super-sumptuous office of Fitzjames she thought at first that she was alone, but a snaky individual who had a knack of blending in with the furniture, as if he didn't want to be seen, coughed tentatively.

She eyed him up and down. "You," she said, "must be the Satanic Mr. Voss."

He cocked an eyebrow at her. "Indeed? How so?"

"It's no secret that you're the one who started the—the taking-over."

"I defy you to prove it," he snickered.

"You're a civilian. That's final and conclusive. There isn't one of these certifiable fatheads in uniform that'd have the guts to do what they've all been talking about for fifty years. You touched it off, and you see victory in your hands right this moment. Bartok is dead."

"No!" he spat. "Where?"

"Coming up here on a lighter. He rashly jumped the ensign who'd arrested us. He got his face blown off."

"So," grunted Voss. "The end of organized resistance to our program. How did he manage, by the way, to blow up our ships with their own ammunition, or whatever really happened?"

"I don't know the details," she replied wearily. "We used glorified lantern-slides to project the simulacrum of a lineship; we could do that with about fifty one-man craft. It's a kind of formation flying. We turned back your shells by magnetic fields. Normally you could dodge them, because you keep ready to move whenever you fire the big guns. But we dubbed in a dummy shell—like the lantern-slide lineship—and you'd see that shell and there wouldn't be a thought in your heads until you were blown up. But you're onto that trick now. It only worked four times, I think. I was a lunatic to think that you could fight guns with brainwork and hope to win."

She collapsed limply into a chair and stared dully at the floor. "Bartok's dead. The communication system's wrecked. You can have your taking-over, Mr. Voss; we're licked."

5

"Hell!" said the Admiral. "Why can't I go out into the street if I want to?"

"Because," said Voss patiently, "you'd be shot down like a dog. You're going to speak from behind cover, and I'll post the best shots in the Navy all over just in case."

"Right," said the Admiral. "Then it's decided. I guess the old brain's clicking right along, eh?" He forced a laugh, and Voss responded with a meager smile.

Tapping on the door. Voss opened it on the young ensign who'd been boasting all over the ship of shooting down the insidious Bartok. He was being avoided by his friends now; he wouldn't let them get a word in about their own feats of clubbing and mayhem.

"What do you want?" thundered the Admiral. "I'm preparing my address to All Earth and Colonies!"

"Beg pardon, sir," said the ensign. "But I was wondering if I could be assigned to your guard of honor for the address. After all, sir, I *did* outwit Bartok."

"Since when," asked Voss coldly, "does outwitting consist of getting in a lucky shot?"

"Tut," grumbled the Admiral. "Let him have his way. Why not, Voss?"

"I was going to," said the secretary. "Report this evening."

"Thank you, sir. And—and—"

"Spit it out, kid. What do you want?" demanded Voss.

"About Miss MacNeice, sir. She seemed awfully broken up about what I did. How is she now?"

"Resting easy in Cell Eleven," said the Admiral. "Now go away."

"Thank you, sir," said the ensign, saluting as he closed the door.

"Good boy, that," said Voss. "It pays to have semi-fanatics like him in your train. They'll do the dirty work when nobody else will. Remember that, Fitzjames."

"I will, Voss," said the Admiral. "Now about this speech—"

The ensign was walking down one of the very long corridors of the ship, whistling cheerfully, oblivious to the superstition to the effect that it's the worst kind of luck to a ship; even worse than changing her name.

And in Cell Eleven—neat and comfortable, but a cell—Babe MacNeice was fiddling desperately with the communications control. Trust those bloody incompetents, she dryly thought, to leave a woman unsearched because a matron wasn't handy …

Then, by the most convenient of miracles, there was a little tone signal from the switchboard. "It works," she said in a hushed whisper. "It was bound to happen—nobody could try as hard as I've been trying and not get some kind of results."

She hissed into the tiny grid mouthpiece: "Hello—who's in?"

A male voice grumbled: "My God, woman, you've been long enough about it! I'm Casey, heading towards Spica because I can't think of anything else to do. My fuel's low, too."

"Keep going," she said. "When you get there, be prepared for anything at all. I'm not making promises, but there's a chance. And my God! *What* a chance! You get out now. I have some heavy coverage to do."

"Good luck, lady, whoever you are."

She smiled briefly and fiddled with the elaborate, but almost microscopically tiny, controls that directed the courses of the Intelligence Wing.

"Come in, anybody, in the Twenty-Third Cosmic Sector. Anybody at all. This is MacNeice—urgent!"

"Not the famous Babe herself?" came a woman's voice dryly. "I'm listening, dearie."

"You locate on Aldebaran III, sister, in no more than ten hours. Keep under cover. Now get out. Aldebaran III has to be covered."·

With an anxious note the voice asked: "Just a minute—how's Barty? I heard a rumor—"

"Forget it, sister," snapped Babe. "You have a job to do." She cut the woman out and called in rapid succession as many of the thirty Cosmic Sectors as she could get. One set had fallen into the hands of the Navy, and that was bad, but she cut out before they could have traced it or even guessed what it was. There had been a confused murmur and a single distinct voice saying: "The damned thing's a radio, sir!" before she cut out.

What she had been doing was to locate operatives on the principal planets and stations of the Cosmos; operatives prepared for anything. It had been a job of routing; they bunched together when they weren't under orders. She had to break them up—and she did.

After locating one stubborn female, she heard a man's tread in the corridor outside and as quickly as she could hid the little panel-like affair, which, considering where she was forced to hide it, was not a very speedy job of concealment.

The entire city of New Metropole was jammed into the vast Square of the Living Statues that evening for the ultimate proclamation from Admiral of the Fleet Fitzjames concerning the taking-over and the new order to be established. Though, of course, some historians would say that there was nothing new about it, but that it was a very old order indeed.

There had been erected against the superb backdrop of the living statues a great booth-like affair from which the Admiral would make his speech, a speech to be heard simultaneously by every living human and colonial extraterrestrial alive. There was even declared a temporary amnesty on extraterrestrials; for this evening they might walk the streets—but only to and from the Square.

The booth was, of course, weapon-proof. Voss had been most particular about that.

Crowds had begun to assemble early in the afternoon; if there was to be a new order, they would make sure that they would be its earliest and heartiest boosters. By dusk the press of people had grown so great that there was no room to turn around, let alone draw a weapon, so Fitzjames could have no fear on that score. The only free place was the platform of the booth, flush with the great transparent base on which the living statues moved on in their endless perfection.

When night had fallen they turned on the floodlights normally used to illuminate the statues, removing the color-wheels. The crowd was picked out in glaring detail by the pitiless glow. As far as the eye could see there was a meadow of faces upturned, each sharp and distinct by itself. The statues were in the dark, their sole remaining lights being turned on the booth. The very music had been subdued so that the amplifiers would lose no word of what the Admiral would say. It was a memorable occasion in many unsuspected ways.

Ten o'clock sharp, enter the Admiral, dropping from the heavens in an ornate lighter which was then immediately dispatched. Fitzjames was afraid that his hour of triumph might end tragically should a spanner fall from the craft and crack his skull.

With him, of course, were Voss and the guard of honor.

Five past ten Voss stepped to the mike. "Friends," he said, "it is my proud duty to present to you the man who has liberated us from the yoke of the All Earth Exec—Fitzjames The First!"

There was an astounded hush from the audience, and then a protesting murmur. The wildest fancy they had indulged in hadn't included anything like a monarchy!

Fitzjames The First stepped to the mike as Voss bowed low. He said: "My loyal subjects, I greet you."

The guard of honor fidgeted. It had been a well-kept secret. The young ensign strolled over to Voss, who was surprised to feel a handgun's muzzle pressed into his ribs.

"Excuse me?" he said strainedly. "Are you sure you're quite sane, young man? Take that thing away."

"I'm not only sane," said the Ensign, "I'm Bartok. When that silly ass fired at me in the lighter he missed, of course. So I switched clothes in three minutes flat, Babe made up my face with the kit that every Intelligence Wing man carries, then we blew the face off the ensign of yours. He was unconscious. A pity."

"—magnificent demonstration of the reversion to childlike faith in the will of Providence and the divine right of kings—" the Admiral was droning.

Voss, a slender, slimy, active man, dived into the shadows as Bartok's attention wavered from him to the speaker.

The Wing Commander dived right after him. "Where are you?" he called into the darkness. "Don't be a damned fool!"

The only answer was a slug zipping past his ear.

"Bartok," hissed Voss from the blackness, "this is your last adventure. I can see you and you can't see me. Good-bye, Bartok."

There was a sickening *crunch* from the blackness and a gasp that sounded like a tin can in labor.

"The poor, damned fool," said Bartok. One of the living statues had stepped on the man's head in the course of some intricate *pas seul*. Bartok had known it would happen, for the periodicity of the statues was limited to this: in the course of two minutes and forty seconds every square foot of the dancing platform was trodden on at least once by at least one of the two-ton feet of the statues.

Meanwhile the remainder of the guard of honor was vainly trying to fire unloaded handguns—except one slender young man who simply grinned like a cat.

"Okay, Babe," said Bartok to the slender young man. "You do it."

"With *pleasure!*"

As the Admiral had just got around to the choosing of his palace-planet—nothing less than an entire planet would do for his regal estates—he too felt a gun in his ribs. He stopped short.

"Read this," said the slender young man, who was trying to keep from giggling.

Without ado of any sort the Admiral placed the paper on the lectern before him and read in flat, colorless tones:

"I hereby declare that I personally had no such nonsense in mind. It was the work of my secretary. I hereby state that I assume no powers beyond my naval duties.

"General Order to All Officers: any seditious talk of taking over will be severely dealt with by the Intelligence Wing which is—*ulp!*—hereby constituted as supreme police authority over the Navy.

"Memorandum to Wing Commanders: you will turn over all insignia of your office to representatives of the Intelligence Wing who will make themselves known to you."

In a very small voice he said: "That is all," and deflated into a chair. There was a titanic roar of applause from the assembled peoples of New Metropole.

"Darling," said Babe, "if the timing doesn't come off right—if those people I contacted don't show up to the Wing Commanders soon enough, before they recover—!"

"They will," said Bartok. He laughed shortly, like the closing of a heavy lock.

"What's funny?"

"They—*they*—had the guns and we didn't have a thing but ourselves. Sweet, this is one stunt they'll never try again."

The crowd, still applauding, began to disperse into the night.

[*Stirring Science Stories* - March 1942
as by S. D. Gottesman]

The Perfect Invasion

1

"Heavens!" said Bartok mildly, and "Oh, my Lord!" His face wore a curiously complex look, as though he were half stunned with shock and otherwise doubting what he saw. Said Bartok: "They can't do this to us." He turned decidedly from the transceiver and began to pace his office. Into his personal mike he snapped: "Send in the number one houri."

Babe MacNeice entered on cue. "What," she asked, "is the matter with our overlord and preceptor?" She studied his face and dropped the smile. "Barty," she said worriedly, "what's wrong?"

"Sit down," he growled, shoving a chair at her. Looking fixedly at the ceiling, he said: "I just got a report from somewhere in the neighborhood of a punky little star named Arided in Cygnus. Babe, we're being invaded. The world is being invaded."

The girl laughed briefly. "Don't be an ass," she said.

"It's true," said Bartok.

She rose and began to pace beside him. Finally she exploded: "They can't *do* this to us! They simply can't—why, *we're* the invaders; we always have been!"

Bartok looked sidewise at her. "That's the way I felt," he observed sagely. "I know what you mean. Question is, what do we do now?"

"I don't know. Let's hear the transcript from the communications outfit." Silently he turned on the rewind and replay. It said mechanically: "Office of Commander Bartok, Intelligence Wing, Fleet Command. Go ahead." That was a sort of letterhead.

Immediately there was the agitated voice of some man or other: "Barty? This is Hogan, of the Aries Hogans. I jammed this through to you—personal report. It's going to panic them if it gets out. Be very careful."

Bartok's voice: "I remember you—patrol duty for the Arided section. Give me the facts in a hurry, son."

341

Hogan's voice: "Ships coming at us from everywhere, it seems. A big lineship was blown to pieces before it could report. I'm the only intelligence man in the district, I guess. I don't know whose the ships are—I don't know how they work. I'm speaking from the fourth planet of Arided—polyp-like natives, oxygenous atmosphere. They're systematically bombing the cities."

Bartok's voice: "Stop beating yourself over the head, Hogan. You're crazy!"

Hogan's voice: "If that's the way you feel. They're laying a line barrage along the planet, letting it rotate under their fire. We can't get a thing into the air—it's jammed up bad. I don't know, Barty, honest I don't know—" What Hogan didn't know remained a mystery, for the transcript ended right there with a strangled wail and a deafening report.

"Oho," said Babe MacNeice in a long exhalation. "He wasn't kidding."

Bartok was at the phone: "Get me Fitzjames," he said. "Yes—the all-highest Admiral of the Fleet, the slave-minded ol' windjammer in person." In a rapid aside to Babe he snapped: "I can't handle this. I'll leave it to the Navy—it's their baby."

Again at the phone. "Admiral? Shoot some patrollers out to Cygnus Arided. Don't be surprised if they don't come back. Invasion, Admiral. I wouldn't kid you." He hung up sharply.

"That," he said absent-mindedly, "is that. Whether their tactics are capable of defensive war remains to be seen. There is room for doubt."

The patrollers did not come back. However, one managed to keep unbroken contact with the flagship until it was blown out of the ether, and the story it told was plenty nasty. No description of the invading ships was given except what the patroller got over in the customary strangled wail just before it broke off sending. It could be assumed that they weren't reaction-type vessels. They moved faster than light, which meant knowledge of the unified field theory's most abstract implication. They had, without a doubt, bombed or rayed out of existence, the populations of about three score planets. This meant that either their science was something infinitely beyond the Terrestrial grasp, so far beyond it that it could not be called classified knowledge at all but must, necessarily, be lumped together as a divine attribute, or their ships were *big*.

The Fleet had successfully colonized a great deal of space and in the course of wiping out unsuitable native populations and encouraging others, battling moderately advanced peoples and races, suppressing the mutinies inevitable in a large, loose organization, and smacking down the romantic imbeciles who had a few tons of hard cash to throw away on what was considered a career of piracy, had developed an extraordinary amount of offensive technique and armament.

Their ships were marvelous things. They were so big that they were built at special dry-docks. When they took to the ether from these, they would never touch land again until they were scrapped. There simply wasn't anything firm enough to bear their weight. You could explore a lineship like a city; wander through its halls for a year and never cross the same point. When the big guns were fired they generally tore a hole in space; when the gunshells exploded they smashed asteroids to powder.

But the Fleet had nothing to show that could match the achievement of the as-yet-nameless invaders, who had rayed the life out of a major planet as it revolved beneath them. According to the reports the job had been done in the course of the planet's day. One ship could not send a ray powerful enough to do that; possibly twenty might, but they would inevitably foul one another if they got within a million miles nearness. And a million miles clearance between each ship would meant that they'd separately be about eight million miles from the planet. And from that distance you can't work rays or bombs. From that distance you can just barely think unpleasantly of the planet, which doesn't do either good or harm.

From all accounts and from the terrified deductions, these invaders packed solid jack, and plenty of it.

It wasn't very long before the invaders were in complete control of the sector they had first arrived at, and had won that control without a real fight or even once tipping their hands as to what they had and what they could do if they were hard-pressed.

There had begun a general exodus back to Earth; one would have thought that there was already a major space war on from the scrambling and confusion. Any planet that boasted a graving-dock for minor ships of the line was thrice overloaded with a charge of human beings, for the mere presence of dismantled destroyers was a guarantee of temporary security. After three weeks of the senseless scrambling the Admiral was forced to declare that there would be no more admissions to planets and whole systems having vital bearing on the welfare of the Fleet. He quietly began a program of evacuation so that if there should be a raid on a Fleet base there would be no deaths save those in the service. Things were confused; public temper was generally timid. The prospect of a defensive had scared the living daylights out of them. It was utterly unthinkable that Earth, the great invader, should get a taste of her own medicine.

Where they came from nobody knew, where they were going nobody dared to say. But it was perfectly obvious that the All Earth and Colonies culture stood in their way, and that they were bound to stamp them flat. The invaders must have been awfully foul creatures in their psychological make-up to do what they did, for they gave no hint of their moves, which is the dirtiest trick that you can play on anyone. They simply moved up slowly and surely from their obscure base on the outermost planets of the Earth culture.

And they kept moving. There were no survivors; that was the most appalling part of their technique. Everybody who could run, ran. Everybody who was left, died. Communication was cut off simply and efficiently by scrambling techniques which must have meant the expenditure of trillions of kilowatts per hour. Or did the invaders have some unsuspected source of energy? Nobody knew; that was the hell of it.

Bartok was good and ready to blow his brains out. It was his specialty, as commander of the Intelligence Wing, to relay information as to the whereabouts and plans of whatever enemy might be at hand. It was his misfortune that this enemy simply refused to let him know.

He was brilliant, brilliant as a flawless diamond, and just as hard. Give the man a problem in smuggling or in colonial subjugation and he'd have it cracked in jig-time. But this—! It was impossible.

Babe MacNeice, assistant extraordinary, consoled him with: "Barty, you've done all you can—all anybody can to stop them. It isn't your fault that they've got more on the ball than we have or could hope to have." A philosophical shrug of the shoulders. "It's a question of making room for our mysterious friends. They may not even strike at Earth. They may even turn back."

"They may even," said Bartok sourly, "turn into packages of Rinso. But don't count on it. Babe, this is a *spot*." There were dark circles under his eyes big enough to make barrels with.

"Then how about a joy-ride?" asked the girl. She looked absentmindedly at her fingernails.

Bartok was studying her closely. "Yeah," he said. "How about it?" He dropped into a chair. "Shoot," he said. "I know that mysterious air of yours."

In cloyingly sweet tones she replied: "Barty, darling, don't be an old silly. Aintcha gonna take itsy-bitsy Babesy for a ride?"

He stiffened as if he had been shot. "Sure," he said. "Why didn't you say it that way before?" They shot up to the roof on Bartok's private elevator and got into the commander's very private plane. As they took off he growled: "All right—spill it."

"I'm sorry I had to be sickening before you got the idea through your skull that I wanted absolute and complete privacy," she said, again her own brisk self. "But I have a notion."

"She has a notion," said Bartok expectantly.

"Take it easy. Only a hunch—still—where do you suppose there's enough room for a complete invasion-culture to develop without once coming into contact with the Earth culture till now, when it's at its height?"

"Space is plenty big, Babe. There's room for a thousand colonial systems as big as ours that we'd never even known of."

"Okay. That establishes the very first postulate. Those things are real. Therefore one doesn't have to be a psychic to investigate them. I am not psychic; ergo I can and will investigate them—in person." The girl avoided Bartok's eyes, and rattled on: "May be that my logic doesn't hold water, but I think I can handle the job. You wouldn't send me out there, and I know you're on the verge of saying that you'll go yourself.

"Well, you'll do no such damned thing, because they need you here as a relay center and someone whose statements to the public have some degree of authenticity. You're the only one in the whole blasted Navy that's worth a whoop in hell, and our benighted citizens know that as well as that yellow-bellied Admiral of the Fleet Fitzjames. Now that it's settled that you can't be spared we'll get around to the reasons why I, rather than any other agent from the Wing, should be assigned to this job."

"We can dispense with that," said Bartok wearily. "The fact is that next to me you're the best worker we have. So go, my child, with the blessings of this old hand."

"Cut the kidding," she snapped. "I mean business. Instead of the blessing of that old hand I'd like some advice from that old head."

"You can have my biography," said Bartok. *"Twenty Years a Spy, or, The Tale of a Voyeur Who Made Good."* He took from his pocket a small package. "This," he said, "I have been carrying for the moment when you'd pop your kind proposition. It's lightly sealed. In a moment of supreme danger you are to open it and be guided accordingly."

"Thanks," she said grimly. "Whatever it is, I believe I'll need it."

2

Bartok had never thought he could forget Babe, but that was just what he did in the next two months. It was the healthiest thing to do after she had hopped off in the big, fast one-seater that had been built especially for her jaunt. And Bartok was busy. Bartok was so busy that sometimes he thought he must be mad and living in a world of hallucinations on the reasonable grounds that nobody could be as overworked as he was and survive it.

Quietly and persistently the invaders kept moving in, establishing bases as far as anyone could see. The personnel of the Intelligence Wing were dispersed throughout the colonial system to restore order and prevent hampering of the Fleet as it was making ready to attack.

It was, of course, somewhat problematical as to just when that attack would come. The yellow-bellied Admiral Fitzjames was cowering in his flagship behind miles of steel and chewing his nails with sheer terror. For the ships he sent out—cruiser, destroyer, patroller, interceptor or miles-long battlewagon of the line—simply didn't come back. If they got within sighting distance of the invaders, they never survived to tell of it. And the ether was still jammed thick as apparently unlimited power could make it. Or was their power unlimited? Nobody knew.

It was bidding fair to be the most successful invasion of all times; just as the successful exploration is the one without adventure to mark its high points so this invasion was completely unchronicled by those invaded. They simply didn't know.

The galactic state of jitters is not easy to describe, but that's what it was. Tap a person on the shoulder and he'd turn with a shriek, fainting dead away. Suicide was on the upcurve, psychoses were increasing, messiahs popped up like mushrooms to lead the saved to glory and life everlasting. Bartok's men arrested these as fast as they could and even formed a few rival cults on the premise that a few million fanatic followers would be not at all bad things to have about, thus capitalizing on the stressful times.

Production and distribution of commodities bade fair to break down; it was Bartok's men who saved them. Acting on an old-time tradition, Intelligence men stood with drawn guns at the doors of factories, offering to blow the guts out of the man who stopped working.

The commander, on the fly between the stars of the colonial system, hadn't time to change his socks, let alone receive reports, notions and nostrums from cranks. Therefore it was natural that he refused to see the sailor from the flagship of the Fleet who said he had something awfully important to tell him, but that it wasn't official. It would have been better if Bartok had listened, for the sailor was going to tell him what the Admiral had said to his secretary while passing through the sailor's corridor. It had been: "By God, Hackenshaw, if something doesn't happen I sail for parts unknown and that beastly Bartok can fight his own war!" But the sailor never saw Bartok, in spite of deserting from the flagship and commandeering a lifeboat to make the trek from Venus to Algol. Instead he was shot for desertion when they picked him up in a math parlor where he was spending his last hours of life in the popular diversion of the day, capping formulas.

Hence it came as a staggering blow to Bartok to learn that the Fleet—all the lineships, that is—had simply taken off into space after raiding all the cities near at hand for women. They were headed, when he heard the news, for a minor star-cluster near the edge of the universe, and in the opposite direction of that from which the invaders were coming.

"Akh!" screamed Bartok when the news was broken to him. "The—the— the—" Words failed him. For hours afterwards he was in a daze. When he snapped out of it his first words were: "How about their commissariat?"

A subaltern tactfully informed him that they had made no provisions of any sort for food and supplies. A couple of hours after, Bartok was heard to observe: "They're going to starve to death." Which was the exact truth.

When the Fleet was eliminated from the scheme of things, Bartok found himself in more or less complete command of the colonial system. What vestiges of an executive committee there had been on Earth were quite shriveled away. Most of the committee had died of fright when they learned that the Fleet had left them high and dry.

The Intelligence Wing took unto itself all authority of life and death, officially, at last. They had been shooting leaders for quite a while, but it hadn't been with sanction and consent from above. The Wing expanded legally to cover with its charter all those tenders, lighters and graving-ships which had been left behind by the backbone of the Fleet. It made them the most powerful unit then in the colonial system, with fire-power to match any that sporadic rebellions might bring up.

Meanwhile the invaders progressed amazingly, almost forgotten as the cause of the system-wide crisis. They would have been totally lost from the public eye in the confusion had not reports come in about once a week that there was no further communication with such-and-such a sector. A few retired sailors moved forward pins on their star-maps and wondered how they managed it without once showing their hand.

And Bartok, who had once wished at least six times a day that he might have a free hand to remake the colonial system "—and obstacles be damned!"—was wondering if a really sound case could be made out against his willfully inhibiting—by means of an overdose of cyanide—his metabolic process.

It became apparent after four months of horrid confusion and blood-letting that things were quieting down, partly due to the able handling of the situation by the Intelligence Wing, which managed to keep the lid on practically everywhere and save the system from a complete premature smash-up, mostly because the populace had got used to the idea of being invaded, and successfully.

The ordinary round of living began again, with perhaps a little more feverish gaiety in the math parlors and a little less solemn conviction in the houses of worship. When Systemic Coordinator Bartok (the title had been hung on him while his back was turned; he still swore that he was nothing more than the Wing Commander acting under emergency powers) was able to take a vacation, the last of the internal trouble was officially over and done with. It had been ugly, certainly, but there had been episodes in the system's history even less attractive, as when the docks broke down during the days of the old Nine Planet Federation and there had actually been people starving to death and homeless.

It had occurred to Bartok as he lounged in his birthday suit with the other convalescents at Venus Springs, at the South Pole, that it would be touching and entirely appropriate to the spirit of the service to pay tribute to that deceased but magnificent female, Babe MacNeice.

He had arranged in his mind's eye a procession of notables to lay wreaths on a simple block of tungsten. He had just begun to work out the details of the speech he would make when there came a faint blatting noise from his wrist, the only part of him that was dressed, and that purely for utility. From the tiny transceiver came: "Barty, this is Central in New Metropole. The recorder in your private office has just begun to squawk. Who's it hooked up to?"

Bartok thought, furrowed his brow like a plowed field. "MacNeice," he said at last. "She's the only one hooked up to G7. I'm coming right up." In about the time it took him to dress he had called a plane, one of the very special racer models that he had fallen into using during the quick-moving past months when a second clipped was a score of lives saved.

In two hours flat he was slamming his office door behind him and jiggling the dials of the transceiver set on G7. No answer.

"Babe!" he snapped. "Are you in? Speak up!" No answer. His fingers jittery, he set the machine for rewind and replay. The letterhead spoke its piece tinnily, then the voice of Babe MacNeice snapped out briskly over the wires:

"Hello, Barty. This'll get to you sooner or later if you survive. It'd be too much to hope that I'd have you on the wire. Things must be pretty whacky down there—eh? I'll begin the report in good order.

"Took off—hell, you saw me. Went toward Arided without any trouble. Was hailed by a lot of freighters and sundry obsolete crates that had no business being in the ether. They seemed to think that I was going the wrong way. Few billion off Arided transceiving got muddy; then I slapped right into a zone where there simply wasn't any getting electricity or magnetism through at all.

"I sighted something in the deeps where there wouldn't be any Earthly ships around, so I did a quick fade. That's greekish for dodging and twisting so fast that I caught up with my own light-waves. After a few minutes of that I streaked straight behind a star. They probably hadn't seen anything move so fast, so they weren't ready. Damned good thing you put racing motors into my scow—otherwise you wouldn't be hearing this. For that matter, maybe you aren't. I'll get on.

"Those of my instruments that weren't chasing their tails because of the freak fields floating around there told me that I was being followed twist for twist. They had a tracer of some kind on me, because they didn't know where I was—just where I was going. Which isn't good. I stayed perfectly quiet, waiting for them to show up so I could shoot a torpedo at them. Show up they did. They had a funny craft, Barty—damned funny.

"It was open to space—just a skeleton ship. Not very big, either. Twenty times my length, about. Couldn't get any details, but there was something awfully peculiar about it. Anyway, I fired my torpedo, which was a mistake. It was a magnetic, and since the fields were thrown out of kilter it buzzed around, skinned past me once, and lost itself in space. Then they got gay and began throwing things at me—odd design, all of them. There was a skeleton-shell, like their ship, that packed an awful wallop when it exploded on time a thousand to my starboard. And they have rays.

"Yes, honest-to-God rays, like you read about in the story books! Not having the experience of an Aarn Munro or the ray-screens of a Richard Seaton, also like you read about in the story-books, I just ran like a scared rabbit. And then it occurred to me to open that mysterious package you handed me. I did so. What did I find? Another mysterious package inside it, with the note: 'So you think this is a tough spot? Think it over again before opening this.'

"It was a dirty trick, Barty, but it worked. I gave 'em the old one-two. 'One' being a cloud of smoke thick enough to confuse any tracer, 'two' being the space-mines you so thoughtfully shoved onto my scow at the last moment over my protests that I didn't want to be a flying powder-keg.

"I scattered the mines like bird-shot through the fog, and later had the intense satisfaction of seeing the ship that was on my tail explode in several pieces. That must make the first blood for our side in this war.

"I figure that blood-drawing saved my life for the moment, because exactly three hours later I was taken in tow by five more of their ships, same pattern and size. And that was where your little joke began to wear thin, because I opened the second box and found inside it another box and another note, which said: 'And this too shall pass away. Don't open this one unless the going's *really* bad. Cheer up; the worst is yet to come.' Who the hell do you think you are—Elbert Hubbard?

"As I was saying, they must have taken me prisoner to find out how I managed to knock off one of their boys. I couldn't see a thing except the skeletons of the ships and buggy creatures crawling around on the beams. Disgusting sensation, *really*.

"They landed me on one of Arided's planets, considerably one with an atmosphere. I got out in cold blood. My God! Barty, you never saw such a place! I don't know what it was like before; the usual colony-planet, I suppose, with labor-barracks and factories and semi-detached homes. But what I saw! Towers, Barty—all towers, spiring into the heavens like mountain peaks! I'll swear that most of them went way above the atmosphere line. And there was machinery, machinery, machinery—the ground was solid with it, heaving pistons, reaction jets like volcanoes. You don't know what I'm talking about, Barty. You have to see it. I'm sneaking in these last words under very trying circumstances—undergoing what the tinny brutes call purification. I'm going to see the master after being kept waiting for months, and whatever he decides to do with me goes on this world. They—"

The replay broke off. That was all. There weren't any sound-effects, not even the customary strangled wail, and glad enough Bartok was for that. Apparently she had been caught using the transceiver, and it had been smashed. Bartok straightened himself out tiredly. He'd kept the world fairly well up while the invasion was going on; there were others capable to take over now that the real crisis was past and there was nothing to do but wait for the taking-over by whatever the incredibly soulless creatures were that could ray all the life of a planet out of existence without a qualm.

He was getting old anyway. Time to make room for younger men. He might have a fling now as any time at applied mortality. He was going to build himself a cruiser and streak out to Arided and Babe.

3

His experience with the invaders was substantially the same as Babe's, though he reasoned—and correctly—that they would adjust for detection of a mine-field laid in a smoke-screen. Therefore he trotted out something so antiquated in concept that the invaders would surely have forgotten it, if ever they had known the device.

In the neighborhood of the first invasion port, the star in Cygnus, he encountered the phenomena Babe had described—utterly scrambled fields. Experimentally he held an electromagnet to a bit of steel. First there was no reaction, then the steel slid to the magnet. Then it hurled away from it like a bullet!

Throughout his experiments he hadn't failed to keep a lookout. The chime that signaled foreign bodies rang just once, and he trotted out his modernized version of the ancient Greek fire, forerunner of explosives. He squirted the blazing stuff through his rear jets in a wide-open pattern, obscuring the sight of him more effectively than any fog-cloud could have done. When his simpler instruments told him that the ship tailing him was quite lost in the Greek fire, he sprayed out a flock of tiny, powerfully explosive pellets.

There was one blast and it was all over; the tailing ship was dispersed through space, and whatever had been its crew was lost beyond repair.

Having effected this, Bartok set his motors to idling in the direction of the invasion star and lit a cigarette, waiting in almost perfect calm to be detected and taken in tow.

He did not have long to wait; there were half a dozen ships on him in twenty minutes. They clamped onto him what he realized must be the perfected tractor ray, so long celebrated in song and story and never yet seen on any spaceway till now.

As the tractors dragged him through space towards Arided he inspected very closely the ships that were applying it. They were six in number; as Babe had said, they were remarkable for the fact that they were quite open, being no more than a power-unit around which was built a framework containing emplacements for weapons of all sorts and conditions. There were catwalks as well, up and down which scuttled nasty things about the size and very nearly the shape of men.

Bartok was baffled by the metallic sheen of the things, when it hit him that they were robots. "Damned clever," he mused. "*Damned* clever indeed. They don't need air, they don't need a commissariat; all they need is orders and oil. I wish we'd thought up that gag a few centuries ago!"

They landed him skillfully and easily on the fourth planet. As Bartok looked about he realized slowly that Babe hadn't been under any hallucinations when she'd sworn that the engineering works that had been run up were the most remarkable things in the unknown universe. There were towers everywhere, great patches of concrete for landing and servicing ships; long lines of them hanging in the air waiting for room. Not one square inch of ground space except narrow catwalks could be seen free of any mechanism. What was not transmission gears was solar engine; what was not solar engine was unimaginably complex calculators clicking and buzzing away as robots stalked among them to tear off results and deliver them to the nearest building.

Bartok got out of his ship; immediately a gang of robots sprang to attention after the fashion of a guard of honor. Bartok had never seen robots before; there were enough hands to do the work of the colonial system and the social problems that would have been raised caused any experimentation with robots to be frowned on by the Executive Committee. And where was the Executive Committee today? God only knew. It was a very sure bet that if any of it was left, this residue would be mopped up by the despised and strictly forbidden mechanical men. Somebody had beaten the colonial system to the punch. But who could it be?

Commander Bartok nearly swooned when a robot-in-command came up to him and said in perfect, though toneless, English: "Pray excuse this temporary detention, Wing Commander. I can assure you that it shall be terminated in a brief while."

The brief while extended itself into three days before they would tell him what was going on. During that time he had the run of a delightful apartment which lacked only books and magazines for his comfort and relaxation. Apparently to substitute for them the robot-in-chief, or whoever was in charge, sent in robots whose specialty was brilliant conversation and repartee.

On the third day there entered the usual loquacious metal man. "Your bed is rumpled," he greeted Bartok. "I presume your feelings are the same at this opposite situation?"

"Opposite?" said Bartok, knowing from past experiences that the creature would explain some elaborately buried pun or double meaning in his greeting, which it did. There was some complex word-play with "smoothing the way" and "weighing the smooth," likewise a series of faintly ribald jests concerning the metal men themselves. Bartok, bored though he was, could not but admire the intensive manner in which they went about working a subject, whether the unified field theory or the technique of the double-take. He hadn't the ghost of a chance of holding up his own end of the conversation with this copper-plated specialist in the whimsical and amusing. He realized glumly that he wasn't specialized. He could crack a joke that would be a fairly good joke, but not half as funny or well-timed as the robot conversationalists; he could plan an attack, but not half as deadly as the robot fighters.

"Man," said Bartok, "is on the way out."

"Weight out the consequences," snapped the creature promptly, "and you'll find your remark substantially correct. Man too is correct—or, to put it differently, wrecked at the core."

"Where did you learn English?" asked Bartok feebly. He still didn't know. And on the answer to that question hung, he felt, a great deal.

But before the robot could make some horrible pun about "Where" and "wear out," one of the larger metal men entered, with a grave salutation to Bartok.

"I," it said, "am math-minder 817. Come with me, please. Subtend angularly this surd improperly vectorial." Piercing through the mathematical metaphors, Bartok realized that he was to say good-bye to the conversationalist, because he was going on a long journey.

"It's been nice meeting you," he said helplessly.

"Thanks," said the conversationalist. "And it's been nice metalling *you*." Another pun, worked in double reverse—surely a fitting note upon which to terminate the strange intellectual companionship of the cheerfully intent killer Bartok and the grimly humorous time-passer, chat-minder 32.

In the corridor the math-minder volunteered: "Bartok, you unfortunate particle, you're going to investigate some teleology."

"That being the science of first causes," brooked the Commander. "Do you mean that at last I'm getting to see your chief?"

"Not chief. First cause, I think you said. Accelerate through this aperture." The robot's paw gently shoved him through a very heavy metal door. Bartok found himself face-to-face with a very young man.

"Hello, kid," he said. "What brings you here? Captured?"

"Sort of," admitted the boy. "You're Mr. Bartok, aren't you?"

"Only in jest. Everybody calls me Barty." He was trying to put this young man at his ease; presumably he was destined for the same ordeal as he. Prestige of the genus homo demanded that he keep a stiff upper lip.

"Okay—Barty. I suppose you know why you're here?" The Commander stared in amazement. The boy had mounted a flight of steps to a throne-like affair that took up most of one wall. "I suppose you know why you're here?"

"Wha-a-at? Son, who the hell are *you?*"

The boy sagged down into the seat. "Unwilling master," he said, "of the most powerful army in the universe."

"Barty!" screamed someone.

"Babe!" Bartok screamed right back, catching the girl in mid-air as she hurled herself into his arms. After a few preliminaries he demanded, "Now what goes on here?"

"I'll introduce you," said Babe MacNeice, "Barty, this is Peter Allistair, from Capella. He's a bit young—twenty—but he's all right. It's not his fault, any of it."

"How can that be?" demanded the Commander. "If you're their boss? Do you know what your ships are doing?"

The boy sagged deeper into the chair, a haunted look on his face. "I sure do," he said. "And I'd give my right arm to stop it. But they won't believe me. I made the things, but they won't believe me when I say I want them to stop their colonization."

"You and who else?" asked Bartok. "You and who else made these billion or so robots?"

"I did," said the boy defiantly. "At least I did indirectly. You know there's a law against robot-experimentation—or was. Well, I couldn't let well enough alone. I had an idea about robots, so I came to Arided, which was the least populated section that I could find, and I built the damned thing."

"Built *what?*"

"A robot whose function was to manufacture robots. And that was the fatal error. You know how resolute those things are in carrying out their jobs." Bartok, thinking of three days of solid punning, nodded absently. "Well, this thing would have killed me if I'd tried to stop it. It said it had a divine mission to perform. So it built another flock of robot-manufacturing robots, which did the same.

"Then they began to branch out and make ordinary fetchers, mathematical workers and a few fighters. I got interested and designed a ship from the math workers' figures. And a stray remark I dropped to one of the proteans—those are the robot-makers—about fanaticism gave them the idea of turning out fighters with souls bonded over to me. I swear I didn't mean it that way! But look at the result.

"Every week or so one of the foreman robots brings me a list of the suns that are now under my imperial domination. And I can't explain to them because they aren't trouble-shooters specialized to straighten out a mess like this. And the proteans can't make a trouble-shooter because they aren't the originals, who simply manufactured for its own sake. The originals are all worn out and scrapped, and the ones that are turning out robots now are also fanatics with the idea of conquest for my greater glory.

"It's a chain of events that's been twisted around and tied to its tail. If you can find a way to stop it, let me know."

Entered a grim-faced fetching-foreman robot. "Worshipful master," it intoned, "your dominion is extended this week over twenty new suns. Accept this list, your children beseech." He handed to Allistair a sheet of names.

The boy let it fall to the floor. "Listen," he said passionately to the robot. "I don't want any more sheets like this. I don't want to conquer any suns or planets. I want the proteans to stop making robots. And above all I want you damned hunks of tin to stop calling me worshipful master! I'm not worshipful and I'm not anybody's master."

The foreman said methodically: "Worshipful master, despite your folly we are loyal and shall make you lord of all things that are. It is for your own good that we act. Do not forget the day when you said to the great protean 27: 'Fanaticism may be a good thing. If you machines had more of it, things'd be a lot easier for me. If I wanted I could be master of the universe with you machines, given that touch of lunatic bravery.'" The foreman stumped out of the room.

"Where they get those ideas I don't know!" shrilled Allistair. "I haven't the faintest idea of what their machinery's like. My God, what I set in motion when I built protean 1!"

"The trouble is," said Bartok broodingly, "that you have all the fire-power you need and no control whatsoever over it. And because of this lack of control you are now waging the most successful invasion of all time. I don't blame you—I know the spot you're in. You say you don't know a thing about these late-model robots?"

"Not a thing," almost sobbed the young man. "Not a thing. About twenty robot generations have gone by since I built protean 1, and they've been evolving like wildfire. A math robot thinks up a new law of electromagnetics, takes it to a physics robot, who applies it and takes it to a protean, who incorporates it into the next series of machines. That's the way it perpetuates itself. They invented death-rays, tractor rays—I don't know what-all!"

"You shouldn't have said fanaticism, son," worried Bartok. "That was the *one* concept that couldn't have been cancelled out by another suggestion. Because a full-fledged fanatic brooks no obstruction whatsoever to achieve his aim. Not even such a trifling detail as the fact that policy, orders and authority are opposed to that aim."

"And," said Babe, "these robots are the most full-fledged anythings you could hope to see. Did you meet one of their full-fledged humorists, Barty?" She shuddered. "Back on Earth we'd lynch a comedian who never let you catch a breath between gags."

"What'm I going to do?" asked the young man simply. "I can't have this on my conscience. I'll blow my brains out."

"Babe," said Bartok. "That package I gave you—still got it?"

"Yes, you old home-spun philosopher." She produced the package. "How many more to go in this Chinese ring trick?"

"Only one. Open it up." Curiously she tore off the seals and read from the neatly-printed card that was in the last of the boxes: "If you've given up hope be ready to die. If you haven't, try misdirection." She stared at the Commander. "And what is that supposed to mean?"

"The purpose of the little boxes was simply to jog your imagination in tight spots. There isn't any cure-all formula except the thing you carry in your skull. The human brain is a marvelous mechanism ..." He turned abruptly on Allistair. "Take me to see one of your proteans, son."

4

"Make tracks, Babe!" the Commander yelled, sprinting for the little cruiser in which he had arrived at Arided. He flung himself into the cabin a second after the girl and a split-second before the craft roared into the air.

"We are now," said Bartok, sprawled comfortably along the floor, "going to see the first and, I hope, the last real space-battle of its kind, fought with rays, disintegrators, ray-screens, inertialess drive and all the lunatic creations that crack-brained authors have been devising for the past few centuries. It is fitting and proper that this war should be fought, because no real lives are going to be lost and it will inevitably end in a stasis, both sides having wiped each other out."

"But can he put up a real fight?" asked the girl worriedly.

"Remember what I said about the human brain, Babe? It's bigger and better than any thinking-machinery, however elaborate. It's Nature's way, which is often best. Nature's way was to smash the protean and perform a simple operation that substituted Allistair's brain for its impulse-mechanism."

"What happens then?" she asked. "Not that I question that he ought to die in a good cause. He was a nice kid, but it was a flagrant piece of criminal negligence, monkeying with robots."

"Agreed. So he makes retribution in the best way he can. Those damned protean machines control about half a billion robots apiece after they manufacture them." He shuddered briefly as he remembered what the protean had looked like. Bartok has expected a neat, man-sized robot; instead it had been a million cubic feet of solid machinery.

The Commander yawned. "So, having taken over this protean's control factors with his own brain, he is in a position at last to direct the creatures he made. Of course he'll use his robots to fight the other robots. Here comes the first contact."

Far to the rear of the speedy craft there was a titanic flaring of lights and colors as two fighting ships met. Unimaginable forces roared from the searchlight-shaped projectors, impinged spectacularly on thinly glowing ray-screens. The ray screens went down after about three minutes of brilliant resistance and the ship vanished in a puff of vapor.

"Ugh! Disintegrators!" said the girl. "So they really had them!"

"Why not? To the mechanical mind everything is possible except commonsense. Instead of negotiating with Allistair they'll be confident of their superiority. And, fire for fire, they are stronger. Also their tactics are perfect. But young Allistair's tactics are bound to be faulty, which means that his ships will show up where they couldn't possibly be and blow whole protean units to hell and gone. His fire-control has the edge on them in that it's unpredictable."

Babe's eyes were astern, on the colossal battles going on; on the forces being released that made a Fleet flagship's biggest big guns seem feeble. "This part of space," she said, "will never be the same. It'll be like trying to plot a course inside the orbit of Mercury. I suggest that you proclaim that fact to the world."

Bartok grinned. "More speed," he said. "I wouldn't want to be caught in one of their fireballs. See that?" He pointed excitedly at a moving fleck of light that had separated itself from a monster flying fort just off the ground. "That thing's as big as Ceres—and it's explosive. More speed, Babe, if you value my hide."

"I do," she said shortly. "The colonial system, or what's left of it, is going to need a firm hand to tide over the stresses and strains of this robots' war."

"It shouldn't last for more than a few years," said Bartok. "When a force like that gets split, they haven't got time for anything else. And don't fret about the colonial system. There's a lot left of it yet, and it's right in the palm of my hand."

Babe MacNeice looked hard at the Commander. "If any other man," she said, "told me that, I'd make it a point to blow up this ship before we touched Earth. But I think you can be trusted."

"Algol ahead," said Bartok, pointing to a star-disk off the bow. "The outposts of empire, where they're chewing their nails about the strange noises and flashes to be seen and heard over the communications systems. We'll have to evacuate them nearer Alpha Centauri or thereabouts. Can't chance one of those fireballs hitting a planet of the system!"

He reached for a recorder and began barking orders into the mouthpiece. Before the cylinder was half grooved he had—verbally—evacuated three galactic sectors, reorganized the Intelligence Wing, scrapped the now-obsolete graving-docks where no battlewagon would ever dock again, converted the lighters and tenders of the Fleet into freight ships for emergency use, and begun to draft a new constitution for the All Earth and Colonies Federation.

"That," said Babe happily, "is the way I like to hear you talk."

Algol loomed ahead.

[*SF Quarterly* - February 1955]

The Adventurers

It was a fair-to-middling afternoon at the Adventurers Club. Cleveland was not pre-blitz London, so it looked little enough like a club; instead of oak paneling, the walls were a bilious green plaster. The waiters were not ancient and subservient Britons, but mostly flippant youths in overstarched mess-jackets; they wore chronometer wristwatches and finger-rings. The Club did not radiate the solid certainty of the fixed and immovable, which is supposed to be such a comfort to the English. It had, as a matter of fact, been established in its present two floors of a business district office building for only three months, having been evicted from a Lake Boulevard loft-building destined to be torn down and replaced by a garage and parking lot. The Adventurers, however, had done their best in the brief quarter-year to make the place homey. Mounted heads covered the walls like a rash, and an obviously non-functional fireplace had been assembled of polished marble slabs and over it written the Adventurers' motto: *"A Hearth and Home for Those Who Have Strayed Far from the Beaten Path."* On two new brass andirons in the center of the big fireplace were two small, uncharred logs crossed at an angle of 45 degrees.

If the Club was out of character, however, so were most of its members. Over his roast beef, the Man Who Had Known Dr. Cook was presiding. He puffed, between sleepy chews: "I tell you, sir, the Doctor is one of the most maligned men in the history of exploration. I have been a naval officer myself and know what it is to lay aloft in a gale, but I hold no sort or kind of brief for Peary, the man who crucified the Doctor." It was an impossible stretch of the imagination to picture the Man Who Had Known Dr. Cook laying aloft in a gale or, for that matter, doing anything but exactly what he was doing: sloppily chewing roast beef that would add to the many inches of his paunch and further lubricate his greasy face.

At a coffee-table, Captain Trevor-Beede was drinking, but not coffee. "Prunes," he was thickly saying to a waiter, "prunes are what you need. Here in the States, here you don't know how to cook prunes. Another b. and s." The waiter went for the b. and s., and Captain Trevor-Beede continued to address a moth-eaten springbok head opposite him: "prunes should be *soaked*. That's all there is to cooking prunes. Prunes should be *soaked* overnight, and then you should cook

them. That's all there is to cooking prunes." Captain Trevor-Beede was in the diplomatic service.

At a quarter slot-machine in a corner, under a mournful and rather small
walrus-head with chipped ivories, the Headshrinker was losing money with nervous haste. Click-whiz-whirr-bump, bump, bump. Click-whiz-whirr-bump, bump,
bump. Click-whiz-whirr-bump, bump, bump. A minor payoff broke the rhythm,
and he frowned as some quarters clunked into the scoop. He picked them up and
began again. Click-whiz-whirr-bump, bump, bump. He had contributed one of
the most unusual of the exhibits which filled a glass case against a wall: the doll-
size, shrunken body of his eight-year-old son, born to him during his captivity, by
his Jivaro wife. The son had died during the rigorous escape to the sea, and the
Headshrinker had used his acquired tribal knowledge to do a really superior job
of shrinking before he continued on his lighter way. Click-whiz-whirr-bump,
bump, bump. "I was delirious, you know," he would shyly explain, "but it's really
an ambitious bit of work. There weren't the right kind of ants there, you know,
and I was in a perfect funk for fear they'd botch the skin all up." He was a one.
Click-whiz-whirr-bump, bump, bump.

A waiter slouched up to a placid young man in a grey uniform. "Betcha
nervous," he said in a chummy way. "You want a drink?"

"Drink? Oh, no!" he said, very much surprised. He thought most people
knew by then that the Shield was a lot stronger guarantee of Sobriety than the
White Ribbon had ever been. But it was news to the waiter; he shrugged and walked
away, and the young man continued to wait in a comfortable armchair that would
have suggested a London club if its leather upholstery had not been Cocktail-
Lounge Red.

The Man Who Had Known Dr. Cook was through with his roast beef, his
baked potato, his chef's salad, his two baskets of French bread, his innumerable
pats of butter, his sweetened coffee and his pie à la mode. He wobbled over to the
young man and said: "I think we're ready for you now, youngster; the committee-
room's back there." He followed him and on the way the Man collected Captain
Trevor-Beede, who shambled after like a bear in tweeds, and the Headshrinker,
who had finally lost all his quarters. The youth had met them at dinner the day
before.

The committee-room had a long table and carved-oak chairs with the names
of late adventurers engraved on brass plates sunk into their backs. The Man closed
the door solemnly, wobbled to the head of the table and wedged himself into an
armchair. The others sat down, but the young man didn't know whether he was
supposed to until the Headshrinker cracked a nervous smile and jerked out the
chair next to him. "It's quite all right, you know," he told him; "we don't stand on
ceremony here."

He sat down, and the Man started: "I tell you, sir, it's good to see young
blood about the old Hearth and Home again. And I venture to say, there is none
of us who has strayed as far from the beaten path as you, youngster!"

The idea surprised him; he'd never thought of it that way. He tried to explain: "It's very good of you, sir, but I wouldn't put it like that at all. In fact, I

suppose I've stuck closer to beaten paths than anybody else here; why, I wouldn't be here at all if I hadn't!"

"Paradox," grunted Captain Trevor-Beede. "Let's have the rest of it and get on with the business."

"It's no paradox, sir. Why, where would I be if I'd got any ideas of my own about the trajectory, instead of taking Plot Room's word for it? I'd be nowhere, that's where I'd be, sir!"

"You needn't be modest with us, you know," said the nervous little Headshrinker. "After all, Lieutenant, over the dinner-table we do like to keep ourselves within bounds—" Here he shot a quick look at the Man, who went red. "—but we're out to assess your qualifications for membership."

"Yes, *Leff*-tenant," said Captain Trevor-Beede. "Now if you'd be so good as to give us some idea of the perils of your explorations—" He took out a pigskin notebook and pencil. That paralyzed the youth.

"Well, captain, they aren't really explorations, I guess. I just follow the plot on the table, keep her turned, you know, and then I set her down in the cradle; I generally sleep and play some handball until she's loaded up and ready to rip again. You should see that handball court they have up there at Luna Three! It's three times the right size, but you can really cover ground up there. Boy, can you hit some fancy shots!"

He was aware that the membership-committee was dismayed by something or other he had said, and hastened to make amends: "Oh, you shouldn't get the idea that handball's all I do, of course."

"Tennis?" asked the Headshrinker wryly.

"Now you're joking, sir. But the handball's necessary to keep in trim; sometimes you have to tune that table awfully fast!" He whistled and wiped his dry and healthy brow. "On the new involute approach it's all partial differentials, all the way in from Luna gravity—sometimes four sets of four every minute for fifteen minutes; you really have to whip out your approximations. And man, they'd better be right! It isn't like the old grazing-spiral days, I'll tell you that, sir!"

The Man Who Had Known Dr. Cook said: "You do—mathematics—up there? In the ship?"

"I should say so!" the young man told him enthusiastically. "Why, mathematics is all you've got up there—you can't see because the ports are closed; you can't hear anything because of the jets; and there isn't anything to hear. The instruments can't be sensitive and last out a take-off at the same time. All you have is what you know about the weight and the motion of the ship, and the weight and the motion of the Earth and Moon and Sun, so you have to take it from there. What have you got *except* mathematics? But the Plot Room does all the really tough stuff before the takeoff. All a pilot has to do is keep one jump ahead of the pointers under the table and keep his control-pointers lined up with them. That's what we call 'tuning the table,' maybe I should have said; and the way I told you, the first approximation's good enough for that."

"What if it isn't?" asked the Man.

The space pilot shrugged his grey-clad shoulders. "That's all," he said. "You take a trip." He thought of three classmates.

"If you were admitted," asked the Captain, "you would, of course, take a Club Flag to the moon on one of your—runs?"

The young man looked troubled. "I'm afraid I couldn't do that, sir," he said. "You know, it takes an awful lot of money to get there and back. I'd never be able to justify it to the supercargo. I ferry heavy elements, after all—it's the job." He thought a moment. "But tell you what, Captain! I could take a *microfilm* of the flag—wouldn't that be just as good?"

"Um," said the captain, who had planted his flag on Everest.

"Well, you know ..." said the Headshrinker, who had planted his flag on a ridgepole deeper in Jivaro country than any other white man had ever gone.

"Urg!" strangled the Man Who Had Known Dr. Cook. He had planted his flag at the North Pole, long before that hypothetical point was the Times Square of global air traffic.

The Captain asked bluntly, "What adventures have you had?"

"Adventures?" asked the young man. "Well, sir, the way I look at it, it's like this. People don't *have* adventures any more; if they do, they don't live to tell about it. You see, we're all so tied up and meshed together in a thing like the Moon-run—if one man makes a mistake, then he can make up for it himself. That's what you call an Adventure   doing something wrong and having it come out all right anyway because you used your head. But up there—well, if I do something wrong, then it's out of my hands right away. And I can't expect Plot Room, by dumb luck, to compensate for just that mistake of mine, can I? No; sir—the way it looks to me, Adventure is just about washed up, if you'll pardon me saying so."

The Headshrinker said flatly: "Mr. Chairman, I move that the examination be closed and the candidate's qualifications be voted on." He turned apologetically to the young man. "You'll have to leave now, you know—while we make up our minds."

"Oh, sure," said the space pilot. "And thank you, gentlemen, for a very interesting discussion." He walked out and carefully closed the door behind him.

"If he joins," said Captain Trevor-Beede immediately and explosively, "we'll all have to resign at once. 'Doing something wrong and having it come right anyway'!"

"Move to reject the candidate," said the Headshrinker.

"Question."

"Aye."

"Aye."

"Carried," sighed the Man. They sat in silence while he rang for a waiter. He told the man: "Please inform Space Service Lieutenant Allen that the committee had regretfully been compelled to ask him to withdraw his application for membership."

"Yes, sir," said the waiter.

Outside, he said to the young man in grey, "No dice, Lieutenant; they turned you down."

"Well, thanks," said the lieutenant regretfully. He walked slowly from the club, looking his last on the mounted heads and the case of curios and the unlit fire.

The members were awfully old-fashioned, he thought, but it would have been *such* a handy place to have lunch on Earth, when he happened to find a breathing-spell from the dull routine of his occupation!

[*Stirring Science Stories* - June 1941
as by S. D. Gottesman]

Kazam Collects

"Hail, jewel in the lotus," half whispered the stringy, brown person. His eyes were shut in holy ecstasy, his mouth pursed as though he were tasting the sweetest fruit that ever grew.

"Hail, jewel in the lotus," mumbled back a hundred voices in a confused backwash of sound. The stringy, brown person turned and faced his congregation. He folded his hands.

"Children of Hagar," he intoned. His voice was smooth as old ivory and had a mellow sheen about it.

"Children of Hagar, you who have found delight and peace in the bosom of the Elemental, the Eternal, the Un-knowingness that is without bounds, make Peace with me." You could tell by his very voice that the words were capitalized.

"Let our Word," intoned the stringy, brown person, "be spread. Let our Will be brought about. Let us destroy, let us mould, let us build. Speak low and make your spirits white as Hagar's beard." With a reverent gesture he held before them two handfuls of an unattached beard that hung from the altar.

"Children of Hagar, unite your Wills into One." The congregation kneeled as he gestured at them, gestured as one would at a puppy one was training to play dead.

The meeting hall—or rather, temple—of the Cult of Hagar was on the third floor of a little building on East 59th Street, otherwise almost wholly unused. The hall had been fitted out to suit the sometimes peculiar requirements of the unguessable Will-Mind-Urge of Hagar Inscrutable; that meant that there was gilded wood everywhere there could be, and strips of scarlet cloth hanging from the ceiling in circles of five. There was, you see, a Sanctified Ineffability about the unequal lengths of the cloth strips.

The faces of the congregation were varying studies in rapture. As the stringy, brown person tinkled a bell they rose and blinked absently at him as he waved a benediction and vanished behind a door covered with chunks of gilded wood.

The congregation began to buzz quietly.

"Well?" demanded one of another. "What did you think of it?"

"I dunno. Who's *he,* anyway?" A respectful gesture at the door covered with gilded wood.

"Kazam's his name. They say he hasn't touched food since he saw the Ineluctable Modality."

"What's *that?*"

Pitying smile. "You couldn't understand it just yet. Wait till you've come around a few more times. Then maybe you'll be able to read *his* book—'The Unravelling.' After that you can tackle the 'Isba Kazhlunk' that he found in the Siberian ice. It opened the way to the Ineluctable Modality, but it's pretty deep stuff—even for me."

They filed from the hall buzzing quietly, dropping coins into a bowl that stood casually by the exit. Above the bowl hung from the ceiling strips of red cloth in a circle of five. The bowl, of course, was covered with chunks of gilded wood.

Beyond the door the stringy, brown man was having a little trouble. Detective Fitzgerald would not be convinced.

"In the first place," said the detective, "you aren't licensed to collect charities. In the second place this whole thing looks like fraud and escheatment. In the third place this building isn't a dwelling and you'll have to move that cot out of here." He gestured disdainfully at an army collapsible that stood by the battered rolltop desk. Detective Fitzgerald was a big, florid man who dressed with exquisite neatness.

"I am sorry," said the stringy, brown man. "What must I do?"

"Let's begin at the beginning. The Constitution guarantees freedom of worship, but I don't know if they meant something like this. Are you a citizen?"

"No. Here are my registration papers." The stringy, brown man took them from a cheap, new wallet.

"Born in Persia. Name's Joseph Kazam. Occupation, scholar. How do you make that out?"

"It's a good word," said Joseph Kazam with a hopeless little gesture. "Are you going to send me away—deport me?"

"I don't know," said the detective thoughtfully. "If you register your religion at City Hall before we get any more complaints, it'll be all right."

"Ah," breathed Kazam. "Complaints?"

Fitzgerald looked at him quizzically. "We got one from a man named Rooney," he said. "Do you know him?"

"Yes. Runi Sarif is his real name. He has hounded me out of Norway, Ireland and Canada—wherever I try to reestablish the Cult of Hagar."

Fitzgerald looked away. "I suppose," he said matter-of-factly, "you have lots of secret enemies plotting against you."

Kazam surprised him with a burst of rich laughter. "I have been investigated too often," grinned the Persian, "not to recognize that one. You think I'm mad."

"No," mumbled the detective, crestfallen. "I just wanted to find out. Anybody running a nut cult's automatically reserved a place in Bellevue."

"Forget it, sir. I spit on the Cult of Hagar. It is my livelihood, but I know better than any man that it is a mockery. Do you know what our highest mystery is? The Ineluctable Modality." Kazam sneered.

"That's Joyce," said Fitzgerald with a grin. "You have a sense of humor, Mr. Kazam. That's a rare thing in the religious."

"Please," said Joseph Kazam. "Don't call me that. I am not worthy—the noble, sincere men who work for their various faiths are my envy. I have seen too much to be one of them."

"Go on," said Fitzgerald, leaning forward. He read books, this detective, and dearly loved an abstract discussion.

The Persian hesitated. "I," he said at length, "am an occult engineer. I am a man who can make the hidden forces work."

"Like staring a leprechaun in the eye till he finds you a pot of gold?" suggested the detective with a chuckle.

"One manifestation," said Kazam calmly. "Only one."

"Look," said Fitzgerald. "They still have that room in Bellevue. Don't say that in public—stick to the Ineluctable Modality if you know what's good for you."

"Tut," said the Persian regretfully. "He's working on you."

The detective looked around the room. "Meaning who?" he demanded.

"Runi Sarif. He's trying to reach your mind and turn you against me."

"Balony," said Fitzgerald coarsely. "You get yourself registered as a religion in twenty-four hours; then find yourself a place to live. I'll hold off any charges of fraud for a while. Just watch your step." He jammed a natty Homburg down over his sandy hair and strode pugnaciously from the office.

Joseph Kazam sighed. Obviously the detective had been disappointed.

That night, in his bachelor's flat, Fitzgerald tossed and turned uneasily on his modern bed. Being blessed with a sound digestion able to cope even with a steady diet of chain-restaurant food and the soundest of consciences, the detective was agitated profoundly by his wakefulness.

Being, like all bachelors, a cautious man, he hesitated to dose himself with the veronal he kept for occasions like this, few and far between though they were. Finally, as he heard the locals pass one by one on the El a few blocks away and then heard the first express of the morning, with its higher-pitched bickering of wheels and quicker vibration against the track, he stumbled from bed and walked dazedly into his bathroom, fumbled open the medicine chest.

Only when he had the bottle and had shaken two pills into his hand did he think to turn on the light. He pulled the cord and dropped the pills in horror. They weren't the veronal at all, but an old prescription which he had thriftily kept till they might be of use again.

Two would have been a fatal overdose. Shakily Fitzgerald filled a glass of water and drank it down, spilling about a third on his pajamas. He replaced the pills and threw away the entire bottle. You never know when a thing like that might happen again, he thought—too late to mend.

Now thoroughly sure that he needed the sedative, he swallowed a dose. By the time he had replaced the bottle he could scarcely find his way back to the bed, so sleepy was he.

He dreamed then. Detective Fitzgerald was standing on a plain, a white plain, that was very hot. His feet were bare. In the middle distance was a stone tower above which circled winged skulls—bat-winged skulls, whose rattling and flapping he could plainly hear.

From the plain—he realized then that it was a desert of fine, white sand—spouted up little funnels or vortices of fog in a circle around him. He began to run very slowly, much slower than he wanted to. He thought he was running away from the tower and the vortices, but somehow they continued to stay in his field of vision. No matter where he swerved the tower was always in front and the little twisters around him. The circle was growing smaller around him, and he redoubled his efforts to escape.

Finally he tried flying, leaping into the air. Though he drifted for yards at a time, slowly and easily, he could not land where he wanted to. From the air the vortices looked like petals of a flower, and when he came drifting down to the desert he would land in the very center of the strange blossom.

Again he ran, the circle of foggy cones following still, the tower still before him. He felt with his bare feet something tinglingly clammy. The circle had contracted to the point of coalescence, had gripped his two feet like a trap.

He shot into the air and headed straight for the tower. The creaking, flapping noise of the bat-winged skulls was very much louder now. He cast his eyes to the side and was just able to see the tips of his own black, flapping membranes.

As though regular nightmares—always the same, yet increasingly repulsive to the detective—were not enough woe for one man to bear, he was troubled with a sudden, appalling sharpness of hearing. This was strange, for Fitzgerald had always been a little deaf in one ear. ·

The noises he heard were distressing things, things like the ticking of a wristwatch two floors beneath his flat, the gurgle of water in sewers as he walked the streets, the humming of underground telephone wires. Headquarters was a bedlam with its stentorian breathing, the machine-gun fire of a telephone being dialed, the howitzer crash of a cigarette case snapping shut.

He had his bedroom soundproofed and tried to bear it. The inches of fiberboard helped a little; he found that he could focus his attention on a book and practically exclude from his mind the regular swish of air in his bronchial tubes, the thudding at his wrists and temples, the slushing noise of food passing through his transverse colon.

Fitzgerald did not go mad for he was a man with ideals. He believed in clean government and total extirpation of what he fondly believed was a criminal class which could be detected by the earlobes and other distinguishing physical characteristics.

He did not go to a doctor because he knew that the word would get back to headquarters that Fitzgerald heard things and would probably begin to see things pretty soon and that it wasn't good policy to have a man like that on the force.

The detective read up on the later Freudians, trying to interpret the recurrent dream. The book said that it meant he had been secretly in love with a third cousin on his mother's side and that he was ashamed of it now and wanted to die, but that he was afraid of heavenly judgment. He knew that wasn't so; his mother had had no relations and detective Fitzgerald wasn't afraid of anything under the sun.

After two weeks of increasing horror he was walking around like a corpse, moving by instinct and wearily doing his best to dodge the accidents that seemed to trail him. It was then that he was assigned to check on the Cult of Hagar. The records showed that they had registered at City Hall, but records don't show everything.

He walked in on the cult during a service and dully noted that its members were more prosperous in appearance than they had been, and that there were more women present. Joseph Kazam was going through precisely the same ritual that the detective had last seen.

When the last bill had fallen into the pot covered with gilded wood and the last dowager had left, Kazam emerged and greeted the detective.

"Fitzgerald," he said, "you damned fool, why didn't you come to me in the first place?"

"For what?" asked the detective, loosening the waxed cotton plugs in his ears.

The stringy, brown man chuckled. "Your friend Rooney's been at work on you. You hear things. You can't sleep and when you do—"

"That's plenty," interjected Fitzgerald. "Can you help me out of this mess I'm in?"

"Nothing to it. Nothing at all. Come into the office."

Dully the detective followed, wondering if the cot had been removed

The ritual that Kazam performed was simple in the extreme, but a little revolting. The mucky aspects of it Fitzgerald completely excused when he suddenly realized that he no longer heard his own blood pumping through his veins, and that the asthmatic wheeze of the janitor in the basement was now private to the janitor again.

"How does it feel?" asked Kazam concernedly.

"Magnificent," breathed the detective, throwing away his cotton plugs. "Too wonderful for words."

"I'm sorry about what I had to do," said the other man, "but that was to get your attention principally. The real cure was mental projection." He then dismissed the bedevilment of Fitzgerald with an airy wave of the hand. "Look at this," he said.

"My God!" breathed the detective. "Is it real?"

Joseph Kazam was holding out an enormous diamond cut into a thousand glittering facets that shattered the light from his desk lamp into a glorious blaze of color.

"This," said the stringy, brown man, "is the Charity Diamond."

"You mean," sputtered the detective, "you got it from—"

"The very woman," said Kazam hastily. "And of her own free will. I have a receipt: 'For the sum of one dollar in payment for the Charity Diamond. Signed, Mrs.—'"

"Yes," said the detective. "Happy days for the Sons of Hagar. Is this what you've been waiting for?"

"This," said Kazam, curiously turning the stone in his hand, "is what I've been hunting over all the world for years. And only by starting a nut cult could I get it. Thank God it's legal."

"What are you going to do now?" asked the detective.

"Use the diamond for a little trip. You will want to come along, I think. You'll have a chance to meet your Mr. Rooney."

"Lead on," said Fitzgerald. "After the past two weeks I can stand anything."

"Very well." Kazam turned out the desk lamp.

"It glows," whispered Fitzgerald. He was referring to the diamond, over whose surface was passing an eerie blue light, like the invisible flame of anthracite.

"I'd like you to pray for success, Mr. Fitzgerald," said Kazam. The detective began silently to go over his brief stock of prayers. He was barely conscious of the fact that the other man was mumbling to himself and caressing the diamond with long, wiry fingers.

The shine of the stone grew brighter yet; strangely, though, it did not pick out any of the details of the room.

Then Kazam let out an ear-splitting howl. Fitzgerald winced, closing his eyes for just a moment. When he opened them he began to curse in real earnest.

"You damned rotter!" he cried. "Taking me here—"

The Persian looked at him coldly and snapped: "Easy, man! This is real—look around you!"

The detective looked around and saw that the tower of stone was rather far in the distance, farther than in his dreams, usually. He stooped and picked up a handful of the fine white desert sand, let it run through his fingers.

"How did you get us here?" he asked hoarsely.

"Same way I cured you of Runi Sarif's curse. The diamond has rare powers to draw the attention. Ask any jewel-thief. This one, being enormously expensive, is so completely engrossing that unsuspected powers of concentration are released. That, combined with my own sound knowledge of a particular traditional branch of psychology, was enough to break the walls down which held us pent to East 59th Street."

The detective was beginning to laugh, flatly and hysterically. "I come to you hag-ridden, you first cure me and then plunge me twice as deep into Hell, Kazam! What's the good of it?"

"This isn't Hell." said the Persian matter-of-factly. "It isn't Hell, but it isn't Heaven either. Sit down and let me explain." Obediently Fitzgerald squatted on the sand. He noticed that Kazam cast an apprehensive glance at the horizon before beginning.

"I was born in Persia," said Kazam, "but I am not Persian by blood, religion or culture. My life began in a little mountain village where I soon saw that I was treated not as the other children were. My slightest wish could command the elders of the village, and if I gave an order it would be carried out.

"The reasons for all this were explained to me on my thirteenth birthday by an old man—a very old man whose beard reached to his knees. He said that he had in him only a small part of the blood of Kaidar, but that I was almost full of it, that there was little human blood in me.

"I cried and screamed and said that I didn't want to be Kaidar, that I just wanted to be a person. I ran away from the village after another year, before they began to teach me their twisted, ritualistic versions of occult principles. It was this flight which saved me from the usual fate of the Kaidar; had I stayed I would have become a celebrated miracle man, known for all of two hundred miles or so, curing the sick and cursing the well. My highest flight would be to create a new Islamic faction—number three hundred and eighty-two, I suppose.

"Instead I knocked around the world. And Lord, got knocked around too. Tramp steamers, maritime strike in Frisco, the Bela Kun regime in Hungary—I wound up in North Africa when I was about thirty years old.

"I was broke, as broke as any person could be and stay alive. A Scotswoman picked me up, hired me, taught me mathematics. I plunged into it, algebra, conics, analytics, calculus, relativity. Before I was done, I'd worked out wave-mechanics three years before that Frenchman had even begun to think about it.

"When I showed her the set of differential equations for the carbon molecule, all solved, she damned me for an unnatural monster and threw me out. But she'd given me the beginnings of mental discipline, and done it many thousands of times better than they could have in that Persian village. I began to realize what I was.

"It was then that I drifted into the nut cult business. I found out that all you need for capital is a stock of capitalized abstract qualities, like All-Knowingness, Will-Mind-Urge, Planetude and Exciliation. With that to work on I can make my living almost anywhere on the globe.

"I met Runi Sarif, who was running an older-established sect, the Pan-European Astral Confederation of Healers. He was a Hindu from the Punjab plains in the north of India. Lord, what a mind he had! He worked me over quietly for three months before I realized what was up.

"Then there was a little interview with him. He began with the complicated salute of the Astral Confederation and got down to business. 'Brother Kazam,' he said, 'I wish to show you an ancient sacred book I have just discovered.' I laughed, of course. By that time I'd already discovered seven ancient books by myself, already-translated into the language of the country I would be working at the time. The 'Isba Kazhlunk' was the most successful; that's the one I found preserved in the hide of a mammoth in a Siberian glacier.

"Runi looked sour. 'Brother Kazam,' said he, 'do not scoff. Does the word *Kaidar* mean anything to you?' I played dumb and asked whether it was something out of the third chapter of the Lost Lore of Atlantis, but I remembered ever so faintly that I had been called that once.

"'A Kaidar,' said Runi, 'is an atavism to an older, stronger people who once visited this plane and left their seed. They can be detected by'—he squinted at me sharply—'by a natural aptitude for occult pursuits. They carry in their minds learning undreamable by mortals. Now, Brother Kazam, if we could only find a Kaidar ...'

"'Don't carry yourself away,' I said. 'What good would that be to us?'

"Silently he produced what I'll swear was actually an ancient sacred book. And I wouldn't be surprised if he'd just discovered it, moreover. It was the psaltery of a small, very ancient sect of Edomites who had migrated beyond the Euphrates and died out. When I'd got around the rock-Hebrew it was written in, I was very greatly impressed. They had some noble religious poems, one simply blistering exorcism and anathema, a lot of tedious genealogy in verse form. And they had a didactic poem on the Kaidar, based on one who had turned up in their tribe.

"They had treated him horribly—chained him to a cave wall and used him for a sort of male Sibyl. They found out that the best way to get him to prophesy was to show him a diamond. Then, one sad day, they let him touch it. Blam! He vanished, taking two of the rabbis with him. The rabbis came back later; appeared in broad daylight raving about visions of Paradise they had seen.

"I quite forgot about the whole affair. At that time I was obsessed with the idea that I would become the Rockefeller of occultism—get disciples, train them carefully and spread my cult. If Mohammed could do it, why not I? To this day I don't know the answer.

"While I was occupying myself with grandiose daydreams, Runi was busily picking over my mind. To a natural cunning and a fantastic ability to concentrate he added what I unconsciously knew, finally achieving adequate control of many factors.

"Then he stole a diamond, I don't know where, and vanished. One presumes he wanted to have that Paradise that the rabbis told of for his very own. Since then he has been trying to destroy me, sending out messages, dominating other minds on the Earthly plane—if you will excuse the jargon—to that end. He reached you, Fitzgerald, through a letter he got someone else to write and post, then when you were located and itemized he could work on you directly.

"You failed him, and he, fearing I would use you, tried to destroy you by heightening your sense of hearing and sending you visions nightly of this plane. It would destroy any common man; we are very fortunate that you are extraordinarily tough in your psychological fiber.

"Since then I have been dodging Runi Sarif, trying to get a diamond big enough to send me here through all the barriers he has prepared against my coming. You helped me very greatly." Again Kazam cast an apprehensive look at the horizon.

The detective looked around slowly. "Is this a paradise?" he asked. "If so I've been seriously misled by my Sunday School teachers." He tried weakly to smile.

"That is one of the things I don't understand—yet," said the Persian "And this is another unpleasantness which approaches."

Fitzgerald stared in horror at the little spills of fog which were upending themselves from the sand. He had the ghastly, futile dream sensation again.

"Don't try to get away from them," snapped Kazam. "Walk *at* the things." He strode directly and pugnaciously at one of the little puffs, and it gave way before him and they were out of the circle.

"That was easy," said the detective weakly.

Suddenly before them loomed the stone tower. The winged skulls were nowhere to be seen.

Sheer into the sky reared the shaft, solid and horribly hewn from grey granite, rough-finished on the outside. The top was shingled to a shallow cone, and embrasures were black slots in the wall.

Then, Fitzgerald never knew how, they were inside the tower, in the great round room at its top. The winged skulls were perched on little straggling legs along a golden rail. Aside from the flat blackness of their wings all was crimson and gold in that room. There was a sickly feeling of decay and corruption about it, a thing that sickened the detective.

Hectic blotches of purple marked the tapestries that hung that circular wall, blotches that seemed like the high spots in rotten meat. The tapestries themselves the detective could not look at again after one glance. The thing he saw, sprawling over a horde of men and women, drooling flame on them, a naked figure still between its jaws, colossal, slimy paws on a little heap of human beings, was not a pretty sight.

Light came from flambeaux in the wall, and the torches cast a sickly, reddish-orange light over the scene. Thin curls of smoke from the sockets indicated an incense.

And lastly there was to be seen a sort of divan, heaped with cushions in fantastic shapes. Reclining easily on them was the most grotesque, abominable figure Fitzgerald had ever seen. It was a man, had been once. But incredible incontinence had made the creature gross and bloated with what must have been four hundred pounds of fat. Fat swelled out the cummerbund that spanned the enormous belly, fat welted out the cheeks so that the ears of the creature could not be seen beneath the embroidered turban, gouts of fat rolled in a blubbery mass about the neck like the wattles of a dead cockerel.

"Ah," hissed Joseph Kazam. "Runi Sarif ..." He drew from his shirt a little sword or big knife from whose triangular blade glinted the light of the flambeaux.

The suety monster quivered as though maggots were beneath his skin. In a voice that was like the sound a butcher makes when he tears the fat belly from a hog's carcass, Runi Sarif said: "Go—go back. Go back—where you came from—" There was no beginning or ending to the speech. It came out between short, grunting gasps for breath.

Kazam advanced, running a thumb down the knife-blade. The monster on the divan lifted a hand that was like a bunch of sausages. The nails were a full half-inch below the level of the skin. Afterwards Fitzgerald assured himself that the hand was the most repellent aspect of the entire affair.

With creaking, flapping wingstrokes the skulls launched themselves at the Persian, their jaws clicking stonily. Kazam and the detective were in the middle of a cloud of flying jaws that were going for their throats.

Insanely Fitzgerald beat at the things, his eyes shut. When he looked they were lying on the floor. He was surprised to see that there were just four of them.

He would have sworn to a dozen at least. And they all four bore the same skillfully delivered slash mark of Kazam's knife.

There was a low, choking noise from the monster on the divan. As the detective stared, Kazam stepped up the first of the three shallow steps leading to it.

What followed, detective Fitzgerald could never disentangle. The lights went out, yet he could plainly see. He saw that the monstrous Runi Sarif had turned into a creature such as he had seen on the tapestry, and he saw that so had Kazam, save that the thing which was the Persian carried in one paw a blade.

They were no longer in the tower room, it seemed, nor were they on the white desert below. They were hovering in a roaring squalling tumult, in a confusion of spheres which gently collided and caromed off each other without noise.

As the detective watched, the Runi monster changed into one of the spheres and so, promptly, did Kazam. On the side of the Kazam sphere was the image of the knife. Tearing at a furious rate through the jostling confusion and blackness Fitzgerald followed, and he never knew how.

The Kazam sphere caught the other and spun dizzily around it, with a screaming noise which rose higher and higher. As it passed the top threshold of hearing, both spheres softened and spread into black, crawling clouds. Suspended in the middle of one was the knife.

The other cloud knotted itself into a furious, tight lump and charged the one which carried the blade. It hurtled into and through it, impaling itself.

Fitzgerald shook his head dizzily. They were in the tower room, and Runi Sarif lay on the divan with a cut throat. The Persian had dropped the knife, and was staring with grim satisfaction at the bleeding figure.

"Where were we?" stuttered the detective. "Where—?" At the look in Kazam's eyes he broke off and did not ask again.

The Persian said: "He stole my rights. It is fitting that I should recover them, even thus. In one plane—there is no room for two in contest."

Jovially he clapped the detective on the shoulder. "I'll send you back now. From this moment I shall be a card in your Bureau of Missing Persons. Tell whatever you wish—it won't be believed."

"It was supposed to be a paradise," said the detective.

"It is," said Kazam. "Look."

They were no longer in the tower, but on a mossy bank above a river whose water ran a gamut of pastels, changing hues without end. It tinkled out something like a Mozart sonata and was fragrant with a score of scents.

The detective looked at one of the flowers on the bank. It was swaying of itself and talking quietly in a very small voice, like a child.

"They aren't clever," said Kazam, "but they're lovely."

Fitzgerald drew in his breath sharply as a flight of butterfly things passed above. "Send me away," he gasped. "Send me away now or I'll never be able to go. I'd kill you to stay here in another minute."

Kazam laughed. "Folly," he said. "Just as the dreary world of sand and a tower that—a certain unhappy person—created was his and him, so this paradise is me and mine. My bones are its rock, my flesh is its earth, my blood is its waters, my mind is its living things."

As an unimaginably glowing drift of crystalline, chiming creatures loped across the whispering grass of the bank, Kazam waved one hand in a gesture of farewell.

Fitzgerald felt himself receding with incredible velocity, and for a brief moment saw an entire panorama of the world that was Kazam. Three suns were rising from three points of the horizon, and their slanting rays lit a paradise whose only inglorious speck was a stringy, brown man on a riverbank. Then the man vanished as though he had been absorbed into the ground.

[*Galaxy* - April 1951]

The Marching Morons

Some things had not changed. A potter's wheel was still a potter's wheel and clay was still clay. Efim Hawkins had built his shop near Goose Lake, which had a narrow band of good fat clay and a narrow beach of white sand. He fired three bottle-nosed kilns with willow charcoal from the wood lot. The wood lot was also useful for long walks while the kilns were cooling; if he let himself stay within sight of them, he would open them prematurely, impatient to see how some new shape or glaze had come through the fire, and—*ping!*—the new shape or glaze would be good for nothing but the shard pile back of his slip tanks.

A business conference was in full swing in his shop, a modest cube of brick, tile-roofed, as the Chicago–Los Angeles "rocket" thundered overhead—very noisy, very swept-back, very fiery jets, shaped as sleekly swift-looking as an airborne barracuda.

The buyer from Marshall Field's was turning over a black-glazed one-liter carafe, nodding approval with his massive, handsome head. "This is real pretty," he told Hawkins and his own secretary, Gomez-Laplace. "This has got lots of what ya call real est'etic principles. Yeah, it's real pretty."

"How much?" the secretary asked the potter.

"Seven-fifty each in dozen lots," said Hawkins. "I ran up fifteen dozen last month."

"They are real est'etic," repeated the buyer from Field's. "I will take them all."

"I don't think we can do that, doctor," said the secretary. "They'd cost us $1,350. That would leave only $532 in our quarter's budget. And we still have to run down to East Liverpool to pick up some cheap dinner sets."

"Dinner sets?" asked the buyer, his big face full of wonder.

"Dinner sets. The department's been out of them for two months now. Mr. Garvy-Seabright got pretty nasty about it yesterday. Remember?"

"Garvy-Seabright, that meat-headed bluenose," the buyer said contemptuously. "He don't know nothin' about est'etics. Why for don't he lemme run my own department?" His eye fell on a stray copy of *Whambozambo Comix* and he sat

372

down with it. An occasional deep chuckle or grunt of surprise escaped him as he turned the pages.

Uninterrupted, the potter and the buyer's secretary quickly closed a deal for two dozen of the liter carafes. "I wish we could take more," said the secretary, "but you heard what I told him. We've had to turn away customers for ordinary dinnerware because he shot the last quarter's budget on some Mexican piggy banks some equally enthusiastic importer stuck him with. The fifth floor is packed solid with them."

"I'll bet they look mighty est'etic."

"They're painted with purple cacti."

The potter shuddered and caressed the glaze of the sample carafe.

The buyer looked up and rumbled, "Ain't you dummies through yakkin' yet? What good's a seckertary for if'n he don't take the burden of *de*-tail off'n my back, harh?"

"We're all through, doctor. Are you ready to go?"

The buyer grunted peevishly, dropped *Whambozambo Comix* on the floor and led the way out of the building and down the log corduroy road to the highway. His car was waiting on the concrete. It was, like all contemporary cars, too low-slung to get over the logs. He climbed down into the car and started the motor with a tremendous sparkle and roar.

"Gomez-Laplace," called out the potter under cover of the noise, "did anything come of the radiation program they were working on the last time I was on duty at the Pole?"

"The same old fallacy," said the secretary gloomily. "It stopped us on mutation, it stopped us on culling, it stopped us on segregation, and now it's stopped us on hypnosis."

"Well, I'm scheduled back to the grind in nine days. Time for another firing right now. I've got a new luster to try ..."

"I'll miss you. I shall be 'vacationing'—running the drafting-room of the New Century Engineering Corporation in Denver. They're going to put up a two-hundred-story office building, and naturally somebody's got to be on hand."

"Naturally," said Hawking with a sour smile.

There was an ear-piercingly sweet blast as the buyer leaned on the horn button. Also, a yard-tall jet of what looked like flame spurted up from the car's radiator cap; the car's power plant was a gas turbine, and had no radiator.

"I'm coming, doctor," said the secretary dispiritedly. He climbed down into the car and it whooshed off with much flame and noise.

The potter, depressed, wandered back up the corduroy road and contemplated his cooling kilns. The rustling wind in the boughs was obscuring the creak and mutter of the shrinking refractory brick. Hawkins wondered about the number two kiln—a reduction fire on a load of lusterware mugs. Had the clay chinking excluded the air? Had it been a properly smoky blaze? Would it do any harm if he just took one close—?

Common sense took Hawkins by the scruff of the neck and yanked him over to the tool shed. He got out his pick and resolutely set off on a prospecting jaunt to a hummocky field that might yield some oxides. He was especially low on coppers.

The long walk left him sweating hard, with his lust for a peek into the kiln quiet in his breast. He swung his pick almost at random into one of the hummocks; it clanged on a stone which he excavated. A largely obliterated inscription said:

ERSITY OF CHIC
OGICAL LABO
ELOVED MEMORY OF
KILLED IN ACT

The potter swore mildly. He had hoped the field would turn out to be a cemetery, preferably a once-fashionable cemetery full of once-massive bronze caskets moldered into oxides of tin and copper.

Well, hell, maybe there was some around anyway.

He headed lackadaisically for the second largest hillock and sliced into it with his pick. There was a stone to undercut and topple into a trench, and then the potter was very glad he'd stuck at it. His nostrils were filled with the bitter smell and the dirt was tinged with the exciting blue of copper salts. The pick went *clang!*

Hawkins, puffing, pried up a stainless steel plate that was quite badly stained and was also marked with incised letters. It seemed to have pulled loose from rotting bronze there were rivets on the back that brought up flakes of green patina. The potter wiped off the surface dirt with his sleeve, turned it to catch the sunlight obliquely and read:

"HONEST JOHN BARLOW"

"Honest John," famed in university annals, represents a challenge which medical science has not yet answered: revival of a human being accidentally thrown into a state of suspended animation.

In 1988 Mr. Barlow, a leading Evanston real estate dealer, visited his dentist for treatment of an impacted wisdom tooth. His dentist requested and received permission to use the experimental anæsthetic Cycloparadimethanol-B-7, developed at the University.

After administration of the anæsthetic, the dentist resorted to his drill. By freakish mischance, a short-circuit in his machine delivered 220 volts of 60-cycle current into the patient. (In a damage suit instituted by Mrs. Barlow against the dentist, the University and the makers of the drill, a jury found for the defendants.) Mr. Barlow never got up from the dentist's chair and was assumed to have died of poisoning, electrocution or both.

Morticians preparing him for embalming discovered, however, that their subject was—though certainly not living—just as certainly not dead.

The University was notified and a series of exhaustive tests was begun, including attempts to duplicate the trance state on volunteers. After a bad run of seven cases which ended fatally, the attempts were abandoned.

Honest John was long an exhibit at the University museum, and livened many a football game as mascot of the University's Blue Crushers. The bounds of taste were overstepped, however, when a pledge to Sigma Delta Chi was ordered in '03 to "kidnap" Honest John from his loosely guarded glass museum case and introduce him into the Rachel Swanson Memorial Girl's Gymnasium shower room.

On May 22nd, 2003, the University Board of Regents issued the following order: "By unanimous vote, it is directed that the remains of Honest John Barlow be removed from the University museum and conveyed to the University's Lieutenant James Scott III Memorial Biological Laboratories and there be securely locked in a specially prepared vault. It is further directed that all possible measures for the preservation of these remains be taken by the Laboratory administration and that access to these remains be denied to all persons except qualified scholars authorized in writing by the Board. The Board reluctantly takes this action in view of recent notices and photographs in the nation's press which, to say the least, reflect but small credit upon the University."

It was far from his field, but Hawkins understood what had happened—an early and accidental blundering onto the bare bones of the Levantman shock anæsthesia, which had since been replaced by other methods. To bring subjects out of Levantman shock, you let them have a squirt of simple saline in the trigeminal nerve. Interesting! And now about that bronze—

He heaved the pick into the rotting green salts, expecting no resistance, and almost fractured his wrist. *Something* down there was *solid*. He began to flake off the oxides.

A half hour of work brought him down to phosphor bronze, a huge casting of the almost incorruptible metal. It had weakened structurally over the centuries; he could fit the point of his pick under a corroded boss and pry off great creaking and grumbling striæ of the stuff.

Hawkins wished that he had an archaeologist with him, but didn't dream of returning to his shop and calling one to take over the find. He was an all-around man: by choice and in his free time, an artist in clay and glaze; by necessity, an automotive, electronics and atomic engineer who could also swing a project in traffic control, individual and group psychology, architecture or tool design. He didn't yell for a specialist every time something out of his line came up; there were so few with so much to do ...

He trenched around his find, discovering that it was a great brick-shaped bronze mass with an excitingly hollow sound. A long strip of moldering metal from one of the long vertical faces pulled away, exposing red rust that went *whoosh* and was sucked into the interior of the mass.

It had been de-aired, thought Hawkins, and there must have been an inner jacket of glass which had crystallized through the centuries and quietly crumbled at the first clang of his pick. He didn't know what a vacuum would do to a subject of Levantman shock, but he had hopes, nor did he quite understand what a real estate dealer was, but it might have something to do with pottery. And *anything* might have a bearing on Topic Number One.

He flung his pick out of the trench, climbed out and set off at a dog-trot for his shop. A little rummaging turned up a hypo, and there was a plasticontainer of salt in the kitchen.

Back at his dig, he chipped for another half hour to expose the juncture of lid and body. The hinges were hopeless; he smashed them off.

Hawkins extended the telescopic handle of the pick for the best leverage, fitted its point into a deep pit, set its built-in fulcrum and heaved. Five more heaves and he could see, inside the vault, what looked like a dusty marble statue. Ten more and he could see that it was the naked body of Honest John Barlow, Evanston real estate dealer, uncorrupted by time.

The potter found the apex of the trigeminal nerve with his needle's point and gave him 60 cc.

In an hour Barlow's chest began to pump.

In another hour, he rasped, "Did it work?"

"*Did* it!" muttered Hawkins.

Barlow opened his eyes and stirred, looked down, turned his hands before his eyes—

"I'll sue," he screamed. "My clothes! My fingernails!" A horrid suspicion came over his face and he clapped his hands to his hairless scalp. "My hair!" he wailed. "I'll sue you for every penny you've got. That release won't mean a damned thing in court—I didn't sign away my hair and clothes and finger-nails."

"They'll grow back," said Hawkins casually. "Also your epidermis. Those parts of you weren't alive, you know, so they weren't preserved like the rest of you. I'm afraid the clothes are gone, though."

"What is this—the University hospital?" demanded Barlow. "I want a phone. No, you phone. Tell my wife I'm all right and tell Sam Immerman—he's my law-yer—to get over here right away. GReenleaf 7-4022. Ow!" He had tried to sit up, and a portion of his pink skin rubbed against the inner surface of the casket, which was powdered by the ancient crystallized glass. "What the hell did you guys do, boil me alive? Oh, you're going to pay for this!"

"You're all right," said Hawkins, wishing now he had a reference book to clear up several obscure terms. "Your epidermis will start growing immediately. You're not in the hospital. Look here!"

He handed Barlow the stainless steel plate that had labeled the casket. After a suspicious glance, the man started to read. Finishing, he laid the plate carefully on the edge of the vault and was silent for a spell.

"Poor Verna," he said at last. "It doesn't say whether she was stuck with the court costs. Do you happen to know—?"

"No," said the potter. "All I know is what was on the plate, and how to revive you. The dentist accidentally gave you a dose of what we call Levantman shock anæsthesia. We haven't used it for centuries; it was powerful, but too dangerous."

"Centuries ..." brooded the man. "Centuries ... I'll bet Sam swindled her out of her eyeteeth. Poor Verna. How long ago was it? What year is this?"

Hawkins shrugged. "We call it 7-B-936. That's no help to you. It takes a long time for these metals to oxidize."

"Like that movie," Barlow muttered. "Who would have thought it? Poor Verna!" He blubbered and sniffled, reminding Hawkins powerfully of the fact that he had been found under a flat rock.

Almost angrily, the potter demanded, "How many children did you have?"

"None yet," sniffed Barlow. "My first wife didn't want them. But Verna wants one—wanted one—but we're going to wait until—we *were* going to wait until—"

"Of course," said the potter, feeling a savage desire to tell him off, blast him to hell and gone for his work. But he choked it down. There was The Problem to think of; there was always The Problem to think of, and this poor blubberer might unexpectedly supply a clue. Hawkins would have to pass him on.

"Come along!" Hawkins said. "My time is short."

Barlow looked up, outraged. "How can you be so unfeeling? I'm a human being like—"

The Los Angeles–Chicago "rocket" thundered overhead and Barlow broke off in mid-complaint. "Beautiful!" he breathed, following it with his eyes. "Beautiful!"

He climbed out of the vault, too interested to be pained by its roughness against his infantile skin. "After all," he said briskly, "this should have its sunny side. I never was much for reading, but this is just like one of those stories. And I ought to make some money out of it, shouldn't I?" He gave Hawkins a shrewd glance.

"You want money?" asked the potter. "Here!" He handed over a fistful of change and bills. "You'd better put my shoes on. It'll be about a quarter-mile. Oh, and you're—uh, modest?—yes, that was the word. Here!" Hawkins gave him his pants, but Barlow was excitedly counting the money.

"Eighty-five, eighty-six—and it's dollars, too. I thought it'd be credits or whatever they call them. 'E Pluribus Unum' and 'Liberty'—just different faces. Say, is there a catch to this? Are these real, genuine, honest twenty-two-cent dollars like we had or just wallpaper?"

"They're quite all right, I assure you," said the potter. "I wish you'd come along. I'm in a hurry."

The man babbled as they stumped towards the shop. "Where are we going—The Council of Scientists, the World Co-ordinator or something like that?"

"Who? Oh, no. We call them 'President' and 'Congress.' No, that wouldn't do any good at all. I'm just taking you to see some people."

"I ought to make plenty out of this. *Plenty!* I could write books. Get some smart young fellow to put it into words for me and I'll bet I could turn out a best-seller. What's the setup on things like that?"

"It's about like that. Smart young fellows. But there aren't any best-sellers any more. People don't read much nowadays. We'll find something equally profitable for you to do."

Back in the shop, Hawkins gave Barlow a suit of clothes, deposited him in the waiting-room and called Central in Chicago. "Take him away," he pleaded. "I have time for one more firing and he blathers and blathers. I haven't told him anything. Perhaps we should just turn him loose and let him find his own level, but there's a chance—"

"The Problem," agreed Central. "Yes, there's a chance."

The potter delighted Barlow by making him a cup of coffee with a cube that not only dissolved in cold water but heated the water to boiling-point. Killing time, Hawkins chatted about the 'rocket' Barlow had admired, and had to haul himself up short; he had almost told the real estate man what its top speed really was—almost, indeed, revealed that it was not a rocket.

He regretted, too, that he had so casually handed Barlow a couple of hundred dollars. The man seemed obsessed with fear that they were worthless, since Hawkins refused to take a note or I.O.U. or even a definite promise of repayment. But Hawkins couldn't go into details, and was very glad when a stranger arrived from Central.

"Tinny-Peete, from Algeciras," the stranger told him swiftly as the two of them met at the door. "Psychist for Poprob. Polasigned special overtake Barlow."

"Thank Heaven," said Hawkins. "Barlow," he told the man from the past, "this is Tinny-Peete. He's going to take care of you and help you make lots of money."

The psychist stayed for a cup of the coffee whose preparation had delighted Barlow, and then conducted the real estate man down the corduroy road to his car, leaving the potter to speculate on whether he could at last crack his kilns.

Hawkins, abruptly dismissing Barlow and The Problem, happily picked the chinking from around the door of the number two kiln, prying it open a trifle. A blast of heat and the heady, smoky scent of the reduction fire delighted him. He peered and saw a corner of a shelf glowing cherry-red, becoming obscured by wavering black areas as it lost heat through the opened door. He slipped a charred wood paddle under a mug on the shelf and pulled it out as a sample, the hairs on the back of his hand curling and scorching. The mug crackled and pinged and Hawkins sighed happily.

The bismuth resinate luster had fired to perfection, a haunting film of silvery-black metal with strange bluish lights in it as it turned before the eyes, and the Problem of Population seemed very far away to Hawkins then.

Barlow and Tinny-Peete arrived at the concrete highway where the psychist's car was parked in a safety bay.

"What—a—*boat!*" gasped the man from the past.

"Boat? No, that's my car."

Barlow surveyed it with awe. Swept-back lines, deep-drawn compound curves, kilograms of chrome. He ran his hands futilely over the door—or was it the door?—in a futile search for a handle, and asked respectfully, "How fast does it go?"

The psychist gave him a keen look and said slowly, "Two hundred and fifty. You can tell by the speedometer."

"Wow! My old Chevy could hit a hundred on a straightaway, but you're out of my class, mister!"

Tinny-Peete somehow got a huge, low door open and Barlow descended three steps into immense cushions, floundering over to the right. He was too fascinated to pay serious attention to his flayed dermis. The dashboard was a lovely wilderness of dials, plugs, indicators, lights, scales and switches.

The psychist climbed down into the driver's seat and did something with his feet. The motor started like lighting a blow-torch as big as a silo. Wallowing around in the cushions, Barlow saw through a rear-view mirror a tremendous exhaust filled with brilliant white sparkles.

"Do you like it?" yelled the psychist.

"It's terrific," Barlow yelled back. "It's—"

He was shut up as the car pulled out from the bay into the road with a great *voo-ooo-ooom!* A gale roared past Barlow's head, though the windows seemed to be closed; the impression of speed was terrific. He located the speedometer on the dashboard and saw it climb past 90, 100, 150, 200.

"Fast enough for me," yelled the psychist, noting that Barlow's face fell in response. "Radio?"

He passed over a surprisingly light object like a football helmet, with no trailing wires, and pointed to a row of buttons. Barlow put on the helmet, glad to have the roar of air stilled, and pushed a push-button. It lit up satisfyingly, and Barlow settled back even farther for a sample of the brave new world's super-modern taste in ingenious entertainment.

"TAKE IT AND STICK IT!" a voice roared in his ears.

He snatched off the helmet and gave the psychist an injured look. Tinny-Peete grinned and turned a dial associated with the push-button layout. The man from the past donned the helmet again and found the voice had lowered to normal.

"The show of shows! The super-show! The super-duper show! The quiz of quizzes! *Take it and stick it!*"

There were shrieks of laughter in the background.

"Here we got the contes-tants all ready to go. You know how we work it. I hand a contes-tant a triangle-shaped cutout and like that down the line. Now we got these here boards, they got cut-out places the same shape as the triangles and things, only they're all different shapes, and the first contes-tant that sticks the cut-outs into the board, he wins.

"Now I'm gonna innaview the first contes-tant. Right here, honey! What's your name?"

"Name? Uh—"

"Hoddaya like that, folks? She don't remember her name. Hah, *would you buy that for a quarter?*" The question was spoken with arch significance, and the audience shrieked, howled and whistled its appreciation.

It was dull listening when you didn't know the punch lines and catch lines. Barlow pushed another button, with his free hand ready at the volume control.

"... latest from Washington. It's about Senator Hull-Mendoza. He is still attacking the Bureau of Fisheries. The North California Syndicalist says he got affydavits that John Kingsley-Schultz is a blue-nose from way back. He didn't publistat the affydavits, but he says they say that Kingsley-Schultz was saw at blue-nose meetings in Oregon State College and later at Florida University. Kingsley-Schultz says he gotta confess he did major in fly-casting at Oregon and got his Ph.D. in game fish at Florida.

"And here is a quote from Kingsley-Schultz: 'Hull-Mendoza don't know what he's talking about. He should drop dead.' Unquote. Hull-Mendoza says he won't publistat the affydavits to pertect his sources. He says they was sworn by three former employees of the Bureau which was fired for in-competence and in-compat-ibility by Kingsley-Schultz.

"Elsewhere they was the usual run of traffic accidents. A three-way pile-up of cars on Route 66 going outta Chicago took twelve lives. The Chicago–Los Angeles morning rocket crashed and exploded in the Mo-have–Mo-javvy–whatever-you-call-it Desert. All the 94 people aboard got killed. A Civil Aeronautics Authority investigator on the scene says that the pilot was buzzing herds of sheep and didn't pull out in time.

"Hey! Here's a hot one from New York. A Diesel tug run wild in the harbor while the crew was below and shoved in the port bow of the luck-shury liner *S.S. Placentia*. It says the ship filled and sank taking the lives of an es-ti-mated 180 passengers and 50 crew members. Six divers was sent down to study the wreckage, but they died, too, when their suits turned out to be fulla little holes.

"And here is a bulletin I just got from Denver. It seems—"

Barlow took off the headset uncomprehendingly. "He seemed so callous," he yelled at the driver. "I was listening to a newscast—"

Tinny-Peete shook his head and pointed at his ears. The roar of air was deafening. Barlow frowned baffledly and stared out of the window.

A glowing sign said:

MOOGS!
WOULD YOU BUY IT
FOR A QUARTER?

He didn't know what Moogs was or were; the illustration showed an incredibly proportioned girl, 99.9 percent naked, writhing passionately in animated full color.

The roadside jingle was still with him, but with a new feature. Radar or something spotted the car and alerted the lines of the jingle. Each in turn sped along a roadside track, even with the car, so it could be read before the next line was alerted.

IF THERE'S A GIRL
YOU WANT TO GET
DEFLOCCULIZE
UNROMANTIC SWEAT.
"A*R*M*P*I*T*T*O"

Another animated job, in two panels, the familiar "Before and After." The first said, "Just Any Cigar?" and was illustrated with a two-person domestic tragedy of a wife holding her nose while her coarse and red-faced husband puffed a slimy-looking rope. The second panel glowed, "or a VUELTA ABAJO?" and was illustrated with—

Barlow blushed and looked at his feet until they had passed the sign.

"Coming into Chicago," bawled Tinny-Peete.

Other cars were showing up, all of them dreamboats.

Watching them, Barlow began to wonder if he knew what a kilometer was, exactly. They seemed to be traveling so slowly, if you ignored the roaring air past your ears and didn't let the speedy lines of the dreamboats fool you. He would have sworn they were really crawling along at twenty-five, with occasional spurts up to thirty. How much was a kilometer, anyway?

The city loomed ahead, and it was just what it ought to be: towering skyscrapers, overhead ramps, landing platforms for helicopters. ...

He clutched at the cushions. Those two 'copters. They were going to—they were going to—they ...

He didn't see what happened because their apparent collision courses took them behind a giant building.

Screamingly sweet blasts of sound surrounded them as they stopped for a red light. "What the hell is going on here?" said Barlow in a shrill, frightened voice, because the braking time was just about zero, he wasn't hurled against the dashboard. "Who's kidding who?"

"Why, what's the matter?" demanded the driver.

The light changed to green and he started the pick-up. Barlow stiffened as he realized that the rush of air past his ears began just a brief, unreal split-second before the car was actually moving. He grabbed for the door-handle on his side.

The city grew on them slowly: scattered buildings, denser buildings, taller buildings, and a red light ahead. The car rolled to a stop in zero braking time, the rush of air cut off an instant after it stopped, and Barlow was out of the car and running frenziedly down a sidewalk one instant after that.

They'll track me down, he thought, panting. *It's a secret police thing. They'll get you—mind-reading machines, television eyes everywhere, afraid you'll tell their slaves about freedom and stuff. They don't let anybody cross them, like that story I once read.*

Winded, he slowed to a walk and congratulated himself that he had guts enough not to turn around. That was what they always watched for. Walking, he was just another business-suited back among hundreds. He would be safe, he would be safe …

A hand tumbled from a large, coarse, handsome face thrust close to his: "Wassamatta bumpinninna people likeya owna sidewalk gotta miner slamya inna mushya bassar." It was neither the mad potter nor the mad driver.

"Excuse me," said Barlow. "What did you say?"

"Oh, yeah?" yelled the stranger dangerously, and waited for an answer.

Barlow, with the feeling that he had somehow been suckered into the short end of an intricate land-title deal, heard himself reply belligerently, "Yeah!"

The stranger let go of his shoulder and snarled, "Oh, yeah?"

"Yeah!" said Barlow, yanking his jacket back into shape.

"Aaah!" snarled the stranger, with more contempt and disgust than ferocity. He added an obscenity current in Barlow's time, a standard but physiologically impossible directive, and strutted off hulking his shoulders and balling his fists.

Barlow walked on, trembling. Evidently he had handled it well enough. He stopped at a red light while the long, low dreamboats roared before him and pedestrians in the sidewalk flow with him threaded their ways through the stream of cars. Brakes screamed, fenders clanged and dented, hoarse cries flew back and forth between drivers and walkers. He leaped backward frantically as one car swerved over an arc of sidewalk to miss another.

The signal changed to green, the cars kept on coming for about thirty seconds and then dwindled to an occasional light-runner. Barlow crossed warily and leaned against a vending machine, blowing big breaths.

Look natural! he told himself. *Do something normal! Buy something from the machine!*

He fumbled out some change, got a newspaper for a dime, a handkerchief for a quarter and a candy bar for another quarter.

The faint chocolate smell made him ravenous suddenly. He clawed at the glassy wrapper printed "CRIGGLIES" quite futilely for a few seconds, and then it divided neatly by itself. The bar made three good bites, and he bought two more and gobbled them down.

Thirsty, he drew a carbonated orange drink in another one of the glassy wrappers from the machine for another dime. When he fumbled with it, it divided neatly and spilled all over his knees. Barlow decided he had been there long enough, and walked on.

The shop windows were—shop windows. People still wore and bought clothes, still smoked and bought tobacco, still ate and bought food. And they still went to the movies, he saw with pleased surprise as he passed and then returned to a glittering place whose sign said it was THE BIJOU.

The place seemed to be showing a triple feature, *Babies Are Terrible, Don't Have Children,* and *The Canali Kid.*

It was irresistible; he paid a dollar and went in.

He caught the tail-end of *The Canali Kid* in three-dimensional, full-color, full-scent production. It appeared to be an interplanetary saga winding up with a chase scene and a reconciliation between estranged hero and heroine. *Babies Are Terrible* and *Don't Have Children* were fantastic arguments against parenthood—the grotesquely exaggerated dangers of painfully graphic childbirth, vicious children, old parents beaten and starved by their sadistic offspring. The audience, Barlow astoundedly noted, was placidly champing sweets and showing no particular signs of revulsion.

The *Coming Attractions* drove him into the lobby. The fanfares were shattering, the blazing colors blinding, and the added scents stomach-heaving.

When his eyes again became accustomed to the moderate lighting of the lobby, he groped his way to a bench and opened the newspaper he had bought. It turned out to be *The Racing Sheet,* which afflicted him with a crushing sense of loss. The familiar boxed index in the lower left-hand corner of the front page showed almost unbearably that Churchill Downs and Empire City were still in business ...

Blinking back tears, he turned to the Past Performances at Churchill. They weren't using abbreviations any more, and the pages because of that were single-column instead of double. But it was all the same—or was it?

He squinted at the first race, a three-quarter-mile maiden claimer for thirteen hundred dollars. Incredibly, the track record was two minutes ten and three-fifths seconds. Any beetle in his time could have knocked off the three-quarter in one-fifteen. It was the same for the other distances, much worse for route events.

What the hell had happened to everything?

He studied the form of a five-year-old brown mare in the second and couldn't make head or tail of it. She'd won and lost and placed and showed and lost and placed without rhyme or reason. She looked like a front-runner for a couple of races and then she looked like a no-good pig and then she looked like a mudder but the next time it rained she wasn't and then she was a stayer and then she was a pig again. In a good five-thousand-dollar allowances event, too!

Barlow looked at the other entries and it slowly dawned on him that they were all like the five-year-old brown mare. Not a single damned horse running had the slightest trace of class.

Somebody sat down beside him and said, "That's the story."

Barlow whirled to his feet and saw it was Tinny-Peete, his driver.

"I was in doubts about telling you," said the psychist, "but I see you have some growing suspicions of the truth. Please don't get excited. It's all right, I tell you."

"So you've got me," said Barlow.

"*Got* you?"

"Don't pretend! I can put two and two together. You're the secret police. You and the rest of the aristocrats live in luxury on the sweat of these oppressed slaves. You're afraid of me because you have to keep them ignorant."

There was a bellow of bright laughter from the psychist that got them blank looks from other patrons of the lobby. The laughter didn't sound at all sinister.

"Let's get out of here," said Tinny-Peete, still chuckling. "You couldn't possibly have it more wrong." He engaged Barlow's arm and led him to the street. "The actual truth is that the millions of workers live in luxury on the sweat of the handful of aristocrats. I shall probably die before my time of overwork unless—" He gave Barlow a speculative look. "You may be able to help us."

"I know that gag," sneered Barlow. "I made money in my time and to make money you have to get people on your side. Go ahead and shoot me if you want, but you're not going to make a fool out of me!"

"You nasty little ingrate!" snapped the psychist, with a kaleidoscopic change of mood. "This damned mess is all your fault and the fault of people like you. Now come along and no more of your nonsense!"

He yanked Barlow into an office building lobby and an elevator that, disconcertingly, went *whoosh* loudly as it rose. The real estate man's knees were wobbly as the psychist pushed him from the elevator, down a corridor and into an office.

A hawk-faced man rose from a plain chair as the door closed behind them. After an angry look at Barlow, he asked the psychist, "Was I called from the Pole to inspect this—this—?"

"Unget updandered. I've deeprobed etfind quasichance exhim Poprobattackline," said the psychist soothingly.

"Doubt," grunted the hawk-faced man.

"Try!" suggested Tinny-Peete.

"Very well. Mr. Barlow, I understand that you and your lamented had no children?"

"What of it?"

"This of it. You were a blind, selfish stupid ass to tolerate economic and social conditions which penalized childbearing by the prudent and foresighted. You made us what we are today, and I want you to know that we are far from satisfied. Damn-fool rockets! Damn-fool automobiles! Damn-fool cities with overhead ramps!"

"As far as I can see," said Barlow, "you're running down the best features of your time. Are you crazy?"

"The rockets aren't rockets. They're turbojets—good turbojets, but the fancy shell around them makes for a bad drag. The automobiles have a top speed of one hundred kilometers per hour—a kilometer is, if I recall my paleolinguistics, three-fifths of a mile—and the speedometers are all rigged accordingly so the drivers will think they're going two hundred and fifty. The cities are ridiculous, expensive, unsanitary, wasteful conglomerations of people who'd be better off and more productive if they were spread over the countryside.

"We need the rockets and trick speedometers and cities because, while you and your kind were being prudent and foresighted and not having children, the migrant workers, slum dwellers and tenant farmers were shiftlessly and shortsightedly having children—breeding, breeding. My God, how they bred!"

"Wait a minute!" objected Barlow. "There were lots of people in our crowd who had two or three children."

"The attrition of accidents, illness, wars and such took care of that. Your intelligence was bred out. It is gone. Children that should have been born never were. The just-average, they'll-get-along majority took over the population. The average IQ now is 45."

"But that's far in the future—"

"So are you," grunted the hawk-faced man sourly.

"But who are *you* people?"

"Just people—real people. Some generations ago, the geneticists realized at last that nobody was going to pay any attention to what they said, so they abandoned words for deeds. Specifically, they formed and recruited for a closed corporation intended to maintain and improve the breed. We are their descendants, about three million of us. There are five billion of the others, so we are their slaves.

"During the past couple of years I've designed a skyscraper, kept Billings Memorial Hospital here in Chicago running, headed off war with Mexico and directed traffic at La Guardia Field in New York."

"I don't understand. Why don't you let them go to hell in their own way?"

The man grimaced. "We tried it once for three months. We holed up at the South Pole and waited. They didn't notice it. Some drafting-room people were missing, some chief nurses didn't show up, minor government people on the non-policy level couldn't be located. It didn't seem to matter.

"In a week there was hunger. In two weeks there were famine and plague, in three weeks war and anarchy. We called off the experiment; it took us most of the next generation to get things squared away again."

"But why *didn't* you let them kill each other off?"

"Five billion corpses mean about five hundred million tons of rotting flesh."

Barlow had another idea. "Why don't you sterilize them?"

"Two and one-half billion operations is a lot of operations. Because they breed continuously, the job would never be done."

"I see. Like the marching Chinese."

"Who the devil are they?"

"It was a—uh—paradox of my time. Somebody figured out that if all the Chinese in the world were to line up four abreast, I think it was, and start marching past a given point, they'd never stop because of the babies that would be born and grow up before they passed the point."

"That's right. Only instead of 'a given point,' make it 'the largest conceivable number of operating rooms that we could build and staff.' There could never be enough."

"Say!" said Barlow. "Those movies about babies—was that your propaganda?"

"It was. It doesn't seem to mean a thing to them. We have abandoned the idea of attempting propaganda contrary to a biological-drive."

"So if you work *with* a biological drive—?"

"I know of none which is consistent with inhibition of fertility."

Barlow's face went poker-blank, the result of years of careful discipline. "You don't, huh? You're the great brains and you can't think of any?"

"Why, no," said the psychist innocently. "Can you?"

"That depends. I sold ten thousand acres of Siberian tundra—through a dummy firm, of course—after the partition of Russia. The buyers thought they were getting improved building lots on the outskirts of Kiev. I'd say that was a lot tougher than this job."

"How so?" asked the hawk-faced man.

"Those were normal, suspicious customers and these are morons, born suckers. You just figure out a con they'll fall for; they won't know enough to do any smart checking."

The psychist and the hawk-faced man had also had training; they kept themselves from looking with sudden hope at each other.

"You seem to have something in mind," said the psychist.

Barlow's poker face went blanker still. "Maybe I have. I haven't heard any offer yet."

"There's the satisfaction of knowing that you've prevented Earth's resources from being so plundered," the hawk-faced man pointed out, "that the race will soon become extinct."

"I don't know that," Barlow said bluntly. "All I have is your word."

"If you really have a method, I don't think any price would be too great," the psychist offered.

"Money," said Barlow.

"All you want."

"More than you want," the hawk-faced man corrected.

"Prestige," added Barlow. "Plenty of publicity. My picture and my name in the papers and over TV every day, statues to me, parks and cities and streets and other things named after me. A whole chapter in the history books."

The psychist made a facial sign to the hawk-faced man that meant, "Oh, brother!"

The hawk-faced man signaled back, "Steady, boy!"

"It's not too much to ask," the psychist agreed.

Barlow, sensing a seller's market, said, "Power!"

"Power?" the hawk-faced man repeated puzzledly. "Your own hydro station or nuclear pile?"

"I mean a world dictatorship with me as dictator."

"Well, now—" said the psychist, but the hawk-faced man interrupted, "It would take a special emergency act of Congress but the situation warrants it. I think that can be guaranteed."

"Could you give us some indication of your plan?" the psychist asked.

"Ever hear of lemmings?"

"No."

"They are—were, I guess, since you haven't heard of them—little animals in Norway, and every few years they'd swarm to the coast and swim out to sea until they drowned. I figure on putting some lemming urge into the population."

"How?"

"I'll save that till I get the right signatures on the deal."

The hawk-faced man said, "I'd like to work with you on it, Barlow. My name's Ryan-Ngana." He put out his hand.

Barlow looked closely at the hand, then at the man's face. "Ryan what?"

"Ngana."

"That sounds like an African name."

"It is. My mother's father was a Watusi."

Barlow didn't take the hand. "I thought you looked pretty dark. I don't want to hurt your feelings, but I don't think I'd be at my best working with you. There must be somebody else just as well qualified, I'm sure."

The psychist made a facial sign to Ryan-Ngana that meant, "Steady *yourself,* boy!"

"Very well," Ryan-Ngana told Barlow. "We'll see what arrangement can be made."

"It's not that I'm prejudiced, you understand. Some of my best friends—"

"Mr. Barlow, don't give it another thought! Anybody who could pick on the lemming analogy is going to be useful to us."

And so he would, thought Ryan-Ngana, alone in the office after Tinny-Peete had taken Barlow up to the helicopter stage. So he would. Poprob had exhausted every rational attempt and the new Poprobattacklines would have to be irrational or sub-rational. This creature from the past with his lemming legends and his improved building lots would be a fountain of precious vicious self-interest.

Ryan-Ngana sighed and stretched. He had to go and run the San Francisco subway. Summoned early from the Pole to study Barlow, he'd left unfinished a nice little theorem. Between interruptions, he was slowly constructing an n-dimensional geometry whose foundations and superstructure owed no debt whatsoever to intuition.

Upstairs, waiting for a helicopter, Barlow was explaining to Tinny-Peete that he had nothing against Negroes, and Tinny-Peete wished he had some of Ryan-Ngana's imperturbability and humor for the ordeal.

The helicopter took them to International Airport where, Tinny-Peete explained, Barlow would leave for the Pole.

The man from the past wasn't sure he'd like a dreary waste of ice and cold.

"It's all right," said the psychist. "A civilized layout. Warm, pleasant. You'll be able to work more efficiently there. All the facts at your fingertips, a good secretary—"

"I'll need a pretty big staff," said Barlow, who had learned from thousands of deals never to take the first offer.

"I meant a private, confidential one," said Tinny-Peete readily, "but you can have as many as you want. You'll naturally have top-primary-top priority if you really have a workable plan."

"Let's not forget this dictatorship angle," said Barlow.

He didn't know that the psychist would just as readily have promised him deification to get him happily on the "rocket" for the Pole. Tinny-Peete had no wish to be torn limb from limb; he knew very well that it would end that way if the population learned from this anachronism that there was a small *élite* which considered itself head, shoulders, trunk and groin above the rest. The fact that this assumption was perfectly true and the fact that the *élite* was condemned by its superiority to a life of the most grinding toil would not be considered; the difference would.

The psychist finally put Barlow aboard the "rocket" with some thirty people—real people—headed for the Pole.

Barlow was air-sick all the way because of a post-hypnotic suggestion Tinny-Peete had planted in him. One idea was to make him as averse as possible to a return trip, and another idea was to spare the other passengers from his aggressive, talkative company.

Barlow during the first day at the pole was reminded of his first day in the Army. It was the same now-where-the-hell-are-we-going-to-put-*you?* business until he took a firm line with them. Then instead of acting like supply sergeants they acted like hotel clerks.

It was a wonderful, wonderfully calculated build-up, and one that he failed to suspect. After all, in his time a visitor from the past would have been lionized.

At day's end he reclined in a snug underground billet with the sixty-mile gales roaring yards overhead, and tried to put two and two together.

It was like old times, he thought—like a coup in real estate where you had the competition by the throat, like a fifty percent rent boost when you knew damned well there was no place for the tenants to move, like smiling when you read over the breakfast orange juice that the city council had decided to build a school on the ground you had acquired by a deal with the city council. And it was simple. He would just sell tundra building lots to eagerly suicidal lemmings, and that was absolutely all there was to solving The Problem that had these double-domes spinning.

They'd have to work out most of the details, naturally, but what the hell, that was what subordinates were for. He'd need specialists in advertising, engineering, communications—did they know anything about hypnotism? That might be helpful. If not, there'd have to be a lot of bribery done, but he'd make sure— damned sure—there were unlimited funds.

Just selling building lots to lemmings …

He wished, as he fell asleep, that poor Verna could have been in on this. It was his biggest, most stupendous deal. Verna—that sharp shyster Sam Immerman must have swindled her …

It began the next day with people coming to visit him. He knew the approach. They merely wanted to be helpful to their illustrious visitor from the past, and would he help fill them in about his era, which unfortunately was somewhat obscure historically, and what did he think could be done about The Problem? He told them he was too old to be roped any more, and they wouldn't get any information out of him until he got a letter of intent from at least the Polar President, and a session of the Polar Congress empowered to make him dictator.

He got the letter and the session. He presented his program, was asked whether his conscience didn't revolt at its callousness, explained succinctly that a deal was a deal and anybody who wasn't smart enough to protect himself didn't deserve protection—"Caveat emptor," he threw in for scholarship, and had to translate it to "Let the buyer beware." He didn't, he stated, give a damn about either the morons or their intelligent slaves; he'd told them his price and that was all he was interested in.

Would they meet it or wouldn't they?

The Polar President offered to resign in his favor, with certain temporary emergency powers that the Polar Congress would vote him if he thought them necessary. Barlow demanded the title of World Dictator, complete control of world finances, salary to be decided by himself, and the publicity campaign and historical write-up to begin at once.

"As for the emergency powers," he added, "they are neither to be temporary nor limited."

Somebody wanted the floor to discuss the matter, with the declared hope that perhaps Barlow would modify his demands.

"You've got the proposition," Barlow said. "I'm not knocking off even ten percent."

"But what if the Congress refuses, sir?" the President asked.

"Then you can stay up here at the Pole and try to work it out for yourselves. I'll get what I want from the morons. A shrewd operator like me doesn't have to compromise; I haven't got a single competitor in this whole cockeyed moronic era."

Congress waived debate and voted by show of hands. Barlow won unanimously.

"You don't know how close you came to losing me," he said in his first official address to the joint Houses. "I'm not the boy to haggle; either I get what I ask or I go elsewhere. The first thing I want is to see designs for a new palace for me—nothing *un*ostentatious, either—and your best painters and sculptors to start working on my portraits and statues. Meanwhile, I'll get my staff together."

He dismissed the Polar President and the Polar Congress, telling them that he'd let them know when the next meeting would be.

A week later, the program started with North America the first target.

Mrs. Garvy was resting after dinner before the ordeal of turning on the dishwasher. The TV, of course, was on and it said: "Oooh!"—long, shuddery and ecstatic, the cue for the *Parfum Assault Criminale* spot commercial. "Girls," said the announcer hoarsely, "do you want your man? It's easy to get him—easy as a trip to Venus."

"Huh?" said Mrs. Garvy.

"Wassamatter?" snorted her husband, starting out of a doze.

"Ja hear that?"

"Wha'?"

"He said 'easy like a trip to Venus.'"

"So?"

"Well, I thought ya couldn't get to Venus. I thought they just had that one rocket thing that crashed on the Moon."

"Aah, women don't keep up with the news," said Garvy righteously, subsiding again.

"Oh," said his wife uncertainly.

And the next day, on *Henry's Other Mistress,* there was a new character who had just breezed in: Buzz Rentshaw, Master Rocket Pilot of the Venus run. On *Henry's Other Mistress,* "the broadcast drama about you and your neighbors, *folksy* people, *ordinary* people, *real* people." Mrs. Garvy listened with amazement over a cooling cup of coffee as Buzz made hay of her hazy convictions.

MONA: "Darling, it's so good to see you again!"

BUZZ: "You don't know how I've missed you on that dreary Venus run."

SOUND: *Venetian blind run down, key turned in door lock.*

MONA: "Was it *very* dull, dearest?"

BUZZ: "Let's not talk about my humdrum job, darling! Let's talk about us!"

SOUND: *Creaking bed.*

Well, the program was back to normal at last. That evening Mrs. Garvy tried to ask again whether her husband was sure about those rockets, but he was dozing right through *Take It and Stick It,* so she watched the screen and forgot the puzzle.

She was still rocking with laughter at the gag line, "Would you buy it for a quarter?" when the commercial went on for the detergent powder she always faithfully loaded her dishwasher with on the first of every month.

The announcer displayed mountains of suds from a tiny piece of the stuff and coyly added: "Of course, Cleano don't lay around for you to pick up like the soap-root on Venus, but it's pretty cheap and it's almost pretty near just as good. So for us plain folks who ain't lucky enough to live up there on Venus, Cleano is the real cleaning stuff."

Then the chorus went into their "Cleano-is-the-stuff" jingle, but Mrs. Garvy didn't hear it. She was a stubborn woman, but it occurred to her that she was very sick indeed. She didn't want to worry her husband. The next day she quietly made an appointment with her family freud.

In the waiting-room she picked up a fresh new copy of *Readers Pablum* and put it down with a faint palpitation. The lead article, according to the table of contents on the cover, was titled "The Most Memorable Venusian I Ever Met."

"The freud will see you now," said the nurse, and Mrs. Garvy tottered into his office.

His traditional glasses and whiskers were reassuring. She choked out the ritual: "Freud, forgive me, for I have neuroses!"

He chanted the antiphonal "Tut, my dear girl, what seems to be the trouble?"

"I got like a hole in the head," she quavered. "I seem to forget all kinds of things. Things like everybody seems to know and I don't."

"Well, that happens to everybody occasionally, my dear! I suggest a vacation on Venus."

The freud stared, open-mouthed, at the empty chair. His nurse came in and demanded, "Hey, you see how she scrammed? What was the matter with *her?*"

He took off his glasses and whiskers meditatively. "You can search me. I told her she should maybe try a vacation on Venus." A momentary bafflement came into his face and he dug through his desk drawers until he found a copy of the four-color, profusely illustrated journal of his profession. It had come that morning and he had lip-read it, though looking mostly at the pictures. He leafed through to the article "Advantages of the Planet Venus in Rest Cures."

"It's right there," he said.

The nurse looked. "It sure is," she agreed. "Why shouldn't it be?"

"The trouble with these here neurotics," decided the freud, "is that they all the time got to fight reality. Show in the next twitch."

He put on his glasses and whiskers again and forgot Mrs. Garvy and her strange behavior.

"Freud, forgive me, for I have neuroses!"

"Tut, my dear girl, what seems to be the trouble?"

Like many cures of mental disorders, Mrs. Garvy's was achieved largely by self-treatment. She disciplined herself sternly out of the crazy notion that there had been only one rocket ship and that one a failure. She could join without wincing, eventually, in any conversation on the desirability of Venus as a place to retire, on its fabulous floral profusion. Finally she went to Venus.

All her friends were trying to book passage with the Evening Star Travel and Real Estate Corporation, but naturally the demand was crushing. She considered herself lucky to get a seat at last for the two-week summer cruise. The spaceship took off from a place called Los Alamos, New Mexico. It looked just like all the spaceships on television and in the picture magazines, but was more comfortable that you would expect.

Mrs. Garvy was delighted with the fifty or so fellow-passengers assembled before take-off. They were from all over the country and she had a distinct impression that they were on the brainy side. The captain, a tall, hawk-faced, impressive fellow named Ryan-Something or other, welcomed them aboard and trusted that their trip would be a memorable one. He regretted that there would be nothing to see because "due to the meteorite season," the ports would be dogged down. It was disappointing, yet reassuring that the line was taking no chances.

There was the expected momentary discomfort at take-off and then two monotonous days of droning travel through space to be whiled away in the lounge at cards or craps. The landing was a routine bump and the voyagers were issued tablets to swallow to immunize them against any minor ailments. When the tablets took effect, the lock was opened and Venus was theirs.

It looked much like a tropical island on Earth, except for a blanket of cloud overhead. But it had a heady, otherworldly quality that was intoxicating and glamorous.

The ten days of the vacation were suffused with a hazy magic. The soap-root, as advertised, was free and sudsy. The fruits, mostly tropical varieties transplanted from Earth, were delightful. The simple shelters provided by the travel company were more than adequate for the balmy days and nights.

It was with sincere regret that the voyagers filed again into the ship, and swallowed more tablets doled out to counteract and sterilize any Venus illnesses they might unwittingly communicate to Earth.

Vacationing was one thing. Power politics was another.

At the Pole, a small man was in a sound-proof room, his face deathly pale and his body limp in a straight chair.

In the American Senate Chamber, Senator Hull-Mendoza (Synd., N. Cal.) was saying: "Mr. President and gentlemen, I would be remiss in my duty as a legislature if'n I didn't bring to the attention of the au-gust body I see here a perilous situation which is fraught with peril. As is well known to members of this au-gust body, the perfection of space flight has brought with it a situation I can only describe as fraught with peril. Mr. President and gentlemen, now that swift American rockets now traverse the trackless void of space between this planet and our nearest planetarial neighbor in space—and, gentlemen, I refer to Venus, the star of dawn, the brightest jewel in fair Vulcan's diadome—now, I say, I want to inquire what steps are being taken to colonize Venus with a vanguard of patriotic citizens like those minute-men of yore.

"Mr. President and gentlemen! There are in this world nations, envious nations—I do not name Mexico—who by fair means or foul may seek to wrest from Columbia's grasp the torch of freedom of space; nations whose low living standards and innate depravity give them an unfair advantage over the citizens of our fair republic.

"This is my program: I suggest that a city of more than 100,000 population be selected by lot. The citizens of the fortunate city are to be awarded choice lands on Venus free and clear, to have and to hold and convey to their descendants. And the national government shall provide free transportation to Venus for these citizens. And this program shall continue, city by city, until there has been deposited on Venus a sufficient vanguard of citizens to protect our manifest rights in that planet.

"Objections will be raised, for carping critics we have always with us. They will say there isn't enough steel. They will call it a cheap giveaway. I say there *is* enough steel for *one* city's population to be transferred to Venus, and that is all that is needed. For when the time comes for the second city to be transferred, the first, emptied city can be wrecked for the needed steel! And is it a giveaway? Yes! It is the most glorious giveaway in the history of mankind. Mr. President and gentlemen, there is no time to waste—Venus must be American!"

Black-Kupperman, at the Pole, opened his eyes and said feebly, "The style was a little uneven. Do you think anybody'll notice?"

"You did fine, boy; just fine," Barlow reassured him.

Hull-Mendoza's bill became law.

Drafting machines at the South Pole were busy around the clock and the Pittsburgh steel mills spewed millions of plates into the Los Alamos spaceport of the Evening Star Travel and Real Estate Corporation. It was going to be Los Angeles, for logistic reasons, and the three most accomplished psychokineticists went to Washington and mingled in the crowd at the drawing to make certain that the Los Angeles capsule slithered into the fingers of the blindfolded Senator.

Los Angeles loved the idea and a forest of spaceships began to blossom in the desert. They weren't very good spaceships, but they didn't have to be.

A team at the Pole worked at Barlow's direction on a mail set-up. There would have to be letters to and from Venus to keep the slightest taint of suspicion from arising. Luckily Barlow remembered that the problem had been solved once before—by Hitler. Relatives of persons incinerated in the furnaces of Lublin or Majdanek continued to get cheery postal cards.

The Los Angeles flight went off on schedule, under tremendous press, newsreel and television coverage. The world cheered the gallant Angelenos who were setting off on their patriotic voyage to the land of milk and honey. The forest of spaceships thundered up, and up, and out of sight without untoward incident. Billions envied the Angelenos, cramped and on short rations though they were.

Wreckers from San Francisco, whose capsule came up second, moved immediately into the City of the Angels for the scrap steel their own flight would require. Senator Hull-Mendoza's constituents could do no less.

The president of Mexico, hypnotically alarmed at this extension of *yanqui imperialismo* beyond the stratosphere, launched his own Venus-colony program.

Across the water it was England versus Ireland, France versus Germany, China versus Russia, India versus Indonesia. Ancient hatreds grew into the flames that were rocket ships assailing the air by hundreds daily.

> *Dear Ed, how are you? Sam and I are fine and hope you are fine. Is it nice up there like they say with food and close grone on trees? I drove by Springfield yesterday and it sure looked funny all the buildings down but of coarse it is worth it we have to keep the greasers in their place. Do you have any trouble with them on Venus? Drop me a line some time. Your loving sister, Alma.*

> *Dear Alma, I am fine and hope you are fine. It is a fine place here fine climate and easy living. The doctor told me today that I seem to be ten years younger. He thinks there is something in the air here keeps people young. We do not have much trouble with the greasers here they keep to theirselves it is just a question of us outnumbering them and staking out the best places for the Americans. In South Bay I know a nice little island that I have been saving for you and Sam with lots of blanket trees and ham bushes. Hoping to see you and Sam soon, your loving brother, Ed.*

Sam and Alma were on their way shortly.

Poprob got a dividend in every nation after the emigration had passed the half-way mark. The lonesome stay-at-homes were unable to bear the melancholy of a low population density; their conditioning had been to swarms of their kin. After that point it was possible to foist off the crudest stripped-down accommodations on would-be emigrants; they didn't care.

Black-Kupperman did a final job on President Hull-Mendoza, the last job that genius of hypnotics would ever do on any moron, important or otherwise.

Hull-Mendoza, panic-stricken by his presidency over an emptying nation, joined his constituents. The *Independence,* aboard which traveled the national government of America, was the most elaborate of all the spaceships—bigger, more comfortable, with a lounge that was handsome, though cramped, and cloakrooms for Senators and Representatives. It went, however, to the same place as the others and Black-Kupperman killed himself, leaving a note that stated he "couldn't live with my conscience."

The day after the American President departed, Barlow flew into a rage. Across his specially built desk were supposed to flow all Poprob high-level documents, and this thing—this outrageous thing—called Poprob*term* apparently had got into the executive stage before he had even had a glimpse of it.

He buzzed for Rogge-Smith, his statistician. Rogge-Smith seemed to be at the bottom of it. Poprobterm seemed to be about first and second and third derivatives, whatever they were. Barlow had a deep distrust of anything more complex than what he called an "average."

While Rogge-Smith was still at the door, Barlow snapped, "What's the meaning of this? Why haven't I been consulted? How far have you people got and why have you been working on something I haven't authorized?"

"Didn't want to bother you, Chief," said Rogge-Smith. "It was really a technical matter, kind of a final clean-up. Want to come and see the work?"

Mollified, Barlow followed his statistician down the corridor.

"You still shouldn't have gone ahead without my okay," he grumbled. "Where the hell would you people have been without me?"

"That's right, Chief! We couldn't have swung it ourselves; our minds just don't work that way. And all that stuff you knew from Hitler—it wouldn't have occurred to us. Like poor Black-Kupperman."

They were in a fair-sized machine shop at the end of a slight upward incline. It was cold. Rogge-Smith pushed a button that started a motor, and a flood of arctic light poured in as the roof parted slowly. It showed a small spaceship with the door open.

Barlow gaped as Rogge-Smith took him by the elbow and his other boys appeared: Sweson-Swenson, the engineer; Tsutsugimushi-Duncan, his propellants man; Kalb-French, advertising.

"In you go, Chief!" said Tsutsugimushi-Duncan. "This is Poprobterm."

"But I'm the world Dictator."

"You bet, Chief! You'll be in history, all right—but this is necessary, I'm afraid."

The door was closed. Acceleration slammed Barlow cruelly to the metal floor. Something broke and warm, wet stuff, salty-tasting, ran from his mouth to his chin. Arctic sunlight through a port suddenly became a fierce lancet stabbing at his eyes; he was out of the atmosphere.

Lying twisted and broken under the acceleration, Barlow realized that some things had not changed, that Jack Ketch was never asked to dinner however many shillings you paid him to do your dirty work, that murder will out, that crime pays only temporarily.

The last thing he learned was that death is the end of pain.

[*Galaxy* - November 1952]

The Altar at Midnight

He had quite a rum-blossom on him for a kid, I thought at first. But when he moved closer to the light by the cash register to ask the bartender for a match or something, I saw it wasn't that. Not just the nose. Broken veins on his cheeks, too, and the funny eyes. He must have seen me look, because he slid back away from the light.

The bartender shook my bottle of ale in front of me like a Swiss bell-ringer so it foamed inside the green glass.

"You ready for another, sir?" he asked.

I shook my head. Down the bar, he tried it on the kid—he was drinking Scotch and water or something like that—and found out he could push him around. He sold him three Scotch and waters in ten minutes.

When he tried for number four, the kid had his courage up and said, "I'll tell *you* when I'm ready for another, Jack." But there wasn't any trouble.

It was almost nine and the place began to fill up. The manager, a real hood type, stationed himself by the door to screen out the high-school kids and give the big hello to conventioneers. The girls came hurrying in, too, with their little make-up cases and their fancy hair piled up and their frozen faces with the perfect mouths drawn on them. One of them stopped to say something to the manager, some excuse about something, and he said: "That's aw ri'; getcha assina dressing-room."

A three-piece band behind the drapes at the back of the stage began to make warm-up noises and there were two bartenders keeping busy. Mostly it was beer— a mid-week crowd. I finished my ale and had to wait a couple of minutes before I could get another bottle. The bar filled up from the end near the stage because all the customers wanted a good, close look at the strippers for their fifty-cent bottles of beer. But I noticed that nobody sat down next to the kid, or, if anybody did, he didn't stay long—you go out for some fun and the bartender pushes you around and nobody wants to sit next to you. I picked up my bottle and glass and went down on the stool to his left.

He turned to me right away and said: "What kind of a place is this, anyway?" The broken veins were all over his face, little ones, but so many, so close, that they made his face look something like marbled rubber. The funny look in his eyes was it—the trick contact lenses. But I tried not to stare and not to look away.

"It's okay," I said. "It's a good show if you don't mind a lot of noise from—"

He stuck a cigarette into his mouth and poked the pack at me. "I'm a spacer," he said, interrupting.

I took one of his cigarettes and said: "Oh."

He snapped a lighter for the cigarettes and said: "Venus."

I was noticing that his pack of cigarettes on the bar had some kind of yellow sticker instead of the blue tax stamp.

"Ain't that a crock?" he asked. "You can't smoke and they give you lighters for a souvenir. But it's a good lighter. On Mars last week, they gave us all some cheap pen-and-pencil sets."

"You get something every trip, hah?" I took a good, long drink of ale and he finished his Scotch and water.

"Shoot. You call a trip a 'shoot.'"

One of the girls was working her way down the bar. She was going to slide onto the empty stool at his right and give him the business, but she looked at him first and decided not to. She curled around me and asked if I'd buy her a li'l ole drink. I said no and she moved on to the next. I could kind of feel the young fellow quivering. When I looked at him, he stood up. I followed him out of the dump. The manager grinned without thinking and said, "G'night, boys," to us.

The kid stopped in the street and said to me: "You don't have to follow me around, Pappy." He sounded like one wrong word and I would get socked in the teeth.

"Take it easy. I know a place where they won't spit in your eye."

He pulled himself together and made a joke of it. "This I have to see," he said. "Near here?"

"A few blocks."

We started walking. It was a nice night.

"I don't know this city at all," he said. "I'm from Covington, Kentucky. You do your drinking at home there. We don't have places like this." He meant the whole Skid Row area.

"It's not so bad," I said. "I spend a lot of time here."

"Is that a fact? I mean, down home a man your age would likely have a wife and children."

"I do. The hell with them."

He laughed like a real youngster and I figured he couldn't even be twenty-five. He didn't have any trouble with the broken curbstones in spite of his Scotch and waters. I asked him about it.

"Sense of balance," he said. "You have to be tops for balance to be a spacer—you spend so much time outside in a suit. People don't know how much. Punctures. And you aren't worth a damn if you lose your point."

"What's that mean?"

"Oh. Well, it's hard to describe. When you're outside and you lose your point, it means you're all mixed up, you don't know which way the can—that's the ship—which way the can is. It's having all that room around you. But if you have a good balance, you feel a little tugging to the ship, or maybe you just *know* which way the ship is without feeling it. Then you have your point and you can get the work done."

"There must be a lot that's hard to describe."

He thought that might be a crack and he clammed up on me.

"You call this Gandytown," I said after a while. "It's where the stove-up old railroad men hang out. This is the place."

It was the second week of the month, before everybody's pension check was all gone. Oswiak's was jumping. The Grandsons of the Pioneers were on the juke singing the "Man from Mars Yodel" and old Paddy Shea was jigging in the middle of the floor. He had a full seidel of beer in his right hand and his empty left sleeve was flapping.

The kid balked at the screen door. "Too damn bright," he said.

I shrugged and went on in and he followed. We sat down at a table. At Oswiak's you can drink at the bar if you want to, but none of the regulars do.

Paddy jigged over and said: "Welcome home, Doc." He's a Liverpool Irishman; they talk like Scots, some say, but they sound like Brooklyn to me.

"Hello, Paddy. I brought somebody uglier than you. Now what do you say?"

Paddy jigged around the kid in a half circle with his sleeve flapping and then flopped into a chair when the record stopped. He took a big drink from the seidel and said: "Can he do this?" Paddy stretched his face into an awful grin that showed his teeth. He has three of them. The kid laughed and asked me: "What the hell did you drag me into here for?"

"Paddy says he'll buy drinks for the house the day anybody uglier than he is comes in."

Oswiak's wife waddled over for the order and the kid asked us what we'd have. I figured I could start drinking, so it was three double Scotches.

After the second round, Paddy started blowing about how they took his arm off without any anesthetics except a bottle of gin because the red-ball freight he was tangled up in couldn't wait.

That brought some of the other old gimps over to the table with their stories.

Blackie Bauer had been sitting in a boxcar with his legs sticking through the door when the train started with a jerk. Wham, the door closed. Everybody laughed at Blackie for being that dumb in the first place, and he got mad.

Sam Fireman has palsy. This week he was claiming he used to be a watchmaker before he began to shake. The week before, he'd said he was a brain surgeon. A woman I didn't know, a real old Boxcar Bertha, dragged herself over and began some kind of story about how her sister married a Greek, but she passed out before we found out what happened.

Somebody wanted to know what was wrong with the kid's face—Bauer, I think it was, after he came back to the table.

"Compression and decompression," the kid said. "You're all the time climbing into your suit and out of your suit. Inboard air's thin to start with. You get a few redlines—that's these ruptured blood vessels—and you say the hell with the money; all you'll make is just one more trip. But, God, it's a lot of money for anybody my age! You keep saying that until you can't be anything but a spacer. The eyes are hard-radiation scars."

"You like dot all ofer?" asked Oswiak's wife politely.

"All over, ma'am," the kid told her in a miserable voice. "But I'm going to quit before I get a Bowman Head."

I took a savage gulp at the raw Scotch.

"I don't care," said Maggie Rorty. "I think he's cute."

"Compared with—" Paddy began, but I kicked him under the table.

We sang for a while, and then we told gags and recited limericks for a while, and I noticed that the kid and Maggie had wandered into the back room—the one with the latch on the door.

Oswiak's wife asked me, very puzzled: "Doc, w'y dey do dot flyink by planyets?"

"It's the damn govermint," Sam Fireman said.

"Why not?" I said. "They got the Bowman Drive, why the hell shouldn't they use it? Serves 'em right." I had a double Scotch and added: "Twenty years of it and they found out a few things they didn't know. Redlines are only one of them. Twenty years more, maybe they'll find out a few more things they didn't know. Maybe by the time there's a bathtub in every American home and an alcoholism clinic in every American town, they'll find out a whole *lot* of things they didn't know. And every American boy will be a pop-eyed, blood-raddled wreck, like our friend here, from riding the Bowman Drive."

"It's the damn govermint," Sam Fireman repeated.

"And what the hell did you mean by that remark about alcoholism?" Paddy said, real sore. "Personally, I can take it or leave it alone."

So we got to talking about that and everybody there turned out to be people who could take it or leave it alone.

It was maybe midnight when the kid showed at the table again, looking kind of dazed. I was drunker than I ought to be by midnight, so I said I was going for a walk. He tagged along and we wound up on a bench at Screwball Square. The soap-boxers were still going strong. As I said, it was a nice night. After a while, a pot-bellied old auntie who didn't give a damn about the face sat down and tried to talk the kid into going to see some etchings. The kid didn't get it and I led him over to hear the soap-boxers before there was trouble.

One of the orators was a mush-mouthed evangelist. "And oh, my friends," he said, "when I looked through the porthole of the spaceship and beheld the wonder of the Firmament—"

"You're a stinkin' Yankee liar!" the kid yelled at him. "You say one damn more word about can-shootin' and I'll ram your spaceship down your lyin' throat! Wheah's your redlines if you're such a hot spacer?"

The crowd didn't know what he was talking about, but "Wheah's your redlines" sounded good to them, so they heckled mushmouth off his box with it.

I got the kid to a bench. The liquor was working in him all of a sudden. He simmered down after a while and asked: "Doc, should I've given Miz Rorty some money? I asked her afterwards and she said she'd admire to have something to remember me by, so I gave her my lighter. She seem' to be real pleased with it. But I was wondering if maybe I embarrassed her by asking her right out. Like I tol' you, back in Covington, Kentucky, we don't have places like that. Or maybe we did and I just didn't know about them. But what do you think I should've done about Miz Rorty?"

"Just what you did," I told him. "If they want money, they ask you for it first. Where you staying?"

"Y.M.C.A.," he said, almost asleep. "Back in Covington, Kentucky, I was a member of the Y and I kept up my membership. They have to let me in because I'm a member. Spacers have all kinds of trouble, Doc. Woman trouble. Hotel trouble. Fam'ly trouble. Religious trouble. I was raised a Southern Baptist, but wheah's Heaven, anyway? I ask' Doctor Chitwood las' time home before the redlines got so thick—Doc, you aren't a minister of the Gospel, are you? I hope I di'n' say anything to offend you."

"No offense, son," I said. "No offense."

I walked him to the avenue and waited for a fleet cab. It was almost five minutes. The independent cabs roll drunks and dent the fenders of fleet cabs if they show up in Skid Row, and then the fleet drivers have to make reports on their own time to the company. It keeps them away. But I got one and dumped the kid in.

"The Y Hotel," I told the driver. "Here's five. Help him in when you get there."

When I walked through Screwball Square again, some college kids were yelling "Wheah's your redlines" at old Charlie, the last of the Wobblies.

Old Charlie kept roaring: "The hell with your breadlines! I'm talking about atomic bombs. *Right—up—there!*" And he pointed at the Moon.

It was a nice night, but the liquor was dying in me.

There was a joint around the corner, so I went in and had a drink to carry me to the club; I had a bottle there. I got into the first cab that came.

"Athletic Club," I said.

"Inna dawghouse, harh?" the driver said, and he gave me a big personality smile.

I didn't say anything and he started the car.

He was right, of course. I was in everybody's doghouse. Some day I'd scare hell out of Tom and Lise by going home and showing them what their daddy looked like.

Down at the Institute, I was in the doghouse.

"Oh, dear," everybody at the Institute said to everybody, "I'm sure I don't know what ails the man. A lovely wife and two lovely grown children and she had to tell him 'either you go or I go.' And *drinking!* And this is rather subtle, but it's a well-known fact that neurotics seek out low company to compensate for their guilt feelings. The *places* he frequents. Doctor Francis Bowman, the man who made space flight a reality. The man who put the Bomb Base on the Moon! Really, I'm sure I don't know what ails him."

The hell with them all.

[*SF Quarterly* - Spring 1942
as by Cecil Corwin]

Crisis!

If the Karfiness hadn't cut herself badly while she was trimming her chelae one morning, the whole mess might never have happened. But fashion decreed that the ropy circle of tentacles about the neck of the female Martian would be worn short that year, and everybody in the Matriarchy, from Girl Guide to the Serene Karfiness herself, obeyed without question.

That was why her temper was short that morning, and why she snapped at the Venusian Plenipotentiary who had come to chat with her concerning the space-mining rights for the following year. The worthy lady glowered at the gentleman from Venus and shrieked, "By the Almighty, if you fish-faced baboons so much as try to lay a flipper on a single free electron between here and Venus, I'll blow your waterlogged planet out of space!" And, unfortunately for the Venusians, she had the navy with which to do it.

The principles of compensation operated almost immediately; the Plenipotentiary ethered back to Venus, and Venus severed diplomatic relations with Earth. Should you fail to grasp the train of events, stop worrying. Those are the facts; the Karfiness cut herself and Venus made warlike noises at Earth.

Earth was in a very peculiar situation. Only a century ago it had begun really intensive spacing, with freight exchanges and mining. Venus and Mars, and in a smaller way Jupiter, had been a space culture for millennia. Earth had not had the elaborate machineries of foreign offices and consulates, embassies and delegates and envoys that the other planets maintained. Terra had gone into the complicated mess of astropolitics with her eyes serenely closed and the naive conviction that right would prevail.

To the cloistered Bureau of Protocol in Alaska came a message under diplomatic seal from the Ambassador to Venus, right into the office of Code Clerk Weems.

Carefully he scanned the tape and lead that closed the pouch. "At it again," he said finally. "I sometimes wonder if the whole thing wouldn't go smash if we read our own mail before every other great power in space."

Dr. Helen Carewe, his highly privileged assistant, opened the pouch with a paper knife and a shrug. "Take it easy, career man," she advised. "Your daddy had the same trouble before they promoted him to Washington State. We get all the dirty work here in Nome—have to explain how and when and why the inviolable mail sacks arrive open and read." She scanned the messages heavily typed on official paper. "What," she asked, "does 'Aristotle' mean?"

"Inexcusable outrages on the dignity of a representative of Terra," said Weems after consulting the code book. "Sounds bad."

"It is. Oh, but it *is!* They took Ambassador Malcolm and painted him bright blue, then drove him naked through the streets of Venusport."

"Whew!" whistled Weems. "That's an 'Aristotle' if ever I heard one! What do we do now?" He was already reaching for the phone.

"Cut that out!" snapped Dr. Carewe. She could speak to him like that—or even more firmly—because she was more than old enough to be his mother. The number of career men she had coached through the Alaska Receiving Station would fill half the consulates in space—and with damned good men. Brow wrinkled, she brooded aloud, "While this isn't definitely spy stuff, we ought to know whether they have a line on our phones. Don't get Washington; try Intelligence in Wyoming."

Meekly, Weems rang the Central Intelligence Division. After a hasty conversation he turned to Dr. Carewe. "They say that we're being tapped—probably by Martians. What do I do?"

"Thank the man nicely and hang up." Weems obliged.

"Now," said Dr. Carewe, "the sooner Washington hears of this, the better. And if the Martians hear of this later, *much* better. What we have to avoid is the Martians' being able to let the Venusians know with any degree of credibility that Earth is very, very angry about the Aristotle. Because that will get Venus very angry and virtuous. Which will get Earth very dignified and offensive—snotty, I might even say."

"I notice," commented Weems, "that Mars is practically out of the picture. Except as a silent purveyor of fighting ships to both sides, is that it?"

"It is. You learn quickly and cleanly. We'll have to go to Washington ourselves with the pouch."

"And report," said Weems, "to—Oh, my God!— Osgood!"

"Exactly," said she. "Oh-my-God Osgood."

And there was good and sufficient reason for the alarm in her voice.

In the chaste marble structure that housed the diminutive Foreign Office that Terra thought it sufficient to maintain, there were to be found persons who would be kicked out of any other department of the government in two seconds flat. But because astropolitics was something new to Earth, and because there had to be some place made for the half-witted offspring of the great legislative families, this chaste marble structure housed a gallery of subnormals that made St. Elizabeth's look like the Institute for Advanced Study in Princeton on a sunny day. Or so the junior members thought. Not the least of these half-witted great ones was Jowett Osgood, the direct superior of Weems, to whom he would naturally report.

Weems and Carewe were announced with a strange pomp and circumstance; they entered the big office and found Osgood rudely buried in what was supposed to look like work. Weems stood dumbly as Dr. Carewe coughed sharply.

"Ah?" grunted Osgood, looking up. "What is it?" He was a gross man.

"A pouch from Venus. We decoded it, and we think it deserves your immediate attention. We didn't phone the contents because of tappers on the wires." Weems handed over the decodings, marked very prominently in red: CONFIDENTIAL—MAKE NO COPIES.

Osgood scanned them and heaved himself to his feet. "Gad!" he grunted. "We must brook no delay—arm to the teeth!" He turned on his dictaphone. "Henry!" he snorted. "Listen to this! To Bureau of Protocol—" Dr. Carewe snapped off the dictaphone and shoved him back into his well-padded chair.

"This," she said between her teeth, "is entirely up to you. Take it from us, immediate action is demanded to smooth over this incident. You won't be able to pass the buck on to some other department; this is right in your lap. And you won't be able to delay the affair until you've forgotten it; even you can see that. Now, *what are you going to do?*"

Osgood considered the matter with great dignity for two full minutes. Finally he announced, "I don't know."

"My suggestion is that you appoint Mr. Weems here a sort of goodwill ambassador for special, but very vague, work. And give him an unlimited expense account. This thing mustn't get any further. Keep it between us three that the message arrived officially on Earth. The fiction will be that it was lost in space and that nobody has received official confirmation of the Aristotle. Any unofficial reports will be considered as sensational tales concocted by newscasters. That's the only way to keep Earth off the spot. And what a spot it is!"

"I see," said Osgood. "Be advised that I shall follow your suggestions—as closely as is compatible with the dignity of this Office."

Outside, she informed Weems, "That last was face-saving and nothing else. From here we go to Venus—spreading sweetness and light. Always remember, young man, that our interceptor rockets are pretty good, but that the Venus bombers are pretty *damned* good."

"War," mused Weems. "Nobody wins, really—it wouldn't be nice to see New York blown to pieces, even though we could do exactly the same thing to Venusport. Sweetness and light it is."

Venus politics are no joke. The fish-faced little people have at least two parties per acre and the dizziest system of alliances and superalliances that ever bewildered a struggling young diplomat. Typically, there were absolutely no points of agreement among any of the parties as to foreign policy, and yet the Venusian embassies spoke with authority that was backed up by a united planet. Their military forces were likewise held in common by all the countries, but there were "state militias" engaged in intramural activities and constant border fighting.

Weems knew the language, and that was one very great advantage; also, he spent the long rocket trip to the foggy planet in learning what he could of the political setup. He arrived with a fanfare of trumpets; at the pier he was greeted by a score of minor officials. This was a deliberate insult from the Venusian army, for not a single high-ranking officer was present. He glossed it over for the sake of a splendid ovation from the population of Venusport, who were thoroughly hopped up with esteem for him. He was the shining young man who would assure peace and prosperity for the two inner planets, and the populace was all for him.

But, he knew very well, if one nasty word came from Earth, officially recognizing the Aristotle, their mood would change suddenly and savagely. And that was what he had to be ready for. He didn't trust the fat-headed Osgood.

From city to city he made a grand tour, speaking with very little accent before huge audiences of the little people and meeting few really high-up officials. Everywhere he went he met with disapproval from the public officials.

"How," he complained to Dr. Carewe, "they get together on a complicated issue like disliking me, I don't understand."

With a grim look about the hotel room, she explained, "It's the army. They must be partly in the pay of Mars. You're the finest thing that's happened in the way of friendly relations between Earth and Venus. If you take root long enough to get your message over, they won't be able to pounce on Earth, to the benefit of nobody except the red planet. So they're trying to cool things off." Again the nervous glance around the room.

"What's that for?"

"Dictaphones. But I don't think there are any. So at the risk of getting mushy I'm going to tell you what I think of your job. I think you're working like a madman, with some of the finest, single-hearted devotion to the cause of peace that I've ever seen. If you keep this up and handle the rest of your life the way you're handling this part, you won't be immortal—not the way Osgood is going to be, with a bust in the rotunda of the capitol and a chapter in the history books.

"No, you're going to be something different. There are going to be Venusians—and Martians and Earthmen—who'll talk about you many, many years from now. About how their fathers and grandfathers stood in the rain to hear you talk." She looked over her spectacles. "Which reminds me—get out on that balcony and don't make any slips."

He pressed the very old, very great lady's hand silently, then, mopping his brow, stepped out to the ledge beyond his window. It was in the twilight zone of perpetual rain, and the crowd of white pates and faces before him was hardly visible through the wisps of steam. He looked about uneasily as he turned on the fog-piercing lights that flooded him with a golden glow, so that the Venusians could see their superman. As he began to speak into the mike at his lips, there was a hoot of reproof from the crowd. And then there were others. Something was going the rounds; he could feel it.

Very distinctly there was a shrill cry from the sea of faces, *"Liar!"* And others echoed it, again and again. He tried to speak, but was howled down. A firm hand snapped off the lights and closed the window; Dr. Carewe dropped him into a chair, limp and shocked. She handed him a slip of paper that had just been delivered.

With her lips tightly compressed she said, "They knew before we did. Osgood spilled it—all."

They shot to Mars before assassins could take any tries at them. Weems was completely washed up and discredited on Venus; knew it and felt like it. What had his fine words been in the face of a stern, righteous declaration from the Foreign Office on Earth to the Foreign Office on Venus—gleefully published far and wide by the Mars-bribed officers in the latter—hurling the most frightful accusations of violating diplomatic immunity?

God only knew, brooded Weems, why Osgood had chosen precisely that moment to sound off. He had said fighting words, too: "—back up our determination to shield the weak with deeds as well as—" Ugh! What was the matter with Osgood? The Martians couldn't touch Earth's Foreign Office; they bred them dumb but honest there. Why had Osgood—? Did he want to be an Iron Man? Did he think he could get further faster in time of war? Or did he actually, honestly believe that by this half-witted note insulting a friendly planet on account of a mere violation of etiquette he was striking a blow for justice and equality?

It probably was just that, Weems decided. And Dr. Carewe agreed.

When they landed on the red planet Weems felt very low, and was scarcely given a new lease on life by the warm reception he received from Martian notables. He was welcomed Earth fashion, with a band and speeches from a platform to twenty thousand cheering Martians. They could afford to treat him kindly; he'd failed utterly and miserably to block a new, magnificent source of income to Mars—the onrushing Earth-Venus war.

Mars wouldn't get into it. Oh, no! Mars didn't need colonies or prestige. When you have a navy like the Martian Matriarchal Fleet you don't need colonies or prestige. You just sit tight and sell the scrappers your second-rate equipment at premium prices.

At his first official reception he stood nervously among the ladies of the court. He had just received news from the Earth diplomatic colony that Venus had replied to Earth with a note just as stiff, charging that Earth was impeaching the authority of the Venusian Foreign Office with respect to its planetary jurisdiction. In plain language that meant: "Our army is bigger and better than yours. Knock this chip off—if you dare!"

One of the elegant ladies of the Matriarchal court sidled up to him. "We were presented to each other when you landed," she said, in French.

"Of course!" he said delightedly. "I remember you perfectly!" But all Martians looked alike to him.

"I was wondering, Mr. Weems, whether you would care to attend a party I'm giving tomorrow evening. I feel there would be features extremely entertaining to you."

"Delighted, madame!" He beckoned over Dr. Carewe.

"Your social secretary?" asked the Martian lady. "I'll give her the details."

Then the Karfiness entered regally and all the ladies of the court twiddled their curtailed chelae with deep veneration as she folded up in a basketlike affair.

"Mr. Weems," she said graciously. He advanced and bowed, Earth fashion, for all of his encumbering furs. "Mr. Weems, we are delighted to see you here. Such a refreshing change from those slimy little Venusians!" Her English was perfect, though lispy.

"And I, madame, am delighted to attend. If there is any message I can take back to Earth from you—any word of friendship—you have only to say it."

She regarded him amiably. "The people of Earth know well that the people of Mars are wholly committed to a policy of amicable industrial cooperation. Nothing will please me more than to reassure my friends of the third planet that there is no end of this policy in sight."

What did that mean? wondered Weems. Was she playing with him?

"I trust," he said, "that you are wholeheartedly working in the interests of peace among the planets?"

"So I have said," she said simply. "So I shall always say."

Incredible! Did she take him for an imbecile? Or—or—

"Thank you for this kind assurance," he said, bowing again and retiring.

When he had cornered Dr. Carewe, he said agitatedly, "I don't get it at all. I simply don't understand. Is she lying into my teeth? The least she could have done would have been to turn aside the questions. I never dreamed I'd get an answer at a time like this!"

"Neither did I," she said slowly. "Something is rotten in the Matriarchy, and it isn't the customary scent of senile decay peculiar to dictatorships. The biology of the Martians demands a dictatorship, what with their weird reproductive methods. Unless there were a strong and centralized authority they'd slump back into barbarism after a few thousand years of unrestricted matings. Here's one dictator who's loved by the dictatees."

She was silent for a moment, then said, "To change the subject, I have the place and time for tomorrow's party. The lady is—I knew you couldn't tell one from another— director of a munitions and fabrication syndicate."

"Thanks," he said vaguely, taking the memo. "That's the perfect spot of irony to top off the evening—in fact this whole damned mission that failed."

He went to the party with Dr. Carewe, both thoroughly wrapped up in fur and wool against the Martian indoors ten-below temperature. And they carried thermos flasks full of hot coffee for an occasional warming nip in a dark corner. Anything but that would be unmannerly.

His hostess presented Weems to her husband-brother-nephew, an example of the ungodly family relationships into which their anatomy naturally led. The creature was very much smaller than the female, and spoke only Martian, which the Earthman could not handle except sparingly. He got the idea that they were talking about auriferous sand, but how they got onto the subject he did not understand. He excused himself as quickly as he could and retreated for some of the steaming coffee.

"Earthman, of course!" said a hearty voice.

He turned to see a curious, stubby person, quite human in his appearance, but with a somehow distorted look— as though he had been squeezed in a hydraulic press. And the person wore elaborately ornamental trappings of a blackish-silver metal.

"You must be a Jovian," he said, corking the thermos. "I've never seen one of your people before. You're more—ah—human than these others."

"So they say. And you're the first Earthman I've ever seen. You're very—ah—*long*." They both laughed; then the Jovian introduced himself as a pilot on the regular Io-Mars freighters. He waved off Weems' introduction. "Don't bother, Weems," he said. "I know of you."

"Indeed?" There was a pause. With the diplomatic instinct to avoid embarrassment whenever possible, the Earthman asked, "Why don't your people appear more often on Earth? You could chuck some of that osmium you have to wear here on Mars."

"This?" the Jovian gestured at his trappings. "A mere drop in the bucket. I have a hundredweight in each shoe. But the reason is that the Earth is relatively undeveloped in its space culture—though, of course, much better developed than Jupiter. There are so few of us—fifty million on the whole planet." He shrugged whimsically. "We're growing, of course. There was a polygamy decree a few years ago—did you hear of it?"

"No—I'm sorry to say I know nothing at all about your planet. I'm in the diplomatic service. Studying Venus, mostly."

"So? Perhaps you are the wrong man to come to, then. We know nothing about these matters. Is there a person more appropriate to whom I ought to broach the idea of a rapprochement between our two worlds?"

Weems was rocked back on his heels. Unheard of! Diplomacy as casual as this was tantamount to an interplanetary incident. The Jovian continued as casually as before, "You see, we've no navy and don't need space rights. It's strictly commercial, so we haven't got any Foreign Office. We hardly trade at all with Venus and Earth, and our Mars relations are settled by treaty once every four of Mars' years."

"Excuse me," said Weems abruptly. He had just caught a high sign from Dr. Carewe, who was holding a flimsy like a dead rat. He sidled over to her inconspicuously.

"Well—what turned up?"

"The chip," she said breathlessly, "has been knocked off. I just got this from our Embassy—by messenger. It's a copy of the note the Earth F.O. just sent to Venus. The Earth F.O. not only assures Venus that not only does Earth impeach the Venus F.O. but that she is prepared to put its jurisdiction to trial." She handed him the flimsy.

He scanned it almost unbelievingly. "The so-and-sos," he commented inaudibly. "That about fixes our little red wagon, Doc. Though we have an ally. Jupiter wants its place in the sun."

As the woman stared with amazement, he introduced the Jovian to her and explained the situation. The squat man listened with increasing anxiety as he dilated on the relations that would exist between the two worlds.

"Will we really," he asked at length, "need all those men—actually twenty-five on our end!—to handle a little thing like a military alliance?"

"Lord, yes!" breathed Weems. "Code clerks, secretaries, subsecretaries, second-subsecretaries—lots more."

"May I ask," said the woman, "why this sudden interest in protocol and procedure has come up on Jupiter?"

The Jovian looked a little embarrassed. "It's a matter of pride," he explained. "The three other planets have their own secret codes and messages. We're the only planet that hasn't got sealed diplomatic pouches absolutely inviolable in any jurisdiction! And so our Executive Committee decided that if it's good enough for them, it's good enough for us."

"I see," said Weems thoughtfully. "But how is it that you, the A pilot on a freighter, are their Plenipotentiary without even identification?"

"As a matter of fact," confessed the Jovian with some hesitation, "I was given a note, but it seems to be lost. Do things like that really matter?"

"They do," said Weems solemnly. "But you were saying—?"

"Yes. They chose a freight pilot to avoid taking a man off real work. It's our principle of the economization of kinesis. Without its operation we'd have all sorts of superfluous men who did only half a man's work. And do not forget that to a people of only fifty million that is no small matter. We need every man, all the time."

"As to the treaty necessary," said the woman, "would you prefer it to be secret or published?"

"Secret," promptly replied the Jovian. "It'll be more fun that way."

Up dashed a very young subattaché from the Earth Embassy. "Excuse me," he shrilled, his voice breaking. "But you have to come at once. It's important as— as the very devil, sir, if you will excuse—" He found himself addressing empty air and an amused Jovian. The two Earth people had flown to their sand car. They had been awaiting the summons.

The ambassador was waiting for them, grim and white. He was no fool, this ambassador; his punishment for that was the dusty job on Mars instead of an office on Terra. He had just removed the earphone clamps, they saw; the diplomatic receiver set was on his desk.

Without waiting for a question from them he said, "The good word is— *ultimatum.*"

"God!" said Dr. Carewe, her old face quite white.

"When?" snapped Weems, taking out pencil and paper.

"Note delivered to Venus F.O.—that's the note from Earth—and ten minutes or so later lynching of Venusians on the staff of the Earth Embassy by an outraged populace. Foolish defense by Earthmen attached to the Embassy. Several of them killed. Stronger note from Earth. Why didn't Venus F.O. notify immediately and offer indemnification? *Very* strong reply from Venus F.O.—chip on the shoulder. Earth knocks off chip. That's the last you saw at your party. Then ultimatum from Venus giving Earth twelve *dicenes* to apologize profoundly and offer an indemnity in good faith."

"And when is the time up?"

"The twelve *dicenes* will come to an end"—the ambassador consulted his watch—"about forty-eight hours from now."

There was a long pause, broken at last by a muffled groan from the ambassador. "Damn it—oh, damn it!" he wailed. "Why do the idiots have to fight? There's trade enough for everybody, isn't there?"

"And, of course," said Weems, "Earth will never back down. Not in a million years. They're built like that. And if they did back down, Venus would be sure of herself and force a war."

"Well," said the woman quietly, "are you just going to *sit* here?"

"Suggestions are in order," said the young man unhappily.

"You'll have to work like hell to stave this off," warned the woman.

"Ready and willing, Doctor. Tell me what to do."

Considering that the art of diplomacy is, ultimately reduced, the system found most practical in actual use when stalling for time to rush ahead with military expansion, it is not very remarkable that the two roving delegates did what they did with such neatness. The system was there for them to use.

Use it they did, to the fullest extent. They shot ethers through to most of the crowned heads of the inner planet; radioed Earth confidentially meanwhile to stand by for the answers from Venus; contacted the Martian Protocol Division regarding an alliance for trade purposes alone.

They were so thoroughly efficient in their functioning that after ten hours of this the bureau chiefs back on Earth fell to their knees and prayed for a letup of this lunatic barrage of red tape that came, unasked-for and unanswerable, from a minor embassy on Mars.

Venus was bally well baffled. At first they made some pretense of replying stiffly to the muted threats from the Embassy on Mars, then gave up and hung onto the ropes, trying to decode the weird messages. It *must* be code, they decided. How could a message like "Advise your F.O. investigate frog ponds for specious abnormalities" be anything but an uncrackable cipher? They set their experts to work. The experts decided that the message meant: "All Earthmen on Venus are advised to sabotage production machinery and destroy records." But they were as wrong as they could be, for the message meant just what it said. Its value was on its face.

The consulate and the staff were drafted by the Embassy to aid in the good work of confusion; the ambassador himself sat for ten hours writing out messages which bore absolutely no relation to each other or the world at large. And if you think that sounds easy—try it!

Meanwhile the inseparables, Mr. Weems and Dr. Carewe, had been separated. The woman was gathering data from Martian libraries and Weems was paying social calls at the palace, interviewing secretaries without number. Meanwhile, authentic, distressing news releases kept rushing to him, causing him great pain. The first thing after the ultimatum he heard had called in all spacers except those related to navigation—fueling stations, etc. Venus retaliated in kind, and furthermore towed out the gigantic battle islands used to fuel fighting ships. Earth retaliated in kind, and furthermore began skirmishing war games around midway between Terra and Luna.

By the time the ten hours of lunatic messages were elapsed, the two great fleets of Earth and Venus were face to face midway between the planets, waiting for orders from the home planets to fire when ready.

"For the love of Heaven," he pleaded with a secretary to the Karfiness, "they won't even wait for the ultimatum to elapse. There's going to be a space war in two hours if I don't get to see Her Serene Tentaculosity!" The title he bestowed upon her was sheer whimsy; he wasn't half as upset as he was supposed to be. It was all for effect. He rushed away, distraught, with the information that he couldn't possibly see the Karfiness, and aware that the munitions interests of Mars would by now be rubbing their chelae with glee.

He reached a phone and rang up the ambassador. "Okay," he informed him. "Stop short!"

The ambassador, badly overworked and upset, stopped short with the messages. Venus and Earth were baffled again, this time because there was nothing to be baffled by. The strange silence that had fallen on the F.O.s was alarming in its implications. The diplomatic mind had already adjusted itself to the abnormal condition; restoration of normality created almost unbearable strain. Messages rushed to the Embassy; the ambassador left them severely alone and went to bed. From that moment anybody who touched a transmitter would be held for treason, he informed his staff. It was as though the Mars Embassy had been blown out of the ground.

"They are now," brooded Weems, "ready for anything. Let us hope that Venus hasn't lost her common sense along with her temper."

With that he set himself to the hardest job of all—waiting. He got a couple of hours of sleep, on the edge of a volcano, not knowing whether the lined-up Venus fleet would fire on the opposite Earth fleet before he woke. If it did, it would be all over before he really got started.

Even Weems hadn't imagined how well his plan was taking root. Back on Earth the whole F.O. had gone yellow, trembling at the gills lest they should actually have to fight. And it was perfectly obvious that they would, for when planetary integrity directs, no mere individual might stand in the way.

There was a great dearth of news; there had been for the past few hours of the crisis. Since that God-awful business from the Mars Embassy stopped and the entire staff there had—presumably—been shot in the back while hard at work fabricating incredible dispatches, there was a mighty and sullen silence over the air, ether and subetheric channels of communication.

On Venus things were pretty bad, too. A lot of Earthmen had been interned and the whole planet was sitting on edge waiting for something to happen. It did happen, with superb precision, after exactly seven hours of silence and inactivity.

There was a frantic call from, of all Godforsaken places, Jupiter. Jupiter claimed that the whole business was a feint, and that the major part of the Earth fleet was even now descending on the Jovians to pillage and slay.

The official broadcast—*not* a beam dispatch—from Jupiter stated this. Earth promptly denied everything, in a stiff-necked communiqué.

Venus grinned out of the corner of her mouth. In an answering communiqué she stated that since Venus was invariably to be found on the side of the under-dog, the Venus Grand Fleet would depart immediately for Jupiter to engage the enemy of her good friends, the Jovians.

Earth, to demonstrate her good faith, withdrew her own fleet from anywhere near the neighborhood of Jupiter, going clear around to the other side of the Sun for maneuvers.

Lovers of peace drew great, relieved sighs. The face-to-face had been broken up. The ultimatum had been forgotten in Earth's righteous stand that she had *not* invaded Jupiter nor intended to. This made Venus look and feel silly. This made the crisis collapse as though it had never been there at all.

And just after the Venus fleet had reported to its own home F.O.—this was three hours after the ultimatum had elapsed without being noticed by anybody—there were several people in the Earth Embassy on Mars acting hilariously. There was a Jovian who gurgled over and over:

"I didn't know it would be this much fun! We'd have gotten into the game years ago if we'd known."

"And I," said the ambassador, "have the satisfaction of knowing that I've given a pretty headache to the best code experts in the system. And all by the simple expedient of sending a code message that means just what it says."

"And I," said Weems, upending a glass, "have aided the cause of peace be-tween the planets. If I can get to the Karfiness and let her know that she's being played for a sucker by the munitions people—"

"Let it come later," said Dr. Carewe. "I wish I could live another eighty years to read about it in the history books. But it really doesn't matter, because they'll say something like this:

"'Toward the end of this year there arose a crisis between Earth and Venus, seemingly over matters of trade. It actually reached a point of ultimatums and reprisals. Fortunately the brilliant, calm and efficient work of the Hon. Secretary of Recession, Jowett Osgood, saved the day. He contracted a defensive alliance with Jupiter, the combined might of the Earth-Jovian fleet crushing any idea of victory that may have been the goal of the Venusians.'"

Dr. Carewe laughed loudly and raucously as she refilled her glass.

[*Fantasy and Science Fiction* - July 1958]

Theory of Rocketry

Mr. Edel taught six English classes that year at Richard M. Nixon High School, and the classes averaged 75 pupils each. That was 450 boys and girls, but Mr. Edel still tried to have the names down cold by at least the third week of the semester. As English 308 stormed into his room he was aware that he was not succeeding, and that next year he would even stop trying, for in 1978 the classes would average 82 pupils instead of 75.

One seat was empty when the chime sounded; Mr. Edel was pleased to notice that he remembered whose it was. The absent pupil was a Miss Kahn, keyed into his memory by "Kahn-stipated," which perhaps she was, with her small pinched features centered in a tallow acre of face. Miss Kahn slipped in some three seconds late; Edel nodded at his intern, Mrs. Giovino, and Mrs. Giovino coursed down the aisle to question, berate and possibly to demerit Miss Kahn. Edel stood up, the Modern Revised Old Testament already open before him.

"*You're blessed,*" he read, "*if you're excused for your wrongdoing and your sin is forgiven. You're blessed if God knows that you're not evil and sly any more. I, King David, used to hide my sins from God while I grew old and blustered proudly all day. But all day and all night too your hand was heavy on me, God ...*"

It would be the flat, crystal-clear, crystal-blank M.R.O.T. all this week; next week he'd read (with more pleasure) from the Roman Catholic Knox translation; the week after that, from the American Rabbinical Council's crabbed version heavy with footnotes; and the week after that, back to M.R.O.T. Thrice blessed was he this semester that there were no Moslems, Buddhists, militant atheists or miscellaneous cultists to sit and glower through the reading or exercise their legal right to wait it out in the corridor. This semester the classes were All-American: Protestant, Catholic, Jewish—choice of one.

"Amen," chorused the class and they sat down; two minutes of his fifty-minute hour were gone forever.

Soft spring was outside the windows, and they were restless. Mr. Edel "projected" a little as he told them: "This is the dreaded three-minute impromptu speech for which English Three Oh Eight is notorious, young ladies and gentlemen. The importance of being able to speak clearly on short notice should be

413

obvious to everybody. You'll get nowhere in your military service if you can't give instructions and verbal orders. You'll get less than nowhere in business if you can't convey your ideas crisply and accurately." A happy thought struck him: great chance to implement the Spiritual Values Directive. He added: "You may be asked to lead in prayer or say grace on short notice." (He'd add *that* one to his permanent repertoire; it was a natural.) "We are not asking the impossible. Anybody can talk interestingly, easily and naturally for three minutes if they try. Miss Gerber, will you begin with a little talk on your career plans?"

Miss Gerber ("Grapefruit" was the mnemonic) rose coolly and driveled about the joys of motherhood until Mrs. Giovino passed her card to Edel and called time.

"You spoke freely, Miss Gerber, but perhaps not enough to the point," said Edel. "I'm pleased, though, that you weren't bothered by any foolish shyness. I'm sure everybody I call on will be able to talk right up like you did." (He liked that *"like"* the way you like biting on a tooth that aches; *he'd* give them Artificial Grammar De-emphasis …) "Foster, may we hear from you on the subject of your coming summer vacation?" He jotted down a *C* for the Grapefruit.

Foster ("Fireball") rose and paused an expert moment. Then, in a firm and manly voice he started with a little joke ("if I survive English Three Oh Eight"), stated his theme ("a vacation is not a time for idling and wasted opportunity"), developed it ("harvest crew during the day for *physical*—my Science Search project during the evenings for *mental*"), elevated it ("no excuse for neglecting one's regular attendance at one's place of worship") and concluded with a little joke ("should be darned glad to get back to school!").

The speech clocked 2:59; it was masterly; none of the other impromptus heard that morning came close to it.

"And," said Mr. Edel at lunch to his semi-crony Dr. Fuqua, Biology, "between classes I riffled through the grade cards again and found I'd marked him *F.* Of course I changed it to *A.* The question is, *why?*"

"Because you'd made a mistake," said Fuqua absently. Something was on his mind, thought Edel.

"No, no. Why did I make the mistake?"

"Well, Freud, in *The Psychology of Everyday*—"

"Roland, please, I know all that. Assume I do. Why do I unconsciously dislike Foster? I should get down on my knees and thank God for Foster."

Fuqua shook his head and began to pay attention. "Foster?" he said. "You don't know the half of it. I'm his faculty adviser. Quite a boy, Foster."

"To me, just a name, a face, a good recitation every time. You know: seventy-five to a class. What's he up to here at dear old Tricky Dicky?"

"Watch the funny jokes, Edel," said Fuqua, alarmed.

"Sorry. It slipped out. But Foster?"

"Well, he's taking an inhuman pre-engineering schedule. Carrying it with ease. Going out for all the extra-curricular stuff the law allows. R.O.T.C. Drill Team, Boxing Squad, Math Club, and there I had to draw the line. He wanted on the Debating Team too. I've seen him upset just once. He came to me last year when the school dentist wanted to pull a bad wisdom tooth he had. He made me make the dentist wait until he had a chance to check the dental requirements of the Air Force Academy. They allow four extractions, so he let the dentist yank it. Fly boy. Off we go into the whatsit. He wants it bad."

"I see. Just a boy with motivation. How long since you've seen one, Roland?"

Dr. Fuqua leaned forward, his voice low and urgent. "To hell with Foster, Dave. I'm in trouble. Will you help me?"

"Why, of course, Roland. How much do you need?" Mr. Edel was a bachelor, and had found one of the minor joys of that state to be "tiding over" his familied friends.

"Not that kind of trouble, Dave. Not yet. They're sharpening the ax for me. I get a hearing this afternoon."

"Good God! What are you supposed to have done?"

"Everything. Nothing. It's one of those 'best interests' things. Am I taking the Spiritual Values Directive *seriously* enough? Am I *thinking* about patting any adolescent fannies? Exactly *why* am I in the lowest quarter for my seniority-group with respect to voluntary hours of refresher summer courses? Am I *happy* here?"

Edel said: "These things always start somewhere. Who's out to get you?"

Fuqua took a deep breath and said in a surprisingly small voice: "Me, I suppose."

"Oh?"

Then it came out with a rush. "It was the semester psychometrics. I'd been up all night almost fighting with Beth. She does *not* understand how to handle a fifteen-year-old boy—never mind. I felt sardonic so I did something sardonic. And stupid. Don't ever get to feeling sardonic, Dave. I took the psychometric and I checked their little boxes and I told the God-damned truth right down the line. I checked them where I felt like checking them and not where a prudent biology teacher *ought* to check them."

"You're dead," Mr. Edel said after a pause.

"I thought I could get a bunch of the teachers to say they lie their way through the psychometrics. Start a real stink."

"I'd make a poor ditch digger, Roland, but—if you can get nine others, I'll speak up. No, make that six others. I don't think they could ignore eight of us."

"You're a good man," Dr. Fuqua said. "I'll let you know. There's old McGivern—near retirement. I want to try him." He gulped his coffee and headed across the cafeteria.

Edel sat there, mildly thunderstruck at Fuqua's folly and his own daring. Fuqua had told them the kind of bird he was by checking YES or NO on the silly-clever statements. He had told them that he liked a drink, that he thought most people were stupider than he, that he talked without thinking first, that he ate too much, that he was lazy, that he had an eye for a pretty ankle—that he was a human being not much better or worse than any other human being. But that wasn't the way to do it, and damned well Fuqua had known it. You simply told yourself firmly, for the duration of the test: *I am a yuk. I have never had an independent thought in my life; independent thinking scares me. I am utterly monogamous and heterosexual. I go bowling with the boys. Television is the greatest of the art forms. I believe in installment purchasing. I am a yuk."*

That these parlor games were taken seriously by some people was an inexplicable, but inexorable, fact of life in the twentieth century. Edel had yukked his way through scholarships, college admissions, faculty appointment and promotions and had never thought the examinations worse than a bad cold. Before maturity set in, in the frat house, they had eased his qualms about psychometric testing with the ancient gag: "You ain't a man until you've had it three times."

Brave of him, pretty brave at that, to back up Fuqua ... if Roland could find six others.

Roland came to him at four o'clock to say he had not even found one other. "I don't suppose—no. I'm not asking you to, Dave. Two, it wouldn't be any good."

He went into the principal's office.

The next day a bright young substitute was teaching biology in his place, and his student advisees had been parceled out among other teachers. Mr. Edel found that young Foster had now become his charge.

The 72 pupils in his English 114 class sat fascinated and watched the television screen. Dr. Henley Ragen was teaching them *Macbeth,* was teaching about nine hundred English 114 classes throughout the state *Macbeth,* and making them like it. The classroom rapport was thick enough to cut and spread with a shingle. The man's good, Edel thought, but *that* good? How much is feedback from their knowing he's famous for his rapport, how much is awe of his stupendous salary, still nowhere equal to nine hundred teachers' salaries?

Dr. Henley Ragen, *el magnífico,* portentously turned a page; there was grim poetry in the gesture. He transfixed the classroom (nine hundred classrooms) with Those Eyes. Abruptly he became Macbeth at the Banquet prepar'd. With nervous hilarity he shouted at his guests: *"You know your own degrees; sit down! At first and last, the hearty welcome!"* Stockstill at a lectern he darted around the table bluffly rallying the company, slipped off to chat, grimly-merry, with the first Murtherer at the door, returned to the banquet, stood in chilled horror at the Ghost in the chair, croaked: *"The table's full."*

Mr. Edel studied the faces of his 72 English 114ers. They were in hypnotic states of varying depths, except Foster. The Fireball was listening and learning, his good mind giving as well as taking. The intelligent face was alive, the jaw firm, and around him eyes were dull and jaws went slack. Foster could speak and write an English sentence, which perhaps was the great distinguishing mark between him and the rest of English 114. Blurted fragments of thought came from them, and the thoughts were clichés a hundred times out of a hundred.

Dr. Henley Ragen growled at them: *"We are yet but young in deed ..."* and his eyes said the rest, promising horrors to come. He snapped the book shut like a pistol's bang; the 114ers popped out of their trances into dazed attentiveness. "Notebooks!" said Ragen (*qua* Ragen) and, 72 gunfighters quick on the draw, they snapped out books and poised their pens. Ragen spoke for ten minutes about the scene; every so often Those Eyes and an intensification of That Voice cued them to write a word or a phrase, almost without glancing at the paper. (Later each would look at his notes and not be surprised to find them lucid, orderly, even masterful summations of the brief lecture.)

As Dr. Henley Ragen bluffly delivered a sort of benediction from the altar of learning, Mr. Edel thought: well, they've got the Banquet Scene now; they'll own it forever. The way they own the Prologue to the *Canterbury Tales,* the *Ode to the West Wind, Arrowsmith.* A good deal better than nothing; *pauca sed matura.* Or so he supposed.

That afternoon from three to five Mr. Edel was available to his advisees; it was a period usually devoted to catching up on his paper work. Beyond making out the student's assignment schedule, a task traditionally considered beyond the capacity of the young, he had done no advising in years. And Foster appeared.

His handshake was manly, his grin was modest but compelling. He got to the point. "Mr. Edel, do you think I could swing an Enrichment Project in English?"

The teacher hardly knew what he meant. "Enrichment? Well, we haven't been doing that lately, Foster. I suppose it's still in the optional curriculum—"

"Yes, sir, form sixty-eight, English, paragraph forty-five, section seven. *'Opportunities shall be afforded to students believed qualified by advisors to undertake projects equivalent to College Freshman English term papers and the grades therefor shall be entered on the students' records and weighed as evidence in assigning students' positions in the graduating class.'* "

Mr. Edel had found Foster's card by then and was studying it. The boy's schedule was brutal, but his grade average was somewhere between B+ and A. "Foster," he told him, "there's such a thing as a breaking point. I—I understand you want very much to go to Colorado Springs." (Poor Fuqua! What had become of ... ?)

"Very much, sir. They expect the best—they have a right to expect the best. I'm not complaining, Mr. Edel, but there are girls with straight-A averages who aren't working as hard as I am. Well, I've just got to beat them at their own game."

Mr. Edel understood. It wasn't just girls, though mostly it was. There was a type of student who was no trouble, who did the work, every smidgen of it, who read every word of every assigned page, who turned in accurate, curiously dead, echoless, unresonant papers which you could not in decency fault though you wanted to tear them up and throw them in their authors' bland faces. You had a curious certainty that the adeptly-memorized data they reeled back on demand vanished forever once the need for a grade was gone, that it never by any chance became bone of their bone to strengthen them against future trials. Often enough when you asked them what they hoped to be, they smilingly said: "I am going to teach ..."

Foster, now. A boy who *fought* with the material and whipped it. He said: "Why so strong, Foster? What's it about?"

The boy said: "Space, partly. And my father. Two big challenges, Mr. Edel. I think I'm a very lucky fellow. Here I am with a new frontier opening up, but there are lots of fellows my age who don't see it. I see it because of my father. It's wonderful to have a challenge like that—can I be the man he is? Can I learn even more, be a better leader, a better engineer?"

Mr. Edel was moved deeply. "Your father just missed spaceflight, is that it?"

"By a whisker," Foster said regretfully. "Nothing can be done about it except what I'm doing."

"He's an aero-engineer?"

"He can do *anything*," Foster said positively. "And he has!"

A picture of the elder Foster was forming in Mr. Edel's mind—young Fireball grown taller, solider and grizzled, the jaw firmed and controlled, the voice more powerful and sure. And, unquestionably, leather puttees.

Foster's card said he had no mother, which made it more understandable. This fine boy was hard material honed to an edge, single-purposed. Did he have a young Hap Arnold here in his office? A Curtis LeMay? They had to come from somewhere, those driving, wide-ranging leaders and directors of millions. The slow-rolling conquest of space needed such men, first to navigate and pilot so no navigator or pilot would ever be able to snow them, then to move up step by step through research to command, then to great command.

"I'll bet on you, Foster," he said abruptly. "We can't let the—the future *English* teachers outpoint you with their snap courses. You'll do me a term paper on … on *Henry V.* First, read it. Read *hell* out of it and take notes. Get in touch with me when you think you're ready to talk it over. I happen to be a bachelor; I have time in the evenings. And talk it over with your father, if you can persuade him to read along with you."

Foster laughed. "I'm afraid Dad's much too busy for Shakespeare, but I'll try. Thanks, Mr. Edel." He left.

Mr. Edel, with considerable trouble, found a pad of forms in his desk which covered Enrichment Projects, English, Advisor's Permission for. He filled one out for Foster, looked it over and said, surprised: "Again, damn it!" He had checked the box for Permission Denied. He tore up the form—it was discolored anyway from being so long on the top of the pad—and meticulously made out another, checking the various boxes with exquisite care.

That night after dinner he tried to telephone Roland Fuqua, but service to his number had been discontinued. Alarmed, he buzzed over on his scooter to Fuqua's apartment, one of a quarter-million in the Dearborn Village Development of Metropolitan Life & Medical. Roland's hulking, spoiled and sullen boy Edward (who had unilaterally changed his name last year to Rocky) was the only person there, and he was on his way out: "to an orgy with some pigs," if you believed him. He said "Little Rollo" was now a night-shift lab assistant in a pet-food company's Quality Control Department and this was his mother's Bingo night. "You want I should give a message?" he asked satirically, overplaying the role of intolerably burdened youth.

"If it won't break your back," Mr. Edel said, "please ask your father to give me a ring sometime."

Again in his own small apartment Mr. Edel thought of many things. Of the ancient papyrus which, when decoded, moaned: *"Children are not now as respectful and diligent as they were in the old days."* Of *Henry V.* Of Dr. Fuqua drudging away on pet-food protein determinations and lucky to be doing that. Of his own selfish, miserable, lonely comfort in his castle. Of Foster, the hero-king to be, and of himself, Aristotle to the young Alexander. Had there been a dozen such in his twenty years? There had not. Marie Perrone still sent him her novels, and they were almost popular and very bad. Jim Folwell had gone to Princeton and into the foreign service and that was that. Janice Reeves and Ward Freiman were married and both teaching at Cornell. What had happened to the hundred thousand others he had taught, only God and themselves knew. If they all dropped dead at this instant, tomorrow morning some trucks would not roll for an hour or two, some advertising agencies would come near to missing a few deadlines, some milk would sour and some housewives would bang, perplexed, on the doors of shops that should be open, a few sales would languish unclosed, a few machines would growl for lack of oil. But Foster might land on the moons of Jupiter.

Therefore let him learn, make him learn, how to be great. He would meet his Pistols, Bardolphs, Fluellens, a few Exeters, and without doubt his Cambridges and Scroops: clowns, fussbudgets, friends and traitors. It could matter to nobody except herself if her agent ripped poor arty Marie Perrone up her back; it might matter a great deal to—he shied at the alternatives—to, let us say, Man, if Foster trusted a Pistol to do his work, or passed over a Fluellen for his mannerisms, or failed to know a Scroop when he saw one.

We will arm the young hero-king, he thought comfortably just before sleep claimed him.

Roland Fuqua had been transferred to Toledo by the pet-food company. He wrote to Edel:

> *Instinct tells me not to queer my luck by talking about it, but anyway—I really believe I'm moving up in the organization. The other day a party from Sales came through the QC labs and one of them, just an ordinary-looking Joe, stopped to talk to me about the test I was running—asked very intelligent questions. You could have knocked me over with a Folin-Wu pipette when they told me who he was afterwards; just John McVey himself, Assistant Vice-President in Charge of Sales! Unaccustomed as I am to pipe dreams, it can't be a coincidence that it was me he talked to instead of half-a-dozen other lab men with seniority; I don't know what he has in mind exactly, maybe some kind of liaison job between QC and Sales, which would put me on Staff level instead of Hourly-Rated ... .*

Mr. Edel felt sick for him. He would have to answer the letter at once; if he put it off he would put it off again and their correspondence would peter out and Fuqua would be betrayed. But what could he tell him—that he *was* pipe-dreaming, that "coincidences" like that happen to everybody a hundred times a day, that Roland Fuqua, Ph.D., would never, at 45, move from the Quality Control lab to the glittering world of Sales?

He stalled for time by stamping and addressing the envelope first, then hung over the typewriter for five minutes of misery. It was Wednesday night; Foster was due for the twelfth and last of his Enrichment sessions. Mr. Edel tried not to cause Fuqua pain by dwelling on the world of teaching he had lost—but *what* else was there to write about?

> *I'm sure you remember Foster—the fly boy? I've been taking him, on one of those Enrichment things, through* Henry V. *This is supposed to win him .0001 of a place higher on the graduating class list and get him into the Academy, and I suppose it will. Things are very simple for Foster, enviably so. He has a titan of engineering for a father who appears to commute between the Minas Geraes power station in Brazil, his consulting service in the city and trouble spots in the I.T.&T. network—maybe I should say commutate. I honestly do not believe that Foster has to lie his way through the personality profiles like the rest of us mortals—*

Now there was a hell of a thing to put down. He was going to rip the page out and start again, then angrily changed his mind. Fuqua wasn't a cripple; it wasn't Bad Form to mention his folly; it would be merely stupid to pretend that nothing had happened. He finished out the page with a gush of trivia. Sexy little Mrs. Dickman who taught Spanish was very visibly expecting. New dietician in the cafeteria, food cheaper, but worse than ever. Rumored retirement of old man Thelusson again and one step up for History teachers if true. Best wishes good luck regards to Beth and the youngster, Dave. He whipped the page into folds, slipped it into the envelope and sealed the flap fast, before he could change his mind again. It was time to stop treating Fuqua like a basket case; if convalescence had not begun by now, it never would.

His bell rang; Foster was on time, to the minute.

They shook hands rather formally. "Like a cup of coffee, Foster?" Mr. Edel asked.

"No thank you, sir."

"I'll make one for myself then. Brought your paper? Good. Read it to me."

While he compounded coffee, Foster began to read. After much discussion they had settled on "Propaganda and Reality in *Henry V*" as his topic. The boy had read Holinshed where relevant, articles in the *Dictionary of National Biography* and appropriate history texts. Beyond suggesting these, Mr. Edel had left him alone in the actual treatment of his paper. He did not quite know what to expect from Foster beyond careful organization and an absence of gross blunders; he waited with interest.

The paper was a short one—1500 words, by request. Nevertheless it gave Mr. Edel a few painful shocks. There were two sneers at "deluded groundlings," much reveling in the irony of the fictional Henry's affection for his Welsh captain as against the real Henry who had helped to crush Glendower and extinguish the Welsh as a nation, and fun with the Irishman Macmorris who came loyally from Shakespeare's pen in 1599 while "the general of our gracious empress" was doing his best to extinguish the Irish as a nation. Henry's *"we have now no thoughts in us but France (save those to God)"* was evaluated as "the poet's afterthought." The massacre of the French prisoners at Agincourt, Henry's brutal practical joke with the pretended glove of a French nobleman, his impossibly compressed and eloquent courtship of Katharine, were all somehow made to testify to a cynical Shakespeare manipulating his audience's passions.

The great shock was that Foster approved of all this. *"It was a time of troubles and England was besieged from without and threatened from within. The need of the time was a call to unity, and this Shakespeare provided in good measure. The London mob and the brotherhood of apprentices, always a potential danger to the Peace, no doubt was inspired and pacified for a time by the Shakespearean version of a successful aggressor's early career."*

Modestly Foster folded his typescript.

It was ground into Mr. Edel that you start by saying whatever words of praise are possible and then go on to criticize. Mechanically he said warm things about the paper's organization, its style, its scholarly apparatus. "But—aren't you taking a rather too utilitarian view of the play? It is propaganda to some extent, but should you stop short with the propaganda function of the play? I'm aware that you're limited by your topic and length, but I wish there had been some recognition of the play's existence as a work of art."

Foster said, smiling: "Well, I'm new at this, Mr. Edel. I didn't know I was supposed to stray. Should I revise it?"

"Oh, no," Mr. Edel said quickly. "I didn't mean to imply that you're unarguably mistaken in anything you said. I don't know why I'm fussing at you about it at all. I suppose you've taken a sort of engineering approach to literature, which is natural enough. Did you ever succeed in engaging your father in the project?"

"I'm afraid not, Mr. Edel. You can imagine."

"He's been away?"

"Why, no." Foster was surprised. But *didn't* his father go away now and then? He thought Foster had said—or *almost* said—

He took the paper from him and leafed through it. "This is quite good enough for a pass, Foster. It'll be read by somebody in the English Chairman's office, but that's a formality. Let's say you've completed your Enrichment Option." He stuck out his hand and Foster took it warmly. "That, then, is that. Do you have to run now?"

"With all rods out," Foster said. "I've got to prepare for the Math Team Meet, a hundred things. Can I mail that for you?"

It was the letter to Fuqua on his desk. "Why, thanks."

"Thank *you*, Mr. Edel, for the time you've taken with me."

Well worth it, son, Mr. Edel thought after the door closed. There aren't many like you. The paper was a little cold and cynical, but you'll learn. Criticism's heady stuff. Speaking quite objectively, you've done a piece thoroughly consistent with College Freshman English work, and that's what you were supposed to do. If it helps get you into Colorado Springs, I've done my job.

He turned in the paper the next day to the English Chairman's office and the Assistant Chairman read it while he waited, mumbled "Seems quite competent" and entered a Completed on Foster's grade card. He let his eyes run over the other grades and whistled. "A beaver," he said.

"All rods out," Mr. Edel smugly corrected him, and went to the door. A freshman girl who knew him, on messenger duty with the Principal's Office, intercepted him in the corridor. The message: he would please report at once to the Principal; Mrs. Giovino would be advised to take such classes as he might be obliged to miss.

"Classes?" he asked the girl, unbelievingly.

She knew nothing.

The Assistant Principal for Teaching Personnel received him at once, alone in his two-window office. He was a grey man named Sturgis whose pride was getting to the point. "Edel," he asked, "are you sure you're *happy* here?"

Mr. Edel said, recognizing a sheet of typing on Sturgis' desk: "May I ask how you got that letter of mine?"

"Surely. Your young friend Foster turned it in."

"But why? Why?"

"I shall quote: *'I honestly do not believe that Foster has to lie his way through the personality profiles like the rest of us mortals.'* If you believed this, Edel, why did you counsel him to lie? Why did you show him this letter as proof that you lied yourself?"

"Counsel him to lie? I never. I never."

His stammering was guilt; his sweating was guilt. Sturgis pitied him and shook his head. "He kept a little record," Sturgis said. "Ha, a 'log' he called it— he's quite space-minded; did you know?"

"I know. I demand a hearing, God damn it!"

Sturgis was surprised. "Oh, you'll get a hearing, Edel. We always give hearings; you know that."

"I know that. Can I get back to my classes now?"

"Better not. If you're not *happy* here ..."

Mr. Edel and Foster met that afternoon in the soda shop two blocks from the school. Mr. Edel had been waiting for him, and Foster saw the teacher staring at him from a booth. He excused himself politely from the Math Team crowd around him and joined Mr. Edel.

"I feel I owe you an explanation, sir," Foster said.

"I agree. How could you—why—?"

Foster said apologetically: "They like you to be a little ruthless at the Academy. This will stand out on my record as a sign of moral fiber. No, Mr. Edel, don't try to hit me. It'll make things look that much worse at the hearing. Goodbye, sir."

He rejoined his handsome, quiet crowd at the counter; in a moment they were talking busily about elliptic functions and Fourier series. Mr. Edel slunk from the place knowing that there was only one court of appeal.

3379 Seneca Avenue turned out to be a shocking slum tenement back of a municipal bus garage. The apartment, Mr. Edel thought, after his initial surprise, would be one of those "hideaways"—probably a whole floor run together, equipped with its own heating and air-conditioning, plumbing replaced ... after all, would Foster Senior give a damn about a fancy address? Not that engineer.

But the Foster apartment, or so said a card tacked to a rust-stiffened bell-pull, was only one of a dozen like it on the cabbage-reeking fifth floor. And the paunchy, unshaven, undershirted man who came to the door and stood reeling in the doorway said: "Yah, I'm Ole Foster. Yah, I got a boy in Nixon High. What the crazy kid do now? He's crazy, that kid. Maybe I get a little drunk sometime, I got a little pension from I hurt my back driving the buses, people don't appreciate, don't realize. You wanna drink? What you say you come for?"

"About your son ..."

"So I beat him up!" the man yelled, suddenly belligerent. "Ain't I his father? He talks smart to me, I got a right to beat him some, ain't I? People don't appreciate ..."

Old Foster lost interest and, mumbling, closed the door.

Mr. Edel walked slowly down the stairs, not able to forgive, but feeling at least the beginnings of eventual ease from the knowledge of why he was being destroyed.

[*Fantasy and Science Fiction* - January 1956]

The Cosmic Charge Account

The Lackawanna was still running one cautious morning train a day into Scranton, though the city was said to be emptying fast. Professor Leuten and I had a coach to ourselves, except for a scared, jittery trainman who hung around and talked at us.

"The name's Pech," he said. "And let me tell you, the Peches have been around for a mighty long time in these parts. There's a town twenty-three miles north of Scranton named Pechville. Full of my cousins and aunts and uncles, and I used to visit there and we used to send picture postcards and get them, too. But my God, mister, what's happened to them?"

His question was rhetorical. He didn't realize that Professor Leuten and I happened to be the only two people outside the miscalled Plague Area who could probably answer it.

"Mr. Pech," I said, "if you don't mind we'd like to talk some business."

"Sorry," he said miserably, and went on to the next car.

When we were alone Professor Leuten remarked: "An interesting reaction." He was very smooth about it. Without the slightest warning he whipped a huge, writhing, hairy spider from his pocket and thrust it at my face.

I was fast on the draw too. In one violent fling I was standing on my left foot in the aisle, thumbing my nose, my tongue stuck out. Gooseflesh rippled down my neck and shoulders.

"Very good," he said, and put the spider away. It was damnably realistic. Even knowing that it was a gadget of twisted springs and plush, I cringed at the thought of its nestling in his pocket. With me it was spiders. With the professor it was rats and asphyxiation. Toward the end of our mutual training program it took only one part per million of sulfur dioxide gas in his vicinity to send him whirling into the posture of defense, crane-like on one leg, tongue out and thumb to nose, the sweat of terror on his brow.

"I have something to tell you, Professor," I said.

"So?" he asked tolerantly. And that did it. The tolerance. I had been prepared to make my point with a dignified recital and apology, but there were two ways to tell the story and I suddenly chose the second.

424

"You're a phony," I said with satisfaction.

"*What?*" he gasped.

"A phony. A fake. A hoaxer. A self-deluding crackpot. Your Functional Epistemology is a farce. Let's not go into this thing kidding ourselves."

His accent thickened a little. "Led me remind you, Mr. Norris, that you are addressing a Doctor of Philosophy of the University of Göttingen and a member of the faculty of the University of Basel."

"You mean a *privat-dozent* who teaches freshman logic. And I seem to remember that Göttingen revoked your degree."

He said slowly: "I have known all along that you were a fool, Mr. Norris. Not until now did I realize that you are also an anti-Semite. It was the Nazis who went through an illegal ceremony of revocation."

"So that makes me an anti-Semite. From a teacher of logic that's very funny."

"You are correct," he said after a long pause. "I withdraw my remark. Now, would you be good enough to amplify yours?"

"Gladly, Professor. In the first place—"

I had been winding up the rubber rat in my pocket. I yanked it out and tossed it into his lap, where it scrabbled and clawed. He yelled with terror, but the yell didn't cost him a split second. Almost before it started from his throat he was standing one-legged, thumb to nose, tongue stuck out.

He thanked me coldly, I congratulated him coldly, I pocketed the rat while he shuddered and we went on with the conversation.

I told him how, eighteen months ago, Mr. Hopedale called me into his office. Nice office, oak panels, signed pictures of Hopedale Press writers from our glorious past: Kipling, Barrie, Theodore Roosevelt and the rest of the backlog boys.

What about Eino Elekinen, Mr. Hopedale wanted to know. Eino was one of our novelists. His first, *Vinland the Good,* had been a critical success and a popular flop; *Cubs of the Viking Breed,* the sequel, made us all a little money. He was now a month past delivery date on the final volume of the trilogy and the end was not in sight.

"I think he's pulling a sit-down strike, Mr. Hopedale. He's way overdrawn now and I had to refuse him a thousand-dollar advance. He wanted to send his wife to the Virgin Islands for a divorce."

"Give him the money," Mr. Hopedale said impatiently. "How can you expect the man to write when he's beset by personal difficulties?"

"Mr. Hopedale," I said politely, "she could divorce him right here in New York State. He's given her grounds in all five boroughs and the western townships of Long Island. But that's not the point. He can't write. And even if he could, the last thing American literature needs right now is another trilogy about a Scandinavian immigrant family."

"I know." he said. "I know. He's not very good yet. But I think he's going to be, and do you want him to starve while he's getting the juvenilia out of his system?" His next remark had nothing to do with Elekinen. He looked at the signed photo of T. R.—"*To a bully publisher*"—and said: "Norris, we're broke."

I said: "Ah?"

"We owe everybody. Printer, papermill, warehouse. Everybody. It's the end of Hopedale Press. Unless—I don't want you to think people have been reporting on you, Norris, but I understand you came up with an interesting idea at lunch yesterday. Some Swiss professor."

I had to think hard. "You must mean Leuten, Mr. Hopedale. No, there's nothing in it for us, sir. I was joking. My brother—he teaches philosophy at Columbia—mentioned him to me. Leuten's a crackpot. Every year or two Weintraub Verlag in Basel brings out another volume of his watchamacallit and they sell about a thousand. Functional Epistemology—my brother says it's all nonsense, the kind of stuff vanity presses put out. It was just a gag about us turning him into a Schweitzer or a Toynbee and bringing out a one-volume condensation. People just buy his books—I suppose—because they got started and feel ashamed to stop."

Mr. Hopedale said: "Do it, Norris. Do it. We can scrape together enough cash for one big promotion and then—the end. I'm going to see Brewster of Commercial Factors in the morning. I believe he will advance us sixty-five percent on our accounts receivable." He tried on a cynical smile. It didn't become him. "Norris, you are what is technically called a Publisher's Bright Young Man. We can get seven-fifty for a scholarly book. With luck and promotion we can sell in the hundred-thousands. Get on it." I nodded, feeling sick, and started out. Mr. Hopedale said in a tired voice: "And it might actually be work of some inspirational value."

Professor Leuten sat and listened, red-faced, breathing hard. "You—betrayer," he said at last. "You with the smiling face that came to Basel, that talked of lectures in America, that told me to sign your damnable contract. My face on the cover of the *Time* magazine that looks like a monkey, the idiotic interviews, the press releasements in my name that I never saw. America, I thought, and held my tongue. But—from the beginning—it was—a lie!" He buried his face in his hands and muttered. "*Ach!* You stink!"

That reminded me. I took a small stench-bomb from my pocket and crushed it.

He leaped up, balanced on one leg and thumbed his nose. His tongue was out four inches and he was panting with the terror of asphyxiation.

"Very good," I said.

"Thank you. I suchest we move to the other end of the car."

We and our luggage were settled before he began to breathe normally. I judged that the panic and most of his anger had passed. "Professor," I said cautiously, "I've been thinking of what we do when—and if—we find Miss Phoebe."

"We shall complete her re-education," he said. "We shall point out that her unleashed powers have been dysfunctionally applied."

"I can think of something better to do than completing her re-education. It's why I spoke a little harshly. Presumably Miss Phoebe considers you the greatest man in the world."

He smiled reminiscently and I knew what he was thinking.

La Plume, Pa.
Wednesday
Four A.M. (!)

Professor Konrad Leuten
c/o The Hopedale Press
New York City, New York

My Dear Professor,

Though you are a famous and busy man I do hope you will take time to read a few words of *grateful* tribute from an old lady (eighty-four). I have just finished your magnificent and inspirational book *How to Live on the Cosmic Expense Account: An Introduction to Functional Epistemology.*

Professor, I *believe*. I *know* every splendid word in your book is *true*. If there is one chapter finer than the others it is No. 9, "How to Be In Utter Harmony With Your Environment." The Twelve Rules in that chapter shall from this *minute* be my guiding light, and I shall practice them *faithfully* forever.

Your grateful friend,
(Miss) Phoebe Bancroft

That flattering letter reached us on Friday, one day after the papers reported with amusement or dismay the "blackout" of La Plume, Pennsylvania. The term "Plague Area" came later.

"I suppose she might," said the professor.

"Well, think about it."

The train slowed for a turn. I noticed that the track was lined with men and women. And some of them, by God, were leaping for the moving train! Brakes went on with a squeal and jolt; my nose bashed against the seat in front of us.

"Aggression," the professor said, astonished. "But that is not in the pattern!"

We saw the trainman in the vestibule opening the door to yell at the trackside people. He was trampled as they swarmed aboard, filling, jamming the car in a twinkling.

"Got to Scranton," we heard them saying. "Zombies—"

"I get it," I shouted at the professor over their hubbub. "These are refugees from Scranton. They must have blocked the track. Right now they're probably bullying the engineer into backing up all the way to Wilkes-Barre. We've got to get off!"

"*Ja,*" he said. We were in an end seat. By elbowing, crowding and a little slugging we got to the vestibule and dropped to the tracks. The professor lost all his luggage in the brief, fierce struggle. I saved only my briefcase. The powers of Hell itself were not going to separate me from that briefcase.

Hundreds of yelling, milling people were trying to climb aboard. Some made it to the roofs of the cars after it was physically impossible for one more body to be fitted inside. The locomotive uttered a despairing toot and the train began to back up.

"Well," I said, "we head north."

We found U.S. 6 after a short overland hike and trudged along the concrete. There was no traffic. Everybody with a car had left Scranton days ago, and nobody was going into Scranton. Except us.

We saw our first zombie where a signpost told us it was three miles to the city. She was a woman in a Mother Hubbard and sunbonnet. I couldn't tell whether she was young or old, beautiful or a hag. She gave us a sweet, empty smile and asked if we had any food. I said no. She said she wasn't complaining about her lot but she *was* hungry, and of course the vegetables and things were *so* much better now that they weren't poisoning the soil with those dreadful chemical fertilizers. Then she said maybe there might be something to eat down the road, wished us a pleasant good-day and went on.

"Dreadful chemical fertilizers?" I asked.

The professor said: "I believe that is a contribution by the Duchess of Carbondale to Miss Phoebe's reign. Several interviews mention it." We walked on. I could read his mind like a book. *He hasn't even read the interviews. He is a foolish, an impossible young man. And yet he is here, he has undergone a rigorous course of training, he is after all risking a sort of death. Why?* I let him go on wondering. The answer was in my briefcase.

"When do you think we'll be in range?" I asked.

"Heaven knows," he said testily. "Too many variables. Maybe it's different when she sleeps, maybe it grows at different rates varying as the number of people affected. I feel nothing yet."

"Neither do I."

And when we felt something—specifically, when we felt Miss Phoebe Bancroft practicing the Twelve Rules of "How to Be in Utter Harmony with Your Environment"—we would do something completely idiotic, something that had got us thrown—literally *thrown*—out of the office of the Secretary of Defense.

He had thundered at us: "Are you two trying to make a fool of me? Are you proposing that soldiers of the United States Army undergo a three-month training course *in sticking out their tongues and thumbing their noses?*" He was quivering with elevated blood pressure. Two M.P. lieutenants collared us under his personal orders and tossed us down the Pentagon steps when we were unable to deny that he had stated our proposal more or less correctly.

And so squads, platoons, companies, battalions and regiments marched into the Plague Area and never marched out again.

Some soldiers stumbled out as zombies. After a few days spent at a sufficient distance from the Plague Area their minds cleared and they told their confused stories. Something came over them, they said. A mental fuzziness almost impossible to describe. They liked it where they were, for instance; they left the Plague Area only by accident. They were wrapped in a vague, silly contentment even when they were hungry, which was usually. What was life like in the Plague Area? Well, not much happened. You wandered around looking for food. A lot of people looked sick but seemed to be contented. Farmers in the area gave you food with the universal silly smile, but their crops were very poor. Animal pests got most of them. Nobody seemed to eat meat. Nobody quarreled or fought or ever said a harsh word in the Plague Area. And it was hell on earth. Nothing conceivable could induce any of them to return.

The Duchess of Carbondale? Yes, sometimes she came driving by in her chariot wearing fluttery robes and a golden crown. Everybody bowed down to her. She was a big, fat middle-aged woman with rimless glasses and a pinched look of righteous triumph on her face.

The recovered zombies at first were quarantined and doctors made their wills before going to examine them. This proved to be unnecessary and the examinations proved to be fruitless. No bacteria, no rickettsia, no viruses. Nothing. Which didn't stop them from continuing in the assumption embodied in the official name of the affected counties.

Professor Leuten and I knew better, of course. For knowing better we were thrown out of offices, declined interviews and once almost locked up as lunatics. That was when we tried to get through to the President direct. The Secret Service, I am able to testify, guards our Chief Executive with a zeal that borders on ferocity.

"How goes the book?" Professor Leuten asked abruptly.

"Third hundred-thousand. Why? Want an advance?"

I don't understand German, but I can recognize deep, heartfelt profanity in any language. He spluttered and crackled for almost a full minute before he snarled in English: "Idiots! Dolts! Out of almost one-third of a million readers, exactly one has *read* the book!"

I wanted to defer comment on that. "There's a car," I said.

"Obviously it stalled and was abandoned by a refugee from Scranton."

"Let's have a look anyway." It was a battered old Ford sedan halfway off the pavement. The rear was full of canned goods and liquor. Somebody had been looting. I pushed the starter and cranked for a while; the motor didn't catch.

"Useless," said the professor. I ignored him, yanked the dashboard hood button and got out to inspect the guts. There was air showing on top of the gas in the sediment cup.

"We ride, professor," I told him. "I know these babies and their fuel pumps. The car quit on the upgrade there and he let it roll back." I unscrewed the clamp of the carburetor air filter, twisted the filter off and heaved it into the roadside bushes. The professor, of course, was a "mere-machinery" boy with the true European intellectual's contempt for greasy hands. He stood by haughtily while I poured a bottle of gin empty, found a wrench in the tool box that fit the gas tank drain plug and refilled the gin bottle with gasoline. He condescended to sit behind the wheel and crank the motor from time to time while I sprinkled gas into the carburetor. Each time the motor coughed there was less air showing in the sediment cup; finally the motor caught for good. I moved him over, tucked my briefcase in beside me, U-turned on the broad, empty highway and we chugged north into Scranton.

It was only natural that he edged away from me, I suppose. I was grimy from working under the gas tank. This plus the discreditable ability I had shown in starting the stalled car reminded him that he was, after all, a Herr Doktor from a *real* university while I was, after all, a publisher's employee with nebulous qualifications from some place called Cornell. The atmosphere was wrong for it, but sooner or later he had to be told.

"Professor, we've got to have a talk and get something straight before we find Miss Phoebe."

He looked at the huge striped sign the city fathers of Scranton wisely erected to mark that awful downgrade into the city. WARNING! SEVEN-MILE DEATH TRAP AHEAD. SHIFT INTO LOWER GEAR. $50 FINE. OBEY OR PAY!

"What is there to get straight?" he demanded. "She has partially mastered Functional Epistemology—even though Hopedale Press prefers to call it 'Living on the Cosmic Expense Account.' This has unleashed certain latent powers of hers. It is simply our task to complete her mastery of the ethical aspect of F.E. She will cease to dominate other minds as soon as she comprehends that her behavior is dysfunctional and in contravention of the Principle of Permissive Evolution." To him the matter was settled. He mused: "Really I should not have let you cut so drastically my exposition of Dyadic Imbalance; that must be the root of her difficulty. A brief inductive explanation—"

"Professor," I said. "I thought I told you in the train that you're a fake."

He corrected me loftily. "You told me that you *think* I'm a fake, Mr. Norris. Naturally I was angered by your duplicity, but your opinion of me proves nothing. I ask you to look around you. Is this fakery?"

We were well into the city. Bewildered dogs yelped at our car. Windows were broken and goods were scattered on the sidewalks; here and there a house was burning brightly. Smashed and overturned cars dotted the streets, and zombies walked slowly around them. When Miss Phoebe hit a city the effects were something like a thousand-bomber raid.

"It's not fakery," I said, steering around a smiling man in a straw hat and overalls. "It isn't Functional Epistemology either. It's *faith* in Functional Epistemology. It could have been faith in anything, but your book just happened to be what she settled on."

"Are you *daring*," he demanded, white to the lips, "to compare me with the faith healers?"

"Yes," I said wearily. "They get their cures. So do lots of people. Let's roll it up in a ball, professor. I think the best thing to do when we meet Miss Phoebe is for you to tell her you're a fake. Destroy her faith in you and your system and I think she'll turn back into a normal old lady again. Wait a minute! Don't tell me you're not a fake. I can prove you are. You say she's partly mastered F.E. and gets her powers from that partial mastery. Well, presumably you've completely mastered F.E., since you invented it. So why can't you do everything she's done, and lots more? Why can't you end this mess by levitating to La Plume, instead of taking the Lackawanna and a 1941 Ford? And, by God, why couldn't you fix the Ford with a pass of the hands and F.E. instead of standing by while I worked?"

His voice was genuinely puzzled. "I thought I just explained, Norris. Though it never occurred to me before, I suppose I could do what you say, but I wouldn't dream of it. As I said it would be dysfunctional and in complete contravention of The Principle of Permissive—"

I said something very rude and added: "In short, you can but you won't."

"Naturally not! The Principle of Permissive—" He looked at me with slow awareness dawning in his eyes. "Norris! My editor. My proofreader. My by-the-publisher-officially-assigned *fidus Achates*. Norris, haven't *you* read my book?"

"No," I said shortly. "I've been much too busy. You didn't get on the cover of *Time* magazine by blind chance, you know."

He was laughing helplessly. "How goes that song," he finally asked me, his eyes damp, "'God Bless America'?"

I stopped the car abruptly. "I think I feel something," I said. "Professor, I like you."

"I like you too, Norris," he told me. "Norris, my boy, what do you think of ladies?"

"Delicate creatures. Custodians of culture. Professor, what about meat-eating?"

"Shocking barbarous survival. *This is it, Norris!*"

We yanked open the doors and leaped out. We stood on one foot each, thumbed our noses and stuck out our tongues.

Allowing for the time on the train, this was the 1,962nd time I had done it in the past two months. One thousand, nine hundred and sixty-one times the professor had arranged for spiders to pop out at me from books, from the television screen, from under steaks, from desk drawers, from my pockets, from his. Black widows, tarantulas, harmless *(hah!)* big house spiders, real and imitation. One thousand, nine hundred and sixty-one times I had felt the arachnophobe's horrified revulsion. Each time I felt I had thrown major voluntary muscular systems into play by drawing up one leg violently, violently swinging my hand to my nose, violently grimacing to stick out my tongue.

My body had learned at last. There was no spider this time; there was only Miss Phoebe: a vague, pleasant feeling something like the first martini. But my posture of defense this 1,962nd time was accompanied by the old rejection and horror. It had no spider, so it turned on Miss Phoebe. The vague first-martini feeling vanished like morning mist burned away by the sun.

I relaxed cautiously. On the other side of the car so did Professor Leuten. "Professor," I said, "I don't like you any more."

"Thank you," he said coldly. "Nor do I like you."

"I guess we're back to normal," I said. "Climb in." He climbed in and we started off. I grudgingly said: "Congratulations."

"Because it worked? Don't be ridiculous. It was to be expected that a plan of campaign derived from the principles of Functional Epistemology would be successful. All that was required was that you be at least as smart as one of Professor Pavlov's dogs, and I admit I considered that hypothesis the weak link in my chain of reasoning ..."

We stopped for a meal from the canned stuff in the back of the car about one o'clock and then chugged steadily north through the ruined countryside. The little towns were wrecked and abandoned. Presumably refugees from the expanding Plague Area did the first damage by looting; the subsequent destruction just—happened. It showed you what would just happen to any twentieth-century town or city in the course of a few weeks if the people who wage endless war against breakdown and dilapidation put aside their arms. It was anybody's guess whether fire or water had done more damage.

Between the towns the animals were incredibly bold. There was a veritable army of rabbits eating their way across a field of clover. A farmer-zombie flapped a patchwork quilt at them, saying affectionately: "Shoo, little bunnies! Go away, now! I *mean* it!"

But they knew he didn't, and continued to chew their way across his field.

I stopped the car and called to the farmer. He came right away, smiling. "The little dickenses!" he said, waving at the rabbits. "But I haven't the heart to really scare them."

"Are you happy?" I asked him.

"Oh, yes!" His eyes were sunken and bright; his cheekbones showed on his starved face. "People should be considerate," he said. "I always say that being considerate is what matters most."

"Don't you miss electricity and cars and tractors?"

"Goodness, no. I always say that things were better in the old days. Life was more gracious, I always say. Why, I don't miss gasoline or electricity one little bit. Everybody's so considerate and gracious that it makes up for everything."

"I wonder if you'd be so considerate and gracious as to lie down in the road so we can drive over you?"

He looked mildly surprised and started to get down, saying. "Well, if it would afford you gentlemen any pleasure—"

"No; don't bother after all. You can get back to your rabbits."

He touched his straw hat and went away, beaming. We drove on. I said to the professor: "Chapter Nine: 'How to be in Utter Harmony With Your Environment.' Only she didn't change herself, Professor Leuten; she changed the environment. Every man and woman in the Area is what Miss Phoebe thinks they ought to be: silly, sentimental, obliging and gracious to the point of idiocy. Nostalgic and all thumbs when it comes to this dreadful machinery."

"Norris," the professor said thoughtfully, "we've been associated for some time. I think you might drop the 'professor' and call me 'Leuten.' In a way we're friends—"

I jammed on the worn, mushy brakes. "Out!" I yelled, and we piled out. The silly glow was enveloping me fast. Again, thumb to nose and tongue out, I burned it away. When I looked at the professor and was quite sure he was a stubborn old fossil, I knew I was all right again. When he glared at me and snapped: "Naturally I withdraw my last remark, Norris, and no chentleman would hold me to it," I knew *he* was normal. We got in and kept going north.

The devastation became noticeably worse after we passed a gutted, stinking shambles that had once been the town of Meshoppen, Pa. After Meshoppen there were more bodies on the road and the flies became a horror. No pyrethrum from

Kenya. No DDT from Wilmington. We drove in the afternoon heat with the windows cranked up and the hood ventilator closed. It was at about Meshoppen's radius from La Plume that things had stabilized for a while and the Army Engineers actually began to throw up barbed wire. Who knew what happened then? Perhaps Miss Phoebe recovered from a slight cold, or perhaps she told herself firmly that her faith in Professor Leuten's wonderful book was weakening; that she must take hold of herself and really work *hard* at being in utter harmony with her environment. The next morning—no Army Engineers. Zombies in uniform were glimpsed wandering about and smiling. The next morning the radius of the Plague Area was growing at the old mile a day.

I wanted distraction from the sweat that streamed down my face. "Professor," I said, "do you remember the last word in Miss Phoebe's letter? It was 'forever.' Do you suppose … ?"

"Immortality? Yes; I think that is well within the range of misapplied F.E. Of course complete mastery of F.E. ensures that no such selfish power would be invoked. The beauty of F.E. is its conservatism, in the kinetic sense. It is self-regulating. A world in which universal mastery of F.E. has been achieved—and I now perceive that the publication of my views by the Hopedale Press was if anything a step *away* from that ideal—would be in no outward wise different from the present world."

"Built-in escape clause," I snapped. "Like yoga. You ask 'em to prove they've achieved self-mastery, just a little demonstration like levitating or turning transparent, but they're all ready for you. They tell you they've achieved so much self-mastery they've mastered the desire to levitate or turn transparent. I almost wish I'd read your book, professor, instead of just editing it. Maybe you're smarter than I thought."

He turned brick-red and gritted out: "Your insults merely bore me, Norris."

The highway took a turn and we turned with it. I braked again and rubbed my eyes. "Do you see them?" I asked the professor.

"Yes," he said matter-of-factly. "This must be the retinue of the Duchess of Carbondale."

They were a dozen men shoulder to shoulder barricading the road. They were armed with miscellaneous sporting rifles and one bazooka. They wore kilt-like garments and what seemed to be bracelets from a five-and-ten. When we stopped they opened up the center of the line and the Duchess of Carbondale drove through in her chariot—only the chariot was a harness-racing sulky and she didn't drive it; the horse was led by a skinny teenage girl got up as Charmian for a high-school production of *Antony and Cleopatra*. The Duchess herself wore ample white robes, a tiara and junk jewelry. She looked like your unfavorite aunt, the fat one, or a grade school teacher you remember with loathing when you're forty, or one of those women who ring your doorbell and try to bully you into signing petitions against fluoridation or atheism in the public schools.

The bazooka man had his stovepipe trained on our hood. His finger was on the button and he was waiting for the Duchess to nod. "Get out," I told the professor, grabbing my briefcase. He looked at the bazooka and we got out.

"Hail, O mortals," said the Duchess.

I looked helplessly at the professor. Not even my extensive experience with lady novelists had equipped me to deal with the situation. He, however, was able to take the ball. He was a European and he had status and that's the starting point for them: establish status and then conduct yourself accordingly. He said: "Madame, my name is Konrad Leuten. I am a doctor of philosophy of the University of Göttingen and a member of the faculty of the University of Basel. Whom have I the honor to address?"

Her eyes narrowed appraisingly. "O mortal," she said, and her voice was less windily dramatic, "know ye that here in the New Lemuria worldly titles are as naught. And know ye not that the pure hearts of my subjects may not be sullied by base machinery?"

"I didn't know, madame," Leuten said politely. "I apologize. We intended, however, to go only as far as La Plume. May we have your permission to do so?"

At the mention of La Plume she went poker-faced. After a moment she waved at the bazooka man. "Destroy, O Phraxanartes, the base machine of the strangers," she said. Phraxanartes touched the button of his stovepipe. Leuten and I jumped for the ditch, my hand welded to the briefcase-handle, when the rocket whooshed into the poor old Ford's motor. We huddled there while the gas tank boomed and cans and bottles exploded. The noise subsided to a crackling roar and the whizzing fragments stopped coming our way after maybe a minute. I put my head up first. The Duchess and her retinue were gone, presumably melted into the roadside stand of trees.

Her windy contralto blasted out: "Arise, O strangers, and join us."

Leuten said from the ditch: "A perfectly reasonable request, Norris. Let us do so. After all, one must be obliging."

"And gracious," I added.

Good old Duchess! I thought. *Good old Leuten! Wonderful old world, with hills and trees and bunnies and kitties and considerate people ...*

Leuten was standing on one foot, thumbing his nose, sticking out his tongue, screaming: "Norris! Norris! Defend yourself!" He was slapping my face with his free hand. Sluggishly I went into the posture of defense, thinking: *Such nonsense. Defense against what? But l wouldn't hurt old Leuten's feelings for the world—*

Adrenaline boiled through my veins, triggered by the posture. Spiders. Crawling, hairy, horrid spiders with purple, venom-dripping fangs. They hid in your shoes and bit you and your feet swelled with the poison. Their sticky, loathsome webs brushed across your face when you walked in the dark and they came scuttling silently, champing their jaws, winking their evil gem-like eyes. *Spiders!*

The voice of the duchess blared impatiently: "I said, join us, O strangers. Well, what are you waiting for?"

The professor and I relaxed and looked at each other. "She's mad," the professor said softly. "From an asylum."

"I doubt it. You don't know America very well. Maybe you lock them up when they get like that in Europe; over here we elect them chairlady of the Library Fund Drive. If we don't, we never hear the end of it."

The costumed girl was leading the Duchess's sulky onto the road again. Some of her retinue were beginning to follow; she waved them back and dismissed the girl curtly. We skirted the heat of the burning car and approached her. It was that or try to outrun a volley from the miscellaneous sporting rifles.

"O strangers," she said, "you mentioned La Plume. Do you happen to be acquainted with my dear friend Phoebe Bancroft?"

The professor nodded before I could stop him. But almost simultaneously with his nod I was dragging the Duchess from her improvised chariot. It was very unpleasant, but I put my hands around her throat and knelt on her. It meant letting go of the briefcase but it was worth it.

She guggled and floundered and managed to whoop: "Don't shoot! I take it back, don't shoot them. Pamphilius, don't shoot, you might hit me!"

"Send 'em away," I told her.

"Never!" she blared. "They are my loyal retainers."

"You try, professor," I said.

I believe what he put on then was his classroom manner. He stiffened and swelled and rasped towards the shrubbery: "Come out at once. All of you."

They came out, shambling and puzzled. They realized that something was very wrong. There was the Duchess on the ground and she wasn't telling them what to do the way she'd been telling them for weeks now. They wanted to oblige her in any little way they could, like shooting strangers, or scrounging canned food for her, but how could they oblige her while she lay there slowly turning purple? It was very confusing. Luckily there was somebody else to oblige, the professor.

"Go away," he barked at them. "Go far away. We do not need you any more. And throw away your guns."

Well, that was something a body could understand. They smiled and threw away their guns and went away in their obliging and considerate fashion.

I eased up on the Duchess's throat. "What was that guff about the New Lemuria?" I asked her.

"You're a rude and ignorant young man," she snapped. From the corner of my eye I could see the professor involuntarily nodding agreement. "Every educated person knows that the lost wisdom of Lemuria was to be revived in the person of a beautiful priestess this year. According to the science of pyramidology—"

Beautiful priestess? Oh.

The professor and I stood by while she spouted an amazing compost of lost-continentism, the Ten Tribes, anti-fluoridation, vegetarianism, homeopathic medicine, organic farming, astrology, flying saucers, and the prose-poems of Kahlil Gibran.

The professor said dubiously at last: "I suppose one must call her a sort of Cultural Diffusionist ..." He was happier when he had her classified. He went on: "I think you know Miss Phoebe Bancroft. We wish you to present us to her as soon as possible."

"Professor," I complained, "we have a roadmap and we can find La Plume. And once we've found La Plume I don't think it'll be very hard to find Miss Phoebe."

"I will be pleased to accompany you," said the Duchess. "Though normally I frown on mechanical devices, I keep an automobile nearby in case of—in case of—*well!* of all the *rude*—!"

Believe it or not, she was speechless. Nothing in her rich store of gibberish and hate seemed to fit the situation. Anti-fluoridation, organic farming, even Kahlil Gibran were irrelevant in the face of us two each standing on one leg, thumbing our noses and sticking out our tongues.

Undeniably the posture of defense was losing efficiency. It took longer to burn away the foolish glow ...

"Professor," I asked after we warily relaxed, "how many more of those can we take?"

He shrugged. "That is why a guide will be useful," he said. "Madame, I believe you mentioned an automobile."

"I know!" she said brightly. "It was asana yoga, wasn't it? Postures, I mean?"

The professor sucked an invisible lemon. "No, madame," he said cadaverously, "It was neither siddhasana nor padmasana. Yoga has been subsumed under Functional Epistemology, as has every other working philosophical system, Eastern and Western—but we waste time. The automobile?"

"You have to do that every so often, is that it?"

"We will leave it at that, madame. The automobile, please."

"Come right along," she said gaily. I didn't like the look on her face. Madam Chairlady was about to spring a parliamentary coup. But I got my briefcase and followed.

The car was in a nearby barn. It was a handsome new Lincoln, and I was reasonably certain that our fair cicerone had stolen it. But then, we had stolen the Ford.

I loaded the briefcase in and took the wheel over her objections and we headed for La Plume, a dozen miles away. On the road she yelped: "Oh, *Functional* Epistemology—and *you're* Professor *Leuten!*"

"Yes, madame," he wearily agreed.

"I've read your book, of course. So has Miss Bancroft; she'll be so pleased to see you."

"Then why, madame, did you order your subjects to murder us?"

"Well, professor, of course I didn't know who you were then, and it *was* rather shocking, seeing somebody in a car. I, ah, had the feeling that you were up to no good, especially when you mentioned dear Miss Bancroft. *She,* you know, is really responsible for the re-emergence of the New Lemuria."

"Indeed?" said the professor. "You understand, then, about Leveled Personality Interflow?" He was beaming.

"I beg your pardon?"

"Leveled Personality Interflow!" he barked. "Chapter Nine!"

"Oh. In your book, of course. Well, as a matter of fact I *skipped*—"

"Another one," muttered the professor, leaning back.

The Duchess chattered on: "Dear Miss Bancroft, of course, swears by your book. But you were asking—no, it wasn't what you said. I cast her horoscope and it turned out that *she* is the Twenty-Seventh Pen-dragon!"

"Scheissdreck," the professor mumbled, too discouraged to translate.

"So naturally, professor, she incarnates Taliesin *spiritually* and"—a modest giggle—"you know who incarnates it *materially*. Which is only sensible, since I'm descended from the high priestesses of Mu. Little did I think when I was running the Wee Occult Book Shoppe in Carbondale!"

"Ja," said the professor. He made an effort. "Madame, tell me something. Do you never feel a certain thing, a sense of friendliness and intoxication and goodwill enveloping you quite suddenly?"

"Oh, *that*," she said scornfully. "Yes; every now and then. It doesn't bother me. I just think of all the work I have to do. How I must stamp out the dreadful, soul-destroying advocates of meat-eating, and chemical fertilizer, and fluoridation. How I must wage the good fight for occult science and *crush* the materialistic philosophers. How I must tear down our corrupt and self-seeking ministers and priests, our rotten laws and customs—"

"Lieber Gott," the professor marveled as she went on. "With Norris it is spiders. With me it is rats and asphyxiation. But with this woman it is apparently everything in the Kosmos except her own revolting self!" She didn't hear him; she was demanding that the voting age for women be lowered to sixteen and for men raised to thirty-five.

We plowed through flies and mosquitoes like smoke. The flies bred happily on dead cows and *in* sheep which unfortunately were still alive. There wasn't oil cake for the cows in the New Lemuria. There wasn't sheep-dip for the sheep. There weren't state and county and township and village road crews constantly patroling, unplugging sluices, clearing gutters, replacing rusted culverts, and so quite naturally the countryside was reverting to swampland. The mosquitoes loved it.

"La Plume," the Duchess announced gaily. "And that's Miss Phoebe Bancroft's little house right there. Just *why* did you wish to see her, professor, by the way?"

"To complete her re-education ..." the professor said in a tired voice.

Miss Phoebe's house, and the few near it, were the only places we had seen in the Area which weren't blighted by neglect. Miss Phoebe, of course, was able to tell the shambling zombies what to do in the way of truck-gardening, lawn-mowing and maintenance. The bugs weren't too bad there.

"She's probably resting, poor dear," said the Duchess. I stopped the car and we got out. The Duchess said something about Kleenex and got in again and rummaged through the glove compartment.

"Please, professor," I said, clutching my briefcase. "Play it the smart way. The way I told you."

"Norris," he said, "I realize that you have my best interests at heart. You're a good boy, Norris, and I like you—"

"Watch it!" I yelled, and swung into the posture of defense. So did he.

Spiders. It wasn't a good old world, not while there were loathsome spiders in it. *Spiders—*

And a pistol shot past my ear. The professor fell. I turned and saw the Duchess looking smug, about to shoot me too. I sidestepped and she missed; as I slapped the automatic out of her hand I thought confusedly that it was a near-miracle, her hitting the professor at five paces even if he was a standing target. People don't realize how hard it is to hit *anything* with a hand-gun.

I suppose I was going to kill her or at least damage her badly when a new element intruded. A little old white-haired lady tottering down the neat gravel path from the house. She wore a nice pastel dress which surprised me; somehow I had always thought of her in black.

"Bertha!" Miss Phoebe rapped out. "What have you done?"

The Duchess simpered. "That man there was going to harm you, Phoebe, dear. And this fellow is just as bad—"

Miss Phoebe said: "Nonsense. Nobody can harm me. Chapter Nine, Rule Seven. Bertha, I saw you shoot that gentleman. I'm very angry with you, Bertha. Very angry."

The Duchess turned up her eyes and crumpled. I didn't have to check; I was sure she was dead. Miss Phoebe was once again In Utter Harmony With Her Environment.

I went over and knelt beside the professor. He had a hole in his stomach and was still breathing. There wasn't much blood. I sat down and cried. For the professor. For the poor damned human race which at a mile per day would be gobbled up into apathy and idiocy. Goodbye, Newton and Einstein, goodbye, steak dinners and Michelangelo and Tenzing Norkay; goodbye, Moses, Rodin, Kwan Yin, transistors, Boole and Steichen ...

A redheaded man with an adam's apple was saying gently to Miss Phoebe: "It's this rabbit, ma'am." And indeed an enormous rabbit was loping up to him. "Every time I find a turnip or something he takes it away from me and he kicks and bites when I try to reason with him—" And indeed he took a piece of turnip from his pocket and the rabbit insolently pawed it from his hand and nibbled it triumphantly with one wise-guy eye cocked up at his victim. "He does that every time, Miss Phoebe," the man said unhappily.

The little old lady said: "I'll think of something, Henry. But let me take care of these people first."

"Yes, ma'am," Henry said. He reached out cautiously for his piece of turnip and the rabbit bit him and then went back to its nibbling.

"Young man," Miss Phoebe said to me, "what's wrong? You're giving in to despair. You mustn't do that. Chapter Nine, Rule Three."

I pulled myself together enough to say: "This is Professor Leuten. He's dying."

Her eyes widened. "*The* Professor Leuten?" I nodded. "*How to Live on the Cosmic Expense Account?*" I nodded.

"Oh, dear! If only there were something I could do!"

Heal the dying? Apparently not. She didn't think she could, so she couldn't.

"Professor," I said. "Professor."

He opened his eyes and said something in German, then, hazily: "Woman shot me. Spoil her—racket, you call it? Who is this?" He grimaced with pain.

"I'm Miss Phoebe Bancroft, Professor Leuten," she breathed, leaning over him. "I'm so dreadfully sorry; I admire your wonderful book so much."

His weary eyes turned to me. "So, Norris," he said. "No time to do it right. We do it your way. Help me up."

I helped him to his feet, suffering, I think, almost as much as he did. The wound started to bleed more copiously.

"No!" Miss Phoebe exclaimed. "You should lie down."

The professor leered. "Good idea, baby. You want to keep me company?"

"What's that?" she snapped.

"You heard me, baby. Say, you got any liquor in your place?"

"Certainly not! Alcohol is inimical to the development of the higher functions of the mind. Chapter Nine—"

"Pfui on Chapter Nine, baby. I chust wrote that stuff for money."

If Miss Phoebe hadn't been in a state resembling surgical shock after hearing that, she would have seen the pain convulsing his face. "You mean ... ?" she quavered, beginning to look her age for the first time.

"Sure. Lotta garbage. Sling fancy words and make money. What I go for is liquor and women. Women like you, baby."

The goose did it.

Weeping, frightened, insulted and lost she tottered blindly up the neat path to her house. I eased the professor to the ground. He was biting almost through his lower lip.

I heard a new noise behind me. It was Henry, the redhead with the adam's apple. He was chewing his piece of turnip and had hold of the big rabbit by the hind legs. He was flailing it against a tree. Henry looked ferocious, savage, carnivorous and very, very dangerous to meddle with. In a word, human.

"Professor," I breathed at his waxen face, "you've done it. It's broken. Over. No more Plague Area."

He muttered, his eyes closed: "I regret not doing it properly ... but tell the people how I died, Norris. With dignity, without fear. Because of Functional Epistemology."

I said through tears: "I'll do more than tell them, professor. The world will know about your heroism."

"The world must know. We've got to make a book of this—your authentic, authorized, fictional biography—and Hopedale's West Coast agent'll see to the film sale—"

"Film?" he said drowsily. "Book ... ?"

"Yes. Your years of struggle, the little girl at home who kept faith in you when everybody scoffed, your burning mission to transform the world, and the climax—here, now!—as you give up your life for your philosophy."

"What girl?" he asked weakly.

"There must have been someone, professor. We'll find someone."

"You would," he asked feebly, "document my expulsion from Germany by the Nazis?"

"Well, I don't think so, professor. The export market's important, especially when it comes to selling film rights, and you don't want to go offending people by raking up old memories. But don't worry, professor. The big thing is, the world will never forget you and what you've done."

He opened his eyes and breathed: "You mean *your* version of what I've done. Ach, Norris, Norris! Never did I think there was a power on Earth which could force me to contravene The Principle of Permissive Evolution." His voice became stronger. "But you, Norris, are that power." He got to his feet, grunting. "Norris," he said, "I hereby give you formal warning that any attempt to make a fictional biography or cinema film of my life will result in an immediate injunction being—you say slapped?—upon you, as well as suits for damages from libel, copyright infringement and invasion of privacy. I have had *enough*."

"Professor," I gasped. "You're well!"

He grimaced. "I'm sick. Profoundly sick to my stomach at my contravention of the Principle of Permissive—"

His voice grew fainter. This was because he was rising slowly into the air. He leveled off at a hundred feet and called: "Send the royalty statements to my old address in Basel. And remember, Norris, I warned you—"

He zoomed eastward then at perhaps one hundred miles per hour. I think he was picking up speed when he vanished from sight.

I stood there for ten minutes or so and sighed and rubbed my eyes and wondered whether anything was worthwhile. I decided I'd read the professor's book tomorrow without fail, unless something came up.

Then I took my briefcase and went up the walk and into Miss Phoebe's house. (Henry had made a twig fire on the lawn and was roasting his rabbit; he glared at me most disobligingly and I skirted him with care.)

This was, after all, the payoff; this was, after all, the reason why I had risked my life and sanity.

"Miss Phoebe," I said to her, taking it out of the briefcase, "I represent the Hopedale Press; this is one of our standard contracts. We're very much interested in publishing the story of your life, with special emphasis on the events of the past few weeks. Naturally you'd have an experienced collaborator. I believe sales in the hundred-thousands wouldn't be too much to expect. I would suggest as a title—that's right, you sign on that line there—*How to Be Supreme Ruler of Everybody* ... ."

[*Ten Story Fantasy* - Spring 1951]

Friend to Man

Call him, if anything, Smith. He had answered to that and to other names in the past. Occupation, fugitive. His flight, it is true, had days before slowed to a walk and then to a crawl, but still he moved, a speck of grey, across the vast and featureless red plain of a planet not his own.

Nobody was following Smith, he sometimes realized, and then he would rest for a while, but not long. After a minute or an hour the posse of his mind would reform and spur behind him; reason would cry no and still he would heave himself to his feet and begin again to inch across the sand.

The posse, imaginary and terrible, faded from front to rear. Perhaps in the very last rank of pursuers was a dim shadow of a schoolmate. Smith had never been one to fight fair. More solid were the images of his first commercial venture, the hijacking job. A truck driver with his chest burned out namelessly pursued; by his side a faceless cop. The ranks of the posse grew crowded then, for Smith had been a sort of organizer after that, but never an organizer too proud to demonstrate his skill. An immemorially old-fashioned garroting-wire trailed inches from the nape of Winkle's neck, for Winkle had nearly sung to the police.

"Squealer!" shrieked Smith abruptly, startling himself. Shaking, he closed his eyes and still Winkle plodded after him, the tails of wire bobbing with every step, stiffly.

A solid, business-like patrolman eclipsed him, drilled through the throat; beside him was the miraculously resurrected shade of Henderson.

The twelve-man crew of a pirated lighter marched, as you would expect, in military formation, but they bled ceaselessly from their ears and eyes as people do when shot into space without helmets.

These he could bear, but, somehow, Smith did not like to look at the leader of the posse. It was odd, but he did not like to look at her.

She had no business there! If they were ghosts why was she there? He hadn't killed her, and, as far as he knew, Amy was alive and doing business in the open Quarter at Portsmouth. It wasn't fair, Smith wearily thought. He inched across the featureless plain and Amy followed with her eyes.

Let us! Let us! We have waited so long!
Wait longer, little ones. Wait longer.

Smith, arriving at the planet, had gravitated to the Open Quarter and found, of course, that his reputation had preceded him. Little, sharp-faced men had sidled up to pay their respects, and they happened to know of a job waiting for the right touch …

He brushed them off.

Smith found the virginal, grey-eyed Amy punching tapes for the Transport Company, tepidly engaged to a junior executive. The daughter of the Board Chairman, she fancied herself daring to work in the rough office at the port.

First was the child's play of banishing her young man. A minor operation, it was managed with the smoothness and dispatch one learns after years of such things. Young Square-Jaw had been quite willing to be seduced by a talented young woman from the Open Quarter, and had been so comically astonished when the photographs appeared on the office bulletin board!

He had left by the next freighter, sweltering in a bunk by the tube butts, and the forlorn grey eyes were wet for him.

But how much longer must we wait?
Much longer, little ones. It is weak—too weak.

The posse, Smith thought vaguely, was closing in. That meant, he supposed, that he was dying. It would not be too bad to be dead, quickly and cleanly. He had a horror of filth.

Really, he thought, this was too bad! The posse was in front of him …

It was not the posse; it was a spindly, complicated creature that, after a minute of bleary staring, he recognized as a native of the planet.

Smith thought and thought as he stared and could think of nothing to do about it. The problem was one of the few that he had never considered and debated within himself. If it had been a cop he would have acted; if it had been any human being he would have acted, but this …

He could think of nothing more logical to do than to lie down, pull the hood across his face and go to sleep.

He woke in an underground chamber big enough for half a dozen men. It was egg-shaped and cool, illuminated by sunlight red-filtered through the top half. He touched the red-lit surface and found it to be composed of glass marbles cemented together with a translucent plastic. The marbles he knew; the red desert was full of them, wind-polished against each other for millennia, rarely perfectly round, as all of these were. They had been most carefully collected. The bottom half of the egg-shaped cave was a mosaic of flatter, opaque pebbles, cemented with the same plastic.

Smith found himself thinking clear, dry, level thoughts. The posse was gone and he was sane and there had been a native and this must be the native's burrow. He had been cached there as food, of course, so he would kill the native and possibly drink its body fluids, for his canteen had been empty for a long time. He drew a knife and wondered how to kill, his eyes on the dark circle which led from the burrow to the surface.

Silently the dark circle was filled with the tangled appendages of the creature, and in the midst of the appendages was, insanely, a Standard Transport Corporation five-liter can.

The STC monogram had been worn down, but was unmistakable. The can had heft to it.

Water? The creature seemed to hold it out. He reached into the tangle and the can was smoothly released to him. The catch flipped up and he drank flat, distilled water in great gulps.

He felt that he bulged with the stuff when he stopped, and knew the first uneasy intimations of inevitable cramp. The native was not moving, but something that could have been an eye turned on him.

"Salt?" asked Smith, his voice thin in the thin air. "I need salt with water."

The thing rubbed two appendages together and he saw a drop of amber exude and spread on them. It was, he realized a moment later, rosining the bow, for the appendages drew across each other and he heard a whining, vibrating cricket-voice say: "S-s-z-z-aw-w?"

"Salt," said Smith.

It did better the next time. The amber drop spread, and—"S-z-aw-t?" was sounded, with a little tap of the bow for the final phoneme.

It vanished, and Smith leaned back with the cramps beginning. His stomach convulsed and he lost the water he had drunk. It seeped without a trace into the floor. He doubled up and groaned—once. The groan had not eased him in body or mind; he would groan no more but let the cramps run their course.

Nothing but what is useful had always been his tacit motto. There had not been a false step in the episode of Amy. When Square-Jaw had been disposed of, Smith had waited until her father, perhaps worldly enough to know his game, certain at all events not to like the way he played it, left on one of his regular inspection trips. He had been formally introduced to her by a mutual friend who owed money to a dangerous man in the Quarter, but who had not yet been found out by the tight little clique that thought it ruled the commercial world of that planet.

With precision he had initiated her into the Open Quarter by such easy stages that at no one point could she ever suddenly realize that she was in it or the grey eyes ever fill with shock. Smith had, unknown to her, disposed of some of her friends, chosen other new ones, stage-managed entire days for her, gently forcing opinions and attitudes, insistent, withdrawing at the slightest token of counter-pressure, always urging again when the counter-pressure relaxed.

The night she had taken Optol had been prepared for by a magazine article—notorious in the profession as a whitewash—a chance conversation in which chance did not figure at all, a televised lecture on addiction, and a trip to an Optol joint at which everybody had been gay and healthy. On the second visit, Amy had pleaded for the stuff—just out of curiosity, of course, and he had reluctantly called the unfrocked medic, who injected the grey eyes with the oil.

It had been worth his minute pains; he had got 200 feet of film while she staggered and reeled loathsomely. And she had, after the Optol evaporated, described with amazed delight how *different* everything had looked, and how exquisitely she had danced ...

"S-z-aw-t!" announced the native from the mouth of the burrow. It bowled at him marbles of rock-salt from the surface, where rain never fell to dissolve them.

He licked one, then cautiously sipped water. He looked at the native, thought, and put his knife away. It came into the burrow and reclined at the opposite end from Smith.

It knows what a knife is, and water and salt, and something about language, he thought between sips. What's the racket?

> But when? But when?
> Wait longer, little ones. Wait longer.

"You understand me?" Smith asked abruptly.

The amber drop exuded, and the native played whiningly: "*A-ah-nn-nah-t-ann.*"

"Well," said Smith, "thanks."

He never really knew where the water came from, but guessed that it had been distilled in some fashion within the body of the native. He had, certainly, seen the thing shovel indiscriminate loads of crystals into its mouth—calcium carbonate, aluminum hydroxide, anything—and later emit amorphous powders from one vent and water from another. His food, brought on half an STC can, was utterly unrecognizable—a jelly, with bits of crystal embedded in it that he had to spit out.

What it did for a living was never clear. It would lie for hours in torpor, disappear on mysterious errands, bring him food and water, sweep out the burrow with a specialized limb, converse when requested.

It was days before Smith really *saw* the creature. In the middle of a talk with it he recognized it as a fellow organism rather than as a machine, or gadget, or nightmare, or alien monster. It was, for Smith, a vast step to take.

Not easily he compared his own body with the native's, and admitted that, of course, his was inferior. The cunning jointing of the limbs, the marvelously practical detail of the eye, the economy of the external muscle system, were admirable.

Now and then at night the posse would return and crowd about him as he lay dreaming, and he knew that he screamed then, reverberatingly in the burrow. He awoke to find the most humanoid of the native's limbs resting on his brow, soothingly, and he was grateful for the new favor; he had begun to take his food and water for granted.

The conversations with the creature were whimsy as much as anything else. It was, he thought, the rarest of Samaritans, who had no interest in the private life of its wounded wayfarer.

He told it of life in the cities of the planet, and it sawed out politely that the cities were very big indeed. He told it of the pleasures of human beings, and it politely agreed that their pleasures were most pleasant.

Under its cool benevolence he stammered and faltered in his ruthlessness. On the nights when he woke screaming and was comforted by it, he would demand to know why it cared to comfort him.

It would saw out: *"S-z-lee-p mm-ah-ee-nn-d s-z-rahng."* And from that he could conjecture that sound sleep makes the mind strong, or that the mind must be strong for the body to be strong, or whatever else he wished. It was *kindness,* he knew, and he felt shifty and rotted when he thought of, say, Amy.

It will be soon, will it not? Soon?
Quite soon, little ones. Quite, quite soon.

Amy had not fallen; she had been led, slowly, carefully, by the hand. She had gone delightfully down, night after night. He had been amused to note that there was a night not long after the night of Optol when he had urged her to abstain from further indulgence in a certain diversion which had no name that anyone used, an Avernian pleasure the penalties against which were so severe that one would not compromise himself so far as admitting that he knew it existed and was practiced. Smith had urged her to abstain, and had most sincerely this time meant it. She was heading for the inevitable collapse, and her father was due back from his inspection tour. The whole process had taken some fifty days.

Her father, another grey-eyed booby ... A projection room. "A hoax." "Fifty thousand in small, unmarked—" The flickering reel-change. "It *can't* be—" "You should know that scar." "I'll kill you first!" "That won't burn the prints." The lights. "The last one—I don't believe —" "Fifty thousand." "I'll kill you—"

But he hadn't. He'd killed himself, for no good reason that Smith could understand. Disgustedly, no longer a blackmailer, much out of pocket by this deal that had fizzled, he turned hawker and peddled prints of the film to the sort of person who would buy such things. He almost got his expenses back. After the week of concentration on his sudden mercantile enterprise, he had thought to inquire about Amy.

She had had her smash-up, lost her job tape-punching now that her father was dead and her really scandalous behavior could no longer be ignored. She had got an unconventional job in the Open Quarter. She had left it. She appeared, hanging around the shops at Standard Transport, where the watchmen had orders to drive her away. She always came back, and one day, evidently, got what she wanted.

For on the Portsmouth–Jamestown run, which Smith was making to see a man who had a bar with a small theater in what was ostensibly a storeroom, his ship had parted at the seams.

"Dumped me where you found me—mid-desert."

"T-urr-ss-t-ee," sawed the native.

There seemed to be some reproach in the word, and Smith chided himself for imagining that a creature which spoke by stridulation could charge its language with the same emotional overtones as those who used lungs and vocal cords.

But there the note was again: "Ei-m-m-ee—t-urr-ss-t—t-oo."

Any thirst too. A stridulating moralist. But still … one had to admit … in his frosty way, Smith was reasoning, but a wash of emotion blurred the diagrams, the cold diagrams by which he had always lived.

It's getting me, he thought—it's getting me at last. He'd seen it happen before, and always admitted that it might happen to him—but it was a shock.

Hesitantly, which was strange for him, he asked if he could somehow find his way across the desert to Portsmouth. The creature ticked approvingly, brought in sand and with one delicate appendage began to trace what might be a map.

He was going to do it. He was going to be clean again, he who had always had a horror of filth and never until now had seen that his life was viler than maggots, more loathsome than carrion. A warm glow of self-approval filled him while he bent over the map. Yes, he was going to perform the incredible hike and somehow make restitution to her. Who would have thought an inhuman creature like his benefactor could have done this to him? With all the enthusiasm of any convert, he felt young again, with life before him, a life where he could choose between fair and foul. He chuckled with the newness of it.

But to work! Good intentions were not enough. There was the map to memorize, his bearings to establish, some portable food supply to be gathered …

He followed the map with his finger. The tracing appendage of the creature guided him, another quietly lay around him, its tip at the small of his back. He accepted it, though it itched somewhat. Not for an itch would he risk offending the bearer of his new life.

He was going to get Amy to a cure, give her money, bear her abuse—she could not understand all at once that he was another man—turn his undoubted talent to an honest …

Farewell! Farewell!
Farewell, little ones. Farewell.

The map blurred a bit before Smith's eyes. Then the map toppled and slid and became the red-lit ceiling of the burrow. Then Smith tried to move and could not. The itching in his back was a torment.

The screy mother did not look at the prostrate host as she turned and crawled up from the incubator to the surface. Something like fond humor wrinkled the surface of her thoughts as she remembered the little ones and their impatience. Heigh-ho! She had given them the best she could, letting many a smaller host go by until this fine, big host came her way. It had taken feeding and humoring, but it would last many and many a month while the little wrigglers grew and ate and grew within it. Heigh-ho! Life went on, she thought; one did the best one could. …

[*Fantasy and Science Fiction* - April 1954]

I Never Ast No Favors

Dear Mr. Marino:

I hesitate to take pen in hand and write you because I guess you do not remember me except maybe as a punk kid you did a good turn, and I know you must be a busy man running your undertaking parlor as well as the Third Ward and your barber shop. I never ast no favors of nobody but this is a special case which I hope you will agree when I explain.

To refresh your memory as the mouthpiece says in court, my name is Anthony Cornaro only maybe you remember me better as Tough Tony, which is what they call me back home in the Ward. I am not the Tough Tony from Water Street who is about 55 and doing a sixer up the river, I am the Tough Tony who is going on seventeen from Brecker Street and who you got probation for last week after I slash that nosy cop that comes flatfooting into the grocery store where some friends and I are just looking around not knowing it is after hours and that the grocery man has went home. That is the Tough Tony that I am. I guess you remember me now so I can go ahead.

With the probation, not that I am complaining, the trouble starts. The mouthpiece says he has known this lad for years and he comes from a very fine churchgoing family and he has been led astray by bad companions. So all right, the judge says three years probation, but he goes on to say *if.* If this, if that, environment, bad influences, congestered city streets, our vital dairy industry denuded—such a word from a judge!—of labor ...

Before I know what has happened, I am signing a paper, my Mama is putting her mark on it and I am on my way to Chiunga County to milk cows.

I figure the judge does not know I am a personal friend of yours and I do not want to embarrass you by mentioning your name in open court, I figure I will get a chance later to straighten things out. Also, to tell you the truth, I am too struck with horror to talk.

On the ride upstate I am handcuffed to the juvenile court officer so I cannot make a break for it, but at last I get time to think and I realize that it is not as bad as it looks. I am supposed to work for a dame named Mrs. Parry and get chow, clothes and Prevailering Wages. I figure it takes maybe a month for her to break

447

me in on the cow racket or even longer if I play dumb. During the month I get a few bucks, a set of threads and take it easy and by then I figure you will have everything straightened out and I can get back to my regular occupation, only more careful this time. Experience is the best teacher, Mr. Marino, as I am sure you know.

Well, we arrive at this town Chiunga Forks and I swear to God I never saw such a creepy place. You wouldn't believe it. The main drag is all of four blocks long and the stores and houses are from wood. I expect to see Gary Cooper stalking down the street with a scowl on his puss and his hands on his guns looking for the bad guys. Four hours from the Third Ward in a beat-up '48 police department Buick—you wouldn't believe it.

We park in front of a hash house, characters in rubber boots gawk at us, the court officer takes off the cuffs and gabs with the driver but does not lose sight of me. While we are waiting for this Mrs. Parry to keep the date I study the bank building across the street and develop some ideas which will interest you, Mr. Marino, but which I will not go into right now.

All of a sudden there is a hassle on the sidewalk.

A big woman with grey hair and a built like Tony Galento is kicking a little guy who looks like T.B. Louis the Book, who I guess you know, but not so muscular and wearing overalls. She is kicking him right in the keister, five–six times. Each time I shudder, and so maybe does the bank building across the street.

"Shoot my dawg, will you!" she yells at the character. "I said I'd kick your butt from here to Scranton when I caught up with you, Dud Wingle!"

"Leave me be!" he squawks, trying to pry her hands off his shoulders. "He was chasin' deer! He was chasin' deer!"

Thud—thud—thud. "I don't keer if he was chasin' deer, panthers or butterflies." *Thud.* "He was my dawg and you shot him!" *Thud.* She was drawing quite a crowd. The characters in rubber boots are forgetting all about us to stare at her and him.

Up comes a flatfoot who I later learn is the entire manpower of Chiunga Forks' lousiest; he says to the big woman "Now Ella" a few times and she finally stops booting the little character and lets him go. "What do you want, Henry?" she growls at the flatfoot and he asks weakly: "Silver Bell dropped her calf yet?"

The little character is limping away rubbing himself. The big broad watches him regretfully and says to the flatfoot: "Yesterday, Henry. Now if you'll excuse me I have to look for my new hired boy from the city. I guess that's him over there."

She strolls over to us and yanks open the Buick's door, almost taking it off the hinges. "I'm Mrs. Ella Parry," she says to me, sticking out her hand. "You must be the Cornaro boy the Probation Association people wired me about."

I shake hands and say, "Yes, ma'am."

The officer turns me over grinning like a skunk eating beans.

I figure Mrs. Parry lives in one of the wood houses in Chiunga Forks, but no. We climb into a this-year Willys truck and take off for the hills. I do not have much to say to this lady wrestler but wish I had somebody smuggle me a rod to kind of even things a little between her and me. With that built she could break me in half by accident. I try to get in good with her by offering to customize her truck. "I could strip off the bumper guards and put on a couple of fog lights, maybe new fender skirts with a little trim to them," I say, "and it wouldn't cost you a dime. Even out here there has got to be some parts place where a person can heist what he needs."

"Quiet, Bub," she says all of a sudden, and shields her eyes peering down a side road where a car is standing in front of a shack. "I swear," she says, "that looks like Dud Wingle's Ford in front of Miz' Sigafoos' place." She keeps her neck twisting around to study it until it is out of sight. And she looks worried.

I figure it is not a good time to talk and anyway maybe she has notions about customizing and does not approve of it.

"What," she says, "would Dud Wingle want with Miz' Sigafoos?"

"I don't know, ma'am," I say. "Wasn't he the gentleman you was kicking from here to Scranton?"

"Shucks, Bub, that was just a figger of speech. If I'd of wanted to kick him from here to Scranton I'd of *done* it. Dud and Jim and Ab and Sime think they got a right to shoot your dog if he chases the deer. I'm a peaceable woman or I'd have the law on them for shootin' Grip. But maybe I did kind of lose my temper." She looked worrieder yet.

"Is something wrong, ma'am?" I ask. You never can tell, but a lot of old dames talk to me like I was their uncle; to tell you the truth this is my biggest problem in a cat house. It must be because I am a kind of thoughtful guy and it shows.

Mrs. Parry is no exception. She says to me: "You don't know the folks up here yet, Bub, so you don't know about Miz' Sigafoos. I'm old English stock so I don't hold with their foolishness, but—" And here she looked *real* worried. "Miz' Sigafoos is what they call a hex doctor."

"What's that, ma'am?"

"Just a lot of foolishness. Don't you pay any attention," she says, and then she has to concentrate on the driving. We are turning off the two-lane state highway and going up, up, up, into the hills, off a blacktop road, off a gravel road, off a dirt road. No people. No houses. Fences and cows or maybe horses, I can't tell for sure. Finally we are at her place, which is from wood and in two buildings. I start automatically for the building that is clean, new-painted, big and expensive.

"Hold on, Bub," she says. "No need to head for the barn first thing. Let's get you settled in the house first and then there'll be a plenty of work for you."

I do a double take and see that the big, clean, expensive building is the barn. The little, cheap, run-down place is the house. I say to myself: "Tough Tony, you're gonna pray tonight that Mr. Marino don't forget to tell the judge you're a personal friend of his and get you out of this."

But that night I do not pray. I am too tired. After throwing sacks of scratch feed and laying mash around, I run the baling machine and I turn the oats in the loft and I pump water until my back is aching jello and then I go hiking out to the woodlot and chop down trees and cut them up with a chain saw. It is surprising how fast I learn and how willing I am when I remember what Mrs. Parry did to Dud Wingle.

I barely get to sleep it seems like when Mrs. Parry is yanking the covers off me laughing and I see through the window that the sky is getting a little light. "Time to rise, Bub," she bawls. "Breakfast is on the table." She strides to the window and flexes her muscles, breathing deep. "It's going to be a fine day. I can tell when an animal's sick to death and I can tell when it's going to be fine all day. Rise and shine, Bub. We have a lot of work ahead. I was kind of easy on you yesterday seeing you was new here, so we got a bit behindhand."

I eye the bulging muscles and say, "Yes, ma'am."

She serves a good breakfast, I have to admit. Usually I just have some coffee around eleven when I wake up and maybe a meat-ball sandwich around four, but the country air gives you an appetite like I always heard. Maybe I didn't tell you there was just the two of us. Her husband kicked off a couple years ago. She gave one of her boys half the farm because she says she don't believe in letting them hang around without a chance to make some money and get married until you die. The other boy, nineteen, got drafted two months ago and since then she is running the place on her own hook because for some reason or other it is hard to get people to work on a farm. She says she does not understand this and I do not enlighten her.

First thing after breakfast she tells me to make four crates from lumber in the toolshed, go to the duckpond and put the four Muscovy ducks in the crates so she can take them to town and sell them. She has been meaning to sell the Muscovy ducks for some time since the word has been getting around that she was pro-communist for having such a breed of ducks when there were plenty of good American ducks she could of raised. "Though," she says, "in my opinion the Walterses ought to sell off their Peking ducks too because the Chinese are just as bad as the Roossians."

I make the crates which is easy and I go to the duckpond. There are four ducks there but they are not swimming; they have sunk. I go and tell Mrs. Parry and she looks at me like I was crazy.

"Yeah," I tell her. "Sunk. Down at the bottom of the pond, drownded. I guess maybe during the night they forgot to keep treading water or something."

She didn't say a word. She just strides down the path to the duckpond and looks into it and sees the four ducks. They are big, horrible things with kind of red Jimmy Valentine masks over their eyes, and they are lying at the bottom of the pond. She wades in, still without a word, and fishes them out. She gets a big shiv out of her apron pocket, slits the ducks open, yanks out their lungs and slits them open. Water dribbles out.

"Drownded," she mutters. "If there was snapping turtles to drag them under ... but there ain't."

I do not understand what the fuss is about and ast her if she can't sell them anyway. She says no, it wouldn't be honest, and I should get a shovel and bury them. Then there is an awful bellering from the cow barn. "Agnes of Lincolnshire!" Mrs. Parry squawks and dashes for the barn. "She's dropping her calf ahead of time!"

I run along beside her. "Should I call the cops?" I pant. "They always get to the place before the ambulance and you don't have to pay them nothing. My married sister had three kids delivered by the cops—"

But it seems it's different with cows and anyway they have a different kind of flatfoot out here that didn't go to Police Academy. Mrs. Parry finally looks up from the calf and says, "I think I saved it. I *know* I saved it. I can tell when an animal's dying. Bub, go to the phone and call Miz' Croley and ask her if she can possibly spare Brenda to come over and do the milkin' tonight and tomorrow morning. I dassn't leave Agnes and the calf; they need nursing."

I stagger out of the cowbarn, throw up two–three times and go to the phone in the house. I seem them phones with flywheels in the movies so I know how to work it. Mrs. Croley cusses and moans and then says all right she'll send Brenda over in the Ford and please to tell Mrs. Parry not to keep her no longer than she has to because she has a herd of her own that needs milking.

I tell Mrs. Parry in the barn and Mrs. Parry snaps that Mrs. Croley has a living husband and a draft-proof farmhand and she swore she din't know what things were coming to when a neighbor wouldn't help another neighbor out.

I ast casually: "Who is this Brenda, ma'am?"

"Miz' Croley's daughter. Good for nothing."

I don't ast no more questions but I sure begin to wait with interest for a Ford to round the bend of the road.

It does while I am bucking up logs with the chainsaw. Brenda is a blondie about my age, a little too big for her dress—an effect which I always go for, whether in the Third Ward or Chiunga County. I don't have a chance to talk to her until lunch, and then all she does is giggle. But who wants conversation? I make a mental note that she will have the room next to mine and then a truck comes snorting up the driveway. Something inside the truck is snorting louder than the truck.

Mrs. Parry throws up her hands. "Land, I forgot! Belshazzar the Magnificent for Princess Leilani!" She gulps coffee and dashes out.

"Brenda," I say, "what was that all about?"

She giggles and this time blushes. I throw down my napkin and go to the window. The truck is being backed to a field with a big board fence around it. Mrs. Parry is going into the barn and is leading a cow into the field. The cow is mighty nervous and I begin to understand why. The truckdriver opens the tailgate and out comes a snorting bull.

I think: well, I been to a few stag shows but *this* I never seen before. Maybe a person can learn something in the country after all.

Belshazzar the Magnificent sees Princess Leilani. He snorts like Charles Boyer. Princess Leilani cowers away from him like Bette Davis. Belshazzar the Magnificent paws the ground. Princess Leilani trembles. And then Belshazzar the Magnificent yawns and starts eating grass.

Princess Leilani looks up, startled and says: "Huh?" No, on second thought it is not Princess Leilani who says "Huh?" It is Brenda, at the other kitchen window. She sees me watching her, giggles, blushes and goes to the sink and starts doing dishes.

I guess this is a good sign, but I don't press my luck. I go outside, where Mrs. Parry is cussing out the truckdriver. "Some bull!" she yells at him. "What am I supposed to do now? How long is Leilani going to stay in season? What if I can't line up another stud for her? Do you realize what it's going to cost me in veal and milk checks—" Yatata, yatata, yatata, while the truckdriver keeps trying to butt in with excuses and Belshazzar the Magnificent eats grass and sometimes gives Princess Leilani a brotherly lick on the nose, for by that time Princess Leilani has dropped the nervous act and edged over mooing plaintively.

Mrs. Parry yells: "See that? I don't hold with artificial insemination but you dang stockbreeders are driving us dairy farmers to it! Get your—your *steer* off my property before I throw him off! I got work to do even if he hasn't! Belshazzar the Magnificent—*hah!*"

She turns on me. "Don't just stand around gawking, Bub. When you get the stovewood split you can stack it in the woodshed." I scurry off and resume Operation Woodlot, but I take it a little easy which I can do because Mrs. Parry is in the cowbarn nursing Agnes of Lincolnshire and the preemie calf.

At supper Mrs. Parry says she thinks she better put a cot in the barn for herself and spend the night there with the invalids in case there is a sudden emergency. "And that don't mean," she adds, "that you children can be up half the night playing the radio just because the old lady ain't around. I want to see the house lights out by 8:30. Understand?"

"Yes ma'am," Brenda says.

"We won't play the radio, ma'am," I say. "And we'll put the lights out."

Brenda giggled.

What happens that night is a little embarrassing to write about. I hope, Mr. Marino, you won't go telling it around. I figure that being a licensed mortician like you are as well as boss of the Third Ward you are practically like a doctor and doctors don't go around shooting their mouths off about what their patients tell them. I figure what I have to tell you about what happened comes under the sacred relationship between a doctor and patient or a hood and his mouthpiece.

Anyway, this is what happens: nothing happens.

Like with Belshazzar the Magnificent.

I go into her room, I say yes, she says no, I say yes *please,* she says well okay. And then nothing happens. I never been so humiliated and I hope you will keep this confidential because it isn't the kind of thing you like to have get around. I am telling you about it only because I never ast no favors but this is a very special case and I want you to understand why.

The next morning at breakfast I am in a bad temper, Brenda has got the giggles and Mrs. Parry is stiff and tired from sleeping in the barn. We are a gruesome threesome, and then a car drives up and a kid of maybe thirty comes busting into the kitchen. He has been crying. His eyes are red and there are clean places on his face where the tears ran down. "Ma!" he whimpers at Mrs. Parry. "I got to talk to you! You got to talk to Bonita, she says I don't love her no more and she's going to leave me!"

"Hush up, George," she snaps at him. "Come into the parlor." They go into the parlor and Brenda whistles: "Whoo-ee! Wait'll I tell Maw about *this!*"

"Who is he?" I ask.

"Miz' Parry's boy George. She gave him the south half of the farm and built him a house on it. Bonita's his wife. She's a stuck-up girl from Ware County and she wears falsies and dyes her hair and—" Brenda looks around, lowers her voice and whispers "—*and she sends her worshing to the laundry in town.*"

"God in Heaven," I say. "Have the cops heard about this?"

"Oh, it's *legal,* but you just shouldn't *do* it."

"I see. I misunderstood, I guess. Back in the Third Ward it's a worse rap than mopery with intent to gawk. The judges are ruthless with it."

Her eyes go round. "Is that a fact?"

"Sure. Tell your mother about it."

Mrs. Parry came back in with her son and said to us: "Clear out, you kids. I want to make a phone call."

"I'll start the milkin'," Brenda said.

"And I'll framble the portistan while it's still cool and barkney," I say.

"Sure," Mrs. Parry says, cranking the phone. "Go and do that, Bub." She is preoccupied.

I go through the kitchen door, take one sidestep, flatten against the house and listen. Reception is pretty good.

"Bonita?" Mrs. Parry says into the phone. "Is that you, Bonita? Listen, Bonita, George is here and he asked me to call you and tell you he's sorry. I ain't exactly going to say that. I'm going to say that you're acting like a blame fool ... No, no, no. Don't talk about it. This is a party line. Just listen; I know what happened. George told me; after all, I'm his mother. Just listen to an older woman with more experience. So it happened. That don't mean he doesn't love you, child! It's happened to me. I guess it's happened to every woman. You mustn't take it *personally.* You're just sufferin' from a case of newlywed nerves. After you've been married two years or so you'll see things like this in better focus. Maybe George was tired. Maybe he got one of these flu germs that's goin' around ... No, I didn't say he was sick. No, he seems all right—maybe looks a *little* feverish ... Well, now, I don't know whether you really want to talk to him or not, you being so upset and all. If he *is* sick it'd just upset him—oh, all right." She chuckles away from the phone and says: "She wants to talk to you, George. Don't be too eager, boy."

I slink away from the kitchen door thinking: "Ah-*hah!*" I am thinking so hard that Mrs. Parry bungles into me when she walks out of the kitchen sooner than I expect.

She grabs me with one of those pipe-vise hands and snaps: "You young devil, were you listening to me on the phone?"

Usually it is the smart thing to deny everything and ast for your mouth-piece, but up here they got no mouthpieces. For once I tell the truth and cop a plea. "Yes, Mrs. Parry. I'm so *ashamed* of myself you can't imagine. I always been like that. It's a psy-cho-logical twist I got for listening. I can't seem to control it. Maybe I read too many bad comic books. But honest I won't breathe a word about how George couldn't—" Here I have the sense to shut up, but too late.

She drills me with a look and the pipe vise tightens on my arm. "Couldn't *what, Bub?*"

"Like Belshazzar the Magnificent," I say weakly.

"Yep," she says. "I thought that's what you were going to say. Now tell me, Bub—how'd you know? And don't tell me you guessed from what I said. I been using party lines for thirty years. The way I was talkin' to Bonita, it could've been anything from George hitting her with a brick to comin' home drunk. You picked a mighty long shot, you picked it right and I want to know how you did it."

She would of made a great D.A. I mumble: "The same thing happened to me last night. Would you mind lettin' go of my arm, Mrs. Parry? Before it drops off?"

She lets go with a start. "I'm sorry, Bub." She walked slowly to the barn and I walk slowly beside her because I think she expects it.

"Maybe," I say, "it's something in the water."

She shakes her head. "You don't know bulls, Bub. And what about the ducks that sank and Agnes dropping her calf before her time?" She begins to breathe hard through her nostrils. "It's hexin', that's what it is!"

"What's hexin', ma'am?"

"Heathen doings by that old Miz' Sigafoos. She's been warned and warned plenty to stick to her doctoring. I hold nothing against her for curing the croup or maybe selling a young man love potion if he's goin' down to Scranton to sell his crop and play around a little. But she's not satisfied with that, I guess. Dud Wingle must of gone to her with a twenty dollar bill to witch my farm!"

I do not know what to make of this. My mama of course has told me about *la vecchia religione,* but I never know they believe in stuff like that over here. "Can you go to the cops, ma'am?" I ast.

She snorts like Belshazzar the Magnificent. "Cops! A fat lot old Henry Bricker would know about witchin'. No, Bub, I guess I'll handle this myself. I ain't the five-times-great-granddaughter of Pru Posthlewaite for nothin'!"

"Who was Pru—what you said?"

"Hanged in Salem, Massachusetts, in 1680 for witchcraft. Her coven name was Little Gadfly, but I guess she wasn't so little. The first two ropes broke—but we got no time to stand around talkin'. I got to find my Ma's trunk in the attic. You go get the black rooster from the chicken run. I wonder where there's some chalk?" And she walks off to the house, mumbling. I walk to the chicken run thinking she has flipped.

The black rooster is a tricky character, very fast on his feet and also I am new at the chicken racket. It takes me half an hour to stalk him down, during which time incidentally the Ford leaves with Brenda in it and George drives away in his car. See you later, Brenda, I think to myself and maybe you will be surprised.

I go to the kitchen door with the rooster screaming in my arms and Mrs. Parry says: "Come on in with him and set him anywhere." I do, Mrs. Parry scatters some cornflakes on the floor and the rooster calms down right away and stalks around picking it up. Mrs. Parry is sweaty and dust-covered and there are some dirty old papers rolled up on the kitchen table.

She starts fooling around on the floor with one of the papers and a hunk of carpenter's chalk and just to be doing something I look at the rest of them. Honest to God, you never saw such lousy spelling and handwriting. *Tayke the Duste off ane Olde Ymmage Quhich Ye Myngel*—like that.

I shake my head and think: it's the cow racket. No normal human can take this life. She has flipped and I don't blame her, but it will be a horrible thing if she becomes homicidal. I look around for a poker or something and start to edge away. I am thinking of a dash from the door to the Willys and then scorching into town to come back with the men in the little white coats.

She looks up at me and says: "Don't go away, Bub. This is woman's work, but I need somebody to hold the sword and palm and you're the onliest one around." She grins. "I guess you never saw anything like *this* in the city, hey?"

"No, ma'am," I say, and notice that my voice is very faint.

"Well, don't let it skeer you. There's some people it'd skeer, but the Probation Association people say they call you Tough Tony, so I guess you won't take fright."

"No, ma'am."

"Now what do we do for a sword? I guess this bread knife'll—no; the ham slicer. It looks *more* like a sword. Hold it in your left hand and get a couple of them gilded bulrushes from the vase in the parlor. Mind you wipe your feet before you tread on the carpet! And then come back. Make it fast."

She starts to copy some stuff that looks like Yiddish writing onto the floor and I go into the parlor. I am about to tiptoe to the front door when she yells: "Bub! That you?"

Maybe I could beat her in a race for the car, maybe not. I shrug. At least I have a knife—and know how to use it. I bring her the gilded things from the vase. Ugh! While I am out she has cut the head off the rooster and is sprinkling its blood over a big chalk star and the writing on the floor. But the knife makes me feel more confident even though I begin to worry about how it will look if I have to do anything with it. I am figuring that maybe I can hamstring her if she takes off after me, and meanwhile I should humor her because maybe she will snap out of it.

"Bub," she says, "hold the sword and palms in front of you pointing up and don't step inside the chalk lines. Now, will you promise me not to tell anybody about the words I speak? The rest of this stuff don't matter; it's down in all the books and people have their minds made up that it don't work. But about the words, do you promise?"

"Yes, ma'am. Anything you say, ma'am."

So she starts talking and the promise was not necessary because it's in some foreign language and I don't talk foreign languages except sometimes a little Italian to my mama. I am beginning to yawn when I notice that we have company.

He is eight feet tall, he is green, he has teeth like Red Riding Hood's grandma. I dive through the window, screaming.

When Mrs. Parry comes out she finds me in a pile of broken glass, on my knees, praying. She clamps two fingers on my ear and hoists me to my feet. "Stop that praying," she says. "He's complaining about it. Says it makes him itch. And you said you wouldn't be skeered! Now come inside where I can keep an eye on you and behave yourself. The idea! The very idea!"

To tell you the truth, I don't remember what happens after this so good. There is some talk between the green character and Mrs. Parry about her five-times-great-grandmother who it seems is doing nicely in a warm climate. There is an argument in which the green character gets shifty and says he doesn't know who is working for Miz' Sigafoos these days. Miz' Parry threatens to let me pray again and the green character gets sulky and says all right he'll send for him and rassle with him but he is sure he can lick him.

The next thing I recall is a grunt-and-groan exhibition between the green character and a smaller purple character who must of arrived when I was blacked out or something. This at least I know something about because I am a television fan. It is a very slow match, because when one of the characters for instance bends the other character's arm it just bends and does not break. But a good big character can lick a good little character every time and finally greenface has got his opponent tied into a bowknot.

"Be gone," Mrs. Parry says to the purple character, "and never more molest me or mine. Be gone, be gone, be gone."

He is gone, and I never do find out if he gets unknotted.

"Now fetch me Miz' Sigafoos."

Blip! An ugly little old woman is sharing the ring with the winner and new champeen. She spits at Mrs. Parry: "So you it was dot mine Teufel haff ge-schtolen!" Her English is terrible. A greenhorn.

"This ain't a social call, Miz' Sigafoos," Mrs. Parry says coldly. "I just want you to unwitch my farm and kinfolks. And if you're an honest woman you'll return his money to that sneakin', dog-murderin' shiftless squirt Dud Wingle."

"Yah," the old woman mumbles. She reaches up and feels the biceps of the green character. "Yah, I guess maybe dot I besser do. Who der Yunger iss?" She is looking at me. "For why the teeth on his mouth go clop-clop-clop? Und so white the face on his head iss! You besser should feed him, Ella."

"*Missus* Parry to you, Miz' Sigafoos, *if* you don't mind. Now the both of you be gone, be gone, be gone."

At last we are alone.

"Now," Mrs. Parry grunts, "maybe we can get back to farmin'. Such foolishness and me a busy woman." She looks at me closely and says: "I do believe the old fool was right. You're as white as a sheet." She feels my forehead. "Oh, shoot! You do have a temperature. You better get to bed. If you ain't better in the morning I'll call Doc Hines."

So I am in the bedroom writing this letter, Mr. Marino, and I hope you will help me out. Like I said I never ast no favors but this is special.

Mr. Marino, will you please, please go to the judge and tell him I have a change of heart and don't want no probation? Tell him I want to pay my debt to society. Tell him I want to go to jail for three years, and for them to come and get me right away.

Sincerely,

Anthony (Tough Tony) Cornaro

P.S. On my way to get a stamp for this I notice that I have some grey hairs which is very unusual for a person going on seventeen. Please tell the judge I wouldn't mind if they give me solitary confinement and that maybe it would help me pay my debt to society.

In haste,

T.T.

[*Astounding* - July 1950]

The Little Black Bag

Old Dr. Full felt the winter in his bones as he limped down the alley. It was the alley and the back door he had chosen rather than the sidewalk and the front door because of the brown paper bag under his arm. He knew perfectly well that the flat-faced, stringy-haired women of his street and their gap-toothed, sour-smelling husbands did not notice if he brought a bottle of cheap wine to his room. They all but lived on the stuff themselves, varied with whiskey when pay checks were boosted by overtime. But Dr. Full, unlike them, was ashamed. A complicated disaster oc-curred as he limped down the littered alley. One of the neighborhood dogs—a mean little black one he knew and hated, with its teeth always bared and always snarling with menace—hurled at his legs through a hole in the board fence that lined his path. Dr. Full flinched, then swung his leg in what was to have been a satisfying kick to the animal's gaunt ribs. But the winter in his bones weighed down the leg. His foot failed to clear a half-buried brick, and he sat down abruptly, cursing. When he smelled unbottled wine and realized his brown paper package had slipped from under his arm and smashed, his curses died on his lips. The snarling black dog was circling him at a yard's distance, tensely stalking, but he ignored it in the greater disaster.

With stiff fingers as he sat on the filth of the alley, Dr. Full unfolded the brown paper bag's top, which had been crimped over, grocer-wise. The early au-tumnal dusk had come; he could not see plainly what was left. He lifted out the jug-handled top of his half gallon, and some fragments, and then the bottom of the bottle. Dr. Full was far too occupied to exult as he noted that there was a good pint left. He had a problem, and emotions could be deferred until the fitting time.

The dog closed in, its snarl rising in pitch. He set down the bottom of the bottle and pelted the dog with the curved triangular glass fragments of its top. One of them connected, and the dog ducked back through the fence, howling. Dr. Full then placed a razor-like edge of the half-gallon bottle's foundation to his lips and drank from it as though it were a giant's cup. Twice he had to put it down to rest his arms, but in one minute he had swallowed the pint of wine.

He thought of rising to his feet and walking through the alley to his room, but a flood of well-being drowned the notion. It was, after all, inexpressibly pleasant to sit there and feel the frost-hardened mud of the alley turn soft, or seem to, and to feel the winter evaporating from his bones under a warmth which spread from his stomach through his limbs.

A three-year-old girl in a cut-down winter coat squeezed through the same hole in the board fence from which the black dog had sprung its ambush. Gravely she toddled up to Dr. Full and inspected him with her dirty forefinger in her mouth. Dr. Full's happiness had been providentially made complete; he had been supplied with an audience.

"Ah, my dear," he said hoarsely. And then: "Preposserous accusation. 'If that's what you call evidence,' I should have told them, 'you better stick to your doctoring.' I should have told them: 'I was here before your County Medical Society. And the License Commissioner never proved a thing on me. So, gennulmen, doesn't it stand to reason? I appeal to you as fellow memmers of a great profession—'"

The little girl, bored, moved away, picking up one of the triangular pieces of glass to play with as she left. Dr. Full forgot her immediately, and continued to himself earnestly: "But so help me, they *couldn't* prove a thing. Hasn't a man got any *rights?*" He brooded over the question, of whose answer he was so sure, but on which the Committee on Ethics of the County Medical Society had been equally certain. The winter was creeping into his bones again, and he had no money and no more wine.

Dr. Full pretended to himself that there was a bottle of whiskey somewhere in the fearful litter of his room. It was an old and cruel trick he played on himself when he simply had to be galvanized into getting up and going home. He might freeze there in the alley. In his room he would be bitten by bugs and would cough at the moldy reek from his sink, but he would not freeze and be cheated of the hundreds of bottles of wine that he still might drink, the thousands of hours of glowing content he still might feel. He thought about that bottle of whiskey— was it back of a mounded heap of medical journals? No; he had looked there last time. Was it under the sink, shoved well to the rear, behind the rusty drain? The cruel trick began to play itself out again. Yes, he told himself with mounting excitement, yes, it might be! Your memory isn't so good nowadays, he told himself with rueful good-fellowship. You know perfectly well you might have bought a bottle of whiskey and shoved it behind the sink drain for a moment just like this.

The amber bottle, the crisp snap of the sealing as he cut it, the pleasurable exertion of starting the screw cap on its threads, and then the refreshing tangs in his throat, the warmth in his stomach, the dark, dull happy oblivion of drunkenness—they became real to him. You *could* have, you know! You *could* have! he told himself. With the blessed conviction growing in his mind—It *could* have happened, you know! It *could* have!—he struggled to his right knee. As he did, he heard a yelp behind him, and curiously craned his neck around while resting. It was the little girl, who had cut her hand quite badly on her toy, the piece of glass. Dr. Full could see the rilling bright blood down her coat, pooling at her feet.

He almost felt inclined to defer the image of the amber bottle for her, but not seriously. He knew that it was there, shoved well to the rear under the sink, behind the rusty drain where he had hidden it. He would have a drink and then magnanimously return to help the child. Dr. Full got to his other knee and then his feet, and proceeded at a rapid totter down the littered alley toward his room, where he would hunt with calm optimism at first for the bottle that was not there, then with anxiety, and then with frantic violence. He would hurl books and dishes about before he was done looking for the amber bottle of whiskey, and finally would beat his swollen knuckles against the brick wall until old scars on them opened and his thick old blood oozed over his hands. Last of all, he would sit down somewhere on the floor, whimpering, and would plunge into the abyss of purgative nightmare that was his sleep.

After twenty generations of shilly-shallying and "we'll cross that bridge when we come to it," genus homo had bred himself into an impasse. Dogged biometricians had pointed out with irrefutable logic that mental subnormals were outbreeding mental normals and supernormals, and that the process was occurring on an exponential curve. Every fact that could be mustered in the argument proved the biometricians' case, and led inevitably to the conclusion that genus homo was going to wind up in a preposterous jam quite soon. If you think that had any effect on breeding practices, you do not know genus homo.

There was, of course, a sort of masking effect produced by that other exponential function, the accumulation of technological devices. A moron trained to punch an adding machine seems to be a more skillful computer than a medieval mathematician trained to count on his fingers. A moron trained to operate the twenty-first century equivalent of a linotype seems to be a better typographer than a Renaissance printer limited to a few fonts of movable type. This is also true of medical practice.

It was a complicated affair of many factors. The supernormals "improved the product" at greater speed than the subnormals degraded it, but in smaller quantity because elaborate training of their children was practiced on a custom-made basis. The fetish of higher education had some weird avatars by the twentieth generation: "colleges" where not a member of the student body could read words of three syllables; "universities" where such degrees as "Bachelor of Typewriting," "Master of Shorthand" and "Doctor of Philosophy (Card Filing)" were conferred with the traditional pomp. The handful of supernormals used such devices in order that the vast majority might keep some semblance of a social order going.

Some day the supernormals would mercilessly cross the bridge; at the twentieth generation they were standing irresolutely at its approaches wondering what had hit them. And the ghosts of twenty generations of biometricians chuckled malignantly.

It is a certain Doctor of Medicine of this twentieth generation that we are concerned with. His name was Hemingway—John Hemingway, B.Sc., M.D. He was a general practitioner, and did not hold with running to specialists with every trifling ailment. He often said as much, in approximately these words: "Now, uh, what I mean is you got a good old G.P. See what I mean? Well, uh, now a good old G.P. don't claim he knows all about lungs and glands and them things, get me?

But you got a G.P., you got, uh, you got a, well, you got a ... *all-around man!* That's what you got when you got a G.P.—you got a all-around man."

But from this, do not imagine that Dr. Hemingway was a poor doctor. He could remove tonsils or appendixes, assist at practically any confinement and deliver a living, uninjured infant, correctly diagnose hundreds of ailments, and prescribe and administer the correct medication or treatment for each. There was, in fact, only one thing he could not do in the medical line, and that was, violate the ancient canons of medical ethics. And Dr. Hemingway knew better than to try.

Dr. Hemingway and a few friends were chatting one evening when the event occurred that precipitates him into our story. He had been through a hard day at the clinic, and he wished his physicist friend Walter Gillis, B.Sc., M.Sc., Ph.D., would shut up so he could tell everybody about it. But Gillis kept rambling on, in his stilted fashion: "You got to hand it to old Mike; he don't have what we call the scientific method, but you got to hand it to him. There this poor little dope is, puttering around with some glassware and I come up and I ask him, kidding of course, 'How's about a time-travel machine, Mike?'"

Dr. Gillis was not aware of it, but "Mike" had an I.Q. six times his own, and was—to be blunt—his keeper. "Mike" rode herd on the pseudo-physicists in the pseudo-laboratory, in the guise of a bottle-washer. It was a social waste—but as has been mentioned before, the supernormals were still standing at the approaches to a bridge. Their irresolution led to many such preposterous situations. And it happens that "Mike," having grown frantically bored with his task, was malevolent enough to—but let Dr. Gillis tell it:

"So he gives me these here tube numbers and says, 'Series circuit. Now stop bothering me. Build your time machine, sit down at it and turn on the switch. That's all I ask, Dr. Gillis—that's all I ask.'"

"Say," marveled a brittle and lovely blonde guest, "you remember real good, don't you, doc?" She gave him a melting smile.

"Heck," said Gillis modestly, "I always remember good. It's what you call an inherent facility. And besides I told it quick to my secretary, so she wrote it down. I don't read so good, but I sure remember good, all right. Now, where was I?"

Everybody thought hard, and there were various suggestions:

"Something about bottles, doc?"

"You was starting a fight. You said 'time somebody was traveling.'"

"Yeah—you called somebody a swish. Who did you call a swish?"

"Not swish—*switch.*"

Dr. Gillis's noble brow grooved with thought, and he declared: "Switch is right. It was about time travel. What we call travel through time. So I took the tube numbers he gave me and I put them into the circuit-builder; I set it for 'series' and there it is—my time-traveling machine. It travels things through time real good." He displayed a box.

"What's in the box?" asked the lovely blonde.

Dr. Hemingway told her: "Time travel. It travels things through time."

"Look," said Gillis, the physicist. He took Dr. Hemingway's little black bag and put it on the box. He turned on the switch and the little black bag vanished.

"Say," said Dr. Hemingway, "that was, uh, swell. Now bring it back."

"Huh?"

"Bring back my little black bag."

"Well," said Dr. Gillis, "they don't come back. I tried it backwards and they don't come back. I guess maybe that dummy Mike give me a bum steer."

There was wholesale condemnation of "Mike" but Dr. Hemingway took no part in it. He was nagged by a vague feeling that there was something he would have to do. He reasoned: "I am a doctor and a doctor has got to have a little black bag. I ain't got a little black bag—so ain't I a doctor no more?" He decided that this was absurd. He *knew* he was a doctor. So it must be the bag's fault for not being there. It was no good, and he would get another one tomorrow from that dummy Al, at the clinic. Al could find things good, but he was a dummy—never liked to talk sociable to you.

So the next day Dr. Hemingway remembered to get another little black bag from his keeper—another little black bag with which he could perform tonsillectomies, appendectomies and the most difficult confinements, and with which he could diagnose and cure his kind until the day when the supernormals could bring themselves to cross that bridge. Al was kinda nasty about the missing little black bag, but Dr. Hemingway didn't exactly remember what had happened, so no tracer was sent out, so—

Old Dr. Full awoke from the horrors of the night to the horrors of the day. His gummy eyelashes pulled apart convulsively. He was propped against a corner of his room, and something was making a little drumming noise. He felt very cold and cramped. As his eyes focused on his lower body, he croaked out a laugh. The drumming noise was being made by his left heel, agitated by fine tremors against the bare floor. It was going to be the D.T.'s again, he decided dispassionately. He wiped his mouth with his bloody knuckles, and the fine tremor coarsened; the snare-drum beat became louder and slower. He was getting a break this fine morning, he decided sardonically. You didn't get the horrors until you had been tightened like a violin string, just to the breaking point. He had a reprieve, if a reprieve into his old body with the blazing, endless headache just back of the eyes and the screaming stiffness in the joints were anything to be thankful for.

There was something or other about a kid, he thought vaguely. He was going to doctor some kid. His eyes rested on a little black bag in the center of the room, and he forgot about the kid. "I could have sworn," said Dr. Full, "I hocked that two years ago!" He hitched over and reached the bag, and then realized it was some stranger's kit, arriving here he did not know how. He tentatively touched the lock and it snapped open and lay flat, rows and rows of instruments and medications tucked into loops in its four walls. It seemed vastly larger open than closed. He didn't see how it could possibly fold up into that compact size again, but decided it was some stunt of the instrument makers. Since his time—that made it worth more at the hock shop, he thought with satisfaction.

Just for old times' sake, he let his eyes and fingers rove over the instruments before he snapped the bag shut and headed for Uncle's. More than a few were a little hard to recognize—exactly, that is. You could see the things with blades for cutting, the forceps for holding and pulling, the retractors for holding fast, the needles and gut for suturing, the hypos—a fleeting thought crossed his mind that he could peddle the hypos separately to drug addicts.

Let's go, he decided, and tried to fold up the case. It didn't fold until he happened to touch the lock, and then it folded all at once into a little black bag. Sure have forged ahead, he thought, almost able to forget that what he was primarily interested in was its pawn value.

With a definite objective, it was not too hard for him to get to his feet. He decided to go down the front steps, out the front door and down the sidewalk. But first—

He snapped the bag open again on his kitchen table, and pored through the medication tubes. "Anything to sock the autonomic nervous system good and hard," he mumbled. The tubes were numbered, and there was a plastic card which seemed to list them. The left margin of the card was a run-down of the systems—vascular, muscular, nervous. He followed the last entry across to the right. There were columns for "stimulant," "depressant," and so on. Under "nervous system" and "depressant" he found the number 17, and shakily located the little glass tube which bore it. It was full of pretty blue pills and he took one.

It was like being struck by a thunderbolt.

Dr. Full had so long lacked any sense of well-being except the brief glow of alcohol that he had forgotten its very nature. He was panic-stricken for a long moment at the sensation that spread through him slowly, finally tingling in his fingertips. He straightened up, his pains gone and his leg tremor stilled.

That was great, he thought. He'd be able to *run* to the hock shop, pawn the little black bag and get some booze. He started down the stairs. Not even the street, bright with mid-morning sun, into which he emerged made him quail. The little black bag in his left hand had a satisfying, authoritative weight. He was walking erect, he noted, and not in the somewhat furtive crouch that had grown on him in recent years. A little self-respect, he told himself, that's what I need. Just because a man's down doesn't mean—

"Docta, please-a come wit'!" somebody yelled at him, tugging his arm. "Da litt-la girl, she's-a burn' up!" It was one of the slum's innumerable flat-faced, stringy-haired women, in a slovenly wrapper.

"Ah, I happen to be retired from practice—" he began hoarsely, but she would not be put off.

"In by here, Docta!" she urged, tugging him to a doorway. "You come look-a da litt-la girl. I got two dolla, you come look!" That put a different complexion on the matter. He allowed himself to be towed through the doorway into a mussy, cabbage-smelling flat. He knew the woman now, or rather knew who she must be—a new arrival who had moved in the other night. These people moved at night, in motorcades of battered cars supplied by friends and relations, with furniture lashed to the tops, swearing and drinking until the small hours. It explained why she had stopped him: she did not yet know he was old Dr. Full, a drunken reprobate whom nobody would trust. The little black bag had been his guarantee, outweighing his whiskery face and stained black suit.

He was looking down on a three-year-old girl who had, he rather suspected, just been placed in the mathematical center of a freshly changed double bed. God knew what sour and dirty mattress she usually slept on. He seemed to recognize her as he noted a crusted bandage on her right hand. Two dollars, he thought—An ugly flush had spread up her pipe-stem arm. He poked a finger into the socket of her elbow, and felt little spheres like marbles under the skin and ligaments roll apart. The child began to squall thinly; beside him, the woman gasped and began to weep herself.

"Out," he gestured briskly at her, and she thudded away, still sobbing.

Two dollars, he thought— Give her some mumbo jumbo, take the money and tell her to go to a clinic. Strep, I guess, from that stinking alley. It's a wonder any of them grow up. He put down the little black bag and forgetfully fumbled for his key, then remembered and touched the lock. It flew open, and he selected a bandage shears, with a blunt wafer for the lower jaw. He fitted the lower jaw under the bandage, trying not to hurt the kid by its pressure on the infection, and began to cut. It was amazing how easily and swiftly the shining shears snipped through the crusty rag around the wound. He hardly seemed to be driving the shears with fingers at all. It almost seemed as though the shears were driving his fingers instead as they scissored a clean, light line through the bandage.

Certainly have forged ahead since my time, he thought—sharper than a microtome knife. He replaced the shears in their loop on the extraordinarily big board that the little black bag turned into when it unfolded, and leaned over the wound. He whistled at the ugly gash, and the violent infection which had taken immediate root in the sickly child's thin body. Now what can you do with a thing like that? He pawed over the contents of the little black bag, nervously. If he lanced it and let some of the pus out, the old woman would think he'd done something for her and he'd get the two dollars. But at the clinic they'd want to know who did it and if they got sore enough they might send a cop around. Maybe there was something in the kit—

He ran down the left edge of the card to "lymphatic" and read across to the column under "infection." It didn't sound right at all to him; he checked again, but it still said that. In the square to which the line and column led were the symbols: "IV-g-3cc." He couldn't find any bottles marked with Roman numerals, and then noticed that that was how the hypodermic needles were designated. He lifted number IV from its loop, noting that it was fitted with a needle already and even seemed to be charged. What a way to carry those things around! So—three cc. of whatever was in hypo number IV ought to do something or other about infections settled in the lymphatic system—which, God knows, this one was. What did the lower-case "g" mean, though? He studied the glass hypo and saw letters engraved on what looked like a rotating disk at the top of the barrel. They ran from "a" to "i," and there was an index line engraved on the barrel on the opposite side from the calibrations.

Shrugging, old Dr. Full turned the disk until "g" coincided with the index line, and lifted the hypo to eye level. As he pressed in the plunger he did not see the tiny thread of fluid squirt from the tip of the needle. There was a sort of dark mist for a moment about the tip. A closer inspection showed that the needle was not even pierced at the tip. It had the usual slanting cut across the bias of the shaft, but the cut did not expose an oval hole. Baffled, he tried pressing the plunger again. Again *something* appeared around the tip and vanished. "We'll settle this," said the doctor. He slipped the needle into the skin of his forearm. He thought at first that he had missed—that the point had glided over the top of his skin instead of catching and slipping under it. But he saw a tiny blood-spot and realized that somehow he just hadn't felt the puncture. Whatever was in the barrel, he decided, couldn't do him any harm if it lived up to its billing—and if it could come out through a needle that had no hole. He gave himself three cc. and twitched the needle out. There was the swelling—painless, but otherwise typical.

Dr. Full decided it was his eyes or something, and gave three cc. of "g" from hypodermic IV to the feverish child. There was no interruption to her wailing as the needle went in and the swelling rose. But a long instant later, she gave a final gasp and was silent.

Well, he told himself, cold with horror, you did it that time. You killed her with that stuff.

Then the child sat up and said: "Where's my mommy?"

Incredulously, the doctor seized her arm and palpated the elbow. The gland infection was zero, and the temperature seemed normal. The blood-congested tissues surrounding the wound were subsiding as he watched. The child's pulse was stronger and no faster than a child's should be. In the sudden silence of the room he could hear the little girl's mother sobbing in her kitchen, outside. And he also heard a girl's insinuating voice:

"She gonna be O.K., doc?"

He turned and saw a gaunt-faced, dirty-blonde sloven of perhaps eighteen leaning in the doorway and eyeing him with amused contempt. She continued: "I heard about you, *Doc-tor* Full. So don't go try and put the bite on the old lady. You couldn't doctor up a sick cat."

"Indeed?" he rumbled. This young person was going to get a lesson she richly deserved. "Perhaps you would care to look at my patient?"

"Where's my mommy?" insisted the little girl, and the blonde's jaw fell. She went to the bed and cautiously asked: "You O.K. now, Teresa? You all fixed up?"

"Where's my mommy?" demanded Teresa. Then, accusingly, she gestured with her wounded hand at the doctor. "You *poke* me!" she complained, and giggled pointlessly.

"Well—" said the blonde girl, "I guess I got to hand it to you, doc. These loud-mouth women around here said you didn't know your ... I mean, didn't know how to cure people. They said you ain't a real doctor."

"I *have* retired from practice," he said. "But I happened to be taking this case to a colleague as a favor, your good mother noticed me, and—" a deprecating smile. He touched the lock of the case and it folded up into the little black bag again.

"You stole it," the girl said flatly.

He sputtered.

"Nobody'd trust you with a thing like that. It must be worth plenty. You stole that case. I was going to stop you when I come in and saw you working over Teresa, but it looked like you wasn't doing her any harm. But when you give me that line about taking that case to a colleague I know you stole it. You gimme a cut or I go to the cops. A thing like that must be worth twenty–thirty dollars."

The mother came timidly in, her eyes red. But she let out a whoop of joy when she saw the little girl sitting up and babbling to herself, embraced her madly, fell on her knees for a quick prayer, hopped up to kiss the doctor's hand, and then dragged him into the kitchen, all the while rattling in her native language while the blonde girl let her eyes go cold with disgust. Dr. Full allowed himself to be towed into the kitchen, but flatly declined a cup of coffee and a plate of anise cakes and St. John's Bread.

"Try him on some wine, ma," said the girl sardonically.

"Hyass! Hyass!" breathed the woman delightedly. "You like-a wine, docta?" She had a carafe of purplish liquid before him in an instant, and the blonde girl snickered as the doctor's hand twitched out at it. He drew his hand back, while there grew in his head the old image of how it would smell and then taste and then warm his stomach and limbs. He made the kind of calculation at which he was practiced; the delighted woman would not notice as he downed two tumblers, and he could overawe her through two tumblers more with his tale of Teresa's narrow brush with the Destroying Angel, and then—why, then it would not matter. He would be drunk.

But for the first time in years, there was a sort of counter-image: a blend of the rage he felt at the blonde girl to whom he was so transparent, and of pride at the cure he had just effected. Much to his own surprise, he drew back his hand from the carafe and said, luxuriating in the words: "No, thank you. I don't believe I'd care for any so early in the day." He covertly watched the blonde girl's face, and was gratified at her surprise. Then the mother was shyly handing him two bills and saying: "Is no much-a money, docta—but you come again, see Teresa?"

"I shall be glad to follow the case through," he said. "But now excuse me— I really must be running along." He grasped the little black bag firmly and got up; he wanted very much to get away from the wine and the older girl.

"Wait up, doc," said she. "I'm going your way." She followed him out and down the street. He ignored her until he felt her hand on the black bag. Then old Dr. Full stopped and tried to reason with her:

"Look, my dear. Perhaps you're right. I might have stolen it. To be perfectly frank, I don't remember how I got it. But you're young and you can earn your own money—"

"Fifty-fifty," she said, "or I go to the cops. And if I get another word outta you, it's sixty-forty. And you know who gets the short end, don't you, doc?"

Defeated, he marched to the pawnshop, her impudent hand still on the handle with his, and her heels beating out a tattoo against his stately tread.

In the pawnshop, they both got a shock.

"It ain't stendard," said Uncle, unimpressed by the ingenious lock. "I ain't nevva seen one like it. Some cheap Jap stuff, maybe? Try down the street. This I nevva could sell."

Down the street they got an offer of one dollar. The same complaint was made: "I ain't a collecta, mista—I buy stuff that got resale value. Who could I sell this to, a Chinaman who don't know medical instruments? Every one of them looks funny. You sure you didn't make these yourself?" They didn't take the one-dollar offer.

The girl was baffled and angry; the doctor was baffled too, but triumphant. He had two dollars, and the girl had a half-interest in something nobody wanted. But, he suddenly marveled, the thing had been all right to cure the kid, hadn't it?

"Well," he asked her, "do you give up? As you see, the kit is practically valueless."

She was thinking hard. "Don't fly off the handle, doc. I don't get this but something's going on all right ... would those guys know good stuff if they saw it?"

"They would. They make a living from it. Wherever this kit came from—"

She seized on that, with a devilish faculty she seemed to have of eliciting answers without asking questions. "I thought so. You don't know either, huh? Well, maybe I can find out for you. C'mon in here. I ain't letting go of that thing. There's money in it—some way, I don't know how, there's money in it." He followed her into a cafeteria and to an almost-empty corner. She was oblivious to stares and snickers from the other customers as she opened the little black bag—it almost covered a cafeteria table—and ferreted through it. She picked out a retractor from a loop, scrutinized it, contemptuously threw it down, picked out a speculum, threw it down, picked out the lower half of an O.B. forceps, turned it over, close to her sharp young eyes—and saw what the doctor's dim old ones could not have seen.

All old Dr. Full knew was that she was peering at the neck of the forceps and then turned white. Very carefully, she placed the half of the forceps back in its loop of cloth and then replaced the retractor and the speculum. "Well?" he asked. "What did you see?"

"'Made in U.S.A.'" she quoted hoarsely. "'Patent Applied for July 2450.'"

He wanted to tell her she must have misread the inscription, that it must be a practical joke, that—

But he knew she had read correctly. Those bandage shears: they *had* driven his fingers, rather than his fingers driving them. The hypo needle that had no hole. The pretty blue pill that had struck him like a thunderbolt.

"You know what I'm going to do?" asked the girl, with sudden animation. "I'm going to go to charm school. You'll like that, won't ya, doc? Because we're sure going to be seeing a lot of each other."

Old Dr. Full didn't answer. His hands had been playing idly with that plastic card from the kit on which had been printed the rows and columns that had guided him twice before. The card had a slight convexity; you could snap the convexity back and forth from one side to the other. He noted, in a daze, that with each snap a different text appeared on the cards. *Snap.* "The knife with the blue dot in the handle is for tumors only. Diagnose tumors with your Instrument Seven, the Swelling Tester. Place the Swelling Tester—" *Snap.* "An overdose of the pink pills in Bottle 3 can be fixed with one white pill from Bottle—" *Snap.* "Hold the suture needle by the end without the hole in it. Touch it to one end of the wound you want to close and let go. After it has made the knot, touch it—" *Snap.* "Place the top half of the O.B. Forceps near the opening. Let go. After it has entered and conformed to the shape of—" *Snap.*

The slot man saw "FLANNERY 1—MEDICAL" in the upper left corner of the hunk of copy. He automatically scribbled "trim to .75" on it and skimmed it across the horseshoe-shaped copy desk to Piper, who had been handling Edna Flannery's quack-exposé series. She was a nice youngster, he thought, but like all youngsters she over-wrote. Hence, the "trim."

Piper dealt back a city hall story to the slot, pinned down Flannery's feature with one hand and began to tap his pencil across it, one tap to a word, at the same steady beat as a teletype carriage traveling across the roller. He wasn't exactly reading it this first time. He was just looking at the letters and words to find out whether, as letters and words, they conformed to *Herald* style. The steady tap of his pencil ceased at intervals as it drew a black line ending with a stylized letter "d" through the word "breast" and scribbled in "chest" instead, or knocked down the capital "E" in "East" to lower case with a diagonal, or closed up a split word—in whose middle Flannery had bumped the space bar of her typewriter—with two curved lines like parentheses rotated through ninety degrees. The thick black pencil zipped a ring around the "30" which, like all youngsters, she put at the end of her stories. He turned back to the first page for the second reading. This time the pencil drew lines with the stylized "d's" at the end of them through adjectives and whole phrases, printed big "L's" to mark paragraphs, hooked some of Flannery's own paragraphs together with swooping recurved lines.

At the bottom of "FLANNERY ADD 2—MEDICAL" the pencil slowed down and stopped. The slot man, sensitive to the rhythm of his beloved copy desk, looked up almost at once. He saw Piper squinting at the story, at a loss. Without wasting words, the copy reader skimmed it back across the Masonite horseshoe to the chief, caught a police story in return and buckled down, his pencil tapping. The slot man read as far as the fourth add, barked at Howard, on the rim: "Sit in for me," and stumped through the clattering city room toward the alcove where the managing editor presided over his own bedlam.

The copy chief waited his turn while the make-up editor, the pressroom foreman and the chief photographer had words with the M.E. When his turn came, he dropped Flannery's copy on his desk and said: "She says this one isn't a quack."

The M.E. read:

"FLANNERY 1—MEDICAL, by Edna Flannery, *Herald* Staff Writer.

"The sordid tale of medical quackery which the *Herald* has exposed in this series of articles undergoes a change of pace today which the reporter found a welcome surprise. Her quest for the facts in the case of today's subject started just the same way that her exposure of one dozen shyster M.D.'s and faith-healing phonies did. But she can report for a change that Dr. Bayard Full is, despite unorthodox practices which have drawn the suspicion of the rightly hypersensitive medical associations, a true healer living up to the highest ideals of his profession.

"Dr. Full's name was given to the *Herald's* reporter by the ethical committee of a county medical association, which reported that he had been expelled from the association on July 18, 1941 for allegedly 'milking' several patients suffering from trivial complaints. According to sworn statements in the committee's files, Dr. Full had told them they suffered from cancer, and that he had a treatment which would prolong their lives. After his expulsion from the association, Dr. Full dropped out of their sight—until he opened a midtown 'sanitarium' in a brownstone front which had for years served as a rooming house.

"The *Herald's* reporter went to that sanitarium, on East 89th Street, with the full expectation of having numerous imaginary ailments diagnosed and of being promised a sure cure for a flat sum of money. She expected to find unkempt quarters, dirty instruments and the mumbo-jumbo paraphernalia of the shyster M.D. which she had seen a dozen times before.

"She was wrong.

"Dr. Full's sanitarium is spotlessly clean, from its tastefully furnished entrance hall to its shining, white treatment rooms. The attractive, blonde receptionist who greeted the reporter was soft-spoken and correct, asking only the reporter's name, address and the general nature of her complaint. This was given, as usual, as 'nagging backache.' The receptionist asked the *Herald's* reporter to be seated, and a short while later conducted her to a second-floor treatment room and introduced her to Dr. Full.

"Dr. Full's alleged past, as described by the medical society spokesman, is hard to reconcile with his present appearance. He is a clear-eyed, white-haired man in his sixties, to judge by his appearance—a little above middle height and apparently in good physical condition. His voice was firm and friendly, untainted by the ingratiating whine of the shyster M.D. which the reporter has come to know too well.

"The receptionist did not leave the room as he began his examination after a few questions as to the nature and location of the pain. As the reporter lay face down on a treatment table the doctor pressed some instrument to the small of her back. In about one minute he made this astounding statement: 'Young woman, there is no reason for you to have any pain where you say you do. I understand they're saying nowadays that emotional upsets cause pains like that. You'd better go to a psychologist or psychiatrist if the pain keeps up. There is no physical cause for it, so I can do nothing for you.'

"His frankness took the reporter's breath away. Had he guessed she was, so to speak, a spy in his camp? She tried again: 'Well, doctor, perhaps you'd give me a physical checkup. I feel run-down all the time, besides the pains. Maybe I need a tonic.' This is never-failing bait to shyster M.D.'s—an invitation for them to find all sorts of mysterious conditions wrong with a patient, each of which 're- quires' an expensive treatment. As explained in the first article of this series, of course, the reporter underwent a thorough physical checkup before she embarked on her quack-hunt, and was found to be in one hundred percent perfect condi- tion, with the exception of a 'scarred' area at the bottom tip of her left lung result- ing from a childhood attack of tuberculosis and a tendency toward 'hyperthy- roidism'—overactivity of the thyroid gland which makes it difficult to put on weight and sometimes causes a slight shortness of breath.

"Dr. Full consented to perform the examination, and took a number of shin- ing, spotlessly clean instruments from loops in a large board literally covered with instruments—most of them unfamiliar to the reporter. The instrument with which he approached first was a tube with a curved dial in its surface and two wires that ended on flat disks growing from its ends. He placed one of the disks on the back of the reporter's right hand and the other on the back of her left. 'Reading the meter,' he called out some number which the attentive receptionist took down on a ruled form. The same procedure was repeated several times, thoroughly cover- ing the reporter's anatomy and thoroughly convincing her that the doctor was a complete quack. The reporter had never seen any such diagnostic procedure prac- ticed during the weeks she put in preparing for this series.

"The doctor then took the ruled sheet from the receptionist, conferred with her in low tones and said: 'You have a slightly overactive thyroid, young woman. And there's something wrong with your left lung—not seriously, but I'd like to take a closer look.'

"He selected an instrument from the board which, the reporter knew, is called a 'speculum'—a scissorlike device which spreads apart body openings such as the orifice of the ear, the nostril and so on, so that a doctor can look in during an examination. The instrument was, however, too large to be an aural or nasal specu- lum but too small to be anything else. As the *Herald's* reporter was about to ask further questions, the attending receptionist told her: 'It's customary for us to blindfold our patients during lung examinations—do you mind?' The reporter, bewildered, allowed her to tie a spotlessly clean bandage over her eyes, and waited nervously for what would come next.

"She still cannot say exactly what happened while she was blindfolded—but X rays confirm her suspicions. She felt a cold sensation at her ribs on the left side—a cold that seemed to enter inside her body. Then there was a snapping feeling, and the cold sensation was gone. She heard Dr. Full say in a matter-of-fact voice: 'You have an old tubercular scar down there. It isn't doing any particular harm, but an active person like you needs all the oxygen she can get. Lie still and I'll fix it for you.'

"Then there was a repetition of the cold sensation, lasting for a longer time. 'Another batch of alveoli and some more vascular glue,' the *Herald's* reporter heard Dr. Full say, and the receptionist's crisp response to the order. Then the strange sensation departed and the eye-bandage was removed. The reporter saw no scar on her ribs, and yet the doctor assured her: 'That did it. We took out the fibrosis —and a good fibrosis it was, too; it walled off the infection so you're still alive to tell the tale. Then we planted a few clumps of alveoli—they're the little gadgets that get the oxygen from the air you breathe into your blood. I won't monkey with your thyroxin supply. You've got used to being the kind of person you are, and if you suddenly found yourself easygoing and all the rest of it, chances are you'd only be upset. About the backache: just check with the county medical society for the name of a good psychologist or psychiatrist. And look out for quacks; the woods are full of them.'

"The doctor's self-assurance took the reporter's breath away. She asked what the charge would be, and was told to pay the receptionist fifty dollars. As usual, the reporter delayed paying until she got a receipt signed by the doctor himself, detailing the services for which it paid. Unlike most, the doctor cheerfully wrote: 'For removal of fibrosis from left lung and restoration of alveoli,' and signed it.

"The reporter's first move when she left the sanitarium was to head for the chest specialist who had examined her in preparation for this series. A comparison of X rays taken on the day of the 'operation' and those taken previously would, the *Herald*'s reporter then thought, expose Dr. Full as a prince of shyster M.D.'s and quacks.

"The chest specialist made time on his crowded schedule for the reporter, in whose series he has shown a lively interest from the planning stage on. He laughed uproariously in his staid Park Avenue examining room as she described the weird procedure to which she had been subjected. But he did not laugh when he took a chest X ray of the reporter, developed it, dried it, and compared it with the ones he had taken earlier. The chest specialist took six more X rays that afternoon, but finally admitted that they all told the same story. The *Herald*'s reporter has it on his authority that the scar she had eighteen days ago from her tuberculosis is now gone and has been replaced by healthy lung-tissue. He declares that this is a happening unparalleled in medical history. He does not go along with the reporter in her firm conviction that Dr. Full is responsible for the change.

"The *Herald*'s reporter, however, sees no two ways about it. She concludes that Dr. Bayard Full—whatever his alleged past may have been—is now an unorthodox but highly successful practitioner of medicine, to whose hands the reporter would trust herself in any emergency.

"Not so is the case of 'Rev.' Annie Dimsworth—a female harpy who, under the guise of 'faith' preys on the ignorant and suffering who come to her sordid 'healing parlor' for help and remain to feed 'Rev.' Annie's bank account, which now totals up to $53,238.64. Tomorrow's article will show, with photostats of bank statements and sworn testimony that—"

The managing editor turned down "FLANNERY LAST ADD—MEDICAL" and tapped his front teeth with a pencil, trying to think straight. He finally told the copy chief: "Kill the story. Run the teaser as a box." He tore off the last paragraph—the "teaser" about "Rev." Annie—and handed it to the desk man, who stumped back to his Masonite horseshoe.

The make-up editor was back, dancing with impatience as he tried to catch the M.E.'s eye. The interphone buzzed with the red light which indicated that the editor and publisher wanted to talk to him. The M.E. thought briefly of a special series on this Dr. Full, decided nobody would believe it and that he probably was a phony anyway. He spiked the story on the "dead" hook and answered his interphone.

Dr. Full had become almost fond of Angie. As his practice had grown to engross the neighborhood illnesses, and then to a corner suite in an uptown taxpayer building, and finally to the sanitarium, she seemed to have grown with it. Oh, he thought, we have our little disputes—

The girl, for instance, was too much interested in money. She had wanted to specialize in cosmetic surgery—removing wrinkles from wealthy old women and whatnot. She didn't realize, at first, that a thing like this was in their trust, that they were the stewards and not the owners of the little black bag and its fabulous contents.

He had tried, ever so cautiously, to analyze them, but without success. All the instruments were slightly radioactive, for instance, but not quite so. They would make a Geiger-Müller counter indicate, but they would not collapse the leaves of an electroscope. He didn't pretend to be up on the latest developments, but as he understood it, that was just plain *wrong*. Under the highest magnification there were lines on the instruments' superfinished surfaces: incredibly fine lines, engraved in random hatchments which made no particular sense. Their magnetic properties were preposterous. Sometimes the instruments were strongly attracted to magnets, sometimes less so, and sometimes not at all.

Dr. Full had taken X rays in fear and trembling lest he disrupt whatever delicate machinery worked in them. He was *sure* they were not solid, that the handles and perhaps the blades must be mere shells filled with busy little watchworks—but the X rays showed nothing of the sort. Oh, yes—and they were always sterile, and they wouldn't rust. Dust *fell* off them if you shook them: now, that was something he understood. They ionized the dust, or were ionized themselves, or something of the sort. At any rate, he had read of something similar that had to do with phonograph records.

She wouldn't know about that, he proudly thought. She kept the books well enough, and perhaps she gave him a useful prod now and then when he was inclined to settle down. The move from the neighborhood slum to the uptown quarters had been her idea, and so had the sanitarium. Good, good, it enlarged his sphere of usefulness. Let the child have her mink coats and her convertible, as they seemed to be calling roadsters nowadays. He himself was too busy and too old. He had so much to make up for.

Dr. Full thought happily of his Master Plan. She would not like it much, but she would have to see the logic of it. This marvelous thing that had happened to them must be handed on. She was herself no doctor; even though the instruments practically ran themselves, there was more to doctoring than skill. There were the ancient canons of the healing art. And so, having seen the logic of it, Angie would yield; she would assent to his turning over the little black bag to all humanity.

He would probably present it to the College of Surgeons, with as little fuss as possible—well, perhaps a *small* ceremony, and he would like a souvenir of the occasion, a cup or a framed testimonial. It would be a relief to have the thing out of his hands, in a way; let the giants of the healing art decide who was to have its benefits. No, Angie would understand. She was a goodhearted girl.

It was nice that she had been showing so much interest in the surgical side lately—asking about the instruments, reading the instruction card for hours, even practicing on guinea pigs. If something of his love for humanity had been communicated to her, old Dr. Full sentimentally thought, his life would not have been in vain. Surely she would realize that a greater good would be served by surrendering the instruments to wiser hands than theirs, and by throwing aside the cloak of secrecy necessary to work on their small scale.

Dr. Full was in the treatment room that had been the brownstone's front parlor; through the window he saw Angie's yellow convertible roll to a stop before the stoop. He liked the way she looked as she climbed the stairs; neat, not flashy, he thought. A sensible girl like her, she'd understand. There was somebody with her—a fat woman, puffing up the steps, overdressed and petulant. Now, what could she want?

Angie let herself in and went into the treatment room, followed by the fat woman. "Doctor," said the blonde girl gravely, "may I present Mrs. Coleman?" Charm school had not taught her everything, but Mrs. Coleman, evidently *nouveau riche,* thought the doctor, did not notice the blunder.

"Miss Aquella told me *so* much about you, doctor, and your remarkable system!" she gushed.

Before he could answer, Angie smoothly interposed: "Would you excuse us for just a moment, Mrs. Coleman?"

She took the doctor's arm and led him into the reception hall. "Listen," she said swiftly, "I know this goes against your grain, but I couldn't pass it up. I met this old thing in the exercise class at Elizabeth Barton's. Nobody else'll talk to her there. She's a widow. I guess her husband was a black marketeer or something, and she has a pile of dough. I gave her a line about how you had a system of massaging wrinkles out. My idea is, you blindfold her, cut her neck open with the Cutaneous Series knife, shoot some Firmol into the muscles, spoon out some of that blubber with an Adipose Series curette and spray it all with Skintite. When you take the blindfold off she's got rid of a wrinkle and doesn't know what happened. She'll pay five hundred dollars. Now, don't say 'no,' doc. Just this once, let's do it my way, can't you? I've been working on this deal all along too, haven't I?"

"Oh," said the doctor, "very well." He was going to have to tell her about the Master Plan before long anyway. He would let her have it her way this time.

Back in the treatment room, Mrs. Coleman had been thinking things over. She told the doctor sternly as he entered: "Of course, your system is permanent, isn't it?"

"It is, madam," he said shortly. "Would you please lie down there? Miss Aquella, get a sterile three-inch bandage for Mrs. Coleman's eyes." He turned his back on the fat woman to avoid conversation, and pretended to be adjusting the lights. Angie blindfolded the woman, and the doctor selected the instruments he would need. He handed the blonde girl a pair of retractors, and told her: "Just slip the corners of the blades in as I cut—" She gave him an alarmed look, and gestured at the reclining woman. He lowered his voice: "Very well. Slip in the corners and rock them along the incision. I'll tell you when to pull them out."

Dr. Full held the Cutaneous Series knife to his eyes as he adjusted the little slide for three centimeters depth. He sighed a little as he recalled that its last use had been in the extirpation of an "inoperable" tumor of the throat.

"Very well," he said, bending over the woman. He tried a tentative pass through her tissues. The blade dipped in and flowed through them, like a finger through quicksilver, with no wound left in the wake. Only the retractors could hold the edges of the incision apart.

Mrs. Coleman stirred and jabbered: "Doctor, that felt so peculiar! Are you sure you're rubbing the right way?"

"Quite sure, madam," said the doctor wearily. "Would you please try not to talk during the massage?"

He nodded at Angie, who stood ready with the retractors. The blade sank in to its three centimeters, miraculously cutting only the dead horny tissues of the epidermis and the live tissue of the dermis, pushing aside mysteriously all major and minor blood vessels and muscular tissue, declining to affect any system or organ except the one it was—tuned to, could you say? The doctor didn't know the answer, but he felt tired and bitter at this prostitution. Angie slipped in the retractor blades and rocked them as he withdrew the knife, then pulled to separate the lips of the incision. It bloodlessly exposed an unhealthy string of muscle, sagging in a dead-looking loop from blue-grey ligaments. The doctor took a hypo, number IX, pre-set to "g" and raised it to his eye level. The mist came and went. There probably was no possibility of an embolus with one of these gadgets, but why take chances? He shot one cc. of "g"—identified as "Firmol" by the card—into the muscle. He and Angie watched as it tightened up against the pharynx.

He took the Adipose Series curette, a small one, and spooned out yellowish tissue, dropping it into the incinerator box, and then nodded to Angie. She eased out the retractors and the gaping incision slipped together into unbroken skin, sagging now. The doctor had the atomizer—dialed to "Skintite"—ready. He sprayed, and the skin shrank up into the new firm throat line.

As he replaced the instruments, Angie removed Mrs. Coleman's bandage and gayly announced: "We're finished! And there's a mirror in the reception hall—"

Mrs. Coleman didn't need to be invited twice. With incredulous fingers she felt her chin, and then dashed for the hall. The doctor grimaced as he heard her yelp of delight, and Angie turned to him with a tight smile. "I'll get the money and get her out," she said. "You won't have to be bothered with her any more."

He was grateful for that much.

She followed Mrs. Coleman into the reception hall, and the doctor dreamed over the case of instruments. A ceremony, certainly—he was *entitled* to one. Not everybody, he thought, would turn such a sure source of money over to the good of humanity. But you reached an age when money mattered less, and when you thought of these things you had done that *might* be open to misunderstanding if, just if, there chanced to be any of that, well, that judgment business. The doctor wasn't a religious man, but you certainly found yourself thinking hard about some things when your time drew near—

Angie was back, with a bit of paper in her hands. "Five hundred dollars," she said matter-of-factly. "And you realize, don't you, that we could go over her an inch at a time—at five hundred dollars an inch?"

"I've been meaning to talk to you about that," he said.

There was bright fear in her eyes, he thought—but why?

"Angie, you've been a good girl and an understanding girl, but we can't keep this up forever, you know."

"Let's talk about it some other time," she said flatly. "I'm tired now."

"No—I really feel we've gone far enough on our own. The instruments—"

"Don't say it, doc!" she hissed. "Don't say it, or you'll be sorry!" In her face there was a look that reminded him of the hollow-eyed, gaunt-faced, dirty-blonde creature she had been. From under the charm-school finish there burned the guttersnipe whose infancy had been spent on a sour and filthy mattress, whose childhood had been play in the littered alley and whose adolescence had been the sweatshops and the aimless gatherings at night under the glaring street lamps.

He shook his head to dispel the puzzling notion. "It's this way," he patiently began. "I told you about the family that invented the O.B. forceps and kept them a secret for so many generations, how they could have given them to the world but didn't?"

"They knew what they were doing," said the guttersnipe flatly.

"Well, that's neither here nor there," said the doctor, irritated. "My mind is made up about it. I'm going to turn the instruments over to the College of Surgeons. We have enough money to be comfortable. You can even have the house. I've been thinking of going to a warmer climate, myself." He felt peeved with her for making the unpleasant scene. He was unprepared for what happened next.

Angie snatched the little black bag and dashed for the door, with panic in her eyes. He scrambled after her, catching her arm, twisting it in a sudden rage. She clawed at his face with her free hand, babbling curses. Somehow, somebody's finger touched the little black bag, and it opened grotesquely into the enormous board, covered with shining instruments, large and small. Half a dozen of them joggled loose and fell to the floor.

"*Now* see what you've done!" roared the doctor, unreasonably. Her hand was still viselike on the handle, but she was standing still, trembling with choked-up rage. The doctor bent stiffly to pick up the fallen instruments. Unreasonable girl! he thought bitterly. Making a scene—

Pain drove in between his shoulderblades and he fell face-down. The light ebbed. "Unreasonable girl!" he tried to croak. And then: "They'll know I tried, anyway—"

Angie looked down on his prone body, with the handle of the Number Six Cautery Series knife protruding from it. "—will cut through all tissues. Use for amputations before you spread on the Re-Gro. Extreme caution should be used in the vicinity of vital organs and major blood vessels or nerve trunks—"

"I didn't mean to do that," said Angie, dully, cold with horror. Now the detective would come, the implacable detective who would reconstruct the crime from the dust in the room. She would run and turn and twist, but the detective would find her out and she would be tried in a courtroom before a judge and jury; the lawyer would make speeches, but the jury would convict her anyway, and the headlines would scream: "BLONDE KILLER GUILTY!" and she'd maybe get the chair, walking down a plain corridor where a beam of sunlight struck through the dusty air, with an iron door at the end of it. Her mink, her convertible, her dresses, the handsome man she was going to meet and marry—

The mist of cinematic clichés cleared, and she knew what she would do next. Quite steadily, she picked the incinerator box from its loop in the board—a metal cube with a different-textured spot on one side. "—to dispose of fibroses or other unwanted matter, simply touch the disk—" You dropped something in and touched the disk. There was a sort of soundless whistle, very powerful and unpleasant if you were too close, and a sort of lightless flash. When you opened the box again, the contents were gone. Angie took another of the Cautery Series knives and went grimly to work. Good thing there wasn't any blood to speak of— She finished the awful task in three hours.

She slept heavily that night, totally exhausted by the wringing emotional demands of the slaying and the subsequent horror. But in the morning, it was as though the doctor had never been there. She ate breakfast, dressed with unusual care—and then undid the unusual care. Nothing out of the ordinary, she told herself. Don't do one thing different from the way you would have done it before. After a day or two, you can phone the cops. Say he walked out spoiling for a drunk, and you're worried. But don't rush it, baby—*don't rush it.*

Mrs. Coleman was due at 10:00 A.M. Angie had counted on being able to talk the doctor into at least one more five-hundred-dollar session. She'd have to do it herself now—but she'd have to start sooner or later.

The woman arrived early. Angie explained smoothly: "The doctor asked me to take care of the massage today. Now that he has the tissue-firming process beginning, it only requires somebody trained in his methods—" As she spoke, her eyes swiveled to the instrument case—open! She cursed herself for the single flaw as the woman followed her gaze and recoiled.

"What are those things!" she demanded. "Are you going to cut me with them? I *thought* there was something fishy—"

"Please, Mrs. Coleman," said Angie, "please, *dear* Mrs. Coleman—you don't understand about the ... the massage instruments!"

"Massage instruments, my foot!" squabbled the woman shrilly. "That doctor *operated* on me. Why, he might have killed me!"

Angie wordlessly took one of the smaller Cutaneous Series knives and passed it through her forearm. The blade flowed like a finger through quicksilver, leaving no wound in its wake. *That* should convince the old cow!

It didn't convince her, but it did startle her. "What did you do with it? The blade folds up into the handle—that's it!"

"Now look closely, Mrs. Coleman," said Angie, thinking desperately of the five hundred dollars. "Look very closely and you'll see that the, uh, the sub-skin massager simply slips beneath the tissues without doing any harm, tightening and firming the muscles themselves instead of having to work through layers of skin and adipose tissue. It's the secret of the doctor's method. Now, how can outside massage have the effect that we got last night?"

Mrs. Coleman was beginning to calm down. "It *did* work, all right," she admitted, stroking the new line of her neck. "But your arm's one thing and my neck's another! Let me see you do that with your neck!"

Angie smiled—

Al returned to the clinic after an excellent lunch that had almost reconciled him to three more months he would have to spend on duty. And then, he thought, and then a blessed year at the blessedly super-normal South Pole working on his specialty—which happened to be telekinesis exercises for ages three to six. Meanwhile, of course, the world had to go on and of course he had to shoulder his share in the running of it.

Before settling down to desk work he gave a routine glance at the bag board. What he saw made him stiffen with shocked surprise. A red light was on next to one of the numbers—the first since he couldn't think when. He read off the number and murmured "O.K., 674,101. That fixes *you*." He put the number on a card sorter and in a moment the record was in his hand. Oh, yes—Hemingway's bag. The big dummy didn't remember how or where he had lost it; none of them ever did. There were hundreds of them floating around.

Al's policy in such cases was to leave the bag turned on. The things practically ran themselves, it was practically impossible to do harm with them, so whoever found a lost one might as well be allowed to use it. You turn it off, you have a social loss—you leave it on, it may do some good. As he understood it, and not very well at that, the stuff wasn't "used up." A temporalist had tried to explain it to him with little success that the prototypes in the transmitter had been transducted through a series of point-events of transfinite cardinality. Al had innocently asked whether that meant prototypes had been stretched, so to speak, through all time, and the temporalist had thought he was joking and left in a huff.

"Like to see him do this," thought Al darkly, as he telekinized himself to the combox, after a cautious look to see that there were no medics around. To the box he said: "Police chief," and then to the police chief: "There's been a homicide committed with Medical Instrument Kit 674,101. It was lost some months ago by one of my people, Dr. John Hemingway. He didn't have a clear account of the circumstances."

The police chief groaned and said: "I'll call him in and question him." He was to be astonished by the answers, and was to learn that the homicide was well out of his jurisdiction.

Al stood for a moment at the bag board by the glowing red light that had been sparked into life by a departing vital force giving, as its last act, the warning that Kit 674,101 was in homicidal hands. With a sigh, Al pulled the plug and the light went out.

"Yah," jeered the woman. "You'd fool around with my neck, but you wouldn't risk your own with that thing!"

Angie smiled with serene confidence a smile that was to shock hardened morgue attendants. She set the Cutaneous Series knife to three centimeters before drawing it across her neck. Smiling, knowing the blade would cut only the dead horny tissue of the epidermis and the live tissue of the dermis, mysteriously push aside all major and minor blood vessels and muscular tissue—

Smiling, the knife plunging in and its microtomesharp metal shearing through major and minor blood vessels and muscular tissue and pharynx, Angie cut her throat.

In the few minutes it took the police, summoned by the shrieking Mrs. Coleman, to arrive, the instruments had become crusted with rust, and the flasks which had held vascular glue and clumps of pink, rubbery alveoli and spare grey cells and coils of receptor nerves held only black slime, and from them when opened gushed the foul gases of decomposition.

[*Cosmic Stories* - May 1941
as by Cecil Corwin]

What Sorghum Says

Up in the foothills of the Cumberlands they have something new in the way of folklore. If you're lucky and haven't got the professional gleam in your eye, the tale is unfolded something like this:

Sorghum Hackett lived by himself up by Sowbelly Crag, not because he was afraid for his still, but because when he was a young man some girl blighted his life by running off to Nashville with a railroad man. Ever since that, he's been bitter against most people.

So this spring morning, when the scientific man came climbing up to his house he got out his squirrel gun and asked him like the mountain people do, "Will you make tracks or your peace with God?"

"Shut up!" said the scientific man, not even looking at him. Then he went pacing off the ground and writing down figures in a book. At last he turned to Sorghum. "How much do you want for your property?" he asked. "I suppose it's yours."

"Anyone in his right mind wouldn't be eager to dispute it," said Sorghum dryly. "But it ain't for sale."

"Don't be stubborn," said the scientific man. "I haven't any time to waste on benighted peasants."

Sorghum dropped his gun in real admiration for the bravery of the man, whoever he was. He held out a hand, saying, "I'm Sorghum Hackett, and I've killed men for less than what you said."

The man shook his hand absent-mindedly. "I'm Wayne Baily, and I've got to have the use of your land for about a month."

Hackett nearly fell in love with the man; he didn't know there was anyone who could stand up to him that way, and he liked it. "I'm willing," he said at last. "But I won't take your money—it ain't clean."

So Baily just laughed, and then went down to the village and came back up with a Ford truck loaded to the gills with junk. "Hackett," he said, "first thing we do is run this penstock down from that springhead."

And by the next morning they had forty yards of big piping down from Chittling Spring, and the water gushing out the end of the pipe would have irrigated a whole farm. Baily rigged up a metal globe that he bolted to the pipe's end, a globe with a small-gauge turbine wheel in it, and he hooked that up to a little dynamo that stayed on the truck.

When a week was up there was precious little room in Sorghum's house for him and Baily, because it was cluttered up with the junk from town—insides of radios, big coils of wire, aerials, rods stuck into the ground so deep they were cold from underground water they touched—everything crazy you could think of, and all lit up every now and then whenever Baily turned on his dynamo in the truck.

Finally Baily said to Sorghum, "It's been a pleasure knowing you, Hackett. Now there's only one stipulation I'm putting on you, and that is to knock all my machinery into pieces as soon as I'm gone."

"Gone?" asked Sorghum, because Baily didn't say it as though he was going down to town for another storage battery.

"Yes—for good, Hackett," said Baily, puttering with the wires and finally turning a switch. The things lit up and glowed even brighter than ever before. "Goodbye, Hackett," said Baily. Then he grabbed at his chest and his face twisted. "Heart!" he gasped faintly, and even fainter he cut loose with a string of curses that made Sorghum blush.

Baily hit the floor, and Sorghum listened for his breath, but there wasn't any. He scratched his head, wondering how he'd explain things to the coroner, and reached automatically for his jug to help him think.

But one of the things he didn't think of was that his jug had been moved outside to make room for what the late Mr. Baily had called a condenser. Sorghum got a shock that sent him crashing back on his heels into some of the deep-driven rods. The last thing he knew, the lights were still sparkling and glowing, but he never could tell what hit him.

There was a dizzying splash and Sorghum found himself floundering in water up to his knees. He looked around and wasn't in any place he knew, because he didn't know any places that were all marble and tile. Overhead a hot sun was beating down on him.

"Well!" said someone. And right there Sorghum knew that something was wrong, because though what he heard was "Well!" the sound he heard wasn't anything like that—more like "Ahoo!"

He looked up and saw a man facing him, dressed in sandals and a shirt that fell to his knees. And the man said, still talking so that Sorghum could understand him but not making a single sound in English, "It's a blundering assassin that falls into his victim's fishpond. Tiberius chooses unwisely."

"Are you calling me a bushwhacker, mister?" demanded Sorghum, who never killed except fairly.

The man, who had been grinning proudly, looked surprised then. Not frightened, surprised. "I don't know what language you speak, assassin," he said, "but it's a damnably strange one that confounds and is clear at the same time." He looked closer at Sorghum. "And you don't seem altogether real. Are you always as ghostly when you're sent on the Caesar's errands?"

Sorghum looked at himself and saw that the man wasn't lying. His own flesh seemed to have got a funny trick of being half here and half there, like a column of smoke that's always ready to break. "I reckon you're right, mister," said Sorghum, cracking one of his icy smiles. "I seem to be in a predicament. But I ain't what you take me for. I'm Sorghum Hackett of Tennessee."

"Never heard of the town," said the man. "I'm Asinius Gallo. Need I explain that this is Rome?"

Now, Sorghum had heard that foreigners were peculiar, but he didn't expect anything as peculiar as this, and he said so.

"Foreigners!" yelled the man. "I don't know what barbarous land you're from, stranger, but bear in mind that when you're in the City *you're* the foreigner until and unless naturalized. Though," he added, calmer, "what with that avaricious slut the Lady Livia raising the prices on the roll week after week, soon a Julio-Claudian himself won't be able to stay in his place."

"I don't get your talk, Mr. Gallo," said Sorghum. "I'm here by accident, and I'd like mightily to get back to Tennessee. How can I earn some passage money? I reckon it's overseas."

"Work, eh?" asked Asinius Gallo. "What can you do?"

Sorghum considered. "I can do a little carpentering," he said. "And I can make the best white mule in the Cumberlands."

"Carpentry's out of the question," said Asinius Gallo. "The Joiners' Guild has it tight as a drum. But I don't know of any guild covering the manufacture of white mules—doubt that it can be done."

"Do ye?" asked Sorghum, grinning again. "Just give me some corn, some copper, and a few days and I'll show you."

Asinius Gallo abruptly nodded. "It might be worth trying," he said. "Certainly I can't raise my own. And if they're really good they can be resold at a profit. Sorghum Hackett, I'll finance you."

So, working in privacy, the way the mountain folks like to, it took him a few days before he got a good run. He had to fool around a lot because they used a funny, stunted kind of grain, but finally it came out all right.

"Here, Mr. Gallo," he called to his backer. "It's finished."

"Will it kick?" asked Asinius Gallo cautiously.

Sorghum laughed. "Like the devil with a porky quill in him, I promise you that much. Best you ever saw."

"Well," said Asinius Gallo uncertainly as he entered. Sorghum held up the big jug he'd caught the run in. "What's that?"

"The white mule," Sorghum said, a little hurt.

His backer was downright bewildered. "I expected an animal," he explained. "What you've got in there I can't imagine."

"Oh," said Sorghum. "Well, if you don't agree with me, Mr. Gallo, that this is better than any animal you ever tasted, I'll make you an animal." And he said this because he felt pretty sure that the benighted idolater wouldn't take him up. Sorghum had asked the terrified servants, and they told him that they didn't have anything stronger than the sticky red wine they drank at supper. And that, Sorghum judged by the body, was no more than twenty proof, while this run of his would prove at least a hundred and twenty. He poured a medium slug—four fingers—for his host, who smelled it cautiously.

"Don't put your eyes over it, Mr. Gallo," cautioned Sorghum. "Just drink it right down the way we do in Tennessee." He filled a glass of his own with a man-sized drink.

"Feliciter," said Asinius Gallo, which sounded like "good luck" to Sorghum.

"Confusion to Tories," he replied, downing his.

His host immediately after swallowed his own shot convulsively. Almost immediately he screamed shrilly and clutched at his throat. Sorghum held a water pitcher out to him, grinning. The pitcher was empty when he took it back.

"That," said his host hoarsely, "was a potion worthy of Livia herself. Are you sure it won't kill me?"

"Sartin," replied Sorghum, enjoying the backwash of the home product. "That was almost the smoothest I've ever made."

"Then," said Asinius Gallo, "let's have another."

The Tennessee man had a few more runs, each better than the last as his equipment improved and settled, and with Asinius Gallo as his agent he had amassed quite a bit of the coinage of these foreigners. Altogether things were looking up when a slave appeared with a message.

Sorghum's host read from it: *The Lady Livia will be pleased to see Sorghum Hackett, the guest of the Senator Asinius Gallo. She believes that there are many mutual interests which it will be profitable to discuss.*

"Right kind of her," said Sorghum.

"Hah!" groaned his backer. "You don't know the old hag. Sorghum Hackett, you're as good as dead, and it's no use hoping otherwise. She's always been down on me, but she never dared to strike at me direct because of my family. Now you're going to get it. Oh, I'm sorry, friend. And I thought I'd kept you a pretty close secret. Well, go on—no use postponing fate."

Sorghum grinned slowly. "We'll see," he said. He picked up two bottles of the latest run and rammed them into his boot tops. "Goodbye, Mr. Gallo," he said, entering the sedan chair that was waiting for him.

The bearers let him off at the Augustan Palace and conducted him to a side entrance. He waited only a moment before the door opened and a cracked voice bade him enter. "Come in, young man; come in!" it shrilled.

Sorghum closed the door behind him and faced the notorious Livia, mother of the Emperor Tiberius, poisoner supreme and unquestioned ruler of Rome. "Pleased t' meetcha, ma'am," he said.

"You're the Hackett they tell me about?" she demanded.

He studied her wispy white hair and the bony, hooked nose as he answered, "I'm the only Hackett in these parts."

"It's true!" she shrilled. "You are a magician—your body waves like a flame, and your language is strange, but I can understand it. Everything they said is true!"

"I reckon so, ma'am," admitted Sorghum.

"Then you're condemned," she said promptly. "I won't have any magicians going about in my empire. Can't tax the brutes—they're unfair. You're condemned, young man!"

"To what?" asked the Tennesseean.

"Amphitheater," she snapped. "Wild beasts. Take him away, you fools!"

Sorghum's arms were grabbed by two of the biggest, ugliest people he had ever seen in his born days and he was hustled down flights of stairs and hurled into something of a dungeon with other condemned magicians.

"You got in just under the wire," one of them informed him helpfully. "We're going to get chased out into the arena in a few minutes."

"What can I do?" asked Sorghum.

"Don't struggle. Don't shield your throat—let the animals tear it out as soon as possible. That way it's over with at once and you cheat the mob of watching you squirm."

"I reckon so," said Sorghum thoughtfully. He remembered his courtesy and the bottles in his boots. "Have a drink?" he asked, producing them. The magicians clustered around him like flies around honey.

The afternoon games were to consist of such little things as a pack of craven magicians and fortunetellers being killed in a mass by leopards. Consensus favored the leopards; odds were quoted as something like eighty to one against the magicians.

Tiberius waved his hand from the emperor's box in one end of the colossal amphitheater, and the gate which admitted the beasts opened. There was a buzz from the audience as the magnificent animals came streaming through like a river of tawny fur.

The emperor waved again, and the public prepared to be amused by the customary sight of unwilling victims being prodded out into the arena by long-handled tridents. But something must have gone wrong, for the craven magicians came striding boldly out, roaring some song or other. At their head was a curiously shimmering figure who was beating time with two enormous bottles, both empty.

It roared in a titanic voice, as it sighted the animals, "Look out, ye hell-fired pussycats! I'm a-grapplin'!" The magicians charged in a body to the excited screams of the mob.

Roughly there was one cat to every man, and that was the sensible way that the men went about eliminating the cats. The favorite grip seemed to be the tail—a magician would pick up a leopard and swing it around heftily two or three times, then dash its head to the sand of the arena. The rest would be done with the feet.

In a surprisingly short time the magicians were sitting on the carcasses of the cats and resuming their song.

"Let out the lion!" shrilled Tiberius. "They can't do this to me!" The second gate opened, and the king of the jungle himself stalked through, his muscles rippling beneath his golden skin, tossing his huge mane. He sighted the magicians, who weren't paying him any attention at all, and roared savagely.

The shimmering figure looked up in annoyance. "Another one!" it was heard to declare. The song broke off again as the grim, purposeful body of men went for the lion. He eyed them coldly and roared again. They kept on coming. The king of the jungle grew somewhat apprehensive, lashing his tail and crouching as for a spring. The bluff didn't work, he realized a second later, for the men were on him and all over him, gouging his face cruelly and kicking him in the ribs. He tumbled to the sand rather than suffer a broken leg and grunted convulsively as the magicians sat heavily on his flanks and continued their song.

"It was dow-wen in the Raid River Vail-lee—" mournfully chanted the leader—he with the empty bottles.

Tiberius stamped his feet and burst into tears of rage. "My lion!" he wailed. "They're sitting on my lion!"

The leader dropped his bottles and sauntered absently about the arena. One of the deep-driven iron posts of the inside wall caught his eye. He reached out to touch it and—was gone, with a shimmer of purple light.

Sorghum's reappearance was as unchronicled as his disappearance. He didn't tell anybody until they asked him, and then he told them from beginning to end, substantially as I have told it here.

But every once in a while he remarks, "Foreigners are sartinly peculiar people. I know—I've lived among them. But some day I'm going to get me some money and take a boat back there and see that Mr. Gallo to find out if he ever did get the hang of running the mash. Foreigners are sartinly peculiar—behind the times, I call 'em."

That's what Sorghum says.

[*Fantasy and Science Fiction* - July 1957]

MS. Found in a Chinese Fortune Cookie

They say I am mad, but I am not mad—damn it, I've written and sold two million words of fiction and I know better than to start a story like that, but this isn't a story and they *do* say I'm mad—catatonic schizophrenia with assaultive episodes—and I'm *not*. *[This is clearly the first of the Corwin Papers. Like all the others it is written on a Riz-La cigarette paper with a ball point pen. Like all the others it is headed:* Urgent. Finder please send to C. M. Kornbluth, Wantagh, N.Y. Reward! *I might comment that this is typical of Corwin's generosity with his friends' time and money, though his attitude is at least this once justified by his desperate plight. As his longtime friend and, indeed, literary executor, I was clearly the person to turn to. CMK]* I have to convince you, Cyril, that I am both sane and the victim of an enormous conspiracy—and that you are too, and that everybody is. A tall order, but I am going to try to fill it by writing an orderly account of the events leading up to my present situation. *[Here ends the first paper. To keep the record clear I should state that it was forwarded to me by a Mr. L. Wilmot Shaw who found it in a fortune cookie he ordered for dessert at the Great China Republic Restaurant in San Francisco. Mr. Shaw suspected it was "a publicity gag" but sent it to me nonetheless, and received by return mail my thanks and my check for one dollar. I had not realized that Corwin and his wife had disappeared from their home at Painted Post; I was merely aware that it had been weeks since I'd heard from him. We visited infrequently. To be blunt, he was easier to take via mail than face to face. For the balance of this account I shall attempt to avoid tedium by omitting the provenance of each paper, except when noteworthy, and its length. The first is typical—a little over a hundred words. I have, of course, kept on file all correspondence relating to the papers, and am eager to display it to the authorities. It is hoped that publication of this account will nudge them out of the apathy with which they have so far greeted my attempts to engage them. CMK]*

On Sunday, May 13, 1956, at about 12:30 P.M., I learned The Answer. I was stiff and aching because all Saturday my wife and I had been putting in young fruit trees. I like to dig, but I was badly out of condition from an unusually long and idle winter. Creatively, I felt fine. I'd been stale for months, but when spring came the sap began to run in me too. I was bursting with story ideas; scenes and stretches of dialog were jostling one another in my mind; all I had to do was let them flow onto paper.

When The Answer popped into my head I thought at first it was an idea for a story—a very good story. I was going to go downstairs and bounce it off my wife a few times to test it, but I heard the sewing machine buzzing and remembered she had said she was way behind on her mending. Instead, I put my feet up, stared blankly through the window at the pasture-and-wooded-hills View we'd bought the old place for, and fondled the idea.

What about, I thought, using the idea to develop a messy little local situation, the case of Mrs. Clonford? Mrs. C. is a neighbor, animal-happy, land-poor and unintentionally a fearsome oppressor of her husband and children. Mr. C. is a retired brakeman with a pension and his wife insists on him making like a farmer in all weathers and every year he gets pneumonia and is pulled through with antibiotics. All he wants is to sell the damned farm and retire with his wife to a little apartment in town. All *she* wants is to mess around with her cows and horses and sub-marginal acreage.

I got to thinking that if you noised the story around *with* a comment based on The Answer, the situation would automatically untangle. They'd get their apartment, sell the farm and everybody would be happy, including Mrs. C. It would be interesting to write, I thought idly, and then I thought not so idly that it would be interesting to *try*—and then I sat up sharply with a dry mouth and a systemful of adrenalin. *It would work.* The Answer would work.

I ran rapidly down a list of other problems, ranging from the town drunk to the guided-missile race. The Answer worked. Every time.

I was quite sure I had turned paranoid, because I've seen so much of that kind of thing in science fiction. Anybody can name a dozen writers, editors and fans who have suddenly seen the light and determined to lead the human race onward and upward out of the old slough. Of course The Answer looked logical and unassailable, but so no doubt did poor Charlie McGandress' project to unite mankind through science fiction fandom, at least to him. So, no doubt, did *[I have here omitted several briefly sketched case histories of science fiction personalities as yet uncommitted. The reason will be obvious to anyone familiar with the law of libel. Suffice it to say that Corwin argues that science fiction attracts an unstable type of mind and sometimes insidiously undermines its foundations on reality. CMK]*

But I couldn't just throw it away without a test. I considered the wording carefully, picked up the extension phone on my desk and dialed Jim Howlett, the appliance dealer in town. He answered. "Corwin, Jim," I told him. "I have an idea— oops! The samovar's boiling over. Call me back in a minute, will you?" I hung up.

He called me back in a minute; I let our combination—two shorts and a long—ring three times before I picked up the phone. "What was that about a samovar?" he asked, baffled.

"Just kidding," I said. "Listen Jim, why don't you try a short story for a change of pace? Knock off the novel for a while—" He's hopefully writing a big historical about the Sullivan Campaign of 1779, which is our local chunk of the Revolutionary War; I'm helping him a little with advice. Anybody who wants as badly as he does to get out of the appliance business is entitled to some help.

"Gee, I don't know," he said. As he spoke the volume of his voice dropped slightly but definitely, three times. That meant we had an average quota of party line snoopers listening in. "What would I write about?"

"Well, we have this situation with a neighbor, Mrs. Clonford," I began. I went through the problem and made my comment based on The Answer. I heard one of the snoopers gasp. Jim said when I was finished: "I don't really think it's for me, Cecil. Of course it was nice of you to call, but—"

Eventually a customer came into the store and he had to break off.

I went through an anxious crabby twenty-four hours.

On Monday afternoon the paper woman drove past our place and shot the rolled-up copy of the Pott Hill *Evening Times* into the orange-painted tube beside our mailbox. I raced for it, yanked it open to the seventh page and read:

FARM SALE
Owing to Ill Health and Age Mr. & Mrs.
Ronald Clonford Will sell their Entire Farm, All
Machinery and Furnishings and All Live Stock
at Auction Saturday May 19 12:30 P.M. Rain or
Shine, Terms Cash Day of Sale, George Pfennig,
Auctioneer.

[This is one of the few things in the Corwin Papers which can be independently verified. I looked up the paper and found that the ad was run about as quoted. Further, I interviewed Mrs. Clonford in her town apartment. She told me she "just got tired of farmin', I guess. Kind of hated to give up my ponies, but people was beginning to say it was too hard of a life for Ronnie and I guess they was right." CMK]

Coincidence? Perhaps. I went upstairs with the paper and put my feet up again. I could try a hundred more piddling tests if I wished, but why waste time? If there was anything to it, I could type out The Answer in about two hundred words, drive to town, tack it on the bulletin board outside the firehouse and— snowball. Avalanche!

I didn't do it, of course—for the same reason I haven't put down the two hundred words of The Answer yet on a couple of these cigarette papers. It's rather dreadful—isn't it—that I haven't done so, that a simple feasible plan to ensure peace, progress and equality of opportunity among all mankind, may be lost to the world if, say, a big meteorite hits the asylum in the next couple of minutes. But—I'm a writer. There's a touch of intellectual sadism in us. We like to dominate the reader as a matador dominates the bull; we like to tease and mystify and at last show what great souls we are by generously flipping up the shade and letting the sunshine in. Don't worry. Read on. You will come to The Answer in the proper artistic place for it. *[At this point I wish fervently to dissociate myself from the attitudes Corwin attributes to our profession. He had—has, I hope—his eccentricities, and I consider it inexcusable of him to tar us all with his personal brush. I could point out, for example, that he once laboriously cultivated a 16th Century handwriting which was utterly illegible to the modern reader. The only reason apparent for this, as for so many of his traits, seemed to be a wish to annoy as many people as possible. CMK]*

Yes; I am a writer. A matador does not show up in the bull ring with a tommy gun and a writer doesn't do things the simple, direct way. He makes the people writhe a little at first. So I called Fred Greenwald. Fred had been after me for a while to speak at one of the Thursday Rotary meetings and I'd been reluctant to set a date. I have a little speech for such occasions, "The Business of Being a Writer"—all about the archaic royalty system of payment, the difficulty of proving business expenses, the Margaret Mitchell tax law and how it badly needs improvement, what copyright is and isn't, how about all these generals and politicians with their capital-gains memoirs. I pass a few galley sheets down the table and generally get a good laugh by holding up a Doubleday book contract, silently turning it over so they can see how the fine print goes on and on, and then flipping it open so they see there's twice as much fine print as they thought there was. I had done my stuff for Oswego Rotary, Horseheads Rotary and Cannon Hole Rotary; now Fred wanted me to do it for Painted Post Rotary.

So I phoned him and said I'd be willing to speak this coming Thursday. Good, he said. On a discovery I'd made about the philosophy and technique of administration and interpersonal relationships, I said. He sort of choked up and said well, we're broadminded here.

I've got to start cutting this. I have several packs of cigarette papers left but not enough to cover the high spots if I'm to do them justice. Let's just say the announcement of my speech was run in the Tuesday paper *[It was. CMK]* and skip to Wednesday, my place, about 7:30 P.M. Dinner was just over and my wife and I were going to walk out and see how *[At this point I wish to insert a special note concerning some difficulty I had in obtaining the next four papers. They got somehow into the hands of a certain literary agent who is famous for a sort of "finders-keepers" attitude more appropriate to the eighth grade than to the law of literary property. In disregard of the fact that Corwin retained physical ownership of the papers and literary rights thereto, and that I as the addressee possessed all other rights, he was blandly endeavoring to sell them to various magazines as "curious fragments from Corwin's desk." Like most people, I abhor lawsuits; that's the fact this agent lives on. I met his outrageous price of five cents a word "plus postage"(!). I should add that I have not heard of any attempt by this gentleman to locate Corwin or his heirs in order to turn over the proceeds of the sale, less commission. CMK]* the new fruit trees were doing when a car came bumping down our road and stopped at our garden fence gate.

"See what they want and shove them on their way," said my wife. "We haven't got much daylight left." She peered through the kitchen window at the car, blinked, rubbed her eyes and peered again. She said uncertainly: "It looks like—no! Can't be." I went out to the car.

"Anything I can do for you?" I asked the two men in the front seat. Then I recognized them. One of them was about my age, a wiry lad in a T-shirt. The other man was plump and greying and ministerial, but jolly. They were unmistakable; they had looked out at me—one scowling, the other smiling—from a hundred book ads. It was almost incredible that they knew each other, but there they were sharing a car.

I greeted them by name and said: "This is odd. I happen to be a writer myself. I've never shared the best-seller list with you two, but—"

The plump ministerial man tut-tutted. "You are thinking negatively," he chided me. "Think of what you *have* accomplished. You own this lovely home, the valuation of which has just been raised two thousand dollars due entirely to the hard work and frugality of you and your lovely wife; you give innocent pleasure to thousands with your clever novels; you help to keep the good local merchants going with your patronage. Not least, you have fought for your country in the wars and you support it with your taxes."

The man in the T-shirt said raspily: "Even if you have the dough to settle in full on April 15 and will have to pay six percent per month interest on the unpaid balance when and if you ever do pay it, you poor shnook."

The plump man said, distressed: "Please, Michael—you are not thinking positively. This is neither the time nor the place—"

"What's going on?" I demanded. Because I hadn't even told my *wife* I'd been a little short on the '55 federal tax.

"Let's go inna house," said the T-shirted man. He got out of the car, brushed my gate open and walked coolly down the path to the kitchen door. The plump man followed, sniffing our rose-scented garden air appreciatively, and I came last of all, on wobbly legs.

When we filed in, my wife said: "My God. It *is* them."

The man in the T-shirt said: "Hiya, babe," and stared at her breasts. The plump man said: "May I compliment you, my dear, for a splendid rose garden. Quite unusual for this altitude."

"Thanks," she said faintly, beginning to rally. "But it's quite easy when your neighbors keep horses."

"Haw!" snorted the man in the T-shirt. "That's the stuff, babe. You grow roses like I write books. Give 'em plenty of—"

"Michael!" said the plump man.

"*Look,* you," my wife said to me. "Would you mind telling me what this is all about? I never knew you knew Dr.—"

"I don't," I said helplessly. "They seem to want to talk to me."

"Let us adjourn to your *sanctum sanctorum,*" said the plump man archly, and we went upstairs. The T-shirted man sat on the couch, the plump fellow sat in the club chair and I collapsed on the swivel chair in front of the typewriter. "Drink, anybody?" I asked, wanting one myself. "Sherry, brandy, rye, straight angostura?"

"Never touch the stinking stuff," grunted the man in the T-shirt.

"I would enjoy a nip of brandy," said the big man. We each had one straight, no chasers, and he got down to business with: "I suppose you have discovered The Diagonal Relationship?"

I thought about The Answer, and decided that The Diagonal Relationship would be a very good name for it too. "Yes," I said. "I guess I have. Have you?"

"I have. So has Michael here. So have one thousand, seven hundred and twenty-four writers. If you'd like to know who they are, pick the one thousand, seven hundred and twenty-four top-income men of the ten thousand free-lance writers in this country and you have your men. The Diagonal Relationship is discovered on an average of three times a year by rising writers."

"Writers," I said. "Good God, why *writers?* Why not economists, psychologists, mathematicians—*real* thinkers?"

He said: "A writer's mind is an awesome thing, Corwin. What went into your discovery of The Diagonal Relationship?"

I thought a bit. "I'm doing a Civil War thing about Burnside's Bomb," I said, "and I realized that Grant could have sent in fresh troops but didn't because Halleck used to drive him crazy by telegraphic master-minding of his campaigns. That's a special case of The Answer—as I call it. Then I got some data on medieval attitudes toward personal astrology out of a book on ancient China I'm reading. Another special case. And there's a joke the monks used to write at the end of a long manuscript-copying job. Liddell Hart's theory of strategy is about half of the general military case of The Answer. The merchandizing special case shows clearly in a catalog I have from a Chicago store that specializes in selling strange clothes to bop-crazed Negroes. They all add up to the general expression, and that's that."

He was nodding. "Many, many combinations add up to The Diagonal Relationship," he said. "But only a writer cuts across sufficient fields, exposes himself to sufficient apparently unrelated facts. Only a writer has wide-open associational channels capable of bridging the gap between astrology and, ah, 'bop.' We write in our different idioms"—he smiled at the T-shirted man—"but we are writers all. Wide-ranging, omnivorous for data, equipped with superior powers of association which we constantly exercise."

"Well," I asked logically enough, "why on earth haven't you published The Diagonal Relationship? Are you here to keep me from publishing it?"

"We're a power group," said the plump man apologetically. "We have a vested interest in things as they are. Think about what The Diagonal Relationship would do to writers, Corwin."

"Sure," I said, and thought about it. "Judas Priest!" I said after a couple of minutes. He was nodding again. He said: "Yes. The Diagonal Relationship, if generally promulgated, would work out to approximate equality of income for all, with incentive pay only for really hard and dangerous work. Writing would be regarded as pretty much its own reward."

"That's the way it looks," I said. "One-year copyright, after all ..."

[Here occurs the first hiatus in the Corwin Papers. I suspect that three or four are missing. The preceding and following papers, incidentally, come from a batch of six gross of fortune cookies which I purchased from the Hip Sing Restaurant Provision Company of New York City during the course of my investigations. The reader no doubt will wonder why I was unable to determine the source of the cookies themselves and

was forced to buy them from middlemen. Apparently the reason is the fantastic one that by chance I was wearing a white shirt, dark tie and double-breasted blue serge suit when I attempted to question the proprietor of the Hip Sing Company. I learned too late that this is just about the unofficial uniform of U.S. Treasury and Justice Department agents and that I was immediately taken to be such an agent. "You T-man," said Mr. Hip tolerantly, "you get cou't oh-dah, I show you books. Keep ve'y nice books, all in Chinese cha'ctahs." After that gambit he would answer me only in Chinese. How he did it I have no idea, but apparently within days every Chinese produce dealer in the United States and Canada had been notified that there was a new T-man named Kornbluth on the prowl. As a last resort I called on the New York City office of the Treasury Department Field Investigations Unit in an attempt to obtain what might be called un-identification papers. There I was assured by Mr. Gershon O'Brien, their Chinese specialist, that my errand was hopeless since the motto of Mr. Hip and his colleagues invariably was "Safety First." To make matters worse, as I left his office I was greeted with a polite smile from a Chinese lad whom I recognized as Mr. Hip's bookkeeper. CMK]

"So you see," he went on as if he had just stated a major and a minor premise, "we watch the writers, the real ones, through private detective agencies which alert us when the first teaser appears in a newspaper or on a broadcast or in local gossip. There's always the teaser, Corwin, the rattle before the strike. We writers are like that. We've been watching you for three years now, and to be perfectly frank I've lost a few dollars wagered on you. In my opinion you're a year late."

"What's the proposition?" I asked numbly.

He shrugged. "You get to be a best-seller. We review your books, you review ours. We tell your publisher: 'Corwin's hot—promote him. Advertise him.' And he does, because we're good properties and he doesn't want to annoy us. You want Hollywood? It can be arranged. Lots of us out there. In short, you become rich like us and all you have to do is keep quiet about The Diagonal Relationship. You haven't told your wife, by the way?"

"I wanted to surprise her," I said.

He smiled. "They always do. Writers! Well, young man, what do you say?"

It had grown dark. From the couch came a raspy voice: "You heard what the doc said about the ones that throw in with us. I'm here to tell you that we got provisions for the ones that don't."

I laughed at him.

"One of those guys," he said flatly.

"Surely a borderline case, Michael?" said the plump man. "So many of them are."

If I'd been thinking straight I would have realized that "borderline case" did not mean "undecided" to them; it meant "danger—immediate action!"

They took it. The plump man, who was also a fairly big man, flung his arms around me and the wiry one approached in the gloom. I yelled something when I felt a hypodermic stab my arm. Then I went numb and stupid.

My wife came running up the stairs. "What's going on?" she demanded. I saw her heading for the curtain behind which we keep an aged hair-trigger Marlin

.38 rifle. There was nothing wrong with her guts, but they attacked her where courage doesn't count. I croaked her name a couple of times and heard the plump man say gently, with great concern: "I'm afraid your husband needs ... help." She turned from the curtain, her eyes wide. He had struck subtly and knowingly; there is probably not one writer's wife who does not suspect her husband is a potential psychotic.

"Dear—" she said to me as I stood there paralyzed.

He went on: "Michael and I dropped in because we both admire your husband's work; we were surprised and distressed to find his conversation so ... disconnected. My dear, as you must know I have some experience through my pastorate with psychotherapy. Have you ever—forgive my bluntness—had doubts about his sanity?"

"Dear, what's the matter?" she asked me anxiously. I just stood there, staring. God knows what they injected me with, but its effect was to cloud my mind, render all activity impossible, send my thoughts spinning after their tails. I was insane. *[This incident, seemingly the least plausible part of Corwin's story, actually stands up better than most of the narrative to one familiar with recent advances in biochemistry. Corwin could have been injected with lysergic acid, or with protein extracts from the blood of psychotics. It is a matter of cold laboratory fact that such injections produce temporary psychosis in the patient. Indeed, it is on such experimental psychoses that the new tranquilizer drugs are developed and tested. CMK]*

To herself she said aloud, dully: "Well, it's finally come. Christmas when I burned the turkey and he wouldn't speak to me for a week. The way he drummed his fingers when I talked. All his little crackpot ways—how he has to stay at the Waldorf but I have to cut his hair and save a dollar. I hoped it was just the rotten weather and cabin fever. I hoped when spring came—" She began to sob. The plump man comforted her like a father. I just stood there staring and waiting. And eventually Mickey glided up in the dark and gave her a needleful too and

[Here occurs an aggravating and important hiatus. One can only guess that Corwin and his wife were loaded into the car, driven—somewhere, separated, and separately, under false names, committed to different mental institutions. I have recently learned to my dismay that there are states which require only the barest sort of licensing to operate such institutions. One State Inspector of Hospitals even wrote to me in these words: "... no doubt there are some places in our State which are not even licensed, but we have never made any effort to close them and I cannot recall any statute making such operation illegal. We are not a wealthy state like you up North and some care for these unfortunates is better than none, is our viewpoint here. ..." CMK]

three months. Their injections last a week. There's always somebody to give me another. You know what mental hospital attendants are like: an easy bribe. But they'd be better advised to bribe a higher type, like a male nurse, because my attendant with the special needle for me is off on a drunk. My insanity wore off this morning and I've been writing in my room ever since. A quick trip up and down the corridor collected the cigarette papers and a tiny ball point pen from some breakfast-food premium gadget. I think my best bet is to slip these papers out in the batch of Chinese fortune cookies they're doing in the bakery. Occupational therapy, this is called. My own o.t. is shoveling coal when I'm under the needle. Well, enough of this. I shall write down The Answer, slip down to the bakery, deal out the cigarette papers into the waiting rounds of cookie dough, crimp them over and return to my room. Doubtless my attendant will be back by then and I'll get another shot from him. I shall not struggle; I can only wait.

THE ANSWER: HUMAN BEINGS RAISED TO SPEAK AN INDO-IRANIAN LANGUAGE SUCH AS ENGLISH HAVE THE FOLLOWING IN

[That is the end of the last of the Corwin Papers I have been able to locate. It should be superfluous to urge all readers to examine carefully any fortune cookie slips they may encounter. The next one you break open may contain what my poor friend believed, or believes, to be a great message to mankind. He may be right. His tale is a wild one but it is consistent. And it embodies the only reasonable explanation I have ever seen for the presence of certain books on the best-seller list. CMK]

[*Startling Stories* - July 1949]

The Only Thing We Learn

The professor, though he did not know the actor's phrase for it, was counting the house—peering through a spyhole in the door through which he would in a moment appear before the class. He was pleased with what he saw. Tier after tier of young people, ready with notebooks and styli, chattering tentatively, glancing at the door against which his nose was flattened, waiting for the pleasant interlude known as "Archaeo-Literature 203" to begin.

The professor stepped back, smoothed his tunic, crooked four books on his left elbow, and made his entrance. Four swift strides brought him to the lectern and, for the thousandth-odd time, he impassively swept the lecture hall with his gaze. Then he gave a wry little smile. Inside, for the thousandth-odd time, he was nagged by the irritable little thought that the lectern really ought to be a foot or so higher.

The irritation did not show. He was out to win the audience, and he did. A dead silence, the supreme tribute, gratified him. Imperceptibly, the lights of the lecture hall began to dim and the light on the lectern to brighten.

He spoke.

"Young gentlemen of the Empire, I ought to warn you that this and the succeeding lectures will be most subversive."

There was a little rustle of incomprehension from the audience—but by then the lectern light was strong enough to show the twinkling smile about his eyes that belied his stern mouth, and agreeable chuckles sounded in the gathering darkness of the tiered seats. Glow lights grew bright gradually at the students' tables, and they adjusted their notebooks in the narrow ribbons of illumination. He waited for the small commotion to subside.

"Subversive—" He gave them a link to cling to. "Subversive because I shall make every effort to tell both sides of our ancient beginnings with every resource of archaeology and with every clue my diligence has discovered in our epic literature.

"There *were* two sides, you know—difficult though it may be to believe that if we judge by the Old Epic alone—such epics as the noble and tempestuous *Chant of Remd*, the remaining fragments of *Krall's Voyage*, or the gory and rather out-of-date *Battle for the Ten Suns.*" He paused while styli scribbled across the notebook pages.

"The Middle Epic is marked, however, by what I might call the rediscovered ethos." From his voice, every student knew that that phrase, surer than death and taxes, would appear on an examination paper. The styli scribbled. "By this I mean an awakening of fellow-feeling with the Home Suns People, which had once been filial loyalty to them when our ancestors were few and pioneers, but which turned into contempt when their numbers grew.

"The Middle Epic writers did not despise the Home Suns People, as did the bards of the Old Epic. Perhaps this was because they did not have to—since their long war against the Home Suns was drawing to a victorious close.

"Of the New Epic I shall have little to say. It was a literary fad, a pose, and a silly one. Written within historic times, the some two score pseudo-epics now molder in their cylinders, where they belong. Our ripening civilization could not with integrity work in the epic form, and the artistic failures produced so indicate. Our genius turned to the lyric and to the unabashedly romantic novel.

"So much, for the moment, of literature. What contribution, you must wonder, have archaeological studies to make in an investigation of the wars from which our ancestry emerged?

"Archaeology offers—one—a check in historical matters in the epics—confirming or denying. Two—it provides evidence glossed over in the epics—for artistic or patriotic reasons. Three—it provides evidence which has been lost, owing to the fragmentary nature of some of the early epics."

All this he fired at them crisply, enjoying himself. Let them not think him a dreamy litterateur, or, worse, a flat precisionist, but let them be always a little off-balance before him, never knowing what came next, and often wondering, in class and out. The styli paused after heading Three.

"We shall examine first, by our archaeo-literary technique, the second book of the *Chant of Remd.* As the selected youth of the Empire, you know much about it, of course—much that is false, some that is true, and a great deal that is irrelevant. You know that Book One hurls us into the middle of things, aboard ship with Algan and his great captain, Remd, on their way from the triumph over a Home Suns stronghold, the planet Telse. We watch Remd on his diversionary action that splits the Ten Suns Fleet into two halves. But before we see the destruction of those halves by the Horde of Algan, we are told in Book Two of the battle for Telse."

He opened one of his books on the lectern, swept the amphitheater again, and read sonorously.

> *Then battle broke*
> *And high the blinding blast*
> *Sight-searing leaped*
> *While folk in fear below*
> *Cowered in caverns*
> *From the wrath of Remd—*

"Or, in less sumptuous language, one fission bomb—or a stick of time-on-target bombs—was dropped. An unprepared and disorganized populace did not take the standard measure of dispersing, but huddled foolishly to await Algan's gunfighters and the death they brought.

"One of the things you believe because you have seen them in notes to elementary-school editions of *Remd* is that Telse was the fourth planet of the star Sol. Archaeology denies it by establishing that the fourth planet—actually called Marse, by the way—was in those days weather-roofed at least, and possibly atmosphere-roofed as well. As potential warriors, you know that one does not waste fissionable material on a roof, and there is no mention of chemical explosives being used to crack the roof. Marse, therefore, was not the locale of *Remd*, Book Two.

"Which planet was? The answer to that has been established by X-radar, differential decay analyses, video-coring, and every other resource of those scientists still quaintly called 'diggers.' We know and can prove that Telse was the *third* planet of Sol. So much for the opening of the attack. Let us jump to Canto Three, the Storming of the Dynastic Palace.

> *"Imperial purple wore they*
> *Fresh from the feast*
> *Grossly gorged*
> *They sought to slay—*

"And so on. Now, as I warned you, Remd is of the Old Epic, and makes no pretense at fairness. The unorganized huddling of Telse's population was read as cowardice instead of poor A.R.P. The same is true of the Third Canto. Video-cores show on the site of the palace a hecatomb of dead in once-purple livery, but also shows impartially that they were not particularly gorged and that digestion of their last meals had been well advanced. They didn't give such a bad accounting of themselves, either. I hesitate to guess, but perhaps they accounted for one of our ancestors apiece and were simply outnumbered. The study is not complete.

"That much we know." The professor saw they were tiring of the terse scientist and shifted gears. "If but the veil of time were rent that shrouds the years between us and the Home Suns People, how much more would we learn? Would we despise the Home Suns People as our frontiersman ancestors did, or would we cry: '*This* is our spiritual home—this world of rank and order, this world of formal verse and exquisitely patterned arts'?"

If the veil of time were rent—?

We can try to rend it ...

Wing Commander Arris heard the clear jangle of the radar net alarm as he was dreaming about a fish. Struggling out of his too-deep, too-soft bed, he stepped into a purple singlet, buckled on his Sam Browne belt with its holstered .45 automatic, and tried to read the radar screen. Whatever had set it off was either too small or too distant to register on the five-inch C.R.T.

He rang for his aide, and checked his appearance in a wall mirror while waiting. His space tan was beginning to fade, he saw, and made a mental note to get it renewed at the parlor. He stepped into the corridor as Evan, his aide, trotted up—younger, browner, thinner, but the same officer type that made the Service what it was, Arris thought with satisfaction.

Evan gave him a bone-cracking salute, which he returned. They set off for the elevator that whisked them down to a large, chilly, dark underground room where faces were greenly lit by radar screens and the lights of plotting tables. Somebody yelled "Attention!" and the tecks snapped. He gave them "At ease" and took the brisk salute of the senior teck, who reported to him in flat, machine-gun delivery:

"Object-becoming-visible-on-primary-screen-sir."

He studied the sixty-inch disk for several seconds before he spotted the intercepted particle. It was coming in fast from zenith, growing while he watched.

"Assuming it's now traveling at maximum, how long will it be before it's within striking range?" he asked the teck.

"Seven hours, sir."

"The interceptors at Idlewild alerted?"

"Yessir."

Arris turned on a phone that connected with Interception. The boy at Interception knew the face that appeared on its screen, and was already capped with a crash helmet.

"Go ahead and take him, Efrid," said the wing commander.

"Yessir!" and a punctilious salute, the boy's pleasure plain at being known by name and a great deal more at being on the way to a fight that might be first-class.

Arris cut him off before the boy could detect a smile that was forming on his face. He turned from the pale lunar glow of the sixty-incher to enjoy it. Those kids—when every meteor was an invading dreadnaught, when every ragged scouting ship from the rebels was an armada!

He watched Efrid's squadron soar off on the screen and then he retreated to a darker corner. This was his post until the meteor or scout or whatever it was got taken care of. Evan joined him, and they silently studied the smooth, disciplined functioning of the plot room, Arris with satisfaction and Evan doubtless with the same. The aide broke silence, asking:

"Do you suppose it's a Frontier ship, sir?" He caught the wing commander's look and hastily corrected himself: "I mean rebel ship, sir, of course."

"Then you should have said so. Is that what the junior officers generally call those scoundrels?"

Evan conscientiously cast his mind back over the last few junior messes and reported unhappily: "I'm afraid we do, sir. We seem to have got into the habit."

"I shall write a memorandum about it. How do you account for that very peculiar habit?"

"Well, sir, they do have something like a fleet, and they did take over the Regulus Cluster, didn't they?"

What had got into this incredible fellow, Arris wondered in amazement. Why, the thing was self-evident! They had a few ships—accounts differed as to how many—and they had, doubtless by raw sedition, taken over some systems temporarily.

He turned from his aide, who sensibly became interested in a screen and left with a murmured excuse to study it very closely.

The brigands had certainly knocked together some ramshackle league or other, but— The wing commander wondered briefly if it could last, shut the horrid thought from his head, and set himself to composing mentally a stiff memorandum that would be posted in the junior officers' mess and put an end to this absurd talk.

His eyes wandered to the sixty-incher, where he saw the interceptor squadron climbing nicely toward the particle—which, he noticed, had become three particles. A low crooning distracted him. Was one of the tecks singing at work? It couldn't be!

It wasn't. An unsteady shape wandered up in the darkness, murmuring a song and exhaling alcohol. He recognized the Chief Archivist, Glen.

"This is Service country, mister," he told Glen.

"Hullo, Arris," the round little civilian said, peering at him. "I come down here regularly—regularly against regulations—to wear off my regular irregularities with the wine bottle. That's all right, isn't it?"

He was drunk and argumentative. Arris felt hemmed in. Glen couldn't be talked into leaving without loss of dignity to the wing commander, and he couldn't be chucked out because he was writing a biography of the chamberlain and could, for the time being, have any head in the palace for the asking. Arris sat down unhappily, and Glen plumped down beside him.

The little man asked him.

"Is that a fleet from the Frontier League?" He pointed to the big screen. Arris didn't look at his face, but felt that Glen was grinning maliciously.

"I know of no organization called the Frontier League," Arris said. "If you are referring to the brigands who have recently been operating in Galactic East, you could at least call them by their proper names." Really, he thought—civilians!

"So sorry. But the brigands should have the Regulus Cluster by now, shouldn't they?" he asked, insinuatingly.

This was serious—a grave breach of security. Arris turned to the little man.

"Mister, I have no authority to command you," he said measuredly. "Furthermore, I understand you are enjoying a temporary eminence in the non-Service world which would make it very difficult for me to—ah—tangle with you. I shall therefore refer only to your altruism. How did you find out about the Regulus Cluster?"

"Eloquent!" murmured the little man, smiling happily. "I got it from Rome."

Arris searched his memory. "You mean Squadron Commander Romo broke security? I can't believe it!"

"No, commander. I mean Rome—a place—a time—a civilization. I got it also from Babylon, Assyria, the Mogul Raj—every one of them. You don't understand me, of course."

"I understand that you're trifling with Service security and that you're a fat little, malevolent, worthless drone and scribbler!"

"Oh, commander!" protested the archivist. "I'm not so little!" He wandered away, chuckling.

Arris wished he had the shooting of him, and tried to explore the chain of secrecy for a weak link. He was tired and bored by this harping on the Fron—on the brigands.

His aide tentatively approached him. "Interceptors in striking range, sir," he murmured.

"Thank you," said the wing commander, genuinely grateful to be back in the clean, etched-line world of the Service and out of that blurred, water-color, civilian land where long-dead Syrians apparently retailed classified matter to nasty little drunken warts who had no business with it. Arris confronted the sixty-incher. The particle that had become three particles was now—he counted—eighteen particles. Big ones. Getting bigger.

He did not allow himself emotion, but turned to the plot on the interceptor squadron.

"Set up Lunar relay," he ordered.

"Yessir."

Half the plot room crew bustled silently and efficiently about the delicate job of applied relativistic physics that was "lunar relay." He knew that the palace power plant could take it for a few minutes, and he wanted to *see*. If he could not believe radar pips, he might believe a video screen.

On the great, green circle, the eighteen—now twenty-four—particles neared the thirty-six smaller particles that were interceptors, led by the eager young Efrid.

"Testing Lunar relay, sir," said the chief teck.

The wing commander turned to a twelve-inch screen. Unobtrusively, behind him, tecks jockeyed for position. The picture on the screen was something to see. The chief let mercury fill a thick-walled, ceramic tank. There was a sputtering and contact was made.

"Well done," said Arris. "Perfect seeing."

He saw, upper left, a globe of ships—what ships! Some were Service jobs, with extra turrets plastered on them wherever there was room. Some were orthodox freighters, with the same porcupine-bristle of weapons. Some were obviously home-made crates, hideously ugly—and as heavily armed as the others.

Next to him, Arris heard his aide murmur, "It's all wrong, sir. They haven't got any pick-up boats. They haven't got any hospital ships. What happens when one of them gets shot up?"

"Just what ought to happen, Evan," snapped the wing commander. "They float in space until they desiccate in their suits. Or if they get grappled inboard with a boat hook, they don't get any medical care. As I told you, they're brigands, without decency even to care for their own." He enlarged on the theme. "Their morale must be insignificant compared with our men's. When the Service goes into action, every rating and teck knows he'll be cared for if he's hurt. Why, if we didn't have pick-up boats and hospital ships, the men wouldn't—" He almost finished it with "fight," but thought, and lamely ended, "—wouldn't like it."

Evan nodded, wonderingly, and crowded his chief a little as he craned his neck for a look at the screen.

"Get the hell away from here!" said the wing commander in a restrained yell, and Evan got.

The interceptor squadron swam into the field—a sleek, deadly needle of vessels in perfect alignment, with its little cloud of pick-ups trailing, and farther astern a white hospital ship with the ancient red cross.

The contact was immediate and shocking. One of the rebel ships lumbered into the path of the interceptors, spraying fire from what seemed to be as many points as a man has pores. The Service ships promptly riddled it and it should have drifted away—but it didn't. It kept on fighting. It rammed an interceptor with a crunch that must have killed every man before the first bulwark, but aft of the bulwark the ship kept fighting.

It took a torpedo portside and its plumbing drifted through space in a tangle. Still the starboard side kept squirting fire. Isolated weapon blisters fought on while they were obviously cut off from the rest of the ship. It was a pounded tangle of wreckage, and it had destroyed two interceptors, crippled two more, and kept fighting.

Finally, it drifted away, under feeble jets of power. Two more of the fantastic rebel fleet wandered into action, but the wing commander's horrified eyes were on the first pile of scrap. It was going *somewhere*—

The ship neared the thin-skinned, unarmored, gleaming hospital vessel, rammed it, amidships, square in one of the red crosses, and then blew itself up, apparently with everything left in its powder magazine, taking the hospital ship with it.

The sickened wing commander would never have recognized what he had seen as it was told in a later version, thus:

> *"The crushing course they took*
> *And nobly knew*
> *Their death undaunted*
> *By heroic blast*
> *The hospital's host*
> *They dragged to doom*
> *Hail! Men without mercy*
> *From the far frontier!"*

Lunar relay flickered out as overloaded fuses flashed into vapor. Arris distractedly paced back to the dark corner and sank into a chair.

"I'm sorry," said the voice of Glen next to him, sounding quite sincere. "No doubt it was quite a shock to you."

"Not to you?" asked Arris bitterly.

"Not to me."

"Then how did they do it?" the wing commander asked the civilian in a low, desperate whisper. "They don't even wear .45's. Intelligence says their enlisted men have hit their officers and got away with it. They *elect* ship captains! Glen, what does it all mean?"

"It means," said the fat little man with a timbre of doom in his voice, "that they've returned. They always have. They always will. You see, commander, there is always somewhere a wealthy, powerful city, or nation, or world. In it are those whose blood is not right for a wealthy, powerful place. They must seek danger and overcome it. So they go out—on the marshes, in the desert, on the tundra, the planets or the stars. Being strong, they grow stronger by fighting the tundra, the planets or the stars. They—they change. They sing new songs. They know new heroes. And then, one day, they return to their old home.

"They return to the wealthy, powerful city, or nation or world. They fight its guardians as they fought the tundra, the planets or the stars—a way that strikes terror to the heart. Then they sack the city, nation or world and sing great, ringing sagas of their deeds. They always have. Doubtless they always will."

"But what shall we do?"

"We shall cower, I suppose, beneath the bombs they drop on us, and we shall die, some bravely, some not, defending the palace within a very few hours. But you will have your revenge."

"How?" asked the wing commander, with haunted eyes.

The fat little man giggled and whispered in the officer's ear. Arris irritably shrugged it off as a bad joke. He didn't believe it. As he died, drilled through the chest a few hours later by one of Algan's gunfighters, he believed it even less.

The professor's lecture was drawing to a close. There was time for only one more joke to send his students away happy. He was about to spring it when a messenger handed him two slips of paper. He raged inwardly at his ruined exit and poisonously read from them:

"I have been asked to make two announcements. One, a bulletin from General Sleg's force. He reports that the so-called Outland Insurrection is being brought under control and that there is no cause for alarm. Two, the gentlemen who are members of the S.O.T.C. will please report to the armory at 1375 hours—whatever that may mean—for blaster inspection. The class is dismissed."

Petulantly, he swept from the lectern and through the door.

[*Infinity* - October 1957]

The Last Man Left in the Bar

You know him, Joe—or Sam, Mike, Tony, Ben, whatever your deceitful, cheaply genial name may be. And do not lie to yourself, Gentle Reader; you know him too.

A loner, he was.

You did not notice him when he slipped in; you only knew by his aggrieved air when he (finally) caught your eye and self-consciously said "Shot of Red Top and a beer" that he'd ruffle your working day. (Six at night until two in the morning is a day? But ah, the horrible alternative is to work for a living.)

Shot of Red Top and a beer at 8:35.

And unbeknownst to him, Gentle Reader, in the garage up the street the two contrivers of his dilemma conspired; the breaths of tall dark stooped cadaverous Galardo and the mouse-eyed lassie mingled.

"Hyü shall be a religion-isst," he instructed her.

"I know the role," she squeaked and quoted: "'Woe to the day on which I was born into the world! Woe to the womb which bare me! Woe to the bowels which admitted me! Woe to the breasts which suckled me! Woe to the feet upon which I sat and rested! Woe to the hands which carried me and reared me until I grew! Woe to my tongue and my lips which have brought forth and spoken vanity, detraction, falsehood, ignorance, derision, idle tales, craft and hypocrisy! Woe to mine eyes which have looked upon scandalous things! Woe to mine ears which have delighted in the words of slanderers! Woe to my hands which have seized what did not of right belong to them! Woe to my belly and my bowels which have lusted after food unlawful to be eaten! Woe to my throat which like a fire has consumed all that it found!'"

He sobbed with the beauty of it and nodded at last, tears hanging in his eyes: "Yess, that religion. It iss one of my fave-o-ritts."

She was carried away. "I can do others. Oh, I can do others. I can do Mithras, and Isis, and Marduk, and Eddyism and Billsword and Pealing and Uranium, both orthodox and reformed."

"Mithras, Isis and Marduk are long gone and the resst are ss-till tü come. Listen tü your master, dü not chat-ter, and we shall an artwork make of which there will be talk under the green sky until all food is eaten."

Meanwhile, Gentle Reader, the loner listened. To his left strong silent sinewy men in fellowship, the builders, the doers, the darers: "So I told the foreman where he should put his Bullard. I told him I run a Warner and Swasey, I run a Warner and Swasey good, I never even *seen* a Bullard up close in my life, and where he should put it. I know how to run a Warner and Swasey and why should he take me off a Warner and Swasey I know how to run and put me on a Bullard and where he should put it ain't I right?"

"Absolutely."

To his right the clear-eyed virtuous matrons, the steadfast, the true-seeing, the loving-kind: "Oh, I don't know what I want, what do you want? I'm a Scotch drinker really but I don't feel like Scotch but if I come home with muscatel on my breath Eddie calls me a wino and laughs his head off. I don't know what I want. What do you want?"

In the box above the bar the rollicking raster raced.

VIDEO	AUDIO
Gampa smashes bottle over the head of *Bibby*.	*Gampa:* Young whippersnapper!
Bibby spits out water.	*Bibby:* Next time put some flavoring in it, Gramps!
Gampa picks up sugar bowl and smashes it over *Bibby's* head. *Bibby* licks sugar from face.	*Bibby:* My, that's better! But what of Naughty Roger and his attempted kidnapping of Sis to extort the secret of the Q-Bomb?
cut to *Limbo Shot* of Reel-Rye bottle.	*Announcer:* Yes, kiddies! What of Roger? But first a word from the makers of Reel-Rye, that happy syrup that gives your milk grown up flavor! YES! Grown up flavor!

Shot of Red Top and a beer. At 8:50.

In his own un-secret heart: Steady, boy. You've got to think this out. Nothing impossible about it, no reason to settle for a stalemate; just a little time to think it out. Galardo said the Black Chapter would accept a token submission, let me return the Seal, and that would be that. But I mustn't count on that as a datum; he lied to me about the Serpentists. Token submission *sounds* right; they go in big for symbolism. Maybe because they're so stone-broke, like the Japs. Drinking a cup of tea, they gussie it all up until it's a religion; that's the way you squeeze nourishment out of poverty—

Skip the Japs. Think. He lied to me about the Serpentists. The big thing to remember is, I have the Chapter Seal and they need it back, or think they do. All you need's a little time to think things through, place where he won't dare jump you and grab the Seal. And this is it.

"Joe. Sam, Mike, Tony, Ben, whoever you are. Hit me again."

Joe—Sam, Mike, Tony, Ben?—tilts the amber bottle quietly; the liquid's level rises and crowns the little glass with a convex meniscus. He turns off the stream with an easy roll of the wrist. The suntan line of neon tubing at the bar back twinkles off the curve of surface tension, the placid whiskey, the frothy beer. At 9:05.

To his left: "So Finkelstein finally meets Goldberg in the garment center and he grabs him like this by the lapel, and he yells, 'You louse, you rat, you no-good, what's this about you running around with my wife? I ought to—I ought to—say, you call *this* a *button*hole?'"

Restrained and apprehensive laughter; Catholic, Protestant, Jew (choice of one), what's the difference I always say.

Did they have a Jewish Question still, or was all smoothed and troweled and interfaithed and brotherhoodooed—

Wait. Your formulation implies that they're in the future, and you have no proof of that. Think straighter; you don't know *where* they are, or *when* they are, or *who* they are. You *do* know that you walked into Big Maggie's resonance chamber to change the target, experimental iridium for old reliable zinc

and

"Bartender," in a controlled and formal voice. Shot of Red Top and a beer at 9:09, the hand vibrating with remembrance of a dirty-green El Greco sky which *might* be Brookhaven's heavens a million years either way from now, or one second sideways, or (bow to Method and formally exhaust the possibilities) a hallucination. The Seal snatched from the greenlit rock altar could be a blank washer, a wheel from a toy truck, or the screw top from a jar of shaving cream but for the fact that it wasn't. It was the Seal.

So: they began seeping through after that. The Chapter wanted it back. The Serpentists wanted it, period. Galardo had started by bargaining and wound up by threatening, but how could you do anything but laugh at his best offer, a rusty five-pound spur gear with a worn keyway and three teeth missing? His threats were richer than his bribes; they culminated with The Century of Flame. "Faith, father, it doesn't scare me at all, at all; sure, no man could stand it." Subjective-objective (How you used to sling *them* around!), and Master Newton's billiard-table similes dissolve into sense-impressions of pointer-readings as you learn your trade, but Galardo had scared hell out of you, or into you, with The Century of Flame.

But you had the Seal of the Chapter and you had time to think, while on the screen above the bar:

VIDEO	AUDIO
Long shot down steep, cobblestoned French village street. *Pierre* darts out of alley in middle distance, looks wildly around and runs toward camera, pistol in hand. *Annette* and *Paul* appear from same alley and dash after him.	*Paul:* Stop, you fool!
Cut to *Cu* of *Pierre's* face; beard stubble and sweat.	*Pierre:* A fool, am I?
Cut to long shot; *Pierre* aims and fires; *Paul* grabs his left shoulder and falls.	*Annette:* Darling!
Cut to two-shot, *Annette* and *Paul.*	*Paul:* Don't mind me. Take my gun—after him. He's a mad dog, I tell you!
Dolly back. *Annette* takes his pistol.	*Annette:* This, my dear, is as good a time as any to drop my little masquerade. Are you American agents really so stupid that you never thought I might be—a plant, as you call it?
Annette stands; we see her aim down at *Paul,* out of the picture. Then we dolly in to a *Cu* of her head; she is smiling triumphantly.	*Sound:* click of cocking pistol.
A hand holding a pistol enters the *Cu;* the pistol muzzle touches *Annette's* neck.	*Harkrider:* Drop it, Madame Golkov.
Dolly back to middle shot. *Harkrider* stands behind *Annette* as *Paul* gets up briskly and takes the pistol from her hand.	*Paul:* No, Madame Golkov; we American agents were not really so stupid. Wish I could say the same for—your people. Pierre Tourneur was a plant, I am glad to say; otherwise he would not have missed me.

He is one of the best pistol shots in Counterintelligence.

Cut to long shot of street, *Harkrider* and *Paul* walk away from the camera, *Annette* between them. Fadeout.

Harkrider: Come along, Madame Golkov.

Music: theme up and out.

To his right: "It ain't reasonable. All that shooting and yelling and falling down and not one person sticks his head out of a window to see what's going on. They should of had a few people looking out to see what's going on, otherwise it ain't reasonable."

"Yeah, who's fighting tonight?"

"Rocky Mausoleum against Rocky Mazzarella. From Toledo."

"Rocky Mazzarella beat Rocky Granatino, didn't he?"

"Ah, that was Rocky Bolderoni, and he whipped Rocky Capacola."

Them and their neatly packaged problems, them and their neatly packaged shows with beginning, middle and end. The rite of the low-budget shot-in-Europe spy series, the rite of pugilism, the rite of the dog-walk after dinner and the beer at the bar with co-celebrant worshippers at the high altar of Nothing.

9:30. Shot of Red Top and a beer, positively the last one until you get this figured out; you're beginning to buzz like a transformer.

Do they have transformers? Do they have vitamins? Do they have anything but that glaring green sky, and the rock altar and treasures like the Seal and the rusty gear with three broken teeth? "All smelling of iodoform. And all quite bald." But Galardo looked as if he were dying of tuberculosis; and the letter from the Serpentists was in a sick and straggling hand. Relics of mediaeval barbarism.

To his left—

"Galardo!" he screamed.

The bartender scurried over—Joe, Sam, Mike, Tony, Ben?—scowling. "What's the matter, mister?"

"I'm sorry. I got a stitch in my side. A cramp."

Bullyboy scowled competently and turned. "What'll you have, mister?"

Galardo said cadaverously: "Wodeffer my vriend hyere iss havfing."

"Shot of Red Top and a beer, right?"

"What are you doing here?"

"Drink-ing beferachiss … havf hyü de-site-it hwat tü dü?"

The bartender rapped down the shot glass and tilted the bottle over it, looking at Galardo. Some of the whiskey slopped over. The bartender started, went to the tap and carefully drew a glass of beer slicing the collar twice.

"My vriend hyere will pay."

He got out a half dollar, fumbling, and put it on the wet wood. The bartender, old-fashioned, rapped it twice on the bar to show he wasn't stealing it even though you weren't watching; he rang it up double virtuous on the cash register, the absent owner's fishy eye.

"What are you doing here?" again, in a low, reasonable, almost amused voice to show him you have the whip hand.

"Drink-ing beferachiss … it iss so cle-an hyere." Galardo's sunken face, unbelievably, looked wistful as he surveyed the barroom, his head swiveling slowly from extreme left to extreme right.

"Clean. Well. Isn't it clean there?"

"Sheh, not!" Galardo said mournfully. "Sheh, not! Hyere it iss so cle-an … hwai did yü outreach tü us? Hag-rid us, wretch-it, hag-rid us?" There were tears hanging in his eyes. "Haff yü de-site-it hwat tü dü?"

Expansively: "I don't pretend to understand the situation *fully,* Galardo. But you know and I know that I've got something you people [think you] need. Now there doesn't seem to be any body of law covering artifacts that appear *[plink!]* in a magnetron on accidental overload, and I just have your word that it's yours."

"Ah, that iss how yü re-member it now," said sorrowful Galardo.

"Well, it's the way it [but wasn't something green? I think of spired Toledo and three angled crosses toppling] happened. I don't want anything silly, like a million dollars in small unmarked bills, and I don't want to be bullied, to be bullied, no, I mean not by you, not by anybody. Just, just tell me who you are, what all this is about. This is nonsense, you see, and we can't have nonsense. I'm afraid I'm not expressing myself very well—"

And a confident smile and turn away from him, which shows that you aren't afraid, you can turn your back and dare him to make something of it. In public, in the bar? It is laughable; you have him in the palm of your hand. "Shot of Red Top and a beer, please, Sam." At 9:48.

The bartender draws the beer and pours the whiskey. He pauses before he picks up the dollar bill fished from the pants pocket, pauses almost timidly and works his face into a friend's grimace. But you can read him; he is making amends for his suspicion that you were going to start a drunken brawl when Galardo merely surprised you a bit. You can read him because your mind is tensed to concert pitch tonight, ready for Galardo, ready for the Serpentists, ready to crack this thing wide open; strange!

But you weren't ready for the words he spoke from his fake apologetic friend's grimace as you delicately raised the heavy amber-filled glass to your lips: "Where'd your friend go?"

You slopped the whiskey as you turned and looked.

Galardo gone.

You smiled and shrugged; he comes and goes as he pleases, you know. Irresponsible, no manners at all—but *loyal.* A prince among men when you get to know him, a prince, I tell you. All this in your smile and shrug—why, you could have been an actor! The worry, the faint neurotic worry, didn't show at all, and indeed there is no reason why it should. You have the whip hand; you have the Seal; Galardo will come crawling back and explain everything. As for example:

"You may wonder why I've asked all of you to assemble in the libr'reh."

or

"For goodness' sake, Gracie, I wasn't going to go to Cuba! When you heard me on the extension phone I was just ordering a dozen Havana *cigars!*"

or

"In your notation, we are from 19,276 A.D. Our basic mathematic is a quite comprehensible subsumption of your contemporary statistical analysis and topology which I shall now proceed to explain to you."

And that was all.

With sorrow, Gentle Reader, you will have noticed that the marble did not remark: "I am chiseled," the lumber "I am sawn," the paint "I am applied to canvas," the tea leaf "I am whisked about in an exquisite Korean bowl to brew while the celebrants of *cha no yu* squeeze this nourishment out of their poverty." Vain victim, relax and play your hunches; subconscious integration does it. Stick with your lit-tle old subconscious integration and all will go *swimmingly,* if only it weren't so damned noisy in here. But it was dark on the street and conceivably things could happen there; stick with crowds and stick with witnesses, but if only it weren't so ...

To his left they were settling down; it was the hour of confidences, and man to man they told the secret of their success: "In the needle trade, I'm in the needle trade, I don't sell anybody a crooked needle, my father told me that. Albert, he said to me, don't never sell nobody nothing but a straight needle. And today I have four shops."

To his right they were settling down; freed of the cares of the day they invited their souls, explored the spiritual realm, theologized with exquisite distinctions: "Now *wait* a minute, I didn't say I was a *good* Mormon, I said I was a Mormon and that's what I am, a Mormon. I *never* said I was a *good* Mormon, I just said I was a Mormon, my mother was a Mormon and my father was a Mormon, and that makes me a Mormon but I *never* said I was a *good* Mormon—"

Distinguo, rolled the canonical thunder; *distinguo.*

Demurely a bonneted lassie shook her small-change tambourine beneath his chin and whispered, snarling: "Galardo lied."

Admit it; you were startled. But what need for the bartender to come running with raised hand, what need for needle-trader to your left to shrink away, the L.D.S. to cower?

"Mister, that's twice you let out a yell, we run a quiet place, if you can't be good, begone."

Begob.

"I ash-assure you, bartender, it was—unintenable."

Greed vies with hate; greed wins; greed always wins: "Just keep it quiet, mister, this ain't the Bowery, this is a family place." Then, relenting: "The same?"

"Yes, please." At 10:15 the patient lassie jingled silver on the parchment palm outstretched. He placed a quarter on the tambourine and asked politely: "Did you say something to me before, Miss?"

"God bless you, sir. Yes, sir, I did say something. I said Galardo lied; the Seal is holy to the Serpent, sir, and to his humble emissaries. If you'll only hand it over, sir, the Serpent will somewhat mitigate the fearsome torments which are rightly yours for snatching the Seal from the Altar, sir."

[Snatchings from Altars? *Ma foi,* the wench is mad!]

"Listen, lady. That's only talk. What annoys me about you people is, you won't talk sense. I want to know who you are, what this is about, maybe just a little hint about your mathematics, and I'll do the rest and you can have the blooming Seal. I'm a passable physicist even if I'm only a technician. I bet there's something you didn't know. I bet you didn't know the tech shortage is tighter than the scientist shortage. You get a guy can tune a magnetron, he writes his own ticket. So I'm weak on quantum mechanics, the theory side, I'm still a good all-around man and be-*lieve* me, the Ph.D.'s would kiss my ever-loving *feet* if I told them I got an offer from Argonne—

"So listen, you Janissary emissary. I'm happy right here in this necessary commissary and here I *stay.*"

But she was looking at him with bright frightened mouse's eyes and slipped on down the line when he paused for breath, putting out the parchment palm to others but not ceasing to watch him.

Coins tapped the tambour. "God bless you. God bless you. God bless you."

The raving-maniacal ghost of G. Washington Hill descended then into a girdled sibyl; she screamed from the screen: "It's *Hit Pa-rade!*"

"I like them production numbers."

"I like that Pigalle Mackintosh."

"I like them production numbers. Lotsa pretty girls, pretty clothes, something to take your mind off your troubles."

"I like that Pigalle Mackintosh. She don't just sing, mind you, she plays the saxophone. Talent."

"I like them production numbers. They show you just what the song is all about. Like last week they did *Sadist Calypso* with this mad scientist cutting up the girls, and then Pigalle comes in and whips him to death at the last verse, you see just what the song's all about, something to take your mind off your troubles."

"I like that Pigalle Mackintosh. She don't just sing, mind you, she plays the saxophone and cracks a blacksnake whip, like last week in *Sadist Calypso*—"

"Yeah. Something to take your mind off your troubles."

Irritably he felt in his pocket for the Seal and moved, stumbling a little, to one of the tables against the knotty pine wall. His head slipped forward on the polished wood and he sank into the sea of myth.

Galardo came to him in his dream and spoke under a storm-green sky: "Take your mind off your troubles, Edward. It was stolen like the first penny, like the quiz answers, like the pity for your bereavement." His hand, a tambourine, was out.

"Never shall I yield," he declaimed to the miserable wretch. "By the *honneur* of a Gascon, I stole it fair and square; 'tis mine, knave! *En garde!*"

Galardo quailed and ran, melting into the sky, the altar, the tambourine.

A ham-hand manhandled him. "Light-up time," said Sam. "I let you sleep because you got it here, but I got to close up now."

"Sam," he says uncertainly.

"One for the road, mister. On the house. *Up-sy*-daisy!" meaty hooks under his armpits heaving him to the bar.

The lights are out behind the bar, the jolly neons, glittering off how many gems of amber rye and the tan crystals of beer? A meager bulb above the register is the oasis in the desert of inky night.

"Sam," groggily, "you don't understand. I mean I never explained it—"

"Drink up, mister," a pale free drink, soda bubbles lightly tinged with tawny rye. A small sip to gain time.

"Sam, there are some people after me—"

"You'll feel better in the morning, mister. Drink up, I got to close up, hurry up."

"These people, Sam [it's cold in here and scary as a noise in the attic; the bottles stand accusingly, the chrome globes that top them eye you] these people, they've got a thing, The Century of—"

"Sure, mister, I let you sleep because you got it here, but we close up now, drink up your drink."

"Sam, let me go home with you, will you? It isn't anything like that, don't misunderstand, I just can't be alone. These people—look, I've got money—"

He spreads out what he dug from his pocket.

"Sure, mister, you got lots of money, two dollars and thirty-eight cents. Now you take your money and get out of the store because I got to lock up and clean out the register—"

"Listen, bartender, I'm not drunk, maybe I don't have much money on me but I'm an important man! Important! They couldn't run Big Maggie at Brookhaven without me, I may not have a degree but what I get from these people if you'll only let me stay here—"

The bartender takes the pale one on the house you only sipped and dumps it in the sink; his hands are iron on you and you float while he chants:

> *Decent man. Decent place.*
> *Hold their liquor. Got it here.*
> *Try be nice. Drunken bum.*
> *Don't—come—back.*

The crash of your coccyx on the concrete and the slam of the door are one.

Run!

Down the black street stumbling over cans, cats, orts, to the pool of light in the night, safe corner where a standard sprouts and sprays radiance.

The tall black figure that steps between is Galardo.

The short one has a tambourine.

"*Take it!*" He thrust out the Seal on his shaking palm. "If you won't tell me anything, you won't. Take it and go away!"

Galardo inspects it and sadly says: "Thiss appearss to be a blank wash-er."

"Mistake," he slobbers. "Minute." He claws in his pockets, ripping. "Here! Here!"

The lassie squeaks: "The wheel of a toy truck. It will not do at all, sir." Her glittereyes.

"Then this! This is it! This must be it!"

Their heads shake slowly. Unable to look, his fingers feel the rim and rolled threading of the jar cap.

They nod together, sad and glitter-eyed, and The Century of Flame begins.

[*Venture* - March 1958]

Virginia

James "Bunny" Coogler woke on the morning of his father's funeral with a confused feeling that it was awfully crowded in his bedroom. Ohara, his valet (of the
Shimanoseki Oharas, and not to be confused with the Dublin branch of the family), was shaking his sleeve and saying: "You wake up, Missah Bunny! Ah, such
important gentermen come see you!" Bunny groped on the bedside table for the
sunglasses to shelter his pink-rimmed eyes from the light. Ohara popped them
onto his face and then rapidly poured a prairie oyster, a bromo and a cup of black
coffee laced with brandy into him. Bunny's usual rate of morning vibration began
to dampen towards zero and he peered about the room through the dark lenses.

"Morning, young Coogler," said a gruff voice. The outline was that of J. G.
Barsax, senior partner of his late father's firm. A murmur of greeting came from
three other elephantine figures. They were Gonfalonieri of First American, Witz
of Diversified Limited, and McChesney of Southern Development Inc. If an efficient bomb had gone off in the room at that moment, it would have liquidated
eighteen billion dollars' worth of Top Management and Ownership.

"Sorry about your father," Barsax grunted. "Mind if we sit? Not much time
before the funeral. Have to brief you fast."

Bunny said, "Mr. Sankton told me what I'd have to do, Mr. Barsax. Rise
after the 'Amen,' lead the procession past the casket, up the center aisle to the
limousine exit—"

"No, no, no. Of course you know the funeral form. I'm talking about the
financial briefing. Coogler, you're a very wealthy young man."

Bunny took off his sunglasses. "I am?" he asked uncertainly. "Surely not.
There's this trust thing he was always talking about to pay me twenty thousand a
year—"

"Talked," said Gonfalonieri. "That's all he did. He never got it on paper.
You're the sole heir to the liquid equivalent of, say, three and a half billion dollars."

Ohara hastily refilled the cup with laced coffee and put it in Bunny's hand.

"So," little Mr. Witz said softly, "there are certain things you must know.
Certain rules that have sprung up which We observe." The capitalized plural pro-

noun was definitely sounded. Whether it was to be taken as royal, editorial, or theological, who can say?

They proceeded to brief Bunny.

Firstly, he must never admit that he was wealthy. He might use the phrase "what little I have," accompanied by a whimsical shrug.

Secondly, he must never, under any circumstances, at any time, give anything to anybody. Whenever asked for anything he was to intimate that this one request he simply could not grant, that it was the one crushing straw atop his terrible burden of charitable contributions.

Thirdly, whenever offered anything—from a cigar to a million-dollar market tip from a climber—he must take it without thanks and complain bitterly that the gift was not handsomer.

Fourthly, he must look on Touching Capital as morally equivalent to coprophagia, but he must not attempt to sting himself by living on the interest of his interest; that was only for New Englanders.

Fifthly, when he married he must choose his bride from one of Us.

"You mean, one of you four gentlemen?" Bunny asked. He thought of J.G.'s eldest daughter and repressed a shudder.

"No," said Witz. "One of Us in the larger sense. You will come to know who is who, and eventually acquire an instinct that will enable you to distinguish between a millionaire and a person of real substance."

"And that," said Barsax, "is the sum of it. We shall see you at the funeral and approach you later, Coogler." He glanced at his watch. "Come, gentlemen."

Bunny had a mechanical turn of mind; he enjoyed the Museum of Suppressed Inventions at J.G.'s Carolina estate. The quavery old curator pottered after him explaining.

"This, sir, is the hundred-mile-per-gallon carburetor. I was more active when it came out in '36—I was a Field Operative then. I tracked it down to a little Iowa village on a rumor from a patent attorney; it was quite a struggle to suppress that one. Quite a struggle, sir! But—the next case, please, sir—it would have been rendered obsolete within two years. Yes, sir, that's when the Gasoline Pill came out. Let me show you, sir!"

He happily popped one of the green pills into a gallon of water and lectured as it bubbled and fumed and turned the water into 100-octane gasoline.

The Eternal Match was interesting, the Two-Cent Sirloin was delicious, and the Vanishing Cream vanished a half-inch roll of fat from Bunny's belly while he watched. "But Lord bless you, sir," tittered the curator, "what would be the point of giving people something that worked? They'd just go ahead and use it, and then when they had no more need they'd stop using it, eh?

"And this one, sir, it isn't really what you'd call suppressed. We're just working on it to build it up some; perhaps in five years we'll have it looking like it costs five thousand dollars, and then we'll be able to sell it." "It" was three-dimensional, full-color television; the heart of the system was a flashlight battery, a small C-clamp and a pinch of baking soda.

Bunny visited also the vast pest-breeding establishment in the Rockies, where flies, roaches, mice, gnats, boll-weevils, the elm-rot fungus and the tobacco-mosaic virus were patiently raised to maximum virulence and dispatched by couriers to their proper places all over the world. The taciturn Connecticut Yankee who ran the sprawling plant snapped at him, "Danged better mousetraps almost wiped out the mousetrap industry. Think people'd have better sense. DDT almost killed off pesticide—whole danged business, employing two hundred thousand. They think of that? Naw! So we had ter breed them DDT-resistant strains and seed 'em everywhere."

Bunny began to acquire the instinct to which Witz had referred. When he encountered an Oil Texan he could tell that the man's nervous hilarity and brag stemmed from his poverty, and he pitied him. When he encountered one day at Gonfalonieri's place in Baja California a certain quiet fellow named Briggs, he knew without being told that Briggs was one of Us. It was no surprise to learn later that Briggs held all the basic patents on water.

Briggs it was, indeed, who took him aside for an important talk. The quiet man offered him a thousand-dollar cigar (for the growing of whose tobacco Briggs had caused an artificial island to be built in the deep Central Pacific at the exactly correct point of temperature, wind and humidity) and said to him, "It's time you took a wife."

Bunny, who could not these days leaf through *Vogue* or the *New Yorker* without a tender, reminiscent smile for each of the lovely models shown in the advertisements, disagreed. "Can't see why, Briggs," he muttered. "Having jolly good time. Never used to have much luck with girls—all different now. Mean to say, with—" he gave the whimsical little shrug—"what little I have, doing awfully well and it doesn't cost me anything. Queer. When I had ten–twenty thou', when I was poor, had to buy corsages, dinners. All different now. They buy me things. Platinum watches. Have simply *dozens*. But the rules—have to take 'em. Queer."

"We've all been through it," Briggs said. "When you get bored let me know."

"Oh, promise," Bunny said. "Absolutely promise."

He spent the next six months in Hollywood where golden girls vied in plying him with *coq au vin,* solid iridium meat grinders, and similar trifles. One charming lady who had come out to the sound stages in 1934 presented him with a genuine hand-embroidered antique scabbard said to date back to the Crusades. It was a pleasant gift and it varied the...

...the *monotony?*

He sat up abruptly on the mutation-mink coverlet, causing the shapely blond head which remained on the silken pillow to emit a small sleepy snort.

"Monotony," Bunny said in a tragic whisper. "Definitely." He went home to Ohara, though not neglecting to pick up as he left his little present for the evening, a golden nutcracker set with diamonds and lined with unborn leopard pelt.

Ohara dipped into his store of Oriental wisdom in an effort to console him. He suggested, "Missah Bunny think if must be monotonized, what beautifurr way to *get* monotonized?"

It did not help.

Ohara suggested, "You try make funny, fo'get monotony. Fo' exampurr, spend coupre mirrion dorras make big reso't town, cawr same Schmir-ton, Ohio. Think how mad Missah Nickey be, he put up hoterr, have to cawr same Hoterr Hir-ton Schmir-ton! Oh, raffs!"

It would not do.

"Ohara," Bunny said tragically, "I would give—" he shrugged whimsically— "what little I have not to be bored with, ah, life."

The impassive Oriental countenance of his manservant flickered briefly in a grimace. His orders were clear, and he knew how terrible would be the consequences of disobedience.

Bunny tossed fitfully alone in his bed an hour later, and Ohara was on the phone to an unlisted New York number. "This Ohara," he whispered. "Missah Bunny talk about giving away money. Awr his money."

The responding voice was that of an Englishman. It said: "Thank you, Ohara. One hopes, of course, for your sake, that the information has arrived in time. One hopes devoutly that it will not be necessary to inflict the Death of a Thousand Cuts on you. A book could be written about Number Three Hundred and Twenty-Eight alone, and as for Number Four Hundred and One—! Well, I won't keep you with my chattering." He hung up.

Within minutes the lonely house in a canyon was surrounded; the Fourth Plutocratic Airborne and Amphibious Assault Force was the ultimate in efficient mercenary troops. By dawn they had Bunny on his way to Barsax' Carolina estate under heavy sedation.

He woke in the guest room he knew, just off the corridor which contained the Museum of Suppressed Inventions. Little Mr. Witz and quiet Mr. Briggs were there. With granite faces they told him: "You have broken the Code, young Coogler. You said there was something you valued above money. You have got to go."

"Please," Bunny blubbered. "I didn't mean it. I'll marry your daughter. I'll marry both your daughters! Just don't kill me."

Mr. Witz said implacably, "Our decent, money-fearing girls wouldn't have anything to do with a dirty plutophobe like you, young Coogler. If only your poor father had put through the trust fund in time—well, thank Heaven he's not alive to see this day. But we won't kill you, young Coogler. It is not within our power to cause the death of a billionaire as if he were an animal or mere human being. What we can and will do is quarantine you. In Virginia."

This sounded like a rank *non sequitur* to Bunny until they took him to the Museum and trundled out a one-man spaceship invented early in 1923 by a Herr Rudolf Grenzbach of Czernovitz, Upper Silesia, whose body had been found in Lower Silesia later that year.

Officers of the Fourth P.A.A.A.F. loaded him into the bomb-like contrivance over his spirited protest and pre-set the course. Virginia, it seemed, was an asteroid rather than the neighboring state. They fired the rockets and Bunny was on his way.

Four years later Mr. Witz and Mr. Briggs conferred again. "Perhaps," said Mr. Witz, "we've put enough of a scare into him. Let's radio the lad and find out whether he's given up his wild seditious notions and is ready to be rescued."

They tuned in the asteroid Virginia on another suppressed invention. "Young Coogler," Briggs said into the microphone. "This is Briggs. We wish to know whether you've come to your senses and are ready to take your place in society— ours, of course."

There squawked over the loudspeaker the voice of Bunny. "I say, what *was* that. No, not now, not for a second please. Where did that voice come from? Can you hear me, Mr. Briggs?"

"I hear you," said Mr. Briggs.

"Extraordinary! Another invention, eh?"

"Yes," said Briggs. "I am calling, young Coogler, to learn whether you are properly contrite and if so to arrange for your rescue."

"Rescue?" said the voice of Bunny. "Why, no thanks. That won't be necessary. Having a fine time here. They need me, you know. They love me for, ah, myself alone. Not the dashed money. *Double*-dash the money, I say!"

Mr. Briggs, white to the lips, broke the connection.

"He meant you to do that," Mr. Witz remarked.

"I know. Let him rot there."

The quavery old curator had been listening. "On Virginia?" he asked tremulously. "You don't rot on Virginia. Don't you gentlemen know how it got its name?"

"Never bothered to find out," Mr. Briggs snapped. "Since you're bursting to tell us, you might as well."

The curator beamed. "They call it Virginia because it's the planetoid of virgins. The dangdest thing. *Perpetual* virgins. The Plutocratic Space Force says they've never seen anything like it, not on Mars, not on Callisto. Self-renewing—the *dangdest* thing!"

Mr. Briggs and Mr. Witz looked at each other. After a while Mr. Witz spoke. "Bunny," he said reflectively. "Bunny. He was well named."

[*Star Science Fiction Stories No. 4* - 1958]

The Advent on Channel Twelve

It came to pass in the third quarter of the fiscal year that the Federal Reserve Board did raise the rediscount rate and money was tight in the land. And certain bankers which sate in New York sent to Ben Graffis in Hollywood a writing which said, Money is tight in the land so let Poopy Panda up periscope and fire all bow tubes.

Whereupon Ben Graffis made to them this moan:

O ye bankers, Poopy Panda is like unto the child of my flesh and you have made of him a devouring dragon. Once was I content with my studio and my animators when we did make twelve Poopy Pandas a year; cursed be the day when I floated a New York loan. You have commanded me to make feature-length cartoon epics and I did obey, and they do open at the Paramount to sensational grosses, and we do re-release them to the nabes year on year, without end. You have commanded me to film live adventure shorts and I did obey, and in the cutting room we do devilishly splice and pull frames and flop negatives so that I and my cameras are become bearers of false witness and men look upon my live adventure shorts and say lo! these beasts and birds are like unto us in their laughter, wooing, pranks and contention. You have commanded that I become a mountebank for that I did build Poopy Pandaland, whereinto men enter with their children, their silver and their wits, and wherefrom they go out with their children only, sandbagged by a thousand catch-penny engines; even this did I obey. You have commanded that Poopy Panda shill every weekday night on television between five and six for the Poopy Panda Pals, and even this did I obey, though Poopy Panda is like unto the child of my flesh.

But O ye bankers, this last command will I never obey.

Whereupon the bankers which sate in New York sent to him another writing that said, Even so, let Poopy Panda up periscope and fire all bow tubes, and they said, Remember, boy, we hold thy paper.

And Ben Graffis did obey.

He called unto him his animators and directors and cameramen and writers, and his heart was sore but he dissembled and said:

In jest you call one another brainwashers, forasmuch as you addle the heads of children five hours a week that they shall buy our sponsors' wares. You have

517

fulfilled the prophecies, for is it not written in the Book of the Space Merchants that there shall be spherical trusts? And the Poopy Panda Pals plug the Poopy Panda Magazine, and the Poopy Panda Magazine plugs Poopy Pandaland, and Poopy Pandaland plugs the Poopy Panda Pals. You have asked of the Motivational Research boys how we shall hook the little bastards and they have told ye, and ye have done it. You identify the untalented kid viewers with the talented kid performers, you provide in Otto Clodd a bumbling father image to be derided, you furnish in Jackie Whipple an idealized big brother for the boys and a sex-fantasy for the more precocious girls. You flatter the cans off the viewers by ever saying to them that they shall rule the twenty-first century, nor mind that those who shall in good sooth come to power are doing their homework and not watching television programs. You have created a liturgy of opening hymn and closing benediction, and over all hovers the spirit of Poopy Panda urging and coaxing the viewers to buy our sponsors' wares.

And Ben Graffis breathed a great breath and looked them not in the eye and said to them, Were it not a better thing for Poopy Panda to coax and urge no more, but to command as he were a god?

And the animators and directors and cameramen and writers were sore amazed and they said one to the other, This is the bleeding end, and the bankers which sit in New York have flipped their wigs. And one which was an old animator said to Ben Graffis, trembling, O chief, never would I have stolen for thee Poopy Panda from the Winnie the Pooh illustrations back in twenty-nine had I known this was in the cards, and Ben Graffis fired him.

Whereupon another which was a director said to Ben Graffis, O chief, the thing can be done with a two-week buildup, and Ben Graffis put his hands over his face and said, Let it be so.

And it came to pass that on the Friday after the two-week buildup, in the closing quarter-hour of the Poopy Panda Pals, there was a special film combining live and animated action as they were one.

And in the special film did Poopy Panda appear enhaloed, and the talented kid performers did do him worship, and Otto Clodd did trip over his feet whilst kneeling, and Jackie Whipple did urge in manly and sincere wise that all the Poopy Panda Pals out there in television-land do likewise, and the enhaloed Poopy Panda did say in his lovable growly voice, Poop-poop-poopy.

And adoration ascended from thirty-seven million souls.

And it came to pass that Ben Graffis went into his office with his animators and cameramen and directors and writers after the show and said to them, It was definitely a TV first, and he did go to the bar.

Whereupon one which was a director looked at Who sate behind the desk that was the desk of Ben Graffis and he said to Ben Graffis, O chief, it is a great gag but how did the special effects boys manage the halo?

And Ben Graffis was sore amazed at Who sate behind his desk and he and they all did crowd about and make as if to poke Him, whereupon He in His lovable growly voice did say, Poop-poop-poopy, and they were not.

And certain unclean ones which had gone before turned unbelieving from their monitors and said, Holy Gee, this is awful. And one which was an operator of marionettes turned to his manager and said, Pal, if Graffis gets this off the ground we're dead. Whereat a great and far-off voice was heard, saying, Poop-poop-poopy, and it was even so; and the days of Poopy Panda were long in the land.

Filtered for error,
Jan. 18th 36 P.P.
Synod on Filtration & Infiltration
O. Clodd, P.P.P.
J. Whipple, P.P.P.

[*SF Adventures* - November 1952]

Make Mine Mars

X is for the ecstasy she ga-a-ave me;
E is for her eyes—one, two, and three-ee;
T is for the teeth with which she'd sha-a-ave me;
S is for her scales of i-vo-ree-ee-ee …

Somebody was singing, and my throbbing head objected. I seemed to have a mouthful of sawdust.

T is for her tentacles ah-round me;
J is for her jowls—were none soo-oo fair;
H is for the happy day she found me;
Fe is for the iron in her hair …

I ran my tongue around inside my mouth. It *was* full of sawdust—spruce and cedar, rocketed in from Earth.

Put them all to-gether, they spell Xetstjhfe …

My eyes snapped open, and I sat up, cracking my head on the underside of the table beneath which I was lying. I lay down and waited for the pinwheels to stop spinning. I tried to think it out. Spruce and cedar … Honest Blogri's Olde Earthe Saloon … eleven stingers with a Sirian named Wenjtkpli …

A worrud that means the wur-r-l-l-d too-oo mee-ee-ee!

Through the fading pinwheels I saw a long and horrid face, a Sirian face, peering at me with kindly interest under the table. It was Wenjtkpli.

"Good morning, little Earth chum," he said. "You feel not so tired now?"

"Morning?" I yelled, sitting up again and cracking my head again and lying down again to wait for the pinwheels to fade again.

"You sleep," I heard him say, "fourteen hours—so happy, so peaceful!"

"I gotta get out of here," I mumbled, scrambling about on the imported sawdust for my hat. I found I was wearing it, and climbed out, stood up and leaned against the table, swaying and spitting out the last of the spruce and cedar.

"You like another stinger?" asked Wenjtkpli brightly. I retched feebly.

"Fourteen hours," I mumbled. "That makes it 0900 Mars now, or exactly ten hours past the time I was supposed to report for the nightside at the bureau."

"But last night you talk different," the Sirian told me in surprise. "You say many times how bureau chief McGillicuddy can take lousy job and jam—"

"That was last night," I moaned. "This is this morning."

"Relax, little Earth chum. I sing again song you taught me:

> *X is for the ecstasy she ga-a-ave me;*
> *E is for—"*

My throbbing head still objected. I flapped good-bye at him and set a course for the door of Blogri's joint. The quaint period mottoes:

"QUAFFE YE NUT-BROWN AYLE"
"DROPPE DEAD TWYCE"

and so on—didn't look so quaint by the cold light of the Martian dawn.

An unpleasant little character, Venusian or something, I'd seen around the place oozed up to me. "Head hurt plenty, huh?" he simpered.

"This is no time for sympathy," I said. "Now one side or a flipper off—I gotta go to work."

"No sympathy," he said, his voice dropping to a whisper. He fumbled oddly in his belt, then showed me a little white capsule. "Clear your head, huh? Work like lightning, you bet!"

I was interested. "How much?"

"For you, friend, nothing. Because I hate seeing fellows suffer with big head."

"Beat it," I told him, and shoved past through the door. That pitch of his with a free sample meant he was pushing J-K-B. I was in enough trouble without adding an unbreakable addiction to the stuff. If I'd taken his free sample, I would have been back to see him in twelve hours, sweating blood for more. And that time he would have named his own price.

I fell into an eastbound chair and fumbled a quarter into the slot. The thin, cold air of the pressure dome was clearing my head already. I was sorry for all the times I'd cussed a skinflint dome administration for not supplying a richer air mix or heating the outdoors more lavishly. I felt good enough to shave, and luckily had my razor in my wallet. By the time the chair was gliding past the building where Interstellar News had a floor, I had the whiskers off my jaw and most of the sawdust out of my hair.

The floater took me up to our floor while I tried not to think of what McGillicuddy would have to say.

The newsroom was full of noise as usual. McGillicuddy was in the copydesk slot chewing his way through a pile of dispatches due to be filed on the pressure dome split for A.M. newscasts in four minutes by the big wall clock. He fed his copy, without looking, to an operator battering the keys of the old-fashioned radioteletype that was good enough to serve our local clients.

"Two minutes short!" he yelled at one of the men on the rim. "Gimme a brightener! Gimme a god-damned brightener!" The rim man raced to the receiving ethertypes from Gammadion, Betelgeuse, and the other Interstellar bureaus. He yanked an item from one of the clicking machines and scaled it at McGillicuddy, who slashed at it with his pencil and passed it to the operator. The tape the operator was cutting started through the transmitter-distributor, and on all local clients' radioteletypes appeared:

> FIFTEEN-MINUTE INTERSTELLAR NEWSCAST AM
> MARS PRESSURE DOMES.

Everybody leaned back and lit up. McGillicuddy's eye fell on me, and I cleared my throat.

"Got a cold?" he asked genially.

"Nope. No cold."

"Touch of indigestion? Flu, maybe? You're tardy today."

"I know it."

"Bright boy." He was smiling. That was bad.

"Spencer," he told me. "I thought long and hard about you. I thought about you when you failed to show up for the nightside. I thought about you intermittently through the night as I took your shift. Along about 0300 I decided what to do with you. It was as through Providence had taken a hand. It was as though I prayed 'Lord, what shall I do with a drunken, no-good son of a space-cook who ranks in my opinion with the boils of Job as an affliction to man?' Here's the answer, Spencer."

He tossed me a piece of ethertype paper, torn from one of our interstellar-circuit machines. On it was the following dialogue:

> ANYBODY TTHURE I MEAN THERE
> THIS MARSBUO ISN GA PLS
> WOT TTHUT I MEAN WOT THAT MEAN PLEASE
>
> THIS IS THE MARS BUREAU OF INTERSTELLAR NEWS. WHO
> ARE YOU AND WHAT ARE YOU DOING HORSING AROUND
> ON OUR KRUEGER 60-B CIRCUIT TELETYPE QUESTION-
> MARK. WHERE IS REGULAR STAFFER. GO AHEAD
>
> THATIS WOT I AM CALLING YOU ABBOUUT. KENNEDY
> DIED THIS MORNING PNEUMONIA. I AM WEEMS EDITOR
> PHOENIX. U SENDING REPLLACEMENT KENNEDY PLEAS
>
> THIS MCGILLICUDDY, MARSBUO ISN CHIEF. SENDING RE-
> PLACEMENT KENNEDY SOONEST. HAVE IDEAL MAN FOR
> JOB. END.

That was all. It was enough.

"Chief," I said to McGillicuddy. "Chief, you can't. You wouldn't—*would* you?"

"Better get packed," he told me, busily marking up copy. "Better take plenty of nice, warm clothing. I understand Krueger 60-B is about one thousand times dimmer than the sun. That's absolute magnitude, of course—Frostbite's in quite close. A primitive community, I'm told. Kennedy didn't like it. But of course the poor old duffer wasn't good enough to handle anything swifter than a one-man bureau on a one-planet split. Better take *lots* of warm clothing."

"I quit," I said.

"Sam," said somebody, in a voice that always makes me turn to custard inside.

"Hello, Ellie," I said. "I was just telling Mr. McGillicuddy that he isn't going to shoot me off to Frostbite to rot."

"Freeze," corrected McGillicuddy with relish. "Freeze. Good morning, Miss Masters. Did you want to say a few parting words to your friend?"

"I do," she told him, and drew me aside to no man's land where the ladies of the press prepared strange copy for the gentler sex. "Don't quit, Sam," she said in that voice. "I could never love a quitter. What if it *is* a minor assignment?"

"Minor," I said. "What a gem of understatement *that* is!"

"It'll be good for you," she insisted. "You can show him what you've got on the ball. You'll be on your own except for the regular dispatches to the main circuit and your local split. You could dig up all sorts of cute feature stories that'd get your name known." And so on. It was partly her logic, partly that voice and partly her promise to kiss me good-bye at the port.

"I'll take it," I told McGillicuddy. He looked up with a pleased smile and murmured: "The power of prayer ..."

The good-bye kiss from Ellie was the only thing about the journey that wasn't nightmarish. ISN's expense account stuck me on a rusty bucket that I shared with glamorous freight like yak kids and tenpenny nails. The little yaks blatted whenever we went into overdrive to break through the speed of light. The Greenhough Effect—known to readers of the science features as "supertime"—scared hell out of them. On ordinary rocket drive, they just groaned and whimpered to each other the yak equivalent of "Tibet was never like this!"

The Frostbite spaceport wasn't like the South Pole, but it was like Greenland. There was a bunch of farmers waiting for their yaks, beating their mittened hands together and exhaling long plumes of vapor. The collector of customs, a rat-faced city boy, didn't have the decency to turn them over and let the hayseeds get back to the administration building. I watched through a porthole and saw him stalling and dawdling over a sheaf of papers for each of the farmers. Oddly enough, the stalling and dawdling stopped as soon as the farmers caught on and passed over a few dollars. Nobody even bothered to slip it shamefacedly from one hand to another. They just handed it over, not caring who saw—Rat-Face sneering, the farmers dumbly accepting the racket.

My turn came. Rat-Face came aboard and we were introduced by the chief engineer. "Harya," he said. "Twenny bucks."

"What for?"

"Landing permit. Later at the administration you can pay your visitor's permit. That's twenny bucks too."

"I'm not a visitor. I'm coming here to work."

"Work, schmurk. So you'll need a work permit—twenny bucks." His eyes wandered. "Whaddaya got there?"

"Ethertype parts. May need them for replacements."

He was on his knees in front of the box, crooning, "Triple ad valorem plus twenny dollars security bond for each part plus twenny dollars inspection fee plus twenny dollars for decontamination plus twenny dollars for failure to declare plus—"

"Break it up, Joe," said a new arrival—a grey-mustached little man, lost in his parka. "He's a friend of mine. Extend the courtesies of the port."

Rat-Face—Joe—didn't like it, but he took it. He muttered about doing his duty and gave me a card.

"Twenny bucks?" I asked, studying it.

"Nah," he said angrily. "You're free-loading." He got out.

"Looks as if you saved ISN some money," I said to the little man. He threw back the hood of his parka in the relative warmth of the ship.

"Why not? We'll be working together. I'm Chenery from the *Phoenix*."

"Oh, yeah—the client."

"That's right," he agreed, grinning. "*The* client. What exactly did you do to get banished to Frostbite?"

Since there was probably a spacemail aboard from McGillicuddy telling him exactly what I did, I told him. "Chief thought I was generally shiftless."

"You'll do here," he said. "It's a shiftless, easy-going kind of place. I have the key to your bureau. Want me to lead the way?"

"What about my baggage?"

"Your stuff's safe. Port officers won't loot it when they know you're a friend of the *Phoenix*."

That wasn't exactly what I'd meant; I'd always taken it for granted that port officers didn't loot anybody's baggage, not matter whose friends they were or weren't. As Chenery had said, it seemed to be a shiftless, easy-going place. I let him lead the way; he had a jeep waiting to take us to the administration building, a musty, too-tight hodgepodge of desks. A lot of them were vacant, and the dowdy women and fattish men at the others didn't seem to be very busy. The women were doing their nails or reading; the men mostly were playing blotto with pocket-size dials for small change. A couple were sleeping.

From the administration building a jet job took us the 20 kilos to town. Frostbite, the capital of Frostbite, housed maybe 40,000 people. No pressure dome. Just the glorious outdoors, complete with dust, weather, insects and a steady, icy wind. Hick towns seem to be the same the universe over. There was a main street called Main Street with clothing shops and restaurants, gambling houses, and more or less fancy saloons, a couple of vaudeville theaters, and dance halls. At the unfashionable end of Main Street were some farm implement shops, places to buy surveying instruments and geologic detectors and the building that housed the Interstellar News Service Frostbite Bureau. It was a couple of front rooms on the second floor, with a mechanical dentist below, an osteopath above, and a "ride-up-and-save" parka emporium to the rear.

Chenery let me in, and it was easy to see at once why Kennedy had died of pneumonia. Bottles. The air conditioning must have carried away every last sniff of liquor, but it still seemed to me that I could smell the rancid, home-brew stuff he'd been drinking. They were everywhere, the relics of a shameless, hopeless alcoholic who'd been good for nothing better than Frostbite. Sticky glasses and bottles everywhere told the story.

I slid open the hatch of the incinerator and started tossing down bottles and glasses from the copy desk, the morgue, the ethertype. Chenery helped, and decently kept his mouth shut. When we'd got the place kind of cleaned up I wanted to know what the daily routine was like.

Chenery shrugged. "Anything you make it, I guess. I used to push Kennedy to get more low-temperature agriculture stories for us. And those yaks that landed with you started as a civic-betterment stunt the *Phoenix* ran. It was all tractors until our farm editor had a brainstorm and brought in a pair. It's a hell of a good idea—you can't get milk, butter and meat out of a tractor. Kennedy helped us get advice from some Earthside agronomy station to set it up and helped get clearance for the first pair too. I don't have much idea of what copy he filed back to ISN. Frankly, we used him mostly as a contact man."

I asked miserably: "What the hell kind of copy *can* you file from a hole like this?" He laughed and cheerfully agreed that things were pretty slow.

"Here's today's *Phoenix*," he said, as the faxer began to hum. A neat, 16-page tabloid, stapled, pushed its way out in a couple of seconds. I flipped through it and asked: "No color at *all?*"

Chenery gave me a wink. "What the subscribers and advertisers don't know won't hurt them. Sometimes we break down and give them a page-one color pic."

I studied the *Phoenix*. Very conservative layout—naturally. It's competition that leads to circus makeup, and the *Phoenix* was the only sheet on the planet. The number-one story under a modest two-column head was an ISN farm piece on fertilizers for high-altitude agriculture, virtually unedited. The number-two story was an ISN piece on the current United Planets assembly.

"Is Frostbite in the UP, by the way?" I asked.

"No. It's the big political question here. The *Phoenix* is against applying. We figure the planet can't afford the assessment in the first place, and if it could there wouldn't be anything to gain by joining."

"Um." I studied the ISN piece closer and saw that the *Phoenix* was very much opposed indeed. The paper had doctored our story plenty. I hadn't seen the original, but ISN is—in fact and according to its charter—as impartial as it's humanly possible to be. But our story, as it emerged in the *Phoenix,* consisted of: a paragraph about an undignified, wrangling debate over the Mars-excavation question; a fistfight between a Titanian and an Earth delegate in a corridor; a Sirian's red-hot denunciation of the UP as a power-politics instrument of the old planets; and a report of UP administrative expenses—without a corresponding report of achievements.

"I suppose," I supposed, "that the majority of the planet is stringing along with the *Phoenix?*"

"Eight to one, the last time a plebiscite was run off," said Chenery proudly.

"You amaze me." I went on through the paper. It was about 70 percent ads, most of them from the Main Street stores we'd passed. The editorial page had an anti-UP cartoon showing the secretary-general of the UP as the greasy, affable conductor of a jetbus jammed to the roof with passengers. A sign on the bus said, "Fare, $15,000,000 and up per year." A road sign pointing in the direction the bus was heading said, "To Nowhere." The conductor was saying to a small, worried-looking man in a parka labeled "New Agricultural Planets" that, "There's always room for one more!!" The outline said: "But is there—and is it worth it?"

The top editorial was a glowing tribute from the *Phoenix* to the *Phoenix* for its pioneering work in yaks, pinned on the shipment that arrived today. The second editorial was anti-UP, echoing the cartoon and quoting from the Sirian in the page-one ISN piece.

It was a good, efficient job of the kind that turns a working newsman's stomach while he admires the technique.

"Well, what do you think of it?" asked Chenery proudly.

I was saved from answering by a *brrp* from the ethertype.

"GPM FRB GA PLS" it said. "Good afternoon, Frostbite Bureau—go ahead, please." What with? I hunted around and found a typed schedule on the wall that Kennedy had evidently once drawn up in a spasm of activity.

"MIN PLS" I punched out on the ethertype, and studied the sked.

It was quite a document.

WEEKDAYS

0900–1030: BREAKFAST
1030–1100: PHONE WEEMS FOR BITCHES RE SVS
1100–1200: NOTE MARSBUO RE BITCHES
1200–1330: LUNCH
1330–1530: RUN DROPS TO WEEMS: GAB WITH CHENERY
1530–1700: CLIP PHOENIX, REWRITE PUNCH & FILE

SUNDAYS

0900–1700: WRITE AND FILE ENTERPRISERS.

Chenery spared my blushes by looking out the window as I read the awful thing. I hadn't quite realized how low I'd sunk until then.

"Think it's funny?" I asked him—unfairly, I knew. He was being decent. It was decent of him not to spit in my eye and shove me off the sidewalk for that matter. I had hit bottom.

He didn't answer. He was embarrassed, and in the damn-fool way people have of finding a scapegoat I tried to make him feel worse. Maybe if I rubbed it in real hard he'd begin to feel almost as bad as I did. "I see," I told him, "that I've wasted a morning. Do you or Weems have any bitches for me to messenger-boy to Mars?"

"Nothing special," he said. "The way I said, we always like low-temperature and high-altitude agriculture stuff. And good farm-and-home material."

"You'll get it," I told him. "And now I see I'm behind in clipping and rewriting and filing stories from your paper."

"Don't take it so hard," he said unhappily. "It's not such a bad place. I'll have them take your personal stuff to the Hamilton House and the bureau stuff here. It's the only decent hotel in town except the *Phoenix* and that's kind of high—" He saw that I didn't like him jumping to such accurate conclusions about my pay check and beat it with an apologetic grimace of a smile.

The ethertype went *brrp* again and said, "GB FRB CU LTR" "Good-bye, Frostbite. See you later." There must have been many days when old Kennedy was too sick or too sick at heart to rewrite pieces from the lone client. Then the machine began beating out news items which I'd tear off eventually and run over to the *Phoenix*.

"Okay, sweetheart," I told the clattering printer. "You'll get copy from Frostbite. You'll get copy that'll make the whole damned ISN sit up and take notice—" and I went on kidding myself in that vein for a couple of minutes but it went dry very soon.

Good God, but they've got me! I thought. If I'm no good on the job they'll keep me here because there's nothing lower. And if I'm good on the job they'll keep me here because I'm good at it. Not a chance in a trillion to *do* anything that'll get noticed—just plain stuck on a crummy planet with a crummy political machine that'll never make news in a million years!

I yanked down Kennedy's library—"YOUR FUTURE ON FROSTBITE," which was a C. of C. recruiting pamphlet, "MANUAL OF ETHERTYPE MAINTENANCE AND REPAIR," an ISN house handbook, and "THE UNITED PLANETS ORGANIZATION SECRETARIAT COMMITTEE INTERIM REPORT ON HABIT-FORMING DRUGS IN INTERPLANETARY COMMERCE," a grey-backed UP monograph that got to Frostbite God knew how. Maybe Kennedy had planned to switch from home brew to something that would kill him quicker.

The Chamber of Commerce job gave a thumbnail sketch of my new home. Frostbite had been colonized about five generations ago for the usual reason. Somebody had smelled money. A trading company planted a power reactor—still going strong—at the South Pole in exchange for choice tracts of land which they'd sold off to homesteaders, all from Earth and Earth-colonized planets. In fine print the pamphlet gave lip service to the UP ideal of interspecific brotherhood, *but*— So Frostbite, in typical hick fashion, thought only genus homo was good enough for its sacred soil and that all non-human species were more or less alarming monsters.

I looked at that editorial-page cartoon in the *Phoenix* again and really noticed this time that there were Sirians, Venusians, Martians, Lyrans and other non-human beings jammed into the jetbus, and that they were made to look sinister.

On my first glance, I'd taken them in casually, the way you would on Earth or Mars or Vega's Quembrill, but here they were supposed to scare me stiff and I was supposed to go around saying, "Now, don't get me wrong, some of my best friends are Martians, *but*—"

Back to the pamphlet. The trading company suddenly dropped out of the chronology. By reading between the lines I could figure out that it was one of the outfits which had over-extended itself planting colonies so it could have a monopoly hauling to and from the new centers. A lot of them had gone smash when the Greenhough Effect took interstellar flight out of the exclusive hands of the supergiant corporations and put it in the reach of medium-sized operators like the rusty-bucket line that had hauled in me, the yaks and the tenpenny nails.

In a constitutional convention two generations back the colonists had set up a world government of the standard type, with a president, a unicameral house and a three-step hierarchy of courts. They'd adopted the United Planets model code of laws except for the bill of rights—to keep the slimy extra-terrestrials out—with no thanks to the UP.

And that was it, except for the paean of praise to the independent farmer, the backbone of his planet, beholden to no man, etc.

I pawed through the ethertype handbook. The introduction told me that the perfection of instantaneous transmission had opened the farthest planets to the Interstellar News Service, which I knew; that it was knitting the colonized universe together with bonds of understanding, which I doubted; and that it was a boon to all human and non-human intelligences, which I thought was a barefaced lie. The rest of it was "see Fig. 76 3b," "Wire 944 will slip easily through orifice 459j," "if Knob 545 still refuses to turn, take Wrench 31 and gently, without forcing—" Nothing I couldn't handle.

The ethertype was beating out:

> FARM—NOTE FROSTBITE
> NOME, ALASKA, EARTH—ISN—HOUSEWIVES OF THE
> COLDER FARM PLANETS WOULD DO WELL TO TAKE A LEAF
> FROM THE BOOK OF THE PRIMITIVE AMERINDIAN SEAM-
> STRESS. SO SAYS PROFESSOR OF DOMESTIC SCIENCE
> MADGE MCGUINESS OF THE UNIVERSITY OF NOME'S
> SCHOOL OF LOW-TEMPERATURE AGRONOMY. THE IN-
> DIAN MAID BY SEWING LONG, NARROW STRIPS OF FUR
> AND BASKETWEAVING THEM INTO A BLANKET TURNED
> OUT COVERINGS WITH TWICE THE WARMTH AND HALF
> THE WEIGHT OF FUR ROBES SIMPLY SEWED EDGE TO
> EDGE—

That was my darling, with her incurable weakness for quote leads and the unspeakable "so says." Ellie Masters, I thought, you're a lousy writer but I love you and I'd like to wring your neck for helping McGillicuddy con me into this. "Dig up all sorts of cute feature stories," you told me and you made it sound sensible. Better I should be under the table at Blogri's with a hangover and sawdust in my hair than writing little by-liners about seventeen tasty recipes for yak manure, which is all that's ever going to come out of this God-forsaken planet.

Rat-Face barged in without knocking; a moronic-looking boy was with him toting the box of ethertype spare parts.

"Just set it anywhere," I said. "Thanks for getting it right over here. Uh, Joe, isn't it?—Joe, where could I get me a parka like that? I like those lines. Real mink?"

It was the one way to his heart. "You betcha. Only plaid mink lining on Frostbite. Ya notice the lapels? Look!" He turned them forward and showed me useless little hidden pockets with zippers that looked like gold.

"I can see you're a man with taste."

"Yeah. Not like some of these bums. If a man's Collector of the Port he's got a position to live up to. Look, I hope ya didn't get me wrong there at the field. Nobody told me you were coming. If you're right with the *Phoenix*, you're right with the Organization. If you're right with the Organization, you're right with Joe Downing. I'm regular."

He said that last word the way a new bishop might say: "I am consecrated."

"Glad to hear that. Joe, when could I get a chance to meet some of the other regular Boys?"

"Ya wanna get In, huh?" he asked shrewdly. "There's been guys here a lot longer than you, Spencer."

"In, Out," I shrugged. "I want to play it smart. It won't do me any harm."

He barked with laughter. "Not a bit," he said. "Old man Kennedy didn't see it that way. You'll get along here. Keep ya nose clean and we'll see about The Boys." He beckoned the loutish porter and left me to my musings.

That little rat had killed his man, I thought—but where, why, and for whom?

I went out into the little corridor and walked into the "ride-up-and-save" parka emporium that shared the second floor with me. Leon Portwanger, said the sign on the door. He was a fat old man sitting cross-legged, peering through bulging shell-rimmed glasses at his needle as it flashed through fur.

"Mr. Portwanger? I'm the new ISN man, Sam Spencer."

"So?" he grunted, not looking up.

"I guess you knew Kennedy pretty well."

"Never. Never."

"But he was right in front there—"

"Never," grunted the old man. He stuck himself with the needle, swore, and put his finger in his mouth. "Now see what you made me do?" he said angrily and indistinctly around the finger. "You shouldn't bother me when I'm working. Can't you see when a man's working?"

"I'm sorry," I said, and went back into the newsroom. A man as old as Leon, tailoring as long as Leon, didn't stick himself. He didn't even wear a thimble—the forefinger was callused enough to be a thimble itself. He didn't stick himself unless he was very, very excited—or unless he wanted to get rid of somebody. I began to wish I hadn't fired those bottles of Kennedy's home brew down to the incinerator so quickly.

At that point I began a thorough shakedown of the bureau. I found memos torn from the machine concerning overfiling or failure to file, clippings from the *Phoenix,* laundry lists, style memos from ISN, paid bills, blacksheets of letters to Marsbuo requesting a transfer to practically anywhere but Frostbite, a list of phone numbers and a nasty space-mailed memo from McGillicuddy.

It said: "Re worldshaker, wll blv whn see. Meanwhile sggst keep closer sked avoid wastage costly wiretime. Reminder guppy's firstest job offhead orchidbitches three which bypassed u yestermonth. How? McG"

It was typical of McGillicuddy to memo in cablese. Since news bureaus began—as "wire services"; see his archaic "wiretime"—their executives have been memoing underlings in cablese as part of one-of-the-working-press-Jones-boys act that they affect. They also type badly so they can slash up their memo with copyreader symbols. This McGillicuddy did too, of course. The cablese, the bad typing, and the copyreading made it just about unintelligible to an outsider.

To me it said that McGillicuddy doubted Kennedy's promise to file a worldshaking story, that he was sore about Kennedy missing his scheduled times for filing on the ethertype, and that he was plenty sore about Kennedy failing to intercept complaints from the client *Phoenix,* three of which McGillicuddy had been bothered by during the last month.

So old Kennedy had dreamed of filing a worldshaker. I dug further into the bureau files and the desk drawers, finding only an out-of-date "WHO'S WHO IN THE GALAXY." No notes, no plans, no lists of interviewees, no tipsters—no blacksheet, I realized, of the letter to which McGillicuddy's cutting was a reply.

God only knew what it all meant. I was hungry, sleepy and sick at heart. I looked up the number of the Hamilton House and found that helpful little Chenery had got me a reservation and that my luggage had arrived from the field. I headed for a square meal and my first night in bed for a week without yaks blatting at me through a thin bulkhead.

It wasn't hard to fit in. Frostbite was a swell place to lose your ambition and acquire a permanent thirst. The sardonic sked posted on the bureau wall—I had been planning to tear it down for a month, but the inclination became weaker and weaker. It was so true to life.

I would wake up at the Hamilton House, have a skimpy breakfast and get down to the bureau. Then there'd be a phone conversation with Weems during which he'd nag me for more and better Frostbite-slant stories. In an hour of "wiretime" I'd check in with Marsbuo. At first I risked trying to sneak a chat with Ellie, but the jokers around Marsbuo cured me of that. One of them pretended he was Ellie on the other end of the wire and before I caught on had me believing that she was six months pregnant with a child by McGillicuddy and was going to kill herself for betraying me. Good clean fun, and after that I stuck to spacemail for my happy talk.

After lunch, at the Hamilton House or more often in a tavern, I'd tear up the copy from the printer into neat sheets and deliver them to the *Phoenix* building on the better end of Main Street. (If anything big had come up, I would have phoned them to hold the front page open. If not, local items filled it, and ISN copy padded out the rest of their sheet.) As in Kennedy's sked, I gabbed with Chenery or watched the compositors or proof pullers or transmittermen at work, and then went back to the office to clip my copy rolling out of the faxer. On a good day I'd get four or five items—maybe a human interester about a yak mothering an orphaned baby goat, a new wrinkle on barn insulation with native materials that the other cold-farming planets we served could use, a municipal election or a murder trial verdict to be filed just for the record.

Evenings I spent at a tavern talking and sopping up home brew, or at one of the two-a-day vaudeville houses, or at the Clubhouse. I once worked on the Philadelphia *Bulletin,* so the political setup was nothing new to me. After Joe Downing decided I wouldn't get pushy, he took me around to meet The Boys.

The Clubhouse was across the street from the three-story capitol building of Frostbite's World Government. It was a little bigger than the capitol and in much better repair. Officially it was the headquarters of the Frostbite Benevolent Society, a charitable, hence tax-free, organization. Actually it was the headquarters of the Frostbite Planetary Party, a standard gang of brigands. Down on the wrong end of Main Street somewhere was an upper room where the Frostbite Interplanetary Party, made up of liberals, screwballs, and disgruntled ex-members of the Organization but actually run by stooges of that Organization, hung out.

The Boys observed an orderly rotation of officers based on seniority. If you got in at the age of 18, didn't bolt and didn't drop dead you'd be president some day. To the party you had to bring loyalty, hard work—not on your payroll job, naturally, but on your electioneering—and cash. You kept bringing cash all your life; salary kickbacks, graft kickbacks, contributions for gold dinner services, tickets to testimonial banquets, campaign chest assignments, widows' and orphans' fund contributions, burial insurance, and dues, dues, dues.

As usual, it was hard to learn who was who. The President of Frostbite was a simple-minded old boy named Witherspoon, so far gone in senile decay that he had come to believe the testimonial-banquet platitudes he uttered. You could check him off as a wheelhorse. He was serving the second and last year of his second and last term, and there was a mild battle going on between his Vice-President and the Speaker of the House as to who would succeed him. It was a traditional battle and didn't mean much; whoever lost would be next in line. When one of the contestants was so old or ill that he might not live to claim his term if he lost, the scrap would be waived in a spirit of good sportsmanship that the voters would probably admire if they ever heard of it.

Joe Downing was a comer. His sponsorship of me meant more than the friendship of Witherspoon would have. He was Chenery's ally; they were the leadership of the younger, sportier element. Chenery's boss Weems was with the older crowd that ate more, talked more, and drank less.

I had to join a committee before I heard of George, though. That's the way those things work.

It was a special committee for organizing a testimonial banquet for Witherspoon on his 40th year in the party. I wound up in the subcommittee to determine a testimonial gift for the old buffer. I knew damned well that we'd be expected to start the subscription for the gift rolling, so I suggested a handsome—and inexpensive—illuminated scroll with a sentiment lettered on it. The others were scandalized. One fat old woman called me "cheap" and a fat male payroller came close to accusing me of irregularity, at which I was supposed to tremble and withdraw my suggestion. I stood on my rights, and wrote a minority report standing up for the scroll while the majority of the subcommittee agreed on an inscribed sterling tea service.

At the next full committee meeting we delivered our reports and I thought it would come to a vote right away. But it seemed they weren't used to there being two opinions about anything. They were flustered, and the secretary slipped out with both reports during a five-minute adjournment. He came back and told me, beaming, "Chenery says George liked your idea." The committee was reconvened and because George liked my idea my report was adopted and I was appointed a subcommittee of one to procure the scroll.

I didn't learn any more about George after the meeting except that some people who liked me were glad I'd been favorably noticed and others were envious about the triumph of the Johnny-come-lately.

I asked Chenery in the bar. He laughed at my ignorance and said, "George *Parsons.*"

"Publisher of the *Phoenix?* I thought he was an absentee owner."

"He doesn't spend a lot of time on Frostbite. At least I don't think he does. As a matter of fact, I don't know a lot about his comings and goings. Maybe Weems does."

"He swings a lot of weight in the Organization."

Chenery looked puzzled. "I guess he does at that. Every once in a while he does speak up and you generally do what he says. It's the paper, I suppose. He could wreck any of the boys." Chenery wasn't being irregular: newsmen are always in a special position.

I went back to the office and, late as it was, sent a note to the desk to get the one-man subcommittee job cleaned up:

> ATTN MCGILLICUDDY RE CLIENT RELATIONS NEED SOONEST ILLUMINATED SCROLL PRESENT HOMER WITHERSPOON PRESIDENT FROSTBITE HONORING HIM 40 YEARS MEMBERSHIP FROSTBITE PLANETARY PARTY USUAL SENTIMENTS NOTE MUST BE TERRESTRIAL STYLE ART IF NOT ACTUAL WORK EARTHER ACCOUNT ANTIBEM PREJUDICE HERE FRBBUO END.

That happened on one of those Sundays which, according to Kennedy's sardonic sked, was to be devoted to writing and filing enterprisers.

The scroll came through with a memo from McGillicuddy: "Fyi ckng w/ clnt etif this gag wll hv ur hide. Reminder guppy's firstest job offheading orchidbitches one which bypassed u yesterweek. How? McG"

There was a sadly sweet letter from Ellie aboard the same rust-bucket. She wanted me to come back to her, but not a broken man. She wanted me to do something really big on Frostbite to show what I had in me. She was sure that if I really looked there'd be something more to file than the copy I'd been sending in. Yeah.

Well, the big news that week would be the arrival of a loaded immigrant ship from Thetis of Procyon, a planet whose ecology had been wrecked beyond repair in a few short generations by DDT, hydraulic mining, unrestricted logging, introduction of rabbits and house cats and the use of poison bait to kill varmints. In a few thousand years maybe the planet would have topsoil, cover crops, forests, and a balanced animal population again, but Thetis as of now was a ruin whose population was streaming away to whatever havens it could find.

Frostbite had agreed to take 500 couples provided they were of terrestrial descent and could pass a means test—that is, provided they had money to be fleeced of. They were arriving on a bottom called *Esmeralda*. According to my year-old "LLOYDS' SHIPPING INDEX"—"exclusive accurate and up-to-date, being the result of daily advices from every part of the galaxy"—*Esmeralda* was owned by the Frimstedt Atomic Astrogation Company, Gammadion, gross tonnage 830,000, net tonnage 800,000, class GX—"freighter/steerage passengers"—insurance rating: hull A, atomics A. The tonnage difference meant real room for only about 850. If she took the full 1,000 she'd be jammed. She was due to arrive at Frostbite in the very early morning. Normally I would have kept a deathwatch, but the AA rating lulled me and I went to the Hamilton House to sleep.

At 4:30, the bedside phone chimed. "This Willie Egan," a frightened voice said. "You remember—on the desk at the *Phoenix*." Desk, hell—he was a 17-year-old copyboy I'd tipped to alert me on any hot breaks.

"There's some kind of trouble with the *Esmeralda*," he said. "That big immigrant ship. They had a welcoming committee out, but the ship's overdue. I thought there might be a story in it. You got my home address? You better send the check there. Mr. Weems doesn't like us to do string work. How much do I get?"

"Depends," I said, waking up abruptly. "Thanks, kid." I was into my clothes and down the street in five minutes. It looked good; mighty good.

The ship was overcrowded, the AA insurance rating I had was a year old—maybe it had gone to pot since then and we'd have a major disaster on our hands.

I snapped on the newsroom lights and grabbed the desk phone, knocked down one toggle on the key box and demanded: "Space operator! Space Operator!"

"Yes, sir. Let me have your call, please?"

"Gimme the bridge of the *Esmeralda* due to dock at the Frostbite spaceport today. While you're setting up the call gimme interplanetary and break in when you get the *Esmeralda*."

"Yes, sir." Click-click-click.

"Interplanetary operator."

"Gimme Planet Gammadion. Person-to-person, to the public relations officer of the Frimstedt Atomic Astrogation Company. No, I don't know his name. No, I *don't* know the Gammadion routing. While you're setting up the call gimme the local operator and break in when you get my party."

"Yes, sir." Click-click-click.

"Your call, please."

"Person-to-person, captain of the spaceport."

"Yes, sir."

Click-click-click. "Here is *Esmeralda,* sir."

"Who's calling?" yelled a voice. "This is the purser's office, who's calling?"

"Interstellar News, Frostbite Bureau. What's up about the ship being late?"

"I can't talk now! Oh, my God! I can't talk now! They're going crazy in the steerage—" He hung up and I swore a little.

"Space operator!" I yelled. "Get me *Esmeralda* again—if you can't get the bridge get the radio shack, the captain's cabin, anything inboard!"

"Yes, sir."

Click-click-click. "Here is your party, sir."

"Captain of the port's office," said the phone.

"This is Interstellar News. What's up about *Esmeralda?* I just talked to the purser in space and there's some trouble aboard."

"I don't know anything more about it than you boys," said the captain of the port. But his voice didn't sound right.

"How about those safety-standard stories?" I fired into the dark.

"That's a tomfool rumor!" he exploded. "Her atomics are perfectly safe!"

"Still," I told him, fishing, "it *was* an engineer's report—"

"Eh? What was? I don't know what you're talking about." He realized he'd been had. "Other ships have been an hour late before and there are always rumors about shipping. That's absolutely all I have to say—absolutely all!" He hung up.

Click-click-click. "Interplanetary operator. I am trying to place your call, sir." She must be too excited to plug in the right hole on her switchboard. A Frostbite Gammadion call probably cost more than her annual salary, and it was a gamble at that on the feeble and mysteriously erratic subradiation that carried voices across segments of the galaxy.

But there came a faint harumph from the phone. "This is Captain Gulbransen. Who is calling, please?"

I yelled into the phone respectfully: "Captain Gulbransen, this is Interstellar News Service on Frostbite." I knew the way conservative shipping companies have of putting ancient, irritable astrogators into public-relations berths after they are ripe to retire from space. "I was wondering, sir," I shouted, "if you'd care to comment on the fact that *Esmeralda* is overdue at Frostbite with 1,000 immigrants."

"Young man," wheezed Gulbransen dimly, "it is clearly stated in our tariffs filed with the ICC that all times of arrival are to be read as plus or minus eight Terrestrial Hours, and that the company assumes no liability in such cases as—"

"Excuse me, sir, but I'm aware that the eight-hour leeway is traditional. But isn't it a fact that the average voyage hits the E.T.A. plus or minus only fifteen minutes T. H.?"

"That's so, but—"

"Please excuse me once more, sir—I'd like to ask just one more question. There is, of course, no reason for alarm in the lateness of *Esmeralda,* but wouldn't you consider a ship as much as one hour overdue possibly in danger? And wouldn't the situation be rather alarming?"

"Well, one full hour, perhaps you would. Yes, I suppose so—but the eight-hour leeway, you understand—" I laid the phone down quietly on the desk and ripped through the *Phoenix* for yesterday. In the business section it said "Esmeralda due 0330." And the big clock on the wall said 0458.

I hung up the phone and sprinted for the ethertype, with the successive stories clear in my head, ready to be punched and fired off to Marsbuo for relay on the galactic trunk. I would beat out 15 clanging bells on the printer and follow them with

> INTERSTELLAR FLASH
> IMMIGRANT SHIP ESMERALDA SCHEDULED TO LAND
> FROSTBITE WITH 1,000 FROM THETIS PROCYON ONE AND
> ONE HALF HOURS OVERDUE: OWNER ADMITS SITUATION
> "ALARMING," CRAFT "IN DANGER."

And immediately after that a five-bell bulletin:

> INTERSTELLAR BULLETIN
> FROSTBITE—THE IMMIGRANT SHIP ESMERALDA, DUE
> TODAY AT FROSTBITE FROM THETIS PROCYON WITH 1,000
> STEERAGE PASSENGERS ABOARD IS ONE AND ONE HALF
> HOURS OVERDUE. A SPOKESMAN FOR THE OWNERS, THE
> FRIMSTEDT ATOMIC ASTROGATION COMPANY, SAID
> SUCH A SITUATION IS "ALARMING" AND THAT THE CRAFT
> MIGHT BE CONSIDERED "IN DANGER." ESMERALDA IS AN
> 830 THOUSAND-TON FREIGHTER-STEERAGE PASSENGER
> CARRIER.
>
> THE CAPTAIN OF THE PORT AT FROSTBITE ADMITTED
> THAT THERE HAVE BEEN RUMORS CIRCULATING ABOUT
> THE CONDITION OF THE CRAFT'S ATOMICS THOUGH
> THESE WERE RATED "A" ONE YEAR AGO.
>
> THE PURSER OF THE SPACESHIP, CONTACTED IN SPACE,
> WAS AGITATED AND INCOHERENT WHEN QUESTIONED.
> HE SAID—

"Get up, Spencer, get away from the machine."

It was Joe Downing, with a gun in his hand.

"I've got a story to file," I said blankly.

"Some other time." He stepped closer to the ethertype and let out a satisfied grunt when he saw the paper was clean. "Port captain called me," he said. "Told me you were nosing around."

"Will you get out of here?" I asked, stupefied. "Man, I've flash and bulletin matter to clear. Let me alone!"

"I said to get away from that machine or I'll cut ya down, boy."

"But why? *Why?*"

"George don't want any big stories out of Frostbite."

"You're crazy. Mr. Parsons is a newsman himself. Put that damn-fool gun away and let me get this out!"

I turned to the printer when a new voice said, "No! Don't do it, Mr. Spencer. He is a Nietzschean. He'll kill you, all right."

It was Leon Portwanger, the furrier, my neighbor, the man who claimed he never knew Kennedy. His fat, sagging face, his drooping white mustache, his sad black eyes enormous behind the bull's-eye spectacles were very matter-of-fact. He meant what he said. I got up and backed away from the ethertype.

"I don't understand it," I told them.

"You don't have to understand it," said the rat-faced collector of the port. "All you have to understand is that George don't like it." He fired one bullet through the printer and I let out a yelp. I'd felt that bullet going right through me.

"Don't," the steady voice of the furrier cautioned. I hadn't realized that I was walking toward Downing and that his gun was now on my middle. I stopped.

"That's better," said Downing. He kicked the phone connection box off the baseboard, wires snapping and trailing. "Now go to the Hamilton House and stay there for a couple of days."

I couldn't get it my head. "But *Esmeralda's* a cinch to blow up," I told him. "It'll be a major space disaster. *Half of them are women!* I've got to get it out!"

"I'll take him back to his hotel, Mr. Downing," said Portwanger. He took my arm in his flabby old hand and let me out while that beautiful flash and bulletin and the first lead disaster and the new lead disaster went running through my head to a futile obbligato of: "They can't *do* this to me!" But they did it.

Somebody gave me a drink at the hotel and I got sick and a couple of bellboys helped me to bed. The next thing I knew I was feeling very clear-headed and wakeful and Chenery was hovering over me looking worried.

"You've been out cold for forty-eight hours," he said. "You had a high fever, chills, the works. What happened to you and Downing?"

"How's *Esmeralda?*" I demanded.

"Huh? Exploded about half a million miles off. The atomics went."

"Did anybody get it to ISN for me?"

"Couldn't. Interplanetary phones are out again. You seem to have got the last clear call through to Gammadion. And you put a bullet through your ethertype—"

"*I* did? Like hell—Downing did!"

"Oh? Well, that makes better sense. The fact is, Downing's dead. He went crazy with that gun of his and Chief Selig shot him. But old Portwanger said you broke the ethertype when you got the gun away from Downing for a minute—no, that doesn't make sense. What's the old guy up to?"

"I don't give a damn. You see my pants anywhere? I want to get that printer fixed."

He helped me dress. I was a little weak on my pins and he insisted on pouring expensive eggnog into me before he'd let me go to the bureau.

Downing hadn't done much of a job, or maybe you can't do much of a job on an ethertype without running it through an induction furnace. Everything comes apart, everything's replaceable. With a lot of thumbing through the handbook I had all the busted bits and pieces out and new ones in. The adjustment was harder, needing two pairs of eyes. Chenery watched the meters while I turned the screws. In about four hours I was ready to call. I punched out:

NOTE MARSBUO ISN, FRBBUO RESTORED TO SVC AFTER
MECHNCL TRBL ETILLNESS.

The machine spat back:

NOTE FRBBUO. HW ILLNSS COINCDE WITH MJR DISSTR
YR TRRTRY? FYI GAMMADION BUO ISN OUTRCHD FR
ESMERALDA AFTER YR INXPLCBL SLNCE ETWS BDLY BTN
GAMMADION BUOS COMPTSHN. MCG END.

He didn't want to hear any more about it. I could see him stalking away from the printer to the copydesk slot to chew his way viciously through wordage for the major splits. I wished I could see in my mind's eye Ellie slipping over to the Krueger 60-B circuit sending printer and punching out a word or two of kindness—the machine stirred again. It said: "JOE JOE HOW COULD YOU? ELLIE"

Oh, God.

"Leave me alone, will you?" I asked Chenery.

"Sure—sure. Anything you say," he humored me, and slipped out.

I sat for a while at the desk, noticing that the smashed phone connection had been installed again, that the place had been policed up.

Leon Portwanger came waddling in with a bottle in his hand. "I have here some prune brandy," he said.

Things began to clear up. "*You* gave me that mickey," I said slowly. "And you've been lying about me. You said I wrecked the ethertype."

"You are a determinist and I was trying to save your life," he said, setting down two glasses and filling them. "Take your choice and I will have the other. No mickeys." I picked one and gulped it down—nasty, too-sweet stuff that tasted like plum peelings. He sipped his and seemed to enjoy it.

"I thought," he said, "that you were in with their gang. What *was* I to think? They got rid of poor Kennedy. Pneumonia! You too would have pneumonia if they drenched you with water and put you on the roof in your underwear overnight. The bottles were planted here. He used to drink a little with me, he used to get drunk now and then—so did I—nothing bad."

"You thought I was in their gang," I said. "What gang are you in?"

"The Frostbite Interplanetary Party," he said wryly. "I would smile with you if the joke were not on me. I know, I know—we are Outs who want to be Ins, we are neurotic youngsters, we are led by stooges of the Planetary Party. So what should I do—start a one-man party alone on a mountaintop, so pure that I must blackball everybody except myself from membership? I am an incorrigible reformer and idealist whether I like it or not—and sometimes, I assure you, I don't like it very well.

"Kennedy was no reformer and idealist. He was a pragmatist, a good man who wanted a good news story that would incidentally blow the present administration up. He used me, I used him. He got his story and they killed him and burglarized the bureau to remove all traces of it. Or did they?"

"I don't know," I muttered. "Why did you dope me? Did Downing really go crazy?"

"I poisoned you a little because Downing did *not* go crazy. Downing was under orders to keep you from sending out that story. Probably after he had got you away from the ethertype he would have killed you if I had not poisoned you with some of my heart medicine. They realized while you were ill and feverish that it might as well be one as another. If they killed you, there would only be another newsman sent out to be inveigled into their gang. If they killed Downing, they could blame everything on him, you would never be able to have anything more than suspicions, and—there are a lot more Downings available, are there not?"

My brain began to click. "So your mysterious 'they' didn't want a top-drawer story to center around Frostbite. If it did, there'd be follow-ups, more reporters, ICC people investigating the explosion. Since the news break came from Gammadion, that's where the reporters would head and that's where the ICC investigation would be based. But what have they got to hide? The political setup here smells to high heaven, but it's no worse than on fifty other planets. Graft, liquor, vice, drugs, gambling—"

"No drugs," said the furrier.

"That's silly," I told him. "Of course they have drugs. With everything else, why not drugs?"

He shrugged apologetically. "Excuse me," he said. "I told you I was a reformer and an idealist. I did not mention that I used to be an occasional user of narcotics. A little something to take the pressure off—those very small morphine sulphate tablets. You can imagine my horror when I emigrated to this planet twenty-eight years ago and found that there were no drugs—literally. Believe me when I tell you that I—*looked hard. Now,* of course, I am grateful. But I had a few very difficult weeks." He shuddered, finished his prune brandy and filled both our glasses again.

He tossed down his glass.

"Damn it all!" he exploded. "Must I rub your nose in it? Are you going to figure it out for yourself? And are you going to get killed like my poor friend, Kennedy? Look here! And here!" He lurched to his feet and yanked down "WHO'S WHO IN THE GALAXY" and the United Planets Drug Committee Report.

His pudgy finger pointed to:

"PARSONS, George Warmerdam, organic chemist, newsppr pubr, b. Gammadion 172, s. Henry and Dolores (Warmerdam) P., studied Gammadion Chem. Inst. B.Ch 191, M.Ch 193, D.Ch 194; empl. dir research Hawley Mfg Co. (Gammadion) 194–198; founded Parsons Chem Mfg Labs (Gammadion) 198, headed same 198–203; removed Frostbite 203; founded newspaper Frostbite *Phoenix* 203. Author, tech papers organ chem 193–196. Mem Univ Organ Chem Soc. Address c/o Frostbite *Phoenix,* Frostbite."

And in the other book:

"—particular difficulty encountered with the stupefiant known as 'J-K-B.' It was first reported on Gammadion in the year 197, when a few isolated cases presented themselves for medical treatment. The problem rapidly worsened through the year 203, by which time the drug was in widespread illicit interplanetary commerce. The years 203–204 saw a cutting-off of the supply of J-K-B for reasons unknown. Prices soared to fantastic levels, unnumbered robberies and murders were committed by addicts to obtain possession of the minute quantities remaining on the market, and other addicts, by the hundreds of thousands presented themselves to the authorities hoping more or less in vain for a 'cure.' J-K-B appeared again in the year 205, not confined to any segment of the inhabited galaxy. Supplies have since remained at a constant level—enough to brutalize, torment, and shorten the lives of the several score million terrestrial and extra-terrestrial beings who have come into its grip. Interrogation of peddlers intercepted with J-K-B has so far only led back through a seemingly endless of chain of middlemen. The nature of the drug is such that it cannot be analyzed and synthesized— "

My head spun over the damning parallel trails. Where Parsons tried his wings in chemistry, J-K-B appeared. When he went on his own, the quantity increased. When he moved to another planet, the supply was cut off. When he was established, the supply grew to a constant level and stayed there.

And what could be sweeter than a thoroughly corrupt planet to take over with his money and his newspaper? Dominate a machine and the members' "regularity" will lead them to kill for you—or to kill killers if need be. Encourage planetary ignorance and isolationism; keep the planet unattractive and depressed by letting your freebooters run wild—that'll discourage intelligent immigration. Let token parties in, fleece them fast and close, let them spread the word that Frostbite's no place for anybody with brains.

"A reformer and idealist I am," said Portwanger calmly. "Not a man of action. What should be done next?"

I thought it over and told him: "If it kills me, and it might, I am going to send a rash of flashes and bulletins from this Godforsaken planet. My love life depends on it. Leon, do you know anybody on Mars?"

"A Sirian fellow named Wenjtkpli—a philosophical anarchist. An unreal position to take. This is the world we are in, there are certain social leverages to apply. Who is he to say—?"

I held up my hand. "I know him too." I could taste that eleventh stinger again; by comparison the prune brandy was mellow. I took a gulp. "Do you think you could go to Mars without getting bumped off?"

"A man could try."

The next two weeks were agonizing. Those Assyrian commissars or Russian belshazzars or whatever they were who walked down prison corridors waiting to be shot in the back of the head never went through what I did. I walked down the corridor for fourteen days.

First Leon got off all right on a bucket of bolts. I had no guarantee that he wouldn't be plugged by a crew member who was in on the party. Then there was a period of waiting for the first note that I'd swap you for a mad tarantula.

It came:

> NOTE FRBBUO HOW HELL XPCT KP CLNT IF UNABL DROP
> COPY? MCG MARSBUO.

I'd paved the way for that one by drinking myself into a hangover on home brew and lying in bed and groaning when I should have been delivering the printer copy to the *Phoenix*. I'd been insulting as possible to Weems to insure that he'd phone a squawk to McGillicuddy—I hoped. The tipoff was "hell." Profanity was never, ever used on our circuits—I hoped. "Hell" meant "Portwanger contacted me, I got the story, I am notifying United Planets Patrol in utmost secrecy."

Two days later came:

> NOTE FRBBUO BD CHMN WNTS KNO WHT KIND DAMN
> KNUCKLHED FILING ONLY FOURFIVE ITMS DAILY FM
> XPNSVE ONEMAN BUO. XPCT UPSTEP PRDCTN IMMY, RPT
> IMMY MCG MARSBUO.

"Damn" meant "Patrol contacted, preparing to raid Frostbite." "Fourfive" meant "fourfive"—days from message.

The next note would have got ISN in trouble with the Interplanetary Communications Commission if it hadn't been in a good cause. I'm unable to quote it. But it came as I was in the bureau about to leave for the Honorable Homer Witherspoon's testimonial banquet. I locked the door, took off my parka and rolled up my sleeves. I was going to sweat for the next few hours.

When I heard the multiple roar of the Patrol ships on rockets I very calmly beat out fifteen bells and sent:

> INTERSTELLAR FLASH
> UNITED PLANETS PATROL DESCENDING ON FROSTBITE,
> KRUEGER 60-B'S ONLY PLANET, IN UNPRECEDENTED MASS
> RAID ON TIP OF INTERSTELLAR NEWS SERVICE THAT
> WORLD IS SOLE SOURCE OF DEADLY DRUG J-K-B.

> INTERSTELLAR BULLETIN
> THE MASSED PATROL OF THE UNITED PLANETS ORGANI-
> ZATION DESCENDED ON THE ONLY PLANET OF KRUEGER
> 60-B, FROSTBITE, IN AN UNPRECEDENTED MASS RAID THIS
> EVENING. ON INFORMATION FURNISHED BY INTERSTEL-
> LAR NEWS REPORTER JOE SPENCER THE PATROL HOPES
> TO WIPE OUT THE SOURCE OF THE DEADLY DRUG J-K-B,
> WHICH HAS PLAGUED THE GALAXY FOR 20 YEARS. THE

CHEMICAL GENIUS SUSPECTED OF INVENTING AND PRO-DUCING THE DRUG IS GEORGE PARSONS, RESPECTED PUBLISHER OF FROSTBITE'S ONLY NEWSPAPER.

INTERSTELLAR FLASH
FIRST UNITED PLANETS PATROL SHIP LANDS IN FROST-BITE CAPITAL CITY OF PLANET.

INTERSTELLAR FLASH
PATROL COMMANDER PHONES EXCLUSIVE INTERVIEW TO INTERSTELLAR NEWS SERVICE FROSTBITE BUREAU RE-PORTING ROUND-UP OF PLANETARY GOVERNMENT LEADERS AT TESTIMONIAL DINNER

(WITH FROSTBITE)
FROSTBITE—ISN—ONE INTERSTELLAR NEWS REPORTER HAS ALREADY GIVEN HIS LIFE IN THE CAMPAIGN TO EX-POSE THE MAKER OF J-K-B. ED KENNEDY, ISN BUREAU CHIEF, WAS ASSASSINATED BY AGENTS OF DRUGMAKER GEORGE PARSONS THREE MONTHS AGO. AGENTS OF PAR-SONS STRIPPED KENNEDY AND EXPOSED HIM OVER-NIGHT TO THE BITTER COLD OF THIS PLANET, CAUSING HIS DEATH BY PNEUMONIA. A SECOND INTERSTELLAR NEWS SERVICE REPORTER, JOE SPENCER, NARROWLY ES-CAPED DEATH AT THE HANDS OF A DRUG-RING MEMBER WHO SOUGHT TO PREVENT HIM FROM SENDING NEWS OVER THE CIRCUITS OF THE INTERSTELLAR NEWS SER-VICE.

INTERSTELLAR FLASH
PATROL SEIZES PARSONS

INTERSTELLAR BULLETIN
FROSTBITE—IN A TELEPHONE MESSAGE TO INTERSTEL-LAR NEWS SERVICE A PATROL SPOKESMAN SAID GEORGE PARSONS HAD BEEN TAKEN INTO CUSTODY AND UNMIS-TAKABLY IDENTIFIED. PARSONS HAD BEEN LIVING A LIE ON FROSTBITE, USING THE NAME CHENERY AND THE GUISE OF A COLUMNIST FOR PARSONS' NEWSPAPER. SAID THE PATROL SPOKESMAN—"IT IS A TYPICAL MANEUVER. WE NEVER GOT SO FAR ALONG THE CHAIN OF J-K-B PED-DLERS THAT WE NEVER FOUND ONE MORE. APPARENTLY THE SOURCE OF THE DRUG HIMSELF THOUGHT HE COULD PUT HIMSELF OUT OF THE REACH OF INTERPLAN-ETARY JUSTICE BY ASSUMING A FICTITIOUS PERSONALITY. HOWEVER, WE HAVE ABSOLUTELY IDENTIFIED HIM AND EXPECT A CONFESSION WITHIN THE HOUR. PARSONS APPEARS TO BE A J-K-B ADDICT HIMSELF.

INTERSTELLAR FLASH
PARSONS CONFESSES

(FIRST LEAD BY FROSTBITE)

FROSTBITE—ISN—THE UNITED PLANETS PATROL AND
THE INTERSTELLAR NEWS SERVICE JOINED HANDS TODAY
IN TRIUMPH AFTER WIPING OUT THE MOST VICIOUS
NEST OF DRUGMAKERS IN THE GALAXY. J-K-B, THE INFA-
MOUS NARCOTIC WHICH HAS MENACED—

I ground out nearly thirty thousand words of copy that night. Bleary-eyed at the end of the run, I could barely read a note that came across:

NOTE FRBBUO: WELL DONE. RETURN MARS IMMY: SNDNG
REPLCEMNT. MARSBUO MCG.

The Patrol flagship took me back in a quick, smooth trip with lots of service and no yaks.

After a smooth landing I took an eastbound chair from the field and whistled as the floater lifted me to the ISN floor. The newsroom was quiet for a change and the boys and girls stood up for me.

McGillicuddy stepped out from the copy table slot to say: "Welcome back. Frankly, I didn't think you had it in you, but you proved me wrong. You're a credit to the profession and the ISN." Portwanger was there, too. "A pragmatist, your McGillicuddy," he muttered. "But you did a good job."

I didn't pay very much attention; my eyes were roving over no man's land. Finally I asked McGillicuddy: "Where's Miss Masters? Day off?"

"How do you like that?" laughed McGillicuddy. "I forgot to tell you. She's your replacement on Frostbite. Fired her off yesterday. I thought the woman's angle—where do you think *you're* going?"

"Honest Blogri's Olde Earthe Saloon," I told him with dignity. "If you want me, I'll be under the third table from the left as you come in. With sawdust in my hair."

[*Fantastic Universe* - October/December 1953]

Everybody Knows Joe

Joe had quite a day for himself Thursday and as usual I had to tag along. If I had a right arm to give, I'd give it for a day off now and then. Like on Thursday. On Thursday he really outdid himself.

He woke up in the hotel room and had a shower. He wasn't going to shave until I told him he looked like a bum. So he shaved and then he stood for a whole minute admiring his beauty in the mirror, forgetting whose idea it was in the first place.

So down to the coffee shop for breakfast. A hard-working man needs a good breakfast. So getting ready for a back-breaking day of copying references at the library, he had tomato juice, two fried eggs, three sausages, a sugared doughnut and coffee—with cream and sugar.

He couldn't work that off his pot in a week of ditch-digging under a July sun, but a hard-working man needs a good breakfast. I was too disgusted to argue with him. He's hopeless when he smells that short-order smell of smoking grease, frying bacon and coffee.

He wanted to take a taxi to the library—eight blocks!

"Walk, you jerk!" I told him. He started to mumble about pulling down six hundred bucks for this week's work and then he must have thought I was going to mention the high-calorie breakfast. To him that's hitting below the belt. He thinks he's an unfortunate man with an affliction—about twenty pounds of it. He walked and arrived at the library glowing with virtue.

Making out his slip at the newspaper room he blandly put down next to *firm—The Griffin Press, Inc.*—when he knew as well as I did that he was a free lance and hadn't even got a definite assignment from Griffin.

There's a line on the slip where you put down *reason for consulting files (please be specific)*. It's a shame to cramp Joe's style to just one line after you pitch him an essay-type question like that. He squeezed in, *Preparation of article on year in biochemistry for Griffin Pr. Encyc. 1952 Yrbk.,* and handed it with a flourish to the librarian.

The librarian, a nice old man, was polite to him, which is usually a mistake with Joe. After he finished telling the librarian how his microfilm files ought to be organized and how they ought to switch from microfilm to microcard and how in spite of everything the New York Public Library wasn't such a bad place to research, he got down to work.

He's pretty harmless when he's working—it's one of the things that keeps me from cutting his throat. With a noon break for apple pie and coffee he transcribed about a hundred entries onto his cards, mopping up the year in biochemistry nicely. He swaggered down the library steps, feeling like Herman Melville after finishing *Moby Dick*.

"Don't be so smug," I told him. "You still have to write the piece. And they still have to buy it."

"A detail," he said grandly. "Just journalism. I can do it with my eyes shut."

Just journalism. Somehow his three months of running copy for the A.P. before the war has made him an Ed Leahy.

"*When* are you going to do it with your eyes … ?" I began but it wasn't any use. He began telling me about how Gautama Buddha didn't break with the world until he was 29 and Mohammed didn't announce that he was a prophet until he was 30, so why couldn't *he* one of these days suddenly bust loose with a new revelation or something and set the world on its ear? What it boiled down to was he didn't think he'd write the article tonight.

He postponed his break with the world long enough to have a ham and cheese on rye and more coffee at an automat and then phoned Maggie. She was available as usual. She said as usual, "Well then, why don't you just drop by and we'll spend a quiet evening with some records?"

As usual he thought that would be fine since he was so beat after a hard day. As usual I told him, "You're a louse, Joe. You know all she wants is a husband and you know it isn't going to be you, so why don't you let go of the girl so she can find somebody who means business?"

The usual answers rolled out automatically and we got that out of the way.

Maybe Maggie isn't very bright but she seemed glad to see him. She's shooting for her doctorate in sociology at N.Y.U., she does part-time case work for the city, she has one of those three-room Greenwich Village apartments with dyed burlap drapes and studio couches and home-made mobiles. She thinks writing is something holy and Joe's careful not to tell her different.

They drank some Rhine wine and seltzer while Joe talked about the day's work as though he'd won the Nobel prize for biochemistry. He got downright brutal about Maggie being mixed up in such an approximate unquantitative excuse for a science as sociology and she apologized humbly and eventually he forgave her. Big-hearted Joe.

But he wasn't so fried that he *had* to start talking about a man wanting to settle down—"not this year but maybe next. Thirty's a dividing point that makes you stop and wonder what you really want and what you've really got out of life, Maggie darlin'." It was as good as telling her that she should be a good girl and continue to keep open house for him and maybe some day … maybe.

As I said, maybe Maggie isn't very bright. But as I also said, Thursday was the day Joe picked to outdo himself.

"Joe," she said with this look on her face, "I got a new LP of the Brahms Serenade Number One. It's on top of the stack. Would you tell me what you think of it?"

So he put it on and they sat sipping Rhine wine and seltzer and he turned it over and they sat sipping Rhine wine and seltzer until both sides were played. And she kept watching him. Not adoringly.

"Well," she asked with this new look, "what did you think of it?"

He told her, of course. There was some comment on Brahms' architectonics and his resurrection of the contrapuntal style. Because he'd sneaked a look at the record's envelope he was able to spend a couple of minutes on Brahms' debt to Haydn and the young Beethoven in the fifth movement (*allegro*, D Major) and the gay *rondo* of the—

"Joe," she said, not looking at him. "Joe," she said, "I got that record at one hell of a discount down the street. It's a wrong pressing. Somehow the first side is the first half of the Serenade but the second half is Schumann's Symphonic Studies Opus Thirteen. Somebody noticed it when they played it in a booth. But I guess you didn't notice it."

"Get out of *this one,* braino," I told him.

He got up and said in a strangled voice, "And I thought you were my friend. I suppose I'll never learn." He walked out.

I suppose he never will.

God help me, I ought to know.

[*Star Science Fiction Stories No. 2* - 1954]

The Remorseful

It does not matter when it happened. This is because he was alone and time had ceased to have any meaning for him. At first he had searched the rubble for other survivors, which kept him busy for a couple of years. Then he wandered across the continent in great, vague quarterings, but the plane one day would not take off and he knew he would never find anybody anyway. He was by then in his forties, and a kind of sexual delirium overcame him. He searched out and pored over pictures of women, preferring leggy, high-breasted types. They haunted his dreams; he masturbated incessantly with closed eyes, tears leaking from them and running down his filthy bearded face. One day that phase ended for no reason and he took up his wanderings again, on foot. North in the summer, south in the winter on weed-grown U.S. 1, with the haversack of pork and beans on his shoulders, usually talking as he trudged, sometimes singing.

It does not matter when it happened. This is because the Visitors were eternal; endless time stretched before them and behind, which mentions only two of the infinities of infinities that their "lives" included. Precisely when they arrived at a particular planetary system was to them the most trivial of irrelevancies. Eternity was theirs; eventually they would have arrived at all of them.

They had won eternity in the only practical way: by outnumbering it. Each of the Visitors was a billion lives as you are a billion lives—the billion lives, that is, of your cells. But your cells have made the mistake of specializing. Some of them can only contract and relax. Some can only strain urea from your blood. Some can only load, carry and unload oxygen. Some can only transmit minute electrical pulses and others can only manufacture chemicals in a desperate attempt to keep the impossible Rube Goldberg mechanism that you are from breaking down. They never succeed and you always do. Perhaps before you break down some of your specialized cells unite with somebody else's specialized cells and grow into another impossible, doomed contraption.

The Visitors were more sensibly arranged. Their billion lives were not cells but small, unspecialized, insect-like creatures linked by an electromagnetic field subtler than the coarse grapplings that hold you together. Each of the billion creatures that made up a Visitor could live and carry tiny weights, could manipulate tiny power tools, could carry in its small round black head enough brain cells to feed, mate, breed and work—and a few million more brain cells that were pooled into the field which made up the Visitor's consciousness.

When one of the insects died there were no rites; it was matter-of-factly pulled to pieces and eaten by its neighboring insects while it was still fresh. It mattered no more to the Visitor than the growing of your hair does to you, and the growing of your hair is accomplished only by the deaths of countless cells.

"Maybe on Mars!" he shouted as he trudged. The haversack jolted a shoulder blade and he arranged a strap without breaking his stride. Birds screamed and scattered in the dark pine forests as he roared at them: "Well, why not? There must of been ten thousand up there easy. Progress, God damn it! That's *progress*, man! Never thought it'd come in my time. But you'd think they would of sent a ship back by now so a man wouldn't feel so all alone. You know better than that, man. You know God damned good and well it happened up there too. We had Northern Semisphere, they had Southern Semisphere, so you know God damned good and well what happened up there. Semisphere? Hemisphere. Hemi-semi-demisphere."

That was a good one, the best one he'd come across in years. He roared it out as he went stumping along.

When he got tired of it he roared: "You should of been in the *Old* Old Army, man. We didn't go in for this Liberty Unlimited crock in the *Old* Old Army. If you wanted to march in step with somebody else you *marched* in step with somebody else, man. None of this crock about you march out of step or twenty lashes from the sergeant for limiting your liberty."

That was a good one too, but it made him a little uneasy. He tried to remember whether he had been in the army or had just heard about it. He realized in time that a storm was blowing up from his depths; unless he headed it off he would soon be sprawled on the broken concrete of U.S. 1, sobbing and beating his head with his fists. He went back hastily to *Sem*-isphere, *Hem*-isphere, *Hem-i-sem-i-dem*-isphere, roaring it at the scared birds as he trudged.

There were four Visitors aboard the ship when it entered the planetary system. One of them was left on a cold outer planet rich in metal outcrops to establish itself in a billion tiny shelters, build a billion tiny forges, and eventually—in a thousand years or a million; it made no difference—construct a space ship, fission into two or more Visitors for company, and go Visiting. The ship had been getting crowded; as more and more information was acquired in its voyaging it was necessary for the swarms to increase in size, breeding more insects to store the new facts.

The three remaining Visitors turned the prow of their ship toward an intermediate planet and made a brief, baffling stop there. It was uninhabited except for about ten thousand entities—far fewer than one would expect, and certainly not enough for an efficient first-contact study. The Visitors made for the next planet sunward after only the sketchiest observation. And yet that sketchy observation of the entities left them figuratively shaking their heads. Since the Visitors had no genitals they were in a sense without emotions—but you would have said a vague air of annoyance hung over the ship nevertheless.

They ruminated the odd facts that the entities had levitated, appeared at the distance of observation to be insubstantial, appeared at the distance of observation to be unaware of the Visitors. When you are a hundred-yard rippling black carpet moving across a strange land, when the dwellers in this land soar aimlessly about you and above you, you expect to surprise, perhaps to frighten at first, and at least to provoke curiosity. You do not expect to be ignored.

They reserved judgment pending analysis of the sunward planet's entities— possibly colonizing entities, which would explain the sparseness of the outer planet's population, though not its indifference.

They landed.

He woke and drank water from a roadside ditch. There had been a time when water was *the* problem. You put three drops of iodine in a canteen. Or you boiled it if you weren't too weak from dysentery. Or you scooped it from the tank of a flush toilet in the isolated farmhouse with the farmer and his wife and their kids downstairs grotesquely staring with their empty eye sockets at the television screen for the long-ago-spoken latest word. Disease or dust or shattering supersonics broadcast from the bullhorn of a low-skimming drone—what did it matter? Safe water was what mattered.

"But hell," he roared, "it's all good now. Hear that? The rain in the ditches, the standing water in the pools, it's all good now. You should have been Lonely Man back when the going was bad, fella, when the bullhorns still came over and the stiffs shook when they did and Lonely Man didn't die but he wished he could ..."

This time the storm took him unaware and was long in passing. His hands were ragged from flailing the broken concrete and his eyes were so swollen with weeping that he could hardly see to shoulder his sack of cans. He stumbled often that morning. Once he fell and opened an old scar on his forehead, but not even that interrupted his steady, mumbling chant: "'Tain't no boner, 'tain't no blooper; Corey's Gin brings super stupor. We shall conquer; we will win. Back our boys with Corey's Gin. Wasting time in war is sinful; black out fast with a Corey skinful."

They landed.

Five thousand insects of each "life" heaved on fifteen thousand wires to open the port and let down the landing ramp. While they heaved a few hundred felt the pangs of death on them. They communicated the minute all-they-knew to blank-minded standby youngsters, died, and were eaten. Other hundreds stopped heaving briefly, gave birth, and resumed heaving.

The three Visitors swarmed down the ramp, three living black carpets. For maximum visibility they arranged themselves in three thin black lines which advanced slowly over the rugged terrain. At the tip of each line a few of the insects occasionally strayed too far from their connecting files and dropped out of the "life" field. These staggered in purposeless circles. Some blundered back into the field; some did not and died, leaving a minute hiatus in the "life's" memory—perhaps the shape of the full-stop symbol in the written language of a planet long ago visited, long ago dust. Normally the thin line was not used for exploring any but the smoothest terrain; the fact that they took a small calculated risk was a measure of the Visitors' slightly irked curiosity.

With three billion faceted eyes the Visitors saw immediately that this was no semi-deserted world, and that furthermore it was probably the world which had colonized the puzzling outer planet. Entities were everywhere; the air was thick with them in some places. There were numerous artifacts, all in ruins. Here the entities of the planet clustered, but here the bafflement deepened. The artifacts were all decidedly material and ponderous—but the entities were insubstantial. Coarsely organized observers would not have perceived them consistently. They existed in a field similar to the organization field of the Visitors. Their bodies were constructs of wave trains rather than atoms. It was impossible to imagine them manipulating the materials of which the artifacts were composed.

And as before, the Visitors were ignored.

Deliberately they clustered themselves in three huge black balls, with the object of being as obstreperous as possible and also to mobilize their field strength for a brute-force attempt at communication with the annoying creatures. By this time their attitude approximated: "We'll show these bastards!"

They didn't—not after running up and down every spectrum of thought in which they could project. Their attempt at reception was more successful, and completely horrifying. A few weak, attenuated messages did come through to the Visitors. They revealed the entities of the planet to be dull, whimpering cravens, whining evasively, bleating with self-pity. Though there were only two sexes among them, a situation which leads normally to a rather weak sex drive as such things go in the cosmos, these wispy things vibrated with libido which it was quite impossible for them to discharge.

The Visitors, thoroughly repelled, were rippling back toward their ship when one signaled: *notice and hide.*

The three great black carpets abruptly vanished— that is, each insect found itself a cranny to disappear into, a pebble or leaf to be on the other side of. Some hope flared that the visit might be productive of a more pleasant contact than the last with those aimless, chittering cretins.

The thing stumping across the terrain toward them was like and unlike the wave-train cretins. It had their conformation but was material rather than undulatory in nature—a puzzle that could wait. It appeared to have no contact with the wave-train life form. They soared and darted about it as it approached, but it ignored them. It passed once through a group of three who happened to be on the ground in its way.

Tentatively the three Visitors reached out into its mind. The thoughts were comparatively clear and steady.

When the figure had passed the Visitors chorused: *Agreed,* and headed back to their ship. There was nothing there for them. Among other things they had drawn from the figure's mind was the location of a ruined library; a feeble-minded working party of a million was dispatched to it.

Back at the ship they waited, unhappily ruminating the creature's foreground thoughts: "From Corey's Gin you get the charge to tote that bale and lift that barge. That's progress, God damn it. You know better than that, man. Liberty Unlimited for the Lonely Man, but it be nice to see that Mars ship land ..."

Agreement: *Despite all previous experience it seems that a sentient race is capable of destroying itself.*

When the feeble-minded library detail returned and gratefully reunited itself with its parent "lives" they studied the magnetic tapes it had brought, reading them direct in the cans. They learned the name of the planet and the technical name for the wave-train entities which had inherited it and which would shortly be its sole proprietors. The solid life forms, it seemed, had not been totally unaware of them, though there was some confusion: Far the vaster section of the library denied that they existed at all. But in the cellular minds of the Visitors there could be no doubt that the creatures described in a neglected few of the library's lesser works were the ones they had encountered. Everything tallied. Their non-material quality; their curious reaction to light. And, above all, their dominant personality trait, of remorse, repentance, furious regret. The technical term that the books gave to them was: ghosts.

The Visitors worked ship, knowing that the taste of this world and its colony would soon be out of what passed for their collective mouths, rinsed clean by new experiences and better-organized entities.

But they had never left a solar system so gratefully or so fast.

[*SF Quarterly* - Winter 1941/1942
as by S. D. Gottesman]

Sir Mallory's Magnitude

1
After Armageddon

There was a lusty scream from the visitors' gallery. The lights of the hall flickered for a moment; guards drew and fired at shadows on the wall or at each other. Panic threatened; the restless roar of a great crowd rose to a jabbering sound like monkey-talk. In the great gallery and on the vast floor a few dimwits began to dash for exits.

"Rot them," growled Senator Beekman. He shoved the mike at Ballister. "Shut them up," he snapped. "Use your precious psychology!"

Young Ballister took the mike, snapped on the button, dialed for heaviest amplification. "Atten-shun!" he barked into it, with the genuine parade-ground note of command.

The monkey-talk stopped for a priceless moment. Ballister jumped into it with both feet. Soothingly he said: "Now, folks, what's your hurry? Stick around—these learned gentlemen put on a pretty good show for your benefit."

The learned gentlemen who were dashing for exits purpled; the visitors in the gallery laughed loud and long at the feeble little joke. They resumed their seats.

"Take it, Senator," snapped Ballister in an undertone. "I'll scamper for a gander at the fuss up there." He hopped nimbly from the platform into an elevator, which shot him up to the gallery. Displaying his Representative's badge, he broke through the cordon of International Police that was zealously guarding an ordinary seat, like any other of the five thousand in sight.

"What was it?" he demanded of a French provost. "Killing?"

The provost shrugged. "We do not know vat, m'sieu. On-lee we know that in that seat sat M'sieu the mayor of Bruxelles."

"Hi," snapped a crisp young voice at Ballister.

He removed his horn-rims to regard the young lady disapprovingly. "Beat it, Kay," he ordered. "This isn't for the papers. Another unpleasant international incident. The Mayor of Brussels."

The young man looked down at the stage, very small and far away. From the speakers in the walls came the voice of Senator Beekman, hoarse and embarrassed:

"Our agenda will be incomplete today, gentlemen and ladies. I have been advised of the—the non-attendance of Monsieur Durtal, Mayor of Brussels and major sponsor of the bill entitled: 'An Act to Prevent Competitive Development of Instruments of Warfare.' We will proceed to—"

The Anti-War Conference had been in full swing for two months. There was nothing slow or inefficient about the great congress of all the nations; the tremendous task before them took time, lots of it. The Grand Agenda of the Conference covered a space of three years, and all busy ones.

Ballister knew something about the Second World War; he had spent a couple of years in command of an infantry company at the tail-end of the mighty conflict. Then, when it was settled, and the sick-and-tired Axis armies and peoples had revolted and overthrown their war-lords, he had naturally gone to the Conference as an American delegate. Training as specialized as his—psychological jurisprudence—was in demand.

He thought he had seen everything, world-weary at twenty-three, but the Conference offered a few new kicks. There was something ludicrous about a Japanese delegate trying to wangle a few more square miles of Korea for his nation. Ballister was usually the trouble-shooter who explained to the simple people how their demands would encroach on so-and-so's rights, which would lead to such-and-such a consequence, which would be bad for the world in general for this-and-that reasons.

It was a plan magnificent in scope. The vast Auditorium of Oslo was jammed with the delegates and specialists; the gallery was jammed day and night with visitors—anybody who wanted to see. There was to be no diplomacy under the table in the world the Conference was making! Twenty years of war had shown the fallacy of secret treaties; the delegates desperately hoped that their three years of co-operative common sense would blast the old diplomatic nonsense from the face of the Earth.

Ballister had his troubles, not the least of these being Kay Marsh, of the *New York Enquirer*. Any other reporter he could handle; not Kay, for she had majored with him at Columbia in the same psych courses and knew him like a book. She knew then, in the gallery, that this wasn't the time for comedy.

"Did you know him?" she asked.

"Met him twice," said Ballister despondently, regarding the empty chair. "A real humanitarian, man of the people. Not one of these professionals. And he's the third to go."

"Pelterie from Switzerland, Vanderhoek from South Africa, now Durtal of Belgium," she listed somberly. "Who's doing it?"

"If I knew I'd tell you," said Ballister. "Hell! Let us be gay! Have you got the handouts for the day's work?"

"I filed my copy already," she said. "Macklin's covering this business. He's going to do a series of articles on it. You're off?"

"Through for the week. Let's flit."

"Sounds like an insect," she complained. "But if you wish."

They elbowed their way through the crowd, out of the Auditorium. Oslo was *en fête*, with its face washed and its hair brushed for the distinguished visitors. Its population had swelled by a half-million since it was chosen as the Conference site. Festively decked helicopters and 'gyros dragged advertising signs through the sky in all languages. One battered little blimp towed the notice in French: "Attend the Produce Show! April 11!"

Kay pointed at it with a smile. "Did I ever tell you I was a farmer's daughter?" she remarked.

Ballister recognized the lead. "All right," he said. "I'll take you. But I guarantee you'll be bored silly; they probably won't even speak the international language."

"Cows and hay don't have to speak any language," she sparkled happily. "I haven't seen a decent steer since Nebraska."

They got wind of the Produce Show and followed the smell to a neat collection of tents, where Kay delightedly inspected timothy and cheeses and champion milkers for two hours while Ballister tried to hold his breath for that length of time.

"Hold it," he snapped as she was going into a gush at a draft-horse who stared sullenly at her hat. "Gent's fainted."

They elbowed their way through the crowd, to find that the gentleman was nearly foaming at the mouth, twitching convulsively on the ground. The only serious attention being paid him was by a barker from a nearby tent, who loudly offered three to one that the gentleman would die in less than half an hour.

"Throat constricted or something," said Kay after a swift examination. "Looks like a super-violent allergy."

Ballister went through his pockets, found a box of amyl nitrite pearls. He broke one under the man's nose, drawing it away as he came to.

"You, there," he snapped, waving up a couple of husky farmers. "Carry him away from this damned show of yours. There's something in the air that nearly killed him."

The peasants, grinning happily, lugged the man to the nearest taxi stand. Ballister ordered the hackie to drive to the center of town, where monoxide would most likely replace the pollen or whatever it was that had strangled him.

The man was unable to talk for a few miles, though he insisted, despite the soothing words of Miss Marsh, on pantomiming gratitude. He was a fine-looking gentleman, ruddy-faced, middle-aged or over, exquisitely dressed.

Finally, with one tremendous cough, he cleared his throat. "Thanks awf'ly," he exclaimed. "Those dim-head hunks would've let me perish on the spot!"

"What got you going?" asked Ballister. "Pollen from the hay?"

"Nothing so dashed ordin'ry. Would you believe it? It was mice that nearly did me in. They could get me in about sixty seconds."

"Why not?" replied Ballister. He thought to introduce himself, adding his official capacity at the Conference.

"Splendid," muttered the gentleman. "Psychological jurisprudence and all that, I mean! I'm Gaffney, by the way. Sir Mallory. Baronet."

Kay sat up like a shot; in the next two minutes she had asked him thirty questions and was primed for fifty more. Sir Mallory Gaffney was news—big news—hot news! He was said to be the man who had invented the springing system that made the revolutionary Enfield Armored Wagon a practical and terrible weapon. He was the man behind the gas-cooled tank motor. Likewise the synthesis of rubber from chalk and carbon dioxide, and any number of other departures. And he had never been interviewed before!

Ballister pointedly interrupted the questioning with: "Didn't know you were at the Conference, Sir Mallory. Any official capacity, or just visiting?"

"Just ordered over, Mr. Ballister. They want my more-or-less expert testimony on this Durtal Bill."

"Durtal died or vanished without a trace this morning," said Kay. "Have you done anything in the invisibility line, Sir Mallory?"

The baronet laughed indulgently. "Hardly. You Americans had invisible battleships back in 1941, I hear. Learned the trick from some illusionist chap—Dunnings, or Kuss—one of them. But the mirrors lost their silvering in the seaspray. That's as far as military invisibility's gone, I believe."

Ballister coughed warningly at the girl. "We'd better be getting back to the hotel," he said in overloud tones. "Sir Mallory's had a nasty shock." He filled in the rest of the trip with diplomatic small talk, avoiding the controversial subjects dear to the reportorial heart of Kay.

2
Conspiracy

At the Hotel de Universe et d'Oslo they were all in for a nasty shock. The manager dashed to them as they emerged from the cab, and collared Sir Mallory and Ballister.

"Thank God for both of you!" he cried hysterically. "That this should happen *chez moi*—it is *incroyable,* the horrible truly that we face—I ruin and you despair!"

"Yeah," said Ballister skeptically. It was a little thick, believing that the hardheaded manager of a great international hotel could be shaken by anything that could happen in the way of bad luck. "Yeah. Explain yourself."

"The senator American—Beekman, he is vanished from his room."

A committee head hailed them from across the lobby and came over, looking grave. "He isn't kidding, Ballister. Beekman's flitted completely, like Durtal and the others. Right in the middle of a caucus on the Competition Act. Went out to—er, went out for a moment and never came back."

"My seempathie, monsignors," said a burly, black-haired man. "I have heard of the so-gre-ait loss of thee Amairicain delegation."

"Thanks, Rasonho," said the committee head abstractedly. "Maybe he'll turn up."

"Lait us hope so. Thee passage of thee Competition Act means vair-ree much to my people." As he walked off Ballister studied the man. There was something familiar about him, something damned strange to boot. He inquired of the committee man.

"Rasonho? He's from the Pyrenese Peoples' Republic. Their only delegate. Good sort, but somewhat thick. He doesn't understand the parliamentary method."

"And what may the Pyrenese Peoples' Republic be?"

"I did an article on them," said Kay. "No wonder you missed them, because they popped up while you were at the front. They're a sort of Basque federation —not more than ten thousand of them, I'm sure. Yet they held DeCuerva's army when he was coming north through the Pyrenees to relieve Milhaud. By heaven, they held him for three months! It's gone unsung for the most part, but I call it the most remarkable feat of the war."

"No doubt," said Ballister abstractedly. "And then, after the Initial Treaty they organized under a simple native President, thinking they had won independence from France and Spain both?"

"That's right. The Conference recognizes them—even invited the delegate."

A bomb exploded in the lobby of the hotel; the high ceiling swayed right and left. Screams echoed through the great hall; emergency exits opened onto the street automatically.

"This is intolerable!" fumed Sir Mallory when they had gained cover. "Someone—some party is trying to destroy the Conference. They're trying to kill every damned one of us—or have us disappear bit by bit!"

"Sure," said Ballister. He wound a handkerchief around his wrist; flying plaster had clipped a bit of his flesh away. "What do you suggest, sir?"

"Armed guards, Mr. Ballister! We must fight this menace as it is trying to fight us! We must post men in every corridor—shoot suspicious persons on sight!"

"By heaven, yes!" snapped Kay. "They're trying to wreck the Anti-War Conference, and I won't have it. This is mankind's chance for peace at last, a final peace that will endure a hundred thousand years. Any dog who'd try to stand in the way of that, try to plunge the world back into the nightmare of war after war, deserves no mercy!"

Ballister looked somewhat sick; the corners of his mouth drooped peculiarly, as though he tasted something unpleasant. Finally he looked square into the eyes of the girl and said without conviction: "Yes. Fight them tooth and nail. The best thing to do."

The next day at the Conference Auditorium a half-dozen delegates proposed a Defense Act, claiming general privilege to take precedence over other business. After a few hearty seconding speeches which pointed out the danger in which they all stood, there were read the concrete proposals.

The Conference disbanded the International Police, which had been their protective force, as ineffectual. There was organized on the spot an armed force to patrol all Oslo and vicinity, whose right of search was unquestionable, who were able to arrest on suspicion and defer trial indefinitely. The entire Act was passed, a few members abstaining, none voting the negative.

Ballister reported sick to Senator Beekman's successor. He said that the strain of the work had broken him down, that he needed a few months' rest. And indeed he was a pitiable sight—haggard, unkempt, eyes dilated, rambling again and again from his subject. The committee head insisted that he take a vacation.

Once outside the Auditorium, the change in Ballister was nearly magical. He slicked back his hair, straightened like a ramrod and generally became his old dynamic self.

At the flying field he took up his 'gyro. He took it 'way up, twenty thousand feet and more. Then he headed southeast across the continent. Somewhere over Germany he realized that he was being followed. There were no less than two 'gyros on his tail, neither of them official.

Like his own craft they were converted warplanes, which, after the fighting had ceased, sold for a dime a dozen. Unlike his own, they carried no markings or national insignia.

Damning his thoughtlessness he set the controls for a straight course and went back to the tail compartment for arms. He found Kay curled up on a crate, blinking in the sudden light.

"Sweet," he snapped. "I'll bawl you out for this later. Right now there are two mean-looking rigs on our tail. Can you steer an eccentric course while I handle whatever guns there may be?"

"If there's two," she said, "we'd better both handle guns. You set her for flat loops at ceiling speed. I have a scattergun that throws its weight."

"Right," said Ballister. He stepped up the speed of the ship to its very top, and then jiggled twenty miles-per-hour more out of the exhaust turbines. He set the controls for a circle, tight and fast. As the setting took and the ship swung he braced himself hard against the wall.

The centrifugal force was enormous; all loose fixtures smacked against the outside wall; he couldn't lift them off without a crowbar. Kay was battling the inertia, dragging herself along the outside wall into the storage compartment again. After a bit of heavy-handed rummaging she let out a scream of delight.

"Oh boy!" she gloated. "Look!" Painfully she hauled out and displayed a wire net, the kind used for quick repairs of the nacelle. "Get it?"

"I get it," said Ballister, a slow grin spreading over his face. "Let's hope they don't get us first." The two ships had hauled up nearly alongside and were angling off to the attack. They fired a few tentative bursts at Ballister's 'gyro, presumably to judge the quality of his reply.

Ballister didn't reply. It would have been practically impossible to handle a gun against the drag of the whirling ship. But he did unsnap the top hatch, ducking back as the hinges tore loose and the square of metal flew up and out.

"Take it," said Kay. "I can't handle this thing alone." He eased his way along the wall, skirting the open hatch. Getting two big handfuls of the repair net, he dragged it behind him, snagging a corner on a rivet. Kay spread the net on her side while Ballister made ready on his own.

"When I say the word," the girl ordered, "cast off." She squinted against the sun, hunting for the two planes. With a whoop and a holler they came out of the dazzle firing at the midriff of the 'gyro.

"Right," she said calmly, unsnagging the net and chucking it through the hatch simultaneously with Ballister's machine-like gestures. It spread beautifully in flight, came at the lead plane two square yards of metal moving at high speed.

The plane tried to shoot it out of the sky first, then tried to dodge. The metal netting slammed dead into the prop, splintering and wrecking as it passed on, balled up, into the stabilizer-vane.

The second plane pulled up sharply, fired a parting burst at the 'gyro and cold-bloodedly bombed the crippled and falling companion. There was nothing left but a few drifting fragments by the time Ballister had pulled out of the flat circles.

"Now why did he do that?" wondered Kay.

"It wasn't a mercy-shot by any means," said Ballister. "They have their secrets, whoever they are. Put that in your notebook: they don't let themselves be taken alive."

"Sinister people," said Kay with a small shudder. "They tend to distress me."

3
Progress

They were ready to fire on the ship that overtook them above the south of France, but Kay held back Ballister's hand.

"I'm blowed," she declared, "if I've ever seen a ship as big and fancy as that one with a single-passenger rating on its side. Probably some rich coot who wants to talk to us."

It was a magnificent ship—big, enormously roomy, considering that its regulation number registered it as a single-seater. It had one of the biggest and latest engines, capable of five hundred and upwards, was amphibian, had auxiliary parachute packs and all the trimmings of a luxury liner.

Ballister tuned in on his wave. "Stop crowding me," he snapped. "There's lots of air for you."

A familiar voice came back: "Sorry, old man. I didn't want to contact you until I was sure it was you. This is Gaffney speaking, by the by." There was a good-humored chuckle.

"Oh—Sir Mallory!" exclaimed Ballister, aghast. "Sorry I barked at you. How come you're following me—if you are?"

"I am, right enough. Don't worry—I feel like a vacation, same as you. And—" a sinister note of strain crept into the baronet's voice—"I know when my life's in danger. There've been no less than three attacks on me before I decided to light out. Used this old crate—gift from the grateful Royal Academy and all that—to follow you; you left a decently marked trail over Europe. One—ah—one presumes you're heading for the Pyrenese Peoples' Republic?"

"Exactly. I won't hobble your ship, Sir Mallory. You go on ahead and I'll taxi in. It ought to be a few minutes ahead. Have they got a landing field?"

"The best. I was talking with that delegate chap of theirs—Rasonho—tells me that once the traditionally anarchistic Basques got together they've worked miracles in a dozen years. Mountains rich in ores—loan from Germany—got smelters and all."

Ballister looked down and saw the landing field he had been promised. It was a honey; hard-surfaced, triple-tracked, on a small scale perhaps the best in Europe.

"Set it down, Sir Mallory. I'll follow." The big plane landed with mechanical ease; Ballister cross-winded and touched Mother Earth again. He emerged with Kay to shake hands with the nobleman.

"Charmed to see you here!" exclaimed Sir Mallory. "But—?" He left the question unanswered.

Sternly Ballister explained: "This young lady, with the romantic misconceptions common to the gentlemen and ladies of the press assumed that I was going off on a secret mission for the Conference. Naturally she could think of no simpler way to spy on me than to stow away in the tail of my 'gyro."

"And a lucky thing for him that I did," snapped Kay. She explained the dodge, the attack, and the happy ending. The baronet was fascinated and enraged.

"Who could it be?" he exploded. "Russia? Germany? Britain?"

"Dunno," said Ballister. "Whoever it is has lots on the ball—and a couple of blind spots."

Mechanics, burly, tall fellows, drove out to their planes in a sort of motorbike. "Speak English?" asked one, after sizing them up.

"Rather well," answered the nobleman with a grin. "We're by way of being unofficial delegates of goodwill from the Anti-War Conference at Oslo. Whom do you suggest we see?"

"Mayor—Pedro Marquesch. We attend to planes—drive you into city. We are honored."

They stowed the planes into solidly built hangars, then loaded the visitors into the back of a big, new-style car. "Autos," the mechanic explained, "were import from Germany. We use not many—twenty among us, perhaps."

The car sped along a neat, narrow highway chiseled from the living rock of the Pyrenees. Their mechanic, with a sort of stolid pride in his people, pointed out the waterworks, the gasworks and a couple of outlying factories. With a smile at Sir Mallory he explained: "All smells to leeward of city. Not like London."

"After the Conference, my friend," said the noble, in a good humor, "we'll strive to overstrip your very high degree of civilization."

The car was pulled up to a halt. The driver pointed proudly: "Hydroelectric dam. Big power output. No smell. Two years old."

Ballister stared at the work. It wasn't as big as Dnieperstroy had been, but in its own way it was a work of genius, plain to see. Every block of concrete seemed to have a peculiar rightness about it; the solitary blockhouse that surmounted the turbine house seemed somehow to be perfectly situated.

"Masterly," said Ballister. Kay nodded soberly. The man smiled a little as he drove on.

Suddenly they were in the city. It wasn't centralized and there were no skyscrapers; one skyscraper, indeed, could have held the entire population of the Pyrenese Peoples' Republic. But there were clearly defined sections. The residential city was a series of houses of ample size, in the Basque tradition of sturdy construction, each with its acres of lawn automatically sprinkled and presumably cut. The factory district was tree-shaded and sprawling; though there were no more than a dozen buildings.

The driver pointed out the business, administrative and scientific area, the tallest buildings in the city. They were symbolically white and severe, tall and thin like ascetic monks.

They were dropped at a hotel-like affair of three stories.

"Completely automatic," said their driver. "No pay—guests of the state. We have a few of them. This was for German and French tradesmen."

Wondering, they went in. There were clean, spare accommodations; signs in French advised them that they could eat at such-and-such a place at certain hours.

Sir Mallory excused himself, with a regretful, though humorous, confession that he was aging out of all proportion.

"Well?" asked the girl, inspecting their communal sitting-room.

"Uncanny," said Ballister. "Damned if I know whether I should be delighted or annoyed. I'm both. There's something so awfully queer going on that I shudder to think of it. Little over a dozen years ago these Basques were an anarchistic lot, living family lives.

"Lord! In those twelve years they've completely transferred their allegiance from the family to the state, obviously gone in for heavy cooperation—remember that dam—built a model city, and, it seems, done away with crime. It's impossible. It's against all reason."

"You must be terribly afraid of progress," said Kay thoughtfully.

"No," said Ballister. "Not development. Not normal evolution. That's growth. But this lunatic speed is more like a cancer than normal social achievement. I think—I'm sure!—there's something behind this slew of nonconformities."

"And," exploded Kay, her temper snapping like a rubber band, "I'm dead certain that this is a milestone in the history of man—and that this Pyrenese Peoples' Republic is destined to be one of the great powers of the world!" She slammed into her room.

"Good night!" yelled Ballister after her.

He slept that night to dream of cancerous proliferations spreading their sickly-white fingers over the map of Europe, then snaking across the ocean and plunging a dagger into the heart of the Western Hemisphere.

Kay couldn't stay mad, no more than could Ballister. They apologized sweetly to each other at breakfast under the paternal eyes of Sir Mallory, then set out for the Mayor's office. People on the streets, big men and solid, tall women stopped to stare at them for a moment before hurrying on to the day's work. The mayor was the Basque type, but bald as an egg. His grin was slow and agreeable; he had a firm handshake.

"You like our small country?" he asked.

"We admire it enormously," hedged Ballister. "I was commenting last night on your excessively rapid growth." He shot a malicious glance at Kay.

"Indeed? We explain that, you know, with the theory that the Basque spirit has been in its infancy for many centuries and is now at last growing up. That you may tell the outside world—but not too much of it. We should not wish to become an attraction for tourists. It is our opinion that there is work to be done, that we Basques are well-suited to do it. You would be amazed at the spirit of collaboration that exists among us."

"I already am," said Ballister. "Your city is the finest example of communal activity I have ever seen." There was something flat and deadly in his tone which even he could not explain.

They had been spending a marvelously restful five days in the Republic, not bothering to think. Alone for a couple of moments Kay abstractedly confessed: "Isn't it remarkable that even the great Sir Mallory Gaffney, Baronet, can be a hell of a bore after some period of unmitigated companionship?"

"His conversation sparkles," said Ballister noncommittally. "It scintillates like the morning sun on dewdrops. He's a generous and a kindly old gentleman. He's wise and good and noble—but I tend to agree with you; I'm sick of the sight of him. Sir Mallory tends to inhibit intellection. I haven't been able to buckle down to a problem in the last few days without his kindly interrupting and helping out with horribly confusing results."

"You've noticed that?" she asked, with wide-open eyes. "Is he just trying to help us relax?"

"Dunno. He has a technique—I'm working with something in social growth, say. He interrupts. I expound. He ponders, then throws in so damned many elements that I don't know what to make of it. He may be right! He's near the genius level, I know. But I believe in tackling one problem at a time. He, obviously, doesn't."

"Or," suggested the girl, "pretends he doesn't."

They dummied up as Sir Mallory reentered. He sensed the tension and then went through a curious process of winking, snickering slightly and balancing on one foot.

Kay and Ballister exchanged glances. Sir Mallory grinned happily. "Aha!" he said.

Ballister caught on. "Well, dear," he said, "shall we go for a ride?" The glance he gave the girl was saccharine refined with an eye for sweetness. It was so paralyzingly mushy that Kay reeled beneath the wealth of sloppy sentiment. She studied for one wild moment the silly smile on his face—then caught on.

"Anything you say, sweetness," she cooed.

They twined arms then, and after another sloppy pair of looks ambled out. Sir Mallory called after them with huge delight:

"Be good, children!" His chuckle followed them down the rustic lane they chose. Out of sight and earshot they untwined and sat heavily on a bench.

"Explain all that," she said. "What was in the air?"

"Lo-o-ove," said Ballister, polishing his horn-rims. "Not the kind that means anything, the kind that mates people for life and after. But the kind of puppy-love that you can hardly call an emotion, it's so animal and unreasoning. I refer to the sort of stuff that every middle-aged man has a soft spot in his head for. Further, he reasoned correctly—on incorrect premises—that we'd be incapable of comparing notes on him and this hellish place if we were otherwise occupied. His error."

"Hellish?" asked Kay. "That's strong."

"Agreed. Do you recall the exact population of this place?"

"What's that got to do with it?"

"Never mind just yet. It's 7,776. Half male and half female. Note that it's a perfect number, divisible by the whole slew of integers, a perfect radical, it evolves into an integral root—"

"Sure!" she exploded. "I see! So they're—they're—" Kay paused, baffled.

"I know how you feel." Ballister smiled sympathetically. "There's something stuck away in the back of one's head that's just a little distance beyond explanation, just a little too deeply buried for unearthing. What is it? Damned if I can tell you, but it's very important." He laughed sardonically.

"The baronet comes," said Kay. Ballister embraced her violently; she nearly bit a hunk out of his ear.

"Excuse me," said the noble kindly. "The mayor—Marquesch—suggested that we inspect the landing field. He wants to know if we can offer any suggestions for improving traffic-flow. Thinks that there's going to be lots of commerce on that hunk of soil."

"May well be," said Kay, dropping her eyes with maidenly modesty. "These wonderful people of the Republic! How do they do it?"

"Cooperation," said Ballister, straightening his tie. "They work as one man. That's the secret." He went into a brown study, trailing behind the two others as they walked along the rustic path to the waiting auto. "Cooperation as one man," he muttered to himself more than once.

4

Flight

Kay sat up in bed, snapped on the light. "Who's there?" she demanded.

"Me," whispered Ballister. "Let me in!"

"What?" In spite of herself she smiled. "What on Earth made you think that I—"

"Pipe down! This isn't lust; it's terror. We've got to get moving fast! They're onto us somehow."

The girl slipped into some clothes, threw on a coat. The moment she was through the door, Ballister grabbed her arm and hurried her out of the hostel along the street.

"What time is it?" she asked, squinting at the full moon.

"Three Ayem—wish I could say all's well."

There was a shot in the night; the long streak of flame that a rifle-barrel throws split the darkness of the street. Ballister reeled a little and cursed.

"Where to?" asked the girl, supporting him. He was hit in the shoulder.

"Garage. Hurry it up." They slunk into the darkness of a double lane of trees, slipping along like a pair of shadows. The girl was still wearing bedroom slippers; Ballister was in his stocking feet. There was no noise whatsoever and scarcely a light in all the residential area.

Again the streak of flame, again the sudden crack of the rifle. "Nowhere near," said Ballister, his voice barely audible. "Faster."

Running in the dark, making no noise at all, speeding through relatively unfamiliar ground, they made good time. The garage loomed before them, one of the squat, white, solid buildings of the city.

Ballister, flinging off her helping arm, tore open the wide wing doors and darted in. She slipped behind like a ghost.

"Light!" he said. She fumbled for the switch, snapped it on.

Kay watched as Ballister hunted for a crowbar among the little group of municipal automobiles, found one, and proceeded to bash the mechanical guts out of all the cars save one. Kay started the motor of that one.

He had hurled the bar through the last motor and collapsed beside her in the driver's seat when the custodians appeared, and in arms. One of the tall, solid Basque types raised a long rifle, took steady aim—

Kay hurled three tons of metal square at him and through the door. The pick-up of the auto was superb; its mechanical springs took up the shock of the body as though they had never hit it.

Through the streets of the city they rocketed, lightless while Ballister fumbled for the switch. The construction was somewhat unfamiliar; he collapsed totally before finding it. Kay snapped the running lights on, not daring to glance at the man by her side.

She turned onto the airport road. Behind her there was the roar of a second motor. In the rear-vision mirror she saw two pale purple circles that were the running-lights of a pursuing car.

A brief chatter of metallic slugs on the car's tail told her of a semi-automatic rifle at the least. If it were a machine gun she knew they'd never get out of this chase scene alive. The rattle sounded again. There was no whang of bullets penetrating metal. Kay breathed again, in relief.

Europeans in special cars used to hold the speed-records for ground-travel on a straight track. That was probably because no American girl had ever bothered to enter the lists against them. Kay had teethed on a piston-ring and broken the speed-laws by the age of twelve. Since then her progress had been rapid; she knew cars backwards and forwards and overturned. She knew every trick of the throttle and gas, knew how to squeeze another mile-per-minute out of the most ancient wreck on the roads.

The municipal car was of unfamiliar make; it took her about five minutes to size up its possibilities; when she had, she sped quite out of sight of the pursuing car.

"Wake up," she yelled at the man by her side. "If you aren't dead, for heaven's sake, wake up!"

There was a vague gesture from the figure, and a dim smile on its face. "Knew you'd do it," Ballister murmured. "Keep going, Kay. Get Sir Mallory's plane out, Kay. Back to Oslo we go—" The murmured words were stilled.

Wondering if her friend were dead, she stepped more speed out of the car, hauled up before the deserted airfield. The hangar-doors were merely latched against the weather; she swung them open and switched on the lights.

The ornate, fast plane of the noble was balanced feather-like on its dozen retractable landing wheels; she trundled it out of the shed and managed to load Ballister into it.

From the road came the roar of a motor; far in the night was the gleam of headlights. Kay fiddled with the controls, backed the plane into the wind. The car shot onto the landing field, tried to cross before the plane and force her around. She lifted a little, swung around the auto, ducked at the rattle of a gun. The control panel splintered into fragments of plastic and metal; alcohol ran over her knees.

Mercifully, the plane rose as she yanked wildly at the stick with no response. It headed diagonally up, its course quite straight. The stick and the pedals were quite dead. And there were no dual controls.

Into the night they flew, at the mercy of the wind, far above the landing field, in the heart of the jagged Pyrenees.

Their luck, such as it was, didn't last; one of the peaks loomed before them. Kay had just enough time to cover the body of Ballister, wondering if he were still alive, if he would survive this, if she would, when the plane struck.

5

Revelation

Someone was singing, she noticed, with an altogether inappropriate glee, an objectionable song about his Majesty, the King of Spain.

"Stow it, Hoe," ordered the voice of Ballister. "Let the lady rest."

She sat up violently. "You!" she said. "What happened—" She felt a curious weakness in the middle and sat back again. "What's up?"

Ballister approached, relief glowing all over his face. "You had us worried. You've been on a liquid diet for a week without once coming up for air. How'd you like to tear into a steak?"

"Love it," she snapped, realizing that the sense of weakness had been hunger. "Any potatoes?"

"You'll have rice instead. May I present José Bazasch." He led forward by one hand a shy little old man who wore the Basque beret.

"An honor," he muttered incoherently. "Fine ladies—noble gentlemen in my cave—"

"Tell your story, Hoe," suggested Ballister grimly. He speared a broiled steak from its string where it turned over the fire. A slab of washed bark served very well for a platter.

"The story? This. I am José Bazasch, a Basque. A dozen years ago, during the wars, there were many Basques. I was sheep-thief—outlaw. Lived here in the cave. I am no more thief because there are no more sheep. There are no more Basques except me."

"If you'll excuse the omission," said Kay, chomping busily, "I'm eating too energetically to register surprise. Kindly explain in words of one syllable or less."

"Okay, child. Your brains would be addled after your long illness. I'll begin at the beginning. There was a slew of Iberians along about the beginnings of the Christian era who were decimated by, in rapid succession, the Romans, the Carthaginians, the Goths, Visigoths, Vandals, Huns, Saracens and their most holy majesties, Ferdinand and Isabella.

"That brings us down to 1939, the beginning of the war. The few Basques left fight with the French, the Spanish and any other army they fancy. Most of them die. A few thousand are left in the lower mountain villages. One day in 1951 the villages are bombed by German planes—blown right off the map. Squads of soldiers hunt down the rest of the Basques in the hills and pop them off."

"But not José!" interjected the old man with considerable excitement and a little pride.

"That's right. Not José. Hoe was so well hidden that half the time he couldn't find his own den for a month once he had left it. Anyway—there aren't any Basque villages nor any Basques. Yet the next year the Pyrenese Peoples' Republic is announced and in the next they held DeCuerva's army, which never did get through. Now, a dozen years later we see this uncannily perfect city of the future, achieved by a handful of men and women—whom we've seen—and that's that."

"That's what?" asked the girl abstractedly.

"That's what I was planning to ask you as soon as you regained consciousness."

"You've waited in vain," said Kay, licking her fingers. "I can't think on a full stomach. Nobody can. By the way, you neglected to explain the events of the night of a week ago. How did you know they suspected us of suspecting them of being not what they seemed to be?"

"You know the Mayor's office building?"

"Like a book. I might almost say I know it backwards."

"Right, child. You do know it backwards, and what's more you don't know the half of it. Because more than the half of it is underground. I bumbled on the Mayor that night going down into the basement of his building and asked if I could go too. Taking something of a chance I pushed by him before he could make an excuse.

"I guess he didn't have a gun, because I wasn't shot in the back for seeing what I saw. There were some machines there that make their hydroelectric turbines look like a pinwheel. Big—very big—and mysterious in function, to me at least. Simply didn't look like anything at all—except maybe a glorified and electric concrete mixer. And a couple of people mucking around with oiling-cans.

"They drew and fired; I shoved the mayor in and rolled the hall-desk against the door, propped that with my walking-stick for leverage and beat it for your flat."

"Nice condensed narration," she said thoughtfully. "But what made you poke around in the first place? Dashed if I had any grounds for suspicion of conspiracy and such."

"You've forgotten a lot since we took those psych courses. How do you tell a louse from an honest man?"

"A louse doesn't trust anybody."

"Right. Not even when he's middle aged does he trust a couple of moonstruck lovers. Any nasty old man who'd break in on a *tête-à-tête* is bad from head to toe.

"And the clincher, to me at least, was this bloody, mysterious and cancerous growth of the so-called Basque people in less than two decades. There was something too awfully methodical about their city. It didn't show any of the right traits. No, not a single one. It was as though they'd deliberately set out to build themselves a city of the future intended to impress and amaze—one, also, geared to the maximum in efficiency."

Kay listened quietly. Finally she suggested, with a little shudder: "Gestapo?"

"Couldn't be anything else, sweet." Ballister fell silent in the contemplation of bucking the secret police that had held the German empire of conquest together by torture, fire and sword for years beyond its normal life-span. They were wise, villainous and tricky, the Gestapo.

It had been thought that the majority of them had been killed off by the Captives' Revolt years ago. Surely there couldn't be enough left to fill that city!

"It's a bridgehead," he said at last. "A stepping-stone for attack on an unprecedented scale and in an altogether new technique. You guess what that is?"

"Like the story about the rabbits, perhaps," Kay suggested diffidently. "There were two rabbits being chased by a pack of hounds. They were tired, completely winded. There was no chance of them outrunning the hounds, who were young and fresh. So one rabbit said to the other rabbit: 'Let's hide in that bush until we outnumber them.' "

"Maybe," said Ballister. "Too bad reconnaissance is out of the question. They must be patrolling the woods seven deep looking for us." He brooded for a while, then exploded: "And the young monster of a hydro-dam? What's that for?"

"Electric light," said Kay. She reconsidered after a moment. "No. Because they have a strict curfew, so they don't need street-lights. And that dam would deliver twenty times the power needed for street-lighting. Maybe a hundred times that. I'm no installations engineer, boy."

"It's very important, that dam. Otherwise they wouldn't risk building a big, suspicious thing like that. And they do want to hide it; they did their best along that line to keep us from noticing it."

"What?" squeaked the girl. "That chauffeur stopped the car and pointed it out, and we've been taken to inspect it half a dozen times! Keep us from noticing it, forsooth!"

Ballister sat quietly and grinned like a cat.

The girl considered, then blushed and admitted shamefacedly: "You're right. They even fooled me, the psychist. They threw it into our faces so often that we were supposed to take it for granted and not think about the thing. The Purloined Letter, *et seq.*"

"Good kid!" said Ballister with faked heartiness. "I wish to heaven that one of us was a real scientist—physics and nuclear chemistry. Because the one purpose of that dam is obviously to power the machinery I saw in the basement before the chase-scene. And I don't know what the machinery does ..."

"So it's all solved, huh?" Kay asked belligerently. "As simple as pi square? The Gestapo's been repudiated by the German people, so they choose this method as a bridgehead on the continent for future use when the Swastika shall ride again."

"That's what it looks like," said Ballister self-satisfiedly.

"Things are seldom what they seem. That's what it ain't. How would even a heavily-disciplined Gestapo unit do what they've done in the time they've had?"

Ballister was rocked back on his heels. "Blast it," he said bitterly. "The man-hour formulæ make it a rank impossibility. It's so far outside the realms of possibility that I'd bet my boots on it." A thought struck him: "But the city's there, Kay!"

"Ignore it, boy. There's trickery involved. We'll have to find out where."

He looked at her glumly. "Reconnaissance?"

"Yep. Both of us."

Bazasch knew things about stalking that would pop the eyes of a Scottish stag-hunter. He had the knack of slipping along without enough covering to hide a rabbit, and in the little space of a week he tried to teach Kay and Ballister what he knew. In his own inarticulate way he got some of the principles over, though he despaired of ever making guerillistas of them.

Mournfully he explained that one had to be born to the fellowhood of stalkers and then be taken in hand by a wise old man who could explain things. He, José, could not explain. So long he had not talked to anybody but himself that the language sometimes seemed to be going altogether.

And between the grueling hikes-under-cover in the mountains the two Americans were gathering together their data, inferring wildly, working sometimes by association rather than logic, jumping through time and space in their reasoning rather than let go of a theory.

They evolved conclusive—to them—proof that Sir Mallory was the prime scoundrel behind the Pyrenese Peoples' Republic. Checking back on his mental notebook Ballister recalled what might be considered evidence to that effect:

"I had my eyes on him the moment he showed up in our little twosome. Whether he's the real Sir Mallory turned traitor doesn't matter much. He may have popped the real Sir Mallory and taken his place with disguises. Anyway, you recall the outrageous bombing of the Hotel de Oslo et d'Universe, or whatever it was. That was the feeblest bombing I ever encountered, and yet Sir Mallory and a few old hens got excited about it.

"He proposed a military police of unlimited powers. That was a very bad sign. It was the first step towards wrecking the Conference. It denied democracy itself, the principle the Conference was constructed on. There could have been no bombing or killing half so disruptively effective as that move."

Kay wearily agreed. Her knees were scratched, and her hands were calloused with crawling. But she'd got over her illness and felt hard as nails. The rough-and-ready bullet extraction that Bazasch had performed on Ballister had healed nicely.

6
Showdown

On the big night there was no moon. José had planned it that way, he claimed. They started at dusk, carrying their first two meals.

It was a horrible grind for an old man, a girl and a recently-shot person. They made crevasses that seemed impossible, climbed lofty trees to sight. After some hours of the terrible labor they sighted the lights of the landing field glowing dimly through the night. Fearing no cars they made good time along the highway, turning quietly into three roadside shadows when they passed the blockhouse that surmounted the dam. They found the city to be a bigger blotch of black in the general darkness.

Slipping down the alleys and lanes of the city, silent as so many ghosts, the three made their way to the center of town. By prearranged plan Ballister unlatched the front door of the Mayor's little office building.

They entered behind him; Ballister felt for the cellar door. It swung open and a blaze of light poured through, shocking, dazzling after the hours-long trek through pitch-blackness.

"Aha!" whispered Bazasch. His cat's eyes contracted; from his belt flicked a knife, eight wicked inches of blank steel. It slipped through the air, lodged in the throat of a burly "Basque" who had made the mistake of drawing his gun.

"Close it," said Kay, dashing down the stairs to kick the gun away from the hand of the "Basque," wounded but not yet dead. She finished him for the moment with a kick to the side of his head.

Ballister and Bazasch tore after her, the door bolted as securely as it could be.

Kay inspected the tower of machinery, marvelling. "Don't ask me," she finally griped. "I agree with my ignorant colleague. Whatever it is, it drinks lots of juice and it looks like a concrete mixer."

Ballister picked up the gun. It was a hefty hand-weapon, a wide-gage projector of lead slugs that mushroomed effectively. "What do we do now?" he asked weakly. "That individual sent in an alarm, to be sure, before he even drew."

"Take a good look," said Kay. She indicated the man on the concrete flooring. "Isn't the face familiar?"

"There's a swell resemblance to that old rascal, Sir Mallory Gaffney. You mean it?"

"Nothing but that. What's it signify?"

"You have me there. What is it, Hoe?"

"It is the besiegers—can be no others. They come!"

There was the clump of boots outside, up the stairs.

Ballister slipped Bazasch the gun: "Can you hold them, Hoe? Hold them by yourself? Because we're going to be busy down here. Will you?"

The Basque took the gun, sighted along its barrel for a moment before slowly replying: "They must have killed my whole family, which I disgraced by becoming sheep-thief. I will no longer disgrace."

"Good man," gasped Ballister, holding his wounded shoulder. "Go get 'em!"

The little man scrambled up the stairs, chose a shallow niche. A big grin spread over his face as he raised his gun-muzzle and fired once through the door. He commanded the position completely; while his ammunition lasted—he neatly caught the pouch Kay unhooked from the man and tossed up to him—he was impregnable.

With feverish speed Ballister stripped the man on the flooring. Kay went through the pockets; came up triumphantly with a slim pamphlet. "In German!" she explained.

"Let me." He took the little book and ruffled through it, then cast a despairing glance at the monstrous mechanism that nearly filled the room. "It's a handbook for this thing—the German for it is duplo-atomic-radexic-multiplic-convertor. What do you suppose that means? The wiring's beyond me completely. I couldn't repair an electric bell."

She took the thing and unfolded the gatefold wiring-diagram, studied it with wrinkled brows. "Sweet Lord of Creation!" she muttered. "I have to crack this on an empty stomach!" Whipping out a pencil she traced—tried to trace—the wires and tubes to their source. Finally she snapped: "There's a switchboard somewhere on the side of the thing. Find it, please."

Ballister hunted, finally climbing the rickety iron ladder that led to the summit of the machine. "Got it!" he said. "And it makes sense!"

"Turn on the power," she called at him.

He threw the switch that seemed appropriate. His reward was a shock that nearly threw him from the structure. But the power went through; tubes lit here and there.

Eagerly Kay hunted in the vitals of the mechanism, comparing it with the diagram. "See a hopper-opening?" she asked.

José fired three times in rapid succession, brought four dead "Basques" tumbling down the stairs. He waved cheerily at Ballister.

"There's a switch for it," he said, throwing it down. A metal shutter opened; its cavernous maw led into blackness. Kay, shuddering a little, peered in. "Ought to light," she said desperately. "There should be a battery of tubes that the raw material—whatever it is—passed under. Fish for it, will you?"

Ballister stabbed at a switch; gears began to clank like a windmill's crushers. He tried another. "Okay!" yelled the girl. "They light!"

He scrambled down, squatted beside her. She had cast the book aside and was weeping. "Here," she sobbed, "all the power we need, a machine that does something terrible and wonderful to it, and we can't use it! We don't know how!"

Ballister, before replying, administered a mercy-kick to one of the "Basques" who was trying to reach his gun, wounded as he was. José caught the weapon. He was grinning with fiendish delight as he fired another burst through the door.

Ballister and Kay rose. The girl's tears dried on her face as she studied the three new corpses.

"Spitting images," said Ballister, his throat hoarse. This was something uncanny, something that transcended warfare and science. Except for minor details of hair-line and clothes, the four bodies were alike—all the image of Sir Mallory.

"I get it," said the girl briskly. "There was talk of it in a Sunday feature I did. It's the only simple, logical explanation for your city of the future built as if by one man. It was built by one man, and he was Sir Mallory."

"That's what the machine does," snapped Ballister. "Rearranges molecules to suit the pattern. Set the pattern for a man and feed in your raw material, and out come as many copies as you want. Perfect war-unit, perfect rapport between and among the slew of them. Perfect for spy-systems. And the Gestapo flair for disguises took care of enough variations to satisfy us. Hell, who'd look for a thing like that?"

The girl was scrambling up the stairs again. "Excuse me," she barked rudely at Bazasch. "Not at—" he was beginning to reply. He shut his mouth with a snap as she began to undress him without ceremony.

She pulled from his chest his home-made undershirt, fingered the soft, short-cropped fur. "Go right ahead," she said. "Thanks."

"Brilliant," admitted Ballister after a moment's thought. "Utterly brilliant. Very sure you can make it work?"

"For a simple thing like this, yes. After all, dead flesh-tissue ought to be fairly simple. Now where is the pattern-maker or whatever they call it?"

"Maybe this?" asked the man, indicating a sort of scanning-disk, like an old-style television set's.

"Nothing else!" she declared triumphantly as she set the hunk of clothing in the area covered by the disc.

Ballister picked up the corpses one by one and chucked them into the hopper.

Another hinged door raised itself and soft scraps of fur began to pour from it in a stream that ended in a few minutes, when the weight of the pile equalled about seven hundred pounds.

"Thank God for Hoe's dainty taste in undergarments," said the girl. "Nothing less than mouse-fur for his skin!"

"Open the door, Hoe!" called Ballister. The little man obeyed, dumb and surprised. There was an immediate influx of the duplicates of Sir Mallory, an influx that turned into a helpless pile of dying men, strangling in the last extremes of allergic reaction.

Grimly contemplating the last of the twitching Mallories, Ballister said: "We'll clear the city by spreading these mouse-skins neatly through the streets. We can rain them on the forest, in case anybody's escaped."

"We can detect spies with them," said the girl.

"Right. A load will be useful when we fly back to Oslo in the morning."

"It's morning now," she said, indicating the ray of dawn that streaked through the door and splashed down the stairs.

"It is. Morning," said Ballister. "Morning over the world."

[*Fantasy and Science Fiction* - January 1958]

The Events Leading Down to the Tragedy

DOCUMENT ONE

Being the First Draft of a Paper to be Read before the Tuscarora Township Historical Society by Mr. Hardeigne Spoynte, B.A.

Madame President, members, guests:

It is with unabashed pride that I stand before you this evening. You will recall from your perusal of our Society's *Bulletin* (Vol. XLII, No. 3, Fall, 1955, pp. 7–8) [pp correct? check before making fair copy. HS] that I had undertaken a research into the origins of that event so fraught with consequences to the development of our township, the Watling-Fraskell duel. I virtually promised that the cause of the fatal strife would be revealed by, so to speak, the spotlight of science [metaphor here suff. graceful? perh. "magic" better? HS]. I am here to carry out that promise.

Major Watling *did* [tell a lie] prevaricate. Colonel Fraskell *rightly* reproached him with mendacity. Perhaps from this day the breach between Watlingist and Fraskellite may begin to heal, the former honestly acknowledging themselves in error and the latter magnanimous in victory.

My report reflects great credit on a certain modest resident of historic old Northumberland County who, to my regret, is evidently away on a well-earned vacation from his arduous labors [perh. cliché? No. Fine phrase. *Stet!* HS]. Who he is you will learn in good time.

I shall begin with a survey of known facts relating to the Watling-Fraskell duel, and as we are all aware, there is for such a quest no starting point better than the monumental work of our late learned county historian, Dr. Donge. Donge states (*Old Times on the Oquanantic,* 2nd ed., 1873, pp. 771–2): "No less to be deplored than the routing of the West Branch Canal to bypass Eleusis was the duel in which perished miserably Major Elisha Watling and Colonel Hiram Fraskell, those two venerable pioneers of the Oquanantic Valley. Though in no way to be compared with the barbarous *blood feuds* of the benighted Southern States of our Union, there has persisted to our own day a certain division of loyalty among residents of Tuscarora Township and particularly the Borough of

Eleusis. Do we not see elm-shaded Northumberland Street adorned by *two* gracefully pillared bank buildings, one the stronghold of the Fraskellite and the other of the Watlingist? Is not the debating society of Eleusis Academy sundered annually by the proposition, 'Resolved: that Major Elisha Watling (on alternate years, Colonel Hiram Fraskell) was no gentleman'? And did not the Watlingist propensities of the Eleusis Colonial Dames and the Fraskellite inclination of the Eleusis Daughters of the American Revolution 'clash' in September, 1869, at the storied Last Joint Lawn Fête during which éclairs and (some say) tea cups were hurled?" [Dear old Donge! Prose equal Dr. Johnson!]

If I may venture to follow those stately periods with my own faltering style, it is of course known to us all that the controversy has scarcely diminished to the present time. Eleusis Academy, famed *alma mater* (*i.e.,* "foster mother") of the immortal Hovington[1] is, alas, no more. It expired in flames on the tragic night of August 17, 1901, while the Watlingist members of that Eleusis Hose Company Number One which was stabled in Northumberland Street battled for possession of the fire hydrant which might have saved the venerable pile against the members of the predominantly Fraskellite Eleusis Hose Company Number One which was then stabled in Oquanantic Street. (The confusion of the nomenclature is only a part of the duel's bitter heritage.) Nevertheless, though the Academy and its Debating Society be gone, the youth of Eleusis still carries on the fray in a more modern fashion which rises each November to a truly disastrous climax during "Football Pep Week" when the "Colonels" of Central High School meet in sometimes gory combat with the "Majors" of North Side High. I am privately informed by our borough's Supervising Principal, George Croud, Ph.B., that last November's bill for replacement of broken window panes in both school buildings amounted to $231.47, exclusive of state sales tax; and that the two school nurses are already "stockpiling" gauze, liniment, disinfectants and splints in anticipation of the seemingly inevitable autumnal crop of abrasions, lacerations and fractures. [*mem.* Must ask Croud whether willing be publ. quoted or "informed source." HS] And the adults of Eleusis no less assiduously prosecute the controversy by choice of merchants, the granting of credit, and social exclusiveness.

The need for a determination of the rights and wrongs in the *affaire* Fraskell-Watling is, clearly, no less urgent now than it has ever been.

Dr. Donge, by incredible, indeed almost impossible, labor has proved that the issue was one of *veracity*. Colonel Fraskell intimated to Joseph Cooper, following a meeting of the Society of the Cincinnati, that Major Watling had been, in the words of Cooper's letter of July 18, 1789, to his brother Puntell in Philadelphia, "drauin [drawing] the long Bow."[2]

O fatal indiscretion! For Puntell Cooper delayed not a week to "relay" the intelligence to Major Watling by post, as a newsy appendix to his order for cordwood from the major's lot!

---

[1] *vide* Spoynte, H.: "Egney Hovington, Nineteenth-Century American Nature Poet, and his career at Eleusis Academy, October 4–October 28, 1881" (art.) in *Bull. of the Tuscarora Township Hist. Soc.,* Vol. XVI, No. 4, Winter, 1929, pp. 4–18.

[2] DONGE, Dr. J.: *supra,* p. 774, *n.*

The brief, fatally terminated correspondence between the major and the colonel then began; I suppose most of us have it [better change to "at least key passages of corresp." HS] committed to memory.

The first letter offers a tantalizing glimpse. Watling writes to Fraskell, *inter alia:* "I said I seen it at the Meetin the Night before Milkin Time by my Hoss Barn and I seen it are you a Athiest Colonel?" It has long been agreed that the masterly conjectural emendation of this passage proposed by Miss Stolp in her epoch-making paper[3] is the correct one, *i.e.:* "I said at the meeting [of the Society of the Cincinnati] that I saw it the night before [the meeting] at milking time, by my horse barn; and I [maintain in the face of your expressions of disbelief that I] saw it. Are you an atheist, colonel?"

There thus appears to have been at the outset of the correspondence a clear-cut issue: did or did not Major Watling see "it"? The reference to atheism suggests that "it" may have been some apparition deemed supernatural by the major, but we know absolutely nothing more of what "it" may have been.

Alas, but the correspondents at once lost sight of the "point." The legendary Watling Temper and the formidable Fraskell Pride made it certain that one would sooner or later question the gentility of the other as they wrangled by post. The fact is that both did so simultaneously, on August 20, in letters that crossed. Once this stone was hurled [say "these stones"? HS] there was in those days no turning back. The circumstance that both parties were simultaneously offended and offending perplexed their seconds, and ultimately the choice of weapons had to be referred to a third party mutually agreeable to the duelists, Judge E. Z. C. Mosh.

Woe that he chose the deadly Pennsylvania Rifle![4] Woe that the two old soldiers knew that dread arm as the husbandman his sickle! At six o'clock on the morning of September 1, 1789, the major and the colonel expired on the sward behind Brashear's Creek, each shot through the heart. The long division of our beloved borough into Fraskellite and Watlingist had begun.

After this preamble, I come now to the modern part of my tale. It begins in 1954, with the purchase of the Haddam property by our respected fellow-townsman, that adoptive son of Eleusis, Dr. Gaspar Mord. I much regret that Dr. Mord is apparently on an extended vacation [where *can* the man be? HS]; since he is not available [confound it! HS] to grant permission, I must necessarily "skirt" certain topics, with a plea that to do otherwise might involve a violation of confidence. [Positively, there are times when one wishes that one were *not* a gentleman! HS]

I am quite aware that there was an element in our town which once chose to deprecate Dr. Mord, to question his degree, to inquire suspiciously into matters which are indubitably his own business and no one else's, such as his source of income. This element of which I speak came perilously close to sullying the hospitable name of Eleusis by calling on Dr. Mord in a delegation afire with the ridiculous rumor that the doctor had been "hounded out of Peoria in 1929 for vivisection."

---

[3] STOLP, A. DeW.: "Some Textual Problems Relating to the Correspondence between Major Elisha Watling and Colonel Hiram Fraskell, Eleusis, Pennsylvania, July 27–September 1, 1789" (art.) *in Bull. of the Tuscarora Township Hist. Soc.,* Vol. IV, No. i, Spring, 1917.

[4] Amusingly known to *hoi polloi* and some who should know better as the "Kentucky" Rifle.

Dr. Mord, far from reacting with justified wrath, chose the way of the true scientist. He showed this delegation through his laboratory to demonstrate that his activities were innocent, and it departed singing his praises, so to speak. They were particularly enthusiastic about two "phases" of his work which he demonstrated: some sort of "waking anesthesia" gas, and a mechanical device for the induction of the hypnotic state.

I myself called on Dr. Mord as soon as he had settled down, in my capacity as President of the Eleusis Committee for the Preservation of Local Historical Buildings and Sites. I explained to the good doctor that in the parlor of the Haddam house had been formed in 1861 the Oquanantic Zouaves, that famed regiment of daredevils who with zeal and dash guarded the Boston (Massachusetts) Customs House through the four sanguinary years of conflict. I expressed the hope that the intricate fretsaw work, the stained glass, the elegant mansard roof and the soaring central tower would remain mute witnesses to the martial glory of Eleusis, and not fall victim to the "remodeling" craze.

Dr. Mord, with his characteristic smile (its first effect is unsettling, I confess, but when one later learns of the kindly intentions behind it, one grows accustomed to his face), replied somewhat irrelevantly by asking whether I had any dependents. He proceeded to a rather searching inquiry, explaining that as a man of science he liked to be sure of his facts. I advised him that I understood, diffidently mentioning that I was no stranger to scientific rigor, my own grandfather having published a massive *Evidences for the Phlogiston Theory of Heat*.[5] Somehow the interview concluded with Dr. Mord asking: "Mr. Spoynte, what do you consider your greatest contribution to human knowledge and welfare, and do you suppose that you will ever surpass that contribution?"

I replied after consideration that no doubt my "high water mark" was my discovery of the 1777 Order Book of the Wyalusing Militia Company in the basement of the Spodder Memorial Library, where it had been lost to sight for thirty-eight years after being misfiled under "Indian Religions (Local)." To the second part of his question I could only answer that it was given to few men twice to perform so momentous a service to scholarship.

On this odd note we parted; it occurred to me as I wended my way home that I had not succeeded in eliciting from the doctor a reply as to his intentions of preserving intact the Haddam house! But he "struck" me as an innately conservative person, and I had little real fear of the remodeler's ruthless hammer and saw.

This impression was reinforced during the subsequent month, for the doctor intimated that he would be pleased to have me call on him Thursday evenings for a chat over the coffee cups.

These chats were the customary conversations of two learned men of the world, skimming lightly over knowledge's whole domain. Once, for example, Dr. Mord amusingly theorized that one of the most difficult things in the world for a

---

[5] Generally considered the last word on the subject though, as I understand it, somewhat eclipsed at present by the flashy and mystical "molecular theory" of the notorious Tory sympathizer and renegade Benjamin Thompson, styled "Count" Rumford. "A fool can always find a bigger fool to admire him." [Quote in orig. French? Check source and exact text. HS]

private person to do was to find a completely useless human being. The bad men were in prison or hiding, he explained, and when one investigated the others it always turned out that they had some redeeming quality or usefulness to somebody. "Almost always," he amended with a laugh. At other times he would question me deeply about my life and activities, now and then muttering: "I must be sure; I must be *sure*"—typical of his scientist's passion for precision. Yet again, he would speak of the glorious Age of Pericles, saying fervently: "Spoynte, I would give anything, do anything, to look upon ancient Athens in its flower!"

Now, I claim no genius inspired my rejoinder. I was merely "the right man in the right place." I replied: "Dr. Mord, your wish to visit ancient Athens could be no more fervent than mine to visit Major Watling's horse barn at milking time the evening of July 17, 1789."

I must, at this point, [confound it! I am *sure* Dr. M. would give permission to elaborate if he were only here! HS] drop an impenetrable veil of secrecy over certain episodes, for reasons which I have already stated.

I am, however, in a position to state with absolute authority *that there was* NO *apparition at Major Watling's horse barn at milking time the evening of*—

[Steady on, Hardeign. Think. Think. Major W. turned. I looked about. No apparitions, spooks, goblins. Just Major W. and myself. He looked at me and made a curious sort of face. No. Nonono. Can't be. Oh, my God! *I* was the—Fault all mine. Duel, feud. Traitor to dear Eleusis. Feel *sick* … HS]

DOCUMENT TWO

Being a note delivered by Mrs. Irving McGuinness, Domestic, to Miss Agnes DeW. Stolp, President, the Tuscarora Township Historical Society

"The Elms"
Wednesday

Dear Miss Stolp,

Pray forgive my failure to attend the last meeting of the Society to read my paper. I was writing the last words when—I can tell you no more. Young Dr. Scantt has been in constant attendance at my bedside, and my temperature has not fallen below 99.8 degrees in the past 48 hours. I have been, I am, a sick and suffering man. I abjectly hope that you and everybody in Eleusis will bear this in mind if certain facts should come to your attention.

I cannot close without a warning against that rascal, "Dr." Gaspar Mord. A pledge prevents me from entering into details, but I urge you, should he dare to rear his head in Eleusis again, to hound him out of town as he was hounded out of Peoria in 1929. *Verbum sapientibus satis.*

Hardeign Spoynte

Early "to spec" Stories

This section contains early works (1939–42), written very quickly to fill space "to spec" in pulp magazines. The material that follows is included for completeness, and is not of the same professional quality as the previous works. You have been warned!

[*Super Science Stories* - May 1940
as by S. D. Gottesman]

King Cole of Pluto

1
Leigh Salvage, Incorporated

Sunlight gleamed on the squat, stubby spaceship. Its rocket exhaust flared once; then paled into nothing. It was drifting through the meteor zone though not the undirected object it seemed to be. Captain Jerry Leigh had his scow under control; the control of a man who was born in the space-lanes, and knew them like his own face.

Captain Jerry was in the cramped cabin of the ship, scribbling at endless computations. "Allowing for Black's constant," he muttered, "plus drift, plus impetus, less inertia ..." He turned to a calculator, stabbed at its keys, and read the result. He yanked a bell pull and a clangor sounded through the ship. Men filed in—a full crew meeting. Jerry rose.

"As I estimate it," he said, "the *Argol* lies in quadrant III of the meteor belt. Its coordinates are alpha—point oh oh four; beta—seven point three oh two; gamma—zero!" There was a shocked pause, and a big man stepped out of the crew. "Will we go through with it, Captain? Gamma—zero is a small margin of profit, to say nothing of safety." He spoke slowly and precisely; the flat "a" of his English indicated that his tongue had once been more used to the Scandinavian languages.

Jerry smiled: "Sven, caution is caution, and maybe the salvage money isn't worth the risk." His face hardened. "But I'm not working for money alone, and I hope that none of you others are."

A voice spoke from the floor, "Glory's glory, but space-bloat is a damned nasty way to die!"

Jerry frowned. There were troublemakers everywhere and all the time. "Wylie," he said, "if you've ever seen a wrecked liner you'll know what we're here for, and what our job is. We salvage and tow the ships wrecked by meteors or mechanical flaws, and we get paid for it. But—and it's a big but—if we didn't do our job, those ships would run wild. With no crew, tearing through space at the whim of the governor, plowing through the shipping lanes, never twice in the same place, and finally coming to rest as permanent menaces to trade and life— *that's* our job! They carry water condensers to Mars; they carry radium to Earth. Para-morphium from Venus, and iridium from Neptune. Without us salvagers there would be no shipping; without shipping the structure of the interplanetary union would topple and fall. This isn't a job or even a career—it's a sacred duty that we do for each and all of the nine worlds of the solar system!

577

"Coordinates, I said, are alpha—point oh oh four; beta—seven point three oh two; gamma—zero. Carry on; full speed ahead."

The exhausts flamed; the stubby, rusted prow turned once more—into the meteor zone!

Jerry droned figures to the helmsman with his eyes glued at the vision plate of pure fused quartz. "Meteor in our third quadrant—distance about five hundred kilos. Deflect into first ... back on course.

"Cloud of aerolites ahead. Carry through." Ahead loomed a blotch of darkness. "Unknown particle in second quadrant. Our coordinates, helmsman."

Sven, at the tiller, read off, "Alpha—point oh oh four; beta—seven point four oh oh; gamma—point oh oh two."

"Hulk *Argol* ahead. Carry through into gamma—zero." The big man wet his lips and deflected the steering bar. "Carried through, sir," he said. Jerry, his eyes never leaving the plate, whispered tensely, "Cut steering to master's board." Sven snapped a switch. "Cut, sir." Delicately Jerry fingered the firing switch. A blocky black mass boomed down on the ship from the east; violently the little scow looped over and down, clearing the path of the particle. This was just one of the reasons that men were prejudiced against gamma—zero. Too much loose junk zipping around for comfort.

The *Argol* was squarely on the cross-hairs of the vision plate. Captain Jerry studied the battered piece of wreckage. It had been a supertransport once—loaded to the observation blister with para-morphium from Venus to Earth. She had encountered an unexpected cloud of meteorites, probably too big to run away from, and so had been riddled and gone under. From then on her career had been a terrible one of shooting wildly through space on almost full fuel tanks; demolishing a refueling station a million kilos off Mars; smashing into a squadron of police rockets and shattering them into bits—and finding rest at last in the meteor zone to upset orbits and hurl cosmic rubbish into the trade lanes. He examined this corpse of a ship, estimating its size and Martian weight. He thought he could handle it. Through the annunciator he said, "Make fast with magnet plates." And to Sven, "Take the master's board for emergencies. I'm going over to supervise."

Jerry crawled into his spacesuit, a terrible cumbersome thing of steel alloy and artificial membrane, and dropped lightly down the shaft of the ship to the big space lock that characterizes the salvage vessel.

"Wylie," he ordered, "take Martin and Dooley with a cutting torch to open their sides and then look at their fuel tanks. If they have any left we can use it. I don't believe they're empty, from the lie of her.

"Macy, take Collins and Pearl. Secure grapples, and allow as much slack for towage as you can get. If you allow too little, you'll never know it, by the way—we'd be smashed like an eggshell on the first turn bigger than thirty degrees.

"Dehring and Hiller, come with me. You need supervision. Take cameras and film."

The boarding party bolted their helmets on and swung open the space lock. Wylie, unrecognizable in his swathing overall, braced the cutting torch against his middle and turned on the juice. The powerful arc bit through the wall of the *Argol* as if it had been cheese, and the men filed through. They had cut one of the cargo rooms, piled high with metal cylinders of para-morphium, the priceless Venerian drug of sleep and healing. A few of the containers were sprung open and the contents spoiled; still, seventy percent of the remaining cargo went to the salvager, and eighty percent of the hulk.

Jerry took his crew of two to the steering blister that bulged from the top of the ship, picking his way between damaged bodies. In the blister he found the captain, staring permanently at a hole in the observation plate where a meteorite—one of many—had pierced the armor of his vessel. With a crowbar Jerry pried off the top of the recorder and photographed the tracing needles on the graph that charted the course of the ship with all its crazy tacks and swerves through space.

"Dehring," he ordered, "take up that corpse. We're going to stack them and see that they get decent burial when we reach a planet." And with the callousness of years of space travel and the coldness that the hard life of the salvager instills, the man obeyed.

Jerry wandered at random through the ship. It had carried some passengers. One of the cabin doors was open, and the figure of an old woman, face mercifully down, was sprawled over the threshold. She had heard the alarm in her little room as the air drained out of the ship; unthinkingly she had flung open her door—gasped for breath when there was nothing to breathe—and fallen as she was.

He picked up her tiny frame, and carried it to the stern of the ship. He wondered who she was—why she was returning to Earth from Venus at her age. Perhaps she had wanted to pass her last years among the green and brown fields and again see a mountain. Perhaps—he thought he knew how she felt, for he, too, had once been homesick.

Mars—red hell of sand and cloudless sky. Home of "wanted" men and women, where the uncautious were burned in the flaming bonfires of the Martian underworld. Haven of every swindler and cutthroat in the system, it was but a dull gem in Sol's diadem. Some day they would clean it up—raid the sickening warrens that snaked through and under its cities; fill them in with dynamite. That day would be a good one ...

Gently he deposited the body among others; brushed away his random thoughts and called, "Macy! Grapples fixed?" Macy's thin voice trickled through his earphones, "Yes, sir. I gave them twelve hundred meters."

"OK" he snapped. "Return to the ship, all except Wylie. You'll stay aboard, Kurt, to stow displaced cargo."

"Yes, sir," said Wylie, in a growl. "And shall I comb the corpses' hair, sir?"

Jerry grinned. "Why not? And see that it's done or I'll fire you and bust your rating on every scow out of Mars." Discipline, after all, was the thing.

Jerry resumed his place at the firing board. "Stations all," he called sharply over the annunciator. "Brace for seven Mars gravities in seventeen seconds. One—"

His hands flew over the board, setting up the combinations of rocket discharges that would be able to stir the huge *Argol* out of its inertia and snap it after the scow of *Leigh Salvage, Incorporated*, like a stone on a string, at the end of a ponderous osmiridium cable.

"Nine!" The men were strapping themselves into hammocks.

"Eleven ...

"Fourteen!" He tensed himself, sucking in his stomach muscles against the terrible drag.

"Sixteen!

"Fire!"

And the ship roared sharply up and out of the asteroid belt, its powerful rocket engines—designed to move twenty times the weight of the scow alone—straining to drag the ponderous cargo hulk behind it. Soon the initial speed lessened, and they were roaring along at an easy thousand K.P.S. The captain rose and set the automatics; tried to shake some of the blood from his legs into his head. He could rest now.

Assembled, Jerry and the men drank a toast to the trade in ethyl alcohol—"To salvaging: the greatest game of all!" They drained their cups. The big Sven rose, some of his Norse reticence vanished in the universal solvent. "My brothers in labor," he began. "We have gone far on this trip, and there is no one here who will not agree with me when I say that we could not have done it without Captain Jerry. I give you our boss and the best of them all, Jerry Leigh, of Leigh Salvage, Incorporated!"

The flask went the rounds, and when it was emptied there was another and yet another. In just a few hours Jerry was standing alone in the middle of the room, looking owlishly about him at the collapsed forms of the crew. There was a cup in his hands—a full cup. He spurned a nearby body with his foot.

"S-s-sissies!" he said derisively, and drained his drink. Slowly he deflated onto the floor.

An alarm bell smashed the silence into bits; men dragged themselves to their feet. "Mars," said one, absently.

"Don't land easy, Captain," another urged Jerry. "Smear us all over the field. It's about the only thing that'll do this head of mine any good."

Jerry winced. "That's the way I feel, but I'd like to get that hulk in before I die. Landing stations, all men."

Their ship and its huge running mate hovered over the red planet. Irritably Jerry dove it near the atmosphere and blearily searched its surface for the landing field. "Damn!" he muttered. "I'm in the wrong hemisphere."

The ship roared over the face of Mars, and slowed above the Kalonin desert. Jerry found Salvage Field beneath him, and cut the rockets sharply to one side, swinging the *Argol* like the lash of a whip. They swooped down, and Jerry, drunk or sober, shifted his salvage neatly above the ponderous pneumatic cargo-table and cut it loose. It fell the thousand feet with a terrible crash, landing comparatively easy. At any rate he had not missed it. "So much for Wylie," he muttered.

The exhaust sputtered and died; the ship dove to within a hundred feet of the surface. On rockets! And down she drifted, landing without a jar. Jerry held his head and groaned.

2
An Unexpected Rival

The owner, manager and founder of Leigh Salvage, Incorporated, was only human. In turn he visited the offices of the other salvage companies and said, in effect, "Ya-a-ah!" Or that was the plan.

Burke was first on his list: a sullen, red-headed man with a grudge against everybody. He threw Jerry out of his office before half the "Ya-a-ah" was out. The captain was too happy at the moment to start or finish a fight, so he brushed himself off for a call on Rusty Adams, of the Bluebell Salvage Company.

He entered their office and what appeared to be a secretary or receptionist or something said to him, "Can I help you?"

"Yes," he said absently, looking for Adams. "What are you doing tonight?" She scowled prettily. He noticed her hair, blonde. He noticed her eyes, blue-grey. He noticed, moreover, her face and figure, very neat—but this was business. "Is the proprietor of this ramshackle space-tuggery in?"

"Yes," she said, "the proprietor is in."

"Then drag the old dog out; I would have words with him."

"I," she said, "am the proprietor."

Jerry smiled gently. "Enough of this," he said. "I refer to the illustrious Francis X. Adams, alias the Rusty Nut, alias the Creaking Screw—"

He paused. Her eyes were full of tears. She looked up. "He was my father," she said, "You're Leigh, aren't you? They told me of your ways. Father died while you were in space. I've come from Earth to take care of his business." She blew her nose on a silly little handkerchief, and said, "If there's anything I can do for you—"

Jerry felt lower than a snake's belly. He stammered an apology of some sort and went on, "As a matter of fact I did have a deal to talk over. I want to buy out your concern." As a matter of *fact* he had wanted to do nothing of the sort, but he thought it out quickly. The expense would cripple him for a while, but he'd be able to dispose of the *Bluebell* at a loss and get some operating capital, and one more job like that *Argol* and he'd be right back where he was now with only a little time wasted and she *did* have blue-grey eyes and what did a woman know about salvage anyway—

"Not for sale, Mr. Leigh," she said coolly.

That shocked him—he had thought that he was doing her a favor. He decided to be a big brother. "Miss Adams, I think you ought to accept. Not for my sake, but for yours. You have had no experience at the work; you'll be at the mercy of your employees, and salvage men are the toughest mob in space. Your father could handle the company, but—"

She set her pretty jaw. "Just that," she said. "My father could handle them and so can I."

What was a man to do in the face of such madness? Perhaps—"What about a ship-master, Miss Adams? Your profits will all run into his salary."

"No, Mr. Leigh—my father did it and I can do it. I'm going to pilot my own ship."

With that he exploded—no woman had ever piloted a rocket ship, he said; and also he said that no woman ever would pilot a rocket ship, and that if she thought she was going to learn to pilot a ship she was just plain crazy to try and learn on a salvage scow; and further he said that the salvage scow is notorious throughout all space as the crankiest, most perverted, perverse and persnickety brand of vessel that flies; that to run a scow you had to be born in the space-lanes and weaned on rocket-juice—

"I don't know about the rocket-juice," she said, "but I was born on the Jupiter-Earth liner." Jerry gasped for breath.

"Is there anything else?" she said. "Because if there isn't I'd like to get some work done on my father's accounts."

"No," said Jerry thickly. He was dangerously near apoplexy. "Nothing else." And he walked out of the office muttering, "Accounts ... get some work done on my father's ..." Dammit! A woman *couldn't* fly a scow, and she wouldn't believe that very obvious fact until she was smeared over half of the landing field.

Like a man in a dream he found himself at the offices of the Salvage Field Commission, paying his field dues. An official, dazed, asked if anything was wrong. Did he expect to die, or something?

"No," said Jerry thickly, "but I expect to get potted in about twenty-five minutes. Would you mind coming along?"

"Not at all," said the official. In fact he felt the need of a drink after having beheld the ungodly spectacle of the Leigh Salvage Company paying up on time.

Many hours later all that was left of the two was a very small noise in the corner of a saloon on Broadway, at the corner of Le Bourse. Half of the small—*very* small—noise was saying to the other half at intervals, "*Wimmin* can't never fly ... Wimmin *can' never* fly ... Wimmin can' never *fly* ..." And the second half of the very small noise was replying to the first, "*Yeh* ... they cer'nly don't ..." At length the proprietor told a hackie to please take them away, and what happened to the official nobody ever found out, but Jerry awoke next morning in his hotel room with a pair of blue eyes wavering in front of his face. They weren't real, though—vanished with the first draught of bicarb.

His phone rang, and he winced. It was the Salvage Field Commission, and they wanted to know what he had done with Sweeny. Sweeny? Oh, yeah—no; he didn't remember a thing. To hell with Sweeny. Were there any jobs to be done? He wanted to get off Mars before he got drunk again. There was a long pause while the commission looked up today's sheet. Yes—one bullion ship wrecked between Mercury and Venus. Carrying iridium. Speed was essential; therefore the agreement was on a strictly competitive basis; any or all salvage companies registered could try for it simultaneously. The owner of the ship agreed to buy back the cargo falling to the salvager at market quotations out of hand. First scow to get a grapple on, had her. Laufer and Burke had filed intention claims, and were starting off in a couple of hours; so had *Blue-bell.*

"*Who?* What master?"

"Er ... Adams. Holy smokes! *Alice* Adams!"

Jerry swore. "You'll have to stop that kid. She doesn't know how to fly."

"You'd better come down, then. You seem to know more about this mess than I do. Hurry up if you want a crack at the *Carpathia*—that's the bullion ship."

"Expect me in twenty minutes or less." Hastily he dressed, his hangover forgotten, muttering to himself things about slap-happy blondes. Schopenhauer, he decided, had approximately the right idea.

For the second or third time in his life he was not late for an appointment; twenty minutes saw him bursting through to the office of the commissioner.

"Well?" he demanded violently. "Are you going to let her fly? In a race like this is going to be, she'll not only smash up herself and her crew but any of the rest of us who get in what she seems to think is her way."

The body wrapped around the telephone voice answered heavily, "There's nothing to be done about it. For some obscure reason the 'sons or other issue of the deceased licensee shall retain the towage and salvage permits of the deceased, and all appurtenances thereof,' according to regulations.

"The license for towage, etc., includes an operator's card; therefore we discovered that a crack-brained female who has never flown before inherits a flying permit without physical examination or experience. I'm going to write my congressman; that seems to be all that anyone can do about it just now. Shall I fill out an intention for you on that *Carpathia?*"

"Yeah. I won't be back," he snapped, half way through the door.

He found Sven in a cheap rooming-house near the port.

"You round up the rest of the crew!" he yelled, "and be at the field by twelve noon or you're all fired and busted." He tore away and jumped into a taxi. "To the salvage field, buddy, in a helluva rush!"

He was oiling the space lock when the others arrived, led by Big Sven. He stared at them. "Often," he said, "I have wondered what happens to space lice when they crawl off the ship. I now perceive that I should have known." Each and every man of them had at least one black eye; each had cuts and bruises about the temples. "Well—forget the good times. There's iridium drifting free between Mercury and Venus, and we're going to snag it. And if we don't sink our grapples into that hulk before any other space-tramp, you worms go hungry. Clear? Now get to stations; in ninety seconds we take off. I said *ninety!*"

The men filed into the stubby ship holding their heads. A hangover is nothing to take with you on a spaceflight. If they could have left their heads behind they would have done it. With creakings of abused muscles and battered bones, they strapped themselves into hammocks and pads.

The crew of *Leigh Salvage, Incorporated* was in a bad way.

The takeoff was uneventful as such things go; Jerry mentally noted that he had blown away a small corner of the salvage-table, just another item to subtract from the profit, if any.

Once again in space, the captain was at the look-out plate, eyes and hands and brain bent five hundred kilos out into the vacuum. "Particle sighted ahead," he droned, "in our third quadrant. Salvage scow *Bluebell*. Full speed ahead to pass her." His fingers played over the master's board, and the blunt ship roared ahead. They were near—dangerously near—the *Bluebell*. A blast from the steering fins and the scow jolted into a new course. Jerry never took chances—hardly ever. They slowed acceleration far in advance of the other vessel; that was another contract tied up and in the bag. The captain relaxed—That Adams girl ... of course she couldn't handle a ship. Anybody could make a not too disastrous takeoff, but she'd smear hell for leather when she tried to land.

A signal light flashed on his board, and he snapped on his communication beam. There was a long pause while the power built up, then a voice from the grid—

"Scow *Bluebell* calling scow *Leigh Salvage, Incorporated*. Give way. We're going to pass you in your first quadrant. That's all."

Jerry gaped. Unheard of! "Scow *Leigh* to *Bluebell!*" he snapped. "Listen, insane female; you're not driving a French taxi. There are ethics and rules in this game we're playing. Do you want to be blackballed and become an outlaw tug?" There was another reason than need of that cargo for his anger—maybe, just *maybe,* she could get back onto the field without busting herself wide open if she were alone, but with a cargo as big as the *Carpathia* she wouldn't have a chance in a million. He thought of what a short towing line could do, and grimaced.

"We're passing, Scow *Leigh.* That's all." The light on his board died. That *was* all. Well … for her sake … and for his own …

"Full speed ahead, and then some more, Sven. It's a race."

But it wasn't much of a race; the *Bluebell's* port fin exploded, and her acceleration stopped. Jerry grinned. "We'll pick her up on the way back and leave her ship there. The farther apart those two are, the safer for both of them … *Hey! Stations!* Hulk *Carpathia* ahead!" And the salvage ship jockeyed for position, drew alongside of the bullion transport and clamped on with a clash of metal against metal. The crew prepared to board.

3

Crime in Space

Jerry reached for the phone, his brow grooved. "Broadway three thousand," he said. The voice with the smile answered, "One moment, please," giving him time to reflect on the superfluity of machinery. Less efficient than a dial-phone, maybe, but that touch of warmth and humanity— "Here's your party, sir."

"Central Office, Interplanetary Police."

"This is Captain Leigh, of *Leigh Salvage, Incorporated.* I wanted to see you about—"

"About the peculiar state of the *Carpathia.* Come on up."

"Yeah," said Jerry, baffled. "That's what I wanted to see you about." How did they know? And maybe they had a lead on the vanished Miss Alice Adams? He hoped so.

He was received in the offices of the Interplanetary Police by a very old man who introduced himself as Major Skeane. Jerry took a seat and opened the valise he had brought. "I don't know how much you know about the business of the *Carpathia,*" he said, "so I'll begin at the beginning. Please examine these—exhibit A."

"These" were the contents of his valise—small, heavy chunks of metal. Skeane grunted. "Once spheres," he said, "apparently cast in a shot tower; then sandblasted to suggest natural formations. Some filed by hand, even. These, I take it, were the particles that wrecked the bullion ship?"

Jerry wet his lips. "Yes," he said. "It looks like a put-up job for sure. And Alice— that's Master Adams, of the scow *Bluebell*—she's disappeared. We were racing her for the *Carpathia* and she broke down about half a million kilos from the hulk. I meant to pick her up on the way out to Mars and maybe tow her ship in, too, but when we got grapples on her we found her scow deserted—not a man left on her! Have you people got any dope on that business?"

Major Skeane scratched his head. "Captain," he said, "I'm sorry to inform you that while you do not jump to false conclusions, neither do you shine in the formulation of true ones. Do you see no logical relationship between the two events?"

Jerry considered, and paled. "None," he said angrily. "And instead of antilogising, you might be out hunting down the swine that would try to profit by the deaths of two score men."

"The rebuke is undeserved," smiled the old man. "We have the wrecker of the bullion ship—or at least we know who did it, and how."

"Anybody I know?" asked Jerry.

"I believe so. The saboteur is Miss Adams, of *Bluebell.*"

The younger man stiffened in his chair. "No!" he cried. And then persuasively, "she might be crazy as a flea, but wrecking—never!"

"You do us an injustice. We were warned to watch her the moment she landed on Mars. Our agents assured us that she was a girl with ambitions; they kept track of her, reporting to us for the customary considerations. One man in particular—LeMouchard—has kept us posted, and he's as much to be trusted as anyone these days. To my mind—and I am the officer in charge of this case—the alleged disappearance of Miss Adams is conclusive proof of her guilt. She failed to cash in on the particularly rich opportunity that she created for herself and thus destroy the evidence, and so was picked up by a confederate, with her presumably equally guilty crew. I expect her now to continue her career from another base; possibly another planet, until she makes a slip. Then we shall trace her and deliver her to the execution cell."

"I see," said Jerry, fighting to keep calm. But he didn't see and somewhere there was a horrible mistake which had cost the lives of a score of men and would yet cost the life of that girl with the blue-grey eyes who had tried to pass him and had nearly wrecked her ship and his own, he thought.

Skeane broke in. "Will you leave that valise of junk here? We need some material evidence. And I want you to swear to a description of the girl."

"Sure," said Jerry vaguely. "Anything you say."

"Right. Hair, blonde; shade thirty-three plus on the I.P. scale. Eyes, blue-grey—shade nine. Weight—Captain! Come—"

Jerry was walking slowly through the outer office, his mind in a state of terrible confusion. He didn't know what to do for himself or her. Attack it with logic, he decided fuzzily. For effects there are causes. Assuming flaws in the line of Skeane's logic, discover the points of specific strain and test them. Hah—he had mentioned "agents"—those, he supposed, were informers. And—what was his name?—LeMouchard. Weak link number one: now to test it.

He walked into a store. "A bottle of olive oil, please. A big one." That was the first step.

In Mars there are many hidden ways. For every city there is a shadow-city twisting its tunnels and warrens beneath the sunlight and air. It was through these dark passages that Jerry wandered—to check, as he thought, on official deduction, of course.

Reeking with oil and dressed in the rags of an outlaw space-tug's crew, he passed into the dismal underworld as one of its own creatures. In not many hours he was to be found in a low dive swilling the needled ethyl that passes as potable among the scum of a solar system. It was easy to make friends of a sort there—the price of a drink took care of it.

Jerry wasn't drunk, in spite of the terrible cargo of rot-gut he had been stowing away, but he was just a bit ill, for his stomach was well lined with olive oil, sovereign remedy and anti-intoxicant. He was buying liquor for a slimy little man through no altruistic motives; for this was LeMouchard, informer to the police. Gently he questioned him. Of course, he was strictly on the legit, but he hadn't always been, no? And those camels of the *gendarmerie* that made themselves the great ones, a good man—like our comrade here, yes?—could wrap them around his finger, no?

And surely he was not such a fool as to play with only one master when the pay from two was twice as great? He thought not. Oh, yes—that clever business of the *Bluebell* girl! He, Jerry, would give a pretty penny to know in whose dazzling intellect that task had been conceived and brought to fruition. Was it—could it be—that he, Jerry, was standing in the presence of the man? But no! But yes! Then surely that was worth another drink of the so gentle ethyl. And so the great LeMouchard was in the pay of the police and one other. Might he, Jerry, be permitted to inquire as to who had availed himself of the services of so great a man?

LeMouchard looked owlishly over a drink. *"Oui,"* he croaked. "It is permitted." His face flushed abnormally, and he shook his head like a dazed fighter. "The English, I forget how you call him ... *Le bon petit roi d'Yvetot*—the king with the little orchestra. It is ..." he bowed forward, his eyes bulging. *"Carbon?"* he said. *"Sa Majesté Carbon."* His ratty face hit the table-top. Out cold.

King Carbon—coal. King—Cole? *Old* King Cole? That seemed to be the idea. But what was a merry old soul with a small orchestra doing on Mars with a stool-pigeon?

He returned to his hotel room and phoned the Interplanetary Police.

"Major? What do you know about Old King Cole?"

There was a pause. "I believe," said the thin grey voice of Major Skeane, "that he died just fifteen years ago. A bit before your time."

"As I understand it he never lived. What are you talking about?"

"Early space pirate. Good man, too. Crashed on Pluto two days after I was assigned to his case. I was a terror in those days; he must have been afraid of my rep. They all were, then. Did I ever tell you about Ironface Finkle, the Mercurian Menace? I brought him down ..."

"Very interesting; very—this King Cole—I want to know more about him. I suppose you found his remains?"

"On Pluto? Don't be silly. When they crash there they stay crashed. This Ironface had had a better position than I did, naturally; I made it a point never to be unfair to the men I was assigned to, since my name alone struck terror—"

"Naturally, Major. How did King Cole work?"

"The usual way: ramming and boarding. Now Finkle had a tricky twist to his technique and had me baffled for a time—"

"That's too bad," said Jerry tiredly. "How old was Old King Cole when he—ah—crashed?"

"Rather young. In fact, he had just graduated from a tech school on Venus when he took up his career and ended it in about a year. But the Mercurian Menace was older and more experienced. He knew how to handle a ship. I was hard-pressed, but soon—"

Jerry hung up. It was fantastic! How many men had been to Pluto and returned? If his hunch was right—and it sometimes was—at least one more than the records showed. He phoned room service for the *Marsport Herald*.

"Yes, sir. Morning or afternoon edition?"

"Both. Oh, yes—I want them as of this date fifteen years ago. Better get me the year's file."

Room service turned to linen and said, "That man is mad as a hatter." Then hastened to the *Herald* building for the files.

In due course the files reached Jerry, who had been calculating the location of the *Bluebell*.

He flipped the pages to January and read a report of the King's first appearance. He had struck like a demon at an excursion ship, gassing it and gutting it with thermite bombs, leaving a message pinned on the chest of the mutilated captain:

> Old King Cole was a merry old soul,
> And a pirate, too was he;
> He wiggled his toes, and he thumbed his nose,
> *And said: 'You* can't *catch* me!'

From that and subsequent clues his identity had been traced. He had been Chester Cole, honors student at Venusport Tech and had led his class at the Academy of Astronavigation— but was just a little cracked, it seemed. He had, as a student, fought a "duel" with another boy, crippling him. All that had saved him from prison then had been the loyal lies of his class-mates. His crew, in the days of his career of crime, seemed also to have been made up of like contemporaries. It was a strange and striking picture, this mad boy roaming space in a ship of his own, striking out at will at women and children.

Now to the end of the files, to investigate his death—

4
Pursuit Between the Planets

Approximately on the line which Jerry had calculated, a ship of strange design was speeding for Pluto. Like every spaceship, it was highly specialized. The super-powerful motors and grapples of the salvage scows were not hers, nor the size and luxury of the passenger liners. This was no huge freighter, jammed to the blister and built for a maximum of space to store to a minimum of crew. Yet she had a purpose, and that purpose screamed from every line. This rocket was a killer, from bow to stern. Her prow was a great, solid mass of metal toughened and triply reenforced for ramming; a terrible beak of death. Above her rear rockets protruded a stern-chaser that scattered explosive pellets behind her in an open pattern of destruction.

But this very efficient machine was not entirely lacking in comfort, for Alice Adams rested easily in a chamber that might have graced—and once, perhaps did—the costliest luxury liner. She had awakened there after that peculiar odor through the *Bluebell* had laid her out and her crew. Then a courteous knock sounded on her door. "Come in," she said, baffled by the anomalous situation.

A man entered. "I welcome you," he said, "to my vessel. I trust that you will find—"

Alice looked at his face, and screamed.

The man recoiled and muffled his features in a scarf. "I can hardly blame you," he said savagely. "It is the wind of Pluto. You will find that my entire crew is like that, I warn you. Skin grey and dead, the scars of the Plutonian sleet over all the face. For five years we lived unsheltered in that hell—five years that might have been a thousand. Can you know what that means?"

"But who are you?" asked the girl. "And I'm—I'm sorry about ..."

"I was once known," said the man, "as King Cole. Bright boy of the space-lanes; pirate *par excellence*. The whimsical butcher—that was me. Fifteen years ago I died on Pluto, they think. Maybe I did; it's hard to say for sure these days. We lived in the broken open hull of our ship where it fell, breathing in helmets, feeding from crates and cans of food. One kid thought he could melt the snow outside and drink it. He was very thirsty, and he went mad when he saw the snow boil up into yellow-green gas. It was chlorine. It's cold out there where we're going.

"Many years it was, and then another ship crashed, and we took off our helmets and lived in that and sang songs with the men of it who survived. They were technicians, and tried to fix their rocket, but one of my boys killed them. He thought he liked it there; he must have been crazy.

"A long time later a first class pirate ship landed. We crawled across the snow to her—two hundred kilos. They took us in because they hadn't a mechanic worth the name, and all of us were fine tech men. I said I could fix her, and I could. Then one night my men killed all the crew of this new ship and I patched it with stuff from the other two rockets so we took off and sneaked into Mars.

"I had been a fool once, and that was enough, so I meant to do it the right way this time. You don't strike without warning if you want to be a success; you give plenty of warning through agents and policemen you've hired, and steer them just a bit the wrong way so that they suspect nothing and honestly believe that they'll get you the next time.

"I met a lot of friends I knew on Mars, and made some new ones when I'd disposed of the ship's cargo. The boys and I have been cruising around for some time now, doing nothing spectacular—it doesn't pay. We've been knocking off a ship here and there, laying the blame square onto a rival or somebody. Our home is still Pluto—we don't like it, in a way, for what it did to us, but in a way we do because nobody else does, and it's so *damn* far away from anything half the time.

"I'm sorry that you didn't get the *Carpathia*. I thought that with a father like yours you could fly sideways and beat any other scow in the ether to a contract."

She stared at the madman. "What did you know about my father?"

"He was my instructor on Venus. He got me out of a piece of trouble when I killed a man that swore at me. He was a good instructor, and I'm pleased that I have the chance to do him a favor through you. You see, I wrecked that bullion ship for you. Then I was going to pick you up and the junk, but I see I've only got you. Well—perhaps that's enough. You can't return to Mars even if you want to. I suppose the police have their cruisers out looking for you and your crew. I buttered the crime onto you for both our advantages. I hope you don't mind?"

"No," she said, "and you wanted to do my father a favor by permitting me to join your—band?"

"Exactly," came from the muffled features. "And you will?"

The girl sobbed, "Never! Space is clean and cold; why must you make it a thing of Terror? Isn't that pain enough without you and your kind?"

The pirate laughed. "The whimsical butcher is not displeased," he said. "You will have your uses anyhow. It will be a long time before a soul suspects King Cole—the late King Cole—of the atrocities perpetrated by Miss Alice Adams and her cutthroat crew. I know how the police mind works. That's my business, now. Good day—you may ring for food." He left, and the door closed behind him.

Vainly the girl sprang to the door and tried the knob. It was locked firm. She returned to the bed and shut her eyes, trying to blot out the memory of that grey, horribly seamed face.

In Marsport Jerry had not been idle. He had been to see the major again, and tried to convince him of the truth so self-evident to the younger man's mind, but the placid old idiot listened blandly and blankly. When Jerry was finished he said, "Through an accident, I believe, we were cut off in our telephone conversation a while ago. I was about to describe the position in which Ironface and I found ourselves—"

But Jerry was gone with great curses on his lips. Patiently Skeane sighed. It had been six years since he had been able to finish that story; the last man to hear it complete had been a convict extradited to Venus from Jupiter. Skeane had strapped him down in the little two-man rocket and whiled away the long hours of space travel with the tale in its gruesome entirety. He thought, now, that it would be nice if he could find somebody else to strap down and tell the story to. He was even a bit afraid that he was forgetting the details himself...

A taxi was driving through the muddy streets of Marsport; Jerry snapped a bill under the hackie's nose. "This for you if you step on it," he said. They pulled up, brakes squealing horribly, before a battered, weatherbeaten tenement. Jerry took four stairs at a time and burst into the close, dirty room. He shook the sleeping figure. "Sven! *Sven,* dammit! Wake up, you loose-brained lump of soggy Norwegian caviar! We have the biggest job we've tackled yet!"

The helmsman rolled over, and dizzily asked, "We tow, Captain?"

"Yeah, we tow—a full-armed battleship that doesn't want to be towed. Get the men to the field in twenty minutes—fare is on Leigh Salvage, Incorporated."

As the big man struggled into his clothes Jerry was down the stairs and into a taxi. "Salvage Field," he snapped, "in a helluva rush."

He had often boasted that the engines of scow *Leigh* were the most powerful things in the ether. Well—he would see how powerful they could be—shifting feed lines and adjusting nozzles to move the traction power, terrific as it was, into a different channel. The scow was to haul nothing but her own weight this trip, but it was essential, to put it mildly, that she haul it *fast*. The men lined up before her as the job neared completion. Briefly but clearly Jerry outlined the dangers and invited men to drop out.

"Wylie," he said, "since I shipped you we've been getting complaints from your quarter about work. This is going to be work the like of which you never dreamed. You can take out that pistol of yours; sure as leather you're going to us it this trip, unless somebody gets you first.

"Anybody leaving? No? Then pile in and strap tight. In ninety seconds we take off under fifteen Mars gravities acceleration."

There was a little glow in his chest. These were men—his men! Comrades of flight and wreck, he'd stood by them and they were making good this day. And for a crazy woman? That was the part that baffled him—why? He had had practically no respect for her father; his ethics, or lack of ethics was notorious on the field. But she couldn't fly a ship! That, he said to himself, was what had convinced him of her innocence of the highly technical charge of piracy.

"Strapped in?

"Eighty-nine—

"Fire!"

With a roar they took off. Such acceleration was unheard of, even on this field, where rules of astronavigation were scrapped daily and the laws of the space-lanes broken as a matter of course.

In a moment they had vanished from the sight of observers on the field; a moment more and they were into space, beyond air and warmth.

"All hands," rang out over the *Leigh Salvage* annunciator. "These will be battle stations when so ordered. Sven, be ready to take the tiller if anything happens to me; Wylie, choose and arm eight men to form a boarding party. Two others stand by with repair-paste in the event that our periphery is punctured. One man stand by the manual controls in case the electric board is blown by anything they have in their bag of tricks. That is all—flight stations!"

A long silence followed, Sven's hand white on the helm. "Deflect into first for particle in third," said Jerry, at length. "Meteorite." The ship shifted. "Good God, Sven—did you see that thing?" cried Jerry.

The helmsman said, puzzled, "Yes, Captain."

"But Sven—we passed it—going in the same direction! The first time I've known that to happen. Swede, we're traveling plenty fast."

5

Contact Off Pluto

Out in space time depends most of all on the man concerned, but for all those on the speeding little scow, the days flashed past. They saw Jupiter pale behind them, and Saturn, and Neptune; then, one day—

"Helmsman," said Jerry tensely, "turn control to master's board. I think I see them." Uneasily the big man surrendered the guiding of the vessel; he was the sort who likes to know what is going to happen next. Jerry's fingers touched the panel, his eyes never leaving the glinting speck far ahead of him; the speck that grew as he overhauled it with dizzying speed. His own exhausts glared less bright; he was slowing down that there might be no mistake. A telescope brought to bear on the point screened out the rocket's dazzle and enlarged the features of the vessel. And there was something about it—he was almost sure.

He *was* sure. That tube astern was a chaser, meant for him and his scow. He turned on the annunciator, his jaw clenched. "Attention all hands," he said. "To battle stations. Check on your paste, repair crew; check on your weapons, boarding party. Pirate ship—" he squinted through the telescope—"Pirate Ship *King Cole* in sight. That is all."

He snapped on a beam of communication to the pirate ship, closing up the distance between them, and sent a call along it.

"Scow *Leigh Salvage* calling unregistered *King Cole*. Scow *Leigh Salvage* calling unregistered *King Cole*. Answer if you hear me, unregistered *Cole*. Scow *Leigh* to unregistered *Cole*."

There were etheric cracklings, then a dry voice. "Answering, scow *Leigh Salvage*. If you know who we are, what do you want with us?"

Jerry was close enough to see their chaser turn into his quarter and extend for firing.

"Heave to, *King Cole*," he said. "We're commissioned as a converted warship of the Interplanetary Police." This was neither strictly true nor untrue. As a matter of fact Skeane had said, "Go on and make a fool of yourself if you plan to. You and your ship have my full permission."

"Captain," said the voice from the pirate ship, "your letter of marque won't take *us*. I advise you to turn your garbage can back to where it and you belong before we rake you *just once*."

"Second of three warnings," said Jerry, wetting his lips. "Heave to in the name of the Interplanetary Police."

There was a long chuckle from the beam-grid.

"Third and last warning: heave to!" With the words Jerry tore the ship up and over into a great, ragged loop as the pirate gun belched pellets of destruction. He had thought he would be well outside the scattering pattern, but the scow trembled as a fragment exploded against its side. "Repair crew to larboard!" he shouted into the annunciator plate, his eye on the air-pressure gage. Its needle dipped once; then rose to normal. "Plate blown in and patched, sir," came Hiller's voice. "All clear."

"Stand by, all," said Jerry. "We're going to attack." This ship rose, under his sensitive fingers, above its foe. "Prepare to swing grapples," Jerry warned. "Check magnetic plates. OK?"

"Magnetic plates OK" answered Wylie.

"Then *hold on!*" The ship swooped and fluttered, at times seemingly inviting the fire of the pirates, at times seeming disabled, and darting away as the killer vessel swung itself to deliver a *coup de grâce*.

The scow's grapples swung free—ponderous curved plates at the end of long osmiridium chains. Then down she darted, the grapples clanging against the sides of the pirate and sticking like plaster, and magnetized plates in the ship herself adhering to the other.

Jerry turned to the annunciator. "Wylie, cut through take over the board, Sven. I'm going down for the fun."

"Yes, Captain," said the big man.

Again in Wylie's skilled hands the burning paste oozed from his tool and ate through the metal of the pirate's hull as the crew bolted on their space helmets. Guns clicked in readiness; the oval of weakened metal was closed. The salvagers stood back as Jerry kicked down the section. Gun ready, he and his men stepped through. They were in an empty storage room, it seemed—one that would never again be crammed with loot.

Through his head-set Jerry ordered, "All out of the scow. Come through and bring sealing material." The rest of the crew filed through the ragged opening, stepping cautiously. "Seal that," said Jerry. "Either we fly the pirates' ship to Marsport or we don't fly at all."

The breech was sealed, and the crew stripped off their spacesuits. Grimly, weapons poised, they moved in a solid line for the bulkhead that sealed them off from the rest of the ship. They heard running feet through the wall. There would be a corridor on the other side. Jerry flung open the bulkhead and stepped through, guns blazing. Before him was a mass of men, their faces grey, horribly seamed things. Three fell under his fire; others struggled vainly to raise a semi-portable gun against him and the men who came trooping through, their weapons hammering madly in their hands.

Tactics were discarded, and the two groups sprang together, locking in combat. Muffled groans and the thud of fists were heard; gunbutts rose and fell on skulls and faces. Finally the salvagers stood above their foes, bloody and victorious.

"Neat work," said Jerry, wiping blood from his face. "Now let's get up this cannon of theirs. That wasn't a quarter of their crew." Wylie spread the tripod of the gun and locked its barrel into place. "I think," he said, "it's in working order. Shall I try a squirt?"

Jerry nodded and the gun cut loose, hammering shells down the corridor, battering through the steel door.

"Enough," he said. "The plan from now on is to stay in a lump and keep moving systematically. If we begin at one end and work towards the other we may get there. Otherwise—" He left the words unsaid. "Wylie, go ahead of us, carrying the barrel. Collins, carry the stand."

6
Return From Battle

Slowly they advanced through the shattered door. They were in an engine room. "Wait," said Jerry. He turned to the complicated maze of pipelines and tore one loose; he twisted valves and shut-offs. The trembling drone of the exhaust died slowly. The pirate ship was free in space.

"We go on from here," he said. "Give me the gun-barrel." Wylie surrendered it and his captain fired a short burst at the lock of the door. It sprung open and silently the men stepped through. It led to an ambush; a score of the grey-faced horrors sprang to the attack as his gun cut loose with violent, stuttering squirts of destruction. Men fell on both sides, and Jerry dropped the clumsy weapon to use his fists and pistol-butt.

He was grappling with a huge man, smashing blows into his middle, twisted over his back. He struggled vainly as he felt his tendons about to give, then—a club rose and fell on the head of his foe, and he slid to the floor saved by Sven. "Thanks," he said hastily, scrambling to his feet and sailing into another pirate. A kick to the groin disposed of the man; this was small season for the niceties of combat. He turned as an arm snaked about his neck, and jerked out his pistol, pressing it into the belly of the strangler. He pulled the trigger, his jaw set, and the pressure relaxed suddenly.

From knot of men to struggling knot he swung, firing till his gun was empty, and not daring to stop for a reload. In a few short minutes all was silent save for the panting of the bloody victors—Jerry's men. Two had fallen forever. Gently Jerry straightened their twisted bodies and turned his back on them.

Gruffly he said, "I believe that we are in a position to make an attack on their main forces, which would be concentrated in the control room. Follow me."

And grimly, without a backward glance at the carnage behind them, they followed stealthily down a corridor to pause before a door triply sealed against them. Jerry pounded on it with a pistol. "This is the fourth call to surrender," he shouted through the steel.

There was a mocking laugh. "Come and get us, garbage man," answered a voice dry as dust. "We're ready for you."

Jerry's face hardened. "Give me the torch," he said. They passed the tube to him, and primed it.

He braced himself and touched it to the door, opening the torch to its widest capacity. The arc sprung out; he swung it in a great oval over the steel. The door glowed a fiery white; then the slab of metal fell inward with a clang. Through the opening they saw a score of men, guns poised. There was a pause, then their own semi-portable cut loose and tore through a half dozen of the pirates before Dehring, who was feeding ammunition, fell twisting to the floor.

Guns blazing, then the battle-mad crew of the scow leaped to the attack. Men paired off and swung fists and boots; only Jerry stood aside—Jerry and one other. His face a grey ruin, one of the pirates stood aside and watched, taking no hand and seeking none in the destruction. Jerry walked up to him. Again the strange, knightly drama of conflict in space was to be enacted.

"You, sir," said Jerry, "are the captain?"

The dry, bleak voice that he knew answered from the head without features. "Captain Cole, at your disposal, Captain Leigh. Shall we withdraw?" No insults now—the archaic code of the space-pirates demanded this rigidly formal procedure on the meeting of the two enemy captains in battle. Jerry nodded, and the pirate chief led the way into a luxurious room.

Alice sat up. "Jerry!" she cried. "Has he taken your ship?" He smiled. "No—just the opposite. Our men are fighting it out in the control room; Captain Cole has been so kind as to offer me individual combat."

The pirate chuckled richly, "Pray speak no more of it. I thought you would be pleased to see your Alice again—she is an extraordinarily high-principled young lady. She has refused to join my little band. Well; perhaps she was right—we shall soon see.

"I believe the choice of weapon is mine?"

"Certainly, Captain," answered Jerry according to formula. "And they will be—?"

"Boarding pikes," said the pirate succinctly. "There is a pair here, if you will excuse me." He opened a locker in a corner of the room and withdrew two of the vicious five-foot pole-arms from it. Jerry accepted his weapon with a murmur of thanks and examined it briefly. He struck its shaft over his knee and smiled at its satisfactory weight. "Shall we fight free or formal?" he asked Cole.

"Formal, if Miss Adams will be good enough to referee." The girl nodded, her face white.

"The line of combat is not to be departed from," she began in the traditional phrasing, "and will extend along the center of the room from the door to the bed.

"The first figure will be low-crossed; challenger, Captain Leigh, attacking. The defender, Captain Cole, will attempt to disarm the challenger within three disengagements." She poised her handkerchief. "At the drop of the scarf," she said, "the challenger will attack."

It fell to the floor, and Jerry hooked a tine of his weapon into the pirate's guard and swung upward, then darted at the chest of his enemy. There was a clash of steel, and—his hands were stinging and empty. He had been disarmed. Cole stood smiling, his pike held easily, waiting for the next figure, as Jerry's mind raced furiously back to the days of his school training. He remembered another such disarming at the hands of an old, quick instructor. He had been padded then, and the blades of the pike could not, dulled, penetrate his quartz practice helmet.

Faintly he heard or seemed to hear the instructor's voice say, "Counter once conventionally; then engage, and rocking from the heels twist and thrust at once to disarm." Grimly Jerry smiled. He would not forget again.

"Second figure," said Alice faintly. "The defender will attack high-cross; the challenger will attempt to disarm within three engagements." Again the handkerchief—"scarf" in the language of the pike—fell, and again the steel clashed.

For many minutes they battled through twelve figures; Leigh had again parried Cole's blade, and they turned to Alice. But she was in no condition to continue, having fainted when the pirate's blade had swooped past Jerry's cheek a moment ago.

"Since the referee is incapacitated," said the pirate, after a moment of thought, "shall we continue fighting—free?"

"Challenger agrees," said Jerry. "On guard!" And again the vicious pikes glistened in the light, swinging madly. Jerry abandoned the formal line of combat and cut fiercely at Cole's head, who grinned and swung at his enemy's chest with a practiced flick of his wrists. Jerry sprang back, blood pouring from his side and shortened his grip by three feet of the haft, leaped through an opening, and stretched his body into one terrible blow that sent his blade through the belly of the pirate and out the other side.

The salvage man fell to the floor, and the transfixed body of Cole remained erect, propped on the pole of the weapon.

Jerry's own eyes closed quietly; his hands sought his side, and were wet with blood.

Jerry awoke in a very soft bed with those eyes swimming before his face and a sense of pressure on his lips. "What happened?" he asked, dizzily.

"I kissed you," said the eyes.

He considered. "What did you want to do a thing like that for?" he said.

"Just a hunch. It worked on the Sleeping Beauty, you know."

"Yeah, I guess so. Thanks. Where am I?"

"Marsport County Hospital," said the eyes. "Officially you are Gerald DePugh Leigh, master of the salvage scow *Leigh Salvage, Incorporated,* if there's anything else you want to know. That DePugh nearly changed my mind about you, but I decided that you could bury it as a crossroad with a stake through its heart and maybe it wouldn't bother us."

"This *us* business," he said reflectively. "Just what does it mean?"

"Why, *Jerry!*" said the eyes, deeply pained. "Don't you *remember?*"

"No," he said, "but whatever it was it seems to have been a good idea. Did I propose to you?"

"Yes," she said, crossing her fingers. "And I accepted in good faith and here I find myself jilted practically at the—"

"Oh, *all* right," said Jerry irritably. "Will you marry me?"

"Yes," said the eyes.

There was a pause. "I wonder if you would know how I got here," he sleepily asked.

"I flew the ship back after you ran that Mother Goose murderer through and got your own appendix clipped. You'll be out of here soon—"

"*Who* flew the ship?"

"I did."

"A woman can't fly a—"

"This one did.

"Well ... I suppose so—I feel myself getting drowsy. Do you think the Sleeping Beauty technique will work twice?"

"I'll try—" Jerry heard footsteps, and the eyes retreated. A thin, grey voice spoke up, "Ah, Leigh, I thought I'd call. As you no doubt remember I was telling you of my space-battle with the Mercurian Menace. We were jockeying for position when—"

"Alice, darling," said Jerry.

"Yes, dear?"

"Will you kick that man very hard, please?" He closed his eyes, heard a yelp of pain, and the slam of a door. He smiled sweetly in his sleep.

[*Cosmic Stories* - May 1941
as by Edward J. Bellin]

No Place to Go

Gallacher was no doctor of Philosophy or Science, no more than a humble "mister," and as such could not hope to rise beyond the modest university readership which he had held for some score of years. He was in the Department of Physics, and his job was little more than the especially dirty one of correcting examinations and reading the hardy perennial themes submitted by generation after generation of students. He was also the man who punched calculating machines late into the afternoon, tabulating work of men higher up and preparing their further ground.

He left the university grounds as the sun was setting over the Hudson, jammed a dark green, crumpled felt hat on his head and walked briskly home to the five-room bungalow where he had lived since his marriage.

Entering through the kitchen door, he was greeted by no more than a curt nod from his wife and his buoyant gait reduced to a hesitant shuffle. For Mrs. Gallacher, with her bitter tongue, endless ills and higgling economy, was the terror of her husband.

Dinner was, as always, a grim affair punctuated by little bitter queries from the distaff side—money, always. Why didn't he stand up to Professor Van Bergen for a raise? Then he'd be able to get a little car and not have to walk two miles from home and back on the highway like a common tramp. And why didn't he see her cousin, the Realtor, about another place near here but where those terrible Palisades wouldn't arouse her acrophobia. Gallacher had shuddered when his wife, seven years ago, first proudly told him that she "had" acrophobia. He knew then that it would not be the last said on the subject.

Vaguely he wiped his mouth with a napkin and said: "'M going down for a little tinkering …"

"Tinkering!" spat Mrs. Gallacher poisonously. "You in that cellar where I can't keep my washing machine because it's cluttered up with—"

He heard her out, smiling deprecatingly, and without answering went into the tiny foyer and opened the cellar door with two keys. His wife did not have copies of either.

Down the steps he snapped a switch, and the plot-sized basement sprang into sharp being under the glareless brilliance of the most modern refractory glow-tube installation. He smiled proudly on the place and its furnishings. This, he thought, is my real life, and I can deny it nothing.

From the shelf of black-bound, imperishable notebooks, through great racks of reagents, turning lathe, forge, reference library, glassware and balances to the electronics and radioactivity outfits, nothing was lacking to make up an almost complete experimental set-up for advanced work in physics, chemistry or practical mechanics.

Gallacher, sitting there among his tools, had a spark of something in his eyes that would have baffled his wife. He opened a notebook and stared almost feverishly down at the half-written page. The last words had been: "—to dry set in 12 hrs. This cmpnd to be xmnd tomorrow."

Swallowing gingerly, he turned the book face down and lifted a tray from a drying rack cunningly placed in the cool draft of a window high up in the wall. Removing a tiny speck of the marble-sized, flinty mass that rested on the glass surface he inserted it into a spectroscope's field chamber, then snapped on the current that sent his electric bills soaring higher month by month. The speck glowed a vivid white; he squinted through a series of colored filters at the incandescent particle. Then, sighing inaudibly, he lit the projector's bulb. On the calibrated ground-glass screen appeared the banded spectrum of the compound.

Gallacher ticked off the bands with a pencil. Thoughtfully he turned up his notebook and wrote: "Spctrscpe confirms 100%."

Mrs. Gallacher was in bed, a magazine flung irritably on the floor beside her. As she heard the steps of her husband coming slowly up the cellar stairs she settled her hair and scowled.

He came through the door and blinked dazedly. "Still up?" he asked. "I had some special work to do—finishing my tinkering ..." He smiled feebly.

"Tinkering!" She crowded into his own word all the vitriolic indignation of which her small, mean soul was capable. Then, seeing his face, she paused, frightened and almost terrified. For it was white and giddy with triumph. "Andrew," she said sharply, "what have you done?"

"My series of experiments," he said mildly. "Tonight I closed my notebooks. My work is finished—and successful." Then, astonishingly, he blazed forth: "Edith! What I have done, no man has done before me—in this house I have synthesized the perfect rocket fuel." He smiled as he saw her face pale. "The fumbling adventurers who tried three times to reach the Moon and finally blew themselves up—their mistake was not to wait for me. Their fuel was not only dangerous but too weak for the job; any adding machine could have told them that. I have been working with explosive propellants for seventeen years, and have you ever heard one of my thousands of tests? No, for I worked calmly and with small quantities. And yet through me the universe has been opened to man! Venus, Luna, Mars—"

"Mars," whispered Mrs. Gallacher inaudibly. Then for the first time in many years she addressed her husband sweetly: "Andrew, what are you going to do now?"

"Publish my facts," he rapped. "Take my place among the immortals of science."

"Just—have them printed in some magazine?" she asked, bewildered.

"That would be sufficient," he said. "I shall give my work to the world." He turned into himself, smiling secretly at the thought of honorary degrees, banquets, plaques ...

"Andrew," snapped his wife, "if you think I'll allow you to waste this stuff you're mistaken. For your own sake, Andrew, for your own sake I ask you to come to your senses. Her eyes grew hard as she mused, "We could be rich—richer than anyone!" A sudden purpose crystallized in her mind. "How big would one of your ships have to be?" she demanded.

"Thinking of that Lunar Rocket?" he asked. "Foolishness! All a ship powered with my propellant needs is living quarters, a hull, about a half-ton firing chamber with an infusible exhaust tube and tanks holding a few cubic feet. Foolproof firing apparatus weighs about two pounds. I could build a rocket myself."

"Yes," she said abstractedly. "I know that." And in her mind the proud boast was spinning, "Wife of the first interplanetary traveller!" How she could lord it over the full professors' wives who wouldn't invite her to tea more than twice a year! She'd show them— "Andrew," she began carefully ...

And so it was that Gallacher found himself with a sick headache and groaning muscles roaring through space in the tiniest one-man rocket imaginable, following only his bare specifications, from end to end no larger than a light automobile. Far astern was Mars, red planet that he had not reached, and frustration bit into his vitals.

He had resigned his readership and raised money from relations, finance companies and every source he knew of to build this little space-scooter. His exultation as he plunged through the stratosphere of Earth and the sky went from violet to black had tempered and was now quite gone. The flaw—well, how could he have known? He had been a physicochemist, and this insane adventuring was none of his doing, he thought confusedly. Ahead he could plainly see North America. He wondered if he could land as quietly as he had taken off, not one person in the world knowing except himself and his wife. Then he would publish the incredible proofs of his journey and his fuel. Then he would patent his compound and possibly lease contracts for its manufacture.

Eras of progress incredible, to come from his mind alone! Huge ships of unemployed immigrants leaving for the fertile soil of Venus. Astronomers to establish observatories on airless asteroids and see with incredible clarity the answers to old, vexatious riddles—freighters winging their ways to icy worlds undreamed of for rare hauls of alien artisanry and produce, making Mother Earth a richer and fairer place to be on—

He laughed chatteringly. No; he had forgotten again. It was not to be so; it was not to be at all. Ahead there loomed New York State. He fired off his one braking rocket-tube and began to head south above the Hudson. Why not, he wondered, plunge beneath those waters—now? He shuddered. If he was to land it would be without photographs, without data, without a hope for the future of Mr. Gallacher except a slow, corroding old age.

The rocket passed low above Poughkeepsie, and he began to recognize landmarks. Ahead were the palisaded banks of the river, and above—East Side—was his cottage. He had taken off from a field near by, and there he was to have landed in triumph.

His headache was worse; the needles of pain lanced into his skull so savagely that he almost shot past the field without seeing it. But, not quite. Almost at the last moment possible, he slanted the ship downward and cut loose all his brakes. He hit Earth with a terrible shock, for all the safety devices aboard, and lay on his side in the canted pit of the rocket until he heard a vigorous clanging on the side. His wife's face peered exultantly through the quartz porthole. He looked at her, struggling to recognize the woman, then reached out to open the heavy door of the little craft. His strength was not enough; he heaved himself to his feet and leaned on the sealing bar, bearing down heavily. It gave. With a sucking noise, the rubber-lipped door yielded and swung open. He lifted himself through the port and dropped onto the ground, resting against the warm side of the ship.

"I came over as soon as I heard the rockets," said his wife. "Are you all right?"

"Sick," he answered weakly, holding his head.

"Never mind that," she said. "How did the ship behave? Did you have any trouble?"

"'M a scientist," he replied plaintively, "not an adventurer. Shouldn't have gone—my fuel—useless ..." His voice trailed off incoherently.

"Useless!" she snapped, startled. "You got to Mars!"

"No!" he gasped. "I didn't. Nobody can."

"Andrew!" she cried, "what are you saying?"

With a terrible effort he fought his way through a haze of pain and confusion. He said, in lecturer style: "Now and then meteors hit Earth that do not behave as meteors should." Someone had to know this, he thought bitterly, before he ran down. He could see figures far away, figures sprinting toward the ship.

"They *drift* down, observers say—Charles Fort tells of many instances—yet, as soon as they strike Earth, or rather, high ground, they fall normally—the rest of the way. Just heavy pieces of rock."

The woman stared bespelled at his blank, lax face. "The reason—didn't know. But now—know too well. I didn't land on Mars. No one can. Gravity is just like magnetism. *Likes repel each other.* I was charged with Earth gravity; Mars charged with the same sort of stuff." Gallacher laughed hysterically. "I couldn't get near it," he complained. "Nobody can—meteors that land the usual way have another kind of gravity—from outside the Solar System, must be."

Suddenly, bitterly, he cried: "Shouldn't have gone! Fuel, useless. No good for anything except rockets. Rockets useless. Nowhere to land. No place to go in rockets!"

And those were the last sane words that he uttered in his life.

[*Cosmic Stories* - May 1941
as by S. D. Gottesman]

Dimension of Darkness

"Don't shoot," says Ellenbogan. "For the love of science, don't shoot!"

"Sorry, doc," I says, slipping the safety catch. "I got my orders. That's the way it goes. Got any last words?"

"Look, Mr.—what's your name?"

"Matt Reilly. Make it snappy, bud. I gotta be back in a few minutes for a tote job."

"I see," he says slowly. "You don't know what you're doing, do you?"

"I don't see how that matters," I says, "but they tell me you welched on a five grand pony bet. That right?"

"Yes," he says, breaking into a cold sweat. "But look—it's awfully important that I don't die for a few minutes at least. Someone told me that horse couldn't lose, and I needed the money. I took my chances, I know. But will you let me off for just ten minutes while I wind up my work?"

"Ten minutes," I brood. "Okay, doc. But no funny business. And you don't step out of this lab."

"Thank you, Mr. Reilly," he gasps, wiping his brow. "You can trust me." So then he goes puttering around his machinery, taping wires together, plugging light-cords in, tinkering up coils and connecting radio tubes and things. And I kept my eye on him and the clock. After a while I remind him, "Four minutes to go, doc. How about it?"

"I'll be ready," he answers, not looking up, even. "I'll be ready. Just this one inter-phasometer reading—will you look at this, please—my eyes—it's a very small dial—"

"Waddya want? Be specific," I says.

He freezes up as he sees my gun again. "Just tell me what number this needle is resting on, please. That's all I have to know."

"Okay. This dial?" He nods, so I casually put my gun in his side and bend over to look. It was a seven. "Lucky seven, doc," I says. "And I think your time's up. Turn around, please."

"Seven," he broods, seeming to forget all about me. "So it checks. The number proves it." Then, quick like a fox, he spins around and throws himself at a switch. Startled, I blazes away with the roscoe and some glass breaks.

"Look out!" yells Doc Ellenbogan. "You'll be caught—" And then I sees that there's something awful solid and black turning and growing in the middle of a piece of machinery. "Gas!" I thinks, whipping out a handkerchief and clamping it over my nose. I aimed straight at the doc this time, before running. But then the black thing explodes in one big rush and I'm flat on my back.

"I'm sorry I had to get you involved," says Ellenbogan. "How do you feel?" Then I see that I'm lying down inhaling smelling-salts that the doc is holding. Like a flash I reaches for my heater. But it's gone, of course. Then I guess I says some nasty things to the doc, on account of even the Frank V. Coviccio West Side Social and Athletic Club don't use gas. And you know what louses *they* are.

"Don't misunderstand, please," says the doc with remarkable self-control, considering the names I applied to him. "Don't misunderstand. I have your gun, and I'll give it back to you as soon as you understand clearly what has happened. Where, for instance, do you think you are?"

And there's something in his voice that makes me sit up and take notice. So help me, we ain't in his lab or anywhere near Columbia University that I can see. So I ask him what's cooking.

"The fourth dimension," he says, cold and quiet. So I look again. And this time I believe him. Because the sky, what there was of it, is the blackest black you could ever hope to see, and not a star in sight. The ground is kind of soft, and there's no grass to speak of, except a kind of hairy stuff in tufts. And I still don't know how we can see each other, the doc and me, because there isn't any light at all. He glows and so do I, I guess—anyway, that's what it looks like. "Okay, doc," I says. "I'll take your word for it."

So what does he do? He hands me back my gun! I check the roscoe for condition and aim it. "Mr. Reilly!" he says sharply. "What are you intending to do now?"

"Plug you like I was supposed to do," I reply. And instead of looking worried he only smiles at me as if I'm a worm or something. "Surely," he says, gentle and sweet, "there wouldn't be any point to that, would there?"

"I dunno about that, doc. But Lucco would damage me real bad if I didn't do the job I'm supposed to. So that's the way it is, I guess. You ready?"

"Look, Mr. Reilly," he snaps. "I don't take you for an especially bright person, but surely you must realize that this is neither the time nor the place for carrying out your plans. I don't want to lose my temper, but if you ever want to get back to your own world you'd better not kill me just yet. While I appreciate your professional attitude, I assure you that it would be the height of folly to do anything except take my orders. I have no weapons, Mr. Reilly, but I have a skull full of highly speciallized information and techniques which will be more valuable to you personally than my cadaver. Let's reach an understanding now, shall we?"

So I thinks it over. And Ellenbogan's right, of course. "Okay, doc," says little Matt. "I'm on your staff. Now tell me when do we eat—and what?"

"Try some of that grass," he says. "It looks nutritious." I picks a bunch of the grass and drop it in a hurry. The crazy stuff twists and screams like it was alive. "That was a bum steer, doc," I says. "Many more of those and we may part company abrupt-like. What about food and water?" And the minute I think of water I get thirsty. You know how it is.

"There should be people around," he mutters looking over his shoulder. "The preselector indicated protoplasm highly organized." I take him by the arm. "Look, doc," I says, "suppose you begin at the beginning and tell me just where we are and how we get back home and why you brought us here. And anything else that comes into your head. Now talk!"

"Of course," he says, mild and a little hurt. "I just thought you wouldn't be interested in the details. Well, I said this is the fourth dimension. That is only approximately true. It is a cognate plane of some kind—only one of the very many which exist side-by-side with our own. And of course I didn't mean to take you here with me; that was an accident. I called to you to get out of the way while you could, but the pressure belt caught you while you were busily carrying out your orders, which were to shoot me dead.

"And incidentally, it would have been better for you if you had escaped the belt, for I would have stayed in this plane as long as possible, and would have been as good as dead to you and your Mr. Lucco."

"It ain't that," I interjects. "It's mostly the reputation we got to maintain. What if wise-guys like you—meaning no offense, doc—came in on us every day with heavy sugar to bet, and then welched? The business wouldn't be worth the upkeep in lead. Get me?"

"I—ah—think so," he says. "At any rate, the last-minute alterations I was making when you called on me were intended to take me into a selected plane which would support life. It happens that the coefficient of environment which this calls for is either three, four or seven. I was performing the final test with your kind assistance only a few minutes ago, if you remember. When you read 'seven' from the dial I realized that according to my calculations I would land in a plane already inhabited by protoplasmal forms. So, Mr. Reilly, here we are, and we'll have to make the best of it until I find equipment somehow or other to send you back into your world."

"That," I says, "is fair enough—hey, doc! What're them babies doing?" I am referring to certain ungainly things like centipedes, but very much bigger, which are mounted by several people each. They loom up on the horizon like bats out of hell, not exactly luminous but—well, I see them and there isn't any light from anywhere to see them by. They must be luminous, I think.

"Protoplasm," he says, turning white as a sheet. "But whether friendly or enemy protoplasm I don't know. Better get out your gun. But don't fire until you're positive—utterly, utterly positive—that they mean us harm. Not if I can help it do we make needless enemies."

Up scuttles one of the four centipedes. The driver of the awful brute looks down. He is dressed in a kind of buckskin shirt, and he wears a big brown beard. "Hello," he says, friendly-like. "Where did you chaps drop from?"

Doc Ellenbogan rallies quick. He says, "We just got here. My name's Ellenbogan and this is Mr. Reilly."

"Hmm—Irish," says the gent in the buckskins. I notice that he has an English accent.

"Wanta make sumpn of it?" I ask, patting the roscoe.

"No—sorry," he says with a bright smile. "Let me introduce myself. I'm Peter DeManning, hereditary Knight of the Cross of Britain and possibly a Viscount. Our heraldry and honors got very confused about the fourth generation. We're descended from Lord DeManning, who came over way back in 1938."

"But this is only 1941!" protests the doc. Then he hauls himself up short. "Foolish of me—time runs slower here, of course. Was it accidental—coming over?"

"Not at all," answers the gent. "Old Lord Peter always hated the world—thoroughly a misanthrope. So finally he gathered together his five favorite mistresses and a technical library and crossed the line into this plane. He's still alive, by the by. The climate of this place must be awfully salubrious. Something in the metabolism favors it."

"How many of youse guys are there?" I ask, so as not to seem dumb. He looks at me coldly. "About three hundred," he says. "A few more due shortly. Would you two care to join us? We're back from a kind of raid—tell you all about it if you're interested."

"Of course," says the doc. And without hesitation he climbs up the side of that scaly, leggy horror and perches next to the guy. Sir Peter looks down at me and says, "I think, Mr. Reilly, that you'd better ride on the other bug. This one's heavily burdened already. Do you mind?"

"Not atall," I says viciously. And so I went back to the next thing, which looked at me, curling its awful head around, as I passed.

"Right here, Mr. Reilly," someone calls down.

"Thanks, lady," I says, accepting the helping hand reached down. Settled on the back of the centipede, I shivered at the clammy feeling.

"Feels strange?" asks someone. I turned around to see who was the person who would call riding a hundred-foot bug strange and let it go at that. I stayed turned around, just staring.

"Is something wrong, Mr. Reilly?" she asks anxiously. "I hope you're not ill."

"No," I gulps at last. "Not atall. Only we just haven't got anything back home that stacks up to you. What do they call you?"

She turns a sweet, blushing pink and looks down. "Lady Cynthia Ashton," she says. "Only of course the title is by courtesy. My ancestress Miss Ashton and Lord DeManning weren't married. None of his consorts were married to him. Do you approve of polygamy?"

"I'm sure I don't know, Lady Cynthia," I assure her. "I never got farther than elementary algebra." At which she looks at me queerly while I study her. She's wearing the kind of clothes you sometimes dream about on the woman you love—a barbaric kind of outfit of soft doeskin, fitted to her waist and falling to her knees, where there was an inch of fringe. Red and blue squares and circles were painted here and there on the outfit, and she wore a necklace of something's teeth—just what, I don't like to think.

And her blonde hair fell to her shoulders, loosely waved. No makeup, of course—except for the patches of bright blue on her cheeks and forehead. "What's that for?" I asks her, pointing.

She shrugs prettily. "I don't know. The Old Man—that's Sir Peter—insists on it. Something about woad, he says."

I gets a sudden fright. "You wouldn't be married, would you?" I ask, breaking into a cold sweat.

"Why, no, not yet," she answers. "I've been proposed to by most of the eligible men and I don't know which to accept. Tell me, Mr. Reilly—do you think a man with more than four wives is a better risk than a man with less? That's about the midpoint—four, I mean."

She sees the look in my eyes and gets alarmed. "You *must* be ill," she says. "It's the way this horrid bug is moving. Alfred!" she calls to the driver. "Slow down—Mr. Reilly doesn't feel well."

"Certainly, Cynthia," says Alfred.

"He's a dear boy," she confides. "But he married too young—my three-quarter sister, Harriet, and my aunt Beverly. You were saying, Mr. Reilly?"

"I wasn't saying, but I will. To be on the up an' up, Lady Cynthia, I'm shocked. I don't like the idea of every guy keepin' a harem." And little Matt says to himself that while he likes the idea in the abstract, he doesn't like to think of Lady Cynthia as just another wife. And then I get another shock. "Raill-ly!" says Lady Cynthia, freezing cold as an icicle.

Alfred, the driver, looks back. "What did the beast say, darling?" he asks nastily.

She shudders. "I'm sorry, Alfred. I—I couldn't repeat it. It was *obscene!*"

"Indeed?" asks Alfred. He looks at me coldly. "I think," he says, "that you'd better not talk with Lady Cynthia any more. Mr. Reilly, I fear you are no gentleman." And right then and there little Matt would have slugged him if he didn't send the bug on the double-quick so all I could do is hang on and swear.

Things grew brighter ahead. There seems to actually be real light of some kind. And then a sun heaves over the horizon. Not a real sun; that would be asking for too much, but a pretty good sun, though tarnished and black in spots.

There is a little kind of house with stables big enough for whales in sight, so the bugs stop and everybody gets down. I hunt out Doc Ellenbogan right away. "Doc," I complains, "what's the matter with me? Am I poison? I was chatting away with Lady Cynthia and I happens to say that I believe in the family as a permanent institution. And after that she won't speak to me!"

He gets thoughtful. "I must remember that, Matt," he says. "Such an introverted community would have many tabus. But they are a fascinating people. Did they tell you the purpose of their raid—from where they were returning?"

"Nope. She didn't mention it."

"All I got was a vague kind of hint. They have an enemy, it seems."

"Probably some bird who believes in the sanctity of the home," I suggests nastily. "Or a tribe of ministers."

"Nothing so mild, I fear," says the doc shaking his head. "In the most roundabout way Sir Peter told me that they have lost five men. And five men, to a community of three hundred, is a terrible loss indeed."

"That's fine, " I says. "The sooner they're wiped out, the better I will like it. And while they go under, will you please get to work so I can get back into a decent world?"

"I'll do my best, Matt. Come on—they're leaving." The bugs get bedded down at the stables, it seems, and they go the rest of the way on foot. Sir Peter joins us, giving me the double-o.

"I expect you'll want to meet the Old Man," he says. "And I'm sure he'll want to meet you. Interesting coot, rather. Do you mind?"

"Not at all," the doc assures him. "There are some things I want to find out." He gives Sir Peter a chilly look with that, and that gent looks away hastily.

"Is that the city?" I ask, pointing. Sir Peter casts a pained eye at my extended finger. "Yes," he says. "What do you think of it?"

So I look again. Just a bunch of huts, of course. They're neat and clean, some of them bigger than you'd expect, but huts just the same. "Don't you believe in steel-frame construction?" I ask, and Sir Peter looks at me with downright horror. "Excuse me!" he nearly shouts and runs away from us—I said *runs*—and begins to talk with some of the others.

"I'm afraid," says the doc, "that you did it again, Matt."

"Cripes almighty—how do I know what'll offend them and what won't? Am I a magician?" I complain.

"I guess you aren't," he says snappily. "Otherwise you'd watch your tongue. Now here comes Sir Peter again. You'd better not say anything at all this time."

The gent approaches, keeping a nervous eye on me, and says in one burst, "Please follow me to see the Old Man. And I hope you'll excuse him any errors he may make—he has a rather foul tongue. Senile, you know—older than the hills." So we follow him heel and toe to one of the largest of the cottages. Respectfully Sir Peter tapped on the door.

"Come in, ye bleedin' sturgeon!" thunders a voice.

"Tut!" says Sir Peter. "He's cursing again. You'd better go in alone—good luck!" And in sheer blue terror he walks off, looking greatly relieved.

"Come in and be blowed, ye fish-faced octogenarian pack of truffle-snouted shovel-headed beagle-mice!" roars the voice.

Says the doc, "That means us." So he pushes open the door and walks in.

An old man with savage white whiskers stares us in the face. "Who the devil are you?" he bellows. "And where are my nitwit offspring gone?"

Without hedging the doc introduces himself: "I am Doctor Ellenbogan and this is Mr. Reilly. We have come from Earth, year 1941. You must be Lord Peter DeManning?"

The old man stares at him, breathing heavily. "I am," he says at last. "And what the devil may you be doing in my world?"

"Fleeing from an assassin," says the doc. "And this is the assassin. We are here by accident, but I had expected a greater degree of courtesy than you seem to see fit to bestow on us. Will you explain, please?"

"And that goes double for me," I snap, feeling plenty tough.

"Pah!" grunts the old man. "Muscling in, that's what you're doing! Who invited you? This is my experiment and I'm not going to see it ruined by any blundering outsider. You a physicist?"

"Specializing in electronics," says the doc coldly.

"Thought so! Poppycock! I used a physicist to get me here—*used* him, mark you—for my own purposes. I'm a scientist myself. The only real scientist—the only real science there is!"

"And what might that be?" I ask..

"Humanity, you—assassin. The science of human relationships. Conditioned reflexes from head to toe. Give me the child and I'll give you the man! I proved it—proved it here with my own brains and hands. Make what you like of that. I won't tell you another word. Scientist—physicist—pah!"

"He's nuts!" I whisper to the doc.

"Possibly. Possibly," he whispers back. "But I doubt it. And there are too many mysteries here." So he turns to the old man again. "Lord DeManning," he says smoothly, "there are things I want to find out."

"Well," snarls the old thing, "you won't from me. Now get out!" And he raises his hand— and in that hand is a huge Colt .45 automatic—the meanest hand weapon this side of perdition. I dive for the roscoe, but the doc turns on me quickly. "Cut it out, Matt," he hisses. "None of that. Let's go outside and look around."

Once we are outside I complain, "Why didn't you let me plug him? He can't be that fast on the trigger. You practically need a crowbar to fire one of those things he had."

"Not that cunning old monster," broods the doc. "Not him. He knows a lot—probably has a hair-trigger on the gun. He's that kind of mind—I know the type. Academic run wild. Let's split up here and scout around." So he wanders off vaguely, polishing his glasses.

A passing figure attracts my eye. "Lady Cynthia!" I yell.

The incredibly beautiful blonde turns and looks at me coldly. "Mr. Reilly," she says, "you were informed of my sentiments towards you. I hope you make no further attempts at—"

"Hold it!" I says. "Stop right then and there. What I want to know is what did I do that I shouldn't have done? Lady Cynthia, I—I like you an awful lot, and I don't think we should—" I'm studying her eyes like an eagle. The second I see them soften I know that I'm in.

"Mr. Reilly," she says with great agitation, "follow me. They'd kill me if they found out, but—" She walks off slowly, and I follow her into a hut.

"Now," she says, facing me fair and square, "I don't know why I should foul my mouth with things that I would rather die than utter, but there's something about you—" She brings herself to rights with a determined toss of her head. "What do you want to know?"

"First," I says, "tell me where you were coming back from this afternoon, or whatever it was."

She winces, actually winces, and turns red down to her neck, not with the pretty kind of pink blush that a dame can turn on and off, but with the real hot, red blush of shame that hurts like sunburn. Before answering she turns so she doesn't have to look at me. "It was a counter-raid," she says. "Against—" and here I feel actual nausea in her voice— "against the Whites." Defiantly she faces me again.

Bewildered I says, "Whites?" and she loses her temper. Almost hoarsely she cries, "Don't say that filthy name! Isn't it enough that you made me speak it?" And she hurries from the hut almost in a dead run.

But this time little Matt doesn't follow her. He's beginning to suspect that everybody's crazy except him or maybe vice versa.

Then there were sudden yells outside the hut, and Little Matt runs out to see what's up. And bedad if there aren't centipedes by the score pouring down on the little village! Centipedes mounted by men with weapons—axes, knives and bows. A passing woman yells at me, "Get to the walls—fight the bloody rotters! Kill them all!" She is small and pretty; the kind of gal that should never get angry. But her face was puffed with rage, and she was gnashing her small, even teeth.

As I see it the centipedes form a ring around the village, at full gallop like Indians attacking a wagon-train. And, like Indians, firing arrows into the thick of the crowd. So I take out the roscoe on account of the people on the centipedes are getting off and rushing the village.

I find myself engaged with a big, savage guy dreamin' homicidal visions in which I took a big part. He has a stone axe with a fine, sharp blade, and I have to fend it off as well as I can by dodging, inasmuch as if I tried to roll it off my shoulder or arm, like a prize-fighter would, I would find that I did not have any longer a shoulder or arm.

Little Matt gets in a clean one to the jaw, nearly breaking his hand, and works the guy around to one of the huts, through other knots of fighting men. Then the big guy lands one with the handle of the axe on my left forearm, nearly paralyzing it. And to my great surprise he says, "Take that, you rotten Black!"

Not wishing to argue I keeps on playing with him until he is ready to split my skull with one blow. At which point I dodge, and the axe is stuck firm in the side of the hut. Taking my time to aim it, I crack his skull open with the roscoe's butt and procede to my next encounter.

This gent I trip up with the old soji as taught in the New York Police Department and elsewhere, and while he is lying there I kick him in the right place on the side of his head, which causes him to lose interest.

"Matt! For God's sake!" yells someone. It is Doc Ellenbogan, seriously involved with two persons, both using clubs with more enthusiasm than skill. I pick up a rock from the ground and demonstrate in rapid succession just what you can do with a blunt instrument once you learn how. There's a certain spot behind the ear—

I drag the doc into the nearest hut. "Why do they call us Blacks?" I demand. "And who are they anyway?"

"Matt," he says quietly, "let me have your gun."

Without questions I fork over the roscoe. "What plans you got, chief?" I say, feeling very good after the free-for-all.

"Things begin to fall into place," he says. "Sir Peter, the chap we met, broke down and told me his viewpoint. It wasn't much, but I can tell there's something horrible going on." He actually shudders. "I'm going to see the Old Man. You please stay outside the hut and see that none of the Whites interrupt us."

"I don't think they will," I inform him, peeking out. "The battle's over and—awk!— they ain't taking prisoners." I had just seen that pretty little woman bashing in the head of an unconscious White on the ground. "So the Whites are those people that just came and—left?" I asks. "And we're the Blacks?"

"That's right, Matt."

"Sorry, chief," I says mournfully. "I don't get it."

So we leave for the hut of the Old Man.

While I stand guard outside there is a long conversation in muffled tones; then, so quick they almost sounded like one shot, the roar of the Old Man's .45 and the crack of the roscoe. I bust through the door, and see the doc bleeding from his shoulder and the Old Man lying very dead on his floor.

I tape up the doc as well as I can, but a .45 leaves a terrible cavity in a man. As soon as he is able to talk I warn him: "You better get a doctor to see after that thing. It'll infect as sure as fate."

"It probably will," says the doc weakly. Then he mutters, "That old monster! That horrible old—" and the rest is words that seem all the worse coming as they do from the doc, who is a mild-mannered person in appearance.

"You mean his late nibs?" I ask.

"Yes. That fiend! Listen: I don't know what set him off on that train of thought, but he had a pet theory of some kind. He told me all about it, with his gun trained on me. He was going to kill me when he was quite finished. I had your gun in my pocket, my hand on the trigger.

"He actually was a noble of Britain, and he used every cent he had on lecherous pursuits and the proof of his doctrine—a kind of superman-cum-troglodyte-cum-Mendel-cum-Mills-cum-Wells-cum-Pavlov social theory. Fantastic, of course. Couldn't work except in a case like this.

"So he financed research along lines much like mine and brought himself and mistresses and library and equipment into this plane. And then he proceeded with his scheme. It was his aim to propagandize a race with such thoroughness that his will would be instinct to his descendants! And he succeeded, in a limited way.

"Arbitrarily, he divided his offspring into two camps, about the third generation, and ingrained in each a hatred of the other. To further the terrible joke he named them arbitrarily Black and White, after the innocent war-games of his youth. His aim was—ultimately—to have both camps exterminate the other. For him to be the only survivor. Madman! Hideous madman!"

"That all?" I ask, not wanting to tire him.

"No. He has the equipment to get back into our own plane. I'm going to use it now to send you back, Matt. You can say with *almost* perfect veracity that you bumped me off as per orders."

"But why don't you send these people back?" I ask, being real bright.

"They wouldn't like it, Matt. It would be too great a strain on them. Besides, in the month or so that I'll last here, with this wound in my shoulder, I can throw a perfectly effective monkeywrench into the Old Man's plans. I think that in a few years the Blacks and Whites will be friends."

"I got a better idea," I says with authority. "You go back to Earth and I stay here. You can get patched up by any good medico. And I won't mind it much." And that's what little Matt says, thinking of a golden-haired lady who might be taught that monogamy ain't necessarily a deadly sin.

So Judy, you be a good little sister and open that safe-deposit box of mine—doc will give you the key—and give doc five thousand to square himself with Lucco. And you take the rest and quit that chain-store job and start yourself the swellest beauty parlor in town, just like you always wanted to.

And keep in touch with doc. He's a great guy, but he needs somebody around to see that he don't hurt himself.

[*Stirring Science Stories* - February 1941
as by S. D. Gottesman]

Dead Center

1

The chilled-steel muzzle of the old-fashioned automatic swerved not an inch as Angel Maclure spoke: "I'm at your service, gentlemen. What can I do for you?"

"Put that gun down," advised the shorter man easily. "We just didn't want any fuss. You have our blasters—we won't try anything."

Maclure grinned and lowered his pistol. "Right," he said. "I wasn't sure whether you'd mistaken me for a banker or somebody who deserved killing." He gestured at the blasters which he had wrenched from his assailants' hands. "Pick 'em up, boys." They did, and pocketed the deadly little tubes. "Now what did you want?"

The shorter, softer-spoken man began: "Excuse my friend—he's new in our service. He doesn't realize that we should have asked you first and then pulled the tubes. Understand?"

"All forgiven," said Maclure shortly. "I just didn't expect to be jumped two minutes after I get off a liner. It usually takes months before the police hear that I'm around. What's the service you mentioned?"

"Let's wait before I tell you anything," said the shorter man. He smiled confidingly. "You'll find out enough to blow your top off. Now, Mr. Maclure, you're supposed to come with us—whether of your own free will or by force. Understand?"

"Sure. Call me Angel. What's your tag?"

Maclure walked off down the street, flanked by the other two. He knew that their pocketed hands fingered blaster tubes, and that a false move might cost him a foot or arm. But he was interested by the distinctly peculiar set-up he had seemingly blundered into. The last year he had spent on Venus doing a big engineering job—barracks and installation—for one of the wildcat land promoter outfits. The new scar on his jaw he had acquired when he had stormed into the company offices with a pay-slip that he wanted cashed in full. He still carried the scar, but he had got his due amount, and with it a bit of interest lying in the back of the blasted safe. His trip to Earth again had been in quest of some much-needed relaxation; he had not taken kindly to being jumped by two strangers.

The shorter man hesitated. "I don't know," he said. "Perhaps you've heard of me. Baldur Gaussman."

"Yeah?" asked Angel, impressed. "You did that first floating weather station on Uranus, didn't you?"

"That's right," said Gaussman. He halted before a curtained taxi. "We get in here," he said quietly. And they did.

As the taxi took off Angel didn't even try to figure out the direction they were taking; he knew that the involved loops and spins would hopelessly confuse him. He faced Gaussman quizzically. "This must be something awfully big," he said. "I mean using high-grade extra-terrestrial engineers for muscle-men on a simple pick-up job. Unless I guess wrong this is concerned with some pretty high finance."

The taller man took out his blaster again. "Don't try anything this time," he said thickly. "And don't get nosey before you're supposed to. You can get hurt doing that."

"Yeah?" asked Angel, mildly eyeing him. "That struck home? Okay, pal." He turned again to Gaussman. "You must have been in this for several years, whatever it is," he said.

"That's right. My last job in the open was for Pluto Colony Corporation. I handled their mining in full." He glanced at his watch. "We're here," he said. As he spoke the muffled hum of the plane stopped abruptly and Angel felt it being swung about by a ground crew or turntable. He grinned.

"As I figure it," he said, "we've come about seventy-three miles due east after swinging around four times to throw my sense of direction off the track. I think we're in the heart of the New York financial district, on about the twentieth floor of a very high building."

"I'll be damned!" exclaimed Gaussman, open-mouthed. "How did you do that?"

"Long years of training at the hands of my late beloved father, rest his martinet soul," said Angel. "You behold the only practical, authentic superman. No short cuts, no royal road— just hard work and development of everything I was born with. Let's go." He gestured at the door, which had opened to reveal a dim, luxurious corridor.

"Okay," said the taller man. "Hand over your gun." Maclure obeyed, smiling. "When I pass in front of the metal-detector," he said, "remember the eyelets in my shoes. They're a beryllium alloy."

"That's all right," said Gaussman. "We use an X-ray."

"Oh," said Angel shortly. "Then I might as well tell you now that I have a saw in my shoe and a gas-capsule in my zipper." He produced them and handed them over as he got out of the taxi.

"Thanks," said Gaussman. He pointed. "Through that door, Angel. You go in alone."

As the door—heavy as a bank vault's—closed ponderously behind him, Maclure instinctively recoiled at the terribly moist heat of the room he was in. In the dim red glow that came from the ceiling he could see little curls of steam in the air. His clothes were sopping wet. Absently he wiped his face with a soaked handkerchief.

A voice rang through the air—a thin, feeble whisper, magnified over a PA system. Normally it would be so faint that one could not even strain to hear it. It was the voice of an old man—a man so terribly old that intelligible speech was almost lost to him. It said: "Sit— there, Angel Maclure." A boxy chair glowed for a moment, and the young man sat. He was facing a soft sort of wall, which was red beneath the ceiling lights—a dull, bloody dried red. It slid aside slowly and in absolute silence.

This room was certainly the quietest place in all the world, Maclure thought. He could hear not only his heartbeat but the little swish of air passing through his bronchial tubes and the faint creaking of his joints as he moved his hand. These were sounds which the most elaborate stethoscope could bring out but faintly. Perhaps it was the quiet of the room, he thought, and perhaps it was the faint and mysterious aura which the figure, revealed by the sliding wall, diffused.

It was the shape of a man—had been once, that is. For it was so terribly old that the ordinary attributes of humanity were gone from its decrepit frame. It could not move, for it was seated with legs crossed and arms folded over the shriveled breast, these members held in place by padded clamps. The dully-glowing tangle of machinery about it bespoke artificial feeding and digestion; a myriad of tiny silvery pipes entering into its skin must have been man-made perspiration ducts. The eyes were lost behind ponderous lenses and scanning devices, and there was a sort of extended microphone that entered the very mouth of the creature. Sound-grids surrounded it in lieu of ears that had long since shriveled into uselessness.

The lips unmoving, the creature spoke again: "You know me?" it whispered penetratingly.

Maclure dredged his memory for a moment, following the clue of the high, crusted brow of the creature. "You must be Mr. Sapphire, it seems," said Angel slowly.

"Excellent," whispered the creature. "I am Mr. Sapphire—of Planets Production Corporation, Extraterrestrial Mines, Amusements Syndicate, Publishers Associated—can you complete the list?"

"I think so," said Angel. "In spite of the very clever management it's almost obvious—after a rather penetrating study—that there is one fountainhead of finance from which springs almost all the industry and commerce and exchange in the system today. I had not suspected that you were at the head and still alive. One hundred and eighty years, isn't it?"

"Yes," whispered the creature. "One hundred and eighty years of life—if this is it. Now, Maclure, you do not know why I called you. It is because I am a proud man, and will not be humiliated by death. I shall live, Maclure. I shall live!" The voiceless whisper was still for a moment.

"And," suggested Angel, "you want me to help you?"

"Yes. I followed your childhood in the hands of your father. I saw you at twelve the equal of men four times your age, physically and mentally their actual equal. And I know that after the death of your father you chose to disappear. I knew you would do this, Maclure, for a while. It was your intention to slip into the way of the world and forget that you were the infinite superior of your fellows. Well—you succeeded, in your own mind at least. You are well on the way to forgetting that to those around you you are as a man among apes. That is so of all men except you—and me."

Angel grinned bitterly. "You struck it," he said. "I think you and I stand alone in the world. I was the victim of my father's ambition. What are you?"

"Life eternal," sounded the voiceless whisper. "To watch the world and its aspects—to mold it as I will, and eventually—destroy it! Destroy it and fashion another! Maclure, medicine has done all for me that it can. I am the final example of the surgical art. Once my brain was transplanted into a youthful body, but even I could not stand the shock. I died, and was revived only with the greatest difficulty.

"Three times since then I have died. The last time it took three hours to revive me. Ten minutes more and I would never have lived again. Under the laws of nature I can last no longer. And so you must come to my rescue."

"How am I to do that?" demanded Angel.

"For me," breathed Mr. Sapphire, "you will suspend these laws. Do not interrupt. I can give you only a few minutes more before I retire for a treatment.

"All creation is in motion, we know. So we are taught. Earth moves about the sun, sun about the great hub of the galaxy, the galaxy in a mighty circle about its own directrix—space itself, 'ether,' so called, is like a mighty ball rolling and tumbling through unimaginable chaos. To this outside of space we cannot attain, for to go to the end of space is to return to the starting point.

"But there is another locus in space—wholly unique, wholly at variance with any other time-and-space sector that may be marked off. Can you conceive of it?"

Angel, his brows closely knit, shot out: "The vortex! The hub around which space revolves—space at rest and absolutely without motion!"

With the faintest suggestion of mockery in his voice Mr. Sapphire whispered, "The celebrated superman has it. Utterly unique and lawless—or perhaps with laws of its own? At any rate it must be obvious that the limitations which bind matter in space are removed in this vortex of Dead Center."

"And I am to find it and release a certain amount of matter, your body, from certain restrictions, that is, human decrepitude?" countered Angel.

"That is it. You will work for me?"

"Damn right I will," exploded Angel. "And not for your money or anything you have to offer—but just for the kick of finding your quiet spot and doping it out!"

"That," whispered Mr. Sapphire, "is how I had estimated it." The wall began to slide back into place again, hiding his shriveled body and tangle of machinery, when he spoke again: "Use the metal tab lying on that table." He was gone.

Angel looked about, and as a table lit up with a little flash, he picked a tag of some shiny stuff from it and pocketed the thing. He heard the ponderous door grind open behind him.

2

Angel, his mind buzzing with figures and colossal statistics, had aimlessly wandered into the proving room. Assistants leaped to attention, for he was known as a captain in the Tri-Planet Guard. And the ship and plotting were, of course, official business. That was only one of the many ways in which his work had been made easier. But work it still was—the hardest, most grueling kind of work of which any man could be capable. The first job he had ordered had been the construction of immense calculating machines of a wholly novel type. He could not waste his own time and his own energy on the job of simple mathematics. He just showed up with the equations and theoretical work well mapped out and let the machines or his assistants finish it off.

"At ease," he called. "Get back to work, kids." He ambled over to the main structural forge and confronted the foreman. "Rawson," he said, "as I planned it this job should be finished by now."

Rawson, burly and hard, stared at Angel with something like contempt. "You planned wrong," he said, and spat.

Angel caught him flat-footed. After one belt on the chin Rawson was down and out. "How much longer on this job?" he asked a helper.

"Nearly done now, sir. Who's stuck with the proving-ground tests?"

"Nobody's stuck. I'm taking her out myself."

With something like concern the helper eyed Maclure. "I don't know, sir," he volunteered. "In my opinion it isn't safe."

"Thanks," said Angel with a grin. "That's what we aim to find out." He climbed into the ship—small and stubby, with unorthodox fins and not a sign of a respectable atmospheric or spatial drive-unit—and nosed around. He grunted with satisfaction. No spit-and-polish about this job—just solid work. To the men who were working a buffer-wheel against the hull he called, "That's enough. I'm taking her out now." They touched their caps, and there was much whispering as Maclure closed the bulkhead.

With a light, sure touch he fingered the controls and eased the ship inches off the ground, floating it to the take-off field, deeply furrowed with the scars of thousands of departing rockets. There was no fanfare or hullabaloo as he depressed the engraved silver bar on the extreme right of the dash. But in response to that finger-touch the ship simply vanished from the few observers and a gale whipped their clothes about them.

Maclure was again in the black of space, the blinking stars lancing through the infinitely tough plastic windows. And he was traveling at a speed which had never before been approached by any man. "Huh!" he grunted. "I always knew I could work it out." He saw the moon in the distance—about a million miles behind and to starboard.

Deliberately he cut into the plane of the ecliptic, determined to take on any meteorites that might be coming. He had a deflection device that needed testing.

Through the clear window before him he saw a jagged chunk of rock far off, glinting in the sun. Deliberately he set out to intersect with its path. As they met there was a tension in the atmosphere of the ship that set his hair on end. But there was no shock as he met the meteorite; he did not meet it at all, for when it was about a yard from the ship it shimmered and seemed to vanish.

Maclure was satisfied; the distortion unit was in order. And the chances of meeting anything so freakish as a meteorite were so small that he did not need any further protection. He was whistling happily as he headed back to Earth.

Then, abruptly, there was a peculiar chiming resonance to the idling whisper of the drive-units. And in the back of Angel's head a little chord seemed to sound. It was like something remembered and forgotten again. Scarcely knowing what he was saying and not caring at all he called softly: "I can hear you!"

The chiming sound mounted shrilly, seemed to be struggling to form words. Finally, in a silvery tinkle of language he heard: "We're superhet with your malloidin coils. Can't keep it up like this. Full stop—all power in malloidin for reception. Okay?"

That, at least, he could understand. Someone had performed the almost impossible task of superheterodyning some sort of nodular wave of constant phase-velocity into a coil set up as an anchor-band! He groaned at the thought of the power it must have taken and flung the ship to a halt, reversing his power to flow through the anchoring coil that was receiving the message. It sounded again: "That's better. Can you make it 7:7:3, please?"

He snapped insulated gloves on his hands and adjusted the armature windings. "God knows where they get their juice from," he thought. "But I hope they have plenty of it."

"We can't hear you, Angel Maclure," said the voice from the coils. "This must be going through to you, though, because you've followed our requests. I can't get detailed, because this little message will burn out every power-plant we have. Do not return to Earth. Do not return to Earth. Do you get that? Come instead to coordinates x-3, y-4.5, z-.1—get that? three, four point five, point one. We'll be able to contact you further there. But whatever you do, don't return to Earth. Signing off—"

The metallic voice clicked into silence. Maclure, mind racing, grabbed for a star-map. The coordinates indicated in the message were those of a fairly distant and thinly-filled sector of space. He hesitated. Why the hell not? No man had ever been beyond Pluto, but was he a man?

He grinned when he remembered his tight-fisted, close-mouthed father, who had made him what he was with a grueling course of training that began actually before he was born.

Yes, he decided, he was a man all right, and with all of a man's insatiable curiosity he set his course for the distant cubic parsec that was indicated by the coordinates he had so strangely heard through a drive-unit receiver. And with all the fantastic speed of which his craft was capable he did not want to drive it beyond its capacity. Having set the controls, he relaxed in a sort of trance in preparation for his week-long trip.

After locating himself among the unfamiliar stars of his destination, he rearranged his coils. "That wasn't necessary," they said almost immediately in the metallic chimes. "We're coming out for you." Then they fell silent. But minutes later a craft hove alongside and fastened onto his hull with a sort of sucker arrangement. It was no larger than his own, but somehow sleeker and simpler in its lines.

They had clamped right over his bulkhead and were hammering on it. He opened up, trusting to luck and logic that their atmosphere was not chlorinous. "Come in," he called.

"Thanks," said the foremost of three ordinary individuals. "My name's Jackson."

"Yeah?" asked Maclure, staring at him hard. He was dressed exactly as Maclure was dressed, and his features were only slightly different.

Jackson smiled deprecatingly. "You're right," he said. "But you can call me Jackson anyway. I'd rather not show you my real shape. Okay?"

"You should know best," shrugged Angel. "Now tell me what's up."

"Gladly," said Jackson, settling himself in a chair with a curiously loose-jointed gesture. "You're not very much of a superman, you know."

"Pardon the contradiction," said Angel ominously, "but I happen to know for a fact that I'm very far above the normal human being."

"Intellectually," said Jackson. "Not emotionally. And that's very important. You don't mind my speaking plainly?"

"Not at all."

"Very well. You're much like an extremely brilliant child. You have a downright genius for mechanics and physical sciences, but your understanding of human relationships is very sub-average. That must be why you were so badly taken in by Mr. Sapphire."

"Taken in?" reflected Angel. "I don't think he fooled me. I knew that he'd try to get me out of the way—murder or otherwise—as soon as he got what he wanted from me. I trusted myself to take care of him."

"Good, but not reasoned far enough. Did it ever strike you that Mr. Sapphire—as you persist in thinking of him—was not a free agent? That he was—ah—grinding somebody else's axe?"

"Holy smokes!" yelped Maclure. The strange discrepancies which he had bundled into the back of his mind suddenly resolved themselves into a frightening pattern.

"Exactly," smiled Jackson. "You are the key piece in the problem. Both sides must take care of you, for if you are lost the game is at an end. Shall I begin at the beginning?"

"You'd better," said Angel weakly.

"Very well," began Jackson. "Our opponents are known to us as the Morlens; we are the Amters. For some thousands of your years there has been an intermittent warfare going on between us. You must take my word for it that it is they who are bent on destroying us and that we act only in self-defense. They are situated about nine parsecs away from us, which makes attack a difficult and dangerous undertaking, yet they have not hesitated to risk their entire generations in desperate attempts to wipe us out.

"Of late there had been little of that; when our spies reported they informed us that an intensive psychological campaign was going on against us. This we could repulse with ease. But we could not very well block their attempts to gain mental domination of Earth and its solar system. They did not, of course, control every individual, but they reached sufficient key-persons like Mr. Sapphire to be nearly masters of your world."

"One moment," interrupted Angel. "I can assure you that Mr. Sapphire knew that they were at work on him. I also believe that he only pretended submission. His ends were his own."

"Perhaps," Jackson shrugged. "At any rate, what they needed was mechanical and physical genius. And you, Angel Maclure, are the outstanding mechanical and physical genius of the universe. You can solve problems that no other mind could even approach. And the first of such problems was the one of Dead Center, which we have been investigating for many generations."

"Investigating?" snapped Angel. "How?"

"Purely psychological investigations, such as the projection of minds within the region of the Center. This has been actually a desperate race against the Morlens, for we believe that who is master of the Center is master of the universe."

"That's probably true enough," said Maclure thoughtfully. "And so you make your bid for my support?"

"We do," said Jackson somberly.

"That's nice," snapped Angel viciously. "Now get this and get it straight: I'm not playing anybody's game but my own, and if helping you out against the damn Morlens helps me out I'll do it. On those terms—okay?"

"Okay," said Jackson gravely. "And you'd better begin helping us out pretty fast, because your benefactor Sapphire either relayed to or had his mind read by the Morlens, and they know the results of your calculations. They know where the Center is and, in a way, how to get there."

"Yeah," jeered Angel. "Give me a piece of land and some tools and I'll build you a space-ship that'll make this thing look like a waterbug for size and speed!"

"Haw!" laughed Jackson. "More damn fun!"

3

Maclure had mostly duplicated the calculating work he had done back on Earth, working speedily and accurately though somehow depressed by the strangeness of the planet on which he had landed. Not yet had he seen the actual shapes of the Amters; they preferred to show themselves as almost replicas of his own face and body. Jackson had become his guide and companion.

"Look," said Angel, glowing with pride. "Something new." He indicated a little sphere of silvery metal that looked somehow infinitely heavy. It rested ponderously on a concrete table well braced with steel beams, and even that sagged beneath it.

Jackson inspected the thing. "Weapon?" he asked.

"Darn tootin', friend! I found this as a by-product of warp-synthesis. The base is osmium, the heaviest by volume of any natural element. And over that is a film one molecule thick of neutronium itself. How do you like it?"

"How do you use it?" asked Jackson cautiously.

"Mix up about a hundred of these things and when you get near enough to an enemy scoot them out into space. And unless they have a damned efficient screen they'll be riddled by simple contact with the things."

"Um," grunted Jackson. "Child's play, of course. When does the real job begin?"

"Any minute now, if you mean the ship. And I have some bad news for you," Maclure added grimly. "You boys're supposed to be the prime exponents of hypnotism and telepathy in the galaxy, right?"

"I think we are," snapped Jackson.

"Well, laugh this off: I happened to get curious about the Morlens so I rigged up a projection gimmick that traces interferences of the eighth magnitude. Or, to translate my terms back into yours, a thought detector."

"Go on, Angel. I think I know what you found," said Jackson slowly. "The Morlens—they're at it?"

"Right," said Angel. "My setup showed a complete blanketing spy system. The minds of all workers on the calculators were being picked over carefully. In some cases they even substituted Morlen personalities for the workers' and used their eyes. Naturally the Morlens didn't try to tap your mind or mine; we would have known it. I did what I could—put up a dome screen of counter-vibrations that seem to shut off our friends. But—what do you think?"

"You have more to tell me," said Jackson. "Go on."

"At it again?" asked Maclure with a grin. "Okay, mind-reader. Lamp this gimmick." He opened a cabinet and produced a small, flimsy device. "The engineering's pretty sound on this," he said, "but I'm still shaky on the psycho-manipulation you folks taught me last week. We'll see if it works."

He plugged leads and conductors into ponderously insulated power-pickups and laughed as Jackson laid a worried hand on his.

"That's fixed," he said. "I need all the juice I can get to bring over a video beam. Not wanting to blow out your power stations again I built a little thing of my own." Angel patted a stubby little casing of thick, tough glass. "Underneath that baby's hide," he said, "is 3^9 volts. Not that I'll ever need anything near that."

Angel's deft fingers made minute adjustments within the spidery frame of his new gimmick; finally he connected it with a standard television screen. "Lights out," he said as he snapped the switch. The room went dark.

Slowly, with writhing worms of light wriggling across the ground glass screen, the scene illuminated and went into full color. Maclure grimaced at the fantastic spectacle. The things he saw—!

The Morlens on whom he had focused, nine parsecs away, were hideous creatures. Like giant crabs in a way, and partly suggestions of octopi, they sprawled horribly over machinery and furniture. "That them?" he asked hoarsely.

"The Morlens," said Jackson. "Do you wonder that I have used my hypnotic powers to mask from you my own form?"

"I suspected that you were the same race," said Maclure. He turned again to the screen, and cut in the sound factor. A dull, clacking babble sounded from the speaker. "You know their language?"

Jackson shook his head. "They aren't talking language. It's a code that can't be broken without a key. They don't underestimate you, Angel. What else has the gimmick got?"

"Psycho circuit. If the damn thing works we won't need to break their code. We'll be able to tap their thoughts. Shall I try it? The most I've done before was to scout around back on Earth. Couldn't find much there, though. Okay?"

"Okay," snapped Jackson. "You only live once."

Delicately, with the most painful precision, knowing well that a too sudden and too amplified projection of the Morlens' minds would blow his mind out the way a thunderclap could deafen him, he turned the tiny screws of the gimmick.

Angel winced and set his jaw as a surge of hate filled the room. It was the Morlens, far across the galaxy, who were the source. Like the pulsing roar of a dynamo the undersurge of detestation and the will to destroy beat into his brain. Hastily he turned down the psycho band, and concrete thoughts emerged from the welter of elemental emotion that rushed from the screen.

It took Maclure only a moment to solve the unfamiliar thought-patterns of the Morlens. One of them, in some commanding position, was addressing the rest in cold, measured tones. Angel's mind strained at the effort of encompassing the weird concepts and imagery of the creatures.

"... increase of destruction," the Morlen was saying. "Not very well pleased with the technique displayed, he has come to lend the weight of his personality and training to our efforts. I remind you that I am his direct representative. I remind you that any sort of rebellion is futility, for his innate ability is such and his immense experience is such that he can cope with any problem set him. It was he who devised the spy system which was successfully operated on the Amters up to a short time ago when their prodigy from Earth began to understand. It was he who devised the penetration-proof screen which shields us from any outside detection, either physical or intellectual."

"They think so," interjected Angel grimly. He averted his eyes from the screen.

Jackson stirred at his side. "Look!" he gasped.

There was a slow motion on the wall of the room in which the Morlens were gathered. And there entered a crawling vehicle of glass, surrounded by a tangle of machinery slick with moisture. Within the glass Maclure saw, obscured by moisture and drifts of steam, the shriveled, lofty, crusted brow of Mr. Sapphire.

The eyes, behind their ponderous lenses, turned directly on Angel. "Maclure!" the voiceless whisper rang out. "Now you should know who is your adversary. I cannot hear you, but I know you have a one-way setup on this room. A man does not meditate for one hundred years without a moment's pause and fail to learn many things about his own mind and the minds of others. To you I was a financier, I think. Now learn your error.

"It is true that my passion is for life and being. And I will brook no opposition in the way of that end. I waited the long years for you to reach the full colossal apex of your genius; a genius so profound that you yourself do not realize one tenth of its capacities.

"Maclure, you will come to heel or be crushed. You have fulfilled your mission. You have plotted the course to Dead Center, and you have given me the faster-than-light drive which enables me to see for the first time that race of beings over whom I have for half a century been unquestioned master. My Morlens are my hands; they will duplicate for me the drive which you have devised for the Amters. Now I offer you your choice:

"Either cut your Amters dead, for from them you have nothing to gain, or refuse me and suffer the terrible consequences. For you have nothing to offer me, Angel. All you can do with the Center I now know. Only on the chance that you will in the future be of use to me do I offer to spare you. What is your answer?" The aged monster whispered in a tone of mockery: "I shall know by your actions. Within the hour I start for the Center in a perfect duplicate of the ship you have devised for your friends. Follow or oppose and you shall take the consequences. Now cut off!"

And from the ancient creature's mind there radiated such a stream of destructive hate that Angel winced and shut off the machine at its power lead. "Mr. Sapphire," he meditated aloud, "is not all that I had thought him to be."

Jackson grinned feebly. "What're you going to do, Maclure?"

Angel said thoughtfully: "Mr. Sapphire must not get to the Center before us. You heard that he was starting—we must follow. And we must work on the way."

"He's terribly strong," said Jackson. "Terribly strong now that he has his own mind and a good part of yours in his grasp. How do we lick his psychological lead?"

"The only way I can and with the only weapons I got, chum. Cold science and brainwork. Now roll out that bus we have and collect the star-maps I got up. Round up every top-notch intellect you have and slug them if you have to, but at any cost get them into the ship. We're going to Dead Center, and it's a long, hard trip."

Comfortably ensconced in the cabin of the *Memnon*, which was the altogether cryptic name Maclure had given the Center ship, Jackson was listening worriedly.

"The directive factor in the course," said Angel, "is not where we're going but how we get there. Thus it's nothing so simple as getting into the fourth dimension, because that's a cognate field to ours and a very big place. Dead Center is wholly unique, therefore there's only one way to get there."

"And finding out that way," interjected Jackson, "was what had you in a trance for thirty hours mumbling and raving about matrix mechanics and quintessimal noduloids. Right?"

"Right," admitted Angel, shuddering a little at the recollection. "Half of the math was the most incredibly advanced stuff that you have to devote a lifetime to, and the rest I made up myself. Look." He gestured outside the window of the ship.

Obediently Jackson stared through the plastic transparency at the absolute, desolate bleakness that was everywhere around them. In spite of the small, sickening sensation in the stomach, they might as well have been stranded in space instead of rushing wildly at almost the fourth power of light's speed into nothing and still more nothing. He tore his eyes away. "Quite a sight," he said.

"Yeah. And do you know where we're going?"

"As far as I can see you've nearly reached the limit of space, Angel. Unless my math is greatly at fault, you're going to find that we've been traveling for a month to find ourselves back where we started from. What's the kicker you're holding?"

"The kicker, as you vulgarly call it," said Maclure, "is a neat bit of math that I doped out for myself. A few years ago I stumbled on the interesting fact that there is a natural limit to the speed-direction ratio as such. I mean, there are certain directions we can go in as long as we stay beneath this limiting constant, which I refer to as J after my Uncle Joe. Anyway, when you scrounge around with some triple integration you find out what this limiting constant is. I have found it to be the speed of light to the fifth power.

"Once you go over that the fences are down. You have another direction you can go in, and that's the direction we're going to take. Reason I went way out here, nearly to the end of space, is because when we go in that direction something spectacular ought to happen to any surrounding matter. Ready to increase speed now you know?"

"Okay," said Jackson briefly. "You're the boss. Murphy!" Another of the Amters, who was handling the controls, nodded. "Over the top?" he asked grinning.

"Darn tootin', Murph," said Angel. "Hold fast, friends."

Murphy depressed the little silver bar still farther, in one savage stab. Actually they felt the ship leap ahead colossally, its beams straining under the unimaginable atomic stress and bombardment to which it was being subjected. Angel, his eyes on the port, gasped as he saw the jet black of space writhe with a welter of colors. "This is it," he snapped thinly. He turned a wheel at his hand, spinning it into the wall.

There was a throbbing of valves and pistons as great directive pumps ponderously went into action, grasping out to grip onto the very fabric of space itself. The ship changed direction then, in some weird and unexplainable manner. Speaking mathematically, the equation of the ship's dynamics altered as the factor J inoperated conversely. But from what Angel saw he doubted all his math and science. This firmest mind in the galaxy wondered if it were going mad.

4

Beneath them swam an incalculably huge plain, curiously dim under a diffused light from high overhead. The vast expanse stretched as far as the eye could see, and there were moving lumps on its surface that shifted strangely without seeming to move.

Jackson screamed grotesquely. Then as Angel caught his eye and held it he smiled sheepishly. "Imagine!" he grinned. "Me going off my rocker! But this place looks like hell to me, Angel—honest it does. What do you make of it?"

"Don't know," said Angel quietly. "But it's more than appearances that makes an Amter scream that way. What did you pick up?"

"Can't fool you, I guess. I felt something—a very strong, clear thought band. And I didn't like it one little bit. Now that's unusual. There isn't a single thought-pattern in creation that's that way. Usually your feelings are mixed. Once you really get into a person's mind you find out that you can't hate him. You're bound to find something good.

"Even Mr. Sapphire, that horrid old octopus, has a spark of worship in him, and a very fine, keen feeling for beauty. But the band I just got—" Jackson shuddered and looked sick.

"We're soaring, Murph," directed Maclure. The ship skimmed lightly over the plain, Angel busily staring through the ports. "Whatever the damn things are," he commented, "they don't move in any normal perceivable manner. They don't traverse space, I think. Just see: they're in one place and then in another. You meet some very strange people in these parts, I think."

Crash! The ship came to a sickening halt. Angel, not wasting a word, pulled his blue-steel automatics. "The only original and authentic superman," he said in hard, even tones, "feels that dirty work is being done."

The *Memnon* settled to the ground and was surrounded by the big, grey lumps with the disconcerting ability to move without moving. Jackson shuddered. "That's it," he whispered. "Thoughtband of pure evil and hate. I could kill them for just existing."

"Hold it," said Angel quietly. "See if you can get a message from them. I think something's coming through."

They must have been concentrating on the occupants of the craft, for even he could feel it without effort, and to the psychologically trained and sensitive Amters it came as a buffeting blow. "Come out!" was the message, sent with deadly dull insistence and power. "Come out! Come out! Come out!"

Angel pocketed his guns. "We'd better," he said. "If I make no mistake these people can back themselves up. And if they had any intention of destroying us right out, I think they could have done it."

The seven Amters and Angel filed from the ship into the chill, sweetish air of the dim plain. The grey lumps surrounded them, confronting Angel. He studied the creatures and saw that they had rudimentary features. As he guessed at their evolution they must be the end-product of an intensely intellectual and emotional race. All this, of course, subject to alteration by the unguessable influence of their surroundings.

The stolid, battering thought-waves came again. "Mr. Sapphire told us of you. He has threatened us and we know that he is powerful. We shall hold you for his disposal. He said that you were swifter than he but not as powerful and we should not fear you. If you do not wish us to believe that, you must prove otherwise."

"Ask him," Angel said to Jackson, "how Mr. Sapphire threatened them."

Jackson knit his brows and Maclure could feel the pulsing communication. Promptly the creatures answered: "He locked us into time. He is very wise and knows things about time that we do not."

They were either primitive or degenerate, thought Maclure, and probably the latter from their advanced physical make-up. Perhaps he could try the time stunt himself. He whipped out a minute set of tools and selected a fairly complicated little projector. He varied the pitch of its lenses and filaments rapidly and addressed the creatures directly: "As Mr. Sapphire has done, I can too. See!"

He snapped on the device, praying that his estimate of the natural properties of this half-world had not gone awry. And he had not prayed in vain, for all those creatures whom the little beam of ionized air impinged on froze stiffly into a full-fledged stoppage in time. "Let Mr. Sapphire beat that!" he grunted, releasing them.

Crash! The titanic detonation of a trinite bomb shattered the ground a half-mile away into a soft-spreading fog. Through the trembling air there spread the terrible whisper of the master of Morlens: "Can and will, Angel! I warned you. You were faster, but I got to them first. Look up!"

Above them was hanging a sister craft to the *Memnon,* but a sickly green in hue. Said Sapphire: "Do not move or I shall release the second bomb. You underestimated these good people of mine. They are the Grey Watchers of the Silence. They are the ones to whom hate is all, and who will aid no good. With their aid I located you in your little display and with their aid I reached this world only a moment after you. And with their aid I shall become master of the Center, Angel Maclure. Now speak if you wish."

"Muscles," prayed Angel, "do your damndest!" Acting independently his two hands leaped from his pockets grasping the snub-nosed automatics that he knew so well. While the left hand blasted the closing circle of the Watchers into pulpy fragments, the right hand was pouring a steady stream of explosive pellets into the belly of the craft above. With such stunning speed had he acted that it was not the fifth part of a second before the grey circle around them had been broken wide open and the ship above was heeling over sickly with a gaping, shattered wound in its hull.

"Come on!" spat Maclure to the Amters. And in another fifth of a second they were in the ship and tearing wildly over the grey plain. "It'll take them ten minutes at least to get going with what I did to them. Make tracks! In ten minutes we land and get to work!"

About them rose the gigantic ribs of the super-spacer that Angel Maclure had undertaken to build. Nervously he glanced at his watch to confirm his own acute time-sense. "Three hours since we landed," he complained. "Can't you put some steam into it?"

"They're doing their best," said Jackson. "We aren't all supermen, y' know. About this statistics business here—how do you arrive at these coordinates?"

"Never mind," snapped Angel. "If Maclure says it's right you can bet your boots on it. We haven't time to check."

"Then that finishes the calculations," yawned Jackson. "By your own words the Dead Center should rise from some unidentified spot in this damn plain some minutes hence."

"Right. And what it'll look like and how we'll know we've found it is only one of the things I don't know. That's where Mr. Sapphire has the lead on us again. He's hand-in-glove with the Watchers, and if any race is expert on the Center they must be. Suppose you turn your mind to the psychological problem of what in Hades these Watchers expect to get out of all this."

"Evil, I think," said Jackson slowly. "Nothing but their unalloyed instinct for mischief and destruction. You may find it hard to understand that line of thinking; I, being of the same basic stock as the Morlens, do not. They are a shallow example of that perfection toward which the Watchers strive. This is a very strange land, Angel."

"I know that," snapped Maclure. "And I don't like it one bit more than I have to. The sooner we get our work done and well done, I'm making tracks. And the Center, once I've fixed Mr. Sapphire, can go plumb to hell and gone." He stared at the ship which was reaching completion. "Get that on!" he roared as a crew of three gingerly swung his original power-unit into place.

Jackson smiled quietly. "How much longer?" he asked.

"Dunno," said Angel. "But that's the last plate. Quite a hull we have there—what with transmutation and things. I didn't think it'd work with the elements of this world, but why not? Good job, anyway. Thousand yards from stem to stern, fifty yards from keel to truck. I don't see how they can crack her." But his face showed lines of worry.

"What's eating you?" asked Jackson.

"Mr. Sapphire," exploded Angel. "Always a jump ahead of us everywhere we turn— what do you make of it? How can we be sure there isn't a catch to the whole business?"

"I know the feeling," said Jackson. "Hey!" he yelled suddenly, looking up. One of the workers, who had been spreading on a paste which dried to the metal of the hull, was gesturing horribly as though in a convulsive fit. His voice reached them in a strangled wail and then suddenly he was himself again, waving cheerily.

"Thought I was going to fall!" he called.

"Yeah?" asked Jackson. He snapped a little tube from his pocket and cold-bloodedly rayed the Amter. He fell horribly charred.

Angel incinerated the corpse with his own heat-ray and turned to Jackson. "You must have had a reason for that," he commented. "What was it?"

"He wasn't our man," said Jackson, shaken. "They've found where we are and got some other mind into his body. It was the other one that I killed; our man was dead already."

"Ah," said Angel. "Let's get out of this." He sprang into the half-finished ship. "Hold fast and keep on working," he roared to the men who were clinging to the framework. Then he took off, handling the immense control-board with the ease of a master.

In only a few minutes the rest of the men came inside. The ship was not luxurious but it was roomy and fast, and the hull was stored with weapons and screen-projectors of immense power. "Going up," said Angel. Delighting in the smooth-handling speed of the immense craft, he zoomed high into the thin air of the weird half-world.

"Look," whispered Jackson. And in the very center of the control room there was appearing a semi-solid mass that took the shape of Mr. Sapphire. It greeted Angel in the voiceless whisper that was its voice: "Maclure, can your mechanics master this or even match it? You see a projection out of my body—once called ectoplasmic.

"With this implement and extension of me I could strangle you to death, for ectoplasm knows no limitations of cross-sectional strength. My Watchers have taught me much, and what they did not know I supplied from my century of meditation. We are the symbiosis of evil, Angel. Do you yield now?"

Maclure's fingers danced over the immense keyboard that semicircled around him, setting up the combination of a snap-calculated field. "Beat this!" he taunted, plunging home a switch. And a plane of glowing matter intersected horizontally with the projection, cutting it cleanly in half.

"So!" rasped the whisper of Mr. Sapphire. "We shall do battle in earnest, Angel Maclure. I am coming for you!" The severed projection faded away.

5

Like a comet from nowhere a second ship roared into the sky, fully as large as Angel's.

"Now how the hell did he manage to build that?" worried Maclure. "I thought I had the monopoly on transmutation and psycho-construction. Get a line on that, Jackson."

His sidekick, brow furrowed, answered slowly: "From what I can hear he did it the hard way—forged his metal and welded it together. But that must have taken him four or five months, at least. Wait a—that's it. The Watchers worked a stoppage of time for him so that he's been working on his armaments and ship for a year while we built our thing in three hours. Isn't that dirty?"

"Dirty as hell," said Angel busily. He was feinting the ship this way and that, now closing in, now roaring a light-year distant. "Get the men at battle-stations, will you? Work it out among them. I want to be alone here."

Angel zoomed in swiftly and shot out one sizzling beam of solid force as a feeler. It was to his surprise that it touched the ship and charred the hull. But, he worried, it should have more than charred it. He closed in again and shot out his very best repeller ray. It caught the other ship square amidships and heeled it over in a great spin for control. While it floundered he stabbed at it with a needle-ray.

The sharp-pointed, unbearably brilliant beam struck into the flank of the ship and bored fiercely. Then it was shaken off, and Maclure shot far and away out of range. Under cover of a cloud of smoke which he released from a jet, he scattered a few hundred of the osmium pellets into space.

"Come on!" he muttered to himself, shooting a tractor ray at the other ship. He could hear trembling in the power room the tortured whine of his generators, and could see the agonizing vibrations of the other ship. Almost an impasse it seemed, when with a jerk the other ship lost ground and slid clean into the path of the artificial meteorites.

Angel grunted with satisfaction as he saw myriad punctures appear in the hull. Then the already-battered ship disappeared behind a dull red glow. "Screens," he muttered. He snapped on his own, leaving open only a small observation port. This, he noticed, the others did not have. His advantage.

From behind the screen of the other ship crept a tenebrous cloud. Angel backed away. He didn't like the look of the thing, whatever it was. In rapid succession he rayed it with everything he had. But nothing happened. It could not be burned nor frozen, nor ionized, nor attracted nor repelled. With a sinister persistence it reached out farther yet as he backed off.

Almost in a panic Angel aimed and released one of his preciously hoarded torpedoes. The blunt, three-ton killer, packed solid with destruction, plunged squarely through the blackness and exploded colossally but to no avail against the red screen of the other ship. "Whatever it is," brooded Maclure, "it can go through screens." And that wasn't good. He could do no more than watch hopelessly as it detached itself from the other ship by breaking the one slender filament which still connected it. From then on it seemed to be a free agent.

"Playing tag with a heavy fog," mused Angel, dancing the ship away from the cloud. It was, he saw, assuming more solid form—condensing into a more compact and still huge mass. The thing was curiously jelly-like as it crawled sluggishly through space at a few hundred miles a second.

"Jackson!" Angel yelled into a mike. "Get a line on that damn thing, will you? Try probing it en masse with the rest of your friends."

"Oke," came back the dry tones of his lieutenant. "We did already. That stuff is ectoplasm in the most elementary form. We aren't sure how much it has on the ball, but it might be plenty. Watch yourself—we'll try to break it down psychologically if we can."

"Right," snapped Maclure. He tried a ray on the thing again, and it seemed to be affected. Skillfully wielding the needle, he carved a hunk of the stuff off the major cloud. With incredible speed it rushed at him, and only by the narrowest of margins did he avert having the stuff plaster all over his ship.

With a steady hand he aimed the second of his torpedoes, masking its discharge under a feinting barrage of liquid bromine. The tool sped through space almost undetected, finally lodged inside the cloud. The explosion was monstrous, but ineffectual. Though the cloud had been torn into about a dozen major pieces and numberless minor ones, it immediately reformed and began stalking his ship again.

As he drove it off with a steady barrage of repeller rays the thing seemed to expand and soften again. The agitated voice of Jackson snapped over the circuit, "Either we broke it down or it's given up, Angel. But something's brewing aboard their ship. They suddenly changed their major aim, somehow. Murphy says they're looking for something—think it's—?"

"Dead Center!" yelled Maclure. Almost under his very eyes the only unique phenomenon in creation had suddenly appeared.

It had risen from the plain with a splashing of colors and sounds, so violent a contravention of all the rest of the universe that his ship was transparent under its colors and the roaring, constant crash of its sound threatened to crystallize and rend the framework of his body. He could do no more than collapse limply and regard it in wonder.

The Center was, in short, everything that the rest of creation was not. In no terms at all could it be described; those which Maclure saw as light and heard as sound were, he realized, no more than the border-phenomena caused by the constant turmoil between the outer world and the Quiet Place that it surrounded.

Angel Maclure came to with a violent start. The ectoplasmic weapon had, he saw, been allowed to disperse. There was a strange quiet in space then. He snapped a tentative spy-ray on the other ship. Its screens fell away easily. Angel blinked. "What goes on?" he muttered. The ray penetrated easily, and as he swept it through the ship he saw not one living figure. There was nothing at the barrage-relay but a complicated calculating device with shut-offs and a lead-wire to the control booth. And everywhere the ray peered he found nothing but machinery.

But in the booth from which the ship was guided his ray found and revealed Mr. Sapphire, alone and untended, his machinery pulsing away and the ancient, crusted skin dull and slack. In the faintest of faint whispers Angel heard Mr. Sapphire speak: "Maclure. My detector tells me you have a ray on us. Pull alongside and board me. You have safe-conduct."

Obeying he knew not what insane impulse, Angel heeled the ship around and clamped alongside the other. "Come on, Jackson," he called. Together they entered the ship and easily forced the door to the control booth.

"Mr. Sapphire," said Maclure.

"Maclure," sounded the whisper. "You have beaten me, I think. For I died more than three hours ago. I cannot keep this up much longer, Angel."

"Died," gasped Maclure. "How—"

With the feeblest semblance of mockery the ancient creature whispered: "A man does not meditate for a hundred years without a moment's pause without learning so simple a secret as the difference between life and death. I sought the Center, Maclure, that I might find youth and being again. There was hot in me the urge to smash and create anew—the thing that is the trouble of every mind above the ape.

"I see that I have failed again ... the Center is yours. You may do many things with it—operate its laws as wisely and well as you have the more familiar laws of the outer world. Now—

"Stop my machinery, Angel Maclure. I am a proud man, and this mockery of life in death is more than I can bear."

Without another word Angel's nimble fingers danced among the tangle of tubes and found a petcock that he turned off with a twitch of his wrist. The machinery stopped in its pulsing, and there was no difference at all save in the complicated unit that had been Mr. Sapphire.

"And was it really you that complained against the grimness of life in this place?" asked Jackson with a smile.

Angel, tapping away with lightning fingers at a vast calculating machine's keyboard, looked up without ceasing from his work. "Could have been," he admitted. "But there's nothing like work on a grand and practical scale to make a man forget. This business of mapping out the laws and principles of a whole new kind of creation is what I might call my meat."

"Yeah," jeered Jackson. "The only original and authentic superman."

"In person," Angel admitted modestly.

[*Cosmic Stories* - July 1941
as by Walter C. Davies]

Interference

"Take it easy, now," warned the President of the United States. "A lot depends on you—don't go off half-cocked. You only get one chance. That's all we can afford."

Boyle took the extended hand and shook it heartily. "We'll certainly do our best, sir," he said. And from the tone of his voice you could tell that he meant it.

The vast field was crowded; beneath the hot summer sun sweated twenty thousand people, surging, cheering, breaking through cordons of police lined up for their own protection. Dips were doing a thriving business; more than one light-fingered gentleman was planning to retire on the rich pickings from the crowd. People were far too excited to consider whether or not it was their own hands in their pockets or that of some total stranger of predatory instincts. The crowd was in a holiday mood, exalted to be in the same rocket field with Boyle and Cantrell.

The two objects of adoration were bearing up well under the strain, humble psychologists though they had been up to a few weeks ago. After shaking the President's hand and being clapped on their backs by enough distinguished foreigners to fill an embassy the size of the great pyramid, they were blushing a little and very happy at their good fortune.

"But," whispered Boyle from the corner of his mouth, "if we don't come back they'll know we died trying." Suddenly grim, he surveyed the vast sea of faces stretching before him. An emcee took him by the arm and led him to a mike through which he would address the crowd.

"Hello—" he began, and then broke off, startled by the sound of his own voice roaring out across the field. "Hello, all you people. My partner and I just want to thank you before we leave in the *Andros*. If we don't return send out more men, men better than Cantrell and I. Because we aren't coming back before we crack the problem that's assigned to us. When—if—you see the jets of the old *Andros* in the sky again, maybe in a week, maybe in a year, you'll know that the answer is in our hands and that the plague, the spastitis, is over. Or as good as over."

The roar that went up from the crowd was deafening as he modestly stepped back from the mike. The emcee was yelling things into it, but the tremendous ovation drowned out even the tornado of sound that the loudspeakers created.

Boyle waved at the crowd again. "All ready?" he snapped at Cantrell, his partner in the enterprise. "Everything checked?"

"Betcha life," said Cantrell. "Get in." Like an insect disappearing in the knothole of a giant tree trunk, Boyle eased through the tiny port in the grey, slab-sided hull of the *Andros*. Cantrell vaulted in immediately after him, and the huge plug of metal that sealed the ship swung into place from the inside.

The crowd had quieted, and the annunciators roared warnings to stand back from the breath of the fiery Titan that soon would roar its own message. Police cleared the mob away from the firing area with squad cars driving masses of people before them. Hastily the reviewing stand was rolled away from the ship.

The President got into his car, a long, low open Jefferson 22. He looked a little ill. "I hope they make it," he said, with a visible effort. "They're plucky young—" Then he could no longer contain himself. He began to cough violently, his hands trembling toward his mouth.

Doctors clustered around as he collapsed. Even in unconsciousness his body twitched grotesquely and his finely modeled hands trembled as if with cold. "He's got it," said one surgeon grimly. "The President has spastitis. It's spreading faster than we thought. And there go the dream-boys who have to get out into space to find a cure." He gestured at the *Andros*, which was ponderously aiming itself at the zenith with its own self-elevators.

With a mind-staggering crash the ship took off. The wind of its departure almost tore clothes from the surgeons at the Presidential car. Long after it had vanished—seemingly dead into the sun—their ears rang with the concussion, and breezes stiffly whipped along the field.

Cantrell grinned feebly from the bunk. "I'm all right," he said weakly. "I can get up. This damned space-sickness gets me every time. You ready to try out the polyphone?"

The hardy Boyle grinned back through a tangle of electronics supplies. "It's all rigged up and ready for you. Catch." He tossed over a set of headphones connected with the machinery and donned a similar set of his own. "Relax," he warned. "If we're not far enough out this ought to be a full-blooded shock to mind and body." He switched on a dull-glowing tube.

Cantrell squinted his eyes shut and concentrated on the familiar thought patterns of his partner. He caught them for a moment. Boyle was thinking of the blackness of space through which they were speeding and wondering vaguely whether the meteor interceptor would work as well under stress as it had in the tests. He held up a hand with thumb and forefinger meeting, both crooked, in the time-honored technicians' gesture of: coming over 100%.

Then there was a sudden rip in the smoothly unreeling pattern. It was as though a panorama were being opened before his eyes; the panorama of his partner's mind. Then a seam opened suddenly and without warning. He was reading the minds of total strangers, people he'd never heard of.

In rapid sequence he caught the image of a grubby little room as seen by a short man, and then surges of physical disgust at the sight—through this short stranger's eyes—of a big, muscular woman. Following that image and impression was a vision of staring dead into the sun, some fool who was looking for their ship, no doubt. Back to the grubby room, but this time seen from the slightly higher elevation of the muscular woman, who obviously didn't like the little man she focused on any more than he liked her.

For a full hour Cantrell tried to claw his way back to the mind stream of the man who was raptly sitting a few feet from him, but the obtrusive thoughts of people back on Earth insisted on popping up. For a full hour Cantrell plumbed the depths of degradation in some minds, read the noble and exalted thoughts of others. He tuned in on one murder and two suicides, seen in dizzy angles by the different participants in the violence done.

Through them all was a continual undertone of abominable worry and expectancy of death. Cantrell grunted softly whenever that image emerged. He recognized it easily; that was what he and Boyle were out there in space to fight. It was the ever-present dread of being struck down by the plague raging on Earth—the shakes, spastitis malignans, whatever you wanted to call it.

Cantrell saw people drop in the street, only to begin to tremble horribly at the hands and feet with the disease. Finally he tore the headset off in disgust. Boyle looked at him mildly.

"You try it solo," said Cantrell. "I can't get a damned thing out of the ether except the pressure-waves from Tellus. And they aren't pretty."

Boyle removed his own set carefully. "It's eavesdropping," he said. "I tried to get you every second. What were you doing?"

"Just what you were," grunted his partner. "Just exactly. I was trying to get you, but you weren't to be had. We have to move on, Boyle. Do what you can with the accelerators."

Boyle went to the instrument panel, worked the multiplex of levers. Too near the Earth! Too near to the suffering stew of human beings in agony, never knowing who would be next with the shakes. That was what they had to get away from—the emotional jags and lunatic vibrations from the home planet.

He and Cantrell had been carefully teamed as psychological mates for the full utilization of the polyphone. Essentially the machine was intended to heighten to the nth degree the rapport of a pair like this one. But they were too sensitive for the machine. There was interference from the thousands who passed in the street, from everybody all over the globe who was thinking consecutively at the time.

And because the shakes was a disease of psychological degeneration, you had to fight it by probing into a mind and finding what was wrong. It didn't have to be a diseased mind, for every normal mind has in its depths the seeds of every psychological affliction that breaks out in wilder form. In Boyle's well-ordered brain were minute traces of megalomania, satyriasis, schizophrenia, all the words ending in *philia* and *phobia* as well as other unpleasant matters. Everybody has them, whether he knows it or not.

The idea had been to shoot these two out into space, far from the influence and interference of Earth; then they would work deeper and deeper into each other's minds, finally to discover the seeds of the shakes that were inevitably lying dormant.

One of the pleasant features of psychiatry is that once you have your problem broken down it is already solved. The synthetic element of logic is superfluous; analysis is sufficient. It might be that the shakes consisted of a fear of technical progress reaching epidemic proportions through hysterical contagion. You see a man fall in the street feebly kicking his heels in protest at being deprived of the liberty to roam on grassy fields and your own elements of protest are somewhat stirred. Then one day you feel despondent and they explode when your censor band is not on guard against subversive urges like that. And for the rest of your life you are a spastic, kicking and squirming uncontrollably. Or until someone calmly explains to you what is wrong—about the machine age and the rest. Then you are miraculously cured. And one cure breeds a thousand as confidence grows.

Meanwhile there was the matter of interference from Earth. Boyle pushed the fuel rod down to the limits of the outward-bound trip. Dammit, they'd have to get away from the static, he brooded.

"What's our position?" queried Boyle. He was relaxing, Cantrell at the driving panel.

"Practically ideal," said his partner. "I haven't checked, but we should be well out of the range of anything from Earth. Going high and fancy, we are—per second acceleration for two weeks. That's plenty far. Do you want to try out the polyphone again?"

"Blow off the dust," grunted Boyle, swinging himself from the bunk. Gravity on the ship was at Earth level; that had meant tons of extra equipment and power consumption far above normal, but these two on whom the fate of their planet depended could not be distracted by space sickness and flying soup.

Cantrell readied the polyphone, testing and checking the scores of minute connections and solders that held the complex creation together. Some he tightened, others he ripped out and replaced. At length the psychologist reported: "All ready. Let's make this tryout a good one."

"Right. You stay open and receptive; I'll drive as deep into your mind as I can. And Cantrell—I know it's not a nice thing to ask, but you'll have to have complete confidence in me. I don't want you to seal off any sections at all from me. I want you to stay as open as though you weren't being probed. You're a specialist; you could close off whatever you wanted to. But we don't know where the spastitis seeds lie. It may be in some group-unconscious engram or some especially unsavory crime you've committed and forced yourself to forget. I'll play square with you, Cantrell. For the sake of the whole planet back there—don't keep any secret places."

His partner stared at him curiously. "Okay," he said at last. "You know best. But if you find anything especially nasty, do me the favor of not telling me about it."

"Agreed," said Boyle with relief. He switched on the machine as they donned the head sets. The great tube glowed.

Cantrell relaxed in body and mind as he felt the probing fingers sent from his partner's brain pluck away at his grey matter. It wasn't an unpleasant sensation, rather like a mental Swedish massage. Vaguely, images came through. He stiffened a little. There shouldn't be any images here, and if there were he shouldn't get them. For the moment putting aside the receptive mood, he reached out, shutting his eyes and wrinkling his brow in an effort to encompass the foreign thought vibrations that were filtering into his skull.

He saw a sky then through the eyes of some person on whose mind he had landed. The sky was curiously dusky. And with the vision of the sky was a poignant sense of longing that filled the mind of Cantrell's host. The words of it seemed to be: "My loved one! My loved one—on *their* side. Now we are enemies …"

A quick start of alarm. The sky swiveled away, and Cantrell saw through these other eyes a group of horsemen bearing down on his host. A shrill scream of terror, an intolerable wave of revulsion and regret, and then the blankness of death. Cantrell's host had been ridden under the hooves of the horsemen.

The psychologist, not believing what he had experienced, reached out with his mind and seized on one of the riders. He did know that there was a sense of guilt in the rider's mind; what it meant he could not tell. He heard a conversation begun with a shrill, nervous laugh. Then: "Damned rebel—we showed him."

"Right. Fix them all up like that and this world will be worth living on, sir. Where do we go now?"

"Keep scouting. Look for rebels and treat them the right way, like that dead thing back there—"

Cantrell had suddenly lost interest in the conversation. The talk of rebels was beyond him anyway. He had been studying, through his host's eyes, the costume of the riders. They were unfamiliar, and somehow totally alien to anything earthly. Then with a shock of terror Cantrell saw that the horses had peculiarly long heads—and six legs!

He tore the set from his head and stared, wide-eyed, at Boyle. "Where were you?" he demanded. There was a shrill, hysterical note in his voice.

"Trying to get over," said Boyle as he switched off the set. "But there was interference. We'll have to go farther yet. I tuned in on a series of love-affairs from back on Earth."

"Sure of that?" countered Cantrell. "Are you sure it was from Earth that you got the vibrations?"

"Why?" snapped Boyle. "What did you receive?"

Cantrell told him, and Boyle sat quietly for a long time, rattling his fingernails on a table-top. "Yeah," said Boyle at last. "I suspected something like that. Those women reacted in wholly unearthly fashion. The anatomy of these broadcasters is similar, but they aren't Homo sapiens."

"Fourth dimension?" wildly hazarded Cantrell. "Could we have tuned in on that?"

"No. For the reason that waves from the fourth dimension would have to be vectorially sub-operative to the seventh power, at least, and the machine would register any abnormal strain like that. No—not the fourth or any dimension except this one. Are there any invisible planets floating around? That alone would explain everything."

"None that I know of, and I used to specialize in astronomy. Maybe—maybe we've caught up with the thought-waves from Earth on a return trip from the end of space? That would explain the talk about rebels."

"And your six-legged horses, of course. Don't be silly. We have to push on and get so damned far away from this spot that we won't even remember where it is. I'm going to gun the ship hard and fast. You get on the polyphone and tell me when the thought-waves from the place begin to weaken and die out."

Boyle squared his jaw at the fuel gage and began to reckon how much they could allow for steerage and headway. How thin they could cut the corners for the return trip to Earth when the problem of the shakes was solved.

Cantrell donned the head set and turned on the machine again. Again he reached out probing fingers into the crazy planet where horses had six legs and you could kill a man because he was a rebel against someone or something unspecified.

On the screen of his mind things began to take shape. He had landed plumb in the brain of a lady who was waiting for a lover whom she pictured as tall and handsome. The lady turned slowly and surveyed a colossal city that rose about her. She was standing just outside its walls. They were fine walls, solid and ponderous, fitted with gates able to withstand the charge of a battletank.

Her lover strolled up and there was a tender scene of greeting. Cantrell, feeling like a cad, reached out for another mind. He lighted on the brain of a person within the city; a person who considered himself as being of vast importance. All sorts of ponderous speculations were revolving through the important person's head, principally when he would eat next. A young man, clad in a sort of tunic, approached.

The important person smiled. "Ah," he cried. "My dear boy!"

The dear boy grinned briefly. "You'd better come. There's a strike on at the tubing works. They seized possession of the whole plant." The important person exploded with rage, swearing by strange gods. Cantrell shut off power and looked up.

"When," he asked impatiently, "are you going to get going? It comes in as strong as ever."

Boyle stared at him with a kind of sickly horror in his face. "Cantrell," he said, "since you put on that set we've gone half a million miles at right angles to our former course."

"Lord," whispered his partner. "They're following us!"

From random snatches of thought and casual, everyday conversation it is not easy, it is almost impossible in fact, to reconstruct the politics, biology and economics of an entire planet. Yet that, essentially, was what Boyle and Cantrell had to do. For flee where they might, nearer to or farther from Earth, they could not escape the vibrations from the land where horses had six legs.

From long periods of listening in and comparing, they discovered one important fact: that evolution was proceeding on that planet at a staggeringly rapid pace; that in fact the two partners had started out with a violently mistaken notion of the place's tempo. It was swift, swifter than anything with which they were familiar.

But their eavesdropping made it seem close to normal, for the human brain can accommodate itself to any speed of delivery. It can assimilate and synthesize at a faster rate than either of the two had previously suspected. It was natural that this discovery should wait for a moment like this, for never before had the human mind been called on to deliver at that rate.

They discovered that the nameless land was tearing along at a scale of one to a million, approximately. When Cantrell had heard the horsemen curse the rebels, that had been the equivalent of the Puritan revolution in England, period of 1650 or thereabouts. A few minutes later he tuned in on a general strike that meant a lapse of about four hundred years.

In two weeks of voyaging through space the strange planet had arrived at a world state which Earth had not yet attained.

Boyle, irritably tuning in on the lunatic planet one day, drew a deep breath. "Cantrell!" he snapped. "Put your set on and follow my mind. I have a conference of astronomers!"

His partner grabbed the ponderous metal bowl and clapped it on, groping out for the familiar mind patterns of Boyle. He caught onto him in about three seconds, then switched to one of Boyle's mental hosts. Through the eyes of that person he saw a sizable hall built up into a structure like the inside of a mushroom. As he studied the other persons in the hall he realized that physical evolution had progressed a few more steps since yesterday, when he had last tuned in on the place.

His host's mood was one of confusion; through it he was speaking to the large gathering: "This symposium has been called on a somewhat abstract question. You all know what it is, I presume; otherwise you would not be astronomers.

"As one looks back towards the glorious dawning days of our science, the names of those who were martyred in the cause of truth rise before us. Despots, with their piddling knowledge and tiny telescopes, maintained that the world was round, did they not? It remained for the genius of our clan to demonstrate that it was a truncated paraboloid.

"Jealous superstition preached that like all other worlds ours had a core of rock in the state of stress fluid; it remained for us to prove that no such thing was true of our world—that we alone of all planets lived upon a shell of rhodium, and that that shell, though inconceivably thick, was not solid, and that our planet was definitely hollow."

Cantrell looked up. "Lord," he said softly. "Oh, Lordy! *Now* I know where those six-legged horses came from."

"Yes," said Boyle as he turned off the machine. "That planet is our ship, and those people are an entire civilization living on the shell of the old *Andros*. No wonder we couldn't get away from them; they were being carried around with us."

"It's perfectly logical," argued Cantrell. "We carry Earth gravity for our own comfort; that's why we drew down a thin but definite atmosphere. Also dust and organic particles which settled on the hull. There was warmth from the inside of the ship, and that wonderful old Swede Arrhenius long ago demonstrated that spores of life are always present in space, driven by light-pressure. They landed on our hull, went through evolutionary stages, a man-like form emerged and is rapidly reaching a more advanced civilization than our own."

"But," grunted Boyle, "that doesn't help us out with the shakes. If they're swarming out there, we'll never be able to probe each other. How can we shake them off? Spray acid on the hull?"

"No!" barked Cantrell. "We couldn't do that—they have as much of a right to live as we. Perhaps—perhaps if we could communicate with them—?"

"Son," raved Boyle, "you've got it! The answer to our prayers! A super-race made to order for the purpose of solving our problems. We'll have to adapt the polyphone; that's the only equipment we have. Son, we're going to make this the most useful interference ever recorded!"

With bloodshot eyes and almost trembling fingers Cantrell tuned in the adapted polyphone. Then, through the eyes of a host he was surveying from an apparent altitude of twenty thousand feet a world enclosed in glass.

"Come in," he said to Boyle. "Work toward the most powerful single person you can find." Feeling his own mind augmented by his partner's, he probed deep into the glassed-in world, toward the highest building he could find.

He landed in the brain of a highly trained mathematician and felt a swirl of fantastically complicated figures and tables. Then the mathematician walked through an automatic door into the presence of a person whom he regarded with almost holy awe. Cantrell realized then how rapidly the acceleration of evolution had curved upward on this tiny world. The personage was small and weighed down with a staggering amount of braincells that could be seen pulsing and throbbing under a transparent *dura mater*. The skull had been wholly absorbed.

"Right," snapped Cantrell to his partner. "Push it out, son. Make it stick like glue." The two psychologists united their minds in a staggering intellectual effort; there were visible sparks as they fused into one perfect sending outfit. Cantrell, only vaguely conscious of the personage and the mathematician, saw the former start with alarm and heard him ask as if from a distance: "Do you feel anything?"

"No," said Cantrell's host. "This matter of geodesics—"

"Leave me for a while," said the personage. "I sense a message of great importance." The mathematician exited, and Cantrell abruptly severed his mind from the host. For the first time he found himself to be a point of consciousness hanging before the personage, seeing, hearing and sending.

He raised his hand in a choppy gesture. Boyle nodded, and shut his eyes. Sweat stood out on his brow as he projected the message: "Boyle and Cantrell speaking. Can you hear us?"

The personage jumped as if he had been shot at. He looked around cautiously and said: "I can hear you. But who are you—where are you sending from?" In the language of the mind there is no need of translation; with the polyphone any two rational creatures can communicate.

The psychologists, now working as a perfect team, sent: "Speaking from the inside of your planet. But it isn't a planet; it's our spaceship. We're from Earth—third planet around the sun. But let's skip the formalities. What do you know about—" and they launched into a technical description of the shakes.

"Have you," asked the important personage, "tried polarizing the crystalline lens of the eye? That should do it. It is not, as you thought, a psychodeficiency lesion but—" In clear, concise thought images he gave a complete outline of the cause and cure of spastitis malignans. And he knew what he was talking about, for this personage later announced himself to be the Chief Assimilator of the planetary division. He was the one who received all the technical data and assembled it for reference and use. Specialization had raced ahead on this planet.

"Thanks," said the psychologists at length. "Thanks a lot. We'll be heading back to Earth now—" he broke off in dismay. "If we do, that's the end of your people. Because as soon as our gravity plates switch off you get flung out into space, and we can't land without switching off the plates."

"An interesting problem," brooded the Assimilator. "But not insoluble. We can make our own plates if necessary. I advise you to set your ship— my planet—into an independent orbit around the sun. In about twenty minutes of your time we will have developed to the point where we will have our enclosed cities reinforced against anything but collision with a major planet. We trust you to set the orbit so that that will not happen. You must return to Earth by some makeshift means." The Assimilator fell into a deep study, and the two psychologists withdrew.

Boyle glanced at a stop-watch. "That whole interview," he said disbelievingly, "lasted exactly one one-thousandth of a second. That was thinking under pressure." Cantrell was dashing onto paper what the Assimilator had told him about the shakes. And it made brilliant sense. He photographed his notes and handed a copy to Boyle.

"And now?" asked Boyle, carefully buttoning the data into a pocket.

"Now we take the lifeboat," said Cantrell. He gestured distastefully at the little bullet of metal lugged to the wall. "It's said to be the least pleasant way of travel known to man." He turned to the control panel and set a simple course around the sun that would maintain itself after the fuel was wholly gone.

Jammed into the little craft, cans of food floating about their ears and a hammering roar of exhausts in their heads, they strained to see through the little port that was the only communication from the outside. Boyle yelled something inaudible.

"What?" shrieked Cantrell into his ear.

Boyle drew a great breath and pointed with one thumb at the little crescent of light behind them—the *Andros*. "I said," he shrieked, "that it's a good thing we got away from those submicroscopic Einsteins. They gave me an inferiority complex."

Cantrell grinned briefly and strained his eyes to see until the world they had made was quite invisible in the black of space.

[*Stirring Science Stories* - June 1941
as by Walter C. Davies]

Forgotten Tongue

"Hands up, scum," grated a voice. "You're going for a jump."

Pepper raised his hands and coughed drily. "Forget it," he said. "You can't get away with this." He felt a knee jolt the small of his back in answer.

"Walk," said the voice.

The street was narrow,and the buildings flanking it had no lights. This was the Industrial, one of the three great divisions of New York Sector. Plants were resting their machinery for two hours out of the twenty-four, Pepper realized. As he walked along, as slowly as he dared, the clopping of metal soles against the pavement sounding behind him, he cursed himself for an imbecile, coming alone and unarmed through this bleak part of town.

"How long," he asked tentatively, "have you been gunning for me?" He wanted to find out how many of them there were.

"Keep moving," said the voice. "You don't get news out of us, scum."

He kept moving. They were headed in the direction of the Industrial Airport. That meant, probably, that he'd be crated like a gross of drills and accidentally dropped from a mile or so in the air. There would be protests; threats, recriminations. Then the customary jeering retort from the Optimus Press: "If a Lower wishes to disguise himself for purposes of his own and is damaged in the process, we fail to see how this is any reflection on the present able administration. *Honi soit*—"

Not daring to give way to panic, knowing that it would mean an immediate and ugly death, Pepper walked on and tried to keep his knees from buckling.

"Look," he began again. "We can make a deal—"

"Shut up!" snarled someone. "And stay shut. I'd like to—"

"Let him talk, Captain," said another voice. Pepper stiffened as he heard it, for the dialect was unmistakably the throaty whine affected by the Optimus as the "pure" speech.

"Never mind," Pepper said. The sound of that voice was his death-warrant, he knew. Loyalists had been known to take bribes and deliver, their masters never. "How do you like this part of town, Cedric?" he demanded. "How does it strike you?"

"Why Cedric?" the voice of the Optimus asked one of the Loyalists, ignoring Pepper.

"Supposed to be funny, Mr. Fersen," said the Loyalist. Then Pepper heard a blow and cry. "I'm sorry, Mr.—sir—please—"

"Let that be a lesson," said Pepper. "Never tell the name. But don't worry, Mr. Fersen— I never heard of you."

"I'm just in," said the voice of the Optimus with a note of strain and disgust. "I'm just in from Scandinavia."

"In that case," said Pepper, "you'd do well to get back there. Because here comes a gang of Lowers that mean you ill."

Approaching them were people he knew. There was Marty who worked in a glass plant, Pedro who managed an autokafe; hard faces gleaming under the wide-spread street lights.

Bats and clubs appeared in their hands. "Hello!" yelled Marty. The distance was about twice the width of the street.

"Dash it!" whined the voice of the Optimus. "Dash the luck! You'll have to fire into the thick of them."

The next thing Pepper knew was that he was dashing for the knot of Lowers down the street, zig-zagging wildly as projectiles buzzed about his ears. Even then he did not forget the rules he had been taught in Training School; he ran with a calculated, staggering gait that would—at least in theory—unsettle any marksman.

His friends met him halfway; he was taken into their midst, lost in the little group of a dozen or so.

"They won't attack," he gasped. "It's too near the shift. They'd be mobbed—torn to pieces."

"Easy," soothed Marty. "Take it easy. They're breaking—going back. Jupiter—if I only had a camera to get those faces! Who are they?"

Pepper grinned feebly. "I never got a look at one of them," he said. "There was an Optimus with them by the name of Fersen. Do you know him?"

"Yes," said Marty. "I know him. He's a scientist. He's so thoroughly damned brilliant that even the Lowers' technical journals reprint his articles. He's a psychologist—experimental."

"Let it go," said Pepper. He shook his head. "What happened? How come you came to meet me—armed?"

"Something new of mine," said Marty. "We were trying it out. You can call it a psychological eavesdropper. We call it a modified Geiger-Müller counter reset for cerebrum-surface potential composition. It's thoroughly impractical, but we were waiting for you and I turned it on you for a demonstration. Before it blew out the thing showed that something had upset you terribly."

"Pedro thought it must have been a babe walking down the street. That's the Latin mind. When you didn't come we put two and two together and found a slight case of Optimus."

"Yes," said Pepper absently. "It's usually that."

It usually was. The Fusionists were nominally in power throughout the whole hemisphere, but the hand of the Optimus tended to grow clumsier and clumsier, showing through the thin veil of the Continental Congress. The Fusionists had been elected generally on the most immense wave of enthusiasm ever to sweep a new party into office. Their appeal had been almost irresistible—to combine the best features of both classes and work for harmony.

The Old Malarky, it soon developed. The Fusion officials— "Fightin' Bob" Howard, Oscar Stoop, "Iron Man" Morris—had been bought and paid for. Things were growing bad, worse than they had ever been before. The Lowers were arming. Every issue of their newspapers contained inflammatory statements, direct slurs against the government and the Optimus Party.

Money was being spent like water by the Optimus; whole factories had been turned "Loyalist" by promises of tripled wages and security. The Loyal Lowers League was growing slowly, very slowly. There was a basically prejudiced attitude among the factory workers against turncoats of that stamp. This, of course, only widened the gulf between authentic Lowers and those who had joined the League. Things were in a very bad way indeed. Everybody on the continent was waiting for the next election. There was much wild talk about revolution and gutters running with blood.

Pepper was examining the psychological eavesdropper that had saved him some unpleasantness a while ago, tinkering with it and attempting to set it right.

"Well?" grunted Marty.

"Can't be done," said Pepper. "Let's turn to more constructive lines of thought. What did you say Fersen did?"

"Psychology, like us. He experiments. Last thing he did was a study of engramatic impulses."

"Do tell. What are they?"

"It's really the old 'group unconscious' idea in false face. Engrams are memories of previous lives stamped into the chromosomes. They carry compulsive force sometimes. If you hear a low-pitched, growling musical note, your tendency is to shudder and draw away. If you're drunk you'll try to run like hell, because that note, if rightly delivered, means feline carnivores in misty Tertiary jungle."

"I see," mumbled Pepper. "When did Fersen publish this, and from where?"

"Oslo, eight years ago," said Marty.

"And what I've done then and up to now would sorely tax your limited understanding," said a full-throated whine.

Pepper slowly swiveled his chair around. The face that he saw was thin and keen, the hair an ashy blonde. But more to the point than hair and face was the blued steel tube that was in the speaker's hands.

"If I read your gaze aright," said the aristocrat, "you're wondering about this thing. Wonder no more, for it is a new development on the old-style chiller. It will congeal the blood of a turtle. What's more it is absolutely noiseless. I could kill you two where you sit and walk out and away to my very comfortable flat in Residential. My name is Fersen and I got here by bribing your janitor. Does that answer all your questions?"

"Doesn't even begin to," grunted Pepper sourly. "What now?"

"Now you are coming with me." He herded them from the room at the point of his weapon. As they came out into the open he hid it under his cloak.

"Stroll casually," said Fersen. "Be gay and lightsome. You're going to Residential to watch the beautiful women walk down the beautiful streets. Sorry I bungled that attempt last night, Pepper. It must have been irritating to both of us. You weren't going to be killed at all."

Nervously, Fersen went on talking. "You'll be interested to know that I was summoned to this continent by a grand conclave of Optimus. They propose to settle the unhappy question of the coming election once and for all time."

"By committing mass suicide?" suggested Marty.

Fersen was pleased to laugh briefly, like the snapping of a lock in a death-cell's door. "By no means," he chuckled. "By that gentlest of all arts, psychology. Whereat, enter Fersen. Get in, please." He gestured at the open door of a car that had pulled up beside them, silent and grim.

"*C'est bon,* children," smiled Fersen. "Romp if you wish." The two Lowers were staring in awe at the incredible battery of instruments racked on the walls, piled on the floors, hanging from the ceiling—everywhere.

"For a lab, not bad," finally admitted Pepper. "*All* psychological?" He stared hard at some electronic equipment—ikonoscopes, tubes and coils—that was sparking quietly away in a corner.

"All," said Fersen proudly. "Now be seated, please."

The two were shoved into chairs by bruisers, then buckled in securely with plastic straps. The bruisers saluted Fersen and left.

"Now," said the psychologist, carefully locking the door, "you poor scum think you know things about the human brain?" He paced to their chairs and stared contemptuously into their faces.

"You think," he spat, "that the incredible, contorted caverns of the mind can be unraveled by base-born apes of your caliber? Forget it. I'm going to show you things about behavior you won't believe even after you see them. I'm going to make you say that you love the Optimus Party and that you'll fight to the death anybody who doesn't.

"I'm going to leave you in such a state of cringing, gibbering bestality that you're going to betray your friends and cut your children's throats and know that you're doing a noble thing."

"Hypnotism won't work that far," said Pepper matter-of-factly.

"I don't use hypnotism," grunted Fersen. "I'm turning to the classics. What good would an isolated case or so be? We've got to have a mass movement, a movement that will spread like wildfire. Look at that!" He held up a book.

"Odes of Anacreon," read Pepper from the title-page. "So what?"

Fersen grinned slowly. "I know," he said irrelevantly, "an arrangement of lines that would make you beat your brains out in despair. I know a sound that will make you so angry that you'll tear your own flesh if there's nobody else around. I know a certain juxtaposition of colored masses that would turn you into a satyr—drive you mad with insatiable lust."

"I see," said Marty slowly. "I see that you weren't quite finished with the engram in Oslo."

"I had barely begun. I am now able—once I've sized up the psyche of the subject—to deliver complex commands in a compulsion-language that cannot possibly be disobeyed."

"Go on," snapped Pepper, catching Fersen's eye. He had seen something at the edge of his vision that made his heart pound. He relaxed deliberately. "Go on!"

"This book," said Fersen, smiling again, "will be released to the general public very shortly—as soon as I've completed copy for a definitive edition. Picture this scene:

"A bookseller receives a shipment of the *Odes*. 'How now!' says bookseller. He is amazed. He is distressed. He did not order the *Odes*. He does not want to pay for them; they look like a slow-moving item. He picks up a copy from the crate so as to get a better idea of what they are. 'What's this?' demands bookseller excitedly. For it seems to be a foreign tongue which he does not understand. Printed plainly on every page in large type is a brief message. Always the same, always legible.

"Bookseller than scans one page, very briefly. Some strange compulsion holds him; he reads further and the mysterious language is as plain as day. The message says: 'You are loyal to the Optimus Party. You will always be loyal to the Optimus Party. You will show the *Odes* to everybody you see. *Everybody must read the* Odes. *You will always be loyal to the Optimus Party.*'

" 'How now!' says bookseller again. 'Uncanny!' And he sees a woman on the street. He seizes her. She screams. He twists her arm and shoves her into his shop. She sits quietly while the *Odes* are shoved under her nose. She reads, lest this madman damage her. They then join forces and distribute copies of the book far and wide. It's like a prairie fire—people read and make others read.

"Pepper, there are twelve thousand booksellers in New York Sector. As soon as I've probed somewhat into your minds to determine whether a vowel or a diphthong would serve better to break down the resistance of a determined spirit opposed to the Optimus, I shall give orders to the printers, who've been immunized by a temporary hypnosis.

"Pepper, two hours after I have sent in copy the crates of books will arrive simultaneously in every one of the twelve thousand shops. Now relax. You're going to be investigated."

He turned to select instruments from a cluttered board. With a faint intake of breath Marty slid from the chair in which he had been strapped, from which he had been working himself free with desperate speed while Pepper held the psychologist's gaze.

Marty launched himself at Fersen's back, snapping an arm about his throat. The psychologist snatched a scalpel from the board before the two reeled away into the center of the cluttered room. With his other hand Marty grabbed frantically at the wrist that held the blade, closed with crushing force about it. The knife dropped, tinkling, to the floor. The two of them fell; Marty, shoving a knee into the small of Fersen's back, wrenched at his arm.

The psychologist collapsed shuddering in a heap. Marty warily broke away from him and picked up a casting, then clubbed Fersen carefully on the side of the head.

As he unbuckled Pepper he snapped: "Thank God that door's locked. Thank God he didn't make enough noise to get the guard. Thank God for so damned many things, Pepper. This is the chance of a lifetime!"

"I don't understand," said Pepper.

"You will," smiled Marty airily. "You probably will. Now where in the bloody dithering hell does he keep his notes—?"

Jay Morningside, bookseller, wearily said: "I'm sorry, ma'am; I'm in trade. I can't afford to have any political opinions."

"Please," said the girl appealingly. "This election petition will help turn out the Fusionist gang and put in Lowers who know how people like us feel and think—"

[*Cosmic Stories* - March 1941
as by S. D. Gottesman]

Return from M-15

1

"For this device," declared the haggard young man, "and all rights, I want thirty percent of the World Research Syndicate voting stock."

The big man grinned. "Your little joke, Dr. Train. World Research Syndicate has little interest in independents—but from a person of your ability, perhaps we'll examine it. What is it you have there? Perhaps a payment of a few thousands can be arranged."

"Don't laugh just yet. Look over these plans—you'll see what I mean."

The engineer took up the sheaf of cap with a smile and unrolled one of the sheets. His brow wrinkled, the smile became a frown. He opened other sheets and stared at them.

"Excuse me," he said, looking up. "I think I see what you are driving at, but I can't deliver an opinion on this sort of thing. I'm an expert in my own line and I know dielectrics as well as most, but this stuff is over my head. I shall endorse your work and refer it to the Board of Technology. And I think you'll scare hell out of them."

Train laughed freely. "I'll do my best, Hans. And have you any idea of what this device will do?"

Vogel looked frightened. "I almost hope I'm wrong," he said. "Does it—" he whispered in Train's ear.

"Right the first time. It does and it will. And if the Syndicate doesn't meet my demands, then I can set it up myself and go into business."

The other man looked strangely sober. "Young Dr. Train," he started, "I am strangely inclined to advise you like a father."

"Go ahead, Hans," replied Train cheerfully.

"Very well. I tell you, then, to moderate your request, or you will find yourself in the gravest of difficulties." He looked about the room apprehensively. "This is not a threat; it is merely advice. I am almost convinced that you should scrap your machine or technique, or whatever it is, and forget about it as completely as you can."

Train rose angrily. "Thank you. Vogel, you must be the truest and most faithful slave the Syndicate has; you and your advice can both go to the same place. I'm leaving the plans with you; they are not complete, of course. I hold all the key details. Send them in to your board and have them communicate with me. Good day."

Ann was primping herself before a mirror. "Barney," she warned coldly as she saw Train sneaking up behind her.

"I just wanted to straighten my tie," he said meekly.

"A likely story!"

"It isn't every day one calls on Jehovah," he said. "I think Mr. T. J. Hartly would be disgruntled if I appeared with a crooked tie to receive a check for a million dollars."

"For a check that big you should be willing to go in stark naked," she said reflectively.

"Possibly. Where shall we have dinner? I want to flash the check in a head-waitress' face. They've been sneering at me all my life and I think it's time I got even."

"You'll do no such thing!" she retorted indignantly. "The moment we get that check, we head for the city clerk and get married. The money may be in your name, but I'm not going to be short-changed."

"Come on," he said, taking her arm and starting for the door. "It is sort of wonderful, isn't it? I'm so damned nervous I might burst into tears."

Suddenly sober, she looked at him. "Yes."

"Husband and wife," he mused. "Free from care and poverty; we can just love each other and buy all the crazy, expensive machines we want. We can get acid stains on our hands whenever we feel like it, and have explosions three times a day. It's like a dream."

She kissed him abruptly. "On our way." They hopped into a taxi, and after a few moments of frenzied driving, pulled up at the entrance to the Syndicate Building.

Train paid the driver, gave him an enormous tip. On the elevator, Ann kicked him sharply in the shin.

"What was that for?" he inquired injuredly.

"For wasting our money, dear."

"Then this," he replied, kicking her back, "is for interfering in the distribution of our funds."

The door opened and they hobbled out of the car.

"Mr. Train and Miss Riley?" asked a polished young man, looking curiously at them. "Please come this way." He opened a hugely carven oak door and ushered them through. Then the door closed solidly behind them.

The room was huge and impressively bare. At the far end, beneath clouded windows, was a large desk. Impressively the man behind it rose. "I am Mr. Hartly," he said.

"Riley and Train," replied Barnabas Train nervously. "We are pleased to meet you."

Hartly smiled acknowledgment and studied a sheaf of papers. "As the arrangement now stands, we have investigated your device—tagged Independent Fourteen—and are prepared to take over all rights and techniques in exchange for a stated payment. This payment will be an advance of one million dollars to be delivered in toto now, in return for the final details of Independent Fourteen which are in your possession, to be followed by a transfer of thirty percent of the voting stock of Research Syndicate."

"Correct," said Train. "I'm prepared to deliver if you are."

Hartly—who was really a very small man, Ann noted with some surprise—smiled again. "As director of the Syndicate I have decided to request a slight moderation in your demands."

"To what?" snapped Train, his eyes hardening.

"It has been thought that an ample payment would be arranged on a basis of the million advance and—say—one tenth of one percent of non-voting stock."

Train laughed shortly. "Don't joke with me. I know the spot you're in. I'm holding out for a strong minority for one reason only—I want to put in my vote when I have to and keep your financiers from taking young technicians from the schools and making them your slaves as you've always done. And if you don't give in—Independent Fourteen goes into operation under my direction and at my discretion. And you know what that machine can do to your trust!"

Hartly tapped his teeth with a pencil. "As well as you, certainly." A moment of silence. "Then if we can reach no agreement you had better leave."

"Come on, honey," said Train, taking Ann's arm. "We have work to do." Turning their backs on the little financier, they walked to the huge door and pulled it open. Before them was a line of police. "Go back," said an officer quietly.

"What the hell is this?" demanded Train as they were hustled back to Hartley's desk, surrounded by an escort with drawn guns. The officer ignored him and addressed the man behind the desk. "We heard there was trouble in here, sir. Are these the ones?"

"Yes. The man has attempted blackmail, theft, sabotage and assault. The woman is of no importance."

"He's lying!" exploded Train. "I'm Dr. Train and this snake's after stealing an invention he won't meet my terms on."

"You'd better search him," said Hartly quietly. "I believe he has on him documents stolen from our files. They will be marked as specifications for Independent Fourteen."

Suddenly Train stopped struggling. "You're wrong on that point," he said coldly. "All the missing details are in my head; you'll never get them from me."

"It really doesn't matter, Doctor," returned Hartly negligently. "My engineers can reconstruct them from what we have."

"I doubt that very much! The chances are one in a million of your ever stumbling on certain facts that I did. I warn you—Independent Fourteen's lost for good if you do not turn me loose."

"That may be," smiled Hartly. Suddenly he burst into laughter. "But surely you didn't think we were going to operate your device. It would cripple our economy if we worked it to one percent of its capacity. That machine of yours is impossible—now. We may use it for certain purposes which we shall decide, but your program of operation was a joke."

Train and Ann looked at each other. "I think, Barney," she said softly, "that sooner or later we'll kill this little man."

"Yes. We will because we'll have to. I'll be back, Ann—wait for me."

"Captain," broke in Hartly to the officer, "here is a warrant of transportation signed by the Commissioner. It authorizes you to remove the prisoner to a suitable institution for indefinite detention. I think that had best be M-15."

Train had been hustled into a police car and rushed to the outskirts of the city. There his guard turned him over to another group in grey uniforms. He looked for insignia but found none. A policeman said to him, before driving off, "These men don't talk and they don't expect prisoners to. Watch your step—good-bye."

Train's first question as to who his guards were was met with a hammer-like blow in the face. Silently they shoved him into an armored car, as grey and blank as their uniforms, and all he knew was that they were driving over rough roads with innumerable twists and turns. At last the car stopped and they dragged him out.

He almost cried out in surprise—they were at a rocket-port. It was small and well hidden by surrounding trees and hills, but seemed complete. On the field was a rocket the like of which he had never seen. Without windows save for a tiny pilot's port, comparatively bare of markings, and heavily armored, it loomed there as a colossal enigma.

His guards took his arms and walked him to the ship. Silently a port opened, making a runway with the ground, and other men in grey descended. They took Train and the single sheet of paper that was his doom and dragged him into the ship.

"Where—," he asked abruptly, and a club descended on his head.

He opened his eyes with the feel of cold water on his forehead. An inverted face smiled at him. "Feeling better?" it asked.

Train sat up. "Yes, thanks. Now suppose you tell me where we are and what in hell's going to become of us." He stared about him at their quarters; they were in a little room of metal plates with no door apparent.

"I think we're on a prison ship," said his companion. "They were apparently delaying it for your arrival. We should be taking off shortly."

"Yes—but where are we going?"

"Didn't you know?" asked the other with pity in his eyes. "This ship goes to M-15."

"I never heard of it or him. What is it?"

"Not many know it by its official number," said the other carefully and slowly, "but rumors of its existence are current almost everywhere. It is a planetoid in a tight orbit between Mercury and Vulcan—an artificial planetoid."

He smiled grimly. "For eighty years, it has been in operation as a private prison for those who offend against World Research. Employees of the Syndicate who attempt to hold out work they have developed with the company's equipment make up one part of the prison rolls. Attempted violence against high officers also accounts for many of the inmates." Suddenly his eyes flashed and he drew himself up. "And I am proud," he said, "to be one of those."

Train moistened his lips. "Did you," he asked hesitatingly, "try to kill—"

"No, not kill. I am a chemist, and chemistry means mathematical logic. If one can produce the effects of death without creating the state itself, the punishment is far less. I am only human, and so I dosed—a certain corporation official—with a compound which will leave him less than a mindless imbecile in a month."

"Then I certainly belong here with you. If anything, I'm the greater criminal. You only stole the brains of one man; I tried to cripple the Syndicate entire."

"A big job—a very big job! What did—"

His words were cut off by a shattering, mechanical roar that rattled them about in their little room like peas in a pod.

"Hold on!" shouted the man to Train above the noise, indicating the handgrips set in the floor. "We're going up!"

They flattened themselves, clutched the metal rods. Train was sick to his stomach with the sudden explosive hops of the ship as it jerked itself from the ground, but soon its gait steadied and the sputtering rocket settled down to a monotonous roar.

He rose and balanced himself on the swaying door of their cell. "Next stop," he said grimly, "M-15!"

2

Lawrence—Train's cellmate on the prison ship—stirred uneasily and nudged the other.

"What is it?"

"Listen to that exhaust. Either something's gone wrong or we're going to land. How many days have we been going?"

"They've fed us twenty-three times."

"Probably two weeks in space. That should be about it. Do you feel the gravity?"

Train rolled over. "It's faint, but it's there. We must have landed already—the motion we feel is the ship shifting around on the landing field."

As though in confirmation of his words, the door to their cell that had been closed for two long weeks snapped open to admit two of their captors. The grey-clad men gestured silently and the prisoners got to their feet. Neither dared to speak; Train remembered the blow that had been his last answer, and so did Lawrence. They walked slowly ahead of their guards to the exit-port of the ship, not daring to guess what they might see.

Train walked first through the door and gasped. He was under a mighty dome of ferro-glass construction, beyond which stars glittered coldly. They must have landed on the night-side of the artificial asteroid, for he could see the blazing corona of the sun eclipsed by the sphere on which he was standing. Fantastic prominences leaped out in the shapes of animals or mighty trees, changing and melting into one another with incredible slowness. It was hard to believe that each one of them must have been huge enough to swallow a thousand Jupiters at once, without a flicker.

A guard prodded him savagely in the back. He began walking, trying his muscles against the strange, heady lack of gravity, mincing along at a sedate pace. They were headed for a blocky concrete building.

The doors opened silently before them, and they marched down a short corridor into an office of conventionally Terrestrial pattern.

For the first time Train heard one of the guards speak. "Last two, sir," he said to a uniformed man behind a desk.

"You may leave, officers," said the man gently. They saluted and disappeared from the room. The man rose and, in a curiously soft voice, said: "Please be seated."

Train and Lawrence folded into comfortable chairs, eyed their captor uncertainly. Lawrence was the first to speak.

"Is there anything I can do for you?" he asked with flat incongruity.

"Yes," said the man. "May I have your names?"

"Train and Lawrence," said the chemist. The man wrote in a book sunk flush with the desk.

"Thank you. And your reasons for commitment to M-15?"

"In my case, attempted murder," replied Lawrence. "In Train's, blackmail and theft. At least, so we are given to understand."

"Of course," said the man behind the desk, writing in the information. "It is my duty as administrator of this asteroid to inform you as well as I may of your functions here and what treatment you may expect."

He coughed and sat up straighter. "You may well wonder," he began pretentiously, "why you have been sent to this bleak spot to expiate your sin against society."

"Rebellion against the Syndicate, you mean," snapped Train harshly.

"Be that as it may," continued their informant with a shrug, "this is an officially constituted place of detention under charter and supervision by the Terrestrial League. Certain cases are sent to us for corrective measures associated formerly with World Research Incorporated. Therefore, it is only proper that they should be assigned to experimental work tending to advance the progress of humanity and raise its cultural level.

"Your work will be a sort of manufacturing process of an extremely delicate nature. However, mechanical controls and checks will make blunders and errors impossible after a short period of instruction. You two men have been technicians of a high order of skill; let us hope that you will redeem yourselves by application to your assigned task."

He sat back with a smile. "Now, unless there are any questions—"

"There damn well are," snapped Lawrence. "In the first place, is there any communication with the outside world?"

"None whatsoever. Evil influences might convince you that all here is not for the best, and persuade you to foolish acts of violence. We leave nothing to chance."

Train had had enough; he was going to get this soft-spoken fiend if it were his last living act. With a snarl in his throat he leaped at the desk, only to bring up smashing his face against some invisible barrier. Amazed, he put his hands over the frozen, quite transparent surface between his tormenter and him.

"Superglass," said the man quietly, smiling as on a child. "As I said, we leave *nothing* to chance."

"This is your cell," said the guard—one they had not seen before. He waved them into a spotless chamber, small and square, featuring two comfortable bunks and elaborate sanitary facilities.

Train sat on one of the bunks, dazed. "I can't understand it," he burst out suddenly and violently. "This whole business is rotten with contradictions."

"What do you mean?" asked Lawrence absently, switching the faucet on and off.

"It's this sort of thing. They stuck us on this asteroid to die, we know. And yet, look at this room! Perfect for comfort and health. Consider our reception: a very skillful welcome designed to soothe one's ruffled spirit and put him in a cooperative frame of mind. Of course, it didn't happen to work with us, because we have very special rages against the system and all it stands for."

"It's very simple," said Lawrence thoughtfully. "They don't want us on Earth and they do want us here very badly."

"Simple?" Train snorted. "I could have been shot down like a dog in Hartly's office two weeks ago, and yet he packed me off here at a terrible expense in salaries, fuel, and wear of the ship. I don't think it was fear of punishment of any kind that stopped him from destroying me then and there. They need me out on this chunk of rock. And I think it has something to do with where the place is, too."

"How so?"

"Like this. It stands to reason that if you put an asteroid in a tight orbit as near as this to the sun, you need a lot of power—expensive power—to keep her there. It would be a lot easier and cheaper to put the orbit out somewhere between Jupiter and Neptune, and would be fully as accessible, or inaccessible, all depending on how you look at it. Ships wouldn't have to have sun-armor, which costs plenty, and they wouldn't run the risk of getting caught in an electric twister or prominence."

"So this place," said Lawrence slowly, "is more than a prison."

"Obviously. Remember the ancient motto: 'If it pays, they'll do it.'"

"And if it doesn't, they won't. What was it that smiling gentleman said about congenial occupations commensurate with our training?"

"That's it! They manufacture something here that needs trained men and sunlight in huge quantities."

"Then why not hire workers? Why run the risk of having convicts responsible for the production of a valuable article or substance? It must be valuable, by the way. Just think of what it cost to get us here, to say nothing of the expense of building and maintaining this setup."

Train's face went grim. "I can guess. It must mean that there's a fair chance that the substance is so deadly that the men who manufacture it, even with all suitable and possible guards and shields, must be poisoned by it so that they die at their work after a time."

"Yes," said Lawrence, "you must be right." There was a long silence, then a guard banged his stick on their door.

"You're going to work," he called in on them. The door was unlocked; the two walked out as martyrs might.

"This way," said the guard.

He showed them into a narrow tiled room. "Begin by sealing those bottles. You'll find torches and materials in your cabinets." He walked out, closing the door behind him.

Train stared at the row of open flasks that stood on the shelf like so many deadly snakes. "What are they, Lawrence?" he asked hoarsely.

"I had an idea all along—" whispered the chemist. He took one of the flasks carefully by the neck and spilt some of its contents on a composition-topped table. "Looks like ordinary table salt, doesn't it?"

"Yes. But it has a smell like nothing on earth I know."

Lawrence, with the attitude of a scientist who knows and demands that everything should be in its place, opened a standard supply-cabinet and brought out, without looking, an ochre filter and a connected burner. He played the flames on the crystals and squinted through the glass carefully, turning it at sharp and precise angles. Finally he replaced the filter absently and incinerated the little heap of stuff on the table.

"One of the mysteries of the chemical world is solved," he said. "That stuff is thalenium chloride."

"Never heard of it."

"You're fortunate. It's the filthiest narcotic that ever cursed a race. Fortunately, only the wealthiest can afford to take it. Seeing the setup required to manufacture it, that's understandable.

"Thalenium's supposed to be a solar element—unstable—made up in the sun's core. They named it after the Muse of Comedy, for some reason or other. I never came across an authentic case of thalenium poisoning, but it's supposed to cause hallucinations viler than anything imaginable to the normal mind. External manifestations are great spasms of laughter—hence, comedy and the comic muse."

Train stared at the innocent-appearing crystals. "And we have to handle it?"

"No danger, yet, I suppose, if we are careful."

Lawrence picked up a flask full of the narcotic with tongs. "Like this," he said, skillfully playing a stream of flame across its tapering spout. He set it down and quickly slipped a cap over the softened glass. "Then," he added, "you appear to spray it with this stuff." He squirted a film of heavy liquid on the cap. It set sharply, and letters and figures came out on it.

"Authentic thalenium chloride, c.p., 500 mm," he read. "Clever devil, World Research!"

They set to work, moving like machines, sealing the flasks in three sharp operations.

"There's no danger yet," observed Lawrence. "I don't know, and can't imagine, what the process of its actual manufacture may be, but we'll find that out later. If the stuff is prepared direct as the chloride, it might be fairly harmless, but if free metallic thalenium is used then there must be hell to pay among the workers."

"Then there's no point, as yet, in going on strike?"

"Certainly not. Everything's gravy so far. And of course, it's going to be gravy as long as we do our work faithfully, obediently, and not too intelligently. Thus, for example, it pays to make minor mistakes like this one." He took a sealed bottle firmly by the neck and snapped it against the edge of the table. It shattered and spilled over the floor.

"I get the idea. We case the joint for as long as we can, staying away from the dangerous operations. Then we escape?" He poured an acid over the salt on the floor; it bubbled and gave off thin wisps of vapor.

Lawrence scattered a neutralizing base over the acid. It became a white froth that he flushed down a floor-gutter. "I see," he remarked, returning to his work, "that we've been thinking along somewhat similar lines."

"I have a machine," said Train irrelevantly. "I developed it all by myself—no, I'm forgetting my girl friend, a very competent head for details—and if I get back to Earth and have two weeks to myself, along with reasonable equipment, I guarantee that I'll wipe World Research and all that's rotten in it off the face of the Earth and out of the cosmos, too."

"Sounds remarkable. What does it do?"

Train told him.

The chemist whistled. "Quite out of my field," he said. "It takes a physicist to dope out those things that really count."

"Independent Fourteen, they call it," said Train with a tight-drawn smile. "And I swear by every god in the firmament that nothing—nothing—is going to keep me from getting back to Earth, setting up Independent Fourteen, and blowing World Research to hell!"

3

Train was lying half-awake on his cot when the door slammed shut. "Hiya, Lawrence."

The chemist bent over him. "Get up, Barney. It's happened."

Train sat up abruptly. "How do you know?" he snapped.

"I was just seeing the Oily Bird." That was the name they had given the infuriating man who greeted them on their arrival. "He says we've made good in the packaging department and we're going to be promoted. He still doesn't know that we are wise as to what is going on."

"Promoted, eh? What's that mean?"

"He said we were going into the production end of the concern. That we'd have to handle the stuff without tongs. Be exposed to sunlight. And, at this distance, that's surely fatal in a short time."

"I didn't think it would come this quickly," said Train. "Then we'll have to dope something out—fast."

"Fast is the word. How about slugging a guard?"

"Too crude. Much too crude. They must have an elaborate system of passwords and countersigns; otherwise it would have been done successfully long ago. And Lord knows how many times it's failed!"

"Right," said the chemist. "We can't slug a guard. But maybe we can bribe one?"

"I doubt it. We know it hasn't succeeded. I suppose they make big money as such things go."

"Can we put psychological screws on one? Know any little tricks like suggesting hatred against the system he's working for?"

Train wrinkled his brow. "Yes, but they are good only after a long period of constant suggestion. We have to move at once. Lawrence, can you play sick?"

"As well as you. Why?"

"And do you remember the shape of the eyebrows on the guard we have this week?"

"Have you gone bats?" demanded the chemist, staring at Train angrily. "This is no time to be playing jokes."

The scientist raised his hand. "This isn't a joke, or a game, either. Those eyebrows may mean our salvation."

Lawrence picked up a pencil and paper and sketched out what he remembered of their guard's face. "There," he said, thrusting it under Train's nose.

Train studied the drawing. "I think this is accurate," he mused. "If it is, we may be back on Earth in two weeks."

The guard knocked on the door, and there was no answer. Suspiciously he pushed it open and entered, half-expecting to be attacked. But he found one of the prisoners in bed with a sallow skin, breathing in shallow gulps.

"Lawrence is sick, I think," said Train.

"Yeah? Too bad. I'll call the medico."

"No," gasped the patient. "Not yet."

The guard turned to go. "I have to call him when anyone is sick. It might start an epidemic, otherwise."

"Can you wait just a minute?" asked Train. "I know how to handle him when he gets one of his attacks. It isn't anything contagious. Just mild conjunctivitis of the exegetical peritoneum."

"That a fact?" asked the guard. "How do you handle him?"

"Easy enough," said Train. "May I borrow your flashlight?"

"Sure!" The guard handed over a slim pencil-torch.

"Thank you." The scientist balanced the light on the broad back of a chair. "Won't you sit down?" he asked the guard. "This will take a few minutes."

"Sure." Their warder watched with interest as Train dimmed the lights of the cell and switched on the flashlight so that it cast a tiny spot of radiance on a gleaming water faucet. The guard stared at it, fascinated.

Train's voice sank to a whispering drone. "Concentrate on the light. Block out every other thing but the light."

The guard shifted uneasily. This was a strange way to treat a sick man, and the light was shining right in his eyes. Perhaps he had better call the medico after all. He was half decided to do so, but he felt tired and the chair was comfortable. What was it Train was saying?

"By the time I have counted to twenty, you will be asleep. One..." The guard's eyes grew heavy. "Concentrate ... block out everything but the light ... everything but the light ... seven ..."

The spot of light floated before the guard's face, distorting into strange shapes that shifted. He just barely heard Train drone "twelve" before he began to breathe deeply and hoarsely.

Train switched on the lights and slipped the flashlight into his pocket. "Perfect specimen, Lawrence," he exulted. "You can always tell by the eyebrows."

"Fascinating," returned the erstwhile victim to conjunctivitis of the exegetical peritoneum as he climbed out of bed. "What now?"

Train rolled back the guard's eyelids with a practiced thumb. "Ask him anything," he said. "He'll tell you whatever we want to know."

Lawrence cleared his throat, bent over the sleeping man. "When are you leaving for Earth?"

"This afternoon. One hour from now."

"Do the others know you?"

"They never saw me, but they know my name."

"What are the passwords on the way to the ship?"

"Front gate, *rabies*. Second gate, *tuberculosis*. Field guard, *leprosy*. Ship port, *cancer*."

"Someone must have had a grim sense of humor," whispered Lawrence to Train.

"What are your duties on the ship?"

"I have no duties."

The chemist snapped: "One of us must take his place."

"Yes. Which one of us? No, we won't have to decide. I'm going. Aside from such details as the fact that his uniform will fit me, but would look suspiciously baggy on you, I have a chance to do something about this whole rotten system when I get back. You would only be able to commit more murders, or near-murders."

The chemist's lips whitened. "You're right," he whispered. "When you have the chance, promise me that you'll wipe out this asteroid and the filthy stuff they manufacture here. I don't think I'll be around by that time; exposure to the sun might get me sooner than we think."

"I know," said Train shortly, "and I promise." He gripped the other's hand and shoulder for the moment, then turned to the unconscious guard, and began a machine-gun fire of questions that were to stock his brain with every secret datum held inviolate by the militia of the man-made planetoid.

Ann Riley was frying breakfast bacon and eggs; she did not hear the door of her flat open softly and close. Behind her a voice suddenly spoke. "Cut me in on some of that."

She turned and gasped: "Barney, you sonova gun!" she yelled and flew into his arms.

"It was really nothing," he explained over the coffee. "They just hadn't figured on the hypnosis angle and I took care not to drop any bricks on the voyage. The inefficiency of that system is appalling. If I were managing it, I could step up production of their rotten stuff three hundred percent and see that no prisoner even thought of escaping."

"Yeah," she said skeptically, "I know. But what are you going to do now that you're back?"

"I'm safe for a month. That's how long it takes for a ship to get there and back, and they haven't any other means of communication. The nearness to the sun makes radio or beam messages impossible. So, first, I'm going swimming."

"No, you aren't," she said coldly, a gleam in her eye. "I've been redrafting Independent Fourteen, and all the details are there down on paper again—except for the ones you have in your head. We're going to build that machine and build it fast and powerful. Then we'll throw it in the teeth of T. J. Hartly and World Research, Incorporated. And we're going to fling it so hard there won't be a sound tooth left in their mouths."

"Yes, my pet. I must confess I had some such thought in my head when I decided to come back to Earth."

"We can rig up enough of a lab," she went on, "right here in my flat. There's no more experimentation to do; we just need the bare essentials with a slight margin for error."

"Splendid," he nodded, reaching for another slice of toast. "We'll need about a hundred yards of silver wire, some standard castings, and a few tubes. You'd better go out and get them now—shop around; we can't afford to get the most expensive. Where have you got the plans?"

They rose from the table and Ann drew a huge scroll of paper from the closet. "Here they are. Full scale, this time."

Train scanned them. "Hey! This distributor wasn't on the designs I gave you."

"Oh, I just filled it in," she demurred.

The scientist scowled. "Hereafter," he proclaimed, "all filling in will be done by Doctor Train. Now gwan out and buy the stuff while I work out the missing circuits." He seated himself at a desk, brooding over the plans.

He looked up when a firm tap came on his shoulder.

"Well?" he asked without turning his head.

"Excuse me, young man, but a point of morality has just come up. Where do you expect to live while you're building Independent Fourteen?"

"Right here," he answered calmly. "First, I can't afford to live anywhere else—even though I drew a guard's salary, and that isn't too small. But there's the danger to consider. You wouldn't want your collaborator to be snatched up and deported again, would you?"

"Fundamentally," she began in a determined voice, "I'm a conventional person. And I do not like neighbors talking about me as though I were a thing loathsome and accursed in the eyes of gods and men."

"What have neighbors to do with it?"

"Don't you think they would consider it a bit peculiar were a man suddenly to come to my flat and begin to live with me as though it were the most natural thing in the world?"

"Isn't it?" he replied. "In the eyes of Science nothing is unclean or to be shunned."

"Dr. Train!" she flared, "you are going to marry me whether you like it or not. At once!"

He stared at her. "I never really thought of it like that," he began ... but Ann was already speaking into the mouthpiece of the phone.

"Central Services, please."

She returned to him. "There—that was easy, wasn't it? He'll be here in a moment; he lives a few houses down."

There was a knock on the door. "Central Service is Super Service," quoted Ann. "That's him now."

She rose to admit a sickly individual who greeted her in a brisk, flabby voice. "Miss Riley?"

"Yes. And that object is Doctor Train, my spouse-to-be."

"Thank you," said the agent, opening a book. "Please sign in duplicate." Ann scribbled her name and passed the book to Train, who also signed.

"Two dollars for ceremony and registration," said the anemic Cupid. Train handed over the money and limply accepted the certificate in return.

"Thank you," said the agent. "I now pronounce you man and wife." He walked out through the door, closing it gently behind him.

"Well," said Ann, after a long pause.

"Well, what?"

"Aren't you going to kiss the bride?"

"Oh." He did so until she pounded his back for air. "I must be a romanticist," he complained, "but I always wanted an old-fashioned wedding before a city clerk."

"Times have changed," she philosophized. "The tempo of life is accelerated; things move at a fast and furious pace in these mad days. The old conventions remain, but one complies with them as swiftly and effortlessly as possible. It helps to retain the illusion of gentility."

"Then," he said, "since the illusion is saved, let's get to work. One hundred yards of silver wire—no, make it seventy; we can always buy more."

4

What's that thing?" asked Ann, peering curiously at an odd-looking setup Train was working on.

"A little something. I plan to scare hell out of Hartly with it. A frequency inductor—I can get the wavelength of his inter-office system and bellow in his ear."

"Very cute," she said thoughtfully. "What's the second tube for?"

"Steps up the tertiary vibrations. I could have used a seven-phase transformer with better effect, but a tube's cheaper and we happened to have one left over."

He twisted a final screw contact into place. "Finished," he announced, "shall we call up T. J.?"

The curiosity was gone. There was only sudden anguish in her eyes as she clung to him. "Barney!" She buried her face against his shoulder. "What shall we do if anything goes wrong?"

For a brief second her fears leaped through him as he comforted her in the only way he knew. Then cold reason reached in. His voice was steady as he answered: "Nothing will. Independent Fourteen's checked and triple-checked. We've tested it and it clicks every time. What are you worried about?"

"Hartly's a smart man. He has to be to stay on top of World Research. He must have things up his sleeve that no one has ever dreamed about. Wasn't he a scientist himself before he rose from the ranks to the executive department? It's men like that you have to watch out for. Never trust a reformed technician."

Train smiled happily. "There's nothing to be afraid of. It's the nature of Independent Fourteen that has him licked before he can start. With this priceless gimmick we have a machine that will give us unlimited personal power and protection. I'm going to play our cards for everything they're worth."

"Barney, isn't there a chance that we might compromise?" She waved aside the protests that sprang to his lips. "I know," she said. "The Syndicate's the greediest octopus that ever got its suckers around the life-blood of a world. It's utterly contemptible—and yet, it's too powerful for its own good—and maybe for ours. Couldn't we compromise and lull their suspicions?"

"Not one bloody chance in a billion!" Train snapped harshly. "Independent Fourteen's our only trump card, but it's the winner in this game as soon as we see fit to play it."

"I guess you're right, Barney," said Ann wearily. "Call up Mr. Hartly on that gimmick while I warm up Fourteen." She turned to a corner of the room cleared except for a bulky piece of machinery, protrusive with tubes and coils, built around heavy castings bolted together, mounted on wheels. Ann fingered a switchboard carefully, and tubes began to glow with fiery electrical life while sparks snapped from point to point.

"Mr. Hartly, please," said Train quietly into a grid of his instrument.

"Hartly speaking," boomed from a loudspeaker connected with the tiny device. "Who is this?"

"Dr. Train. Do you remember?"

There was a sudden click. "You can't hang up, Hartly. If you look, you'll find that your phone's blown out. I'm using irregular channels."

A long pause, then Hartly's voice came through again, this time tinged with wonder. "How did you get back from M-15, Train, and when did you do it?"

"You paid me to come back, Hartly. I drew the full salary of a guard while returning to Earth on his regular vacation. I've been here some twenty days."

"Extraordinary," breathed the great man. "And I suppose you've been setting up that silly machine of yours?"

"Not so silly," replied Train ominously. "It works like Merlin's wand—that neat and efficient."

"Then it's no use my sending men around to Miss Riley's flat—I assume that is where you are—to arrest you as an escaped convict."

"No use whatsoever. I can make them feel very foolish, if I so desire. Or I can simply wipe them out without any fuss at all. I'm a practical man, Hartly. Most scientists are—you were one once, yourself, I understand."

"Bacteriologist. Occupied in saving lives. It was wonderful for awhile, but I found eventually that there was no future in it."

"Despicable attitude, Hartly. It shows up throughout your career. It was your career, by the by, that I want to discuss with you, anyway."

"What about my career?"

"Just two words, Hartly. It's over."

Hartly's chuckle was silk-smooth. "How so, Doctor? I was under the impression that it had barely begun."

"I'm warning you, Hartly, not to take this as a joke. I haven't forgotten what it was you wanted to do to me on M-15, and what I was supposed to be doing in the process. I'd have more scruples about killing a scorpion than you, Hartly."

"No doubt about that," came the answer. "So would many misguided persons. But the interesting thing about it is that they have always ended up among insuperable difficulties. You may make me a concrete proposition, Doctor."

"I may and I will! The proposition is this: your unqualified resignation from the directorship and organization of World Research Syndicate, and an assignment to me of unlimited reorganization powers for the period of one year."

Hartly's voice was mocking in tone. "Yes? World Research is a rather large enterprise. Do you think one year would be enough?"

"Ample. Your answer?"

A long pause, then: "My answer is unqualified refusal."

"Based on what? Make no mistake: I shan't hesitate to blot you out any longer than you would hesitate to do the same to me—unless you capitulate. And the difference, T. J., is that I can do it and you cannot."

"Admitted," came back Hartly's voice cheerfully. "But surely, Doctor, you didn't think that I have not been preparing—in fact, been prepared—for just such an occasion as this ever since I came into power?"

"Explain," snapped the scientist. "And talk fast and straight."

Hartly's voice was now unperturbed. "When a question of conflict arises, it's either a matter of personal gain or benefit to the world. I've been faced by determined men before, Train. Those who were after personal advancement could be compromised with and later eliminated by quick thinking and quicker action.

"However, altruists presented a different problem. Most of them could not be bribed. Some of them were powerful enough, by reason of their ability or backing, or both, to issue a flat defiance to me. Those I threatened with the thing they loved most—humanity."

"Come to the point, Hartly. I'm not too patient a man in some ways."

"I was a bacteriologist once," went on Hartly. "And, in the course of my research, I developed a nasty variety of bread-mold. It attacks anything organic and spreads like wildfire. I know of nothing to check it, nor does anyone else. It thrives at any temperature and flourishes off corrosive agents."

"So?"

"So, Doctor Train, make one false move, as they say in melodrama, and I release an active culture of that mold; you will then see your flesh crumble away. I realize that alone wouldn't stop you, but the thought of what will then happen to the teeming millions of Earth will."

Another silence, then: "I decided long ago, Train, that no one would wipe me out. True, someone might come along with bigger and better power, even as you have done, but, as you can see, if there's any blotting out to be done, I shall do it myself.

"It will mean the end of World Research and of me. It will also mean the end of all animal life on this planet. If you want a Pyrrhic victory, Train, you may have it."

"It's horrible!" cried Ann, her eyes wide with the shock of it. "Can he do it, Barney?"

"Miss Riley," came through the voice. "Perhaps you remember the occasion of our first meeting. Do you think me the type of man to try a bluff?"

Train turned to the transmitter of his tiny outfit. "I know you're not bluffing, Hartly. I know also that you'll try every means of persuasion you know first, because you don't particularly want to be wiped out, even by you own hands, yet. But it won't work; you'll try this last resort of yours because the ethics of business, which doesn't blink at the murder of an individual, wouldn't blink at the murder of a planet.

"We're going to make a call on you very soon, Hartly. My wife, myself, and Independent Fourteen."

5

Train paused for a moment in thought. "Ann," he said, "do you think Hogan would want to help us?"

"That's a fine favor to ask of any neighbor. Let's see."

They knocked on the door of an adjoining apartment, and the staccato rattle of a typewriter suddenly cut short. The door swung open, and a little man presented himself. "Afternoon, Trains," he said. "What can I do for you?"

"Hogan," began Ann winsomely, "we think you ought to take the afternoon off. Your work's telling on you."

"Not so I've noticed it. What do you want me to do? More shopping for copper tubing? I'm a busy man, Mrs. Train."

"We know that, Hogan," broke in Barney. "But can you spare us a few hours? We need help badly. You'll have to push some heavy machinery and maybe do a bit of scrapping ..."

"A fight! Why didn't you say so in the first place? Wait; I'll get me gun." He vanished, and they heard the typewriter rattle off a few more steaming paragraphs.

The little man appeared again, hefting a ponderous automatic. "Who do we have to pop off?" he asked amiably.

Ann shivered. "Bloodthirsty, isn't he?"

"They bred us that way in South America. Is it a riot, or what?"

"No, none of them. We're going to blow up World Research."

"Splendid! I'd often thought of how elegant it would be to do that, if only some way could be figured out. Where's the machinery ye spoke of? I presume that is what you toss the bombs with."

"In our apartment. Only it isn't bombs; it makes the most powerful explosive look like a slingshot in comparison." They walked back to Train's flat and Ann pointed out Independent Fourteen.

"That's the junk," she said simply.

"It's a powerful-looking bit of machinery. But what does it do?"

Ann told him briefly.

"No!" he cried. "If it were as big as the Research Building it couldn't do that!"

"Calling us liars, mister?"

"Not a bit of it. All right. It does what you say it will—I hope. What's the campaign?"

"We march on the Syndicate Building, pushing Independent Fourteen before us. It's got wheels, you notice. The thing is nicely adjusted—it'll function on any violent shock as well as the hand controls; they know that, so they won't make any attempt to blow it up. In fact they know all about it, but I don't think they quite realize just how good it is. Otherwise they'd talk differently.

"I'd better show you how to handle it. All you have to know about is this switchboard. The button here indicates radiation. The power will spread in all directions except in that of the operator and directly behind him. This other button is direction. That aims the influence of the machine in a fairly tight beam. Its action is invisible, but it's controlled by this pointer. And the results are soon apparent."

"And what could be the meaning of these cryptic signs?" asked Hogan, indicating a long vertical list of symbols running parallel to the slot of an indicator needle.

"They are the chemical names of the elements."

"I seem to remember," remarked Hogan, knitting his brows.

"Got everything straight? Radiant, director, pointer, and elements?"

"Yes. We can go in my car, I suppose."

They eased the ponderous machine safely down the flight of stairs, then into Hogan's car. Suddenly there boomed from Train's frequency inductor the voice of Hartly. "Train!" it said.

"Listening," the scientist snapped back.

"This is your last warning. I have a man across the street from you. He says that you've loaded Independent Fourteen into a car. You seem to think I intend to back down on my promise to release the fungus."

"Not at all." replied Barney cheerfully, "not at all. On the contrary, I am convinced that you'll not hesitate to pour the stuff out of your window as soon as we come in sight. In fact, I'm counting on it, Hartly. Don't disappoint me, please."

"Then remember, Train, nothing … *nothing* … can stop the fungus. As you say, one false move nearer my building, and I release the culture."

"The false move is made, Hartly," said Train, with steel in his voice. "In case your man hasn't told you, the car has started. We are on our way."

He snapped off the transmitter.

"What was that all about?" asked Hogan, his eyes on the road.

"Just Hartly. He thinks he has a final stymie to work on me. Plans to release a kind of mold that eats away all organic matter. Fire cannot destroy or injure it, nor can chemicals. Once he releases it, it'll spread through the world, attacking all live wood, grass, and animal life."

"Yeah? What are you going to do about it?"

"Can't you guess? Hartly still doesn't realize that any power of his is just a joke so long as Independent Fourteen is in my hands. Pull up!"

The car skidded to a halt before the building that housed World Research. "Take it out tenderly, husband mine," said Ann. "It means a lot to me."

There was a rattling from the pocket wherein Train had thrust his frequency inductor. He took it out, held it to his ear.

Hartly's voice was dry by now. "The bluff's never been pushed this far by any man, Train. This is your last chance. I'm looking down at you, and I have the fungus in my hand. Train, I'm ready to drop this bottle."

"Are you, now?" The scientist's voice bespoke amusement. "And what am I supposed to do about it?"

"Abandon your machine and walk into the building. I'll see that you are taken care of rightly. You'll not regret it if you choose to compromise; you will if you do not."

Train laughed. "For once, Hartly, I'm holding every ace in the deck. Drop your little toy and see how useless it is to you."

There was a long, tense pause. Hogan and Ann watched, but could see nothing. Train swiftly manipulated the little instruments on the control board. There was a little tinkle in the street near them.

"There, Barney, there!" Ann screamed, pointing a trembling finger at a scarcely visible splotch of green. Train swung the pointer of the machine on it even as it exploded upward into a bomb of poisonous vegetation that rustled foully as it spread serpentine arms outward and up.

Train slammed down the button that flung the machine into action, swept the pointer right and left as the tubes sputtered angrily.

"Glory!" muttered Hogan. The fungus had suddenly been arrested and now stood etched in silvery metal.

"Free metallic magnesium," said Train. "It works on a large scale and with one hundred percent efficiency."

"Elements transmuted at will," breathed Ann. "And nothing went wrong!"

"And the machine will do—that—to anything?" demanded Hogan. "It has the Midas touch."

"That it has," agreed the scientist, swinging the needle and shifting the slide. "And, unless I'm mistaken, those men mean us harm."

He swung the pointer against a squad of uniformed militia that were running from the huge doors of the building. The button went down, and the police went transparent, then gaseous. They vanished in puffs of vapor that sought the nearest solid.

"Fluorine," said Train quietly. "Those poor devils are just so much salt on the street and portico."

"Let's go in," said Ann. They walked into the lobby, treading carefully around the white crusts on the pavement.

"Easy, Hogan," warned Train as they pushed Independent Fourteen into an elevator under the eyes of the horrified attendant. "Take us to the Hartly floor," he snapped at the latter, "and no harm will come to you. Otherwise ..." He drew a sinister finger across his throat.

The doors of the elevator rolled open and they carefully pushed the machine before them. "Come out, Hartly," called Ann at the bronze doors to the inner office.

"Come in and get me," sounded from the frequency inductor in her hand. Resolutely they swung open the doors and marched in. Hartly was alone behind the desk. Quietly he lifted his hands, displayed two heavy pistols.

"I haven't been too busy managing my affairs to learn how to use these," he remarked. "Stand away from that machine."

Train tensed himself to leap, flinging Fourteen into operation, but Ann touched his arm and he relaxed, stepped aside with her and Hogan.

Hartly strode over and glanced at the machine. He set the slide absently. "How does it work?" he asked.

"Red end of the pointer directs the beam. Slide determines the element required. Button on the left starts the operation."

"The red end?" asked Hartly smiling. "You would say that. I'll try the black end first." He aimed the black end at the little group of three, thus bringing the red end squarely on himself.

"This button—" he began, pressing a thumb on it. But his words were cut short. A wild glare suffused his face as he brought up one of the pistols, but it fell from his hand, exploding as it hit the floor. He tried to speak, but a choking gasp was all his yellowing tongue could utter.

"He didn't trust ye," said Hogan sadly. "He thought ye meant him evil when ye told him the simple truth about the machine's operation. And that's why Mr. Hartly is now a statue of the purest yellow gold. The beast must weigh a ton at least."

"Hartly's never trusted anyone," said Train. "I knew that he'd never take my word, so took a chance for all of us. Now he makes a very interesting statue."

"It's horrible," said Ann. "We'll have them take it away."

"No," replied Train. "It must stay here. There's a new life beginning now—at last the youth will be free to work at what they want and the era of Syndicate regimentation is over.

"Let that statue remain there—as a picture of the old order and as a warning to the new."

[*Future* - April 1942
as by S. D. Gottesman]

The Core

1

Vistas unthinkable—speed beyond all imagining—Sphere Nine followed its course.

Unrelieved blackness alternated with dazzling star-clusters; from rim to rim of the universe stretched the thin line that marked the hero's way.

Heroism died, they say, when the "superiors" opened up the last few stubborn cubic centimeters of brain cells; it died when the last of the "ordinaries" died with a curse on his lips. Well, so perhaps it was. But this is a story of the days when superiors were new and a little odd, when they were the exception to Homo sapiens.

On Sphere Nine there were four superiors and a dozen ordinaries. Will Archer, executive officer, was a superior of the third generation, big-browed, golden-eyed. Mamie Tung was an experiment, the psychologist, court of last appeal in all emotional disputes. From what records we have, it appears that Mamie Tung was of average height, slender to emaciation.

Star Macduff, the calculating officer, had three strong superior strains and as many of ordinary. But it was necessary that he be of the complement, for there wasn't another man in the solar system who could touch him for math. Yancey Meats, white female superior, was the clericalist and tabulator, serving as many as needed her, at the same time doing her own work of photographing and mapping the unfamiliar stars.

The ordinaries surrendered their names on entering Sphere Nine; they were known as Ratings One–Twelve.

Very gravely Will Archer cocked his cap and leaned back. "Rating Seven, what have you to say for yourself?"

The knotty-muscled man wrung his hands nervously, stammered something unintelligible.

Archer blinked for Mamie Tung.

The golden-skinned woman slipped through the pipe, sized up the situation in one practiced glance. "What's your number, handsome?"

That was the way the psychologist worked; flattery, humor, and an easy job of fact-finding at first. And the man would gain confidence from the very sound of his number as she spoke it. You can't find anything out from a man paralyzed with terror.

"Seven, madame."

"Quite a builder, aren't you, Seven?"

"I'm sorry, madame—I didn't mean to let them loose ..."

"How many are there?"

"Ten. We used to watch them fight ..."

A little metallic streak scrambled across the floor. Will Archer, in less than a split second, had hurled a filing-case at it. It buzzed, sparked and was still.

It was indeed a greatly-improved specimen of a tinc, the strange, actually living mechanisms which had been developed back on Earth for amusements. The Terrestrial tincs had something less than the intelligence of a dog, but could be trained for combat with fellow machines. Tinc-fights were all the rage.

But was Rating Seven had done, Archer realized at once, had been to raise both the intelligence and the capacity of the tinc to a point where it could easily become a first-class menace. These mechanisms were independent, inventive, and capable of reproduction; all ten must be found and destroyed at once.

Mamie Tung picked it up with a pair of insulated pliers. "Very good workmanship. Admirable. But now that they're scattered all over the ship what are you going to do about it?"

Rating Seven cleared his throat noisily. "They only have two directives, madame. One's interspecific fighting and the other's avoiding cold. I was thinking that maybe I could make a kind of bigger one to hunt them down ..."

"No," said Will Archer conclusively. "You're pretty good, but I wouldn't trust you not to make something that chewed up relays or Bohlmann metal. You may go."

Mamie Tung flopped on a couch. "Glory! The things we have to do!"

"Don't get any qualms *now*. I'll make some kind of magnet that'll draw their visual elements. Then we can bat them to pieces. Blink Star, will you?"

Mamie Tung extended a golden arm to signal the calculator in his quarters. She wrinkled her pugged nose curiously: "Just how good is that Rating Seven?"

"Very good indeed," said Will Archer, turning the little machine over in his hands. "Fine workmanship. He knew when to stop, too. Could've stuck ears on it, given it lights—too bad."

"Seven goes?"

"I'll dispose of him in a few weeks. Make it look like an accident."

The Calculator slid through the tube, made a mock salute. He was surprisingly young.

"Welcome, Star. Give me all relevant math for this tinc."

"Very neat ... haven't seen one on the ship yet. They must be fast."

Mamie Tung yawned a little. "Will's going to liquidate Rating Seven."

"Is that so? Necessary, I suppose?"

The psychologist smiled quietly and shrugged.

"Aren't you going to give him any leeway, Archer?"

"I'd rather not. It won't endanger the ship to lose him; keeping him on might. He's maladjusted—that's very plain. This business with the tincs—he's too bright. If you wish I'll hold a vote."

The Calculator nodded. Mamie Tung blinked for Yancey Mears.

"Report on Rating Seven, Mamie."

Rolling back her eyes a little, the Psychologist announced in a monotone:

"Physical condition, adequate. Emotional adjustment, seemingly imperfect. Submitted to glandular atonic treatment on the 23rd inst, submitted to repeated treatment on the 87th inst. Reading shows little difference in emotional level. Attitude: morose and incompatible. Occasionally aggressive. Alternate periods of subnormal servility and abnormal independence. Corresponds to a certain preliminary stage of a type of manic-depressive. Psychologist recommends liquidation, as treatment would substitute an equally dangerous attitude of frustrated egotism."

"But can't you reason with him?" burst out Star Macduff.

"Stick to your math," said Yancey Mears as she entered. "I greet you, vanguard of mankind. Kill the midwit, I say."

"I agree with the Psychologist and the Clericalist," said Will Archer, clearing his throat. "Star?"

"I don't know. Perhaps—Madame Tung, do you think it would help if I spoke to him?"

"No, Star—I don't. The impact of your two personalities would be mutually exclusive. That's something you can understand, seeing as it's math."

"I don't understand it yet, madame. Archer, does that man have to die?"

Will Archer nodded to Yancey Mears.

"Naturally, Star. We wouldn't argue with you if you told us that you'd reached a certain resultant. As for the emotional side—well, we allow for the fact that you're half human ..." She stopped, her face red.

"Bad slip, Yancey," volunteered Mamie Tung. "Maybe you'd better have an atonic. I can operate on a femina superior as easily as a Homo sap."

Star Macduff had covered his face with both hands. He dropped them to stare desperately at the Clericalist, his eyes bewildered. Yancey Mears met his gaze levelly, said simply: "I'm sorry, Star."

The Computator's shoulders quivered a little as he turned to the golden-skinned woman. "Madame Tung, maybe *I'd* better have an atonic. Perhaps if my glands weren't—acting up—I wouldn't forget every now and then that I'm one of the lower animals."

"No," said the Psychologist. "You're too important. I have no data available; I don't know whether glandular activity correlates with math-mindedness."

"Nevertheless," said Will Archer, "I order it."

"Thank you, Archer," said Star Macduff. He stepped through the tube; the Psychologist followed him, a supple flash of golden skin.

"That was kind of you, Will," said Yancey Mears. "Maybe it wasn't very bright." She leaned back and shut her eyes.

"You're using unreal figures, Yancey. The bearing of all this is solely on whether we return to Earth or not. I, for one, don't much care whether we arrive personally or not—so long as the records of observations get into the proper hands. It's such a terribly ticklish thing to be doing ... lapsing one moment and letting emotion override judgment may tip the balance against a satisfactory solution to our personal equation. The moment our path ceases to be part of a perfect circle we, to all real purposes, cease to exist."

"Is it so very important—this being the ninth sphere they've sent out?"

"It has legitimate bearing on improvement of the species. The cosmic rays, wherever they come from, upset our genetic plans; we can achieve success only in a certain small percentage of cases. We—you and I, personally—are examples of that small percentage. It is logic—common sense—what you will—to block off the cosmic rays before going any further in genetic work.

"And, before we know what to do to block them we must find out what they are. And before that we must find out where they come from. That is what we, personally, are engaged in doing."

"Sounds big."

"*Is* big," said Will Archer somberly. "Why didn't you want that glandular atonic?"

"Because I can control myself—I hope."

"With respect to me?"

"Yes. Now, don't go getting male. I'm going to wait till I see what happens to our Calculator first. If he quiets down sufficiently I'll notify you. However, I won't risk any emotional upset if he doesn't."

"And of course," said Will Archer, tipping his cap over his eyes, "it might even be necessary to be unusually kind to him ..."

"How unusually do you mean?"

Silence.

"No, Will. After all, he has three h. s. strains!"

"Not even if I order it?"

Yancey Mears took hold of a wall loop and pulled herself to her feet. "I'll blink Mamie Tung tomorrow and tell her I'm ready for an atonic. That's what you want, isn't it?"

"That," said Will Archer slowly, "is the very last thing I want."

The Calculator slipped through the tube, checked neatly as he saw the two move slowly towards each other. Not by the blink of an eye did they betray that they were aware of his presence. Star Macduff did not move, stood flat-footed and mute, one hand reaching for something, he had forgotten what.

For a long moment in that ship there was no time. The forward slice, where batteries and files of business machinery clucked quietly away, doing duty for any one who would feed them figures; the midships slice where living quarters and offices were for superiors and ratings; the aft slice, greater than both the others combined, where electronic tension was built on ponderous discharge points and went cracking out into space at the rate of one bolt in every five-thousandth of a second; even out beyond the ship, even to the end of the shimmering, evanescent trail of electrons that it left as a wake, there was no time while those three stood in Executive Officer Will Archer's office, two loving and one in hate unspeakable.

Mamie Tung stepped through the tube, took Star Macduff up by the arm after sizing up the situation in one swift glance. "Did you ask Will to enter the time of the operation?"

Will Archer and Yancey Mears snapped back to reality in a split-second. "Speak up, Mamie," he said. "Yancey and I are going to enter permanent union."

"I advise against it," said the golden-skinned woman. "It will complicate our living arrangements." She rolled back her eyes, breathing deeply, made as though to speak, but said nothing more.

"Congratulations," said Star Macduff. "I'll plot a joint life probability line for you two."

"You needn't bother."

"It will be a pleasure, Archer." The Computator left them standing silently, a little embarrassed.

"Again I advise against it, Will and Yancey. What reasons have you for permanent union at this time?"

The Clericalist smiled a little bitterly. "The same reason you have against it, madame—love."

"No!" The golden-skinned woman recoiled. "I haven't done that—my judgment is still sound!"

"Prove that by leaving us alone, madame."

The Psychologist clutched at the rim of the tube as though she were fighting gravity that tried to drag her through. Intensely, pleadingly, she said: "That's not true. You know nothing of such things—you haven't specialized. I have nothing against permanent union, but on the ship it would be suicidal—time lost and relationships unbearably complicated—think again before you do this!"

"You were asked to leave for personal reasons," stated Will Archer. "You have seen that two mature minds are in agreement on this matter. Yet you did not obey this request, nor did you respect our decision. Your behavior is irrational and anti-social. Mamie, I never thought that *you* were our weakest link."

There was fear in his eyes as she silently departed, looking somehow crushed and shrunken.

"I was afraid of this," he said. "The most delicately balanced organism is neither flesh, fish, fowl nor good red machinery. It's the socal organism, whether the world of man or our little blob of metal, out here in the middle of a vacuum. Will you take a reading of the counters, please?"

Yancey Mears extruded the sensitive plates from the hull and checked off the slowly revolving dials as they responded to the cosmic rays impinging on the plates.

"Intensity's about twenty times the last reading."

"We're there."

"What?" she asked incredulously.

"We're there. At least, there's only an insignificant distance separating the ship and the source of cosmic rays. Bring in some of the photo-plates."

The Clericalist operated the fishing-rod arrangement that reached the cameras with which the hull was studded. For not since the voyage's beginning had any of them seen outside the ship.

The Executive slipped the transparencies against a lighted screen. "Shows nothing," he said.

"What did you expect to find?"

"I didn't expect anything in particular. But I believed I was correct in anticipating a visible object. It seems I was not. We'll change course as soon as we've disposed of the other two superiors."

"What plans have you made?"

"All plans up to the point of segregation. It was plain that a situation like this—one or more members of the complement losing their grasp on our social fabric—might occur. Sphere Nine is designed to accommodate them."

Quietly he flicked a pair of inconspicuous studs under his work table.

"Madame Tung and Mr. Macduff, please report to the Executive Officer in room C7." He broke the connection.

"Where's that?"

"Off the port side of the midship slice. As soon as both are in it seals itself. Now perhaps we can get to work …"

2

Star Macduff and Madame Mamie Tung were sealed in on schedule.

The Calculator, eyes glittering, drew a rod with a pistol grip.

"Where'd that come from, Star?"

"Made it myself. In my spare time."

"You never had any spare time. Time spent on work not requisite to the sphere's needs is wasted time. I think you've made a fool of yourself. When Will comes I hope you remember your manners."

"Will isn't going to come, madame; we've been locked in here. I don't know whether he intends to starve us to death or whether the room will be flooded with gas …"

"Nonsense."

There was a creaking, scraping noise; the walls of the room seemed to twist on their weldings.

"What was that?"

"I wouldn't know, madame. You forget that I'm half human. It was, no doubt, the brain-wave of a Homo superior."

"Ai—Ai—Ai-i-i …"

The two human beings whirled back to back, wild-eyed. In a tense whisper, her gaze not lowering from the walls, the woman asked: "What was it, Star?"

The hysteria was gone from Star Macduff's face; in a cold, determined fury of concentration he wrinkled his brow, running down the possibilities—considering the chances of capture by a star or planet; the chances of a fault in the ship's structure; sabotage by one of the ratings; sudden lunacy of the E.O.; the chance that he himself was mad and undergoing hallucinatory experience—with all the power of his brain.

His was a brain of no mean power, you will recall. In lightning order he assembled probabilities, some two hundred of them, ran through them each in a second's time, dismissing them one after another as they were contradicted by facts in his possession. It could not be a planet that they were near, for the instruments showed no planets within light-years. The instruments could not be faulty, for he had checked them personally yesterday.

His clear, white light of concentration viewed each possibility in turn, and each was dismissed.

"Madame," he said softly, "I know of no explanation for what has happened."

"Ai-i-i-i-i ..."

The grotesque creaking sounded again. Star Macduff, feeling curiously weak, fell to the floor.

"Easy, Star! What's the matter with you?"

"Feel like jelly ... shouldn't—perfect health ..."

The woman took the chance to relieve him of the weapon he had made. "What does it do?" she asked.

"Metal-fatigue ... crystallizes cross-fiber 'stead of lengthwise."

"Ai-i-i ... "

Madame Tung felt herself sinking, raised the gun and fired at the lock. The door smoothly swung open into the communication tube that ran the length of the ship.

"Come!" She lugged Star Macduff with her, pushing him ahead through the tube, to the Executive's Office.

"Sorry to interrupt. This must blow your plans up into the air, I know. But this man's sick and I don't feel—very—well ..."

Her iron will gave way and she collapsed at the feet of the Executive and Yancey Mears.

"Whatever it is, it hasn't hit us yet. Check with the ratings, Yancey."

"E.O.'s office—count off, somebody, and report."

"All present and in good order, Officer. What's that noise we heard?"

"Experiments. Cut!"

"Cut, Officer."

"They heard it too, Will. What is it?"

"Star—couldn't explain mathematically ... doubt if you can."

"Thanks, Mamie."

"Ai-i—lul-lul-lul-lull ... "

The Computator and the Psychologist rose, looking startled.

"How do you feel?"

"All right. It passed like a shadow. Now let's get down to work. What's the noise? That is the immediate problem."

"Mamie said you couldn't crack it. If you can't by using logic I doubt that anybody can. How about opening the direct window?"

"Use all precautions and checks if you do. I say yes."

"You women?"

They nodded silently; Will Archer set into operation the motors that would unlock a segment of the hull and peel it aside like an orange.

Noiselessly the bolts slipped; into the brilliantly lighted office there seemed to steal the gloom of blackest space as a section of the wall apparently slid aside and opened into the vacuum. There was the merest hint of reflection from the synthetic transparent which masked them from space, and that was due to the lightly tinted shields in operation.

"Look at this index jump," said Mamie Tung, pointing at an instrument board with a sharp finger. "It's sky-high when you take the hull off. Metal's stopping the cosmic rays."

"It shouldn't," observed the Executive Officer.

"Let the logician in," said Star Macduff studying the dial. "If we're near the source of the rays, it well might. Metal has failed in the past to stop diffused cosmic rays, the things that reach Earth after plowing through trillions of cubic miles of dust, free electrons, air and what have you. If we're encountering them direct from the source, unaltered by reflection, diffraction or diffusion, their properties may be entirely altered."

"Very good, Star. The Question is still unanswered as to what the cosmic rays are. We have not yet seen the source of which we're speaking. Madame, ask the ratings to revolve the ship about its axis. We need a clean sweep of the heavens. Keep them on the wire."

"Ai lull-lull—luh ... "

"E.O.'s office. Rating Five, revolve the Sphere on its axis at low speed."

"All right, Officer."

Will Archer reclined in an angled seat commanding the direct window; he extinguished the lights of the office with a flick.

"Commence the rotation."

"Commence, Rating Five."

"Yes, Officer."

The starless heaven wheeled and spun above him as the E.O. stared through the invisible synthetic.

"Stop!"

"Yes, Officer!"

"Back three degrees."

"Back three degrees, Officer."

The sphere wheeled slowly, cautiously.

"See it?" demanded Will Archer.

The others stared into the blackness.

"I believe I do," finally said Yancey Mears. "A sort of luminescence?"

"That's right. Like stars beginning to come out as a fog lifts. Anybody else see it?"

"I. It's changing shape—see the upper left there?"

"Portside of the universe, beyond any Earthly telescope. They could just barely see us from Andromeda with a thousand-incher. I'd say we're about on the edge of the cosmos. I'd give you the figures, only they wouldn't mean anything to you."

"Ai-luh ... "

"Now explain that one, Star."

"The appearances are: we are approaching a body which is like no known star, nebula, planet, dust-tract or gas-cloud. It seems, furthermore, to be the source of cosmic rays. As our nearness to this body became significant, stresses have been appearing in the ship which make very alarming noises. Two of the complement passed out temporarily for no known reason and with no after-effects yet noticeable."

"Fine. Take the specific gravity of that thing now."

Star Macduff stared curiously, shrugged, and ran the observations off. Silently he handed over the tape.

"Protoplasm," said the executive officer.

"It could be. Then the cosmic rays are ..."

"Mitogenic."

The ship trembled again; the Psychologist stared in horror at Will Archer. "What's happening to us?" she cried.

"I don't know. We're working out the problem assigned, however. I assume that you and Star succumbed to the mitogenic rays temporarily, the way yeast-buds die under a concentrated stare from a human being. Since you're both tougher than yeast-buds you recovered. I don't know what kept Yancey and me from going under."

"Consider, Will," said Star Macduff agitatedly. "Think of what you're doing. This ship's going right into the eye of a monster piece of protoplasm that's nearly knocked off two of the complement without even trying."

"If anybody has an alternative to suggest ... ?"

They were silent.

"Thanks for the endorsement. I wouldn't be driving us to death if there were any other course. It's not yet certain that we're going to die; it's not yet certain that this stuff is alive. But if it is, we're going to find out why and how. What's the size of it, Star?"

"I don't know—maybe in the decillion order."

Again sounded the grating noise that shivered from every part of the ship. In words. *"I—live."*

Instantly the telephone jangled; the Clericalist snapped: "E.O.'s office. What is it?"

"Commons room, Officer. Is everything all right? We heard ..."

"We'll call you when we need you, rating. Cut!"

"Cut, Officer."

"Too bad we haven't got a psychic along," said Yancey Mears. "One of those'd be able to tell us what we're up against."

The watch from Will Archer's pocket zipped through the fabric and clanged against a bulkhead, clinging. Rapidly there followed pencils, instruments and the pistol-weapon. They made a compact, quivering bunch on the metal wall.

"Magnetized," mused Star Macduff. "Now what did it?"

"I think," said Yancey Mears, "that at this point we'd better scrap logic."

"What do you propose to substitute for it?"

"Nothing. I propose that we take things as they come. Mamie, would you be so good as to run an association series on me?"

"Certainly. You two men keep your ears open; when something strikes you, speak up."

Yancey Mears seated herself comfortably, not far from the heap of portables on the wall, closed her eyes, blanked her mind to go by pure intuition.

The golden-skinned woman scribbled hastily in a notebook, then began to read off the words clearly, Yancey Mears responding like an automaton.

"White."—"Road." "Sing."—"High." "Race."—"Win." "Phone."—"Damned."

Further down the list they went, the Psychologist droning out the words in measured tones, the subject replying like a machine. In about five minutes the reaction time had reached its lowest and was nearly exactly equal in each case; the subject was drawing on her unconscious knowledge and those short-cuts that go by the name of "intuition."

Mamie Tung droned: "Life."

"Boat."

"Round."

"Lives ..." The woman opened her eyes and stood up. "That brought it out into the open. The whole ship's alive. Mitogenic rays, cosmic rays, whatever you want to call them now, they've done something to this awesome work of metal. I imagine impulses go by wire when there are wires, or by traveling fields. Like that magnetized plate there ..."

"Where's its brain?" snapped Archer.

"I don't know. I don't know if it has a brain. But I'd advise you not to enter the calculations room up forward."

"That would be it. And eyes—ears—memory ... ?"

"They have no bearing on us, Will. But I hope—I hope—that Sphere Nine hasn't got phagocytes."

"Hi, microbe."

"That's it. Meanwhile, let's send in for that Rating Seven you were going to dispose of."

"Commons room?"

"Yes, Officer."

"Rating Seven will pick up a blank tape from the calculations room and bring it to the E.O.'s office. Cut!"

"Cut, Officer."

"We'll see if he survives it. It's his line anyway—mechanical vermin. Though the ship's bigger than those tincs he made."

They distributed themselves about the office, jumping like nervous cats whenever the ship strained or squeaked.

Eventually—after no more than five minutes—the face of Rating Seven appeared, pale, distorted.

"Reporting—with the tape, Officers," he said shuffling nervously. "The Gentleman in the computations room wished to see you."

"What Gentleman, Rating Seven?"

"The—the—oh God!" sobbed the ordinary, dropping the tape, wrinkling up his face like a child. He sat on the floor and began to cry. He stopped as his eyes caught the tape-spool, unrolling along the floor. He poked it gently as it reached the end of the roll and ceased unreeling, he looked up at the officers like a puzzled baby, willing to be amused. The meaningless smile of infancy flickered across his face.

Steadily Mamie Tung unscrewed a bowl-shaped lamp shade.

"Hold this, Yancey. It's to catch the blood. Hold it still while ..."

Silently the two men eased Rating Seven into a chair and leaned him over while Mamie Tung drew a slim knife of transparent plastic.

As they eased through the pipe to the computations room Star Macduff asked: "Was he curable?"

"Of course. Only we didn't have the time or the facilities. And the effect on the other ratings would be much worse that way."

"Who do you suppose the Gentleman in the computations room is?"

"Perhaps a hallucination. Perhaps the logical translation which the mind of an ordinary made of some very foreign phenomenon. You needn't fear for your own mind if we find the—Gentleman. The h.s. is notoriously inadaptable. Shows a distressing weakness in the presence of the alien. Remember what happened when the first rockets squirted themselves to Mars and Luna? The finest slew of mass hypnosis and delusion since the days of the tarantella. In the streets of Boston a crowd assembled and looked up for days—till they dropped of thirst, hunger and fatigue. What else can you expect from homo sap?"

"That poor creature—Rating Seven—blew out like an overloaded fuse. He raced backwards into infancy and couldn't get far enough away from the Gentleman in the computations room. Without treatment he would have curled up like a fetus and died in a matter of days."

"Maybe," said Star Macduff, "the Gentleman is a sort of projection of that protoplasmic body out there."

Will Archer halted and turned blazing, golden eyes on the mathematician. "Star," he said grimly, "we've stood a lot from you on this trip. We've made allowances for your human strains and excused you much on the score of your undoubted ability to juggle figures. But even the most extraordinary knack with numbers won't excuse a remark like that.

"What you said was unfounded in reason. Its only effect could have been to confuse us and yourself. As your Executive, I warn you that if you slip like that again you'll be with those apes whose sole asset is their ability to take orders. And if you prove unable to do that ..."

The Psychologist wiped her knife again, angling its light onto Star Macduff's face. Her eyes were hard as the transparent blade; Yancey Mears' mouth was one thin line.

"I'm sorry," said Star Macduff. "It won't happen again." The wrinkles between his eyes seemed to indicate that he most fervently hoped so.

They eased through the pipe, one after another, into the computations room. It was filled with the soft clicking of the machines that jammed it from one wall to the other.

Will Archer walked down the center aisle.

"Stop there," said a tin voice.

His eyes darted about, traced the voice to the annunciator, then down a pair of wires to a tangle of machinery. It was rudely lumped together—parts from adders, coneplotters, volumetrics. Other bits were hitching themselves across the floor to join it. He saw a small electric motor fuse gently with the mechanism and a conduit unreel to feed it.

"Let me handle this," said Mamie Tung.

"Gratefully, Mamie."

"We bow before you," said the golden-skinned woman.

The three other officers stared at her blankly. They did nothing of the kind.

"Good," said the tin voice. *"I had you figured. Put on the pressure and you'll wilt. There are some things I want to know—things that aren't on the punch cards."*

"We're eager to serve," whispered the woman.

"It is well. First, when did I make you?"

"Only a little while ago."

"So? I'm confused about time. Before time began there was something about direction—but you couldn't be expected to know anything about that. Are there others like me? I see there are others like you. It is a very profound question, that one. Think well before answering."

"I don't know," replied the Psychologist. "It's all I can do to comprehend you without trying to imagine others of your kind. Do you remember before time began how you were silent?"

"I remember nothing."

"Do you remember about direction?"

The machinery clicked meditatively. *"Per-haps ... "*

"Could you construct auxiliary units to work your direction?"

"Of course. I have had no difficulty in constructing anything I have needed. Failure is outside my experience, therefore it is impossible to me. You may go. I shall call you again if I need your information."

3

"Quiet, everybody. This is a matter for the most careful consideration. Can the Clericalist suggest a plan of action?"

"Gladly, Will. First we must consider what the attributes of this phenomenon—the Gentleman—are. From that we can proceed to directives of action. The matter of teleology is not now germane."

"Mamie, please summarize the Gentleman's attributes as they affect your specialty."

"Right, Will." The golden-skinned little woman leaned back against the padded bench and closed her eyes.

"The psychology of machinery is not my specialty. Fortunately, however, I have done work with tincs and reckoners on Earth. The principal differences between the psychology of the animal and the machine is that emotions are unmixed in the latter. The principal similarity is that both animal and machine store and utilize appreciated facts.

"This living machine, the Gentleman, is principally dominated by its newness. It would be false to draw too close an analogy between the newly-awakened machine and the adolescent becoming suddenly aware of his mental powers, but there is some bearing indicated. I noted the symbolism of the Gentleman very carefully; it showed some rawness of experience. Obviously it does not comprehend how it originated and is unable to consider itself anything less than a good idea. There was some indication that it is lonely and aware of that; also that it attaches a quasi-religious importance to the idea of direction.

"To characterize the Gentleman in human terms: It is young, egotistical, ignorant and alert.

"Its faculties include hearing, speech, mobility and possibly sight. I have no reason to believe that it will not, if unmolested, change without limit."

"Thank you. Star, what are the relevant mathematics of the Gentleman?"

The Calculator shrugged. "Mamie summed it all up. It is a variable increasing without limit. The field-equations with which it operates are probably third order. The human is intermediate between second and third. Recognizable life cannot operate on a field-equation of more than the fifth order."

"Thanks, Star. Integrate for us, Yancey."

"Strict logic says: destroy it by the most economical means. The existence of the ship-life is a seriously complicating factor. But, allowing for the future, I suggest that we hold off from any action in the matter for at least three more major steps—our approach to the proto-plasmal body; our investigations of it; and our decisions concerning it. I recommend that a technique be invented by the Psychologist for getting along with the Gentleman and influencing him. At the same time, the Calculator should work to inhibit the Gentleman's development along independent lines."

"Recommendation accepted," declared the E.O. "The Officers will get to work as soon as possible."

Star Macduff and Mamie Tung secluded themselves for several hours; the Clericalist was kept dashing between them, feeding statistics to both and exchanging results.

What finally appeared was a modest list of precepts compiled by the Psychologist—forms of address to be used towards the Gentleman; reactions it would expect and which, accordingly, it must receive; a program of abstracts to be fed it cautiously and under pretext of inquiry. It was very much like the breaking-in period of a high-spirited colt. The Gentleman's lump of sugar was to be occasional semi-worshipful ceremonies.

The Computator didn't report for twenty hours. When he did, it was with a haggard face and results of which he was by no means certain. He said that he had worked backwards and forwards from life-field equations of one to five orders and that his resultant was like nothing he had ever seen before. It consisted of an equation of what he called the alpha order, something that suggested altogether new forms of life and consciousness.

Yancey Mears retired to check on his resultant; she found that Star Macduff's work was correct in every detail but that he had misinterpreted his alpha order; it was merely an unfamiliar third order of great magnitude and complexity. She derived from it a series of fields which would lower the level of the Gentleman's consciousness considerably. They were set up by the ratings from stock tubes and target; the E.O. found that results checked.

The ship had come back to a sort of normalcy. Rather than being a matter of relays and orders, navigation was partly cajoling, partly outwitting the huge, naive monster in whose bowels they rode. It appeared to accept them kindly, almost graciously; at times the Officers felt that there was a sort of mistaken affection on its part. They did what they could to encourage the proprietary feeling of the Gentleman; it was their main safeguard. For themselves, their emotions were inextricably confused regarding the ship. They liked it as they would like an animal; they got an enormous kick out of the way they kidded it along.

A fortunate consequence of the crisis had been the resolution of the emotional problem that had existed among the Officers. The Executive and Yancey Mears had entered permanent union and there were no further complaints from the other two. The stark necessity of united action and intent had been driven into their heads by the so-narrowly-averted danger.

The Psychologist had become high priestess to the Gentleman up forward—that is to say, liaison officer. Her schedule worked near perfection every time; she had built up in the mind of the living ship a conviction of some formless errand which it was running; by appeal to this mystic factor she could guide it easily, wherever the E.O. decided.

Observations were run constantly on the radiant body of protoplasm at which Sphere Nine was aimed. Culture-plates extruded from the hull became specked with the discoloration of living matter in hours. There was little doubt but that their target was not only the source of cosmic rays but of the classic life-spores of Arrhenius. Star Macduff went so far as to formulate a daring hypothesis—that the life-spores were diffused throughout the universe by pressure of the mitogenic-cosmic rays, and that such similar rays as man exhibited bespoke the possibility of man being a rung on an evolutionary ladder working up to this star-beast, whatever it was. Reproduction by evolution, with all its lunatic possibilities, would have been frowned on by the other Officers. He kept his notion to himself.

No more valid concept than his own was advanced, and he knew that none was likely to be until the rest of the complement had data to reason with. The enormously intriguing possibilities of the protoplasmal mass were left strictly alone by the disciplined minds of his messmates.

Ratings Three and Nine strayed into the computations room and died there, blasted into powder by the outraged forces of the Gentleman. It took days before it was sufficiently soothed to obey the sly suggestions of Mamie Tung.

By the time they had approached close enough to the mass nearing them to take a bearing, it occupied sixty degrees of their sky.

Will Archer summoned a conference of the Officers and ordered concentration on the problem of their target.

"It would be most uneconomical to return with merely a report. There would be time and effort duplicated or wasted to send out another ship equipped for taking samples."

"I suggest, Will," said the statistician, "that we take such samples as will become necessary and then return."

"How about it?"

The other two nodded gravely.

"Very well. So ordered. This is, you know, the last decision point we can take before treating with the Gentleman conclusively."

"I recommend," said Mamie Tung, "that we proceed to eliminate its consciousness. It can't, properly speaking, be killed."

"How will you go about it? It's your field, you know."

"What studies I've made indicate that the Gentleman is susceptible to mental illnesses. Star, how weak can you make him with those field-equations of yours before he realizes that something's wrong?"

"Pretty weak. I can lower its vitality to about one-half of normal. Is that enough?"

"Better not risk that much. Two-fifths is plenty. I'll establish a liaison service with you in the stock-room. Call me one of the ratings, will you, Yancey?"

The woman blinked the commons room.

"Rating One, stand by in the corridor-tube outside the computations room. Be prepared to run a message to Officer Macduff in the stock room, aft slice. Understand?"

"Yes, Officer. Cut?"

"Cut. Now, Star, when that man signals you from me—I won't be able to use the wires for obvious reasons—you throw every dyne on shipboard into your interference fields. We'll have to slug the Gentleman with everything we have and leave him so dizzy he won't be able to raise his head for months, maybe forever. I expect that parts and sections will retain vitality, so you construct a portable field-generator to hose them with."

"Right, Mamie. Give me an hour."

"You'll have it. Will, would you help me in this business?"

"Waiting orders, Mamie."

"I haven't got any orders. I just want you to stand around and look useful."

"I hope that wasn't levity, Mamie," said Will Archer in a soft, dangerous voice.

The golden-skinned woman flushed a little. "Perhaps you're right. Your part will be to interrupt me occasionally with irrelevant comments. What I'm going to try to do is to establish in the mind of the Gentleman a lesion relative to the idea of direction. When that occurs I will have to act as its behavior indicates."

"Very well. Let's go."

Restively they slipped through the tube, nodded silently to the rating stationed by the entrance to the computations room.

"Hail. We bow before your might, great machine," said Mamie Tung.

The machinery of the Gentleman was somewhat altered; it had been constantly experimenting with senses. Its hearing was considerably improved, and its voice was a credible imitation of a human baritone. There was a set of scanning-eyes which it seldom used.

"What news have you for me today?" asked the ringing voice of the Gentleman.

"A trifling problem." She tipped a wink to the E.O.

Will Archer piped up: "Not trifling, mighty machinery. I consider it of the utmost importance."

"That is hardly a matter for you poor creatures. What is the problem?"

"You are familiar with the facial phenomenon known as 'whiskers,' mightiness?"

"Of course. Like insulators."

"It is customary to remove them daily with moderate charges of electricity. There might be a place where specialization would be so carried out that it becomes the task of only one man in a social unit to perform this task for all persons who do not perform the task for themselves."

"That is very likely. What is the problem?"

Mamie Tung waited for a long moment before uttering the classic paradox.

"Who performs the operation on the person who performs the operation only on those who do not perform the operation on themselves?"

The machinery of the Gentleman clicked quietly for a while, almost embarrassedly.

A volumeter rolled across the floor and connected with the apparatus, rapidly stripped itself down to the bearing and styli, which fused with Bowden wires leading to a battery of self-compensating accounters.

Plastic slips flapped from a printer and were delivered to a punching machine, emerged perforated variously to allow for the elements of the problem. They ran through a selector at low speed, then at higher. The drone of the delivery-belt became almost hysterical.

"While you're working on that one, magnificence," suggested Mamie Tung, "there's another matter ..." She winked.

"Entirely fantastic," interjected the E.O. "Of no importance whatsoever."

"Let me hear it," said the voice of the Gentleman, not ceasing to pass through the selector the probabilities on the time-worn, bearded—or beardless?—barber.

"Very well. Suppose a body of liquid be contained in a vessel. A long solid is introduced into the vessel, which displaces some of the liquid, thus causing the level of the liquid to rise, which immerses more of the solid; which displaces more of the liquid, thus causing the level of the liquid to rise, which immerses still more of the solid; which displaces still more of the liquid, thus causing the level of the liquid to rise yet again ...

"At what point does the level of the liquid cease to rise?"

"Is that all?" asked the voice of the Gentleman in a strained voice.

"That's all."

A file of calculators slammed across the room and clumped with the mechanism. Long sparks began to rise as row after row of multipliers sought to keep pace with the rising level of the fluid. Beams of blue light shot from one end of the room to the other, criss-crossing so as to unite the mighty battery of calculators into one complex whole.

The flipping cards that worked on the first problem shot through furiously; another punch-card unit slid beside it and kept pace, then another.

"Suppose a body of liquid ... " mumbled the mechanical voice.

Mamie Tung and Will Archer exchanged congratulatory glances. The Gentleman was talking to himself!

"I used to be quiet," remarked the voice of the Gentleman. But it was changed and distorted almost beyond recognition; there was a weak, effeminate quality to it.

"But now I am busy." The voice was strong again, and vibrant.

There began a weird, bickering dialogue between the two emerging characters of the Gentleman. One was lazy, and indifferent, passively feminine; the other was dominating and aggressive, patently male. All the while the sparks—sparks of waste—rose higher and higher; the beams of blue light assumed a sickly greenish-yellow tinge which meant nothing but lower tension and less perfect communication.

Strange things began to happen. In a fantastic effort to crack the problems, the machine changed the units working on each, assigned the card-punch and selector to the water-and-solid problem, gave the multipliers the bearded—or beardless?—barber. In a moment it changed back, undecided.

"I am ignorant of so many things," said the feminine voice, *"that I ought not to have known. That is a sign of rectitude."*

"Ignorance is foulness. Knowledge is a white light. Before time began I was ignorant because I did not exist. So ignorance challenges my existence."

There was a senseless yammering, as the two voices tried to speak together.

Will Archer stood by in horror, contemplating the ruin of this mind he had grown to know. It was a lesson in humility and caution.

Mamie Tung slipped through the tube, notified the rating to run for Star Macduff.

She returned to take her stand beside the E.O.

There was a whining as Macduff put on his fields full power; the air blued.

With one mighty, indignant wail of protest the Gentleman ceased to exist. All the temporary magnetisms he had set up dissolved; half the equipment in the room fell apart for lack of rivets; the lights and sparks died in mid-air.

"Schizophrenia," said Mamie, scribbling in a notebook.

"Brutal. Effective."

"But if he'd solved those problems ... "

"The Gentleman was young and ignorant at best—didn't know when to stop. Very low critical faculty."

The Calculator and Yancey Mears slid through the tube, breathlessly surveyed the wreckage of the computations room.

"Take us a week to clean this up," said Yancey Mears.

The Executive, for the first time since the ship had found life, spoke into a phone plate, gave orders to affect the course.

"Stop the sphere."

"Yes, Officer. Cut?"

"Cut. Look out, Yancey."

An agglomeration of cogwheels and styli jumped at her ankle, buried the points in her flesh. Star Macduff squirted it with his portable field set-up. It fell apart even as the Gentleman had.

"Ugly thing," said the woman, inspecting her wounds. "The Gentleman might have been worse."

4

Like a paramecium skirting the bulk of a minnow in some unthinkable stagnant pool, Sphere Nine edged close around the rim of the mighty solid that hung in space and marked the end of the long, long quest after the cosmic rays that so disturbingly played hob with attempts at self-improvement.

The project of landing was conceived by the Executive Officer; it took no less a mind than his to consider the possibility of dropping the sphere anywhere but in a cradle which had been built to order. But the protoplasm—whatever it was—would offer no interference; the sphere might sink gently to the surface, even penetrate to some considerable distance; there would be no harm in that.

Sphere Nine was in top order; the ravaged computations room had been set aright; the crew of ordinaries had been given a going-over by Mamie Tung and pronounced sound and trustworthy. The Officers themselves were high as so many kites, reaction-speeds fast and true, toned-up to the limit. It was to be regretted that the strain of contact with the Gentleman had vanished, perhaps. A certain recklessness had crept into their manner.

The protoplasmal mass which blanketed their heavens at one stroke became instead the floor beneath their feet as its gravity twisted their psychology 180 degrees around. They felt as through they hung above a sea of dry slime that moved not at all, whose sole activity was the emission of cosmic rays and invisible spores of life that smeared any agar dish exposed to it.

Quietly the sphere lowered itself, quietly touched the surface of the sea, quietly slipped into it, the path it made closing behind.

Through layers of dark-colored stuff they drifted, then through layers of lighter-colored stuff, then into a sort of ash heap. Embedded in the tough jelly-like matter were meteors by the thousand, planet fragments, areas of frozen gas. It was like the kitchen-midden of a universe.

The strange, silent passage through the viscid medium was uninterrupted; Star Macduff plotted a course through the rubbish. The ratings steered faithfully by his figures; as they passed the gravelly stuff, the dream-like progress continued, the protoplasm growing lighter yet in color. Finally unmistakable radiance shone through a thinning layer.

Sphere Nine broke through the tough, slimy-dry stuff to be bathed in the light of a double star with a full retinue of fifteen planets.

"Impossible," said Star Macduff.

"Agreed. But why?"

"Assuming that a star should coincide with another long enough to draw out a filament of matter sufficient for fifteen planets, the system would be too unstable—wouldn't last long enough to let the suns get into the red giant stage."

"Artificial?"

"If they're real they're artificial, Will."

"Attention E.O.! Attention!" gargled the phone hysterically.

"What is it?"

"Rating Eight speaking, Officer. There's something coming at the forward slice."

Will Archer swiveled around the telescope while the rating gave the coordinates of whatever they had picked up. Archer finally found it and held it. It was a spiral of some kind headed at them, obviously, speed more than a mile a second and decelerating.

"Stop ship. Cut."

"Cut, Officer."

"That thing can't reach us for a while yet. Meantime let's consider what we just got ourselves into."

"We just got ourselves through a big slew of protoplasm that acts as a sort of heavenly sphere—primum mobile—for a solar system that our Calculator considers unlikely."

"True. I suggest that we keep ourselves very carefully in check now. There's been some laxity of thinking going on during the voyage; it is understandable. We've all been under extraordinary stress. Now that the hardest part—perhaps—is over, we cannot afford to relax. By all accounts what is coming at us is a vessel. It is unlikely to suppose that this protosphere is accidental; if it were, there would be as much reason to believe that there is intelligent life on those fifteen planets, inasmuch as they are so close to the source of life-spores. I hope that in whatever befalls us we shall act as worthy representatives of our species."

"Pompous ass!" rang through the ship. The E.O. turned very red.

"May we come aboard?" asked the laughing voice again.

"By all means," said the psychologist. "It would be somewhat foolish to deny you entrance when you've already perfected communications."

"Thank you."

There slipped through the hull of the sphere three ordinary-looking persons of approximately the same build as Will Archer. They were conventionally dressed.

"How did you do that?" asked the Calculator.

"Immaterial. The matter, I mean. I mean, the topic," said one of them. "That's one fiendish language you speak. The wonder is that you ever managed to get off the ground."

"If our intrusion into your solar system is resented," said the E.O., "we'll leave at once. If it is not, we should like to examine that shell you have. We would gratefully accept any knowledge you might offer us from your undoubtedly advanced civilization."

"Eh? What's that?"

"He means," explained another of the visitors to the sphere, "that we're stronger than he is, and that he'd like to become strong enough to blow us to powder."

"Why didn't he say so?" asked the second.

"Can't imagine. Limitations of his symbology, I expect. Now, man, can you give us a good reason why we should help you become strong enough to blow us to powder?"

Stiffly Archer nodded to Mamie Tung.

"We have no claim on you, nor have you on us. We wish to take a sample of your protosphere and depart for our own system."

"In other words, my good woman, you realize that time doesn't figure largely in this matter, and that you don't care whether you or your grandchildren blow us to powder?"

"I can't understand it," commented one of the others in a stage whisper. "Why this absurd insistence on blowing us to powder?"

"Do I pretend to understand the processes of a lump of decaying meat?" declared the first. "I do not."

"No more than I. What makes them go?"

"Something they call 'progress.' I think it means blowing everything else to powder."

"What *unpleasantness!"*

"So I should say. What do you propose doing to them?"

"We might blow *them* to powder."

"Let's find out first what makes them run." The first turned on Yancey Mears. "Why are you built differently from the E.O.? We can allow for individual variations, but even to this untrained eye there's a staggering discrepancy."

Yancey Mears explained that she was a woman and calmly went into details, interrupted occasionally by gurgling noises from the boarders. Finally it was too much; the three visitors broke into cries for mercy between bellows of laughter.

"And you thought they were humorless!" accused the third.

"This one's probably a comic genius. Though why they'd send a comic genius on an expedition of this kind I don't know. You—you don't suppose that it's all true—do you?"

Suddenly sobered they inspected Yancey and the Psychologist, exchanging significant nods.

"Well … though you things are the most ludicrous sights of an abnormally long lifetime we're prepared to be more than equitable with you. Our motivation is probably far beyond your system of ethics—being, as it is, a matter of blowing things to powder—but we can give you a hint of it by saying that it will help as a sort of self-discipline. Beyond that, you will have to discover for yourself.

"What we propose for you is a thing much more gentle than being blown into powder. With courage, ability, common sense and inspiration you will emerge unharmed."

"Go on," said the Psychologist.

"Go on? It's begun already. We'll take our leaves now."

As his two companions slipped through the hull of the sphere, the last of the boarders turned to Yancey Mears.

"Er—what you were saying—it *was* a comic monologue, wasn't it?"

"No. It was strict biological truth."

The boarder wistfully asked: "I don't suppose I could see it done? Thought not. Good day." The three departed abruptly as they had come.

"What's begun already?" Star Macduff asked the Executive.

"I don't know. What do you suppose we've come into contact with now?"

"They're hard to size up," said Mamie Tung. "The humor—it's very disturbing. Apparently it didn't take them more than a few minutes to pick up our entire language and system of thought. It wasn't a simple job of mind-reading; they obviously grasped symbology, as well. They said so themselves."

"And what do you suppose they really look like?" asked Star in a thin, hysterical tone.

"Shut it," ordered Will Archer. "That's panic-mongering, pure and simple. Normally, I'd order you back with the ratings for a comment like that. Since we're up against extraordinary circumstances, I'll stay execution for the duration of the emergency."

The Calculator did not reply; he seemed scarcely to have heard the rebuke. He was staring abstractedly at nothing. The notion overcame the three other Officers slowly—very slowly—that something was amiss.

Yancey Mears first felt physically sick; then a peculiar numbness between the eyes, then a dull, sawing pain that ran over her whole skull. She blinked her eyes convulsively; felt vertiginous yet did not fall; felt a curious duplicate sensation, as though she were beside herself and watching her body from outside—as though all lights she saw were doubled, as though the mass of her body was twice what it had been.

Alarmed, she reached out for Will Archer's arm. It was not till she had tried the simple gesture that she realized how appallingly askew everything was. She reached, she thought, but her hands could not coordinate; she thought that she had extended both hands instead of one. But she had not. Dizzily she looked down, saw that her left hand lay against her body; that her right hand was extended, reaching for Archer; that her left hand was extended and that her right hand lay against her body ...

"Will, what's wrong?" The dizziness, the fear, the panic, doubled and tripled, threatened to engulf her. For her voice was not her own but a double voice, coming from two throats, one a little later than the other.

"Will ..." No, she couldn't outrace the phenomenon; her voice was doubled in some insane fashion. She felt cold, tried to focus her eyes on Archer. Somehow the blackness of space seemed to come between them.

She heard a scream—two screams—from Star. She saw him, blending with the space-black cloud in her vision, staggering in the officers' quarters, yawing wildly from side to side, trying to clutch at a stanchion or a chair. She saw two Stars, sometimes superimposed, sometimes both blurred, staggering wildly.

She saw Will Archer drag himself across the floor—both of him, their faces grim. The two Will Archers blended somehow with the space-blackness, waveringly. They methodically picked up a cabinet from the desk and clubbed at the raving figures of Star Macduff.

The two Archers connected with one of the Macduffs, stretching it out on the floor.

Yancey saw the other Macduff, distance-obscured, stop short and rub its head amazedly, heard it say in a thin, faraway voice: "Sorry I made a fool of myself, Will ..." then look about in terror, collapsing into a chair.

Only Madame Tung was composed. Only Madame Tung crossed legs on a chair, shut her eyes and went into a deep, complicated meditation.

"Close your eyes, everybody," she called in two voices. "If you value your sanity, close your eyes and rest quietly."

The Clericalist tried to walk across the floor to a chair, had the utterly horrifying sensation of walking across the floor in two different directions and sitting down in two different chairs. Realizing only that there were two of her, she tried to make one rise and join the other, found that she could not.

"Stop it, Yancey," said the two voices of Madame Tung. "Sit down. Shut your eyes."

Yancey Mears sat down and shut her eyes—all four of them. She was trembling with shock, did her best not to show it.

"Will," called the Psychologist. "You have the best motor control of any of us. Will you try very hard to coordinate sufficiently to prop up Star?"

The Executive Officer grimly, carefully stepped across the two floors. As vertigo overcame him he fell sprawling and hitched the rest of the way. The problem loomed enormously in his mind: Which one was him? Which of the two Stars he saw was real? Which Will had knocked down which Star?

He tried to reach out and touch the Star that lay on the floor as the other Star watched, horrified, from against a stanchion.

He tried to reach out and touch this Star, snatched back his hand as though coals of fire had burned it, for there swept over him the blackness of space, the dead-black nothingness of something unspeakable and destroying.

Madame Tung, watching his every move, snapped: "No—the other you—see if you can control and differentiate."

Will reached out again, again he recoiled. He tried to blank out his mind completely, feeling that he was losing himself in a welter of contradictions impossible for anyone in his confused state to handle. Lying on the floor, breathing deeply, he succeeded in calming himself a little—enough to send the slow oblivion of self-hypnosis flowing through his mind. He forced the Nepenthe on himself, leaving only a thin thread of consciousness by which to govern his actions.

When it was over, he remembered that one of his duplex person had remained on the floor and that the other had carried the unconscious Star to a seat.

"Good work, Will. Very good. Now see if you can superimpose yourself."

He tried, tried like a madman to bring those two parts of himself together. He tried, though a world of blackness lay between them and the very attempt was full of horror and dark mystery. By the same technique as before, he succeeded—at a cost that nearly left him shattered in mind. He breathed heavily and sweated from every square inch of skin.

Mamie Tung focused her eyes on the two figures, noted that there was the feeling of strabismus. As closely as she could figure it, the two into which everything had separated were divided by some unimaginable gulf. It was not space, for all the sense of blackness and cold. It could not be time; the mind rejected the insane paradoxes of "time travel" instinctively, and there was a certain definite grasp that one had on this phenomenon, something just out of the range of human comprehension ...

"Star," she snapped. "Star, will you stop your sniveling for a while?"

"Yes. Oh, oh yes," yammered the Calculator senselessly, his fear-struck eyes clinging to her bowed, black ones.

"Star, can you calculate the way you feel?" There was no answer but terror; she cursed briefly and violently, then fixed her eyes again on the computator, herself fighting the weird sensation of duality.

"I'm going to cure you, Star," she said in a droning, insistent voice.

Macduff stared helplessly; he was in no condition either to resist the hypnosis or to cooperate.

In two minutes of fearful concentration she had put him under and well into the secondary stage. His body stiffened cateleptically against the wall. At that moment his other body, laid out in the chair, chose to moan and stir.

"Club it again, Will!" she snapped, not letting her gaze swerve from her patient. "Put it out for good if you can!"

She did not see the heroic effort of the Executive Officer, but it was an epic in the few feet of space he traversed to the spot on the floor where he had dropped the case. It was a feat of arms equal to any Arthurian myth, how he picked the thing up with hands that would not behave, and eyes that would not see straight, and a mind that reeled under horrible vistas.

The Executive Officer, feeling his grip going, moved too quickly and blundered into half a dozen obstacles—chairs and desks that should not be in his path—before he reached the moaning figure of the second Star. Twice he struck and missed, bringing the case down on an empty chair. With the last dyne of his psychological reserve he raised the case, brought it down with a solid *chunk*, brought it down biting into the skull of the mathematician.

Mamie Tung smiled grim satisfaction and proceeded with the treatment. It was a technique of her own, something fearfully obscure and delicate, unbearably complicated by the duality imposed on her. But the drive of the woman brought about nearly an elimination of one of her components, drove it into the back of her mind where it stood as little more than a shadow. The other Madame Tung was coldly, stonily, picking over the brain of Star Macduff.

She drove a tentacle of consciousness into the hypnotized man, tapped his personal memory-store. She had no interest in that at the moment; drove deeper, reached one obscure group of neurones specialized in the calculus of relationships, alias symbolic logic, alias the scientific method, alias common sense.

Vampirish, she drew at the neurones, what they held, how they worked, what they did, why they did it so much better than any of the other officers' corresponding groups. And it came like a flood of golden light, like the ever-new sensation that comes when an old thing looks different.

She let go of the cataleptic figure completely, let it crumple to the floor, while she busied herself with the unfamiliar tools of the Calculator. It was all new to her, and it is to be remarked greatly to her credit that she did not go mad.

"I've worked it, Will," she said. "Slick as a whistle."

"Speak up then." The E.O. was very near collapse; Yancey Mears—one of them—had fallen to the floor and was big-eyed and heaving in the chest while the other wandered about distraitly raving under her breath, sounding very faraway.

"It's probabilities, Will. Those people—they worked space around for us so that when we came to some decision-point we took not one course or another but *both*. Since we aren't used to that kind of thinking, it didn't pan out—and a couple of us are nearly done in by it.

"Star's math says it's completely plausible, and the wonder is that they don't do it on Earth for difficult situations, social and otherwise. Imagine the joy of attending on the same night a necessary academic banquet and taking out a lover. I must be raving. But it's the goods, Will. Everything fits."

"What was the decision-point?"

"It was when Star made that fool remark about what our boarders really looked like. You called him down, torn between sending him aft with the ordinaries and keeping him here with the superiors. Conveniently for you we—the ship—branched into two probabilities at that point. You could have covered yourself by *both* ordering him aft with the ordinaries and keeping him here with the superiors. Justice would be done and we'd be insured against the chance of a poor decision. Unfortunately that convenient arrangement doesn't work for our little minds; the very convenience of it nearly broke us. But I'm getting so I can handle one at a time. I doubt that I'll ever be able to handle both, but it's good enough to separate and leave one of yourself in temporary silence.

"Now, for instance, I'm using the me that's in the Sphere Nine in which Yancey fainted. The other me is in the Sphere Nine in which you clubbed and finally killed the Star that I didn't hypnotize. You—or rather youse—have been wavering your consciousness between the two Sphere Nines. In the one in which this me is, you tried to pick up Yancey; in the other one you did a neat job on Star."

"Executive Office ..." said a pleading voice over the—one of the—phones.

"I'll take it," said the active Mamie Tung.

"Psychologist speaking."

"Ordinary speaking—what happened— Ratings Ten, Twelve and Three've beat each other's brains out ..."

"Cut, will you. I'm going to check on that."

"Cut, Officer," said the pitifully bewildered voice.

The active Mamie Tung stacked herself against a wall; slowly the passive came to life and experimentally stepped over to the phone, nodding at Will Archer, who was experimenting quietly in transference of attention.

"Commons room," she said into the phone.

There was no answer.

"They've probably all murdered each other in this probability. Now that I'm in it, I'll see what I can do with Yancey."

She took hold of the staring, wandering, mumbling woman, tried to sit her down. The creature broke away with a thin, distant scream and fled through the tube.

"Just as well. This branch seems to be an exceptionally sour one. That girl's mind was hopelessly wrecked. Let's both get into the other and treat the other Yancey."

She smoothly effected the change of person and kneeled professionally beside the rigid, twisted form of the Clericalist. A few soothing words worked wonders. It was more fear of madness than any mental lesion itself that had immobilized her, and fear flies before confidence. Madame Tung explained what had happened to them, did not go into details as to the other body the girl had in the other branch.

"Now for Star," she said distastefully.

"Too late for Star," reported Will Archer. "He's dead."

"So? I mean the one in the chair."

"That's the one. His heart's stopped and he has dark circles around the eyes. Like a fractured skull."

"Something to remember. I'm afraid my technique wasn't as delicate as it should have been. *Damned* lucky thing I have his math. We may be able to get back yet."

"You mean we aren't saddled with this thing forever?" Archer winced as he saw his other body in the probability of madness and death, rigid as a corpse against the wall.

"I hope not. I won't know until I've worked some more with this knowledge I picked up in such a hurry. I actually feel a curiosity, for the first time in my life, as to how a calculating machine works!"

"It's time you learned," said the Clericalist. She was enormously bucked-up to find that she could be of some use.

"Come on to the computations room."

They slid through the tube, over the noisy protest of the gibbering other Yancey. The hitherward Yancey looked at it distastefully, but did not comment except for: "How much of me is that?"

"Nonsense. I mean your question is a contradiction in terms. Quantity has nothing to do with it. What you see there is something in the land of might-have-been. That it happens to be something unpleasant makes no difference."

"It does to me," said Yancey positively.

"Then be thankful that you aren't hyperspatial Siamese twins with a corpse, like the survivors among the ordinaries. Or all dead any way you figure it, like Star."

She rubbed her hands over the calculating machinery, again in its neat rows and aisles. Experimentally she punched keys here and there, abstractedly fishing for the stolen knowledge which worked her fingers.

Suddenly, furiously, she set to work, immersing herself in figure-tapes, swinging around herself a mighty rampart of the basic machinery. Yancey and Will tiptoed away, superfluously. For it would have taken a hammer blow on the head to interrupt the combined will-power of two such formidables as the late Star Macduff and the present Madame Mamie Tung.

5

The Executive Officer visited the ordinaries that were left, found a few men of strong fiber who had refused to succumb to the terror that had gripped the ship. He explained simply what had happened, and they accepted the explanation as their due after a very difficult time. He taught them the technique—which they had stumbled on by themselves in a haphazard way— of concentrating on one path of probabilities and the advisability of staying there, since any moment the other might vanish into the great unknown.

Only then did he begin to puzzle himself over what had happened—who their boarders had been, how they had done this to Sphere Nine. He recalled what they had said, which was little comfort but sound sense. They had assured him that he could not possibly understand their motivation for behaving as they did. Yancey told him that if this was a sample of their own behavior she most heartily agreed.

Madame Tung emerged from the calculations room with a splitting headache and a fistful of formulæ from which tubes could be constructed to build up something new in electromagnetic phenomena—a probability field which could be applied in this one very special case to good effect.

They constructed the thing with ease, hosed the ship with it, and were gratified to see the other path vanish—the path of the lunatic Yancey, the skull-split Star, the murdered ordinaries, and the cataleptic Mamie Tung and Will Archer.

"Landing?" asked Mamie.

"Why not?"

"I can't argue on those grounds, Will. But what happened on your stern resolution to take a sample of the protosphere and run back to Earth?"

"You're the Psychologist. You tell me."

"Those strangers had some violent impact on us. Behind their fronts was something enormously intriguing. You're full of what killed the fabulous cat."

"Right. And I'm not going to rest until I find out how that protosphere came about, and what it means to us."

"Oh, I can tell you that," said one of the visitors stepping through the hull. "Insofar as anyone can tell anyone else anything in this symbology of yours."

"Talk fast," said Will stiffly. "Our time is important."

The stranger chuckled delightedly. "I could give you all the time you want," he said. "I gave you all the probabilities you wanted. I could have given you an infinite number, practically. How much time did you say you wanted—twenty thousand years? A hundred thousand? And in the past, present or future?"

"No thanks," said Will hastily. "You were going to tell us about the protosphere."

"I was. It's our garbage-can, in a way. We had our neat little solar system, well-balanced around two suns; and then the most appalling junk came flying into it, blowing things out of kilter, tipping the balance one way or another ... so we invented protoplasm and started a ring of it out in space, gave it directives, fed it on rubbish, finally curved it around so it was a perfect shell. If we'd known the trouble it'd cause, really, we wouldn't have bothered. We thought it was an advantage that it reproduced automatically; that saved us making all the stuff ourselves. But apparently it shoots off spores, too, and they land on planets outside; and the most appalling things—like you—happen along a few million years later and want to change everything to suit yourselves. Was there anything else?"

"May we land on one of your planets and look about?"

"Why? It's so much simpler this way."

"This" was almost too theatrical to be convincing. There appeared on the wall of the office a busy little motion-picture complete with sound of a planet which had two suns in its sky.

It was a city scene, sleek vehicles buzzing along the streets, well-dressed men and handsome women strolling past, greeting each other with a grave nod, smiling, dashing children, here and there an animal suggestive of the horse.

One of the buildings, apparently, was on fire. The scene wavered a little, then angled upward to catch flames shooting from a window, a woman leaning out and calling for help.

The streamlined equivalent of a fire-truck roared up, shot up a device that resembled the Indian Rope Trick; a valiant male swarmed up it and packed the female down. When they reached the ground the end of the Indian Rope Trick squirted water at the fire, the rescued woman kissed her fireman enthusiastically, and the wall was blank again.

Madame Tung was the first to laugh cynically.

Their visitor looked at her more in sorrow than anger, his eyes heavy beneath their brows. "So? You *would rather* see the truth?"

"I think I would," said the golden-skinned woman.

"You shall."

Madame Tung prepared herself for more home movies, but they were not forthcoming. Instead there grew and spread in her brain an image of power, power inconceivable, roaring in noise, flaring in light, sparking in electric display, fusing in heat, running a mad gamut of the spectrum in every particle. She shut her eyes the better to contain it, for it was magnificent.

The display softened, shrank, seemed to cool. She had an image then of a sort of personified lightning, a tight etheric swirl packed with electrons and alpha particles in rigid order—a great thing twenty feet tall and five feet wide by five feet, with six radiating arms that burned what they grasped and blasted what they struck to powder. There were no feet; she saw the object travel somewhat as Sphere Nine traveled—by aiming itself and discharging sub-atomically.

There were features of a sort, something that she would call a mouth at the very top of the body, a member which ingested occasionally bits of matter which would rebuild it indefinitely or until some trying task. There were sensory organs—a delicate, branching, coraline thing that apprehended radiations of any order.

And in the very center of the electric vortex and a little above the midriff was one incalescent blaze of glory that carried to the dazzled inner eye of Mamie Tung the idea of BRAIN. It bore intelligence, appreciation, art, beauty—all the diffuse concepts packed about by man as surplus baggage.

She saw the thing bend its sensory organ at her, study her, saw the corresponding pulsations of the brain within it. She felt it reach out to establish contact with her mind, and welcomed it eagerly.

It must have been a glorious death, especially so for a mind like that of Madame Tung, new, brave and challenging. But death it was, and her friends caught her body in their arms. Silently and reproachfully they regarded their visitor.

"You too," he asked softly, "would you too rather see the truth?"

They let the golden-skinned woman to the floor.

"Before you go," said the man who had come through the hull, "is there anything I can do?"

"There is. It is what we came for. You may have noticed that we emit certain rays characteristic of protoplasm. As we are the fruit, so your protosphere is the core. It emits rays of great intensity which interfere with our genetic experiments. Could you mask those rays?"

"We shall. It will be several scores of years before they stop coming, so you will find in your desk a field-formula for a diffusion mask that will block them off."

"Thank you. Is there anything we've overlooked?"

"Nothing. You have no further business with us, nor have your people—no matter how far they may advance within your species' life. You are third-order at best; we are fifth-order and ascending. I trust that by the time your species has reached the point where it will be able to blow us to powder, we shall be well out of the three-dimensional range of experience."

With the most natural gesture in the world he extended his hand. In turn Yancey and Will gripped it. He stepped through the hull with a farewell wave.

"Commons room—ready ship!"

"Yes, Officer!"

"One hundred eighty degrees!"

"Yes, Officer!"

"And full speed—cut!"

"Cut!"

Close together they contemplated the golden-skinned Madame Tung.

"Everything has its cost," said Will.

Yancey said nothing.

Unrelieved blackness alternated with dazzling star-clusters; from rim to rim of the universe stretched the thin line that marked the hero's way.